"A MONUMENTALLY DOCUMENTED WORK ... PROVIDES FASCINATING INSIGHTS ... CONTRIBUTES WORTHILY TO THE UNDERSTANDING OF AN ENIGMATIC MAN AND HIS CREATIONS."
—*Booklist*

His imagination took countless millions where none had dared dream of going before. They went on voyages that roamed the farthest reaches of space, yet at the same time illumined the inner depths of the heart and mind of the captain, the crew, and the quests of the Starship *Enterprise*. Now a book that at last lets you share on the lifelong journey of discovery and creation that produced and powered the immortal *Star Trek* saga against all odds and opposition to reach heights of glory and lasting greatness unrivaled still today.

Even the most fervent fan will find startling new illumination about the series that made TV history, and how and why Gene Roddenberry did what he did so uniquely and so well. *Star Trek Creator* is riveting with a galaxy of fascinating revelations, incidents, anecdotes, insights, and personal testimonies.

"SHOWS RODDENBERRY AS A BRAVE AND ADVENTUROUS MAN WHO PROVED TO BE HARDWORKING AND TENACIOUS AS WELL."
—*Publishers Weekly*

DAVID ALEXANDER is an ex-private detective, investigative journalist, and magazine editor, who was chosen by his friend Gene Roddenberry to tell his extraordinary life story.

STAR TREK CREATOR

THE AUTHORIZED BIOGRAPHY OF
GENE RODDENBERRY

DAVID ALEXANDER

With an Introduction by
Majel Barrett Roddenberry
and a Foreword by Ray Bradbury

A ROC BOOK

Grateful thanks to the following for permission to print their remarks at Gene Roddenberry's memorial service: Whoopi Goldberg, Christopher Knopf, E. Jack Neuman, and Patrick Stewart.

To Gene Roddenberry,
who proved Gandhi was right:
One man can shake the world gently.

CONTENTS

INTRODUCTION BY MAJEL BARRETT RODDENBERRY

Whenever I make personal appearances, people always ask me, "What was Gene Roddenberry like?" It is a difficult question to answer quickly or simply. Gene was different things to different people.

First, in his own view of himself, Gene was a storyteller. He had a story for all occasions, and as self-effacing as he was, it wasn't uncommon for him to create a convenient story to dramatize some aspect of his life or career to divert attention away from his innate shyness.

Gene loved watching people, and he loved seeing their reactions to his stories. He loved a good debate and would encourage a good argument at the drop of a hat, often ending up, in the intellectual push and shove, on the opposite side from which he began. Gene and Chris and Sam (his closest writing buddies) would play the devil's advocate with each other and this spurred him (and them) on to creative heights. They would dissect, discuss (and cuss) each other's work until it was perfect. It was part of the process that made them good writers.

Gene was a voracious reader and insatiable when it came to learning. That, perhaps more than anything, was the key to his success as a writer. An intense and highly intelligent man, Gene's public persona was often seen, but there was a part of him he carefully guarded.

About six months before his untimely death in 1991, Gene asked his friend David Alexander to begin work on this biography. The two had become acquainted a number of years earlier, and David had written what Gene considered to be the best interview he had ever given. They met frequently at our house in Bel Air and down at our retreat in northern San Diego County. Gene became comfortable with David and shared many of his private thoughts and letters.

Throughout the entire process, Gene had but one rule: the biography must be honestly told. In order to tell his story completely, Gene insisted that his warts were just as important as everything else if the reader were to truly understand him.

Gene was a complex man with a penchant for life, for love, and mostly for humanity, but a man who needed to be loved in return. He was fair, with a few exceptions, and his insistence on avoiding confrontation was apparent not only in his work, but in his personal life.

Gene had an uncanny ability to choose the best people available for a job, then sit back and watch them do it. It was a pattern repeated often in his life. So it was for this book. When Gene died unexpectedly, David forged ahead and produced this work. Not only is it a thorough and honest look at Gene's life, but it is entertaining as well, and filled with many surprises.

David has read between the lines of Gene's life and has discovered all of these things. He has captured Gene's "essence." David is an incredible sleuth and could put Sherlock Holmes to shame. I can say that this book is true to Gene's wishes.

Some of the fascinating aspects of Gene's life that David has uncovered are the roots of Gene's philosophies, the important people in his life, and how Gene's experiences came together to mold the man known as the "Great Bird of the Galaxy." Above all, this book is the story of my "true and gentle knight," the wonderfully charming and loving man I was fortunate to call my husband.

This book is a comprehensive study of a complex man. It cuts right through the B.S. and the jealous dissidents and gives you an insight into a man whose biggest fault may have been his unshakable love and trust of humanity. Indeed, he loved humanity.

—Majel Barrett Roddenberry
Bel Air, California
March, 1994

FOREWORD
BY RAY BRADBURY

(From his remarks at Gene Roddenberry's memorial service)

Every time I've ever talked at Cal Tech, when the question period comes, they don't ask me about my stories. They say, "Do you know Gene Roddenberry?" I say, "Yes" and they say, "What is he like?" And then I tell them.

I think a lot of you know that for the last ten years, everywhere I went people mistook me for Gene. I was over in Scottsdale last year and three men in their early thirties ran up to me and cried, "Oh, Mr. Roddenberry, you're wonderful! We love you and we love your show and we hope it goes on forever." I said, "Thank you, I'm glad you like my work."

I learned not to disappoint, because to tell them the truth would be terrible. Their faces would have been destroyed. I let them go away happy. It made me happy too.

When I told some of my friends this week that I was going to be here today, two of them said, "What an honor!" I hadn't thought of it until that moment. I was sad, first of all—it was going to be a burden, a sweet burden. And when they said that twice, I said, "Yes! It is an honor, a great honor to speak of an honorable man."

So here we are, with his family. How rare it is to come to a gathering like this and look out at all the people and realize that you're here for the best reason. You're not here because you're obligated; you're here because you're part of his family, one way or another, small family, large family outside the doors and beyond in the city, the state, and the whole country. . . . It is rare that one man whom we trusted and knew, had a family this large. It's going to continue beyond the end of this century. That's the great thing about motion pictures and television—we'll be around a long time if we do fine work.

Gene, to me, symbolized what Schweitzer said years ago: Do excellent work: someone may imitate it. Every time I was at Cal Tech, I saw all these young science students dealing with the morality that he taught, and taught in a very quiet way—he didn't pontificate with his stories in his show—but he showed by example. In the midst of so much violence and so many shows we don't care about, *Star Trek* stands out as a nice, quiet, moral example in a time when we need it.

Over the years I've accepted being mistaken for him. Gene would send me the mail he got about *The Martian Chronicles,* and I'd send him the mail about *Star Trek.* Last year I threatened to start cutting in on the percentages! We need all the humor we can gain on a day like this. A gentle humor, and very heartfelt.

Years ago, the thing about *Star Trek* that a lot of people have missed, those of you who really care know long before I say it, but the producers at the studios, it's taken them years to catch on, about a really good space film having something to do with the universe. You know, when you get up in the morning and you look out, the simplest thing, the gift of the eye—which was invented how many billions of years ago?—commencing with the simplest animalcules and the swamps and the flowers that followed the sun.

As a result of the eye being invented, mankind discovered the stars, and wanted them, for tens of thousands of years now. All of the inventions that were connected with motion pictures and television had to do with the eye. The wonderful magic of just seeing, being alive each morning and looking out at the simplest thing—finding the grass and the trees.

It sounds banal, but Gene took it that extra step with all of his compatriots into the universe where we want to live. It's basic with us. Once we see the stars, we want the stars. So at the center of *Star Trek* for me, time and again, was the whole problem of the universe itself—the mystery of life. Very mysterious. We know little about it. I've had arguments with experts at the Smithsonian and the Planetarium about the "Big Bang" theories. The "Big Bang" was seven billion years ago. The "Big Bang" was *ten* billion years ago. I said, "Prove it!" Of course, they couldn't, because the universe has been here forever, which is impossible, yes?

So we're dealing with two impossibilities: the impossibility of your all being here today, and Gene having been among us and enjoying life to the fullest. No matter how poor you are, and most of us came from poor families, but didn't know we were poor because we knew how to scan the universe.

I fell in love with the stars when I was in high school, when I was seventeen. The mystery of life and the mystery of death. We ponder on these things constantly. We go to the dentist to have a tooth pulled, and for the rest of the day we can't take our tongue out of the socket because it's a small death. We taste our own mortality.

Gene's show time and again dealt with these two miracles. The fact that we have one time, so we must be celebrants. No matter how poor, no matter what the conditions, we must be celebrants of life belonging to no one particular religion, but glad to have been here once. So we're here today, glad to have lived with Gene over a long period of time.

Years ago, if you'll allow, I wrote a short story about my great-grandmother who lived to be around eighty-two and died when I was about three. A very practical woman—was always up on top of the house nailing shingles in place—that kind of creative person in the midst of our life. When she died, she called all of us in one by one. She made the decision herself one day. She just went to bed, and said, "I've had it. I'm tired. I need the rest. Nice long rest." And she called us in one by one and talked to us. At the end of this short story, I'd like to read you some of her thoughts and hope that they evoke something for you.

My great-grandmother says, "I don't want any Halloween parties here tomorrow. Don't want anyone saying anything sweet about me. I said it all in my time and my pride. I've tasted every vittle and danced every dance. Now there's one last tart I haven't bit on. One tune I haven't whistled. But I'm not afraid. I'm truly curious. Death won't get a crumb by my mouth I won't keep and savor, so don't you worry over me. So, all of you go and let me find my sleep."

"Somewhere a door closed quietly. That's better, she thought. Alone she snuggled luxuriously down through the warm snowbank of linen and wool, sheet and cover, and the colors of the patchwork quilt were bright as a circus banner of old time. Lying there she felt as small and secret as on those mornings eighty-some-odd years ago when wakening she comforted her tender bones in bed.

"A long time back, she thought, I dreamed a dream, and was enjoying it so much, when someone wakened me and that was the day when I was born. And now, now, let me see. . . . She cast her mind back. Where was I? she thought. Ninety years!

"How to take up the thread and the pattern of that lost dream again. She put out a small hand. There, there. Yes. That was it. And she smiled, deeper in the warm snowhill, she turned her head upon her pillow. That was better. Yes. Now. She saw it shaping in her mind quietly, and with serenity like a sea moving along an endless and self-refreshing shore, now she let the old dream touch and lift her from the snow and drift her above the scarcely remembered bed.

"Downstairs, she thought, they are polishing the silver and rummaging in the cellar, and dusting in the halls. She could hear them living all through the house. It's all right, whispered great-grandma, as the dream floated her. Like everything else in this life, it's fitting. And the sea moved her back down the shore."

I write that for all of you. I write that for myself. I speak that for Gene now. I say it for him, and I end as I began.

Maybe even in the years ahead, strangers will come up to me and will have lost track of time. And they will look at me and say, "Mr. Roddenberry, I thought you were dead!" And you know what my answer will be? "Not as long as *I'm* alive."

AUTHOR'S PREFACE AND ACKNOWLEDGMENTS

In *The Art of Biography,* Paul Murray Kendall suggested that biography may be defined as "the simulation, in words, of a man's life, from all that is known about that man." Well said, but not easily done. A biographer's job is to take the threads of a person's life: the paper trail, the memories of relatives, friends, colleagues and associates, the factual and the conjectured, the thousands of imperfectly remembered moments that come out of human interaction and weave those myriad strings into a recognizable tapestry while keeping the weaver and his opinions out of the design.

It requires time and there is never enough. Even though this book represents two and one-half years of research and writing, I would willingly take an equal amount to do more. A biographer is never finished, a biography never completed. There is always one more fact to check out, one more anecdote to collect, one more bit of insight into the subject's character to develop. Unfortunately, the realistic and not unreasonable demands of my publisher make any longer preparation impracticable. At some point you simply stop and bring your story to a conclusion, knowing there is always more to tell.

With Gene there would always be more to tell, for he was a mercurial character. He showed different aspects of his personality to different people at different times. As he matured and evolved, people moved in and out of his professional and personal lives. Some saw facets that were hidden from others or facets that did not appear until later. Some saw more than others, but almost always Gene decided who saw what. He was, at core, a very private person. Those who knew him best often used the same two terms to describe him: self-effacing and shy.

About his work Gene was protective. About ideas Gene could be an intellectual barroom brawler. He had a habit of saying things for effect, looking to provoke a reaction. Unless you were aware of that habit and of the purpose of the outrageous remark, his words could easily be misinterpreted. An example was his comment one afternoon to several friends, two of whom were gay, that if he had it to do all over again he'd rather be a homosexual. This from a man who celebrated his heterosexuality vigorously. On two occasions he referred to all women with a gutter epithet. It was said to shock, to outrage, but was not an opinion set in stone. Like many other comments it was made for effect or was transitory—coming out of the mood of the moment.

Gene was always, as several friends independently characterized him, "stirring the pot." In researching and writing this book I have attempted to take that trait into account.

As he described himself, Gene was a storyteller: a person with the ability to excite the mind and heart with the power of words. Since before the beginning of recorded history, storytellers have taken us out of the ordinary into the possible, the improbable, and the fantastic. They are as important to our well-being as clean water and wholesome food.

Had he lived a thousand years ago, Gene would be as revered by society then as he is today, for his special genius would have been recognized in any culture, in any time. Gene held up a mirror for us to examine ourselves, to see the best and worst, to understand that we could be better than we are.

Gene was a talented man who lived several lives. He was human on as many levels as he could experience in his short seventy years.

Gene Roddenberry was my friend. He chose me to tell his story, his charge being to "write an honest biography." My great regret is that the one person whose opinion I would have valued above all others did not live to tell me if I succeeded in the task he set before me.

Acknowledgments

A great many people have contributed to this biography. Some shared their memories in interviews, providing invaluable insights into Gene's life; others found old letters and photographs. Many suggested additional places to search for information, while others suggested individuals who had known Gene and could add another tile of remembrance to the mosaic of his life.

First and foremost my deepest debt to Gene Roddenberry for leading such an interesting life and choosing me to chronicle it. Like so many other people he touched, his friendship changed my life.

Deep thanks also to Gene's wife, Majel Barrett Roddenberry, for supporting Gene's decision and for her friendship and candor.

My wife, Cassidy J. Alexander, is the necessary constant in my life and thanks go to her for ongoing support, good advice, and just being there. Her help, especially during the last six months of this project, was invaluable.

This book would not exist without the advice and continuing help of Ernie Over, Gene's personal assistant, now Majel's personal assistant. He has my deepest gratitude. A bonus from this project is Ernie's friendship. Richard Arnold, *Star Trek* archivist and consultant deserves many thanks for both his loyalty to Gene, his prodigious memory, and his support of this book.

Many pleasant hours were spent in the company of Gene's mother, Caroline Glen Roddenberry, who lets me call her "Nana." Appreciation also goes to Gene's brother, Bob, and his wife, Bernice, as well as Gene and Bob's sister, Doris Willowdean. Gene's oldest daughter, Darleen Roddenberry, and her husband, Antoine Bacha, deserve many thanks for friendship and remembering what family is all about. Gene's maternal aunt Doris Willowdean and her late husband, Clint Higgins, are also thanked for their remembrances and hospitality.

Thanks go to Janet Asimov, widow of Isaac Asimov, for permission to reprint Isaac's letters; Mrs. Jean Gardner, widow of Erle Stanley Gardner, for permission to reprint her husband's letters; and Perry A. Chapdelaine of AC Projects, Inc., copyright owners of the letters of John W. Campbell.

Appreciation also to Ronnie Day, East Tennessee State University, College of Arts and Sciences, Department of History, and Helen Morriss Wildasin, widow of Mack Morriss, for excerpts from his diary and unpublished dispatches; and Terry Sweeney for permission and assistance.

Deepest thanks go to Colleen who remembered the dream.

In-depth interviews, stories, opinions, thoughts, impressions, along with photos, letters, and helpful suggestions were freely shared by a small army of Gene's friends, colleagues, and associates. They are listed and thanked in random order: William Ware Theiss, for his generosity of time given when there was so little left; Marta Houske and Nick Agid; Denise and Michael Okuda; Bob and Pat Atchison; Dr. Barry Unger; Penny Unger; Jim Kyle; Morris Chapnick; Bob Lewin; former California governor Pat Brown; Bob Justman; Bill Bixby; Cy Chermak; Oscar Katz; Larry Walton; Vivian Rigler; Carl Mason; Carla Mason; Wilton Dillon; Captain Stanley Sheldon; Chief Daryl Gates; Patrick Stewart; E. Jack Neuman; Chris Knopf; Sam Rolfe; Sam Peeples; Cliff Wynne; Jonathan Frakes; Whoopi Goldberg; Wil Wheaton; Debbie Wheaton; Dr. Paul Logan; Captain Michael Graham; Norman Felton; Tom Gilbert; Marcia Cash; Colonel William Ivey; Ray Johnson; Chris Noel Bassior; Don Ingalls; Betty Ballantine; Katherine Horton; Teresa Victor; Fred Ziv; Pierre Weis; John Dozier; Ed Naha; Michael Greene; Andy Garb; Jeff Loeb; Bill Hamilton; Diane Demers; Vi Smith; Bridget A. Flynn of Guinness Import Co.; Jack F. Raineault at Guinness Import Legal Dept.; Larry Richardson, President of the Marketing Centre Advertising Agency; David B. Gero; Wade Williams; Donna O'Mara; Hubert and Mary Hough; H. G. Burns Ph.D.; Tom Gilbert;

Mary Elizabeth and Colonel Don Prickett; Dr. Gary Wollam; Mo, the perfect woman; Dan Madsen; Duke Campbell; Anita Doohan; Barbara Marx Hubbard; Joe Jacobs; Lottie Berg; Pat White Bradley; Miriam Post; Anthony G. Volpe; Mary Shambra; Babbie Bogue Stull; Karen Kearns; Sara Jane Bray Archer; and Joe D'Agosta.

Members of fandom who were of great help and are due thanks are: Bjo and John Trimble; Allyson M.W. Dyer; Forrest J Ackerman, Lana Brown, David Lomazoff, Joan Winston, Wanda Kendall-La Vita, Tom Lalli, Mather B. Pfeiffenberger, Lana Brown, Rod Summer, Eileen Salmas, and Janet Quarton.

Thanks go to the librarians, archivists, and researchers who provided valued assistance: Professor Morleen Getz of the University of Cincinnati; Brigitte J. Kueppers and her assistant, Paul Camp, UCLA Arts Library Special Collections; Virginia Frey, Manager, Business Affairs, CBS Entertainment, New York; Rita Bottoms, The Robert A. Heinlein Archive at California State University at Santa Cruz; Margaret (Maggie) Roddenbery of the Roddenbery Memorial Library; Joshua Ranger, researcher at the Wisconsin Historical Society; Ben Brewster, Assistant Archivist, University of Wisconsin; Ruta Abolins, Assistant Archivist, University of Wisconsin; Catharine Heinz, Librarian of the National Association of Broadcasters; Adele Askin of Pan Am; Darlis Wood, librarian, Chevron USA, Inc.; Dr. Mamie Clayton, Western States Black Research Center, Los Angeles; The Collings Foundation; Kerri Childress, Mary Noonan, San Dimas Public Library; Dana Bell, Norton Air Force Base; Dorothy Fuhrmann, Los Angeles City College; Colonel Bruce Bell, Public Affairs Officer, West Point Military Academy; Susan P. Walker, Assistant Archivist, U.S. Military Academy Archives; Floyd M. Geery, Fort Bliss Museum; Wayne N. Wallace, Randolph Air Force Base; Mitchell Yockelson, National Archives; Shelly Cagner, Press Relations at Arbitron, Inc.; Dennis East, Associate Dean, Bowling Green State University; Carlisa Carter-Jacobs of the FAA; Janalyn Robnett of the Pomona Valley School District; Sergeant Michael Obert, History Office, Kelly Air Force Base; Suzanne W. Clark, River Bluffs Regional Library, St. Joseph, Missouri; Jonathan Rosenthal, The Museum of Broadcasting; Rick Ewig, Manager of References Services, American Heritage Center, University of Wyoming; Calista and James Bray, Tim Finney, Jim Brown, Susan Hewitt, West Covina Library; Teresa Malinowski, Cal State University Library, Fullerton; Roseanne Macmillan of KTLA; Charron E. Fullerton, Director of Creative Services, MONY; Katherine Plumb at National Public Radio Program Library; Mary Ann Bydlon, Nestlé Company; Lee Benbrooks; Sergeant Barry Spink; Dr. Dennis Casey; Willie Bostick; Bill McKale; George Mathew; Marsha Halley; Roy J. Nirschel, Jr.; Paulette Spyrell; Jim Cooper; Eloisa Marquez; Neil McAleer; Vivian Rigler; Marsha Halley; Phyllis Wheelis; Richard Kyle; Richard Kalk; Hal Fowler; Cathy Henderson, Ken Craven of the Harry Ransom Humanities Research Center, the University of Texas at Austin; Laurel Beckman, State Historical Society of Missouri; Leon C. Metz; and Robert Fleming, Archivist, Emerson College.

Two friends have always been available to supply friendship and advice, and for that my deep thanks go to Gerry O'Sullivan and Michael A. Stackpole.

Thanks also are sent to my good friend Richard Webster for much assistance.

Finally, deserving of deepest gratitude is Russell Galen, literary agent extraordinaire, for being there to guide me through the publishing labyrinth; Amy Stout, my editor at ROC Books, for continued grace under pressure; and Elaine Koster at Dutton Signet, who decided to rush and helped make it all happen, and John Silbersack, who saw enough promise in a new writer to buy the book.

There were a number of people who wished to remain anonymous, but their help is appreciated nonetheless.

—David Alexander,
Los Angeles,
March, 1994

PROLOGUE

Wednesday, October 23, 1991.
Roddenberry home, Bel Air, California
Early evening.

Majel could only make Gene comfortable. Suffering from the effects of diabetes and the gradual buildup of fluid in the brain, Gene's doctor expected him to last no longer than six months. A year would be a miracle.

Gene had little to look forward to except a slow, painful decline that had begun with a small stroke two weeks before. The stroke had paralyzed the muscles of his right arm. They started to atrophy, causing him pain. The stroke had also eliminated much of the right field of vision in both eyes and affected his ability to communicate easily. He could not articulate full sentences except with great difficulty, but Gene did not complain. His smile was as easy and infectious as ever.

The word quietly spread among his inner circle that Gene wasn't in great shape and that now would be a good time to visit. A small, sad parade of friends dropped by in ones and twos to spend a few minutes. In the week before, Gene had visited with his old friend Bob Justman. They laughed and joked; Gene was usually in good spirits around friends, but Bob knew the time was short. When Gene left he said he wanted to come back and visit again. Bob readily agreed, saddened by the sure and certain knowledge he would never see his friend again.

As best he could, Gene had watched *Star Trek VI* the day before. The trip to Paramount, the viewing, and the trip home had been tiring. He was still recovering from the exertion.

The house was quiet. Gene and Majel's son, Rod, was out with friends and Gene's personal assistant, Ernie Over, had left for the day. The night nurse, Ida, was in the master bedroom watching television and the new housekeepers, Grace and Bulock Malczewski were in their private quarters doing the same. The Roddenberrys' three German Shepherds, E.T., Bump, and the newly purchased puppy, Terminator 3, were napping. The three Roddenberry cats were off somewhere attending to cat business. Most of the rooms were dark, their doors closed. A single overhead light illuminated the large floral arrangement on a glass-topped table in the entrance foyer, making it an island of color in a hallway of darkness. The only lit room in the house was the kitchen. Gene, in his wheelchair, sat in the entrance to the garden breakfast room, just off the kitchen, watching Majel prepare dinner. The kitchen was alive, filled with light and the smell of cooking food. It was a simple domestic scene—two people, married for over 20 years, keeping each other company while dinner cooked.

Majel and Gene had a unique relationship. Both possessed powerful, independent personalities that were, in an odd way, complementary. In dramatizing his life, as he liked to do from time to time, Gene played the henpecked husband to Majel's demanding, domineering, spendthrift wife. The truth was more the opposite. Gene was the one who spent money, often freely, and usually got his way. Majel, a child of the Depression, was the one who was financially conservative. At Thanksgiving dinner she proudly told her guests that the turkeys she served were free from the market because she had stocked up on staples. She constantly looked for bargains and rarely bought anything unless it was on sale. She clipped coupons religiously. Her huge walk-in closet seemed to contain everything she had bought since 1955. Majel not only bought quality, she kept it and got full value out of it over the years.

Gene and Majel had been lovers since 1962 and married since 1969, an eternity by Hollywood standards. It hadn't always been a smooth relationship. Gene was a "man in control" and Majel was the archetypical independent woman.

While Gene admired and respected that trait, he worked hard during much of their marriage to bring Majel under "control." It never happened, and that simple fact was part of the glue that bound them together. In a world that easily capitulated to his intellect and will, Gene realized that Majel was the one constant he could not fully dominate. He did not always like it, but he always respected her for her consistency and strength. A few days before his death, he referred to her as "a remarkable woman."

Gene's condition had cut away the nonsense in their relationship. In his last year of life, their deepest feelings surfaced and they grew closer to one another. The game was over; the pretense gone. As Gene learned many years earlier, it is under harsh circumstances that people's real feelings and beliefs emerge. The Roddenberrys had worked through Gene's infirmities and won something priceless.

A gourmet cook, Majel worked hard preparing an extensive dinner for their evening meal. Gene always had a robust appetite that was wide-ranging in its taste. He could have an extensive gourmet French lunch, then a frozen pot pie over rice for dinner, and eat both with equal gusto. Feeding Gene's hearty appetite was one way Majel had of taking care of him. It helped her cope with her own private grief for what was becoming more apparent: Gene was dying by inches. A good dinner would divert their attention from the obvious, and the inevitable.

Unfortunately, today was a repeat of the past several days: Gene was without appetite. By cooking him a favorite meal, Majel thought she could coax him into eating, but he wasn't up to it. In spite of her efforts, Majel could not get him to eat.

Months of frustration started to come to the surface as Majel's inability to stem the unalterable became fixed in that moment. She stood in the kitchen not knowing what to do. Sensing her frustration, Gene pushed himself over to her and took her right hand in his left. For a man who was world-famous for his communication skills, it was a frustrating time, too. He understood what she was going through.

Gene held Majel's hand lovingly for several moments and then with a supreme act of will looked up and said, "I love you." Majel bent down and hugged him for a long time, doing her best to hold back tears.

For the past three months, Majel had been sleeping on the

leather sofa in the downstairs family room. Gene had become a fitful sleeper, and with his nurse nearby watching television through the night it had become impossible for Majel to get a good night's sleep. Although there were several guest bedrooms available upstairs, she wanted to be nearby in case Gene had an emergency in the night.

As comfortable as her couch was, Majel did not sleep well, either. That night she walked into the master bedroom and found Gene on the bed watching television. He wanted her next to him and so, in spite of the discomfort to his atrophying muscles, Majel got into bed and cuddled with him.

Over the next hour, Majel slowly turned down the television's volume and Gene drifted off. As Majel got up to go to her couch, Gene opened his eyes and said, "Sleep." Majel nodded and repeated, "Sleep," and went off to the family room. Gene closed his eyes as Majel left the room. It was their last night together.

Thursday was a perfect day. The sky was populated with a scattering of white clouds that looked like tufts of cotton floating in the clear blue. There was a gentle but persistent cool breeze that made the air feel fresh and clean. The temperature was in the middle-70s.

Gene had a 2 P.M. appointment with Dr. Ronald Rich, a neurosurgeon who would give his opinion on the advisability of a shunt operation to alleviate the buildup of Gene's brain fluid. The procedure could lessen the chance of further strokes, and Gene might regain some of his lost motor control. The downside to the operation was serious: it might not accomplish anything and, worse, there was a chance that Gene would die on the operating table. Understandably, he and Majel had some apprehension about it. Everyone acknowledged that Gene would make the final decision, no matter what family and friends might want. In spite of his deteriorating physical condition, Gene was still very much in control of his life. His ability to speak was impaired, not his ability to think.

I arrived a little after ten in the morning and found Gene sitting in his wheelchair near the pool. He wore one of his favorite shirts, a colorful pastel, a pair of turquoise shorts, white socks, and white canvas shoes. His hair was neatly combed and he looked good, but tired. He was enjoying the weather but his appetite had not returned. He absently drank a glass of milk and nibbled on crackers and cheese Grethel, the day nurse, had left on a nearby table.

A variety of small potted mums, mostly yellow, filled the planter next to the patio. The cool breeze played a tuneless melody on the wind chimes that hung next to the kitchen window. There was a Halloween party planned for that Saturday night, and Gene watched workmen as they erected a tent to cover part of the patio. Gene was going as an English country squire. Bill Theiss, his longtime friend and costume designer on *Star Trek* and *Star Trek: The Next Generation* had been over the week before, fitting him exactly. Ernie made a cup of coffee for Gene and a cup of tea for me—Earl Grey, hot.

Gene, Ernie, and I sat and talked. I knew Gene had seen *Star Trek VI* two days before and I asked what he thought of the film. He replied that it was "okay." There was little excitement in his voice. He held out his left hand with the palm flat to the ground, rocking it back and forth.

"Was it just so-so?" I asked.

Gene replied, "Yeah."

"Are you going to put your name on it?"

"Yeah, sure," he responded without any enthusiasm.

"Well," I said, "after *Star Trek V,* how could you refuse?"

Gene chuckled.

We talked a bit more about the film, about it being well photographed. Gene agreed that it was well photographed, but Ernie and I suspected that Gene had difficulty in seeing much of the film since his stroke had robbed him of much of his vision. We suspected he heard more of the film than he saw.

Near lunchtime, Gene's old friend of 10 or 12 years, Marta Houske, dropped by. She was, as usual, energetic, with a gusto for life that made her invigorating to be around. She sat in front of Gene, where he could more easily see her. She asked him questions, moved him around the house, showed him the arrangement of flowers that had just been delivered, and generally tried to buck up his spirits. Gene responded but seemed strained.

Marta coaxed Gene into having something to eat. She wheeled him through the kitchen, where Grace was preparing New England-style clam chowder and roast beef sandwiches. Marta parked Gene in the sunlit-breakfast room at the end of the glass-topped table. Gene ate half a sandwich and part of a bowl of chowder. He dipped some of the sandwich in the soup and ate the rest straight, using his left hand. He fed himself. No one babied him. After eating a bit, he said he'd had enough. He wanted to go to his bedroom for a rest before the doctor's appointment. Marta pushed him to the bedroom, said goodbye and left. While Ernie prepared the car, I sat in the family room and read.

At 1:30 Ernie pulled the Rolls Royce with the custom license plates, GENE R, around as Grethel pushed Gene to the front door. Ernie got a sweater for him in case the weather cooled. Gene walked the short distance to the Rolls. Good democrat that he was, Gene always rode in the front seat. While Grethel and I found our seats in the Rolls, Majel got in her Mercedes, MAJEL R, to follow. Ernie performed his usual before-drive ritual of opening a tin of Altoids and offering everyone in the car one of the "curiously strong" British mints.

As we rode down Wilshire Boulevard, Gene joked a bit and looked out the window, observing the passing scenery as best he could. He did not seem overly apprehensive. The radio was on, playing "adult-contemporary" music from KBIG-FM, instead of Gene's usual preference, KNX Newsradio. He tapped his left forefinger to the beat of the music, something he did not often do. We talked about making a time to see the film *Blue Planet* at the IMAX Theater. After a 20-minute drive, we entered the medical office building at 15th and Wilshire in Santa Monica, just across the street from the Santa Monica Hospital.

Grethel helped Gene stand as Ernie got the portable wheelchair out of the trunk. Ernie gave a little shout of encouragement to Gene, to which he responded in kind. The doctor's office was on the ninth floor: the car park was on the third.

As we passed the fifth floor, Gene suddenly began to struggle for breath. He turned to his left, the only direction in which he could see well, and looked up at Ernie with fright and confusion. The other passengers had pushed the sixth floor button and as soon as the elevator door opened, they quickly jumped off. Gene's struggle to breathe worsened. The ride from the sixth to the ninth floor probably only took 30 or 40 seconds. It seemed an eternity.

The moment the door opened on the ninth floor, I sprinted around the corner and down the hall to alert the doctor to the emergency. Ernie pushed Gene's wheelchair as fast as he could. Gene was fighting to breathe, making gasping noises. As soon as Ernie had him inside the office, the doctor had him tilt the wheelchair back to elevate Gene's legs. Ernie complied and supported Gene's head and shoulders as he did so. The office nurse came out with an oxygen bottle and slipped the mask over Gene's nose and mouth. Ernie continually reassured Gene that he was going to be all right and that the doctors were right there. It was just two P.M.

I ran off to find Majel, who had never been in this building before, and guided her to the office. Short moments later, she was on the floor holding Gene's head on her lap, comforting him. The doctors and their staff were attentive. The paramedics were on their way. Everyone thought this just another episode, brought on by Gene's overall condition. The office called Gene's regular doctor, Leonard Schwartzman.

Majel continued to reassure Gene, telling him in a quiet voice to breathe. After a few moments, he turned toward her and tried to say something. He only managed to gasp out a sound like "yeah." He gave another gasp; his chest lifted one last time, and then relaxed and became still. Ernie saw that Gene had stopped breathing and said so forcefully.

Majel stood up and got out of the way as the doctor jumped over Gene and immediately started cardio-pulmonary resuscitation (CPR). He said, "Get the family out of here," to which Majel instantly responded with a firm and unalterable, "No!" In the background, Grethel, a native of Jamaica, began a litany of repetitive prayers that beat an odd counterpoint to the noise of the doctor performing CPR. Gene's death became as paradoxical as his birth: a mixture of modern science and ancient superstition.

Gene's left arm was bone white. His eyes were fixed and staring. He was gone then, but hope continued that the magic of CPR and modern medicine would, somehow, bring him back as it had a few months before. Majel and Ernie stood to the side, holding onto each other for comfort and assurance. We watched and hoped. Ernie stepped out for a moment to phone Reinelda Estupinian, Majel's assistant at Lincoln Enterprises, asking her to contact Leonard Maizlish, Gene's longtime lawyer and closest friend, and inform him of the situation.

Within moments the paramedics arrived and began their

procedures, hooking up a cardiac monitor and starting an IV. After searching for a pulse, one of the paramedics took over the CPR from the doctor and continued the rhythm unbroken. Grethel moved to the corner of the waiting room and continued her prayers in a quiet but insistent voice.

The paramedic team prepared Gene for transport across the street to the Emergency Heart Center at Santa Monica Hospital. The CPR continued uninterrupted. Dr. Rich accompanied the three of us to the emergency room. Once there, Majel used the pay phone in the waiting room to contact Harvard-Westlake Preparatory, Rod's school. She gave instructions for the administration to find Rod and have him driven to Santa Monica Hospital immediately.

After a few moments, the emergency room clerk came out and showed everyone to the inside waiting room. We stationed ourselves in the hall outside Gene's trauma room and watched each time the door opened. We could see the trauma team working on Gene with a furious, practiced intensity.

After 30 minutes the door opened one final time. CPR had stopped. The trauma team's intensity was dissipating. Majel knew then what she had suspected earlier—Gene had died in the doctor's office, in her arms. The last thing Gene saw and the last sound he heard was the face and voice of the woman he loved. It was little comfort.

Dr. Rich came out and introduced Dr. Walid Ghurabi, head of the trauma team. Dr. Ghurabi's face betrayed the sad news. In the traditional and caring manner, using timeworn words, he said that the trauma team had done all they could to bring Gene back—but he was gone. The finality of his words hung in the air.

Majel entered the room as the trauma team quietly filed out. Gene's body lay on a stainless steel table, covered with a simple white hospital sheet. If life is movement, then death is a terrible, quiet stillness. Majel faced that stillness. Gene had been larger than life, able to fill a room with his presence. That spark, that vital actuality, was gone. The room was empty.

Majel saw the remains of a great man, the creator of a worldwide phenomenon, the father of her only child, her lover and friend. She walked over to where he lay and, without realizing it, performed one last intimate gesture: she reached out and gently closed his eyes. He looked asleep.

Their 30-year love affair was over. She grieved by quietly talking to Gene, stroking his face and hair, choking back tears.

Other than her gentle sobbing, the room was quiet.

CHAPTER 1

"Why, it's a veiled baby!" With that surprised exclamation, Dr. Herbert Stevenson slapped Eugene Wesley Roddenberry on the rump and welcomed him into life late in the evening of August 19, 1921. When this century was young, popular folklore saw meaning in every deviation from the norm. A "veil" was no more than a part of the placenta that covered the baby's head and shoulders, but tradition dictated that such a veil meant the child was gifted with second sight—the ability to see the future. Gene's mother, Caroline Glen Golemon Roddenberry, was a good Baptist of seventeen who didn't believe such nonsense, but in her eyes the doctor's words would forever set her firstborn son apart from other children.

As was the custom, Dr. Stevenson had only been called to the El Paso home of the new grandparents, William and Lydia Golemon, when their daughter went into labor. There had been no prenatal care, but this wasn't the first time Dr. Stevenson had seen Glen, as her friends called her. As he walked into the bedroom, he looked at the young woman and recognized her instantly. He turned to Lydia Golemon and asked, "She's one of mine, isn't she?" Seventeen years earlier, Stevenson had assisted in the birth of Gene's mother.

The modest three-bedroom wooden house was unusually quiet that warm August night. Glen had ten siblings from her father's two marriages and even with the older children married and away there was still a passle of Golemon siblings living in the household. Glen's mother had sent most of the children to neighbors to give her daughter some degree of privacy during birth. In addition to the doctor, Glen's mother, her younger sister, Willodean, and Gene's father were present for the birth. Cool, calm, and very much in control, Eugene Edward Roddenberry was not going to miss the birth of his first child.

The home birth was part of custom and belief. It would be years before hospital births became commonplace. Besides, Eugene Edward had insisted, as he would with all his children, on a home birth. That guaranteed there would be no hospital mixups and no non-Roddenberry child brought home.

Glen's easygoing nature was reflected in the birth—beginning of labor to delivery was only about an hour—quite surprising given her youth, small stature, this being her first pregnancy, and the baby's size: nearly nine pounds. Glen put it down to her good health and all the hills she'd climbed as a child.

The baby was welcomed into the burgeoning Golemon household with love and affection. His strong-willed maternal grandmother, Lydia, decided that he should be named Eugene Wesley after his father and grandfather. No one argued with her about the choice of names, or her right to choose. Lydia was not one to be questioned.

Naming the baby after his father was prophetic. Eugene Edward Roddenberry, physically, temperamentally, and intellectually, would be the major influence in his son's life. Gene's father was twenty-four at his son's birth, more or less. His age was a guess, because it was learned in later years that he had three birth certificates, each bearing a different date of birth.

In spite of the imprecision of his age, there is no dispute that he was born into a family beset by tragedy, his childhood over almost before it began. His parents, Leon and Clara May Roddenberry, were married in 1892. They lived in Folkston, Georgia, and supposedly had a child every other year straight through to 1900. The second child, Clara Mae, died in infancy. Eugene Edward was their third child.

In 1907, Leon died at the age of forty, leaving Clara with little education and a family to raise. She sought solace in a bottle and the family dissolved. Eugene and his youngest brother, Hilbert, were sent to live across the state line in a north Florida orphanage.

After a year, the two children were taken out of the orphanage, but the family was never fully reunited. Eugene bounced back and forth between relatives and his own family. To help support his family as best he could, Eugene began working. This meant quitting school. He never finished elementary school, his formal education ending at the third or fourth grade.[1]

During his brief exposure to organized education, Eugene had been given the basics of literacy, but he was far from proficient. He knew that to advance in the world he needed to read and write, so he taught himself. Years later, his world-famous son would point to the fact that his father was essentially self-educated: "He was a very intelligent man. He learned much like I learned. He met people and fastened on to what they were saying. My father was a very common man who got his high-school diploma while he was a police officer in Los Angeles. He was very pleased with that."

Big Gene's hatred of Republicans did not diminish with the passage of time or his oldest son's success. Many years later, when "Little" Gene had achieved some degree of success as a free-lance script writer and moved into his first really large house, Papa and Glen were invited in for drinks and dinner. The Beverly Hills house was a big step up from where Gene and family had been living—it even had a wet bar. Papa, uncomfortable and agitated from the time he had entered the house, was offered a drink. With that offer Papa reached his limit. He exploded, forcefully telling his oldest son that he couldn't understand how he could live like a Republican, drinking in the living room rather than drinking in the kitchen like a good Democrat. He and Glen left. This small rift healed over, but Papa could never reconcile himself to the thought of a Democrat with money. For him, it was a contradiction in terms.

On April 10, 1916, Eugene Edward used the birth certificate that said he was 18 to join the U.S. Army. Being tall and smart, he easily passed for the legal minimum.

The Army taught him organization and gave him responsibility. He learned the value of cleanliness and became meticulous in his personal habits. After basic training, he was posted to Fort Bliss, five miles outside El Paso, Texas. He

---

[1] Years later, on his application to the Los Angeles Police Department, he would claim to have completed the seventh grade.

became part of the Army's buildup along the border. Within a short time of his posting, he became one of the 5,000 troopers chasing Pancho Villa.

Fort Bliss and its surrounding camps became the host for the 82nd Field Artillery, the 20th Infantry, the 5th Field Artillery, the 2nd Battalion of the 4th Field Artillery, and regiments from Georgia, South Carolina, New York, Michigan, Pennsylvania, and Illinois. Various national guard units were mobilized. At the buildup's peak there were over 50,000 soldiers in and around Fort Bliss.

Every officer knows that boredom is the enemy of command. Things were not always peaceful between the novice soldiers. The heavy concentration of troops further strained the love-hate relationship between the townspeople and the Army. The troopers thought the local merchants overcharged them and the townspeople were tired of the soldiers' constant fights and public drunkenness.

In an effort to smooth over strained relations, a number of local businessmen and ministers organized dances to which the soldiers were invited. It was at one of these church socials that Gene's father met the lovely but oh-so-young Caroline Glen Golemon. Eugene Edward was in his late teens and Caroline Glen was 12 when they met. She was the daughter of an Alabama-born iron and brass moulder and his second wife, Lydia.

Eugene was tall and imposing in his private's uniform and made a strong impression on the young girl. He called her his "little sweetheart" with an older teenager's indulgence for a young girl obviously flush with her first crush. They did not date, but she did not forget him. When asked about this first meeting, Glen would gently smile, look back across seventy-five years, and quietly but firmly state: "He was the most handsome thing that ever lived," the delight still in her voice.

The Army had a bigger job to handle as President Wilson decided that Germany was a greater threat to peace than Mexico. On April 6th, 1917, the United States declared war on Imperial Germany. Eugene Edward found himself transferred to an artillery unit and on his way to France.

His unit saw combat and the carnage that typified "The War to End All Wars," but further details are unavailable. Like so many men who have gone through combat, Papa rarely talked about his experiences, and what little he did say did not encourage the asking of details.

It is known that near the very end of the war he had been gassed and spent the Armistice lying in a pew in a French country church waiting for medical assistance. After a time in the hospital, he returned to the United States. The only surviving Army document that gives us any information is a faded pay record from 1920. It shows that on October 1, 1919, Eugene Edward Roddenberry was honorably discharged a private and reenlisted at Camp Meade, Maryland, where he was promoted to Sergeant, Fourth Grade. He was sent back to Fort Bliss as part of F Troop, 8th Cavalry.[2]

In El Paso he began dating a local girl. Fortunately for Glen, Eugene's new flame was a friend of hers, and one day she brought him by to show him off. In the three years since their first meeting, Glen had grown and changed. No longer a child, she was a gorgeous young woman of fifteen. The "old" girlfriend was quickly forgotten and the two began dating. What had begun as a child's crush blossomed and grew into adult love.

By October, Eugene, who had considered making the military a career, found himself mustered out almost exactly a year after reenlisting and receiving his promotion. He was again out of a job—thanks, it seemed, to the hated Republicans.

The surviving pay records note that Eugene's commanding officer characterized his service as excellent and found him eligible for a $90 bonus. With accumulated sergeant's pay, travel allowance, and bonus, minus $2.20 he owed to another soldier, Eugene found himself along with thousands of other exsoldiers on the street with minimal skills and $258.60 in his pocket. With his natural intelligence and self-confidence, this temporary setback was not going to change his plans. One month later, on November 3, 1920, Eugene married his "little sweetheart" in a simple ceremony in her parents' home. She was three months shy of her seventeenth birthday. Ten months later, Eugene Wesley Roddenberry was

---

[2]Gene's mother recalled that Gene told her a friend was developing a new television program about the cavalry and needed a name. Gene suggested his father's old troop designation. This is how the television comedy, *F Troop* received its name.

born. As Glen always joked, "At least I had a month, so Gene was perfectly legal."

Economically, times were tough in El Paso. With the Army cutting back, there were fewer soldiers spending money in town. Glen and Eugene lived in a small apartment at the beginning of their marriage, but when Eugene lost his job with the railroad, they had to move in with her parents. He managed to get a lineman's job just before Gene was born, and was listed as such on Gene's birth certificate.[3] While it was gainful employment, neither Gene nor Glen saw any future in working as a lineman, nor did they see much of a future in El Paso. They set their sights on the West and the opportunities they'd heard about in Southern California.

Roddenberry lore has it that in order to save money Eugene rode the rails to California. He wore a suit all the while, doing his best to look the gentleman. This, he hoped, would save him a beating at the hands of the railroad detectives, many of whom took pleasure in harassing hobos. He had been a railway cop himself and knew how they thought.

It took several months but Eugene was successful. In March 1923, he sent for his family. It was an adventure for both the nineteen-year-old mother and her nineteen-month-old son. Neither of them had ever been out of El Paso. Gene, talking baby talk, was dressed up in his finest for the trip. Glen remembers him charming the train employees. The trip was a day and a night, short and relatively comfortable for a coach seat, but Glen and Gene's journey was longer than they thought: they were going from the old world of El Paso to the new world of Southern California.

---

[3]Record-keeping in 1921 El Paso was less efficient than it is today, and Gene was a victim of bureaucratic inefficiency right at the beginning of his life. His middle name was incorrectly spelled as "Westley" and his mother's maiden name incorrectly spelled "Goldman" on his birth certificate.

CHAPTER 2

Los Angeles was Papa Roddenberry's destination. It was a city very different from El Paso, a city constantly reinventing itself, continually reshaping itself into an ever more complex human tapestry. When Papa arrived in 1922, Los Angeles was just coming of age. It had long been a sleepy village, its potential limited by the sparse fourteen-inch annual rainfall.

The city languished until nineteenth-century medicine announced a correlation between health and climate. Thousands of consumptives flocked to the area looking for a cure. Medicine may have suffered a loss in credibility, but the local funeral industry enjoyed a small boom. Regardless of the efficacy of cure, national attention to the area's temperate climate was the beginning of the Southern California myth.

The growth that lured Poppa was the result of careful planning begun years before. In the late 1800's a small oligarchy of powerful local businessmen[1] came together and created The Los Angeles Suburban Homes Company. This company eventually held options on thousands of acres of vacant land in the San Fernando Valley. If Los Angeles was to grow and prosper, these men would see to it that it would grow and prosper on their land.

Their plan was simple. The height of buildings in Los Angeles would be limited—guaranteeing that the city would

---

[1]Principally, Harrison Gray Otis, editor and publisher of the *Los Angeles Times*, E.H. Harriman, president of the Southern Pacific Railroad, Henry E. Huntington of the Pacific Electric Railroad, plus other local businessmen.

expand out instead of up—and a source of cheap water developed.

By the time Poppa Roddenberry arrived, the city had grown to over 600,000 and there were no signs that growth would stop.

The Southern California myth became a new American dream. It did not matter that most of the California myth was nonsense: the opportunities and the climate were real.

Papa found that what he had heard in El Paso was true. Los Angeles was badly in need of policemen. Bodies were needed to patrol the streets, and emergency appointments to the department sped up the normally slow Civil Service process. Because of the need, selection was left to recruiters. Principal requirements for being an emergency policeman were "large" and "intelligent." In the absence of reasonable intelligence, "large" would do. Fortunately, Papa was both smart and almost six feet tall.

On December 7, 1922, Eugene Edward Roddenberry became an emergency appointee to the Los Angeles Police Department. By July 1, 1923, he had taken and passed the Civil Service test and received a proper commission. He wore badge number 991.

With thousands pouring into California, old societal conventions, moral restrictions, and antiquated formalities that were followed in the East and the South were only occasionally applied in Southern California. People could be anything they wanted to be. Some took that more literally than others. Los Angeles became a wide open city and many took full advantage.

It is no small coincidence that the motion picture industry, founded by hard-edged businessmen whose only product was fantasy and make-believe, located and thrived in Southern California. No business better epitomized the new myth. No business capitalized on it more. The small, nearby town of Hollywood became the focal point for the dreams and aspirations of millions of Americans and much of what happened there would affect Los Angeles in no small way.

Just before the Papa arrived, the Los Angeles newspapers carried a story that illustrated the Los Angeles/ Hollywood connection at its sordid best:

William Desmond Taylor had been murdered in his bungalow court home on Alvarado Street, shot in the heart by someone he knew. While Taylor's body lay dead on his living room floor, two of the biggest stars of the day, Mabel Normand and Mary Miles Minter, both former Taylor lovers, searched his house for incriminating love letters. They were assisted by executives from the Famous Players-Lasky Studios.[2] The studio had been notified *before* the police. Once the scene had been sanitized to the studio's and stars' satisfaction, the police were called.

Assimilation into the police department was relatively easy for Papa because of his work as a railroad detective in El Paso and his experience as a cavalry sergeant. Papa became a patrolman, the backbone of every police department. He would stay at that rank for twenty years.

Papa, Glen, and Little Gene lived in a succession of rented houses and the Roddenberry family grew. In 1924, Robert Leon was born, and in late 1925 the third and final Roddenberry child, Doris Willowdean,[3] completed the family. "The first five years I was married," Glen recalls, "all I did was wash diapers."

Wanting to insulate his family from the realities of life in downtown, he kept the family across the Los Angeles River in Glassell Park. Papa and Glen bought their first home, a two-bedroom Craftman-style house that sat on an agriculturally-zoned half acre at 3243 Drew Street. It was two short blocks from the famous cemetery Forest Lawn in a very quiet neighborhood.

In the twenties and thirties, two of the things Los Angeles would later become world famous for, smog and traffic, were virtually nonexistent. The air was clear and clean, and the mountains that surround the L.A. basin were almost always visible. Freeways and gridlock were nonexistent because anyplace you wanted to go was easy to get to and the roads weren't crowded. There was fast, efficient, and inexpensive rapid transit available.[4] Perhaps most important,

---

[2]Lasky Studios later became Paramount Studios.

[3]The name "Willowdean" comes from her maternal grandmother, Lydia. Caroline Glen remembers, "I didn't have my daughter named Willowdean, but when I showed her to my mother she said, 'Well, she's Doris Willowdean.' I had no intention of naming her Doris Willowdean, but my mother wasn't someone you crossed very often. My mother also named Gene after his father and her father, but she didn't name Bob. I got to do that, but only because my mother wasn't around when Bob was born."

[4]Southern California was crisscrossed by rail lines served by Pacific Electric Red Cars. There was virtually no place in the Los Angeles Basin that was not served

there were a lot fewer people living in Los Angeles during Gene's youth. As Gene grew up on Drew Street, the city went from just under 600,000 to double that by 1930. While Gene attended junior high and high school, an additional 300,000 made Los Angeles home. Today, the city's population is over 3.5 million.

Glassel Park was a middle-class/working-class area that had been built just after World War I. It was five miles north of downtown and a world away from its troubles. Or so Papa thought.

But early one morning:

"Mrs. Roddenberry! Mrs. Roddenberry!" the voice cried out, punctuated by a loud and rapid pounding on the side door.

"Mrs. Roddenberry," the voice became more insistent, "your house is on fire!"

Although sound asleep, those urgent words snapped Glen instantly awake. Beyond the voice and the pounding, she could smell smoke and hear the crackling of burning lumber. Her mind focused sharply on one thought: save her children. The responsibility was all hers as Papa was away—his lack of seniority had him working the graveyard shift.

Gene and Bob were toddlers, asleep in their room, Doris in her crib in the living room. Glen hurried—first to Gene and Bob, who were already waking up from the noise of the man pounding on the door. She grabbed Bob, who was too young to walk fast enough. Herding Gene ahead of her, she ran to the living room, scooped Doris out of her crib, and rushed out the front door into the cool safety of the early morning.

The neighbors, awakened by the ruckus, called the fire department, who arrived within minutes. As the sun was peeking over the eastern horizon, Papa came home from work in time to see firemen dousing the last of the flames.

The cause of the fire was a careless match from a pipe-smoking visitor the night before. It had ignited the stuffing in the couch, which had smouldered for hours, finally bursting into flames in the early morning. Tragedy had been averted by the Roddenberry's milkman. He had spotted the

by this system. The city boasted trolley cars and electric buses. All this was dismantled in the late 1940's and 1950's, when the individually owned automobile became king.

smoke and flames while delivering that morning's milk. Without his intervention, Glen and the children would have likely perished. For all the years they lived in that area, the Roddenberry family always ordered an ample supply of milk.

Gene was an unusually self-assured little boy, with verbal skills and intelligence beyond his years. His mother remembered one instance when Gene was four or five:

"Little Gene and I were out for some reason or another near Downtown when Gene saw a policeman.

"Hello," Gene said, and the policeman said hello back. Gene began talking to the officer.

"Do you have anybody down at the police station that looks like me?" he asked very clearly.

The policeman, not quite understanding what this self-possessed little boy was getting at, said, "Well, I don't know."

Gene replied, "Well, you do and he's my daddy. His name is Roddenberry and he looks just like me!"

While Gene's intelligence and self-assurance always made his young mother's life interesting, sometimes it was more interesting than she wanted.

One afternoon, when Gene was five or six, Glen saw that he was drinking a bottle of soda, something she knew she did not have in the house. Glen asked Gene where he got it. "The corner grocery store," was the nonchalant reply. On further questioning, Glen learned that her bright son had decided he wanted a soda. So, while she was busy in the back of the house, he opened the front door and walked down to the corner grocery store.

When Glen asked Gene how he paid for the soft drink, he confidently replied, "I charged it."

Everyone in the neighborhood knew he was the son of a policeman, who would be good for the money. However, lest he develop a habit of charging anything he wanted, Glen took him back to the store and told the owner Gene's charge account was closed.

Gene attended the nearby Estara Avenue School, renamed Fletcher Drive Elementary during his attendance in 1928. School was exciting and interesting for Gene, but it was not always pleasant. Over sixty years later he would remember one elementary school experience in particular, one that permanently resonated in his memory. It was an early lesson for Gene in how to deal with authority and still remain his own person. This experience also set in place a dislike of confrontation which, later in life, would cost him dearly. Here, in one seemingly minor incident, we can see the beginnings of an outlook that allowed Gene to be that most unusual combination—a pragmatic artist:

"I learned fairly early in life that great honesty about things could give you trouble, cause you problems. I started being dishonest in that way quite young.

"I remember a time in about the fourth grade where a teacher got it into her head that I had skipped a stair—a crime. I honestly hadn't, but she kept after me and kept after me. I tried to analyze this in my own young way: what was the point of insisting on honesty? I finally said, ashamedly, 'Well, I guess I didn't notice that I had skipped that stair, but now that I think about it, I did.' She was off my case from then on.

"What was my insistence on total honesty about?

"I had nothing to gain by keeping her on my back. I felt as long as I knew the difference between what really happened and what I said, it was of small import.

"In a strange way, you can be honest and dishonest with your inner self. We are in many ways, I've often thought, two people. As long as the inner person believes and admits that decency is good, the outer person who has to deal with the world, and not always a fair world, is allowed to slip. I suppose that I have thought all my life that the only real person was the inner me."

As the Roddenberry family grew, so did Los Angeles. In 1922, the Los Angeles Philharmonic opened the Hollywood Bowl for its first season, and radio stations KHJ and KFI began broadcasting. That same year the Rose Bowl was completed just outside Pasadena. A year later, the Memorial Coliseum (destined to be the site of two Olympiads) opened in Exposition Park, and the famous Hollywood sign was erected advertising a housing development known as Hollywoodland. (It was shortened years later to read simply: Hollywood.) The University of California at Los Angeles (UCLA) was dedicated in 1926, as was the Los Angeles Public Library on West Fifth Street. The completion of City Hall at 200 North Spring Street took place in 1928. By 1930, the year Gene turned nine, the population of the city had doubled to nearly 1.25 million.

Los Angeles is also called "The City of the Angels." In the Roaring Twenties and days of the Depression this was a striking misnomer. While the chamber of commerce advertised "opportunity in the land of sunshine," Los Angeles also became the background and inspiration for the stories that formed the "hard-boiled dick" genre of fiction, typified by Raymond Chandler and his knight-errant detective, Phillip Marlowe.

Day or night, anyone with the necessary cash could easily obtain sex of any variety, illegal alcohol, cocaine, marijuana, or morphine. There were more than a thousand brothels, bookie joints, and gambling parlors around the city.

All this went on with a wink and a nod from the political and legal establishment of Los Angeles. In essence, there were two police forces: the men on the street who did the real police work, of which the senior Roddenberry was a part—he was commended numerous times for efficiency, courtesy and cooperation by the local citizenry—and the crooks who carried badges, who were mostly downtown in the vice, narcotics, and intelligence squads.

In spite of his many years in the city, Papa remained a country boy. While they lived on Drew Street, he put up rabbit hutches around the backyard and raised chickens. When the rabbits hit a certain age, Papa would box them up and send the kids out to sell them. Standing at the corner of Fletcher Drive and San Fernando Road, Gene and Bob would sell their stock. Business was especially good at Easter, when they would get twenty-five cents for the regular rabbits and thirty-five cents for the Angoras.

The rabbits were the inspiration for Gene's first published writing, a poem written when he was ten, under the watchful eye of Adelia Osborne, his teacher at Fletcher Drive Elementary School. Miss Osborne thought enough of Gene's effort that she had it published in *The Ace,* a tabloid-sized newspaper the school put out twice a year. There, on a page crowded with juvenile prose as "My First Fishing Trip," "Poems from Room 4," "My Big Tree," next to ads for Lester M. Jones, Druggist, the W.W. Freeman Detective Agency, (With Agents All 'Round the World), The Blue Moon Cafe

(Specializing in Chili and Short Orders), is the poem by the fifth grader.

My Greedy Rabbit

My little rabbit
Has a greedy habit
Of eating the hay
When the others play.

—Eugene Roddenberry, B5

For Gene, life in Glassell Park was idyllic, its grass-covered hills provided unlimited places for a young boy to explore and exercise his imagination. One year Gene formed a club with several friends and called it the S.O.S. Club—"Seven Old Saps." Not one of them was over ten. His brother, Bob, was vice-president. Gene, of course, was president.

Even though it was seemingly a world away from the troubles downtown, reality still intruded. During the Depression, members of the LAPD rank and file were forced to take a ten-percent pay cut to avoid layoffs. Papa and Glen bought their home and raised their children on less than $200 a month.

In 1933, when Gene was 12, Bob 10, and Doris 8, the family moved two miles over Mt. Washington, east to Highland Park. Papa and Glen bought another Craftman-style home, a modest, three-bedroom house with detached garage at 4906 Monte Vista. The house was just a hundred yards from where Monte Vista made a sharp curve and turned into Marmion Way, in the shadow of Mt. Washington. The W-Street car line went right past Gene's front door. The neighborhood was middle and working class, similar to Glassel Park and built at about the same time. This neighborhood was also about five miles northeast of downtown and convenient to Papa's work. From this house Gene attended Burbank Junior High School, Franklin Senior High School, and Los Angeles City College. He always considered it the house he grew up in.

What Papa protected his family from by living over the hill from downtown, what he saw happening almost daily, ultimately played itself out on the radio and in the pages of the local newspapers all through Gene's childhood and adolescence. The drama that unfolded was an odd counterpoint to the Andy Hardy/Our Gang childhood Gene lived and added more tiles to the mosaic of his personality.

Papa, then working in the Downtown Traffic Division, watched the scandals happen with amusement and satisfaction. His devotion to his own ethical standard had proved correct. He was untouched by them. His supervisor, Sergeant William H. Parker, became a friend of the Roddenberry family and would figure importantly in both Gene's life and that of the Los Angeles Police Department years later when other scandals would erupt.

None of the morality plays were lost on Gene as he went through school. What happened to those who publicly adhered to strong moral principles was remembered.

The regularity of Papa's income, while modest, made the Roddenberrys one of the more affluent families in their working-class neighborhood. Papa shared the wealth. Rarely did a Sunday go by without a large gathering at the Roddenberry home. Glen often cooked for twenty or more. During the week, Papa would make up boxes of food to give to those who needed it. On one occasion he took a homeless boy off the streets and housed, fed, and clothed him for several months until the young man got on his feet. Papa did not see this as charity. It was something strong men did for those who could not help themselves. It was something he had learned as a child.

Gene Roddenberry was very much his father's son. Perhaps the best illustration of this is Gene's receipt of a letter during the first season of *Star Trek*. It was from two elderly women in Florida. They had seen his name on the show and said they remembered meeting him when he was in New York on his way to fight in World War I. During their meeting he had talked so much about the future and how it would be that the two women weren't a bit surprised to see him producing a program like *Star Trek*. They had mistaken Gene for his father.

Much of Gene's character was formed by emulating the better qualities of his father while rejecting other traits entirely. It was as if Gene were continually watching his father and listening to his own internal voice, weighing one against the other and resolving the conflict through personal experience. In spite of their differences, Glen would describe her husband and son as "two peas in a pod."

Gene could not help but notice the disparity in his father's duty as a policeman and his attitude towards the Volstead Act, commonly known as Prohibition. Passed as the Eighteenth Amendment to the U.S. Constitution in 1919, and in force until its repeal by the Twenty-first Amendment in 1933, the Volstead Act proscribed the importation, sale, and use of alcohol. This "great experiment" in social engineering was a failure from the beginning and many believe it laid the foundation for the establishment of organized crime in this country. People thought it was a good law for everyone except themselves, and this included most of the police sworn to enforce it. The law was widely ignored, and Papa ignored it in a very specific way.

Bob Roddenberry remembers:

"Pop was a social drinker and had a drink every night before dinner, even through Prohibition. He made his own beer and stored it under a rug-covered trap door in the back porch. It was cool down there and out of sight as well. He also made root beer for the kids, partly as a bribe so we wouldn't talk about his beer. Occasionally, on hot summer nights, one of the corks would let go and a loud *pop* would be heard all over the house. The pungent aroma of homemade beer would waft through our house for several hours.

"It was always very funny."

Gene's father had a willingness to play a prank or tell a joke if there was someone convenient to play it on. It was always on someone else. A favorite target was his brother-in-law, Clint Higgins, or "Hickey" as he liked to call him. Papa never missed an opportunity to needle Hickey who was married to Glen's youngest sister, Willowdean. During World War II Papa and Glen lived on an agriculturally zoned half acre on Green Street in Temple City. Papa raised corn, chickens, and had a pig . . . named "Hickey."

Papa was a character. One evening, just as dinner was ending, Glen was putting the dirty dishes in the sink when the phone rang. Clint and Dean were coming over. Papa realized that meant Clint would get some of Glen's great pie, which meant less pie for him. He hurriedly gobbled down all that was left. Sitting in his favorite chair, his belt loosened, his stomach swelling, Papa had a stomachache through the evening, but there was no pie for Hickey.

On other occasions, Clint and Papa would have contests to see who could eat the most cake or pie. Papa invariably won, usually to his stomach's dismay.

Papa was usually right most of the time and would go to great lengths to prove so. He would rarely concede a point, even the most minor. One day, when Bob was about ten, and the family had just moved to Highland Park, Papa and Clint got into an argument over how far away the El Roy Theater was from the new house on Montevista. Papa said he could walk the distance, about two miles, in just fifteen minutes. Clint immediately took the bet. Papa turned to his son and said, "Come on, Bob. Let's go!," and took off walking with his long policeman's stride. Bob remembers the incident: "I'll bet I ran that whole damn two miles just to keep up with my dad. He won the bet but I was one exhausted kid."

There was no question that Papa was the king of his own roost. His attitude was simple: he was the male, he brought home the paycheck, so he expected things to be done his way . . . and they were. Glen wore her hair long all through their marriage because that's the way Papa liked it. Papa drove a 1931 Chevrolet and when he came home to the Montevista house each evening, he would sound the horn as he turned the corner and headed for the garage around back in the alley. Heaven help the Roddenberry child who did not make a quick appearance to open the garage door for him. Physical punishment was unusual, but Papa's displeasure was worse. None of the children wanted a tongue-lashing from Papa.

Papa believed that work made for good character, and he got his boys jobs after school and on Saturdays. One job for Gene was delivering papers. When Gene moved on to working in a gas station, the paper delivery job went to Bob. When Gene graduated high school and went to Los Angeles City College, Bob inherited the gas station job as well. The after-school work gave the boys some cash and kept them from bothering their father for money. It also taught them responsibility and character.

Papa's definition of family fun wasn't necessarily shared. Weekend fishing trips often saw him take Bob or Gene to Lake Hodges, with the boys thinking they were going fishing. In a way, they were. At the lake their father had a small fishing boat with a five-horsepower motor attached, but instead of firing up the engine, he turned to whichever of his two male children were with him and gave them the oars. The lucky youngster, Bob would have been eleven, and Gene, thirteen, at this time, rowed the boat out into the middle of the lake while their father fished. Papa would catch the limit for both of them. The number of fish he caught was only limited by how many of his children he brought along.

When Gene and Bob were in their early teens, Papa took them dove hunting. Papa had a full choke 12-gauge shotgun and Gene and Bob each had small .410-gauge shotguns. After suitable safety instructions, father and sons tramped through the underbrush, hunting the elusive quarry.

Papa directed Bob to go off to the left about a half a mile, and Gene was directed to go about the same distance to his father's right. The boys were told to walk toward their father, all the while making noise. Papa shot doves all afternoon, charging hunting limits to each of the boys as well as himself. Bob and Gene never shot their guns at anything.

The 1930's were in some ways a more innocent time and in other ways a meaner, more intolerant time than today. Much of what one experienced depended on one's ethnic background and sexual orientation.

Gene attended Franklin High School. Pictures in Gene's year books show a few scattered Asian and Latino faces among his schoolmates, but no African Americans in the school population or on the faculty. Indeed, there were few blacks in the population of Los Angeles in the twenties and early thirties, the big influx arriving in the late thirties and during World War II.

The small black population in Los Angeles knew their place, and if they didn't, they were quickly reminded in no uncertain terms. They knew which areas they could freely travel in and what areas were off-limits.

African Americans also knew where they could buy real estate and where they could not. Los Angeles, the place where you could live the American dream, was as segregated as any Southern town.

This matched Papa's outlook on life. While intelligent and farsighted in many ways, Gene's father was a child of the South, who brought his ingrained cultural and racist viewpoint with him to Los Angeles.[5] African Americans were "niggers," Jews were "kikes," and, of course, the worst of all were the detested Republicans. In their home, the word "Republican" was banned entirely. Papa's attitude was not something that was open for debate. It was, for him, a cultural norm—not how things should be, but how they were and would continue to be. He had grown up with this cultural bias and no amount of heated discussion or argument with his oldest son would change it.

The roots of the humanistic philosophy that would prove so appealing on *Star Trek* began here, with Gene's attempt to understand his father's contradictory behavior—Papa's love for his family and his professed intolerance of certain minorities.

Education, travel, rational thought, knowing people of other races and cultures, and his measurement of his father's ideas against his own internal logic had their effect on Gene. He grew up free of his father's burden of bigotry. Over thirty years in the future, Gene would create a program that broadcast television's first interracial kiss.[6] His father lived to see the program, but the two men never discussed the episode.

It was only during the preparation of material for this book that Gene came to understand that his father was a far greater influence on him than he had previously realized or cared to admit.

To see and accept Papa Roddenberry as a complete but flawed human being is a first step towards understanding his son's philosophy. To recognize Papa's ingrained decency to his family is another. Papa was a man who, in twenty years of police work, never became calloused to the suffering of

---

[5]Papa's attitude seemed to be at odds with others in his family still in the Deep South. He was related to the Georgia Roddenberys (spelled with one "r"), a large and distinguished family, and remained in correspondence with them throughout his life. The Georgia-based, family-held company, Roddenbery's, had, since the late 1800's, produced a cane sugar product known as "Nigger In 'De Cane Patch Syrup." The can's label carried a picture of a small black child in a cane patch. In the 1920's they changed the name to "Cane Patch Syrup," fully forty years before the civil rights movement swept the country.

[6]*Star Trek*, the original series, third season, "Plato's Stepchildren," air date 11/22/68. The Enterprise crew encounters the Platonians, a race of strong telekinetics. For their own amusement, the platonians force the crew to "perform" like living puppets. Captain Kirk is forced to kiss Lieutenant Uhura. Ironically, this episode was directed by David Alexander (no relation).

children. Often he would come home and be unable to eat dinner because an incident involving a child had upset him.

Today Papa would be viewed as something of a chauvinist—domineering and self-centered. In the twenties and thirties, when women were only at the beginning of their liberation, Papa was looked upon as a good husband, a good father, and a good provider.

Certainly Glen thought so. Their marriage lasted, until his death, a month short of 49 years.

CHAPTER 3

No one who lived through the trauma of the Great Depression will ever forget the hard times. Intelligent and able-bodied men—one out of four in the work force—men who weren't afraid of hard work, were unable to find any job to support their families. It was a humiliating and humbling time, yet many rose to the occasion. It was in the Depression that Gene learned the meaning of the phrase, "Events don't make the man, they reveal him."

The country had gone from boom to bust, a fact not lost on Gene and his family. Unlike most who lived in their neighborhood, the Roddenberrys were not effected directly. The Depression hurt relatives, friends, and neighbors, but not Papa. He was protected against the vagaries of hard economic times by the Civil Service and his intelligence in keeping away from graft on the police force. The Rodden-berry household was a rare oasis of comparative affluence in an economic desert. Papa Roddenberry wasn't affluent due to the size of his paycheck, but because he *had* a paycheck. Papa and Glen could not ignore what happened to the rest of their family and friends. Papa distributed boxes of food, and every Sunday Glen cooked for a large contingent of family and friends.

Gene, his brother, and later their sister, all went to Luther Burbank Junior High School at the corner of Meridian and Figueroa, two miles north of the house on Monte Vista. The yellow trolley line rumbled down the middle of Monte Vista, right in front of the Roddenberry house. The fare to school was three and a half cents. Each morning Papa gave Gene and Bob seven cents for the two-mile ride to school, but Papa's generosity did not extend to the afternoon. The boys got to walk home. Papa saved seven cents and the walk would build character—or so he claimed—and would be a reminder to the children that they were living through hard times. Another reminder was the occasional classmate who came to school barefoot. Most of the children knew what that meant, knew it could easily be them without shoes in a week or a month, so no unkind comments were made.

Where did Gene's propensity to write strange and unusual stories come from? Most would say it was a combination of his father's influence, Gene's own innate curiosity and intelligence, his omnivorous reading, and exposure to *Flash Gordon* serials at the movies. Gene's lifelong friend, Ray Johnson, tells a different story.

Ray lived on Malta, the next street over from Monte Vista. He and Gene were the same age. Just after Gene and family had moved into the neighborhood, Ray and some other local kids had decided to build a tree house in a large pepper tree on a vacant lot on Monte Vista. Some of the kids scared up the wood from various odd sources. Ray was the carpenter, up in the tree, hammering the boards together as the kids brought them over.

Ray had seen Bob in the neighborhood earlier, but this was the first time he'd encountered Gene, who'd come over to introduce himself and see what was going on. Florence, the girl who lived next-door to Ray, was also in the tree when Gene came by.

Gene wanted a closer look at what Ray was doing.

"I'm coming up," he hollered from below. Florence was protective of Ray's work and wanted no part of Gene in the tree. She told him to stay on the ground. He started to climb anyway.

Florence was adamant. She picked up a hammer, held it aloft, and yelled out, "Eugene, if you try to climb up here, I'll drop this hammer on your head."

Gene paid no attention to the threat and kept coming. Unfortunately for Gene, Florence's aim was as true as her threat. The hammer hit Gene square on the top of his head and he fell back, knocked to the ground, legs splayed out, surprised and hurt. Trying to salvage as much dignity as he could, he went home without saying another word. He ended up with a knot on his head as big as a golf ball.

After Gene became famous, Florence joked that the hammer she dropped had started Gene's career.

In spite of the odd introduction, Ray, Gene, and Bob began a friendship that continued lifelong. Ray came to think of the Roddenberry house as a second home. He remembered learning to play Monopoly there, and another game and a lesson in kindness one afternoon:

"It was a Saturday afternoon and Gene had the idea for us to go to the movies. The matinee only cost a dime. I went home to find a dime, but by the time I got the money and got back to their house, Mrs. Roddenberry was just coming back from dropping them off at the theater. I guess they thought I wasn't going to go with them. Anyway, I was real disappointed and Mrs. Roddenberry could see that on my face. She asked me if I knew how to play cribbage and I told her I didn't know what that was. So, she taught me and we spent the rest of the afternoon playing. We enjoyed it so much we were still playing at 5:30 when Gene and Bob walked in from the theater."

For over sixty years, Ray has remembered Glen's kindness.

From childhood on, Gene was a voracious reader. The twenties and thirties provided him with plenty of material. The pulps were inexpensive magazines, named for their use of the very cheapest paper available, so cheap that readers occasionally found small wood splinters imbedded in the pages. The pulps influenced two generations of American writers, those who wrote for them and those who read them.

Every month hundreds of stories that ranged from the lurid to the fantastic were churned out. There was something for almost every reader's taste. The largest company was Street & Smith, which put out thirty-five titles, including *The Shadow, Doc Savage, Detective Story, Love Story, Western Story, Sport Story, Wild West Weekly,* and many others. The Frank A. Munsey Company, the company that began pulp publishing in 1896, produced *Argosy, All-Story, Railroad Stories,* and *Detective Fiction Weekly.*[1] Popular Publications produced a knock-off of *The Shadow* called *The*

---

[1] Munsey converted the children's magazine, *Golden Argosy* into *Argosy,* an all-adventure publication that was aimed at male readers.

Spider, as well as *Operator #5, Dime Detective, Dime West-ern,* and *Adventure.* There were a dozen other publishers and at least 150 different pulp titles.

The pulps spawned an entire generation of American writers: Dashiell Hammett, Carroll John Daly, H. Bedford-Jones (who wrote under ten names and was called "King of the Woodpulps"), H.P. Lovecraft, Raymond Chandler, Jack London, Tennessee Williams, Sinclair Lewis (the Nobel Prize winning Lewis worked as associate editor of *Adventure*), Frederick Schiller Faust (who wrote under the name Max Brand), Isaac Asimov, Ray Bradbury, and Erle Stanley Gardner, with whom Bedford-Jones happily shared his title.[2]

Decried as anything but literature by the critics, ignored by college English curriculums, the pulps were almost universally reviled . . . until they were gone. Then they became a bastion of American genre writing, part of our social and literary heritage.[3]

Gene could become lost while reading the pulps. One of his favorite places to satisfy his voracious reading appetite was out of the way of the household clamor on the old sofa Papa had put on the front porch of the Monte Vista house. Often Ray would find Gene on the couch, legs curled off to his left, right elbow on the sofa's arm, his right cheek firmly supported by his right hand, a book in his lap, deeply absorbed in *Amazing Stories*[4] or its arch-competitor, *Astounding Stories.*[5] Gene would be off in the stars with Richard

---

[2] By 1933 Bedford-Jones and Gardner were acknowledged by *Life* magazine as the only two "$50,000 a year men" working in pulps. The pulps supported at least 1200 full-time and an unknown number of part-time writers in the depths of the Depression. Gardner's name became a draw on the cover. His creation of Perry Mason led him to become the world's best-selling author with his novels selling hundreds of millions of copies. He also figured prominently in Gene's early writing career.

[3] There was more than a little hypocrisy operating here, as *Black Mask,* the most prestigious of the mystery pulps, was secretly founded by critics George Jean Nathan and H.L. Mencken of *Smart Set* and *American Mercury,* because they needed the money. They never permitted their names to be used in the magazine. They sold the magazine when their $500 investment had grown to $100,000.

[4] *Amazing Stories* was founded by Hugo Gernsback in 1926. His editorial philosophy favored instructional stories that he thought would engender an interest in science through "scientifiction." The term later became "science fiction," or SF.

[5] *Astounding Science Fiction* began principally with action/adventure stories. Many historians of the genre say that the Golden Age of science fiction began in

Seaton, E.E. "Doc" Smith's scientist-hero from the *Skylark of Space,* oblivious to the street cars, traffic, and neighborhood children playing just a few feet away. Ray knew that he could walk up the steps and stand right next to him and Gene would not know he was there until Ray raised his voice or touched him.

This ability to lose himself in his imagination, which would later make him world famous, once almost got Gene killed. He and some friends were out driving when Gene went off thinking about something and lost his focus on the road. He nearly rear-ended a car stopped at an intersection. Only his friends' yelling brought him back to reality before a crash did.

Gene's attention to books also gave him a privacy rarely available in the Roddenberry household. For Papa, family came first, and that meant Glen's family, too. The Depression wreaked havoc on the already depressed economy of El Paso, so the Golemons began moving to Southern California. "My mother was a restless woman," she would remember without a sign of rancor or irritation at her parents' nomadic ways. At one point, the Drew Street household consisted of Glen, Papa, the three children, as well as Glen's parents and her younger sister, Willowdean. For a small, three-bedroom home it was a tight fit, but as it was the Depression and Papa had a steady job, the tight squeeze didn't matter. Gene grew up watching his father act the part of the strong, intelligent head of household, helping those less fortunate because it was the right thing to do—echoing the strong, heroic characters Gene found in the pulps.

Ultimately, Glen's parents bought a house in Redondo Beach. Throughout their childhood, Gene and Bob, sometimes with their sister, Doris Willowdean—"Willie"—visited their grandparents almost every other weekend. Summers would have them there weeks at a time. When the boys were older, they got to ride the streetcar all the way to the exotic confines of Redondo Beach by themselves. Just

---

Astounding, under the editorship of John W. Campbell, in July 1939, when he published A.E. Van Vogt's "Black Destroyer," and Isaac Asimov's "Trends." The next issue featured Robert Heinlein's debut, and the one after that, Theodore Sturgeon's. Asimov, Heinlein, Van Vogt, and Sturgeon, masters of the genre, would become Gene's friends. Sturgeon would write two scripts for Star Trek—"Amok Time" and "Shore Leave."

getting there was high adventure for two boys from Highland Park.

At their grandparent's house, Gene and Bob were usually up with the sun. They rushed through breakfast, much to Nana Golemon's concern, and without slowing their breakneck pace, the boys, sometimes accompanied by their cousin Bill, would run to the beach only blocks away. Their urgency was not a fear of missing any fun—it was business. For several hours the boys would dig and pour sand through a large strainer their grandfather had made, filtering out sand crabs and saving them in a bucket. When they had several dozen, they would walk over to the nearby fishing pier and sell the crabs to fishermen for bait—ten cents a dozen. Split two ways, or three if Bill was along, the boys had spending money for the day. Ice cream cones were a nickel, hot dogs a dime, and a Saturday afternoon matinee was also a dime. For Gene and the members of his generation, going to the movies then was nothing like going to the movies now.

Gene was born before Jolson[6] sang and Garbo[7] talked. His first trips to the cinema were spent watching silent films on his mother's lap. As he grew, so did film.

In Gene's youth, going to the movies was an experience on a grand scale. He saw them in movie palaces, replete with spacious lobbies, opulent wall decorations covered in gallons of gold paint, comfortable, velour-covered seats, spacious aisles, and deep, plush carpets. To people of limited means—which meant almost everyone during the Depression—the movie palaces with their massive crystal chandeliers were, next to what they saw on the screen, the closest the average person would come to wealth and glamour.

Gene, Bob, and Bill, for their ten-cent tickets, would have an entire afternoon of fantasy and adventure. The program

---

[6]It is generally accepted that the first talking picture was 1927's "The Jazz Singer" starring Al Jolson, one of the biggest stage entertainers of his time. Oddly enough, the bulk of the film was a silent with synchronized sound used only when Jolson sang.

[7]When silent films became talkies, a number of strong, virile appearing actors and sensual actresses were found to have small, nasal voices that did not match their screen characters. Many were laughed off the screen, their careers in tatters. Greta Garbo was a Swedish actress with a magnetic screen persona. She began in silents, and there was considerable concern that her heavy Swedish accent would destroy her career. Her first talkie was heralded by posters screaming, "Garbo Talks." It was great hype and audiences accepted her heavy accent.

usually began with a newsreel of the previous week's events, bringing pictures from all over the world to the local neighborhood. Very possibly it would be Fox Movietone News, narrated by the famous deep tones of newsman Lowell Thomas. Then there would be several cartoons featuring popular characters of the day: Popeye, Mickey Mouse, or Betty Boop.[8] A short subject would follow the cartoon—usually with motion picture contract players in disguised commercials for consumer products or a Hal Roach comedy short featuring Laurel and Hardy.

Leisure traveling was out of the question for most people, so a travelogue usually came at this point in the program. A multipart serial came next in 20-minute segments. The hero was always in jeopardy in the last seconds of each installment, creating enough curiosity to lure youngsters back to the theater the following week to see how the hero escaped.[9] Serials were a staple from the beginning of the film industry until the early 1950's.

Previews of coming attractions were next—some lasting as long as ten minutes. Then came not one but two features, the A feature and the B feature. The A feature is self-explanatory, but the B picture was a genre all to itself; they were the second features, with the less-famous actors and smaller budgets. Many fine actors began their careers in B pictures and managed to graduate to A picture work.[10]

---

[8]Betty Boop was the invention of Dave and Max Fleischer. Betty started out as a dog—literally—and evolved into a sexy female. An unlikely hit, Betty had a head that was as wide as her shoulders, no neck, no chin, a brief, sexy outfit that showed off her legs, and a tinkly voice that could shatter glass. Created before movie censorship became widespread, her material, somewhat risqué even today, was freely shown to youngsters of all ages in the thirties.

[9]A popular science fiction serial was *Flash Gordon.* Based on a comic strip begun by Alex Raymond in 1934, the strip featured an elaborate and detailed artistic style with fantastic plots and settings. Flash Gordon inspired a radio serial, a pulp magazine, and three film serials starring Larry "Buster" Crabbe. The first, made in 1936, was budgeted at $350,000, a huge sum for a serial. The second was *Flash Gordon's Trip to Mars* in 1938, followed by *Flash Gordon Conquers the Universe* in 1940. In 1951, Flash Gordon came to television in a mercifully brief run. Dino deLaurentis brought Flash to the movie screen most recently in 1980.

[10]A cowboy actor and USC football player named Marion Morrison is one good example. He changed his name to the more familiar John Wayne and eventually became an American icon.

With the Depression raging, people flocked to the movies for a few hours' escape from the mediocrity and limitations of their lives. When social critics commented that film did not depict real life, Myrna Loy, one of the biggest stars of the day, succinctly responded with the film makers' attitude: "Some people say the movies should be more like life. I say life should be more like the movies." Few who suffered through the Depression would disagree with her.

The 1930's was a decade of great heroes in books: Tarzan and John Carter of Mars were two of Gene's favorites.[11] He would remember E.E. "Doc" Smith's "Skylark" series[12] for over fifty years. Other great heros entered Gene's world through the radio. He learned to visualize his heros' adventures as he read them or heard them: vital, early training for the writer-to-be.

Gene, and many of his fellow writers who worked during television's Golden Age, shared the experience of growing up listening to radio in its Golden Age. Aptly named "the theater of the mind," radio transported listeners to other worlds and other times with nothing more than the spoken word and sound effects. Without the need to provide pictures, the simplest of devices could be used to stimulate the listener's imagination. Buck Rogers was a program not to be missed and Gene rarely did.[13] The other-worldly touch that started each broadcast, a dramatic hollow-echo vibrato

---

[11]Both Tarzan and John Carter were created by Edgar Rice Burroughs.

[12]E.E. "Doc" Smith is often called the "father of the space opera" genre of science fiction. He was influential in the American pulp market between 1928 and 1945. "The Skylark of Space" first appeared in *Amazing Stories* in the same issue as the introduction of Buck Rogers. Other "Skylark" stories appeared in both *Amazing Stories* and *Astounding Stories*.

[13]*Buck Rogers* was important in that it was the first American science fiction comic strip that was moderately adult and sophisticated in nature. It had been inspired by the novel *Armgeddon 2419,* by Philip Francis Nowlan, that appeared in *Amazing Stories* 1928–9. The comic strip began in 1929 and came to radio in 1931. The radio show lasted until 1939, but amazingly enough, the comic strip lasted until 1967. Noted for its futuristic gadgetry, the comic strip featured disintegrator rays and antigravity belts, and the serial had a nicely done matter transporter, predating *Star Trek*'s transporter by 27 years. Buck Rogers also affected other noted writers. Ray Bradbury once told Gene that he would get up early and sit on his front porch waiting for the morning newspaper to see what Buck did that day.

of Paul Douglas shouting, "Buck ... Rogers ... in the twenty-fifth ... CEN ... tury!" was accomplished by the distinguished announcer sticking his head into a grand piano.

Because the action occurred in the listeners' minds, virtually anything could be and was produced on the radio. For adults, radio was an endless fountain of comedy, drama, and culture, but for kids it was the source of great heros. Daily and weekly deeds of daring-do and altruistic heroism were served up to the nation's youngsters in fifteen or thirty-minute doses. Two programs Gene listened to regularly were *The Lone Ranger*[14] and *The Shadow*.[15]

Gene looked forward to Sundays because of the radio line-up, but he also dreaded the Christian Sabbath because it meant church—boring sermons about things he didn't believe in. He did it for his mother, but when it became possible not to go without hurting her feelings, he stopped.

Papa thought that the children should be exposed to religion, so each Sunday off to church they went. This was "do as I say" and not "do as I do," as Papa rarely found his own way to church. When he finally did, it was a unique experience.

On one such occasion, Glen persuaded Papa to attend an early evening church function. They hadn't been inside for more than a few moments when a strong earthquake struck.[16] The building shook and terrorized people ran into the street.

---

[14]*The Lone Ranger* was the brainchild of George W. Trendle and Fran Striker. Trendle imagined a program that was action-packed, a program that would inspire and instruct without emphasis on violence. He hired writer Fran Striker to create the program. The show was broadcast nationally from 1933 until 1954. Who today can listen to Rossini's stirring "William Tell Overture" and not think of The Lone Ranger?

[15]The Shadow, played forcefully on the radio by Orson Welles, and later by Bret Morrison, from 1944 to 1956, was one of the first crimefighters to have a secret identity and a believable "super" power, the ability to cloud men's minds. He was powerful, mysterious, invincible.

[16]March 10, 1933 at 5:55 P.M. and it became known as the "Long Beach Earthquake," as it killed 51 people in that seaside town by destroying many of the unreinforced brick buildings that made up the town. Over $8 million (1933 dollars) worth of private structures were also destroyed there. Years afterwards, the earthquake was determined to have been 6.3 on the Richter Scale. This earthquake was felt for hundreds of miles and forced changes in the state building codes. It was the end of unreinforced brick buildings in California.

While Papa didn't take the earthquake personally, it provided him a convenient excuse. It would be years before he attended church again.

Regardless of the continuing exposure as a child and his mother's firm Baptist beliefs, Gene's attitude towards religion was shaped by his clear understanding of his father's opinion of religion and the ministers who represented it.

"I came from a very religious family. We were from the South. Every Sunday we went to a local Baptist church. I didn't really take religion that seriously. It was obvious to me almost from the first, as a child, that there were certain things that really needed explaining and thinking on, but as life was interesting and pleasant, why bother about it?

"A great deal of my early religious training was due to my father, who, mysteriously, never showed up in church. I can remember now what things he had to say about religion. He did not think the church was particularly the guidance that he would have pushed me to have. He felt that it was good for me to go to church, but that I should be damn careful of what the ministers said.

"I think the first time I really became aware of religion, other than the little things you do as a child because Mom says to do it, was when I had gone to church—I was around sixteen and emerging as a personality—and I decided to listen to the sermon. I had never really paid much attention to the sermons before. I was more interested in the deacon's daughter and what we might be doing between sermons.

"I was listening to the sermon and I remember complete astonishment because what they were talking about were things that were just crazy. It was Communion time where you eat this wafer and you are eating the body of Christ and drinking His blood. My first impression was 'Jesus Christ! This is a bunch of cannibals they've put me down among!' For some time I puzzled over this and puzzled over why they were saying these things, because the connection between what they were saying and reality was very tenuous. How the hell did Jesus become something to be eaten?

"I guess from that time it was clear to me that religion was largely nonsense, was largely magical, superstitious things. In my own teen life I just couldn't see any point in adopting something based on magic, which was obviously phony and superstitious.

"So my thinking about religion sort of stultified at that time and I just decided not to pay any attention to it. I stopped going to church as soon as it became possible to do things on my own as a teenager. I made up my mind that church, and probably largely the Bible, was not for me. I did not go back to even thinking much about it. If people need to do that, ignore them and maybe they will ignore you and you can go on with your own life."

Self-assured as a boy, Gene grew into a self-assured young man. Classmates remember him as slightly apart from his fellows, as if he were always observing what was going on around him "through half-lidded eyes," as one classmate recalled. She expanded: "He moved around less, he sat longer in one place and contemplated more than any of the people that I knew. He was always thinking and observing. He was just a different kind of kid."

Highland Park, circa 1933, was a world apart from its incarnation today. The streets were safe, neighbors knew each other. There was a sense of community, a sense of safety, a sense of belonging to a time and a place.

Gene was daring and experimental. He had a New Year's Eve party when he was around thirteen, inviting a few girls and boys to his parents' home on Monte Vista. It was to be formal, or at least their idea of formal, something his friends had never heard of—ties for the boys and long dresses for the girls. Pat Bradley remembers walking the few blocks from her house to Gene's in an unfamiliar long dress. "Gene was the only one venturesome enough to do anything like this. For him it was quite plausible, what you did on New Year's Eve. None of the rest of us had done anything like this. I remember thinking that he was observing, taking everything in during the party.

"I always thought Gene's personality was operating in its own field. When I would talk to him he was most pleasant, interesting, making appropriate comments, but he truly was in a little bit of a world of his own making."

It was called the "Informal Group," and was an educational experiment, one of the first of its kind. It began with intelligence testing in junior high school and some intellectual segregation in high school. When Gene entered Franklin, he was grouped with twenty or so other students who had also scored well on the tests. Throughout high school, the students who had the highest IQs were kept together, sharing the same homeroom and two-hour social studies period, overseen by two teachers, Mrs. Hughes and Mrs. Stelter.

Babbie Bogue Still, a member of the Informal Group, remembers:

"At Franklin, the halls were safe and orderly, the classrooms controlled, and peer pressure was, aggressively, on the side of the angels. In spite of Dewey's baleful theories and influence, there was enough educational capital left that social promotion and the graduation of functional illiterates would have been totally unthinkable. Latter-day egalitarian attempts to equalize that which cannot be equalized had not overwhelmed Franklin. As we had the information on high authority, we, in the Informal Group, thought we were brighter than most of the rest of the class *but not better.* This is a crucial differentiation but I think we and the rest of the class of W'39 made it."

It was thought of the Informal Group that "peer pressure" and "mutual stimulation" would produce "something," as one of Gene's classmates recalled, but exactly what would come from the experiment, no one was quite sure. While the powers that be waited for something to happen they exposed the members of the Informal Group to a variety of cultural events, often at cut-rate prices. The class got to see a production of *Everyman* at the Hollywood Bowl after reading it in class. They often went to the foreign film theater in downtown; one student remembers seeing *Bolero.* The classmembers also had subscriptions to *Reader's Digest* which would stimulate class discussion. They read *The Melting Pot* and thought it true, and read *Hugh Wynne* and liked it because Cliff Wynne, a descendant, was in their class.

The Great Depression was raging, and Babbie remembered the social conditions that many of their friends lived in:

"There were some very gallant students amongst us, some young people experiencing terribly tough economic times.

Some Franklin students were facing grinding poverty, which they seemed to meet with enormous dignity and even grace. I remember an incident during my brief membership in the Girls' Rifle Club. I was pleased to be elected to their midst until I learned that the fiends expected me to get up at the crack of dawn and shoot a rifle, prone, sitting, and standing. Before I figured out how to resign, I went to a progressive dinner with the club. Our first stop was at the home of one of the officers. It was a tiny place in Highland Park, and the only furniture in the first room was the hostess' narrow metal bed. There was a meager collation in the bleak dining room. However, it *was* better than a stalled ox and I will never forget the pleasure the hostess and her mother took in sharing what they had nor the warmth of their welcome."

A peek inside the 1939 school annual, *The Almanac,* at the extracurricular activities shows how different high school in the late 1930's was from today. In addition to the usual academic clubs—Spanish, French, and Latin—there was the Needlework Guild; the Good Form Club ("a club for girls who wish to improve their poise and social grace"), and its corresponding club for boys, the Hi-Hatters; the Dancing Club ("formerly known as the Little Theater of the Dance, offers an opportunity for tenth-grade girls to learn the fundamentals of the most graceful of arts. . . . Ballroom, natural, ballet, and modern dancing by the sponsor"); and the Hook and Curve Club ("a club primarily for upper-grade commercial students, its purpose is to help solve some of the various social and economic problems, particularly those of interest to commercial majors").

Gene was a member of the International Forum ("Franklin's section of the World Friendship Club, designed to promote a better feeling among nations"), the Junto Club (". . . provides an outlet for students with forensic ability by sponsoring oratorical contests and debates"—Gene was the president for one semester), and the Spanish Club.

In their two-hour daily social studies class, the members of Informal Group were allowed to work on their own projects at their own pace. Gene was remembered as very patriotic by one student, but vigorous patriotism was the norm rather than the exception.

The Informal Group was an educational experiment with

no followup that we can locate today, but one can make this observation: Gene graduated in a class of less than 240, yet from that small group of people we have three world-class achievers: Gene, of course; Dr. Sammy Lee, the Olympic diving champion; and George Pimentel, a well-known chemist that some thought should have won the Nobel Prize.

Bob Atchison, a lifelong friend, remembers one day in the eleventh grade. Gene had not been doing well in school, his grades were down, and he was not living up to his potential. His parents had talked to him—not giving a lecture, but expressing their natural concern. Gene spent some time thinking and reached a conclusion. He turned to his friend and said, "Bob, I'm going to make something of myself."

Franklin High School annuals tell the rest of the story. From an anonymous eleventh grader who participated in few school activities, Gene's personality blossomed in his senior year. He became a social, political, and academic achiever. In the graduating glass of 1939, his picture is prominent as the Boy's Social Chairman. In addition to the other activities previously mentioned, Gene was a member of the Varsity Debate team—its manager for a semester—and a member of the Authors' Workshop.

In English class, and as part of the extracurricular Authors' Workshop, Gene came under the influence of Mrs. Virginia Church, an extraordinary woman who, by 1939, had become an institution at Franklin. Virginia Church was a teacher right out of Central Casting, personifying the classic definition of a teacher in the twenties and thirties: genteel, refined, educated, ever patient, and concerned about each student's progress. She was educated at Smith College and took her masters degree at Boston University. She had additional studies at Columbia, Harvard, and Queen's College, Oxford. She married Colonel John Church who, like her, was a writer, playwright, and critic. She began her teaching career at Franklin in 1920, when she accepted the post of Head of the English Department, a position she held until her retirement in 1945. While she possessed a strong intellectual vigor, she never displayed anything but the kindest of attitudes towards her students. Her literary criticism was precise, yet gently delivered lest young and delicate egos be bruised. It was her goal to inspire self-confidence.

Mrs. Church was the faculty sponsor of the Authors' Workshop and was herself the published author of a novel and two volumes of poetry, as well as a contributor to various magazines of the day. She was a member of the Writers' Guild and the Drama League.

Through Mrs. Church's teaching, Gene was exposed to thinking about writing and literary criticism. Through her he learned that literature can be written on several levels and communicate different messages to readers with varying levels of education and sophistication. The perfect inspiration to encourage budding writers, Gene soaked up her advice like a sponge.

Gene graduated with the winter class of 1939. On page 23 of the school annual, his postage-stamp-sized senior picture sits at the bottom of the page with his high school career summed up in one brief paragraph: "Eugene Wesley Roddenberry—Varsity Debate, Junto Club President, Spanish Club, International Forum, Authors' Workshop." He makes one more appearance on page 74 in the yearbook's coverage of Forensics—The Debate Team.

Oddly, the future world famous writer seemed to have an aversion to cameras in his senior year. The only picture that appears in the yearbook is his official senior picture. He does not appear in any of the group photos.

We remember our lives in moments—brief slices of experience that are emotionally connected to people and places, good times and bad. The little house on Monte Vista was a place of many warm and pleasant moments, simpler times for Gene—it was the last place his family lived as a complete unit. It was the house he grew up in. He never forgot the special times there. Gene remained connected to that house all his life.

The order would come out of nowhere, "Let's go by the old neighborhood." Sitting in the front seat as was his habit, Gene directed Ernie Over, his personal assistant, out the winding, snakelike Pasadena Freeway. Off at Avenue Fifty-two and a left turn at the end of the short, antiquated concrete off ramp built fifty years before. Up a half a mile or so to Monte Vista and then another left and down a few blocks.

It was a familiar trip to Gene, who had driven this route many times before, back when both he and the freeway were young.

Gene's old neighborhood, built just after the first World War, had been a bastion of the white middle and working classes. Now it was a mixture of Latinos and Asians working at their own version of the American Dream, but the neighborhood showed its age. Franklin High School, behind them and up Avenue Fifty-four, sparsely populated with minorities in Gene's day now serves students from fifty different cultures.

Gene wouldn't say much during these trips other than an occasional word directing Ernie where to turn. The stately Rolls Royce made an odd statement as it silently negotiated turn after turn on the old, narrow streets. It was an artifact from an alien world passing through a neighborhood that boasted few new cars.

Gene had Ernie slow down as they drove past the old house. Another left and up the alley past the back of the house and the garage. At the sight of the weathered garage, at least a decade old when he was born, Gene was taken back to his childhood. He could almost hear his father beeping the horn on his old '31 Chevy, demanding the appearance of one of the Roddenberry children to open its doors. The memory was bittersweet—Gene's father had been dead nearly twenty years.

At a word, Ernie would back the car out of the alley and he and Gene would park in front, facing north on Monte Vista. Gene would look at the house quietly, lost in memories of a time long past. Occasionally he would voice a memory, something he had done, something his father or mother had said, moments evergreen in his memory. Often he wouldn't say anything and simply let the memories wash over him, lost, not in the science fiction universe he had created, but lost in the tide of experiences that make a life.

These trips were not the idle ruminations of a man with extra time on his hands. They were visual and emotional anchors, reminders of where he had come from and who and what he was: not just the creator of a world-famous phenomenon, but the son of a policeman, who had come a long way from his beginnings, the man who was the result of an eleventh grader's determination to "make something of himself."

The visits to the old neighborhood always ended the same way. After a few minutes, Gene would quietly say, "Let's go home," and Ernie would drive the big car back over the hill to Gene's other world in Bel Air and the present.

CHAPTER 4

Nineteen thirty-nine was a good year for films and a bad year for Europe. The American film industry produced *Of Mice and Men, Gunga Din, The Hound of the Baskervilles, Beau Geste, The Hunchback of Notre Dame, Wuthering Heights, Stagecoach, Mr. Smith Goes to Washington, Dark Victory,* and two films that used the Technicolor process to its full advantage and would become enduring classics: *Gone With The Wind* and *The Wizard of Oz.*

Politically and economically, the United States was working it way out of the Great Depression under the leadership of Franklin Delano Roosevelt. In Europe, things were not going well. On September 1, 1939, Adolf Hitler taught the world a new word, "blitzkrieg" or "lightning war," when his mechanized divisions invaded Poland and rapidly conquered the antiquated Polish army, officially beginning World War II. But thousands of miles away, safe between two oceans, the U.S. felt secure and remote from Europe's political strife. Isolationists, who had developed great influence after World War I, wanted no part of Europe's wars.

Gene entered Los Angeles City College in February 1939. The intelligence test that was part of his entrance exam put him at or above the ninetieth percentile. His reading comprehension score was extraordinarily high at the 99.9th percentile.

Studio-generated biographies, have Gene taking "pre-law" courses at Los Angeles City College then switching (or planning to switch) to engineering at UCLA. Perhaps to studio publicity hacks "pre-law" sounded more prestigious, but the records show that Gene stayed true to his roots and studied the solidly blue collar Police Curriculum at LACC.

In addition to his studies, at least one of Gene's extracurricular activities had a police orientation: he was president of the LACC Police Club. Through the club he met a number of men who would, after the coming war, serve with him in the LAPD. Gene also met Stanley Sheldon, the LAPD liaison with the club for whom Gene would work eleven years in the future.

On his way to college, Gene also met someone who would figure in his more immediate future. As he rode the bus home one afternoon, he noticed a stunning, long-legged blonde who was going home from Hollywood High School. He wanted to meet her, but she would have nothing to do with him. Gene's friend Bob Atchison thought it very funny that a good-looking, intelligent college man couldn't get to first base with a high school girl.

Gene persevered and eventually began dating Eileen Anita Rexroat, two years his junior. On their first date they doubled with Bob Atchison and his girlfriend, Pat, whom Bob later married. They went to a beach party and had a bonfire. The boys drove, but before they left Papa Roddenberry cautioned them that "if they couldn't be good, they should be careful." He was only half kidding.

Gene and Eileen continued to date. Things seemed to be getting serious when Eileen cooked dinner for Gene at his house from time to time while Gene's parents and siblings vacated the house for a suitable time. While Eileen seemed happy with Gene, her parents were not. More specifically, her mother, Maude, did not approve of her daughter's choice. She had raised Eileen to do better than a common policeman's son and was not shy about voicing her opinion that Eileen was associating with someone beneath her. Maude aspired to better things for her only child, something better than her own working class marriage to a carpenter. Eileen's father, Frank, may have had an independent opinion about his daughter's boyfriend, but no one seems to remember him ever voicing it. Family disapproval notwithstanding, Eileen and Gene continued dating.

At the beginning of his second year at LACC, Gene fell into a net cast large and wide by a farsighted Army Air

Force general, Henry "Hap" Arnold. General Arnold was a rarity in the Army, a fervent believer in air power—not surprising, since in 1911 he had been trained as a pilot by the Wright brothers themselves. Arnold knew a war was coming and that there would be a desperate need for pilots. In late 1939, he set about to create a pool of pilot talent that the Army could tap into.

Arnold instituted the Civilian Pilot Training program, where college men could learn to fly at no cost. Hundreds of colleges adopted the program. Gene started his second year at LACC in February 1940. Two of the classes he took had the nondescript titles of Engineering 166 and 167. They were flight training pure and simple, contracted out by the government to private flight instruction schools.

Gene filled out the student application for vocational flight training, giving his parent's Monte Vista Street address. He listed himself as: single, 170 pounds, 6′1″, with light brown hair and hazel eyes. He was eighteen years old.

The application also elicited answers that showed Gene had no previous flying experience and had not studied anything connected with flying. One question near the bottom of the application gave some suggestion of the program's purpose: "Do you intend to enter Regular Army or Navy flight training?" He answered, "Undecided." The Civil Aeronautics Authority (CAA) issued Student Pilot Certificate No. S 54614 to Gene on June 29, 1940.

Instruction was at the Joe Plosser Air College at the grand Central Air Terminal in Glendale. Plosser used the Porterfield Trainer, a single-engine, high-wing plane similar to the Piper Cub. Plosser liked the Porterfield. He had eight.

Gene drew Flight Instructor George William Hogan—Bill to his friends. Hogan's experience and Gene's progress as a student pilot are best illustrated by Hogan's comments recorded in the student record.

> July 10—"Seems promising."
> July 11—"May improve."
> July 12—"Improving."
> July 18—"Flying rough."
> July 22—"Coordination better."
> July 23—"Flying good at times."
> July 24—"Improving slowly."
> July 26—"Shows improvement."

August 2—"Very rough."
August 3—"Landings and takeoffs poor."
August 5—"Reaction slow on landings."
August 6—"Landings very bad."

Old flight instructors used to brag that they could have someone soloing with three hours of instruction. While that may have been true, it was also dangerous. The CPT program required a minimum of eight hours dual instruction before the student was allowed to solo. Gene received nine hours of dual instruction. He soloed on Tuesday, August 6, thirteen days before his nineteenth birthday. He improved steadily. The only comment Hogan noted on Gene's solo was that it was "good."

For Gene, it was an experience he remembered all his life: "The first time I flew an airplane by myself it was a feeling of great exhilaration. When you get into an airplane by yourself and take off you find yourself in this lovely three-dimensional world where you can go in any direction. There is no feeling any more exciting than that. Freedom, freedom, freedom! That's the feeling you get."

Gene's solo was a psychological breakthrough and a turning point in his flight training. His confidence boosted, he continued to improve.

August 7—"Landings and takeoffs good."
August 12—"Student's landings very good."
August 16—"Spins good—precision not exact."
August 23—"Work improved considerably."
August 29—"Doing well."
August 30—"Doing very well."
September 5—"Dual cross-country o.k."
September 10—"Coordination above average."
September 11—"Student ready for test."
September 11—"Approved for private pilot."

On September 12 he was presented a graduation certificate from the Joe Plosser Air College certifying that he had completed their course of instruction and was eligible to apply for a private pilot's license issued by the CAA. At that time, Gene had eighteen and a half hours dual and almost nineteen hours solo flying time. He took and passed both the written CAA test—scoring "above average" as Plosser char-

acterized it—and the flight test. On September 17, 1940, the
CAA issued Airman Certificate No. 37177-40 to Eugene
Wesley Roddenberry. He was a fully licensed pilot. He had
turned 19 less than a month before.

The fall semester of his second year in college had Gene
back at his police studies. He got an A and a B in Law 85
and Law 82 respectively, as well as a B in Psychology 58,
but his pilot's training was far from over.

In February 1940, Gene started his fifth semester at
LACC. Either he didn't have enough points to graduate or
he purposely did not wish to graduate so he could take advanced flight training. He took Principles of Government,
where he didn't do well, Physical Education and Health, and
three more "engineering" classes: Civilian Pilot Training—
Secondary Ground Course (Engineering 168), and Civilian
Pilot Training—Secondary Flight Training (Engineering
169).

From February through June of 1941, Gene was given advanced flight training by Earl Percy Parkes, Jr., an instructor
at California Flyers, Inc.[1], another government contracted
flight school located at Los Angeles Municipal Airport.[2]
There Gene learned advanced techniques and developed the
skills that make the difference between someone who can fly
a plane and a pilot.

It was under Parkes' supervision that Gene experienced
his second flying memory: "My second experience also had
to do with flying—the first time I flew at night. I remember
it so well. The air was clear and over my head was this canopy of stars like jewels, diamonds in a cathedral and below
me were all the jewels of the earth, the reds and the greens
and the lights of the cars and buildings, piled up, shining and
sparkling. It's a pity the air doesn't stay clear these days because the sheer beauty just takes your breath away."

Gene averaged four days a week flight training until he
completed his Stage D check. On June 18, 1941, he was ap-

---

[1]California Flyers, Inc. started around 1933 by having its flight instructors sell
flying lessons door-to-door to raise the money to buy the planes to teach the people to which they had sold courses.

[2]A small, quiet municipal field, it later became Los Angeles International Airport.

proved by a flight inspector with a passing grade of 89 percent.

Gene also found time during this phase of his training to have some fun. One afternoon he took a training plane and buzzed his house on Monte Vista. Skimming in just over the top of Mt. Washington, a large hill immediately to the south of his parent's home, he revved his engine, repeatedly flying low over the house until his family came outside and waved at him. His brother Bob remembers that Gene kept this up for five minutes or so despite the proximity of Mt. Washington. Had anyone in the FAA learned of Gene's short flight of fancy, he would have found himself lucky to escape with a severe reprimand—he could have had his flight certificate turned into confetti.

While Gene continued his advanced flight training, Army Air Corps recruiters were taking advantage of the seeds planted by the CPT program. They worked the Los Angeles area targeting the campuses of USC, UCLA, and LACC, recruiting bright young pilots, forming what they called the "Los Angeles Squadron." The squadron never really saw action, but it sounded good and gave another reason for the men to join the military.

While the United States was officially neutral, most people knew it was just a matter of time until the country weighed into the European conflict on the side of England and France. Joining the military would give Gene some degree of control rather than taking his chances with the draft.

On June 26, 1941, Gene received his Associate of Arts degree in LACC's twenty-first commencement ceremonies. He was awarded a College Service Honor for his time in the Police Club and was recognized as a member of Sigma Lambda, the Honor Society for Law. The program listed his curriculum as "Police." He was the first member of his family to finish high school and graduate college.[3]

Within weeks of his graduation, on a particularly warm July day, Gene and the other members of the "L.A. Squadron" boarded rented busses and traveled ninety hot, dusty, miles over a narrow two-lane highway to March Air Force Base, just outside Riverside, California. There they were given physicals and administered their oaths, officially mak-

---

[3]His father had earned a high school diploma several years before, encouraged by a policy set by the police department.

ing them cadets in the Army Air Corps. With that formality over, the men were returned to Los Angeles late that evening. While it was a momentous day that signaled a change in the direction of their lives, it was also anticlimactic. The Army was long on recruits and short on places to train them. The War Department notified Gene and his fellow squadron members that they were to hold themselves available until otherwise notified. They could not leave town for more than two weeks at a time.

Gene spent the summer attending the Cal Tech Institute of Peace Officer training at UCLA. He found part-time work from August to October as a wrapping checker for the May Co. department store and then from October 23 to December 18 as a temporary mail carrier for the Post Office.

The L.A. Squad was told they would be hearing from the Army in due course, but they were not contacted until mid-December, a few days after the Japanese attacked Pearl Harbor.

Relations with Japan had been deteriorating,[4] On December 7, 1941, at 7:55 A.M., while most of Hawaii began a lazy Sunday morning, planes from the Imperial Japanese Navy struck Pearl Harbor and Hickam Field in two waves. The U.S. fleet's battleships, then the nucleus of every world navy, were destroyed—with one bomb hitting the powder magazine of the *U.S.S. Arizona*. Over a million pounds of explosives blew up, lifting the old warship out of the water. More than a 1,000 men were killed instantly. Authorities thought pictures of the *Arizona*'s destruction so inflammatory that they placed an embargo on all film of the disaster for a year.

The attack galvanized the nation. Admiral Yamamoto, commander of the Japanese Fleet and architect of the Pearl Harbor attack, had predicted that if Japan did not win

---

[4]The evisceration of the armed services that had caused Papa to leave the service in 1920 also depleted U.S. intelligence. Our code-breaking skills, espionage, and counter-espionage followed Secretary of State Seward's infamous and naive dictum, "Gentlemen do not read other gentlemen's mail." In a perfect world, where all men are gentlemen, perhaps that would be an appropriate sentiment, but the Japanese and American interests had been on a headlong collision course for years. For the ten years preceding the attack at Pearl Harbor, a question on the final exam at the Japanese Naval Academy was how could one go about attacking a harbor exactly like the installation in Hawaii. Because of depleted U.S. intelligence abilities, no one ever noticed this giveaway clue.

quickly and decisively, all the attack would succeed in doing would be to "arouse the sleeping dragon that is the United States." Yamamoto, more than any of his colleagues, understood the industrial potential and internal resolve such an attack would unleash in a country that was only just on the verge of becoming a world power. Yamamoto did not live to see confirmation of his prediction.

Within days of the attack on Pearl Harbor, Gene received a telegram and his orders. He was to report to Kelly Field, Texas, for training. On December 18, 1941, eleven days after Pearl Harbor, he and the other members of his squadron boarded a troop train at Union Station just east of downtown Los Angeles.

Twenty years earlier, Gene's first train ride was from Texas to Los Angeles. Now, his second would be the reverse. The first trip was spent on his mother's lap. Now he sat by himself, a young man leaving home for the first time, on his way to war and an uncertain future. It would be his first Christmas away from family and friends.

The train worked its way south, stopping at every military base and garrison along the way. Even with the draft, there was no shortage of volunteers. Lines formed outside recruiting offices, and the armed services found themselves overwhelmed.

Gene and the members of the L.A. Squad got off at San Antonio, bound for Kelly Field. There he met others from all over the country, eager and patriotic young men who believed in their country and wanted to fly for it. They all had the same story: they had been part of the Civilian Pilot Training program in college and they wanted to fly for Uncle Sam.

There were hundreds of them, but only a handful would graduate as Air Corps pilots. For a variety of reasons—temperament, intelligence, ability to think under pressure—most would not make the cut. Gene's graduating cadet class, #42-G, would number exactly 247 newly commissioned officers: second lieutenants and pilots. It was almost the same size as his graduating class at Franklin High.

Training began as all Army training does, with a month of boot camp. The cadets' welcome to the military began the next morning with a rude awakening—literally. Kelly Field did not use a bugler as a wakeup call. They set off a cannon at 5:30 A.M., a fact no one bothered to tell the new boots.

Daily calisthenics quickly trimmed the new recruits. Hair cuts, uniforms, drill instruction, military protocol and courtesy, weapons training, every aspect of a boot's life became military issue—at least when it was in stock. At one point, the cadets were forced into wearing overalls as the Army did not have enough uniforms on hand.

Boot camp also held other hazards. For several days, the small base hospital was filled with yellow cadets—not cowards, but cadets who were in various stages of jaundice. A group of men had been inoculated with faulty Yellow Fever Serum. Rather than be put back a class, at least one cadet talked a nurse into forging his blood count. Gene's luck held; he had been in another line and had received a different batch of serum.

The one hazard that could not be avoided were upper classmen, who each day provided an hour of hazing to the junior cadets. They would enter the barracks and prescribe the "uniform of the day," which might be dark glasses, jock straps, and feet shined with shoe polish. So attired, the cadets would be ordered to stand at attention by their beds. Cadets were required to recite meaningless poetry and memorize nonsensical answers to questions the upper classmen might ask. Incorrect answers meant the cadet doubletimed it around the exercise area.

After boot camp, the cadets were parceled out to small flight instruction fields all over Texas for primary flight training. Gene and his squad were transferred to tiny Corsicana, Texas, 40 miles south of Dallas. Managed by the military, it used civilian pilot instructors. Primary school architecture in Corsicana was "wartime utilitarian"—hastily constructed wood frames covered with tar paper. The barracks were hot during the day, cold at night, always drafty, and carried the faint odor of tar. They kept the elements out, but just barely.

Primary school was a make or break situation. There were no "second best" and Army pilots were quickly separated out often by nothing more than the whim of an instructor. The instructors were continually seeking to find or instill a sense of coolness under fire, the ability to think and react intelligently while performing under the stress of combat.

One of Gene's classmates, Don Prickett, remembers: "The

instructors were tough. If your instructor figured that you couldn't solo within ten hours, they were wasting their time and you were out. About half the class washed out in Primary.[5] The people who washed out were given the choice of going to Bombardier School or Navigator School. Most chose one or the other because if they washed out completely, their enlistment was over. They had no more commitment, but they were eligible to be drafted."

But some of the instructors were simply cruel. John Dozier, another classmate of Gene's, remembers: "I had a perfectly miserable flight instructor. He was the sort of guy you could really learn to hate. If I saw him today, I would probably walk over and hit him. He beat you with a stick if you made any mistakes. Whack, whack, he would hit your knees inside the plane. It was quite painful.

"He would get out of a flight and look at me and say, 'You're the dumbest son-of-a-bitch I ever saw.' That was my instructor. He was assigned five cadets and within ten days one of them came to him and told him to shove the Air Force up his ass, walked off and quit.

"This instructor washed out three cadets in the first two weeks. The only ones who made it through were the ones who stood up to him. One afternoon we were doing stalls and he didn't like my recovery so he would hit the stick, dropping us 7500 feet. I got so mad I grabbed the stick back and he was so surprised he hit his head on the plane's canopy. I thought I was going to get washed out. I asked for another instructor."

Cadet pilots were trained on one of three single-engine trainers: the Ryan, the BT-19A, and BT-13. The latter was known as the "Vultee Vibrator," an underpowered airplane that rattled a lot. The Vibrator had a nasty habit of stalling, and when it stalled it slipped off on one wing or the other. Alert cadets knew which wing each plane favored. The type of trainer depended strictly on the primary school the cadets drew in the lottery of orders. Gene trained on the relatively modern BT-19A, a low-wing, single-engine plane. He soloed quickly. His ground school grades averaged in the upper eighties.

Primary school at Corsicana was run by an Army Air

[5]Principally people who had not gone through the Civilian Pilot Training program.

Corps major who oversaw the civilian flight instructors. The other military personnel were two Army "check riders." Check riders were feared because it was they who went along on "wash rides," the flights that determined whether or not a cadet had what it took to be an Army pilot. Student flying was nerve-wracking enough, but for many, the wash ride was the last flight they would make as students.

Don Prickett remembers: "It was awful to see some of these kids come back from a wash ride. You knew they hadn't made it and they knew too. Some who washed out were just heartbroken. A lot of bombardiers and navigators came out of this process and some carried a lot of bitterness from the experience."

In the serious business of preparing for war there were some lighter moments. The drill instructors were sergeants whose time in the Army was sufficient for their little-used sense of humor to completely atrophy. Then they met cadet Dutton C. Dutton.

The drill instructors would call out for the cadets' last name and Dutton would respond, "Dutton." The sergeants would then call out for the first name and Dutton would respond truthfully. This would cause a short argument between Dutton and the confused sergeant until the matter was straightened out, but the sergeants were never certain Dutton wasn't, somehow, putting them on. The cadets took to calling him "Dutton C. Dutton C."

Then there was Schifani, the Italian from Albuquerque, New Mexico. Schifani was the company's practical joker, who enraged the cadets by turning on the lights and blowing the sergeant's whistle, waking everyone up and getting them dressed and out on the parade grounds before anyone realized it was two AM. Schifani also had a charicature in the rear of the cadet class book, drawn by another cadet, Disney artist Bill Williams. The charicature was to lurk in the back of Gene's memory for over twenty years and then unconsciously make its contribution, along with the Roman god Pan, to Gene's creation of a pointy-eared Vulcan named Spock.[6]

---

[6]Emmanuell Schifani had every right to be a character. He had been a flyer since 1933. When the war began in Europe, Schifani volunteered and flew 1600 hours with the Royal Air Force, seeing combat well before the United States joined the war. Schifani had more hours as a pilot than his instructors. He took revenge on

By the time he left primary school at the end of March 1942, Gene had sixty hours of flight time, thirty-two of them solo. The next step was Goodfellow Field, Texas, and basic flight training. Basic saw another ten percent of the cadet class wash out. In basic, Gene trained on the BT-13, a simple, single-engine trainer aircraft with fixed landing gear. Goodfellow Field had only been in service for a year, built in five months to accommodate the cadet overflow from Randolph Field. It had over a hundred buildings and could accommodate 1500 enlisted men, 400 cadets, and 200 officers.

Goodfellow Field had been, a year earlier, a farmer's pasture. Now it was a level, sod field, with two long rows of two hundred training planes, all with dark fuselages, white engine cowlings, and white rudders. It was an impressive sight. From a distance, when the sun was right, the planes looked like two parallel rows of white picket fencing stretching out over the flat planes of Texas, meeting and vanishing over the horizon.

Between June and August, Gene moved on to advanced training and it was then that he finally reached Kelly Field. By this time the cadets had been formed into more formal units—Gene was in Group Four, Squadron A. Kelly Field was a World War I facility, built for the Signal Corps and later taken over by the Army Air Corps. Its facilities were modern when compared to the tar paper shacks Gene had up until now spent so much time in. The cadet barracks were brick or stucco, occasionally clapboard, and the hangars were brick buildings with wooden floors. The instruction rooms were a bit cooler during the day, but only a bit. The humid San Antonio summer was no treat for men used to much drier Southern California weather.

Advanced training also meant the possibility of another change in status. Thanks to the pressures of war, the rules had been changed so that cadets in advanced training could be married. Both Gene and Don had become engaged before they left Los Angeles. Both men were certain they would be

---

one particularly irritating instructor by doing a series of aerobatics that made the instructor airsick. Schifani was certain he would be washed out but was only threatened with dismissal when the flight instructor made him promise never to reveal his humiliation. After being called back into the U.S. Air Force for the Korean War, he retired in 1964 as a three-star general.

sent overseas, which would mean almost certain combat, and so they had both already discussed the situation with their fianceés. Everyone agreed: they would be married before the men went overseas.

It was in his friend's attempt to get married that Gene saw arbitrary military pettiness at its worst. The commandant of cadets was incensed that the policy on marriage had been changed. For reasons still unexplained, the commandant did not like Don Prickett. Prickett became the lightning rod for his wrath, the outlet for his frustration. The commandant knew Don's fianceé was coming in by train for a Saturday wedding, so everyone knew Don would have trouble with Saturday morning's inspection. Even with his friends helping, extra hands cleaning his rifle and shining his buttons and shoes, Don could not pass the commandant's malicious eye. He was ordered to extra duty for the morning and had to have fellow cadet, Leo Summers, pick up his fianceé. Gene, leading his charmed life, was also getting married that day but had no trouble with the commandant. Prickett had absorbed all the wrath the commandant could muster.

Because of the sudden change in the rules, there was no base housing for married cadets. Gene and Don rented a two-bedroom apartment over a private home in San Antonio. It was a major expense, costing each man $20 a month—a large portion of their $75 per month cadet pay.

Eileen was already in the apartment, having come down a week in advance of their wedding date. She and Gene applied for the marriage license on Saturday, June 13. Such an arrangement might have been acceptable for Gene and Eileen, but Don's fianceé, Mary Elisabeth Mèsny,[7] (M.E. to her friends) was more traditional. She arrived the night before the ceremony and stayed in a hotel. War or no war, the ring would be on her finger before the honeymoon began.

Don and Gene also had considered a double wedding, but M.E. had other ideas. The future Mrs. Prickett lived in Los Angeles and Eileen called her before either left for San Antonio. Eileen was less than diplomatic as regarding the wedding ceremony, as M.E. recalls:

"She called and introduced herself on the phone. She said

---

[7]In an unusual coincidence, Mary Elisabeth Mèsny (pronounced "meany"), is the daughter of Reginald Mèsny, the French engineer who oversaw the construction of Kelly Field during World War. I.

this is the way it was going to be, that we were getting married together and that we were going to live together. I was thinking, 'Who in the hell are you?' It was very odd, a stranger calling and telling me what I would be doing.

"So I told Don, I'm not having any double wedding and if this is the way it is, just forget the whole damn thing. I didn't know her until I got to San Antonio."

On June 20, 1942, a hot and muggy Saturday, Gene and Eileen stood before Kelly Field Chaplain George W. Shardt and recited their vows. The chapel was standard Army-issue with white clapboard, an unadorned steeple, and three simple wooden steps leading up to the double doors in the back—like the ceremony, simple and utilitarian. Don and M.E. were married in a separate location, and afterward the two couples celebrated with friends at the Kit Kat Klub in San Antonio.

After the excitement of the weekend, training continued for Gene and Don, and the new brides settled into their tiny apartment. From M.E.'s perspective, things did not improve when she began sharing living space with Eileen. The plan was for each of the couples to buy their own food, but M.E. does not remember Eileen living up to the bargain during the four months they lived together:

"She didn't share. She took. She wouldn't do any cleaning or picking up. She wouldn't pay her share of whatever groceries we were supposed to split. Never! Everything had to be her way. As I told Don, I realized she was very, very young and very spoiled."

Then there was Eileen's distinctively avant-garde manner of handling San Antonio's heat. According to M.E., when the boys were on base Eileen would simply remove all her clothes and sit around the apartment in the nude.

M.E. liked to read and did her best while in San Antonio to soak up local culture by visiting museums and reading local history, but she does not remember seeing Eileen open a book or magazine during the four months they shared the apartment. The contrast between the two women was not unnoticed. Three years later, near the end of the war, Gene visited Don and M.E. in Omaha where Don was stationed. Toward the end of the visit, Gene looked at M.E. and spontaneously said, "M.E. I think you are undoubtedly the most cultivated person I have ever known." M.E. has remembered Gene's compliment for nearly fifty years.

M.E. also remembered something else:

"There was another woman that Eileen knew. I don't know how she fit into the picture and if I knew her name I've forgotten it by now. She had a big convertible. Two nights after the four of us were married this girl came over with her convertible saying, 'We'll go to the drive-in movie.' The boys were probably night flying or something so it was just the girls.

"We went to the drive-in movie and she and Eileen were picking up some cadets. I told them they could take me home. I didn't go out with them again."

According to M.E., Eileen and her friend went out "practically every night" during the week when Gene was at the base. M.E., who describes herself as "somewhat mid-Victorian," never asked Eileen where she and her friend went or what they did when they went out. While she was not certain what Eileen and her friend did, M.E. knew she didn't want any part of it.

M.E. summed up her memory of Eileen in one succinct observation: "She wasn't very bright."

When Gene and Don were sent overseas, M.E. moved back to Los Angeles and never saw Eileen again.

Like Goodfellow Field, the runways and taxiways of Kelly Field were large, unbroken expanses of sod. This meant the field was large enough for the squadron to taxi and take off simultaneously in one large, nine-ship formation. It was always an impressive sight.

Advanced training at Kelly was as careful and thorough as the Army could manage. The general rule of thumb was that it took five men to keep one plane in the air. There was a ratio of one instructor, comprised of Army Air Corps lieutenants and captains, for every three students. From them Gene learned instrument flying and navigation. Gene could spend his leisure time (what little there was of it) in the post theater, the four-lane bowling alley, or the Cadet Day Room.

On August 5, 1942, Gene graduated and received his officer's commission as a second lieutenant. Eileen was there to pin his wings on.

Gene remembers: "Flying was a mixture of good things to me and bad things. It was a great victory to me, personally, to get through cadets and not be washed out. So many boys in those days were. It was a great victory to be able to pass the physical as I had had asthma in childhood and a sensitivity to bright sunlight. The miracle of adolescence for me is that all those things went away."

He was going to the South Pacific, but he had not selected what sort of pilot he would be: bomber or fighter. Before he could make the choice, or be chosen, there was a holdup in the Army machinery.[8] Gene and Don would be delayed by a month before they could be transferred to their assigned bases.

They were no longer cadets but second lieutenants, the most junior grade of officer, but the Army would not waste that humble resource even for thirty days. Regardless of experience, the Army assigned its newest officers a variety of duties. A group of South American officers were at Kelly for flight training, and so the Army, in typical fashion, assigned Don Prickett, fresh out of training himself, to be their instructor. Gene, who had studied Spanish in high school, was passed over for this assignment and, of course, Don did not speak a word of the language.

During his extra time at Kelly, Gene was assigned to advanced twin-engine training, spending time on the Cesna AT-17 twin-engine trainer. This extra training on a multiple-engine trainer made Gene a certain candidate for bombers. Years in the future, Gene would contribute to his own mythology by saying that he was assigned to bombers by an accident in Hawaii, but given his nearly six-foot-two-inch height it was unlikely that he would have been assigned to fighters even if he had asked. Gene was simply too large to comfortably fit in the small fighter cockpits.

In September 1942, Gene finally received his first assignment: Bellows Field, Hawaii, where he would join the 394th Squadron, 5th Bombardment Group, along with his friend Don. The 5th Bombardment Group had been a part of the Army Air Corps since it had been authorized as the Second Group (Observation) on August 15, 1919, and organized in Hawaii. Through a number of different incarnations, it was finally designated the 5th Bombardment Group (Heavy) in November 1940.

Bellows Field was a relatively new installation on the

---

[8]An acronym for this sort of situation became famous during World War II— "SNAFU," meaning "Situation Normal, All Fouled Up." The more earthy substituted "fucked" for "fouled," making the acronym even more accurate in application.

STAR TREK CREATOR   63

north side of Oahu, replete with the tar-paper barracks the Army was so adept at constructing, but in the tropics, with their temperate climate, the design was more practical than in the hot and cold open spaces of Texas. Bellows Field was also the least damaged airfield, behind the principle targets of Hickam and Wheeler Fields, during the Japanese attack of December 7.

The 394th was a bomber squadron that flew B-17s. The B-17 was a large, no-nonsense aerial weapon designed to deliver a payload of bombs over enemy territory.[9] It was an impressive weapon of war that went through a number of design changes and improvements as the war progressed. Pilots and crews are nearly unanimous in their praise as the B-17's reliability brought many crews home when a lesser aircraft would not have made it. The B-17 was a very forgiving aircraft; it could sustain tremendous damage and continue to fly. One plane in the European Theater took 3,000 machine gun hits and stayed aloft. Dozens of planes landed with parts of wings and control surfaces missing, and one famous photograph shows a B-17 flying with half its rudder missing. The plane became a well-deserved object of affection.

At the beginning of the war, the heaviest armament the 394th's planes had were 30-caliber machine guns. These were "plug in" guns, installed by shoving the weapon through a rotating ball in the plexiglass windows. B-17 models C and D did not have the top, bottom, and tail gun turrets

---

[9]The B-17 was America's first heavy bomber. There was great debate during and after World War I as to the place and effectiveness of aviation in the military. Part of the debate was the ability for bombers to sink large war ships. Brigadier General Billy Mitchell proved to the Navy brass, that the largest warships afloat were no match for accurate, high-level bombing and helped set the stage for American air power, which would turn the Axis tide in both the European and Pacific Theaters of War. For his dedication to his cause, General Billy Mitchell was court-martialed and suspended from duty for five years in 1925. He resigned his commission in 1926.

Beyond being the greatest aerial weapon the world had known to date the "Boeing Model 299" represented a great gamble for the Boeing Company. Boeing, not the U.S. government, paid the costs for research, development, and construction. Had the plane not performed, it is likely that Boeing would have gone out of business and not been there, ready to tool up, when the war began. At the height of production Boeing's Seattle, Washington, plant turned out 16 finished planes every 24 hours. A total of 12,731 B-17s were built. There are, perhaps, nine left flying in the world today.

the plane would become famous for. It was far from being what would later be called, "The Flying Fortress." The squadron was used for submarine and recon flights, looking for the Japanese task force on sector searches.[10]

The men of the 394th were not assigned a single job description. Major Wrigley, the commanding officer, had the philosophy that any officer in the crew had to be able to handle any job on the plane in case some were wounded and worked out a complete cross-training program. Officers were taught to field strip machine guns, develop skill as bombardiers on the bomb trainers,[11] and practice bomb runs actually dropping 100-pound bombs in the ocean. They also assisted the crew chiefs in aircraft maintenance and engine changes. When they were finished, the officers thoroughly understood everything about their planes.[12]

The new officers were fortunate that the first pilots and most of the enlisted personnel had several years' experience. More than one officer interviewed for this book observed that the experience of the crews "saved their necks." It is a near certainty that Gene survived the war due to his training, innate intelligence, a good supply of luck, and flying B-17s with the experienced men of the 394th.

Bellows Field was not far from Honolulu. Gene bought an old car for $175 and got off base and into town as often as possible. With ready transportation, Gene spent many nights off base, so many that his friends often commented on it and remember it to this day. Gene was rarely around to join his friends on liberty or the inveterate poker games that were played during free time—he was off on his own. He was

---

[10]A sector search consisted of flying out several hundred miles, turning left or right, and flying 200-300 miles, and then heading back to base. Search patterns were in "pie-shaped wedges" of 15°.

[11]One of America's great wartime secrets was the development of the Norden Bombsight. It gave a tactical advantage in that it allowed for accurate, high-level bombing. A rate meter on the bombsight was on the drop mechanism. The pilot had to fly the plane, in the earlier versions, and the bomb run was no better than the pilot's ability to hold air speed, altitude, and accurately follow the direction indicators. Bombardiers were sworn to die to protect the Norden. After the war, it was discovered that the bombsite plans had been stolen by a German-American worker at the Norden offices in 1936.

[12]Gene never forgot this part of his training, so it is not surprising to see his starship captains, Kirk and Picard, thoroughly familiar with all aspects of their ships' functions.

young, good looking, and took advantage of the "pilot's mystique" to feed his large appetites. He usually kept quiet about what he did on his own time, but friends and squadron mates interviewed for this book mentioned that, more than once, when Gene took a shower in the morning, he had scratches down his back. Eileen was living in Southern California with her parents, and some officers interviewed for this book were surprised to learn that Gene had been married while he served with them.

Gene was not overly popular with the other officers of the squadron. While he could be gregarious and friendly, he was something of a loner. He had an "intellectual ego," as Don Prickett described it, that kept him a bit apart from the other squadron members. Occasionally quoting Shakespeare did not endear him to other officers, many of whom had never read, let alone understood, such works. Don Prickett recalls, "Gene always had that little touch of 'artistic snobbery' and it was always tied into literature. Gene would ask, 'Have you read this book?' or like that, and, of course, the other members of the squadron hadn't. We played poker all the time and I don't remember Rod sitting in one poker game with us. He'd probably be off reading something. There wasn't much to read but he had a few books, one or two of poetry, and he wrote a bit of poetry every now and then."

Brief entries in military records and history books state that the 394th was "equipped with B-17s and B-18s." "Equipped" is not a word that clearly explains the squadron's situation. The B-17s that the Army assigned to the 394th were planes that had a history. They had previously been assigned to the 19th Bomb Group, which had been at Corregidor[13] and Cart Field in Manila. The planes that hadn't been destroyed when the Japanese attacked the Philippines had escaped to Port Moresby, on the southern side of New Guinea, just across the Coral Sea from Australia. These planes and crews were on their way back to the mainland for engine changes and complete overhauls. They'd been shot up and had "more discrepancies on their maintenance logs than you could count."

When the planes got to Hawaii, the plan called for the

---

[13]Corregidor is a fortified, rocky island approximately two square miles, at the entrance to Manila Bay in the Philippines. It had been under U.S. control since 1898. It fell to the Japanese in May 1942, after months of ferocious fighting.

394th to get several newer model B-17Es coming in from the States, but "the plan" was open to constant revision. The planes never made it back to the States. They became the "new" planes assigned to the 394th. Major Wrigley got his orders to take his crews to Hickam Field and pick up his planes. The planes, veterans of hundreds of hours of flight and combat, would take Wrigley and his men into combat in the Solomons. Wrigley was not happy.

Don Prickett remembers: "The plane I got, the old 6-3-0, had had a major accident with full landing gear replacements. It had patches all over covering up bullet holes, it had over 500 hours on every engine and that was supposed to be overhaul time. All the planes were pretty similar. That was the condition of the seven B-17s we got. Then we got orders to pick up and head for the Solomons where the fighting was. The Marines were having a real tough time and we were ordered to get down there and help them. That was just before Christmas 1942."

Gene, flying copilot for Captain William Ripley, did not find his plane in any better shape. Within a couple of days of receiving their "new" planes, the 394th was given its orders to ship out. The men loaded their planes with every spare part they could beg, borrow, or steal. The bomb bay of each plane carried a spare engine—plus the crew's gear. Overloaded by 10,000 pounds, everyone hoped their plane would make it into the air.

Early on the morning of November 15, 1942, as dawn was breaking in the east, one by one the ancient B-17s creaked down the runway of Hickam Field. The planes that took off first climbed into the rising sun, circled like giant birds of prey, waiting for their fellows to join them. Once formed up, the squadron flew almost directly south to Christmas Island. The first leg of their trip to the Solomons was an eight-hour flight, though not uneventful.

Captain William Ivey was a first pilot. He had been in the Army Air Corps since 1939 and was a veteran of Pearl Harbor, stationed at Hickam Field when the Japanese attacked. He was a skilled pilot and cool under pressure. About three hours out, his number 2 engine developed trouble. He feathered the engine, taking it off line, but the gearing malfunctioned and the propeller continued to turn, not from the power of the engine, but from the plane's forward momentum through the air. The bearings did not like the strain and sang their protest. Even with three other giant engines roaring away, the bearing's shrill scream could be heard by the whole crew. Gene, in Ripley's plane, and the other men in the formation could also hear the bearings shriek.

Hours passed and the situation worsened. The bearing howl had grown louder and more intense and the bearings were wearing unevenly. The propeller was wobbling as it turned. The prop's deteriorating condition was easy to observe since the number two engine was inboard on the left wing, level with the cockpit and only a few feet away from the pilot sitting in the left-hand seat. Bill Ivey was in a very dangerous position. If the propeller broke off, it would act like a giant buzz saw, ripping into the fuselage on a line even with his seat and the plane would tumble into the sea.

There was no question of turning back and the only help was at their destination, Christmas Island. Ivey did the only thing he could do: he moved his crew, including his flight officers, to the rear of the plane and flew on in the cockpit alone. The safety precaution unbalanced the plane and it flew the remaining miles to Christmas Island with its nose in the air.

When the plane landed, it was found that five of the eight mounting bolts had either broken or worn away. The prop was being held on the plane by three weakening bolts.[14] The whole squadron knew that Ivey and his crew had narrowly escaped certain death.

The next day, the rest of the squadron flew to Canton Island, part of the Line Island group southwest of Christmas Island, while Ivey and his crew worked on repairs. Before he went into combat, Ivey made certain that all four engines on his plane had been changed.

On November 17, the squadron flew seven and a half hours to Nandi, Fiji, on the way to reporting to Admiral Halsey[15] and combat in or around the New Hebrides.

---

[14]Ivey stayed with the military and retired a colonel. In August 1943, he was awarded the Oak Leaf Cluster in lieu of a second Distinguished Flying Cross.

[15]William Frederick "Bull" Halsey, Jr. (1882–1959), was a naval hero in World War I, where he won the Navy Cross for distinguished service. Vice-Admiral Halsey commanded Task Force 2 and was at sea on board his flag ship, the carrier *Enterprise,* when the Japanese hit Pearl Harbor. He was promoted to command of the Pacific Theater. As commander of the 3rd Fleet, he helped destroy the Japanese fleet at Leyte Gulf in 1944. He served as fleet admiral until his resignation in 1947, when he entered private business.

Prepared to take on the Japanese, poor flying conditions, and bad food, the squadron encountered something they weren't prepared for: Brigadier General Owens, the island commander.

General Owen was, by one account, an old World War I balloon pilot who had remained a second lieutenant for many years between the wars. He had his own way of looking at things. The men of the 394th had not been able to fly in with their ground support—it would be six or eight weeks before they caught up—so the air crews were doing their own maintenance. In spite of the dirty work, the heat, and the humidity, the general expected the men to keep their appearance neat and tidy, even going so far as to suggest they wear ties. The men ignored him every chance they got.

The general knew that the Japanese could invade the islands under his command at any time. In order to beef up his defenses and provide early warning of any impending attack, he needed a reconnaissance squadron to fly patrol out of Fiji. The 394th filled his needs precisely. He ordered Major Wrigley to stay at Nandi and not to fly on to the New Hebrides. However, Wrigley's orders were to report to Admiral Halsey. The chain of command was in some disarray and was further complicated by the 394th, an Army Air Force bomber group, being assigned to the command of a Navy admiral. Wrigley had no one to turn to for help, support, or clarification. He was still in the Army, and even though he was described as "fit to be tied," he knew he could only push the situation so far with a superior officer. In the end he was, after all, a major and Owen was a general. Regardless of their desire to get to the war and help the Marines on Guadalcanal, the men and their planes of the 394th stayed on Fiji and flew recon patrols. The Japanese would not sneak up on Fiji if General Owen, with the help of the 394th, could do anything to prevent it.

The town of Nandi was about four and a half miles from the airfield. It was a tiny settlement with one street perhaps two blocks long. The small shops on either side of the short street were run by Indians, who eked out a small living by selling souvenirs of shells, pictures, necklaces, and bracelets they claimed were made of silver.

The English presence had added something to the local

ambiance. The tiny town in the middle of nowhere had an unusual feature best described by Mack Morris, a journalist and correspondent for *Yank* magazine, who covered the war. He wrote in his personal diary:

"Nandi is much the same as any other island town, but I got the impression that it is a little cleaner, perhaps because of the tennis court—grassed—in the middle of town.

"Coming into town on a truck, we saw a native girl by the river do a Sally Rand[16] with her lava-lava, taking it off and re-wrapping it so she could walk into deeper water. After months of Mother Hubbards[17] I was amazed to see a native thigh. The women don't wear the Hubbards, but effect a distinctly novel appearance by a blouse and a long wrap-around skirt which they wrap extremely tight; the costume looks good because the gals are not all 200-pounders—most of them are pleasantly plump but some are built along our lines. The men, who offer a deep 'Boola' in greeting, are big bastards: like the Caledonians in physique but with more refined features.

"Our major experience was meeting Tina, the girl who works in the Chinaman's dimly lit cafe. Tina is a Fijian glamour girl—she wore a blue print dress, low cut, and white anklets with oxfords. She speaks English perfectly with a soft, semi-Southern accent. We didn't know at first whether she could understand us, but there was no more question after we heard her crooning: 'I Don't Want to Walk Without You, Baby.' When she had brought our food—a good dinner of ham and eggs and coffee—she sat down with us and ate Chinese food with chop sticks. We talked. I noticed she had a beautiful set of teeth.

"She told us she loved parties and native dances. 'There's a dance tonight—I'd love to take you boys but the MP's would cause trouble.' She explained troops aren't allowed into the villages because there had been trouble over the women. Sometimes they danced American dances: they play the guitar and mandolin, but when I asked if they had

---

[16]Sally Rand was a famous exotic dancer of the thirties and forties, known for her fan dance. Much of what was seen was in hopes and imagination.

[17]A long-sleeved dress that covered the body completely. Christian missionaries' contributions toward "civilizing" the natives, taught them mostly about modesty and guilt.

drums she smiled and said no, as much as to say, 'you dumb dope.'

"Tina said she had four girl friends who had worked with her, but they were in the hospital now. Naturally we asked their trouble. 'Oh,' said Tina, 'they've just been having too much of a good time.' "

For Gene and his squadron mates, Tina, her girlfriends, and the entire town of Nandi would remain off limits. Several officers interviewed for this book remembered making it into Nandi once or twice but were vague on details. Regardless, there wasn't much time for socializing, as the Army kept the men busy with long recon flights and constant maintenance on the planes when they weren't flying. Though they couldn't get into Nandi, four and a half miles away, they occasionally made it to the capital, Suva, 175 miles away.

Mindful of the future, each of Gene's crewmates and fellow lieutenants had bought a bottle of liquor in Hawaii before they left. Their planning was wise, as it was just about the only liquor they would have during their tour of duty except during those rare visits to Suva.

As the Christmas holidays approached, the feeling of distance from home and family increased. It would be Gene's second holiday in a row away from his family. Gene and Don got to sampling the liquor they had brought with them. Feeling adventurous, they walked to the small, nearby native settlement built by the locals who did laundry and odd jobs around the base. It was not off limits. They came to the large community house in the middle of the settlement and found several dozen native Fijians sitting in a circle on the mat floor, singing Christmas carols. Emboldened with liquid courage, they joined the natives sitting in a circle on the floor and began singing right along with them: natives singing in Fijian and Don and Gene singing in English.

The natives might have lived somewhat primitive lives by American standards, but they were neither stupid nor unsophisticated. The major lesson they seemed to have learned from years of Christian missionaries was, "The Lord helps those who help themselves," and they recognized an opportunity when it presented itself in the persons of Gene and Don. Within a song or two, the chief told them that if they wanted to stay and sing they would have to pay for the privilege—in silver coins. Gene and Don enjoyed themselves, and the natives did well by the two young Americans who had more money than sense.

Nothing goes smoothly in war. In spite of all the effort at training, wars are still fought by fallible humans who make mistakes. This fact contributed to a significant reduction in the number of planes assigned to the 394th.

At the Nandi airfield, the squadron's B-17's were lined up on the right side of the runway, the right side if you faced the ocean. Further off to the right, down near the beach, were a number of four-man tents where a squadron of fighter pilots lived.

One evening, the fighter squadron was scheduled to practice night takeoffs and landings. Nandi field had no lights, blackout rules applied, so a pair of lights were set out at the end of the runway and a pair at the mid-point of the runway. The pilots were to line up on these lights for both takeoffs and landings. It was tricky business under the best of circumstances.

Unfortunately, one of the tents had a light burning, and from the lead pilot's vantage point it looked like one of the lights at the end of the runway. The first pilot lined up on the tent light and accelerated for his takeoff, running 15 degrees off the center of the runway. As he was accelerating into his takeoff, the fighter sliced across the front of one of the 394th's neatly parked bombers.

The second fighter pilot made the same mistake, smashing into the second bomber in line, and a third fighter took out a third bomber before they could be stopped. Everyone was thoroughly embarrassed and not a little irritated.

Recon flights out of Nandi were flown in the same pie-shaped flight plan as they were on Hawaii. Some of the planes had a crude form of radar, but as no one could keep the sets operating, most recon patrols were flown with visual search rules, flying below the clouds. The planes were supposed to fly close enough to one another that they could spot a Japanese task force if it was halfway between. That was the idea, anyway. The flights lasted anywhere from eight to eleven hours, often becoming studies in tedium with nothing to look at but hundreds of thousands of miles of open ocean.

On one such flight, Gene and crew flew directly into a typhoon.[18] That day the B-17 proved how well built and air worthy it was. The B-17's flight controls were cables, so the plane was flown directly from pilot to air surface with no hydraulics between. In strong winds, this caused the pilot to tire quickly. Ripley flew the plane as long as he could and then turned it over to Gene in the right seat. While well designed and thoroughly tested, the B-17 was not designed for aerobatics, but it became a toy tossed about by the typhoon. Gene and crew discovered that it could stand on its nose and fly in a variety of attitudes and still survive.

While everyone else was buckled in as tightly as possible, Jim Kyle, the bombardier, had been moving around, out of his station in the plane's nose. He wanted to get back to his station, but because of the buffeting, was unable to crawl through the tunnel beneath the cockpit. He found the only safe place he could by standing between Ripley and Gene, holding on tightly while the plane was knocked around. Without warning, the men would have the sensation of the floor giving out beneath them as the plane hit a downdraft and dropped several hundred feet, or, just as suddenly, they would feel a great weight on their heads and shoulders and the updrafts moved the plane straight up several hundred feet.

Then, just as suddenly, all was calm and the plane was flying as it was designed to. They had flown into the eye of the storm. Perhaps twenty miles across, the air was calm and clear all the way down to the sea. It was only a few moments respite; Ripley's calm voice informed the crew that they were about to fly out of the storm through the other side.

Kyle stayed put, fearing he would be battered senseless if he returned to his place in the nose.

Flying into the dark clouds at the edge of the eye, they again encountered fierce up and downdrafts with the plane dropping what seemed thousands of feet in just seconds.

Still standing between the pilot and copilot, Kyle looked out the right window just past the back of Gene's head and saw a horrifying sight that would stay with him the rest of his life: just a few feet off the end of the right wing was a

---

[18] 1943 was years before weather satellites, and weather prediction was often just a good guess. There was little warning of bad weather. Suddenly, it was just right in front of the pilot filling the horizon as far as he could see.

wall of water with no top in sight. The B-17 had been blown so low it was flying near the bottom of a giant wave trough.

When the plane and crew made it back to base, they found rivets popped out all over the plane and a bottom hatch cover ripped off by either force of wind or wave action. It was more frightening than meeting Japanese fighters—or so they thought at the time.

Bomber crews are trained to deliver ordnance over targets, and the men of the 394th were anxious to get on with what they were trained to do. January 1943, they began a rotation of flying bombing missions out of Espiritu Santo Island, Guadalcanal, and Nandi.

When they left Nandi on their first assignment, the squadron buzzed the field in formation at an altitude of fifty feet. The combined noise and power of six or eight B-17s rattled every building in the area. It was the airmen's way of thumbing their nose at their overly officious general. Several officers stood outside and saluted as the squadron passed over.

Flying out of Espiritu Santo Island, the 394th would make daylight, dusk, and night bombing runs on a variety of targets. Often they made dusk attacks on Kahili Airport at the southern end of Bougainville flying "up the slot," the ship channel between the Solomon Islands. Though the Air Force would ultimately mount giant raids of a thousand B-17s over Germany, the 394th's missions usually consisted of between four and eight planes. There was no fighter escort.

On at least one of the Kahili raids, the crew could see a small plane following them on a parallel course off to their left: a Japanese spotter craft relaying the bombers' position, guiding the anti-aircraft fire. The sky was dark in the east and the sun beginning to set in the west. With the time of day and the spotter plane's position, the B-17s were neatly silhouetted against the setting sun.

Suddenly, someone was yelling over the intercom, "Two o'clock high! Two o'clock high!" The men were able to see the blinking of the 20-mm cannon as several Japanese fighters were beginning their attack. Joe Jacobs, Gene's navigator, began firing his starboard 50-caliber machine gun, but almost immediately blinded himself with his own muzzle blast. It didn't stop Joe. He kept on firing where he thought the Zero should be, following the fighter curve he had been taught in Hawaii.

The fighters had appeared nearly simultaneously with "bombs away" and so Gene quickly turned and headed east for sanctuary in a large bank of clouds. As Joe's flash blindness cleared, Gene informed him that his training had paid off: the Japanese fighter had exploded almost directly in front of the plane.

Occasionally, during bombing runs, the plane itself seemed as though it wanted to betray the men. Intelligence had reported some night fighter activity around the south coast of Bougainville. Gene was only able to coax his war-weary bomber up to fourteen thousand feet. The effort had made the engines' superchargers glow nearly white hot, a sure sign to a watchful Japanese lookout. Gene took the plane down slowly in an effort to cool down the superchargers, popping through small tufts of stratocumulus clouds as he descended.

Jim Kyle, the bombardier, turned to Joe Jacobs, the navigator, and asked him to point out the target, but all Joe could see was unrelieved black. The Japanese obliged almost instantly by turning on their searchlights, illuminating the darkness, and allowing Kyle to see where to drop his bombs.

Gene witnessed the real ravages of war, and those experiences led to his ultimate antiwar stance. In the South Pacific, Gene observed human stupidity raised to new levels. Captain Slack of the 394th was a victim of such stupidity. The B-24 "Liberator" bomber was being phased in, replacing the B-17. A squadron had been sent to the South Pacific along with the technical manuals describing the limitations of the planes—bomb load, fuel consumption, etc. Once in the South Pacific the planes were modified, so much so that there was additional drag on the plane in flight. Captain Slack was a professional who knew his business. Rather than relying on the tech manuals to tell him what the plane could do, he flight-tested the modified plane. He *knew* what the plane could and could not do. Unfortunately, the Navy brass, who had the tech manuals, paid no attention. They knew what the plane could do: they had it in writing from the manufacturer. Who could be a better authority?

Slack and a number of other men were ordered on a

bombing mission. Slack looked at his orders and said that the plane could not make the round-trip. Slack had tested the planes in flight, he knew their fuel consumption, he protested. Headquarters was adamant and did not listen to a word Slack said. Slack and several other crews went on the mission. The bombs were dropped for whatever effect they may have had, but none of the planes made it back to base. One by one they dropped into the ocean, each over a hundred miles short of home. A few were rescued, but many died, needlessly. Gene's distrust of authority became etched in stone that day.

One of Gene's navigators was Larry Walton, a green kid of nineteen when compared to the mature, combat-experienced crewmen of twenty-one and twenty-two. Larry remembered his first mission with Gene. It was a night bombing run. When the Japanese searchlights pinpointed their plane as it was coming in for its run, Larry announced the obvious to the rest of the crew in a slightly panicky voice. "They've got us in their spotlight. What do we do?"

The calm and reassuring voice of Gene came back over the intercom, "Take a bow."

Gene's writing ambitions began to surface in the South Pacific, as did the lessons learned in Mrs. Church's English class and the Authors' Workshop. Gene's penchant for poetry, and inspiration provided by the situation he and his friends were in, provided the following lyrics.

I WANNA GO HOME
THEME SONG OF THE 394TH. BOMB. SQDN. (H)

I wanna go home
I wanna go home
Ack ack and Zeros are driving me mad
You can't eat the chow and the liquor is bad
Take me back to Frisco
That's where we're longing to go
Oh Ma, I'm too young to die
I wanna go home

I wanna go home
I wanna go home

Our B-17s are breaking to bits
They won't hold together for many more trips
So let's go back and sell Bonds
And cheer the war heroes on
Oh Ma, I'm too young to die
I wanna go home

I wanna go home
I wanna go home
We're thru with Shortland and Bougainville
If the Japs don't get you the weather sure will
Even Texas is better than this
A land of comparitive bliss
Oh Ma, I'm too young to die
I wanna go home

I wanna go home
I wanna go home
The Medicos claim we're still able to fly
Our Chaplain tells us we're ready to die
But we'll take none of that stuff
We know when we've had enough
Oh Ma, I'm too young to die
I wanna go home

I wanna go home
I wanna go home
TIME tells us that ack ack's a beautiful sight
LIFE printed a picture of tracers at night
But the stuff that we see is real
From up close it loses appeal
Oh Ma, I'm too young to die
I wanna go home

Gene's song spread all over the South Pacific.

War throws all sorts of people together and creates unusual situations. One afternoon, Gene was lying on a cot when a large sergeant walked into his tent. The sergeant looked at Gene and said, "Are you Lieutenant Roddenberry?"

When Gene acknowledged that he was, the sergeant then asked, "Do you recognize me?"

Gene, slightly puzzled, said he didn't.

"I'm Buster Nicks," came the reply.

Gene's memory flashed back to a day in twelfth grade when he had a fateful encounter with Buster. It was first period physical education. Gene and Ray Johnson were in the gym with their class and the bell had rung. The teacher asked whoever was nearest the door to close it. Gene started to swing the gym door shut when he saw one of the school toughs and a couple of his friends running across the street to make the class. Gene kept the door open with his foot, which the tough tripped over as he came in, falling face first, sprawled out on the hardwood floor. It was an undignified position for a school tough to be in. He became the object of some laughter by those in the back of the class to whom anonymity had granted momentary courage.

To salvage his bruised ego, the tough guy immediately accused Gene of deliberately tripping him. Gene denied it to no avail and the tough told Gene he would beat him up, possibly hoping, as many bullies do, that his victim would back off. Gene wasn't intimidated, didn't back off, and told the tough he would meet him after school, across the street, in front of the small market.

The fight was short and sweet. Gene landed most of the blows, knocking the bully down several times. The former tough guy was unaware that while Gene may have appeared bookish he had a built-in sparring partner in the person of his younger but good-sized brother Bob. Gene's reputation rose, and Buster Nicks' reputation as a tough guy fell that afternoon. Now, Buster Nicks was back in Gene's life.

Buster was not looking for a fight. He was looking to set things straight. The two men shook hands and talked for the rest of the afternoon. Army training, combat, and the passage of three years had changed Buster. Later, Gene wrote to his sister: "Do you remember the big fight I had in my senior year at FHS? Well, the guy it was with is over here. I met him on one of the islands. He turned out to be a nice sort of fellow. He's a sergeant and works on one of our airplanes." What Gene did not write his sister was what happened the day after his meeting with Buster. Buster went out on a B-17 and never came back.

Gene used to say he participated in eighty-nine missions, but that is only a good guess. Record-keeping was not precise, and often missions were flown but not recorded in the pilot's permanent flight record. The chances are he flew more.

After several months of flying reconnaissance patrols, the 394th began a variety of bombing missions. Sometimes they flew out of Nandi, then they alternated between Espiritu Santo and Guadalcanal.

While conditions were not great on Nandi, and the men quietly grumbled, they couldn't wait to get back to Nandi when they were on Espiritu Santo. Some hated it worse than Guadalcanal, which was unusual because Espiritu Santo Island was a secure base and the front lines on Guadalcanal began 100 yards beyond the end of the runway. It was not unusual for Gene and crew to receive fire as they landed or took off from Henderson Field.

What bothered the men when they were on Espiritu Santo was what happened when they tried to sleep. The palms had been bulldozed to make runways and the fallen trees were pushed into large piles which quickly turned into apartments for rats—hundreds of thousands of rats. The plane crews, sleeping in two-man tents—two cots with a trench between for use as a bomb shelter—would have their sleep continually interrupted by rats scurrying across their faces.

To call conditions on Guadalcanal awful is to give only the faintest inclination of how bad they were. About the time Gene was in and out of Henderson Field, Mack Morris, a correspondent for *Yank* magazine visited. Here is an unpublished dispatch written and filed from Guadalcanal on April 15, 1943, a few days before Gene arrived.

Joe Flanagan, a lean-jawed Oklahoman who used the word "recruit" for anybody who hasn't pulled at least one hitch, is a line chief who takes his troubles philosophically, and one at a time.

In B-17 Engineering on Henderson Field, he administers to all comers. Flying Fortress ground crews in this neck of the woods have their problems in keeping combat weary bombers in commission, and the crew chiefs and flight chiefs come to Joe with more heartaches than sister Janie in third year high.

M/Sgt. Flanagan gives to each his blessing.

"Where's your prop specialist, Joe?" demands a crew

chief. "We got that No. Two engine back in shape and I'd like to finish up so somebody else can use the hoist."

"Prop specialist's sick," Joe tells him. "Hang it on yourself for the time being."

"Hell, Joe," yelps the crew chief, "we might as well fly the airplane."

"For the time being, hang the prop on," Flanagan says evenly. "You can do that all right."

"Sure, Joe, sure," the S/Sgt. grins. "We can do it."

The crew chief turns and walks out. Joe waits till he's gone and then laughs flatly. "Trouble with specialists, you miss 'em when they're gone."

It's hot inside B-17 Engineering and hotter on the bare mat of Henderson Field. Joe says he doesn't sweat much, even here, but he can appreciate the temperature.

"One time at Randolph we were doing work on a bakery oven. Got it heated up to about 170°, cut off the heat and then went inside to shovel out some sand. It was registerin' 155° then.

"I'll swear it feels hotter than that up in the nose of some of these airplanes on the line sometimes." Which is plausible when you consider that Guadalcanal is nine degrees south of the equator. It's almost impossible to breathe inside a Fortress on the ground, but the grease monkeys keep working.

"Between the weather and other things like having a specialist get sick, it's pretty hard to maintain airplanes here sometimes—working conditions being what they are—but we still do fourth echelon work when we have to. And that's fairly regular."

Fourth echelon maintenance is the highest echelon, ordinarily taken care of by well-established air depots. When it becomes necessary that an airplane fly here, it flies—if men must work 24 hours a day and go begging for required spare parts wherever they can find them.

"I don't know which is worse—the heat or the mud. The dust is the worst of all, though. Armorers get all their guns cleaned up and then some monkey backs up to 'em with all four engines turning. They gotta do it all over again." The first and only hangars on Henderson Field were built and bombed out by the Japs. Since then the ground crews have worked in the open, rain or shine, night and day.

"It's like working in the bull's-eye of a target when night raiding Mitsubishis come over, as they are in the habit of doing. Ordinarily a warning is sounded but sometimes, hard at work, the crews' first awareness of a raid is when the ground jumps under them. Decorations have been recommended for men who, on urgent jobs, continued working despite enemy planes over head."

Gene's first visits to Guadalcanal had him and his crew sleeping under the wings of their planes.

Like all groups, large and small, the 394th had people who were more popular than others. Lieutenant Talbert H. Wollam was one such. Likable and easy to talk with, Wollam mixed easily with the other men, officers and enlisted alike. Wollam was an armaments officer and as such had contact with all the crews, and he was constantly trying to learn more about how the bombs he shepherded worked when they were delivered to a target.[19]

August 2, 1943, began like any day on Espiritu Santo Island: generally clear weather, a slight breeze, scattered clouds, and humidity building. It was to be a "first lieutenants' mission," another long and boring 800-mile recon flight where every member of the crew hoped they wouldn't spot the enemy. Nothing foreshadowed the disaster that was about to happen. The majority of the 394th was in New Zealand on a week's leave, but since Gene had had that privilege some months before, he was left behind.

Gene and the other "first louies" were told to fly the standard triangle pattern 800 miles on a side on a heading that was slightly east of true north and report what they saw. Gene was first pilot with a pickup crew and a pickup aircraft, meaning they weren't Gene's regular guys or his regular plane.

Gene and crew did their preflight check and then rumbled down the number two runway—the standard South Pacific military runway of crushed coral and steel mesh he'd be-

---

[19]Wollam learned that bombs dropped on island targets usually buried themselves in the soft ground before exploding, muffling and radically decreasing the force and effectiveness of the explosion. Wollam figured out that by extending the detonator on a spike sticking a couple of feet out of the front of the bomb the bomb would explode at ground level. The 394th tested Wollam's idea and found that it worked with a minimum of problems.

come so used to. The runway was muddy from the previous day's rain, which came as regular as clockwork at 2 P.M. It was 5:50 A.M. and time to go to work.

The plane seemed to have difficulty gathering speed as it rolled down the runway. Today's modern planes, which use long, level, reinforced concrete runways, have everything mapped out and marked for the pilots. They must be at a specific speed by a certain spot on the runway and have increased their speed to a certain level by another checkpoint further on or the takeoff is aborted.

Not so in the wartime South Pacific. Takeoffs and landings were guided by experience and feel. The pilot knew when he could take off and when he couldn't by the feel and sound of the plane.

A third of the way down the runway, Gene knew he didn't have enough speed to get airborne. The engineer, Theophilus Davies, Jr., told him the brakes were dragging and squeaking. Gene began to abort the takeoff as he had been taught: he cut the throttles and applied the brakes.

The brakes on B-17s were notoriously bad. For a plane that was loved by its crews—a plane that was extremely difficult to shoot out of the sky, a plane that was remarkably, even miraculously, forgiving in flight—it had absolutely awful brakes. The brakes were operated by a sensitive hydraulic system engaged by pressing the toes forward against the tops of the rudder pedals.

Gene pressed his toes forward and found no resistance. The brakes were out and the plane continued rolling toward the end of the runway. Gene's next option was to ground loop the plane. That would turn his plane to the side, whipping the tail around, checking its forward momentum.

Gene ordered Second Lieutenant Frank Balosic, his copilot, to release the tail brake, letting the tail wheel turn freely. Balosic tried and failed, then tried again without success. Gene looked up and saw the end of the runway rushing toward him and knew he had run out of time and options. The plane roared on, bounced over a small ditch, barreled past a gun pit, and rumbled another 500 feet past the end of the runway. It crashed into a sea of palm stumps left after the end of the runway was cleared. The plane's plastic nose was crushed and fire broke out immediately. Gene and his men quickly evacuated the plane. At least, seven of them did. Sergeant John P. Kruger, bombardier, and Lieutenant Talbert H. Wollam, navigator, had their stations in the nose. For them, the war was over. They were buried the next day with military honors.[20]

It was wartime and accidents happened. One officer contacted in the course of research for this book commented that in his experience, in some theaters of operation, there were often more operational fatalities than combat fatalities.

There was an official investigation conducted by Captain Edward D. Hemingway. In three brief pages, Captain Hemingway set forth the facts and explained the circumstances: it was an accident, nothing more. Gene reacted as he was trained to do and circumstances did not permit anything past the attempted ground loop . . . and two men died. It was not a black mark against Gene's career and the incident did not even appear on his flying record, but a few men in the squadron felt differently. Just two days before, another B-17 had groundlooped to abort a takeoff. Why couldn't Gene have done the same thing? they wondered. Much of this antipathy was fueled by Gene's manner and Wollams' popularity. No one asked Gene what had happened when they returned from R&R in New Zealand, and Gene was not one to explain himself to justify his actions.[21]

In spite of the crash, Gene was back in the air within two days, flying bombing missions, but everything was rapidly becoming anticlimactic. The Army brass had decided that the B-17 would be phased out in the South Pacific, replaced with the more modern B-24. Gene was checked out on the 24 and flew several missions as copilot in the days after the accident, but the 394th was rotated back to the United States in early September 1943.

The men were going home, but their exuberance was quickly tempered by the mode of transportation: a Dutch freighter that took much of the month of September getting to San Francisco. Without escort on an open and dangerous

[20]Just hours before his crash, a few hundred miles northeast of Espiritu Santo a Japanese destroyer had cut a Navy PT boat in half. Gene's crash precluded his being involved in any air search for the survivors. The destroyed PT boat carried the number 109 and was skippered by Lt. John F. Kennedy.

[21]One of Gene's superior officers, contacted in the course of research for this book, still harbored the misunderstanding that Gene had somehow erred in the handling of the emergency. He did not change his mind until he read a copy of the Army's own investigation, conducted the day after the incident.

sea, the freighter made its way across the South Pacific to the coast of South America, which it hugged as it made its way north to the Golden Gate. The southern, zigzagging route avoided Japanese submarines, but the Dutch captain almost had a mutiny on his hands.

The ship was paid a flat rate to transport the men, and the captain decided that he could make some additional money by scrimping on the enlisted men's food. After several days of endless bologna sandwiches, including breakfast, grumbling came close to action when the men made their unhappiness known to their officers. Shortly thereafter, the food improved after the officers had a friendly chat with the captain.

Gene returned to Los Angeles, Eileen and his family, and was given a thirty-day leave. The *Los Angeles Times* ran his picture and a short description of what he had done in the South Pacific.

Gene did not go overseas again. Ironically, his experience was needed in the States as an investigator of plane crashes. In early October 1943, Gene was transferred to Forth Worth, Texas, and then to the 18th Replacement Wing, Salt Lake City, Utah. A few weeks later, the Army finally decided where his talents could best be used, and he was transferred in mid-December to the Office of Flying Safety, Region Four, Oakland, California. Six weeks after that, in February 1944, he came full circle when he was transferred to March Field, just outside Riverside, California, the same base where he had taken his enlistment physical four years earlier. In April, while stationed at March Field, Gene was promoted to captain. March Field was not the end of his travels, since he would be flying all over the country investigating crashes. There would be several more moves before Gene left the military in the middle of 1945.

In addition to the baggage Gene and Eileen packed and unpacked when they moved, there was the emotional baggage Gene carried from the South Pacific. A strong man who'd had a strong man for a role model, Gene, like his father before him, did not easily articulate his most personal thoughts.

We have only one glimpse of those rarely seen turmoils when he visited with Jim Kyle, then stationed at March Field. Socializing between officers and enlisted men was frowned on, but Gene and Jim's friendship had been forged in combat. Gene wasn't going to let tradition or regulations stand in the way.

During one of their visits, Gene mentioned to Jim that he had been in another accident, this time as a passenger. It was a military flight and Gene was going somewhere in connection with his job—the details are lost to us now—but there had been a crash and a fire. Gene said he'd pulled two or three men to safety. Then, almost as an afterthought, perhaps more to himself than to Jim, he let the emotional door open a crack when he quietly said that perhaps, somehow, it might help make up for what happened in the South Pacific. As far as can be determined, he never spoke of either incident again.

During the last few months of his life, I spent several days each week with Gene at his home. After his surgery in late July 1991 for a subdural hematoma his ability to articulate full sentences was limited. The length of Gene's sentences might have been limited, but not their import. His mind was still sharp.

We were in the family room, watching the large projection television on the pull-down screen. As I moved from channel to channel, we hit on an A&E broadcast of a documentary on a large B-17 raid over Germany. I asked Gene if he wanted to watch it and he said yes. As he watched the grainy black-and-white footage of hundreds of B-17 bombers flying missions over Germany, I watched him. After a few moments it was clear he wasn't watching the broadcast, he was back almost fifty years, remembering. After about ten minutes, I stood up and asked, "Have you seen enough, Gene?"

Sitting in his wheelchair, tired, his body betraying the force of the intellect inside, he looked directly at me and said in a voice firm with conviction, "Yes, quite enough."

CHAPTER 5

In the late 1940's civil authority was being reestablished in Europe, economies were growing, and the world was exhibiting a need for safe, reliable, intercontinental air transport. The war effort had produced new technologies that translated into larger, faster, and longer-ranging aircraft. For the first time, it was now possible to establish true international air service, and Pan American World Airways was on the cutting edge of just such a service.

Gene was discharged a captain from the Army Air Force in July 1945, but had been flying for Pan Am for several months before his official separation. He had planned on the shift to the airline for months, having applied to the CAA in March 1945, for a certificate of pilot status and a commercial rating. After a short test, he was given Airman Rating Record No. 248367 and was certified to fly single and multiengine land planes from 225–1500 HP.

He became a junior pilot with Pan Am. Based first in Miami, Florida, he transferred to New York where he flew the long runs—Pan Am's version of first lieutenant missions—with the danger replaced by boredom: New York to Johannesburg, South Africa, and New York to Calcutta—Pan Am's two longest routes. Gene flew as a third officer or as a copilot.

He and Eileen first lived in Jamaica, Long Island, but moved to River Edge, New Jersey, in early 1946. The life of a pilot, while seemingly glamorous, was most often marked by long absences from home, often weeks at a time. At one point, Gene did a rotation of six weeks on and six weeks off.

This schedule was, of course, barring mechanical break-downs, which often delayed flights for days at a time. Flying to Calcutta could take slightly over a week, but more often circumstances added several more days.

Gene had harbored ambitions of being a writer for years, but he now began to act on his ambition. Even though his single effort at song writing had spread all over the Pacific, he knew he needed education in his craft. He enrolled in three writing classes at Miami University,[1] but was trans-ferred by Pan Am to New York City in November 1945. He withdrew from all three classes with passing grades.

Even though he was unable to complete his classes, they had some effect. Gene wrote a poem and submitted it to the *New York Times,* which published the poetry on June 17, 1945, on the lower right-hand corner of the Op-Ed page:[2]

Sailor's Prayer

Oh, for a glimpse of the sea again,
For the thrill when the ocean spray,
Caught from the crest of a rolling wave,
Is a kiss from a sea bouquet.

Give me the wheel of a sailing ship
And the surge of the briny main.
Bring on the wind till the hawsers sing
And the spars and the lanyards strain.

Sing me the chanteys of sailing men
To the tune of a northern gale.
Sing to the music of anchor chains,
To the beat of a popping sail.

Bury this frame in these fields you must,
But this soul is unfettered and free.

---

[1] From Gene's transcript and the class descriptions in the University of Miami course catalog: English 333—The Modern English Novel, "Wide reading in the twentieth century novelists;" English 353—Individual Problems in Writing, "A laboratory course in creative writing with instruction in descriptive and narra-tive technique. Admission only by consent of the instructor," English 251—Advanced Composition "An advanced course in expository writing with instruction in the composition of the personal essay and the expository article."
[2] Oddly enough, in the middle of the page is an uncredited piece, "Transoceanic Rockets," describing the future of the rocket for interplanetary travel.

I'll set my sails to a western wind
And beat my course to the sea.

Capt. Eugene W. Roddenberry

Gene took advantage of his proximity to New York City and took two Columbia University extension courses—"Structure and Style" and "Workshop for Poets"—in the spring term of 1946, and received an A- in each class. In the autumn term, he again took "Workshop for Poets" as well as "Short Story Writing." Unfortunately, Pan Am was demanding more of his time and his schedule could not accommodate studying, writing, and flying. He withdrew with passing grades on January 14, 1947, but the ambition to write stayed with him.

Pan Am continued to break new ground in world airline service. In June 1947, Juan Trippe, the company's pioneering president, inaugurated the first around-the-world air route by taking a number of leading publishers and editors from the United States to fly the route on the Clipper *America*, the latest model Lockheed Constellation. At that time, Pan American had flown over a billion miles without a passenger fatality; the Lockheed Constellation had been in military and civilian service for over four and a half years with only one accident involving passenger fatalities, and Pan Am had recently won a special award from the National Safety Council for flight safety.

As Trippe and his guests were flying east in the most modern Constellation Lockheed had built, Gene was flying west on an older model, unsuspecting of the events about to turn his life upside down.

He had picked up the Pan Am Clipper *Eclipse* in Karachi, India, sharing a room the night before with Purser Anthony Volpe. Tony and Gene had flown several times before.

The number two engine had given them trouble from the start of the flight out from New York. Between New York and Gander, Newfoundland, the engine had to be shut down because of a drop in brake pressure. Spark plugs were changed on a cylinder at Gander, but the plane was forced to return to Gander a second time due to similar symptoms in the same engine. A complete cylinder was changed and was found to have suffered a top piston ring failure.

A few days later in Rome, Purser Volpe and the captain,

Joe Hart, were walking under the wing when Volpe noticed what he thought was dripping oil. He asked Hart about it and Hart responded that he wished it was oil. It was hydraulic fluid, and a new hydraulic pump was installed because of a leaking seal. It was engine number two again, and another delay. While the passengers were given a tour of the city, Volpe interpreted for Captain Hart in buying gifts for his wife in anticipation of their wedding anniversary, which was only days away.

Two days later, at Instabul, there was a problem with the magneto in engine number two. Then, Gene came on board along with nine crew members and twenty-six passengers in Karachi.

Even though he was flying with his friend Captain Joe Hart, Flight 121 was going to be tedious for Gene because he was deadheading—a pilot reduced to passenger status, an extra hand with no real duties on the long ride home. He could help out, but he was not part of the regular flight crew. He would spend much of his time sitting in a passenger seat with nothing to do but read and occasionally spell the pilot or copilot. Maybe he could flirt with Jane Bray, the gorgeous blond stewardess from Memphis whom he had noticed on his way in. Probably not, he reflected on second thought, as the plane seemed to be full. Stewardess Bray and the purser, Anthony Volpe, would be busy until the passengers went to sleep. Well, Gene thought, he could always work on his assignments for the writing class at Columbia. He turned his attention to what to write for his current assignment.

Everything was routine as the *Eclipse* rolled down the Karachi Airport runway and became airborne at 3:37 on the afternoon of June 18, 1947. The plane slowly climbed to its cruising altitude of 18,500 feet. The schedule called for a ten-and-a-half-hour flight with an arrival at Istanbul at 2:08, local time, the next morning.

Five hours out of Karachi, Gene gave Joe Hart a break at the wheel. With over 12,000 hours and 2.5 million miles in the air, Hart was a Pan Am veteran and one of the most experienced pilots working for the company. During the war, he made thirteen South Atlantic crossings in twelve days. Other pilots thought Joe tended to be in a hurry at times, but by any standard, Joe Hart was an excellent pilot.

While the captain stretched his legs, Gene gave a navigational exercise to one of the flight crew. It was interrupted by a problem with the number one engine. An exhaust rocker arm had broken. Gene feathered the propeller and took the engine off line. Hart came back on the flight deck and evaluated the situation. The Lockheed Constellation was a fine, well-tested plane that had been in both military and civilian service for almost five years. It was easily capable of flying on three engines. Further, Hart knew that local fields did not have the capability of repairing the damaged engine. Landing now would mean a delay of several days while parts and mechanics were flown in. There had been too many delays already on the flight out from New York caused by problems with the number two engine. Hart decided to push on to Istanbul.

Gene knew that flying on three engines was perfectly acceptable, having done it several times himself. In any event, there was nothing more he could do; he decided to take a nap. There were two bunks built into the flight deck. Gene crawled into the lower bunk, pulled the curtains shut, and promptly went to sleep.

For the two hours Gene napped, all was not well on the flight deck. The three functioning engines, doing the work of four, began to overheat, even though the outside temperature was below zero. Hart decided to descend to a lower altitude where the engines would run cooler. It was tense on the bridge. One of the engineers, accepting a cup of coffee from Volpe, asked him when he was planning on serving breakfast. "About two hours before landing," Tony replied. The engineer told him he had plenty of time; they were behind the flight plan, as they had to reduce power to prevent additional overheating. Meanwhile, both flight engineers kept their eyes on the engine readouts.

Hart ordered Radioman Nelson Miles to advise local fields of their position and situation. At 10 P.M. Miles broadcast their position as 14,000 feet, fifty miles east of Baghdad, Iraq, and ninety miles east of the Royal Air Force Field at Habbaniya, Iraq.

Habbaniya Tower reacted conservatively and strongly suggested that an emergency landing be made there but Hart declined, knowing the airport's lack of adequate repair facilities. He asked Habbaniya Tower to advise the civilian airfields in its area that they were proceeding to Istanbul on three engines. He quickly learned that no other airfields on his flight path would be open until dawn, several hours away. In case of trouble, he would have few options.

At 11 P.M., Flight 121 was seventy-five miles northwest of Habbaniya at 10,000 feet. Alerted to Hart's situation, Damascus Airport opened and Damascus Radio went on the air a few minutes past 11 P.M.

Thirty minutes later, all options vanished.

A pilot's response to the cockpit alarm is a conditioned reflex. When the alarm's sound filled the flight deck, Gene was instantly awake, rolling out of the bunk and into the emergency that was only beginning.

No one had to tell him what the problem was: Gene had seen plenty of engine fires during the war. He saw the bright light shining through the cockpit window, illuminating the left side of Joe Hart's face. It was the thing most dreaded by all who fly—fire in flight. The number two engine, the one closest to the fuselage on the left wing, was burning furiously. The flight crew tried the normal fire-extinguishing procedures to no effect. The brightness and intensity of the flames told them that the problem was beyond their control—the magnesium parts of the engine were burning and the built-in fire extinguishers were useless. Captain Hart knew it was just a matter of minutes before the engine burned itself off the wing. How airworthy the plane would be after that was anybody's guess. Hart had to take the plane down. Gene was more pessimistic. He thought the plane would blow up in midair before it could be crash-landed.

Concerned with the passengers and the possibility of panic building in the cabin, Hart told Gene to take charge of the passengers and prepare them for a crash landing just as he put the plane into a steep dive. Hart's confidence in his friend's ability to handle the passengers saved Gene's life. Had he stayed on the flight deck, he would have ridden to his death.

Seconds before Gene entered the passenger cabin, Jane Bray, napping in a seat, had been awakened by the fire's light shining through the cabin windows. Looking out, she saw the engine burning, the fire spreading to the wing and, curiously, for no particular reason, noted a scene that would remain with her: bright stars, serenely distant diamonds set against the black velvet sky, twinkling through the yellow-white flames of the burning engine.

Hart wanted to make for the emergency landing field at

Deir ez Zor, Syria, but the extent of the fire made it impossible to go anywhere except down. Circumstances forced him to undertake the most difficult and frightening maneuver any pilot can ever be called upon to perform: a crash landing, at night, on unknown terrain in a burning plane.

As Gene left the flight deck, making his way to the passenger cabin, Hart ordered Radioman Miles to send an emergency message. Miles sent the following: "To H.A. from K.MO. My callsign is NC.845. Position at 2330Z 34.38'N. 41.04'E. Heading at 298 degs. Ground speed 163 kts., Number 2 on fire." Habbaniya Tower acknowledged the message but received nothing further. A few moments later, all they heard was a continuous tone, as if the plane's Morse key were being held down. Then nothing but silence.

As Gene entered the passenger cabin, he saw there was some hysteria building; the passengers were agitated, not knowing what was happening. Gene knew instinctively what to do. He applied a survival skill learned in childhood: he told the passengers what they wanted to hear. With difficulty he walked down the aisle, keeping his balance by holding onto the seat armrests. Speaking as calmly as he could, he told the passengers, "it looks worse than it is," "we know where we are going to land," and "we know what we are doing"—lies he hoped would reassure the passengers and keep them calm.

He told Jane Bray to stay seated while he and Tony Volpe directed the passengers in crash procedures. Gene knew they had very little time to prepare. Jane rose to assist, but in the urgency of the moment Gene spoke sharply to her, telling her to stay in her seat and to fasten her seatbelt. The passengers were told to do the same. Gene hoped they would have a chance to use the crash procedures, as by now the entire left wing was engulfed in flame. The likelihood of surviving a crash landing seemed to grow more remote with each passing second.

Tony Volpe sat down next to Jane Bray and buckled himself in. He tried to reassure Jane that things would be better once the engine fell off the wing. The same thing had happened recently to a Pan Am Constellation over Connecticut with Janet Leigh and Lawrence Olivier on board. Everything turned out all right there. Gene sat in the third to last row and buckled himself in.

The professional demeanor of Gene and Tony Volpe, com-

bined with Gene's comforting tone of voice and authorata-
tively delivered lies, if not reassuring to the passengers at
least deflected their building panic. An odd calm settled over
the cabin. Everyone sat and waited. No one said a word.
There was nothing more to do. Many had resigned themselves to the idea that they were going to die. Some of the
passengers were praying. Years later, Gene, who had rejected religion and supernatural beliefs as a teenager, reflected on that moment:

"Something happened to me during that crash that had a
big influence on my life. As we were coming down, and
death was absolutely certain, I was thinking all sorts of
things—should I scratch a message to my wife on the metal
of the side of the plane? What was I going to say—'I love
you?' She already knew that. I thought, maybe I just ought
to pray. I remember thinking, 'Wait a minute.' I didn't ordinarily pray and I wouldn't have much respect for a god that
would accept prayers when I was in dire straits like this. He
would be bound to judge you, if he's judging you, on what
you did in ordinary times. He just wouldn't accept prayers at
times like this. I remember making up my mind not to pray.
I thought, 'OK, take me as I am.'

"I've always been rather proud of that. If you believe
something in a dire emergency, that is probably what you
truly believe."

The number two engine burned itself off the left wing and
fell into the Syrian desert below, making the wing unstable.
Survivors described the sensation as if a giant tooth were
ripped from the plane. The falling engine ruptured additional
gasoline lines, feeding more fuel to the flames. The loss of
the engine and the diminishing control over the flight surfaces caused the plane to vibrate uncontrollably. It seemed to
be shaking itself to pieces in midair while it circled, an injured bird looking for a safe haven.

In spite of his minimal control of the aircraft, Captain
Hart distinguished himself by making a smooth approach
and attempted what one passenger, Michael Graham, a
Royal Air Force pilot, later called "a perfect crash landing."
Although Hart circled to pick out the best area to land on,
the unseen surface of the Syrian desert did not cooperate.

A woman forward of Gene screamed, and he loosened his
seatbelt to move forward and see what her trouble was. Seconds later, the plane crashed into the dark Syrian desert.

Gene suffered two broken ribs as a result of not being properly strapped in.

As Hart guided the plane into a wheels-up landing, the left wingtip made the first contact with the ground. The number one propeller hit, and then the left wing at the number two engine position struck an unseen mound of sand. The thundering impact tore the left wing from the fuselage near its root. This sudden impact caused the aircraft to spin violently to the left, revolving in a tight half-circle while continuing to skid backwards for 200 feet before coming to rest in flames 400 feet from where it had first hit the ground. From the beginning of the fire at 10,000 feet to the crash on the desert floor, no more than six minutes had passed. To the participants, it seemed like six lifetimes.

The combination of desert sand and plane fuselage impacting at more than 150 mph produced a roaring, tearing sound. Bodies, baggage, and anything loose flew around inside the cabin as the plane skidded across the sand, spun around, and came to a stop. On impact, the plane's electrical system failed and everything went dark. As the plane revolved and slid backward, the fuselage broke in two just behind the trailing edges of the wing. Four passengers sitting in that row died instantly. The gas tanks ruptured, and a wall of flame enveloped the forward section of the cabin and flight deck. The passengers in the forward section and the crew on the flight deck died horribly—those who weren't killed by the impact were burned to death by the burning oil and aviation fuel that washed over them.

The second the plane came to a rest, Roddenberry, Volpe, and Bray quickly began evacuating their charges through the ruptured fuselage. As the fire in the front of the plane approached their section, they knew they had only seconds to get everyone out. Moving as fast as they could, they pushed open the cabin door and guided the uninjured passengers out. Gene and Tony handed down the injured, then the uninjured passengers on the ground dragged them to safety.

Even with the composed and focused actions of the surviving crew, the evacuation did not go smoothly. After most of the passengers had been removed, the seatbelt of the Majarani of Pheleton would not release, trapping her in the burning wreckage. The large woman was hysterical. Gene forced the belt open and rescued the Indian royal. She and her son, the prince, were put with the others on the sand, away from the plane and the fire.

Gene pulled out several people who were themselves on fire and used a pillow he found on the ground to smother the flames. On board, the flames were growing in intensity, so he could only make a couple of trips into the passenger compartment. The last passenger he pulled out died in his arms. The wind changed, blowing the burning gasoline directly over the ship's wreckage; Gene and Volpe were unable to rescue any more passengers out of the plane.

The other passengers safe for the moment, the trio turned their thoughts to their friends on the flight deck. They ran around the burning fuselage and wings to the front of the plane. Looking in the cockpit windows, they could see the flight crew sitting at their stations, slumped over in their seats, dead or unconscious. Frantically pounding on the windows, Volpe, Bray, and Roddenberry tried to rouse their friends until the flames drove them back.

Many years later, when asked about the crash, Gene's eyes would lose their focus as his memory transported him back to that traumatic time:

"I remember a great, flaming pool of gasoline, a glimpse of bodies writhing in the flames as they were burning." The passage of years never dimmed Gene's horror of that moment nor his frustration at being unable to help his friends.

Gene and Tony Volpe made their way to the tail of the plane and rescued all the first-aid equipment and luggage they could, along with many of the passengers' coats for protection against the cold night air. They also pulled out a twenty-man survival raft. It was nearly 2 A.M. local time.

In a matter of minutes, a model of modern technological wizardry had become a tangled metal funeral pyre for fourteen people. The survivors moved away from the wreckage as the fire continued to blaze. There was no sound except the crackling of the flames and the moans and cries of the injured survivors. The plane burned for hours.

Standing in a slight hollow in the cold desert sands, Gene's feelings of helplessness were replaced by a cold realization: he was the surviving flight officer. Emotions would have to wait for later—he had responsibilities. He turned his attention to the living. It was cold, people were injured, and he was in charge. He was two months short of his twenty-sixth birthday.

The passenger manifest listed three British Army officers, professional soldiers, all captains about Gene's age or slightly older, and all uninjured. Jane Bray remembers that there was no question that Gene was in charge. No one challenged his authority or disagreed with his decisions. Everyone worked together.

The plane had crashed at approximately 1:45 A.M. local time, leaving almost three hours until sunrise. There was no friendly moon to give off light that night. It was as dark and lonely as only a desert at night can be. The three crew members and uninjured passengers did what they could, administering first aid where possible, but with several passengers severely burned, the need was for more than simple first aid. Fortunately, one of the rescued bags was a doctor's kit. (The doctor had survived the crash but was too deep in shock to give assistance.) In the kit, Gene found morphine and sleeping tablets. He gave this to all the burned and injured. He considered this find fortunate; by the time the injured recovered from their shock, they were well sedated.

The surviving crew members had not escaped unscathed. Jane Bray had badly sprained her ankle when she jumped from the ship. After working steadily for several hours, she collapsed. Gene had broken two ribs and sustained a number of contusions and abrasions, but he continued to work through the night. Tony Volpe also had an injured rib and a slightly twisted back.

There was another dimension to their dilemma, which Gene did not discuss with the other survivors. Since he had left the flight deck, he did not know exactly where they had crashed or if their position had been successfully radioed to authorities. Although he knew a search would be made as soon as the sun rose, he had no idea how quickly help would arrive or how long his passengers could survive in the harsh desert conditions.

Although the fire gave off some light, the full extent of the damage was not visible until morning. Sunrise came at 4:24 A.M. Only then did the crew and passengers see that the distinctive Constellation tail, thirty feet of the rear fuselage, and a portion of the right wing and one engine were all that remained intact and unburned.

The left wing lay on the sand 200 feet from the main body of the wreckage and the number two engine was a mile back on the flight path. The superior flying skill of Joe Hart and his crew, and the quick action by the three surviving crew members, accounted for the number of lives saved.

Sunrise brought a new problem: the desert heat. As the sun rose above the horizon, so rose the temperature. Gene, Tony Volpe, and the uninjured passengers inflated the survival raft and propped it up to provide shade. The passengers huddled beneath the makeshift shelter and waited. Volpe overheard one passenger comment to another, "I never thought a life raft would come in handy in the middle of the desert. Good thinking."

Shortly after sunrise, Gene looked up and saw a dozen or so desert tribesmen on horseback on top of a nearby sand dune, silhouetted against the morning sky. Sunlight glinted off the swords they waved above their heads. They were surveying the wreckage, the survivors, and the burned victims. Gene knew they were not there to help. He remembered that years earlier Pan American representatives were supposed to have negotiated agreements with the desert tribes. The tribespeople would receive a reward for every survivor brought in, as opposed to the often more lucrative alternative of killing survivors and looting the wreckage. Gene could almost see these men thinking over which would be more profitable.

Remembering what he called "the American Handshake," Gene approached the man who appeared to be the leader and stuck out his hand. The man took it and shook it vigorously. In spite of the night's ordeal, his torn and dirty uniform and his own injuries, Gene's bearing, his presence, and feigned confidence seemed to work. Even though there was an insurmountable language barrier, some form of mutual respect passed between the two men. While the living were left alone, the horsemen robbed the dead and helped themselves to the unburned luggage. Two hours later, after they had completed their ghoulish task, the tribesmen rode back into the desert, offering little help to the injured beyond leaving a bit of water and food. Perhaps they thought sparing the survivors' lives was a generous enough gesture, but there was more likely another reason.

The crash site was not in the middle of the desert at all. What Gene did not know, and the tribesmen did, was that the *Eclipse* had crashed only four miles northwest of the small village of Mayadine. Spotting telephone wires and poles, Gene knew that there was some civilization nearby;

just how close he had to determine. He formed two parties of two men each and ordered them to walk in opposite directions following the poles until they spotted something. They were to report back what they saw.

The nearby townspeople were not idle either. Even though the crash had occurred in the early morning hours, it had been observed as the plane had dropped flares and flown over the village on its approach. One aged resident of Mayadine described what he saw: "She burned and circled and circled and then she went down into the sands." Sometime after sunrise, after the mounted tribesmen had left, several dozen townspeople descended on the crash scene. They began helping themselves to, as one crash survivor described it, "every bright or metal object that wasn't too hot to conceal in their flowing robes. They made a fight of it if anyone tried to stop them." Within a short time, all the survivors had left were their toilet articles and what they were wearing.

After he determined the correct direction, Gene walked the four miles into the town, located a telephone, and called the emergency field at Deir ez Zor, thirty-eight miles away. It was 8 A.M. Syrian time.

At 10:30 that same morning, Juan Trippe and his guests on the around-the-world flight landed at Istanbul. The first news he was given was of the crash. Trippe made arrangements for a relief plane to fly to Syria. Within hours, the Pan Am Clipper *Racer* took off from Shannon, Ireland, for Damascus to pick up survivors.

The garrison commander at Deir ez Zor dispatched Syrian Army planes, ambulances, jeeps, medical personnel, military police, and gendarmes to the crash site with medical supplies and water. Captain Chazli, the chief instructor of the Syrian Army Air Force, made two landings at the site with medical personnel and supplies and helped evacuate the wounded. Also at Deir ez Zor that morning was a flight of Syrian student pilots in thirteen small training planes. They immediately flew to the crash site and gave what help they could. Later that morning, two C-47s of the Syrian Airways Company left Damascus carrying Pan Am officials, medical personnel, and Robert Evans Cashin, third secretary of the American Embassy.

After making his call, Gene returned to the crash site and supervised the treatment of the injured, gave what comfort he could, and waited for the medical teams to show up.

When the rescuers arrived, they found fourteen dead—seven crew and seven passengers—eleven passengers who needed hospitalization, and eight passengers who were unharmed or only slightly injured. The gendarmes immediately cordoned off the site and protected the survivors and what little was left of the plane and the passengers' belongings.

By noon, all the survivors had been transported by jeep over thirty-eight nearly roadless miles to the Presbyterian mission hospital at Deir ez Zor, where they were treated by the resident physician, Dr. Monroe Bertsch, Jr., and his small staff of nurses. Later that afternoon, the most seriously injured were evacuated by air to Beirut, accompanied by Jane Bray and Tony Volpe. The walking wounded, uninjured passengers, and Gene were flown to Damascus.

Three days after the crash, Gene sent the following short letter to his parents in California.

June 22, 1947

Dear Mother and Dad—

Hello from Damascus. This is an exciting city full of exotic bazaars, Bedouins, Moslems, Roman ruins and biblical places such as the Sea of Galilee, etc. Weather is like S. Cal and a garden in the midst of this desolate desert country. I hope you were not too worried—Dad, that a PAA ship went down out here. I do hope that my letter from Istanbul had not reached you by then or you would have guessed it was my ship. I am very well so don't worry at all.

I have a couple of broken ribs and a bruise or two but all that is very minor and we can consider it as being very lucky. I can tell you all about it sometime later. I'm stuck here several days with the investigation as I am the Airline Pilots Association's man in this area and must assist with the investigation in that capacity. I was very worried about Eileen and hope that Frank and Maude had not left yet. [Maude and Frank Rexroat were visiting their daughter in New Jersey before the crash.] I'll take a vacation when I return and give her plenty of time to relax before I start flying again.

You will be proud to learn that I have received a
personal commendation from the PAA vice-president
here to make the investigation, for saving several lives
and commanding the rescue and hospital operation
in an efficient manner. The real trick of the matter
is that everyone performed wonderfully including the
badly injured and proved what fine people average
human beings are when confronted by a catastrophe
involving life and death.

I'll put this on a homebound plane with a friend
who will mail it in N.Y. I hope to get home on the
1st of July. Will write soon after. Hello to Nana
and love to all the family

Love

Gene

Damascus is the oldest inhabited city in the world. The
year before Gene's crash, it had become the capital of a
newly independent Syria. A city of contrasts, its northern
section is modern and its southern section ancient, with a ba-
zaar of labyrinthine corridors, the Great Mosque, a medieval
citadel, and teeming multitudes of colorful and exotic people
from all over the Middle East. Exciting and mysterious, Damascus was an ever-changing whirlpool of sights, smells
and sounds. The city was the perfect place for an aspiring
writer to soak up background and color—to be exposed to a
thousand stories waiting to be written.

All Gene wanted to do was go home.

His stay in Damascus was longer than expected, but it
wasn't his injuries that delayed his departure. His two broken ribs had been taped in the Presbyterian Mission Hospital
at Deir ez Zor and he felt good enough to copilot the DC-3
that had been sent to take him to Damascus a day or two after the crash.

His delay was due to the Syrian government's conviction
that since he was the surviving flight officer his testimony
was vital to *their* inquiry. It didn't matter to the Syrians that
several highly qualified and experienced agencies of the
U.S. government were conducting in-depth investigations of
the crash. It had happened on Syrian soil, and the newly organized Syrian aeronautics bureaucracy, fueled by national
pride and local ego, would not have its sovereignty usurped

by foreigners. Gene would be available to answer questions until the Syrians had finished their investigation.

Gene stayed with his friend, fellow Pan Am pilot Bill Hamilton, who had flown him up from Deir ez Zor. This would not be the only time Hamilton would fly a plane for Gene. Twenty-two years later, he would be the pilot flying Majel and Gene from Tokyo to Honolulu. Learning who the pilot was, Gene sent his business card to the flight deck. On the back he wrote:

> Bill, Haven't seen you since I survived NC47 crash out of Damascus. Walk back & say hello.
>
> Rod

The two old friends visited, and a few weeks after the flight Gene wrote and exposed some long-held feelings about his experience in Syria in a letter to Bill.

> Dear Bill,
>   Sorry to have missed you in Waikiki as I wanted
> very much to sit down with you and reminisce
> about old times as well as get your attitudes on the
> new jets and air transportation today. Interested partly
> because of my Pan American background but also
> because as a writer almost anything I learn about
> anything can be put to use in a story or script
> someday. The writer who stops watching, asking, and
> wondering is a writer in trouble.
>   As I said on the airplane, my feelings towards
> you have always been remarkably warm since I can
> never forget the "friend in need" you were that day
> I staggered into Damascus with broken ribs and a brown
> spot on my shorts. Man, I needed that drink.
>   I still remember with gratitude your running
> interference for me through the Syrian petty bureaucrats
> who were trying to stage a comic Arab-style "CAA
> investigation." I was in no mood to answer their
> questions such as, "Was it the top or bottom wing
> that came off first?"[3]

---

[3]The Syrian aeronautic bureaucracy was just being put in place, and this crash was an overwhelming beginning for them. Gene in this instance was being humorous, but his frustration at wanting to leave then was quite real. He resented being used as a "teaching example" for the Syrians.

Gene represented the Airline Pilots Association in the investigation. After two weeks of endless questions, he returned home. It is unclear whether he left with the permission of the Syrian government or, having grown tired of their questions, simply walked out before their investigation was completed; but as the State Department file does not mention any problems with the local authorities it may be safe to assume Gene did his duty to the satisfaction of all parties concerned.

For Gene, River Edge, New Jersey, never looked so good. This homecoming was second only to coming back from the war. Gene was a survivor of Pan Am's worst crash in years, returning to the first home he ever owned with a particular mission in mind: starting a family. Years later, he admitted that during the descent in the burning plane he had thought about not having a child, not being able to leave something of himself behind. Additionally, the loss of a baby boy in a miscarriage two years earlier had diminished and Gene felt it was time to try again.[4] His close brush with death sparked a deep-seated drive. He would taste immortality through children.

Gene's two broken ribs notwithstanding, Eileen became pregnant around July 8, 1947, within days of Gene's return.

Over forty years later, he remembered his clarity of purpose in a cryptic inscription written on a photograph of himself that he gave to his firstborn two years before his death. She had not understood what her father had written until research for this book brought meaning to his words. The inscription reads:

> To Darleen—I came back determined to have a child.
> I'm glad it was you.
>
> Love, Dad

At home in New Jersey with Eileen tending to him, Gene rested and healed, pleased and happy to be home. In late July, he testified at an inquiry held by the Civil Aeronautics

---

[4]We have almost no details of this sad fact, but it is a good illustration of how Gene treated deeply personal feelings. He never spoke of it to his family. Caroline Glen knew about it because she was told by Eileen. Gene mentioned it once in a letter to the noted actor, Rip Torn, twenty years later, and once to Majel after the birth of their son, Rod, in 1974.

Board's Safety Division at the Hotel Lexington in New York City. Also testifying were the other two Pan Am crew survivors, Purser Anthony Volpe and Stewardess Sara Jane Bray.

Their stories, calmly recounting their activities before, during, and after the crash, were testaments to individual bravery and heroism. Robert W. Chrisp, who presided over the inquiry for the CAB, read into the record a commendation of the three by the board for their "devotion to duty, their calmness and efficiency in this difficult and hazardous experience." Volpe and Bray also received citations from the Transport Workers Union of America for "heroic conduct in the line of duty."

Gene wrote a report to the Pan Am's Flight Service Department:

> As the senior surviving crew member of Clipper 88845 which crashed at Meyadine, Syria on June 18, 1947, I wish to file with your department this report commending the personal courage and professional ability of both Tony Volpe, Purser, and Miss Jane Bray, Stewardess.
>
> Were this the military service, with which I am more familiar, I am certain they would by this time have received decorations commensurate with the valor and merit they demonstrated. However, the company and the public are well aware of this fact and I request that this report be placed in their personal files as a matter of record.
>
> It would be easy to cover several pages pointing out incidents in which one or the both were involved which would prove their courage again and again. In the performance of rescue and medical aid they demonstrated, beyond coolness and ability, a high degree of training of which your department can be proud. Rather than continue at length, I direct your attention to the survivors' reports of the accident and to the many letters since received from passengers and their families further praising these actions.

Gene got another award, of sorts. Later that month he applied for and was granted Workman's Compensation for injuries suffered in the crash. He received $40—or $20 for each broken rib.

Ribs healed, Gene began flying again, much to Eileen's

displeasure. Over the ensuing months, three incidents caused Gene to rethink his flying career.

In February 1948, Caro Dolan, Special Technical Consultant to the Senate Interstate and Foreign Commerce Committee released the committee's conclusion regarding the cause of the crash. Dolan concluded that Pan Am's failure to change the number two engine after it had exhibited numerous symptoms of malfunctioning during the flight from New York to Karachi was the cause of the crash. Gene realized that in the position of copilot he had little control over maintenance decisions, decisions that were often made under financial and scheduling pressures.

A month after that report was issued, a second event gave Gene pause. On April 4, 1948, almost nine months to the day of Gene's return, the Roddenberry's first child, Darleen Anita, was born in Hackensack, New Jersey. Now it was no longer just Gene and Eileen: they were a family and Gene had to look to the future. Gene was responsible for another life, and Eileen made it clear that she had no wish to raise a baby on a Pan Am widow's pension.

Finally, Gene came close to dying again, and again this close brush with death was from a combination of circumstances beyond his control.

During the early months of 1948, Gene was flying out of La Guardia Field when he relearned a lesson all pilots know: takeoffs and landings are the most dangerous parts of a flight. Gene was copilot on the flight service to the Bahamas. It was snowing, the wind was blowing, and the conditions were icy. The plane was deiced and quickly taxied for takeoff. As the wheels retracted and the plane began to gain altitude, the controls abruptly froze. The plane continued its assent, but it was in danger of stalling, which would have meant almost certain death for everyone on board. There would be no gliding down to a gentle landing. Without forward momentum, the plane would have all the aerodynamic properties of a large, silver stone.

Gene and the pilot only had a very few seconds to do whatever they could. They both applied brute force to their wheels, putting every ounce of strength they could into freeing the frozen controls. With sweat running down their faces from exertion and fear, with only seconds left before the plane went into a stall, the controls suddenly freed up and everything was back to normal.

Pan Am was unable to recreate the circumstances that caused the controls to lock. No cause was determined and no solution offered to prevent it from happening again. By the narrowest of margins, luck, not pilot skill, had prevented another disaster.

It was enough for Gene. He would not become a victim of happenstance if he could help it. He had, for years, entertained the idea of earning a living as a writer. His first thoughts were to be a poet, an expression of his more romantic and impractical nature and the lasting influence of his high school English teacher, Virginia Church. Finding out that most poets either starve or work at something else to earn a living, he quickly dropped that ambition. He decided he wanted to write fiction.

A neighbor on Dorchester had bought a new toy, a television set. It cost almost $1,000 and had a six-inch screen. It was early 1948 and television broadcasting was rarely more than four hours a night, beginning at 7 P.M., but Gene, with his science fiction reading background, saw beyond the tiny screen with the fuzzy, flickering picture. He saw what could become the entertainment medium of the future. With a television in every household, the demand for programming would be enormous—and so would the demand for writers.

On May 15, 1948, Gene resigned from Pan Am. The house on Dorchester was put on the market and plans were made for a cross-country trip to California, where Gene would be a writer in the new medium of television.

Gene had assumed that because California was the center of motion picture production it was also the center of television production. He did not investigate or phone ahead to learn what television's situation was. He had no knowledge of television production, script requirements, or the probabilities of employment for a new writer with no credits and no experience, or even any proven ability to write for the medium. Gene was about to find out that charm, intelligence, ambition, and talent weren't all that he would need to succeed.

In the ensuing years, Gene honed his storytelling ability to a high degree. He was a top free-lance writer well before he created *Star Trek,* writing dozens of screenplays and series pilots, but he never tried to tell the great drama he lived early one morning on the Syrian desert.

Asked why he never turned this gripping experience into

a script, he replied, "I don't think it possible to capture the feeling of the survivors as they experienced the sunrise on that morning so many years ago. There was a small group of us who were alive and thankful that we had survived what was an unsurvivable crash. I could never display the impact surviving had on me and the others. I knew, for all my skills, I could not capture that moment."

CHAPTER 6

When Gene and family arrived in August 1948, postwar Los Angeles was just beginning its long climb to domination of the Pacific Rim. World War II had made Southern California a boomtown. The aircraft plants and other wartime industries had been established to provide airplanes and war materiel had attracted people from all over the country. Skilled workers had flocked to Los Angeles and its neighboring cities. Many stayed after the war and began to raise families.

A revolution in communications was beginning as television moved from its long gestation into infancy. As a technological accomplishment television was a reality, but as a commercial enterprise it was only beginning to invent itself. For a number of reasons, this was the worst time for a fledgling writer to begin a career.

Television had been developed well before World War II[1] but because of the war's voracious appetite for raw materials, the commercial exploitation of television had to wait until the war was over.[2]

By 1946, there were sufficient materials, factories, and

---

[1]Demonstrations of television broadcasting began as early as the late 1920's including experiments with primitive color television in 1929. NBC had an experimental station, W2XBS, in New York City in 1930. CBS had a similar station the next year. NBC televised the official opening of the World's Fair on April 30, 1939, and Franklin D. Roosevelt became the first incumbent president to appear on television.

[2]Neither network could claim a "first." NBC and CBS both received their commercial licenses on July 1, 1941.

workers available to begin the manufacture and sales of television sets,[3] but the high prices, $750 to $1,000 in 1940's dollars, kept sales limited to the well-to-do and the corner tavern.

In 1947, NBC broadcast the World Series. It was carried on stations in New York, Philadelphia, Schenectady, and Washington, D.C., and played to an audience estimated at 3.9 million people, with 3.5 million of them watching from neighborhood bars. The desire to own a television set became contagious.

Even though people were fascinated with the fuzzy, black-and-white pictures produced by the primitive technology, television did not grow as fast as the public's fascination seemed to predict. Three separate government activities combined to hinder television's rapid propagation—which also made it difficult for Gene to secure employment as a writer.

In September 1948, the Federal Communications Commission (FCC) imposed a freeze on all new television channel assignments. This limited growth to the 36 stations then on the air and the 70 that had already received construction permits. The FCC wanted to determine what frequency allocation plan would best provide a competitive nationwide system. They also wanted to develop a policy on color television.[4] The freeze lasted until July 1952.

During that four-year period, Hollywood also went through a major transformation. Post-wartime movie attendance had peaked in 1946, with gross receipts totalling nearly $2 billion—when movie tickets were less than a dollar. The motion picture industry began to change with the 1948 United States Supreme Court decision in *United States* v. *Paramount, et al.* The major motion picture companies—Paramount, Loew's (including MGM), RKO, Twentieth Century-Fox, Warner Brothers, Columbia Pictures, Universal, and United Artists—had violated antitrust laws by own-

---

[3] In the summer of 1946, RCA put its first black-and-white sets on the market.

[4] This was a major reason why CBS entered the network business late in the game. They were pushing to have their color system adopted as the standard. Some television historians believe that if this had occurred, television's development would have been set back several years. The CBS system was not reliable or compatible with the black-and-white system then in common use. Eventually, the RCA all-electronic system, which was compatible, was adopted.

ing their own theater chains. They had to sell their theaters. The studios thought that unless they owned the theaters, they could not find outlets for the 400 to 500 films they produced each year, so they cut back on production. Experienced directors, producers, actors, writers, and technicians found themselves out of work.

Adding to the climate of depression and fear were hearings by the House Committee on Un-American Activities,[5] which began in Washington, D.C., in 1947. It was the beginning of the great Hollywood witch hunts, with the committee examining filmmakers suspected of a "pro-Communist" bias. More than a few careers were destroyed[6] and more than a few boosted[7] in the movie community. Nor did television escape the witch hunters' wrath. The 1950 publication of *Red Channels*—a book carrying no author credit—listed the names of performers, writers, composers, and producers alleged to be "Communists," "fellow travelers," or "dupes of the Communists."[8]

Still, even though television stations were few in number and sets expensive, the public saw something wonderful and fascinating in the little box with the flickering light and grainy black-and-white picture. They bought sets by the hundreds of thousands. Price did not stop them: people took

---

[5]A committee of the House of Representatives organized in 1938 to investigate Fascist, Communist, and other organizations deemed to be "un-American." The committee was criticized for abusing witnesses and proceeding on the flimsiest of evidence, but even with that criticism the committee's status went from temporary to permanent in 1945. Many famous and talented individuals were blacklisted. A prominent member of the committee in the late 1940's was Richard M. Nixon.

[6]Besides destroying careers, the committee's work produced at least one fatality. The lead actor on *The Goldbergs* (a successful transplant from radio to early television), Phillip Loeb, was blacklisted for alleged "left-wing sympathies." When the show aired on NBC for the 1952 season, Loeb was gone. Depressed and embittered, his career in a shambles, Loeb took an overdose of sleeping pills in 1954.

[7]More than one Hollywood "luminary" was willing to demonstrate his "patriotism." Lapsed Liberal Democrat, soon to be ex-actor and spokesman for General Electric (and president), Ronald Reagan was, from 1943 to 1947, a "confidential informant" for the FBI under the code name T-10.

[8]*Red Channels: The Report of Communist Influence in Radio and Television* was published by *Counterattack*. Both were products of American Business Consultants, whose principals were former FBI agents John G. Keenan, Kenneth Bierly, and Theodore Kirkpatrick.

out loans to buy sets. In the late 1940's, a New York banker reported that the most cited reason for new small loans was a "television set." When asked by the banker how they planned on repaying the loan, most applicants gave an answer that sent chills through Hollywood: they would save money by cutting back on the number of times they went to the movies. During the freeze period, television sets sold like no other product in consumer history. Between 1948 and 1952, the number of television sets in the United States rose from 250,000 to over 15 million.

In Los Angeles there was little local production of television programs, the majority being piped in from New York and occasionally Chicago by coaxial cable or sent by kinescope. Gene and his family had unknowingly left the heart of TV production, but he had no intention of going back. Another cross-country move with a wife, small baby, and limited resources was not for him. Besides, his and Eileen's families were in Southern California. With the large number of out-of-work movie craftspeople, Gene realized that a career writing for television was not going to happen right away. Priorities would have to be rearranged.

To save money, he, Eileen, and baby Darleen moved into his parent's home at 2710 Green Street, Temple City, a Los Angeles suburb. Brother Bob was living at home, having returned from his wartime service in 1946. He had followed his father's example and joined the LAPD. Gene's sister, Doris, was married and off on her own. Two additional people and a baby made the two-bedroom house a bit crowded, but Papa and Glen would not have it any other way. Besides, it reminded them of the days when Glen's family lived with them. For Papa and Glen it was always good to have family around.

With money short and television writing prospects nonexistent, Gene ended up combining his winning ways with people and his interest in photography by becoming the sales manager for Tri-Vision Sales Corporation of Alhambra, a company promoting and selling 3-D cameras. Prized today by camera collectors, 3-D photography never caught the American public's fancy in a big way. The vaunted title of "sales manager" was not a position that would advance Gene's writing career or, given the history of 3-D photography, be of great longevity. Gene knew that he would have to do something else.

Early in 1949, Gene was complaining to his lifelong friend Bob Atchison about his lack of prospects and difficulty in earning a living. Bob tired of hearing him complain, so he bundled Gene into his car, drove him down to Los Angeles City Hall at Temple and Spring, and marched him into the Los Angeles Police Department headquarters. Bob got an application and told Gene to fill it out.

Gene saw the wisdom of Bob's action. Not only had Gene's father been a policeman, who was still in contact with a number of highly placed men in the hierarchy of the LAPD, his younger brother, Bob, had three years on the force. Bob Atchison, as well as several other boyhood friends, were all policemen. It made sense. Gene filled out the application on January 10, and terminated his employment with Tri-Vision sales the next day.

The LAPD application did not give room for embellishment or overstatement. In filling out the form Gene reported the following: he had one charge account balance of $240 and had not been a conscientious objector with Selective Service; under military service he wrote that he "served in the Army Air Corps, served in Headquarters Army Air Force (HQAAF), held the rank of Captain and had combat duty and overseas duty." Under the heading "Special Skills, Interests, Knowledge, or Hobbies," he wrote, "Pilot, Navigator and allied skills, writing, photography." Gene listed his parents' house in Temple City as his address, that he had been at that address for four months, and that he shared the home with them. He owned a 1938 Chrysler.

The LAPD sent an inquiry to each of Gene's personal references, receiving the following comments:

He has the interest plus the ability and will to learn. He makes a fine public appearance. I have known Eugene for 12 years and through school and the years that followed, his has been the kind of a friendship I have strived to cultivate. I believe that in so doing, I have elevated myself.
—Robert Atchison
Policeman, LAPD

Outstanding applicant in the Police Course at L.A. City College. An interest in being a policeman since high school. It was largely through the association with his father that I chose to go to City College with Eugene and pursue the Police Curriculum. Mr. Roddenberry Sr is retired from LAPD.

—Harry L. Brown[9]
Sergeant, LAPD

I am acquainted with Mr. Roddenberry intimately and have known him since 1944. His is of fine character, honest, reliable and loyal to his friends and those he works for. I highly recommend him for any position you may be considering him for.

—Major George Andrews
Army Air Force

Intelligent, personable, reasonable, industrious, and highly moral character. I have had close association with the applicant for the past three years in business and socially. From my own experience and remarks made by other associates of his, convince me of his high calibre and steadfastness as a citizen.

—Robert D. Neale, Flight Engineer
Pan American World Airways

Gene took the oath of a policeman on February 1, 1949, receiving Police Commission #11317 and badge number 6089. He entered the police academy and six weeks later, on March 16, finished formal training. The course was not graded. His police file simply notes that his training was "satisfactorily completed."

Rookies had no choice of assignments. Ten days after graduating, Gene was transferred to the Traffic Division. For the next six months, he worked intersection control in downtown Los Angeles.

Gene Roddenberry—former Pan Am pilot, bomber pilot, war hero, genius, and would-be television writer—tall, good looking and resplendent in a navy uniform, was now earning a living standing at the intersection of Fifth and Broadway directing traffic. If Gene thought it was a step down, he gave no outward sign, nor did his supervisors see anything other than a competent rookie doing his job. Lieutenant Jack

---

[9]Several years after Gene had left the department and gone on to success as a writer, his childhood friend Harry Brown developed cancer. Gene quietly saw to it that his friend had a last expenses-paid vacation in Hawaii.

Hawe, writing in Gene's Personnel Rating Report[10] for the period of June 30 to September 26, 1949, reported, "A fine looking officer who seemed very interested in his job and who did a good job on his corner."

Downtown traffic was in good hands in mid-1949. As the eastbound traffic went through Gene's hands at Fifth and Broadway, they were handed off to his younger brother, Bob, directing traffic a block away at Fifth and Spring. The brothers were upholding family tradition, as their father had spent time directing traffic at Seventh and Main years earlier.

Bob benefitted in another way from his traffic job. One afternoon he saw a petite young blonde inattentively step off the curb and attempt to cross against the light. With traffic approaching and the blonde paying little attention to her dangerous situation, Bob blew his whistle, startling her and bringing her attention to her situation. The woman's name was Bernice Love, and she thanked the tall, good-looking traffic officer by marrying him—a marriage that endures forty-three years later.

Bernice had a well-developed sense of humor. She worked

---

[10]A unique look into the LAPD is seen here in their Personnel Rating Report, a continuing policy of the LAPD which rates every police officer twice a year. Today ratings are simply "satisfactory" and "not satisfactory." During Gene's career ratings were more defined.

The definitions used then were:

Unsatisfactory (lower 10%) Inefficient; below minimum standard.

Fair (lower 25%) Satisfactory; passably efficient; up to minimum standard.

Good (middle 50%) Average qualifications; efficient, but to a less degree than "Very Good."

Very Good (upper 25%) Above average: efficient; well qualified.

Excellent (upper 10%) Highly efficient; qualified to a high degree.

Officers were rated under a wide range of criteria. These criteria and their definitions give us a good idea of what the LAPD expected of their officers in those days.

The first category examined was "Performance of duty (based on fact)," and subdivided into five sections: Regular Duties, Administrative Duties, Ability to Organize Work, Handling Subordinates, and Dealing with the Public. These and the following 10 categories were divided into the levels of service described above.

The next section covered 10 different qualifications: "physical fitness," "appearance and neatness," "attention to duty," "cooperation and tact," "initiative," "judgment and common sense," "presence of mind," "force," "leadership," and "loyalty."

at the Rowan building on the North East corner of Fifth and Spring. She loved teasing either of the Roddenberry boys. At just over five feet tall, Bernie would often sneak up behind Gene in the middle of the intersection and tap him on the shoulder, pretending to ask for directions. Gene, at nearly six foot two would turn around, completely overlooking, or pretending not to see, his diminutive future sister-in-law. He would look in all directions until Bernie would say, "I'm down here."

Many, indeed most, policemen go through their entire careers without having to draw and fire their weapons. Gene went eleven months.

It was a quiet Sunday afternoon, and Gene was driving his 1938 Chrysler to work using the country's first "freeway," the winding Arroyo Seco Parkway. Opened nine years before, its novelty was that one could drive from the outskirts of Pasadena to downtown Los Angeles at a steady 45 mph without stoplights or intersections. Today it is the Pasadena Freeway.

Ahead of him Gene saw a car accidentally hit a dog running loose in traffic. The injured dog, a small, dark-colored mutt, lay shivering in the road, blocking traffic. Gene took charge of the situation and tried to rescue the animal, but it would not permit anyone near. The dog was in great pain, crying out in agony and clearly dying.

Even though traffic was light, the potential for an accident was high, and with his inability to help the dog Gene was left with one choice. He drew his service revolver and shot the dog in the head.

A lifelong dog lover, Gene never discussed this incident with anyone.

"What a way to spend a holiday," Gene would later comment.

It was Christmas Day, 1949.

Though it was Gene Roddenberry's first year on the force, 1949 was not a good year for the LAPD. Several police officials had been indicted by the grand jury for giving protection to Brenda Allen, a well-known, Mafia-connected madam. To make matters worse, members of the elite LAPD task force assigned to combat organized crime were eating at Lost Angeles's more expensive restaurants as guests of Mickey Cohen, the city's most famous gangster.

The corruption was not as widespread as that of the late thirties, but it was bad enough. Mayor Fletcher Bowron appointed retired Marine Corps Major General William Worton to clean up the mess. As General Worton was not a sworn police officer, he was limited by the city charter to serve no more than a year in office. In that short time, he had to weed out the crooked cops and help find his successor. He in turn promoted the incorruptible William H. "Bill" Parker to deputy chief and assigned him to head up Internal Affairs. From there, Parker was in the perfect position to weed out the dishonest cops.

Eleven days after Parker became deputy chief, and sixteen months after he joined the department, Gene was transferred to the Traffic Services Division, Education Section, Newspaper Unit.[11] It would be years before he returned to street duty. Gene's new job was to write news releases, give lectures on traffic safety, and make contact with every newspaper editor in Los Angeles. Gene found himself being paid to write.

Parker had known the Roddenberrys for years and had been Papa's supervisor when Parker was a sergeant. The two men liked each other and Parker often visited the Roddenberry home. This friendship validated the senior Roddenberry as an honest cop. If he wasn't, Parker never would have associated with him, much less become his friend.

On August 9, 1950, William H. Parker became chief of police of the City of Los Angeles. He would serve longer than any previous or subsequent chief. Parker was to become one of the most famous lawmen in the United States, second only to J. Edgar Hoover, the longtime head of the FBI. Parker saw police work as public service, something of a calling. With near missionary zeal, he set out to modernize and professionalize the LAPD. Parker saw to it that Gene assisted him in carrying out that mission.

Beyond professionalizing and streamlining LAPD's internal structure, Parker also sought to change the public's per-

---

[11]When asked if the closeness of Parker's promotion and Gene's transfer off the street had anything to do with one another, Bob Roddenberry responded, "I don't know about that, but I do know that Parker thought a lot of Gene. He sure liked him."

ception of policemen and their work. With two major scandals in less than 15 years and on-going petty corruption and lax ethical standards, Parker had a big job. He set out to solidify both his department's and his own standing in the community as a protection against possible problems. For this he relied on personal persuasion and sound argument.

Television was still in its infancy when Parker took office and, while he used the medium whenever possible, its severe time constraints never gave him the time or personal contact he thought he needed to make his argument. So Parker went on the stump, talking directly to the people. An accomplished public speaker with a faint and affected Harvard accent, Parker accepted speaking engagements anywhere and everywhere. Often he would give two speeches during the day, one or two more in the evening and several on weekends.

Parker needed ammunition for his continuing verbal blitz. In October of 1951, a little over a year after he became chief, he upgraded the Newspaper Unit to the status of "division," renaming it Public Information, and placing Captain Stanley Sheldon[12] as its head. For a steady supply of speeches that reflected his thoughts and values Parker relied on Captain Sheldon and two of the men Sheldon supervised: Don Ingalls, and a young policeman Parker watched grow up—Eugene Roddenberry.

Gene threw himself into police work wholeheartedly, retaining in reserve an ambition to write for television. He did not shortchange the department in time, effort, and enthusiasm, but he also looked for opportunities to advance himself. Gene was ambitious, smart, and clever at working within institutions. That cleverness was about to pay off.

Gene began writing speeches, both for Parker and himself. As a member of the Public Affairs Division, Gene gave the occasional speech on traffic safety to public service groups. Civic organizations of all sorts became the proving ground for the young officer's speaking skills. For most people, public speaking is one of the most terrifying things they can do. For Gene, it became an extension of his high school var-

---

[12]Sheldon was no stranger to Gene. During Gene's time at Los Angeles City College, Sheldon was the police liaison with the LACC Police Club. Gene was, of course, the president of the club.

sity debate days, only this time there was no one arguing back.[13]

Parker's continuing goal was to professionalize police work. For Parker, police work had too long been viewed as permanently blue collar, something less than honorable, that didn't require a great deal of intelligence or honesty. As the common wisdom went, if you couldn't get a "real" job, you could always get on at the post office or become a policeman. Parker wanted to change that.

Parker also moved to change the policeman's attitude about himself and his work. His aspiration provided an opportunity for Gene. He still wanted to be a writer, that ambition had never left, but he also knew that the odds against succeeding as a writer were high. Much of a writer's success, especially success in Hollywood, happened out of happy accidents or fortunate circumstances that presented themselves, then were recognized and acted upon. What if circumstances conspired against him? To guard against that, Gene played a double game: he gave his best to the LAPD, but made certain that he benefitted whenever possible. Access to Parker allowed him to sell an idea he had, an idea that would allow him to create a niche at the LAPD that would shelter him from the rigors of street work, a position that would let him beat the LAPD at its own game. Anyone who has climbed the corporate ladder will appreciate Gene's insight into the organizational mentality.

In September 1952, Gene published his first article in *The Beat,* the LAPD's in-house magazine. With Parker's blessing, Gene framed and explored the philosophical aspects of what a profession was, how a profession differed from other groups of skilled workers, and how this applied to the average policeman. Doubtless, these were concepts foreign to many policemen, ideas that many policemen, including the brass, had never been exposed to or never thought of applying to their own work. Gene listed seven basic obligations that, when practiced, put an occupational group into the realm of a profession:

---

[13]Gene's LAPD personnel file contains a number of letters from civic groups thanking the chief for sending "such a fine young officer" to their organization. Gene was the sort of officer Parker wanted the public to envision when they thought about the LAPD.

1 - A duty to serve mankind generally rather than self, individuals or groups.

2 - A duty to prepare as fully as practicable for service before entering active practice.

3 - A duty to continually work to improve skills by all means available and to freely communicate professional information gained.

4 - A duty to employ full skill at all times regardless of considerations of personal gain, comfort or safety, and at all times to assist fellow professionals upon demand.

5 - A duty to regulate practice by the franchising of practitioners, setting the highest practicable intellectual and technical minimums; to accept and upgrade fellow professionals solely upon considerations of merit; and to be constantly alert to protect society from fraudulent, substandard, or unethical practice through ready and swift disfranchisement.

6 - A duty to zealously guard the honor of the profession by living exemplary lives publicly and privately, recognizing that injury to a group serving society, injures society.

7 - A duty to give constant attention to the improvement of self-discipline, recognizing that the individual must be the master of himself to be the servant of others.

For many on the force it was their introduction to Parker's philosophy of police professionalism. The article intimated the question, "How do the police become professional?" The answer was soon in coming.

Less than two months later, on November 12, 1952, *The Beat* announced the formation of the Association for Professional Law Enforcement (APLE) at a Police Academy luncheon. There were nine founding members of the board of governors: two captains, one lieutenant, three sergeants, and three officers from the rank and file, one of whom was named Roddenberry.

Gene, as spokesman for the group, announced that, "The association specifically would not deal with wages, pensions, labor-management disputes, or similar problems. We are of the opinion that professional ethics and practical police work are completely compatible and we intend to meet together to promote this compatibility."

The association was well received and other departments wrote for information on the Los Angeles experiment.

Gene used the organization as a vehicle to meet people he admired and who could do the organization some good. Erle Stanley Gardner was the world-famous creator of Perry Mason. Gene had read an article by Gardner in the August 1953, issue of *Argosy* magazine. Within a few days, Gene began a correspondence with Gardner that would last for years. Gene had learned that Gardner liked to correspond by "audograms," made by sending belts or disks recorded on an Audograph, an early dictating machine.

Gardner liked the device, as it freed him from writing in his office. He had a large ranch in the Fallbrook section of San Diego county. Mornings would find him saddling up a favorite horse and riding around his ranch, dictating his Perry Mason mysteries into a battery-powered Audograph as he rode. Gardner had drop-off points around his ranch for the recording belts, where a team of secretaries could collect the dictated material. The method suited the prolific Gardner, and he regularly dictated ten thousand words a day.

Gene talked Parker into buying one of the expensive machines, ostensibly to record the chief's speeches, but what he really wanted it for was to correspond with Gardner.

In early August 1953, Gene sent his first audogram, introducing himself, offering to provide information to Gardner, and asking for clarification on points made in Gardner's *Argosy* article. Gene also informed Gardner of the formation of APLE, its goals and code of ethics. His words give us a unique insight into Gene's philosophical development at the time. Gene dictated:

> "It happens that I'm also researching the thing that has become known as [the] 'police problem,' and I would like to get your thinking on the subject. I've given the matter quite a bit of thought myself—some of it expressed in writing, and I've come to the opinion that the answer is not improvement in police techniques, for we police of the last quarter century have worked to improve our method and systems and I confess that crime seems to be getting ahead of us.
>
> "It appears to me that we're working in the wrong direction. I think in your twelve paragraphs in *Argosy* you imply a point that I have made and I think it can be very

easily proven. And that point is, despite a most aggressive and enlightened leadership, law enforcement cannot rise above the level set by the electorate, and I would say that a condition precedent to the establishing of efficient, professional law enforcement in any community would be a demand on the part of a resident of the community for that type of law enforcement. A police department can be no better or worse than the people collectively desire it to be. I believe that, to this point, you will agree with me.

"But it appears, to effect that designated demand on the part of citizens, we're going to have to go a little deeper into the problem and, by that, I mean into the philosophy of law enforcement, or rather, its place in the scheme of things. My reasoning goes something like this, Mr. Gardner. The extremes of conduct possible in human affairs are infinite. We manage to exist collectively only because we set up and enforce certain rules of conduct. These are, of course, our laws. We promulgate these rules of laws, not because men agree on ways of conduct, but because they do not agree. Law is an artificial standard which marks the limits of activity beyond which certain society is injured. Law, standing alone, is a fiction. It achieves reality only when it is observed. Now, I believe that the character of every society lies in the method of establishing observance of these laws, and the permanence of every society lies in the success in securing observance of these laws.

"In other words, law enforcement is an elemental, basic part of life together. Of course, in some states it's militaristic type of law enforcement; in others, totalitarian and in others, democratic. I believe it could be proved and can be proved that even the tribal leaders of Pacific Islands have their followers who enforce the laws that the leader makes.

"As a sidelight, I've gone to some trouble exploring the established works and philosophy, and it's amazing that you find absolutely no mention of the place of law enforcement in human affairs. You may be acquainted with Charles Reese of England, his book *The Blind Eye of History,* and it appears that its law enforcement is aptly called 'The Blind Eye' or rather, the philosophers' failure to recognize the importance of law enforcement is their 'Blind Eye.' Here's my point. It appears that it's not enough to tell people—citizens—that we need honest and efficient law enforcement and to instruct them that they should co-operate with officials in raising standards of pay and selection, training, etc.

"In some way, it must be demonstrated to people that law enforcement is an integral or basic component of man's government by man. That it is not merely another modern convenience like garbage collection and sanitation, etc. It's been said that it's up to we police to do that kind of selling but, frankly, I wonder if we really can. In the first place, our motives will be suspected. It will appear that we're trying to build a police empire and secondly, our words do not reach out very far. We seldom have direct access to the magazine, large television programs, and other media of communication. Thirdly, and most important, this type of thinking is bound to meet with a great deal of resistance. People just will not believe that the cop on the corner fills any larger place in society than giving traffic tickets, catching criminals, and so on. They refuse to believe that he is a symbol and a fact of collective existence and refuse to believe the function he represents is really very important."

Gardner was impressed and responded within days with a four-page letter, a week before Gene's thirty-second birthday. He sent a copy of Gene's letter to Harry Steeger, owner of *Argosy*. Gardner wrote:

You and I see eye to eye on this problem, and you have a very fine ability to express your thoughts on the subject.

I have been very much interested in your reasoning of going to the very fundamentals of law and order to consider the proper relation of the problem of law enforcement.

As I see it, there are three or four things that simply need to be done if we are going to keep from losing a battle with organized crime.

For society to wait until law has been violated and then expect the police to apprehend the violator is like turning loose smallpox carriers and expecting the doctors to treat the smallpox "because that's their business."

For society to retain any degree of personal liberty, avoiding a police state, and yet have effective laws, there must be something more than law *enforcement*. There must be an understanding of the law and of the field of the law. There must be a respect for the law and there must be a *compliance* with the law. I think it is important that the citizen generally realize this, and it is important that the police officer realize it.

We must search out the causes of crime and try to cope with them. We must, above all, try to quarantine the casual offender from a contact with the vicious, anti-social criminal.

So long as we consider law enforcement as a political play-thing, so long as citizens are willing to consider the higher police jobs as political plums, we are not going to have satisfactory progress regardless of how much we pay our law enforcement officers.

Somewhere along the line we have to make the whole program of law enforcement an integrated part of our society, as much a bulwark of our liberties as the Constitution itself. To do this we are going to require some change in attitude on the part of the many of the individual police officers, and a very large change in attitude on the part of the public.

Gardner began soliciting Gene's opinion on a variety of subjects. In early February 1954, he sent Gene an advance copy of a revised paperback edition of *The Court of Last Resort,* asking Gene for his comments and suggestions.

Gardner also wrote that he wanted Gene to meet his close friend, Cornwell (Corny) Jackson, head of the J. Walter Thompson Advertising Agency.[14]

Gene responded quickly with a Audogram that has been lost, but which Gardner acknowledged in a letter of February 26th.

---

[14]Jackson was married to Gail Patrick, a film and television actress who later, as Gail Patrick Jackson, produced Perry Mason for television.

I was very much interested in your Audogram.

I certainly appreciate your kind comments about
the chapters on police problems in *The Court of Last
Resort,* and the fact that you and your associates find
they may be potentially beneficial is a source of
great pleasure to me.

Gene had asked for permission to reprint part of Gardner's
work in *The Beat* and Gardner wrote that he had already sent
off a letter to his publisher asking them to do just that.

Gardner then spent several pages discussing the bad experiences his friend Jackson had with traffic cops, to which
Gene would take exception. Finally, Gardner concludes:

In regard to your comments about the philosophy
of law, I think it all boils down to a very simple situation
as far as human nature is concerned.

After all, most of our laws are simply an attempt
to bring about a group good through the surrender of
individual liberties.

The citizen in the aggregate is inclined to believe
that the group good amply warrants the surrender
of the liberties, but when it comes to a showdown he
feels that it is the other fellow's liberty which should
have been surrendered and not is.

Don Ingalls and Gene shared more than cramped office
space on the 27th floor of City Hall. They had common experiences in life that bound them together. Both had been
B-17 pilots and seen extensive combat—Gene in the South
Pacific and Ingalls half a world away in Europe. Like Gene,
Ingalls was an aspiring television writer. They became lifelong friends.

In addition to their writing ambitions, Gene and Don
shared two other things as well: an appreciation of beautiful
women and failing marriages. Gene privately admitted to
friends that his marriage to Eileen was over by the early
1950's, but he stayed for the children, and because it was
what one did. Strong men did difficult things. Strong men
did not abandon their families. Even though Gene had been
raised in Los Angeles, his Southern background and his intense dislike for personal confrontation made a divorce unlikely. Handsome, intelligent, well-spoken, and a good

provider, Gene would seem to have been the ideal husband, but the failure of his first marriage cannot be placed entirely on Eileen's shoulders.

While appearing to be the best of husbands, Gene had always lived by his own code of marriage ethics, a set of standards that did not have sexual fidelity near the top of the list or, perhaps, even on the list. From his experiences in Hawaii, the South Pacific, and New Zealand, with weeks away from home while he was flying for Pan Am, Gene was a man who listened to his own dictates and acted on them. And so it was on the LAPD. The department had a ready supply of pretty clerks, secretaries, and policewomen, and Gene was young, handsome, and in a position of power, even if he had only the rank of policeman. There were plenty of opportunities with willing partners, and Gene had a big appetite. With one colleague, he even discussed the feasibility of the two of them sharing the rent on a downtown apartment to save money on hotels.

One retired lieutenant remembers Gene carrying on a steamy affair with a woman associated with the police department, whose husband had business ties with known criminals. Everyone who knew Gene and this woman knew about the affair except, it seems, the woman's husband and Gene's wife. At least one of Gene's friends commented that, even though the woman was beautiful with a spectacular figure, her husband was the sort that was prone to violence. Gene was playing with fire, but that added to the intrigue and the excitement. Throughout his life Gene craved the experience of the new—thoughts, women, books, ideas. He was forever exploring new territory. One of the things he never sought to experience was sexual fidelity.

Gene was always somewhat suspicious of authority. At times he could be disdainful, other times playful, toward those in control. His time in the military and Pan Am had not given him any reason to change his mind and nothing he experienced during his time at LAPD changed his outlook about the follies of authority. While he did not know it at the time, it was wonderful training for dealing with network and studio executives.

To Gene and Don, their boss, Captain Stanley Sheldon, was "Uncle Captain" after Horatio K. Huffenpuff, a character on a local kid's show *Time for Beany*. Occasionally, when Sheldon was otherwise occupied, Don and Gene would tune their tiny in-office television set to Bob Clampett's sly and witty puppet show, as wildly popular with hip adults as *Pee Wee's Playhouse* was in the eighties and *Rocky and Bullwinkle* were in the sixties. Feet up and coffee cups in hand, Parker's two information officers would spend fifteen minutes of their afternoons guffawing at the antics of a boy named Beany; his friend Cecil, the Seasick Sea Serpent; and the crew of Huffenpuff's boat, the *Leakin' Lena,* overseen by their very own "Uncle Captain."[15]

Gene's disdain for authority often extended to the way he handled the receipt of assignments from the brass. Ingalls always knew when he and Gene had been given something new to do by Sheldon. He knew by the sound Gene made coming down the hall from a visit to Sheldon's office. It was a continuous rhythm of shuffle-and-kick, shuffle-and-kick as Gene worked a wadded-up ball of paper down the long, highly polished corridor with the toe of his shoe. Turning into the office he and Ingalls shared, Gene would line the wadded paper up with a soccer player's precision and send it sailing to his colleague's desk with a sharp kick. "There's another assignment from Uncle Captain," Gene would announce, returning to the project he'd been doing before Sheldon interrupted him.

Yet, because he understood that those in authority were simply flawed human beings, Gene's respect for Parker endured. It did not fade with Parker's dissolution into alcoholism, or his accelerated embrace of extreme right-wing political ideas, or his death; nor was it affected by Gene's liberal outlook.

Writing Parker's speeches became a great learning experience for Gene. It taught him research techniques, the ability to focus on a subject, how to write persuasively, and how to emulate another person's voice and put thoughts on paper in an understandable manner. In later years, he was still very proud of what he wrote for Parker. But Gene was always

---

[15]Gene was in good company with his enjoyment of *Time for Beany*. Stan Freberg, the brilliant satirist, was the voice for several of the characters. In his autobiography, he reported receiving a letter from a physicist at Cal Tech, who described a meeting attended by Albert Einstein. At a certain point, Einstein pulled out a gold pocket watch, studied it for a moment and then stood up, announcing that those assembled would have to excuse him. As he shuffled towards the door he explained, "It's time for Beany."

quick to add that Parker never asked him to write something he, Gene, did not believe in himself. Their relationship was complicated and not easily described. Some have characterized it as a father/son relationship, but Gene never called it that. His solid relationship with his own father precluded him from looking for a substitute. Perhaps older brother/younger brother or mentor/apprentice give some suggestion, but even those are too simplistic and do not suggest the full range of dynamics that passed between two men with equally complicated personalities. One thing that can be said for certain: the relationship was a curious one. The two men could not have been more different.

Parker was short, balding, politically conservative to the core, a devout Catholic, and the imperial chief. His reaction to a subordinate could make or break a man. His displeasure had ended more than one LAPD career.

Gene was a tall, young, good-looking, moderately Democratic, a wet-behind-the-ears policeman with limited street experience, who had, in childhood, rejected belief in the Christian God. Despite their differences in philosophy, theology, professional rank, and virtually everything else, the two men liked each other. Binding them was a powerful respect for each other's minds, ethical standards, the ability to argue on an intellectual level, and their mutual desire to see law enforcement become a recognized profession.

Daryl Gates, fourteen years as Chief of Police (1978–1992), joined the department eight and a half months after Gene. One of his early assignments was almost two years as Parker's driver. Gates remembers:

"I met Gene when he was in Public Affairs, writing speeches for the Chief. I walked into Parker's office and straight into a very strange situation. I was appalled at what I saw. Gene was sitting there, in front of Parker's desk, arguing with the Chief.

"Given the exalted station Parker held in the minds of most of his men, seeing him actually arguing with someone, much less a low-ranking policeman, was unthinkable. I remember thinking, 'Who is this guy so vigorously disagreeing with Parker?' They were going at it, too.

"As I listened I quickly understood that they were having an intellectual argument over the preparation of a particular speech. Parker would pound his fist saying, 'Dammit I didn't want to say that,' and Gene would respond with a reasoned argument of his own, delivered just as vigorously. Gene was clearly not afraid of Parker. He was probably the only person on the department who wasn't.

"I developed respect for Gene right at that moment. I thought, 'My God, there's a guy who is arguing with Parker and getting away with it.'

"Out of that came this remarkable speech that is really a vision for community relations. The speech was not Parker and it was not Gene, it was an amalgamation of both their ideas and thoughts. Parker was always considered to be a very conservative guy, and he was in many respects. On the other hand he was a liberal in many respects as well. Somehow Gene was able to capture just enough of the liberal in Parker to make this speech. It is still a hallmark in the eyes of everyone."[16]

Throughout his life, Gene would rally to the defense of Parker, even writing letters supporting his old boss.[17]

Things went routinely for Gene, researching, writing, refining his skills, making an occasional speech about traffic safety, but there was a need for more money. Both he and

---

[16]The "remarkable speech" he refers to is "The Police Role in Community Relations," delivered by Parker at the National Conference of Christians and Jews, Institute on Police-Community Relations, Michigan State University, May 19, 1955. It earned Parker a standing ovation and became the framework for police-community relations ever since.

[17]In August 1965, Parker made some comments on the Watts Riots, which had just occurred. His comments became controversial and he was not supported by the politicians as quickly as many thought he should. Sam Yorty, then mayor of Los Angeles, finally said something. On August 23, 1965, Gene wrote the following to the mayor: Your recent stand on the subject of our Chief of Police is most gratifying. Almost without exception, it has created among my circle of acquaintances increased respect for you. . . . I was (and still am) a strong liberal, and civil rights partisan. It is no secret to anyone that Bill Parker is an equally strong conservative. We differed strongly and still differ strongly on certain philosophical concepts and issues. And yet, I assure you personally, and would welcome the opportunity to say it more publicly, that despite differences in social and political beliefs I could never find, nor do I believe any reasoning liberal could find, any disagreement or argument with William H. Parker on basic issues of morality, decency, and tolerance. It would be difficult for me to name a man I respect more as a fine professional and outstanding human being.

"As a citizen of Los Angeles, I thank you for your wisdom and strength during this crisis. Please call on me for whatever assistance and support I may be able to give."

Eileen liked nice things—things that could not be easily purchased on a policeman's salary. Like many policemen before and since, Gene decided to supplement his income.

On March 28, 1951, he submitted LAPD Form 1.47, requesting permission for outside employment. Gene was careful in his wording on the application:

"The work is of a dignified nature and does not involve door bell ringing or telephone campaigning but will bring this officer in contact only with established prospects. The name of the police department will enter into no part of the business and employment qualifications involve no union or membership in any such type organization. The firm is unable to fill this part time position from any available labor supply and the income, dependent upon this officer's ability and experience in this field, while well above average, does not deprive any other person of the opportunity of earning a livelihood."

The "dignified work" Gene wanted to do was sell Amana freezers!

Gene's interest in science fiction had not abated. He continued to be the ever-avid reader and filmgoer, but through the war years and just after there were few science fiction films produced. This changed with the release in 1949 of the low budget film *The Man From Planet X*. It was followed in 1950 by *Rocketship X-M* and the George Pal film, *Destination Moon*. In 1951, Robert Wise directed a film that is viewed by some as the *"Citizen Kane* of science fiction films," *The Day The Earth Stood Still*.[18]

While early television did not have the budget or technological sophistication of film, science fiction was present on

---

[18]A "thinking person's" science fiction film, it was adult drama in a science fiction setting. Michael Rennie was "Klatu," an ambassador from a federation of planets bringing a message to Earth—learn to work together or be destroyed by the patroling robots who had complete autonomy over matters of aggression. The film also starred Sam Jaffee, Hugh Beaumont, Patricia Neal, and Billy Gray.

Also released during 1951 were *The Thing*, based on the book *Who Goes There* by John W. Campbell, Jr. and *When Worlds Collide*, based on the novel of the same name by Phillip Wylie and Edwin Balmer. The next several years saw a renaissance of quality science fiction films with the release of such classics as: *It Came From Outer Space, The War Of The Worlds, The Creature From The Black Lagoon, Them!, 20,000 Leagues Under The Sea, This Island Earth, Invasion of the Body Snatchers,* and the science fiction interpretation of Shakespeare's *The Tempest—Forbidden Planet*.

television from the very beginning. *Captain Video* was broadcast by the Dumont[19] network beginning in 1949. It was the first science fiction on television, or "video," as it was more commonly called then. *Captain Video* was shot in a small studio with a matching budget. Interestingly, a number of the early scripts were written by such notable SF writers as Robert Sheckley, Damon Knight, and C. M. Kornbluth.

The second prominent SF program was a thrice-weekly 15-minute serial on CBS, *Tom Corbett, Space Cadet.* Broadcast live, the action and special effects were, again, severely constrained by the show's minimilist budget. It lasted one season. The show's science advisor was noted scientist and science writer Willy Ley.[20]

Both *Captain Video* and *Tom Corbett* were popular, but nothing compared to the first major science fiction show to capture the public's fancy, a show that was to strangely parallel *Star Trek* in the next decade. It was locally broadcast on ABC's Los Angeles affiliate, KECA Channel 7 (now KABC), first airing June 9, 1951, before being picked up by the network.[21] Principally a children's show, it ultimately attracted a much wider audience.

Saturdays at 5:30, the announcer's voice would build to a crescendo with the words: "High adventures in the wild, vast reaches of space. Missions of daring in the name of interplanetary justice. Travel into the future with Buzz Corry, Commander and Chief of the SPAAAAACE PATROL."

Space Patrol was "space opera"[22] brought to television.

---

[19]A television broadcast pioneer, Dumont received its commercial license in 1944. Headed by the brilliant engineer Dr. Allen B. DuMont, the company marketed the first large-screen (14-inch) television set in 1938.

[20]German-born Willy Ley's book *Die Möglichkeit der Weltraumfart* ("The Possibility of Interplanetary Travel") 1928, was one of the inspirations of the seminal SF film and book, *Die Frau im Mond* ("The Woman In The Moon"). He wrote for *Astounding* and *Amazing Stories* and became the science columnist for *Galaxy* in 1952 until his death in 1969. One of his finest books, in collaboration with the beloved space artist Chesley Bonestell, was *The Conquest of Space.*

[21]It was also on the radio several days a week but it was unusual in that this program went from television *to* radio.

[22]A variation of the term "soap opera," coined to describe continuing daytime radio dramas that specialized in endless domestic crisis. Westerns were sometimes described as "horse operas." The name became generalized to mean any corny or hackneyed dramas. "Space opera" was brought into SF by Wilson Tucker in 1941.

For its time it was imaginative, innovative, and done exceedingly well.

The "Space Patrol" had been formed by the "United Federation of Planets" to battle space pirates, renegade scientists, and evildoers all over the galaxy. Their adventures, some complete in each half-hour program and some with continuing story arcs, had kids riveted to their sets each week. By the standards of the day it was exciting adventure and displayed a number of innovative special effects developed without a large budget or sophisticated camera trickery. Nothing like it had been seen on television before. In a curious twist, *Space Patrol,* like *Star Trek,* was the creation of a military pilot: William (Mike) Moser, a Navy veteran.

Space Patrol took the country's children by storm. The clearest evidence of this was the merchandise campaign kicked off at the May Company in downtown Los Angeles where the stars of the program and a mock-up of the show's spaceship made an appearance. A few thousand people were expected. To everyone's surprise, 30,000 video-struck children and their parents showed up. The streets around the store were jammed for blocks and extra police were called in to handle the huge but orderly crowd.

Moser capitalized on his program's popularity. *Space Patrol* developed a series of merchandise tie-ins. Youngsters could buy space helmets, ray guns, model rockets and monorails, cosmic generators, and a host of paraphernalia that bore the *Space Patrol* logo. Fan clubs proliferated. *Life* magazine reported that merchandising brought in an additional $40 million a year in 1950's dollars. Today, *Space Patrol* merchandise is highly collectible and much sought after.

What *Space Patrol* did for children in the fifties, *Star Trek* would attempt to do for them as young adults in the sixties, although it would not find its real success until the mid-seventies. *Space Patrol* helped set the stage for an appreciative generation of science fiction viewers, who would grow up ready for the adult fare Gene would provide them years later. *Space Patrol* was the first of three early television programs that were important to Gene's career.

The second program debuted a little more than six months after *Space Patrol*. On December 16, 1951, viewers watching NBC saw the screen go black. When the picture returned, there was a close-up of an LAPD sergeant's badge, number 714. The first four notes from Walter Schumann's famous

march resounded across the country—*dum-de-dum-dum!*
Dragnet had come to television.[23]

Throughout the 1950's the tried and true formats of radio
were feeding the increasing appetite of television. *Dragnet*
was one of the most successful programs to make the transition from the ear to the eye. It became wildly popular
attracting as many as 17 million viewers each week.[24]

Dragnet drew its stories from "the files of the Los Angeles Police Department." In 1949, the show's production
company had struck a deal with then Chief Jack Horrall, and
the relationship continued on through Chief Parker: the
LAPD would supply information on closed cases for the
program's writers. Parker expanded the LAPD's involvement considerably and saw his department benefit in many
ways. Parker got to know and like the star of the show, who
became a friend of the LAPD.

His name was Jack Webb, and for an entire generation he
would personify what the ideal cop should be—how he
moved, how he dressed, how he talked, and how he carried
out police business. Webb was the program's producer and
director as well as its star, and was a well-known workaholic
who often spent fifteen hours a day at the studio.

The program centered on Detective Sergeant Joe Friday
(Jack Webb) and his partner, played by a succession of actors,[25] and the standard police procedures they went through
to investigate and solve a crime. Each program had them in
a different division: robbery/homicide one week, burglary,
forgery, bunco/fraud, or car theft another. Each step of the
investigative procedure was true to protocol then in place at
LAPD.

Dragnet drew its authenticity from the painstaking attention to detail by Webb and the carefully monitored support
it received from the LAPD. Scripts were checked by Park-

---

[23]*Dragnet,* originally on the NBC radio network, was broadcast on NBC television from December 16, 1951, to September 6, 1959. It returned to television,
again on NBC, as *Dragnet 1967* (advancing the title chronologically each year)
and ran from January 12, 1967, to September 10, 1970.

[24]*Dragnet* won several Emmys and was in the Nielson Ratings Top 25 Shows for
1952–1956.

[25]Barton Yarborough as Detective Sergeant Ben Romero in 1951, Barney Philips
as Sergeant Jacobs in 1952, and Ben Alexander portrayed the best-known partner, Officer Frank Smith, from 1952 to 1959. Harry Morgan, later to star in
M*A*S*H, was the partner when the show came back on the air in 1967.

er's representatives to make certain they contained nothing that would reflect badly on the department. There were often as many as three technical advisors on the set, hired right out of LAPD.

Authenticity extended to the show's props and sets. The finish on the set's wood trim was an exact duplicate of the finish in the squad rooms. Even the ash trays were placed the same. On each day of shooting, a special courier would leave police headquarters carrying a box that contained the two actual badges used by the principal actors in the show. At the end of the day, these badges were returned to headquarters for safekeeping. Their delivery and return each day was an important ritual and a subtle reminder to the production company of the long string attached to each badge—a string held by Chief William H. Parker.

The show was potent propaganda that benefitted both sides. Webb got a program he could not have produced under any other circumstances, and Parker's vision of a professional police force found its way into millions of homes each week.

But Webb was not simply an opportunist. Webb helped create the Police Academy Trust Fund and promised it six percent of the profits from the first showing of each episode. From that fund, several buildings were built at the Police Academy. Today Jack Webb's personal mementos can be found in a glass display case next to the entrance of the restaurant at the academy.

Dragnet had two qualities that were hallmarks of virtually all early television: it was produced quickly and cheaply. To disguise the low budget, the program was filmed in a highly stylized manner which focused on tight dialog and interesting characters, giving it the sort of street grittiness that permeated the entire production. The feeling of realism was helped by Webb's running narrative in the staccato, no-nonsense delivery he perfected, describing police procedural minutiae, punctuated by frequent references to the time.

American writers in the twenties and thirties had the pulp magazine market and gruff but helpful editors as instructors. It was a wonderful school for writers to learn their craft. Unfortunately, the pulps met their match during the 1940's in cheap comic books and twenty-five-cent paperbacks. The pulps were gone, but slowly the pulp market transformed itself into something new, telling the same old stories in a new medium. The pulps had undergone a transmutation to, as Gene later characterized it, "the pulp pages of television." Television in the early fifties was alive with dozens of 30-minute anthology shows, the equivalent of a pulp short story. All the studios producing such shows needed stories. Exactly as was the experience of the previous generation of writers, the new generation of television writers would rely on talent, intuition, the trial and error method, and the assistance of story editors to learn their craft.

For Gene, *Dragnet* was the starting point of his television writing career. Both the radio and television versions of the show announced at the end of each programs, "The story you have just seen is true. Only the names have been changed to protect the innocent." The stories originally came from the files of the LAPD, but as the show progressed, most of the stories came from the officers and detectives who lived them.

Webb's production company, Mark VII Limited, paid $100 for a story, usually five or six paragraphs on a single sheet of paper. They always bought more stories than they shot, as many turned out to be too complicated to convert to the show's stylized and inexpensive format.

Gene cut a deal with friends on the force. They would tell him their stories and he would put them into sellable form. If the story sold, they would split the money fifty-fifty. After talking to a detective about a story and making a few notes, he could pound out the treatment in one or two evenings. Gene developed the two traits necessary for successful writing in early television: he was good and he was fast. Fifty dollars for two nights' work was good money to a policeman making $400 a month.

Gene learned and improved, paid attention to what the producers wanted, and started to sell stories—but he wanted to do more. He wanted to go where the real money was: he wanted to write scripts.[26] In the days of early television,

---

[26] A number of books have reported incorrectly on Gene's association with *Dragnet,* assuming that when he said he wrote for *Dragnet* he meant scripts. A thorough search of the bound copies of *Dragnet* scripts donated by Jack Webb to the UCLA Library did not turn up any scripts written by Gene. Gene wrote stories and treatments as described, but they are not credited or preserved in the Webb archives.

there were no schools that taught script writing, no weekend seminars on television writing, no degrees in screenwriting offered by universities. Everyone wrote by the "seat of their pants."

Gene devised his own practical approach: he borrowed scripts from Jack Webb's company and other sources. He then watched the corresponding programs when they were broadcast, matching each scene with the direction printed on the page. From that he learned the terminology and camera directions needed in scripts: "long shot," "med shot," "three shot," "close two shot," etc. To learn blocking and action, he would watch a program with the sound turned down. To develop his sense of dialog and timing, he would *listen* to dramatic programs, not watch them.

Genius or no, success did not come fast or easy. Gene held himself to a regimen of writing a thousand words a day, producing scripts and program ideas at a furious pace, all the while working full time as Parker's chief researcher and speech writer. To protect his creations he would mail a copy to himself, spending the extra thirty cents to register the letter and having cancellations stamped over the flap to provide proof of the date of creation. The protection was ultimately unnecessary. He sold nothing.

Years later, he reflected on his early days in a short, unpublished article, "Notes On Writing."

Most early problems are due to a lack of experience; and this can be remedied, of course, if one is willing to continue to devote time and study and long hours of *writing* and *writing* and *writing*.

Most people give up at about this point. They nod agreement when experienced writers tell them that this profession takes the same years of apprenticeship as any other craft—but most of them secretly believe this rule does not apply to them. After having tried a manuscript or two without any sales, they rationalize they are as good as any professional writer but haven't had the "break." It simply becomes easier to quit and blame it on politics than to develop writing style, learn the tricks of the craft, and build the mental muscles which they only get after constant and continual exercise. They wouldn't expect to be a goldsmith or an Olympic gymnast without years of learning and toil, but they somehow feel that writing is different. It isn't.[27]

As he honed his skills, Gene realized that his earlier thoughts of a writing career were presumptive. He learned the meaning of the maxim, "The confidence of the amateur is the envy of the professional." He took his own advice and wrote, and wrote, and wrote. His work and study began to pay off when he reached a new level in his writing: he was able to read and criticize his own work as if it were someone else's. This brought him closer to the necessary level of professionalism he was aiming at. As Gene's writing skills improved things were changing in the television business as well.

The industry that in 1948 had no place for a neophyte writer was, by 1953, maturing into a business that had a better idea of who and what it was. Several battles were waged simultaneously in commercial television development. A large part of the fight within television had been the debate between "live versus film," and between the executives in New York and the telefilm entrepreneurs of Hollywood.

In the beginning, film was considerably more expensive than live broadcasts, but as motion picture techniques and cost-cutting measures were applied to telefilm production, the differences in cost changed considerably. Hollywood was becoming increasingly competitive. By 1953, Hollywood was making 78 percent of the films used on television. Eight studios, previously devoted to producing motion pictures, were now devoted almost completely to television production.

The pressures of business shook out many would-be and wanna-be television production companies. Gene lived through this shake-out period refining his skills, learning his

---

[27] In August 1971, Gene responded to an aspiring writer who had written for advice: "Glad to hear you are writing. Whether or not you become a professional writer, it is valuable training in communication which is important in any aspect of life. Let's hope that your first script does sell, but you should go into it aware that the odds are against this happening, just as the odds are against a novice goldsmith or painter selling his first work. It took me six full scripts to get a sale, and I find this to be pretty much the average in the industry. Far too many beginners in writing feel that their time has been lost if their work does not sell. This is foolish, of course. However, again, first scripts do occasionally sell and you should proceed vigorously and optimistically."

craft, and making a living under civil service protection. In 1953, he began sending out query letters and treatments to producers all over town, but opportunity found him in the form of a phone call to his immediate boss, Captain Stanley Sheldon. Ziv Television Productions needed a technical advisor for their new show, *Mr. District Attorney,* and hoped the LAPD could provide one. Sheldon had just the man and *Mr. District Attorney* became the third program to exert a major influence on Gene's early career.

Ziv Television Productions' owner, Frederick W. Ziv, was a radio syndication pioneer. Tough and smart, Ziv had two qualities many of his competitors did not: foresight and imagination. His company had become one of the largest program syndicators during radio's heyday. In mid-1953, he bought the radio and television rights to *Mr. District Attorney,* a long-running radio drama.

In late 1953, Gene became the program's technical advisor and instantly recognized the opportunity before him. Fred Ziv remembered the beginning of Gene's association with his company: "A very large police officer in full uniform—badge, whistle, and gun—was on the set of *Mr. District Attorney* for several days, reading scripts and giving advice. Finally, he looked at Jon Epstein [the head of Ziv's story department] and said, 'I can write scripts as good as this.' " Fred Ziv remembers that Gene was invited to make good on his boast.

On October 22, Gene wrote to Epstein:

Dear John: [sic]
    This is it! MR. DISTRICT ATTORNEY finally has
a story tailored to TV's every need. If you don't
like this you should go back to, you'll pardon the
expression, Longuyland [Long Island].
    P.S. This story is of current interest because gambling
operations are currently giving industry a headache.
Its [sic] been in the news recently. I'm sure Locheed
[sic] or Douglas will give permission for most of the
shooting in their plant, with the appropriate credit tacked
onto the film.

                                                Gene R.

Enclosed with the letter was the following story outline.

October 22, 1953

TO: ZIV Television Programs, Inc.
SUBJECT: MR. DISTRICT ATTORNEY story outline.
FROM: E.W. Roddenberry

Management and labor from a large aircraft company complain to Mr. District Attorney of gambling operations being conducted on the sly in their plant. (Football, baseball pool, or similar) Although it appears to be a penny-ante affair, Mr. DA decides to look into it—he wonders if it is being conducted by organized crime. Investigation proves it to be a big thing—tens of thousands of dollars every month. After starting with minor bets, some workers are now spending food and rent money. *First climax:* a worker is beaten up for non payment of a bet. Everything points to organized crime; the method of operation is identical.

Mr. DA discovers that the parts-room men throughout the plant are set up as takers and receivers. Practically all workers can go to the parts-rooms without arousing suspicion. Betting sheets are discovered in parts books. These men are taken in for questioning. They put the finger on an ex-mobster who services the soft-drink equipment. This furthers their belief of the gambling being directed by organized crime. But they cant [sic] break the ex-con down.

Second climax: Mr. DA discovers that defense secrets are getting out of the plant. He confers with the worried government men. But it doesn't tie-up. Interrogation of the parts men reveal that they were just after the few bucks rake-off. The ex-con is too dumb to handle the sale of classified information. Mr. DA works with the plant's Personnel Director, going over personnel records trying to find the weak spot in the plant. No luck.

Final climax: Mr. DA, although he could find nothing on the individual personnel reports, discovers a pattern in the whole collection. The culprit is the Personnel Director. For years he had given the employment aptitude tests. He had selected men with marked weakness for gambling and gotten them into key spots. After their gambling debts had goot [sic] high enough to worry them, he allowed them to buy their way out with defense secrets.

(Signed)
E.W. Roddenberry

Epstein liked what he read and commissioned the script. Gene had made his first television script sale. It became "Defense Plant Gambling," *Mr. District Attorney* program #9B, Ziv production number 1009.[28] The final master script is dated March 2, 1954, and credited to "Robert Wesley."[29] While Gene was busy cementing his relationship with Ziv, he was also careful to keep his backside covered with his bosses at LAPD. On December 1, 1953, somewhat after the fact, he submitted Form 1.47 requesting permission once again to engage in outside employment. Under description of the work he wrote, somewhat disingenuously: "Free-lance writing—will include some script checking and advising." Reasons given: "Increasing family requires increasing budget." The chief approved the request the next day.[30]

Years later, in his college lectures, Gene would tell a far different story of his career's genesis. With his right hand held high as if taking an oath—and his tongue lodged firmly in his cheek—Gene told his audience of rapt young fans that he became a police officer, not to "gain experience," but because he knew a badge and a gun would help him sell scripts.

He also enjoyed relaying how he happened upon his first

---

[28] For the *Star Trek* trivia buff, one of the characters included in this first script is a "Sergeant Ryker." Gene used this name in several other unsold scripts before conferring it on the Executive Officer of the Enterprise, Commander William Ryker in *Star Trek: The Next Generation.*

[29] Gene also experimented with his brother's first and middle names, Robert Leon, but never submitted anything under this pseudonym. One coworker of Gene's at the LAPD thought that Gene also wrote under the pseudonym "Rod N. Berry." This writer could find no evidence in either Gene's papers, or any other archive I searched, of that name ever being used.

[30] Gene also took advantage of another opportunity. On a second Form 1.47, submitted simultaneously, Gene asked for permission to appear as a "guest or alternate lecturer" in "Police and the Public," a class at Los Angeles State College taught by Captain Sheldon. It paid $4.50 an hour, a nice step up from the $2.50 an hour he earned as a regular policeman, and a nice credit as well. It, too, was approved by Chief Parker the next day.

agent. Knowing that an agent would be necessary, he supposedly studied the list of agents, selected the one he wanted and learned the man's driving habits. Soon thereafter, he caught the agent speeding. As he was about to write the ticket, Gene told the agent that while he looked like a policeman he was really a writer. The agent supposedly suddenly realized how remiss he had been in encouraging new talent and Gene had his first agent.

It was a wonderful and amusing story, especially as told by Gene, but despite his assurances of its veracity, it was nothing more than an imaginative and self-effacing writer entertaining his audience with an imaginative tale. Gene was never one to let facts stand in the way of a good story.

The reality of Gene's success was not so magical or humorous but his allegory did contain a kernel of truth: Gene was prepared to "lay in wait," prepared when he met, or stumbled upon, opportunity. Much of the secret to success in show business is a matter of recognizing or creating opportunity and being prepared to take advantage of it when it presents itself. Gene had what writing teacher Wells Root calls the two essentials for writing: "A gleam of natural talent and a compulsion to write that forbids doubt."

That was the real story of Gene's accomplishment and he was smart enough to understand this.

Don Ingalls, Gene's office partner at LAPD, who would go on to a distinguished writing and producing career of his own (writer, story editor, associate producer, then producer on *Have Gun Will Travel,* writer-producer of *Fantasy Island* and many other shows) remembered Gene getting an agent[31] shortly after he had begun writing and selling scripts. Both men, Don remembers, used the same selection criteria: they went with the first agent who agreed to represent them.

Gene's career was going well, but his marriage was not. Even though his second child, a daughter, Dawn, was born

---

[31] Letters in Gene's files show that his first agent was Lawrence Cruickshank. While Gene was happy with him for a while Cruickshank was a "pound the pavement" type of agent, not the kind who was able to cut the big development and percentage deals Gene wanted. When Gene could move on to that level of the business he dropped Cruickshank for another, more powerful agent. Cruickshank was bitter about this for the rest of his life and Gene confessed to a few friends that while the move was practical and necessary for his career, he still felt guilty about doing it.

in 1954, Gene confided to Don Ingalls that he was unhappy. He mentioned to other friends that he and Eileen never laughed anymore.

Even though he had permission to work outside the department, Gene wrote all his early scripts under the pseudonym "Robert Wesley." His *"nom de video"* gave him some distance from the LAPD which allowed him to explore subjects that Chief Parker might not think appropriate for one of his officers, let alone his chief researcher and writer. The pen name also allowed Gene to disguise exactly how much of his time and energy was going into his script writing as well as how much money he was making. This was an important consideration since then, as now, LAPD officers were expected to give 110 percent. One of the factors each officer was graded on every six months was loyalty. As defined by the LAPD that was "the quality of rendering faithful and willing service, and unswerving allegiance." A talented police officer who was making more in a part-time job than most of his superiors would likely be in for a rough ride.

Compared to the $440 a month he earned as a policeman, television writing paid well. This is illustrated by a letter from Ziv:

Dear Gene:
  We have today given you a writing assignment, Number 1614. Total compensation agreed upon, $700, is payable as follows:
  $100—48 hours after delivery of Outline.
  $250—7 days after delivery of First Draft.
  $200—7 days after delivery of Final Screenplay.
  $150—7 days after delivery of Add'l Revisions.
  Please sign and return to us the enclosed copies of the contract.

Yours very truly,
ZIV TELEVISION PROGRAMS, INC.
Jon Epstein

February of 1954 marked Gene's fifth year in the department. It was also the minimum of time an officer had to put in before he could take the sergeant's exam, a major milestone for a career in the LAPD. Preparing for this test can consume all of a candidate's free time, and some begin studying two years before they are eligible. Many do not pass the exam on their first try; others, knowing the difficulty, never bother taking it at all. Gene prepared by forming a study group of four or five other candidates, meeting on evenings and weekends.

That Gene took the exam and placed among the top candidates on his first try is hardly surprising to those who knew him. What makes this accomplishment extraordinary is that Gene did it while performing his duties as Parker's researcher and script writer, lecturing at Los Angeles State College for Sheldon's class, acting as technical advisor for *Mr. District Attorney,* and writing scripts for Ziv.

Gene took the test in early 1954. The first script for *Mr. District Attorney* was dated March 2, 1954, but that wasn't the only script Gene wrote at that time. His second *Mr. District Attorney* script, "Wife Killer," was dated April 26.

On April 29, Gene's high standing on the elegibility list led to his promotion, and like all new sergeants, he had to serve six months' probation in another division. He requested transfer from the Public Information Division to the Hollywood Division, "to obtain basic field experience prior to appointment as Sergeant of Police." Captain Sheldon, in making out his final rating report, was sorry to see Gene go and rated him as "very good" or "excellent" across the board. Sheldon philosophically noted that "the field experience would probably be beneficial." Gene hadn't been in the field since he transferred inside from traffic investigation in mid-May 1950. He was going back on the street as a sergeant with very little street experience, supervising police who may have had as many years on the street as he had months.

During his six months sergeant's probation, Gene became friends with another probationary sergeant. Gene's friend stayed with the department and retired a lieutenant. Ten years later, Gene took his friend's name and plugged it into the *Star Trek* universe, keeping the pronunciation but changing the spelling. His friend was Wilbur Clingan, and his name became that of the fierce warrior race that battles the Federation: the Klingons. To this day, Lieutenant Wilbur Clingan, LAPD Retired, is always happy to introduce himself as the "original Klingon."

Another aspect of the LAPD lives on in *Star Trek,* an aspect Gene discussed once publicly. Gene's long philosophical and intellectual discussions (and arguments) with Parker, and his observations of Parker's taciturn, emotionally distant nature, helped Gene shape the persona of the show's most popular character: the half-alien, half-human science officer, Mr. Spock.

Gene worked his probation in the Hollywood Division and downtown. Years later, he would joke that when he worked Hollywood he would try and stay out of sight in case any of the producers he tried to do business with spotted him and found out he was a cop. His time on probation became fodder for the myth. In his lectures during the 1970's, he would tell the story of being in a conference with three producers—in some variations it was just one—to whom he was trying to sell scripts. It was a warm day and so the producers took off their coats. Gene did the same. During the rest of his presentation he noticed how attentive the producers were, how closely they were paying attention to what he said. Then he remembered that even though he was off duty he had on a large .38-caliber revolver in a shoulder holster. In variations of the story, the producer eagerly bought his script at the end of the conference.[32] In any event, Gene was one of the few members of the Writer's Guild to legally carry a gun.

In July he sold another script to Ziv for *Mr. District Attorney.* This became "Police Academy" and was also written under the name "Robert Wesley." It would be the last script we have any record of him selling that year. Gene's gross police salary that year was a bit over $5,000 and his income from writing was nearly half that, even though he had sold only three scripts.

Near the end of his probation, in the middle of December 1954, Gene got an idea for a science fiction story. Adhering to his normal procedure, he scribbled his idea on lined yellow paper—making several corrections and strike-outs as he wrote. As usual, he sealed the two handwritten pages in an envelope, registered and mailed it to himself to establish the

---

[32] The wide dissemination of this story seems to have come from NBC publicity during the early days of *Star Trek.* Doubtless it originated with an interview with Gene, who was always ready with a good story.

"poor man's copyright." As he was not yet a member of the Writer's Guild, it was some degree of protection in case his idea was stolen.

The two pages were an outline of a mature science fiction story. The writing is hurried, reflecting Gene's thinking. He composed this story as he wrote, editing and improving as he went along.

A man and woman, middle twenties, purchase a house from a real estate agent. Their manner is just odd enough to arouse interest. Inside the newly purchased house, we learn they are leader-agent from another star group. They are here to contact other agents, check their findings, and arrange ~~destruction of trhoublesom op so that commercial exploitation can be started. colonize~~, destruction & colonization.

~~They belong to a hro~~

Their manner toward each other is cold and efficient. ~~They're members of a perfectly disciplined state society. Actually~~ They exist in bodies which are exact multicellular castings of the typical homo sapiens. They are members of a society with "ant colony" type discipline.

That evening they await the pre-arranged arrival of ~~a pair of eart~~ a pair of agents placed on earth earlier. ~~They~~ The door bell rings and an older pair walks in. For a while there's a strange mix-up of conversation—the visiting pair are not ~~enemy~~ agents, they're neighbors welcoming the new arrivals. They manage to cover up conversational errors & get rid of the neighborly intruders.

(Page 2)
The agents do not arrive.

Concluding there may be some transport difficulties due to the earth's primitive set up, they are prepared ~~for a do~~ to wait awhile. ~~If they're not contacted in a month, they'll proceed alone.~~ The problem given to the other agents—Will earth destroy globe rather than submit to destruction. Earth has some power—the capacity the scope and nature of earth defenses. If they're not contacted within the month they'll form their own conclusions & signal the attack.

He goes to work—atomic agency—perfect references.

They are forced into something like normal life. She slowly falls for him. He responds, somewhat, feeling it unnecessary to appear above suspicion.

At plant he learns they have not yet arrived at the mass-sub-mass equation which makes destruction of earth possible. Elated, he announces to her he will send the signal. She announces a child is on the way. Argument—he leaves.

Time for destruction—he reappears—perfect love casteth out something or other.

In the next week or two, Gene hammered out the script, changing the ending from his original idea to the neighbors being the first team of agents who did not reveal themselves, waiting for "J-117's secret defense," love, to work its magic. The original title was "J-117's Defense," but Gene changed it to "The Secret Defense of 117" when he sold it. Given the vagaries of television production, it would be two years before this script would go out over the airwaves.

The script was sold to Four Star Productions originally for use in *Four Star Theater.* Someone decided otherwise and used it for the second season of the anthology series *Stage 7.* When that series was cancelled before the second season was broadcast, it became part of a syndication package and sold around the country in various markets under a variety of local sponsors' names. In Southern California it was broadcast under the title, *Chevron Hall of Stars,* on March 6, 1956, with a slightly different title, "The Secret Weapon of 117." This was Gene's first adult science fiction script, but it was still sold and broadcast under the name "Robert Wesley."

"Secret Weapon" became the first script for which Gene received professional notice. *Daily Variety* Television Review, March 9, 1956:

Secret Weapon of 117
(Chevron Hall of Stars)

Filmed by Four Star Films for Standard Oil Co. of California (BBD&O). Producer: Warren Lewis; Director, William A. Switer; teleplay and story, Robert Wesley; camera, Nick Musuraca; film editor, Lester Orlebeck; art director, Duncan Cramer.

Cast: Stars Ricardo Montalban,[33] John Litel, Susan Morrow, Sheila Bromley, Lewis Martin, Jack Daly. KTTV, Tues, 7:30 p.m. Running time: 30 min.

A tongue-in-cheek science-fictioner which takes off on a romantic comedy tangent, this "Chevron" proves a gay little romp with sharp philosophical overtones. It also marks the maiden telepic effort of a promising scripter, Robert Wesley, which is the nom de video of an L.A. cop—oops—policeman.

Off-beat tale intro's Ricardo Montalban and Susan Morrow as an unfriendly couple from outer space, sent to spy out the earthling's defenses against eventual destruction. Pair are transformed from their original states to handsome human male and female forms for this chore and soon find that basic biology is interfering with their mission. Predictably they fall in love and abandon their duties, to live human lives.

In this, they are abetted by a friendly, folksy, next-door neighbor couple, done by John Litel and Sheila Bromley. Telegraphed but still effective conclusion reveals that neighbors are a similar pair of spies sent 30 years ago on same mission, who also succumbed.

William A. Switer directed this half-hour adeptly. Montalban and Miss Morrow are a comely couple and display a flair for frothy humor. Litel and Miss Bromley effectively squeeze all the possibilities from respective roles.

KOVE

Gene was hitting his stride and 1955 became a good year for sales. He submitted a steady stream of ideas for stories for other Ziv shows and Ziv bought the occasional script. One idea he submitted was for a show in development at Ziv, *Science Fiction Theater. SFT* was to be an anthology series that based its dramas on scientific fact and speculation, extrapolating the story from the scientific principle or fact introduced each week by Truman Bradley, the program's host. At least that was the premise, backed up in publicity

---

[33] The dignified and charismatic Montalban would pass through Gene's life several more times. He guest-starred on *Star Trek,* the original series, as Khan Noonian Singh in "Space Seed," aired 2/16/67, and reprised the same role in the 1982 feature film, *Star Trek II: The Wrath of Khan.*

releases from Ziv announcing a $75,000 budget for the program's "scientific advisors." In reality, it was standard Hollywood hype. The science advisors were presented with the scripts and asked for scientific principles and demonstrations that could be used as tie-ins, not the other way around as Ziv would have the audience believe.

Each drama often had a clever twist at the end leaving the viewer with a question, often reiterated by Bradley, "Was it possible?" Bradley had been a radio announcer and had a wonderfully resonant voice and commanding yet sincere personality. He was the perfect host for the program's quasi-documentary format.[34]

On January 4, 1955, Gene submitted the following to Jon Epstein, head of the story department at Ziv:

Story idea for *Science Fiction Theater.*
"The Transporter"

ITEM: Recent experiments have identified the sections of the brain which control the various sensations—sight, sound, smell, feel, etc. During surgical operations, these areas have been artificially stimulated by mild electric currents, resulting in highly realistic hallucinations. (One patient "saw" his long dead mother; another reached out to pick up a nonexistent purring kitten.) Eventually it may be possible to stimulate the brain *without surgery* by means of ultra-high frequency radiations. Properly directed and controlled they would transport the recipient to another world, to him a very real world of color, sound, and action—all controlled by the stimulating device.

The proposed story is of the invention of the "Transporter"—a device which is television, smellovision, soundvision, all rolled into one. A device which creates an artificial world for the user, capable of duplicating delight, sensation, contentment, adventure—all beyond the reach of the ordinary person living the ordinary life. With it you can voyage to far-off lands, argue with Socrates, earn and spend a million dollars, or lay Marilyn Monroe. Take your choice.

---

[34] Fans of Star Trek and DeForest Kelly will note with appreciation that he appeared in two episodes of *SFT*: "Y.O.R.D." 5/6/55, and "Survival In Box Canyon," (10/12/56). In both episodes he played a doctor!

And this is the story of the inventor who, after achieving this miracle, suddenly realizes that a commercial, greedy, sometimes inhuman world would take over his miracle. And it might be used as they have used the miracle of radio, television, the motion pictures—with much more devastating results. It could become the most powerful totalitarian enslaving device; it could become the most powerful opiate; it could create wants and desires for which the world would destroy itself—a dying race sitting at their "transporters."

We leave the ultimate question unanswered. Will he destroy the "transporter"—or will someday, somewhere the "transporter" appear? Sooner or later we will have learned enough about the brain to create it.

The story idea was written eleven years before the noted science fiction writer Phillip K. Dick utilized a similar device in his short story "We Can Remember It For You Wholesale," that appeared in *The Magazine of Fantasy and Science Fiction*, April 1966. Dick's story was the basis for the Arnold Schwarzenager film, *Total Recall*. Gene's story idea predated the concept of virtual reality by thirty years or so.

Ziv did not buy the idea as it was too expensive to produce and *SFT* was firmly grounded in the Ziv tradition—the highest possible quality at the lowest possible price, the second consideration being of paramount importance. A syndicated program, *SFT* went on the air in early 1955, airing in 125 markets, including the top 60 stations in the country. Its final episode was broadcast in most markets by February 8, 1957, after a run of 77 episodes. Eight months later the Russians launched Sputnik I, inaugurating the "Space Race" and setting off renewed interest in science fiction. By then it was too late to restart *SFT*, but Ziv followed up with two series designed to tap into the public's renewed interest—*The Man and the Challenge* and *Men Into Space*. The public wasn't *that* interested and both series stopped production after one season.

SFT was the first program to feature adult themes in a science-fiction setting on a continuing basis. The next step, using continuing characters to explore adult themes, would have to wait a few more years for Gene to create *Star Trek*.

* * *

On January 14, 1955, Gene sold "Court Escape" for *Mr. District Attorney.* On April 5, he sold "Patrol Boat," and on July 1, "Police Brutality," both for *Mr. District Attorney.* Then, after a number of rejected story ideas to Ziv for *Highway Patrol,* several clicked and he sold "Reformed Criminal" on August 23, "Human Bomb" on October 24, and "Mental Patient" on December 7. All these scripts were sold and broadcast under his pseudonym of Robert Wesley. It was a good year: Gene made over $4000 as a writer and just under $6000 as a police sergeant.

The next year, 1956, became the "Year of Decision" for Gene. He was in his same routine—daylight hours were spent as the Public Information Division Day Watch commander, researching and writing speeches for Chief Parker, and nights were spent researching and writing television stories and scripts for himself. The quality and pace of his writing continued to improve.

In January, Ziv accepted two story ideas for their series *I Led Three Lives.* This was a departure for Gene from what he had previously written. *I Led Three Lives* was probably the most explicit political progaganda ever broadcast in a popular American dramatic television series. The program opened each week with the announcer setting the tone by seriously delivering the words: "This is the fantastically true story of Herbert A. Philbrick, who for nine frightening years led three lives—citizen, Communist, counterspy."

Today only those with very conservative leanings would take *I Led Three Lives* seriously, but in the 1950's, at the height of the Red Scare, it was accepted with deadly seriousness.[35] The program was based on Philbrick's book of the same name. He served as the series' technical consultant.[36]

---

[35] In the early 1950's much of America believed that a worldwide Communist conspiracy was about to overtake the country. It was the heyday of red-baiting demagogue Senator Joseph McCarthy, whose name has come to symbolize intrusive investigations propelled by fear and a lack of evidence. Later, after he was disgraced by a Senate censure and his behaviour was broadcast on television, McCarthy died of alcoholism.

[36] Herbert Philbrick was an FBI informant—later upgraded to "counterspy"—who had informed on communist front organizations from 1940 on. He broke his cover in 1949 and wrote a book whose title was used for the program.

By the time Gene wrote for the show, the producers had run out of material from Philbrick's book and were relying on writers to make up stories that Philbrick said "could have" happened. These were identified as stories "from the files of Herbert A. Philbrick." The stories were fantasy and exploited the rabid anti-communism then rampant in the country, but Ziv saw the popular series as a money-maker and so, if you could write a good story about the ever-skulking Communists ready to do dirt to honest, God-fearing Americans, Ziv would buy it and dramatize it.

Ziv, mining the anti-Communist fear then current in the country, met unprecedented success with *I Led Three Lives*. In the first four weeks of sales, Ziv placed the program in 58 markets. A month before it began broadcasting, it was scheduled in more markets than any of network television's top-ten rated shows. By September 1953, the show was in 94 markets as opposed to the 79 markets that carried *I Love Lucy* (CBS) and *Groucho Marx* (NBC).

Gene's friends and fans should not be surprised to learn that he wrote for such a program. He explained his attitude toward his writing in a letter to Chief Parker dated August 12, 1965:

Although we differ in philosophy on some matters, as you know, we are closer together on others than you may suspect. And either way, I like to think of myself as a thoroughly professional writer whose many characters can reflect many ideas and whose manuscripts are not a medium of personal propaganda but rather examinations of many things from many points of view.

As Gene's writing skill improved, he began to sell more and more stories. Finally, the pressure became too much. His career on the LAPD offered steady but limited money. Advancement in the department would take years. If he wrote for a living, his income would only be limited by how hard he worked—and writing certainly paid a lot more than being a policeman.

Ziv, gearing up for the major network push on *West Point,* handed a number of writing assignments to Gene. It was time to make a decision.

Gene had done a lot of soul searching, self-examination and analysis. He had decided. He would go into writing full-time. On May 25, he wrote to his friend Erle Stanley Gardner:

Dear Erle:

You may be interested in the following news since you are, in some degree, responsible for it. I recall a story about you—it seems many years ago you asked yourself "Quo vadis?", which lead to an analysis of what you wanted from life—freedom to create, explore, travel, plus a comfortable income and some challenge. True or not, the story goes that you set up a ledger sheet, listing various occupations and their disadvantages and advantages. Everything cancelled out except writing.

You may have guessed from my preoccupation and questions that I have been doing very much the same thing. Although the challenge can be found in police work, not much else is there. During the past seven years, via notebook and considerable research and study, I've learned a big part of what the job teaches—and the remaining education at a cost of 23 more years doesn't look like a good investment.

Of course, Parker wasn't surprised. He smiled and said he'd been expecting it for the last couple of years—as a matter of fact, he'd gone out of his way (unrealized by me) to put me in touch with people in various industries—hoping I'd get an offer I liked. He was kind enough to say that much of what we've accomplished in LA was due to my basic research and creative thinking and said he was truly sorry that he couldn't give his "ghost" proper credit. Of course, I told him that working with him and learning from him was ample repayment. And it certainly was.

The thing that tipped the scale in favor of writing was, of course, the recent success of several scripts which has lead to a number of top-paying assignments. Am working on two pilots now, continuing on *West Point*, which goes on a national hook-up this fall, as well as doing what I can on two other shows. ZIV's head of production was quoted in *The Reporter* the other day naming me as their top writer—this and other things still have me amazed and grateful. Suddenly my agent is asking and getting top prices and I find myself picking and choosing assignments like an old pro. Have been off-duty (vacation and specials) for slightly over a month now. Last work day is May 31.

Anyway, thought you might be interested. No illusions about matching your success but will try to match your hard work, if physically capable of it.

Incidentally, there's one thing I'd like to make clear. I value your friendship as friendship alone. I have no intention of trading upon it to wangle writing assignments, bore you with questions or requests for advice. Like you, I'm sort of a stubborn cuss and like to make it on my own. I know that attitude's considered "old fashioned" in this industry, but I like it.

Gardner responded a few days later:

Dear Gene:

Chief Parker told us in San Diego that you had gone into the writing business exclusively. Congratulations on your success in that business, but don't get away from your police contacts.

If it is at all possible, and you could work out a deal by which you could spend part time in the public relations work of the police, you would be a lot more satisfied in the long run and you would find that the practical background would be a very wonderful anchor which would keep you from being enveloped in the Never Never Land of Hollywood television.

The income tax is such that you can't hope to make enough money to pay your income tax and save enough money to be independent—or at least I've never been able to—because the more you make the harder you work, the harder you work the more help you need, the more help you need the more money you spend, the more money you spend the harder you have to work, etc., etc., etc.

However, there is a great satisfaction in feeling that you are using your creative talents and there is an even greater satisfaction when you can feel that you are using those talents in the interests of law enforcement and the administration of justice.

You are going to find that there are a lot of problems which confront you when you start putting in all of your time on writing. When you are working on a part-time basis you have a tendency to feel that if you could only put in all of your time on writing it would be a cinch. Once you start putting in all of your time, you find that you have troubles.

The big thing you are going to have to fight against is getting written out, or getting in a groove, and in order to avoid that pitfall, you're going to have to do a lot of thinking and remember to keep up an intake of new experiences which can be transformed into new stories.

This is rather a disjointed letter because I'm hitting the high spots at which I am working on a book manuscript and trying to get out enough work to keep my five secretaries banging away at the typewriter. I never can tell whether they're working for me or whether I'm working for them.

Anyhow, Gene, you're always welcome here at the ranch and we regard you as part of the family. If there is anything in my thirty-odd years of writing experience that will be of help to you, I'll be only too glad to give you anything I can.

My best all around, and every wish for your success in this writing field.

On June 7, 1956, Gene handed in a simple written resignation.

I find myself unable to support my family at present on anticipated police salary levels in a manner we consider necessary! Having spent slightly more than seven years on this job, during all of which fair treatment and enjoy-

able working conditions were received, this decision is
made with considerable and genuine regret.

Signed,
E.W. Roddenberry,
Sergeant of Police,
Public Information

CHAPTER 7

The future looked bright. Through Ziv and other independent producers there was a demand for scripts, and Gene was confident of his ability to supply them. Ziv had already assigned him to their new series *West Point,* but Gene's resignation from the LAPD and civil service security was not a great leap into the unknown. As someone who had left the department voluntarily, Gene had a three-year window of opportunity during which he could return at his old rank should the new career not work out. There was only one caveat: part of his base of power in the LAPD was linked to his relationship with Chief of Police William H. Parker. As Parker aged, he became less stable and more right wing in his political thinking, and his drinking increased. He acquired a nickname that said it all: "Whiskey Bill." One former LAPD officer observed, "For the last several years it was well known in the department that Parker's adjutants' main jobs were to get Parker out of sight when he drank too much at lunch or dinner." While he would continue to respect Parker for the rest of his life, Gene always knew he had made the right choice.

Gene's successful plunge into full-time writing was simultaneously celebrated and parodied by his friend Don Ingalls. Ingalls had left the department before Gene to follow his own career and was writing a daily column for the *Valley*

Times newspaper.[1] On June 27, 1957 the following column appeared.

The Valley Roundup
by Don Ingalls

Now, my thinking doesn't operate too much along mercenary lines and I usually hang onto a fairly cheerful way of looking at things—philosophic and all that. But! Take my advice and don't drop in on any old friends you haven't visited for some years.

Gene Roddenberry and I started writing more or less about the same time. In fact, I used to drop him little kind hints as to what was wrong with his stories. Then we drifted apart.

Recently I decided to look up dear old friend Gene and let him know how well I was doing. Daily columnist and all that—you understand.

So, I drove over to his place. That was my mistake.

Gene met me at the door, fat and sleek. Not at all the picture of a struggling writer. Eating too much and not enough work, I thought smugly.

After the usual amenities we settled down in his study to talk.

"Well," I asked, "how are things, old friend?"

The telephone rang.

"Excuse me," said Gene.

The conversation went something like this: "Oh, hello Max. Yes, fine. Oh, sure, I finished all seven of those scripts. What! Only five thousand? I was planning on ten. That'll drop my weekly average to fourteen thousand! My agent will squawk like mad.

"Well, OK. If I get that mystery series contract. Deal. Mail me the checks will you? So long, Max."

His wife came in with some mail, eyeing me with suspicion. "Oh, excuse me," she said, staring at me. "I thought you were the gardener." She hurried out, all flustered.

Gene fingered through the letters. "Checks, checks," he

---

[1] He would later, on Gene's recommendation, be hired by Sam Rolfe as story editor for *Have Gun Will Travel*, rising to producer. Don also produced the last five and a half years of *Fantasy Island*.

muttered absently. "The IRS will murder me next year."
He threw nine or ten of those unwelcome checks onto his
desk top; where I devoured them with my eyes.

He turned to me. "Now—" he sighed.

The phone rang.

"Hello," said Gene. "Oh, Max. Hmm. But I already got
a house in Malibu. A deal, eh? Well, maybe I could sell
off one or two of mine at Newport Beach. Or the small
house in Palm Springs. OK Max—thanks."

He hung up.

"Well," I said, without much hope.

The phone rang.

"Excuse me," said Gene. "Hello. Umm. Sure, Harry.
Another assignment? But I'm already working on fourteen shows, nine series, three movie scenarios, two novels
and a couple of other ideas. Huh? Thirty thousand up
front, eh? Hmm. Well—"

It was about there that I somehow felt that my old
friend Gene didn't need my advice any more. So, I crept
out, stumbling over a bundle of uncashed checks lying
near the doorway.

Man, do I feel down! Take my advice and don't drop in
on any old friends you haven't seen in a while.

Daily columnist indeed!

Say! I wonder how much old friend Gene pays his gardener?

In becoming a full-time writer and accepting the advice of
Erle Stanley Gardner, Gene joined a small, elite fraternity, a
direct line of writers who went back before the turn of the
century.

Gardner's writing career had begun in the pulps, though
he had made the transition to the higher-paying slick magazine market, then books and, in the 1950's, television, when
his most popular character, lawyer–detective Perry Mason,
made the transition to the small screen. Gardner's philosophy of writing was that he wrote to entertain the reader,
nothing more.[2] That he was successful is attested to by his
paychecks. Gardner was described by *Life* magazine as earn-

---

[2]This attitude was passed down to Gene, and while Gene adhered to it in the early
part of his career, he did manage, in *Star Trek,* to include social commentary and
philosophy as part of his writing, à la Jonathan Swift.

ing $50,000 a year in 1933[3]—all at a nickel a word or less. In order to earn that kind of money, he had to write quickly and efficiently.

While others would say that the secret of writing was rewriting, Gene learned through experience the same lesson that Gardner had learned in his early career, a principle validated by tens of millions of written words over seventy odd years: the real secret of profitable commercial writing was to write once and revise minimally. Getting it right the first time only came with constant practice, and Gene put in the time. His output expanded. As he progressed, he analyzed his work, ever improving and refining, listening to Gardner's advice and studying his craft.

Six months after Gene's plunge into full-time writing, Gardner wrote near Christmas and made the following offer: "If you have any trouble getting stale in digging up plots, I have a system which may be of some help to you."

Gardner was unbelievably prolific, regularly dictating 10,000 words a day, keeping five secretaries working fulltime. His lifetime output of words ran into the tens of millions, the result of tremendous energy, iron discipline, and a careful, analytical approach to writing that came directly out of his training as a lawyer.

Gardner developed his own way of creating plots, which he called "The Fluid or Unstatic Theory of Plots." Kept in a simple notebook in his study at Rancho del Paisano, Northern San Diego County, and labeled "Formulae for Writing a Mystery," it was his single most valuable creation, carefully guarded and usually carried while traveling.

By August 1958, Gene was having trouble and called on Gardner for help.

> Dear Erle:
>   Help!
>   As you once advised (and the wisdom becomes more apparent every day), writers have a way of going stale. The battery runs down. You said you had a system of recharging which you were holding until I said I needed it.
>   I need it.
>   Gene Roddenberry

---

[3]Gene's father was making about $200 a month as a policeman.

Going stale at this point may have been understandable, as Gene had written literally dozens of stories and scripts, some sold and produced and others less successful. Gardner, at his retreat in Paradise, California, wrote back on September 4:

> I'm not sure that I can give you exactly what you want but I think I can do you quite a bit of good.
> It's stuff that I don't want to put on paper and stuff I would like to have you regard as being more or less confidential.

Gardner finished the letter by telling Gene he would be back on the ranch in early October and in Hollywood on October 21. Immediately after dictating the letter to Gene and having it sent Airmail–Special Delivery, he dictated the following to himself:

> Gene Roddenberry is having trouble going stale. He can't get plots the way he used to.
> Explain to him the theory of the lowest common denominator in fiction and the theory of combining two conventional gambits, also the theory of overlapping impulses and plot structure, and the theory of picking up a point of contact far removed from the main plot sequence and if absolutely necessary, give him the secret of plot concentration.[4]
>
> ESG

Gardner then dictated a memo to his office instructing them to remind him with the previously dictated note of the substance and tenor of the conversation he was planning on having with Gene when he saw him. Generous as he was in his comments to Gene that "he was family," Gardner was not able to part with the full scope of his closely guarded study. Whatever the extent of the information Gardner whispered in Gene's ear, the problem was solved and Gene's output remained constant for years.

---

[4]For a detailed examination of Gardner's full methodology, including an exposition of his "Formulae For Writing a Mystery," so well hidden during his lifetime, see *Secrets of the World's Biggest Selling Writer: Storytelling Techniques of Erle Stanley Gardner* by Francis and Roberta Fugate (New York: William Morrow, 1980). It is currently out of print but available in libraries and used bookstores.

* * *

Ziv Television had been exploring the feasibility of filming a television series at the U.S. Army Military Academy at West Point since October 1954. By March 1955, the pilot film script had been approved and filming completed both in Hollywood and at West Point, New York. It was an ambitious project for Ziv, the studio's first network program. It required extensive logistics and close interaction with the military. Fred Ziv was against it from the beginning, but ever the pragmatic businessman, he read the situation accurately and acted accordingly:

"I had no desire to ever work with the networks, but as our organization got larger, we had some people who wanted to work with the networks; for example, Jerome Lawrence and Robert E. Lee. While they were happy writing for syndication, when the network came along and made them an offer, they were flattered by it, and there is no question that they wanted to write for the networks.

"I would never have produced a program for the networks had I not been subject to this kind of pressure within the organization. If the only way I could hold my organization together was to do an occasional network show, I would do it. And so when television came long we did a network show called *West Point*."[5]

Ziv also decided that the high cost of filming on the East Coast would be easier to accept if he could film two series at once, and so, with the military's blessing, he created *Men of Annapolis*, a syndicated program with exactly the same operations.

The men responsible for the success of *The West Point Story* knew that the principle ingredient would be authenticity, but the decision wasn't prompted by purely artistic considerations. Ziv had been granted exclusive rights by the Department of Defense to film at the military academy, and that exclusivity brought oversight by a special "TV" committee at West Point. Echoing Jack Webb's experience on *Dragnet* with Chief Parker, nothing would appear on the new program without approval by the military.

---

[5]The network deal was profitable and Ziv later made a number of programs for the networks, including *Tombstone Territory, Rough Riders, Bat Masterson, Men Into Space,* and *The Man and the Challenge.*

The Army assigned principle oversight to young Army officers who reported to the Army Television Board, who oversaw the whole operation. Only a few reports survive. One was written by First Lieutenant Stanley Wielga, Jr. of the 5th Infantry Division at Fort Ord, California, and was directed to Colonel Heiberg, President of the TV Board, West Point, New York.

He wrote in part:

> Sets appeared authentic. Work days were long, with 66 hours work in 5 days. I believe the results will be hightly satisfactory, however.
> One of the writers, Gene Rodenberg (sic), approached me with a story he is writing. It involves cadets doing varius (sic) types of personal service (washing car, cutting grass and hedges, etc.) for an instructor in order to discourage him from resigning from the Army to work for an oil company. I advised strongly against it, but he decided to go ahead with the story, so it will probably be submitted to the board in the near future.

Maurice "Babe" Unger, Ziv's chief of production, considered Gene a bright and rising young writer. He assigned Gene to *West Point*. Ziv and the Pentagon concluded that a visit of the production staff to the academy would be valuable. Unfortunately, at the time of this assignment (late 1955), Gene was still employed full-time by the LAPD, an organization which liked to see its employees appear for work each day. The visit to West Point was scheduled for the end of the first week of March 1956. Gene wasn't the least bit fazed. He had accumulated a large number of days off and was not closely supervised. The Public Information Unit had been organized by a sergeant and three uniformed officers. As one of them remembered, "We pretty much did what we wanted." Gene informed his captain that he was taking a week and a half off and departed for New York.

He visited West Point with Leon Benson, producer and director of the first thirteen episodes, Jon Epstein, Ziv's story supervisor, and Don Brinkley, another writer, where they received the full VIP treatment—meetings with colonels, cadet escorts, and meals with cadets and other VIPs. They received a thorough familiarization with West Point and its environs. Gene even went so far as to live for a day or two in the cadet barracks. He later wrote an episode, "The Operator," that had cadets watching television on a clandestine set. On a subsequent visit to The Point, several cadets quietly told him that they had watched that episode on an illegal set and had gotten a big kick out of art imitating life.

Like LAPD's Chief Parker, the Pentagon realized the power of television and knew that the show, if properly done, would be a 30-minute commercial for the Army running on national television each week. That Ziv assigned Gene to this program was a clear indication of their opinion of his skills and abilities. Gene's history with Ziv was short but solid. He had sold them less than a dozen scripts since beginning his career as a writer.

In less than two years from his first sale, he was writing for a network program. Gene slipped easily into the creative maelstrom that was Hollywood in 1956, near the middle of the "Golden Age of Television." His assignment to the *West Point* program grew and Gene became the program's head writer. He wrote at least ten episodes—roughly one-third of that season's production.

Leon Benson remembers:

"It was a heck of a good operation. The production setup on this was that we did shows in groups of four. Now these were still three-day schedules, and considering the complexity of these productions this was really an achievement. We started in Hollywood where we built replicas of the most important, the most familiar and the most used sets, such as the interior of cadets' rooms, portions of some of the public buildings, classrooms, and stuff like that. . . . We did two of the interiors in the studio for the first of those four shows. Then we traveled to West Point where we did the exteriors for the next two shows, then we returned to Hollywood and did the interiors for the last two shows.

"We took as little cast as possible from Hollywood to West Point and hired actors who could work only in the exteriors at West Point. We hired a lot of actors that have become very big since. We hired Steve McQueen in New York and brought him out to Hollywood. He was a young punk then. . . .

"One of the most important things in making pictures inexpensively is to get the best possible people that you can. You get people on their way up—actors, directors, writers. . . ."

West Point did not consume all Gene's time. He was constantly working on series and story ideas. Television was a growing, ever hungry creature, and Gene worked hard to feed the beast. On June 20, even though he was a member of the Writers' Guild, Gene did not register the following series concept with the WGA but fell back on his old standby, the self-addressed, registered letter, to protect his idea.

I have this date, June 20, 1956, discussed with my agent Lawrence Cruikshank and Mr. Epstein of CBS a series idea created by myself and entitled "Hawaii Passage" along with suggested alternate titles STAR PASSENGER, PACIFIC PASSAGE, SEA PASSAGE, HAWAII CRUISE, HAWAII LINER, OCEANLINER, STEAM SHIP, CRUISE SHIP, SEVEN SEAS, (OF) SHIPS AND STARS, THE LURALINE,[6] HAWAII.

"Hawaii Passage" is a series of stories which take place mainly aboard an ocean liner, a cruise ship which travels between the mainland and Hawaii and possibly other pacific ports. Although the beginning or close of the story might be set in any stateside or island city, the major setting is the ship itself.

The continuing main characters in the series of stories, outside of the ship itself, are the ship captain, purser, and/or deck-officer. The stories are of a general anthology nature. They will concern passengers and the ship personnel, separately or in combination.

A salient feature of the new series idea is the use of an ocean liner (Matson or President lines) in public-relations cooperation with the operating company, for practical-location shots. For example, during the 4½ day trip to Hawaii from Los Angeles, it will be possible to film the exterior sequences of approximately three half-hour shows—including an equal number on the trip back unless production schedules requires the actors and crews to fly back via air. The ship itself provides a stable platform,

[6]The name of one of Matson Line's cruise ships. Later, earning more money, Gene got into the habit of taking a cruise to Hawaii in January.

electrical outlets, storage facilities, and crew accomodations. And, of course, the scene possibilities of an ocean liner are tremendous—in many respects one of these liners is a floating city with everything aboard from beauty parlors, medical facilities and dining rooms to the ship's bridge, swimming pools and deck vistas.

Due to the fact that the conversations at CBS lasted until late afternoon, this memo had to be typed and registered the following day at the post office.

E.W. Roddenberry
9855 Key West Street
Temple City, California

The reader will note the germ of an idea in the interaction between the main characters—the ship's captain, purser, and/or deck officer—and the concept of the ship itself being a "character," something Gene would repeat ten years later. This idea, which CBS did not buy, was 21 years before *The Love Boat* appeared on home screens and ten years before another ship of Gene's creation began making longer voyages.

Eight days later, Ziv's *Highway Patrol* aired the last script sold under Gene's pseudonym, Robert Wesley.

Besides a career as a writer, something else came out of Gene's association with Ziv—the determination to ultimately be a producer. It was Ziv's handling of a script that sparked that drive. Sitting with his family, he watched a *Highway Patrol* episode made from one of his scripts. Gene became irritated, seeing how the producers had changed his ideas. He turned to his brother and told him that he would have to become a producer in order to prevent his work from being changed. It was the irony of ironies as years later, Gene, in producing *Star Trek,* freely rewrote what most writers submitted, earning lifelong enmity from more than one who failed to grasp this fundamental nature of television.

On October 5, 1956, CBS began broadcasting Ziv's first network series, *The West Point Story.* Gene's work was now being seen Friday evenings at 8 o'clock.[7]

---

[7] It would last two seasons, the first on CBS and the second on ABC—October 1956 to September 1957, and October 1957 to July 1958.

* * *

While Gene's writing career was blossoming, his marriage was crumbling. The circumstances of the early years of marriage would have stressed any couple. The young newlyweds had spent only four months together before Gene shipped out to the South Pacific. He was gone a year and returned a mature combat veteran—a man who had seen death and learned responsibility as only those in combat have. During his absence, Eileen had continued to live with her parents. When he returned, the young couple led a nomadic life, moving from base to base, as Gene's stateside assignment in aircraft crash investigation had him assigned to a variety of locations during the remainder of his military obligation. Even when they found themselves someplace semi-permanently, Gene could be gone for days or weeks at a time.

Little changed when he left the Army Air Force and began flying for Pan Am. Gene had no seniority, so he flew the long runs. He often had a schedule that had him gone six weeks at a time. Eileen was beautiful, unsophisticated, in love and eager to please, but was no source of intellectual stimulation for Gene.

In May 1948, when Gene resigned from Pan American World Airways, he and Eileen began living together on a continuous, daily basis. There would be no more multi-week interruptions, no long absences.

As the years wore on and Gene advanced in the LAPD, he confided to a few friends that things weren't going well at home. To many of his friends this was no revelation, as Gene's numerous affairs—at least one quite blatant in the department—were proof enough. One colleague, also active extramaritally, remembered Gene discussing the possibility of them sharing the rent on a downtown apartment for their various liasons, but nothing came of it.

Eileen became pregnant with Dawn late in 1952 and commented to her sister-in-law Bernice that she was unhappy carrying a child again. Dawn Allison Roddenberry greeted the world in Pasadena, California, on August 31, 1953. She grew up asking uncles and aunts, and her paternal grandmother, if she could come and live with them every time she visited. According to the relatives' memories, she rarely wanted to go home after a visit.

With regard to his marriage, Gene's traditional nature asserted itself, or at least part of it did. The 1950's were not a time of easy and simple divorce, there were two children to consider, he had made certain promises in the marriage ceremony plus he had to consider the logistics and financial costs involved. Above everything else was Gene's strict aversion to confrontation in his personal life, especially confrontation with women. From the time he skipped a stair in elementary school to the end of his life, he would work at avoiding confrontations. It was an expensive character flaw that would end up costing him untold emotional turmoil and millions of dollars.

Gene continued his association with Ziv and contracted in April with them for their series *Harbormaster,* story #102, "Coastal Security." Also that same month he signed a contract to develop yet another half-hour show for Ziv, *Junior Executive.* This contract was unusual in that Gene had a collaborator for the first time, Quinn Martin, who was also employed by Ziv. While nothing came of this series, Martin made his name secure in television history by going on to produce *The Untouchables* for Desilu in 1959 and then forming his own independent production company, QM Productions.[8]

Martin, Gene, and a number of other people who started out with Ziv would become successful through their own talents and drives, with no small credit being given for their time working for Ziv. They were men who came to understand what television was in terms of practical matters—what the networks wanted on the screen and the practical considerations that came with production. They also understood that television existed as the most powerful of the mass media because of its pervasiveness and the ability of pictures to quickly convey massive amounts of information and invoke an emotional response.

Gene became a successful part of the Hollywood program creation/production crap shoot, though the odds against being successful in the business were tremendous. Every year thousands of program ideas and story treatments are run past producers who select a small number for development. Of those, a few will have scripts written. The tiny number who

---

[8]QM produced *The Fugitive, The F.B.I., The Invaders, Cannon, The Streets of San Francisco, Barnaby Jones,* and *Bert D'Angelo/Superstar.*

pass through the crucible of development—which means receiving criticism, both constructive and otherwise—will make it to the coveted stage of "ORDER," where a pilot is actually filmed. Finally, after what may seem like endless tinkering by everyone except the studio janitor, the pilot is shown, sometimes to test audiences and/or network executives, or broadcast as a "movie of the week." The ratings are carefully watched and a series order placed for a few programs if the ratings warrant it. There may be more tinkering by network executives, often at odds with the people who created the show. The series may then be bought by the network or sent back for more "fixing." It is a strange process, and often the most successful program is the result of many hands and many contributions.

With his talent, training, experience with Ziv, and ambition, Gene exploded into the television writing market in late 1956 to early 1957.[9]

Gene began selling to other studios. He had learned his craft, polished his skills in the training arena, and now it was time to move on to bigger studios who paid more money. By October 1956, he had signed a contract with Screen Gems to write a 90-minute television movie, *Natchez.* He would be paid $800 for the story ($100 more than a fully completed script for Ziv), $2,173 for the first draft and $1,000 for the final. Previously, three half-hour teleplays to Ziv would have paid only $2,100 total.

The next month, he sold the pilot script for the series *Threshold* to Meriam C. Cooper Enterprises. *Threshold* was to be an anthology of stories centered at the United States Air Force Academy. While Gene was paid for his work, like most series ideas this one did not make it past preliminary development. Screen Gems liked his work and came through with another contract, $2,500 for an episode of *The Man From Texas,* another series in development that was never made.

From late 1956—after his formal resignation from the LAPD—through 1962, Gene became a one-man story and script-writing factory, reminiscent of his friend Erle Stanley Gardner's business, "The Fiction Factory," who had taken

---

[9]When the Writers' Guild of America was contacted for a printout of Gene's recognized credits, even the experienced WGA representative was impressed at his prolificacy.

the title from William Wallace Cook. In 1956, Gene wrote and saw filmed five episodes of *The West Point Story* and an episode of *Dr. Christian*. In 1957 he wrote four episodes of *Boots and Saddles,* four episodes of *Have Gun Will Travel,*[10] an episode of *The Jane Wyman Theater,* five more episodes of *The West Point Story,* and Gene's contribution to the "Golden Age of Television" canon, "So Short a Season" for the *Kaiser Aluminum Hour.* In 1958 he sold an episode each to *Harbor Command, Bat Masterson,* and *Sam Houston,* three more episodes to *Have Gun,* and four episodes to *Jefferson Drum.* In 1959 Gene's produced credits list ten scripts for *Have Gun* and "The Big Walk," a pilot for the unsold series *Nightstick;* 1960 lists a story credit for *The June Allyson Show,* but that may have been written late the previous year, and two episodes of *The Detectives* also very early in the year. He then went to work for Screen Gems, leaving in the middle of 1961, resuming his free-lance work with two scripts for *Shannon,* and one each for *Target: The Corruptors* and *Two Faces West.* These were all produced scripts, work that actually went before the camera. Add to the produced work, dozens more that were credited to Gene by the Writers' Guild and ranged from one-page ideas to finished scripts that did sell but weren't produced. These credits alone would comprise a full career for a number of writers, but Gene was just getting started.

As 1958 rolled in, Gene did not diminish his creative pace. In addition to the previously listed sold and produced scripts he also had a number of ideas for series. On March 13, he registered with the Writers' Guild *The Man From Lloyds,* an action–adventure series about an agent of the famous insurance company, Lloyds of London. He named the main character Anthony Ryker. It is the second time we have record of him using the name "Ryker," (the first being a

---

[10]The next year, Gene won the Writers' Guild Award for best-written script for a TV Western for the *Have Gun Will Travel* episode "Helen of Abajinian," telecast December 28, 1957. He received the award at a presentation in November 1957.

Gene was often described, and on several occasions described himself, as the "head writer" on *Have Gun Will Travel.* In an interview with the program's creator, Sam Rolfe, some months before his death, he wanted it made clear that there was no position of "head writer," and that while Gene may have written a lot of episodes, he was not the head writer, just a reliable free-lance writer whose quality was always very high. Sam spoke well of Gene's ability to create a quality script quickly and never let the producer down.

character in his first script in late 1954 for *Mr. District Attorney*). It wouldn't be the last time he used it. Like most writers' ideas, the series concept found no buyers.

In June, Gene came up with a series idea out of personal knowledge and experience. He wrote to Hunt Stromberg, Jr. at CBS television proposing a half-hour television series called *Footbeat,* stories about a beat cop and his adventures. CBS did not buy the idea. Once again Gene was either ahead of his time or the executives behind the times.[11] Gene was not one to waste a good idea. In May 1960, he attempted to sell the cop-on-the-beat idea again. Using the same letter he had written to Hunt Stromberg, Jr. two years earlier, Gene pitched *Footbeat* to Charles Irving at Hollis Productions. The results, like the letter, were identical. It finally made the grade at Screen Gems and almost made it to the Sunday night lineup, but circumstances prevailed against it. ABC decided to go "all Western" in their Sunday night lineup, and Gene's creation went down for the count.

Although he was making inroads with the bigger and better paying production companies, Gene still knocked off "Pecos Shootdown" for Ziv's network program *Bat Masterson.*

Life did not happen *to* Gene. A forceful individual, he controlled circumstances as much as he could and benefited accordingly. He was quick to recognize opportunity in the oddest of situations. In 1959, he was presented with an award by the American Baptist Convention "for skillfully writing Christian truth and the application of Christian principles into commercial, dramatic TV scripts." Gene, a freethinker and humanist who had rejected the Christian concept of God in his teenage years, graciously accepted the award, and the attendant publicity.[12]

Shortly thereafter, Gene began corresponding with John M.

---

[11]Gene was not the only cop who left the LAPD to pursue a writing career. Years later, LAPD detective Joseph Wambaugh carved out a successful writing career dealing realistically with police subjects.

[12]Also given an award at the same occasion were Roy Rogers and Dale Evans, long known for their evangelical work and deep commitment to Christianity. After his death, he was given an Angel award posthumously by what turned out to be another Christian media group. They gave him the award for *Star Trek: The Next Generation,* the most blatantly humanistic program on the air.

Gunn, head of the broadcasting and film commission of the National Council of the Churches of Christ, producers of the television program *Frontiers of Faith*.[13] Gunn wrote that they were planning "a series on the modern application of the Christian ethic; in searching for theological background, we find ourselves pushed right back to the teaching of Jesus. . . . I'm not looking for modern parables, but stories that will illuminate, however subtly, the teachings. If this appeals and you have the time, please let me know and I'll send along some material and a couple of old scripts."

Gene, ever on the lookout for writing assignments, wrote back:

As you must have guessed, the theme outline in your letter does appeal to me. At the moment, however, you've caught me with a pair of pilots in work plus several promised scripts overlapping.

Waited a week before answering you in the expectation that some might cancel out or fold but the situation just got more grim.

The Beat Cop [previously mentioned as *Footbeat*] thing became *The Big Walk* which sold to L & M, was set to go ABC Sunday night following *Maverick*, then was cancelled out last moment on a policy decision to go all-Western. Ah well . . . At least it may come alive again this Winter but frankly, I've become disenchanted with it now.

In his next undated letter Gunn says:

What I hoped for from you is a story which will illuminate the meaning of the Cross. If this is an impossible assignment, as it may well be, do what you will within the area.

Our limitations are those of low budget, public service shows, notably space. We generally are given a studio which allows four sets, and perhaps a flat. Because the program is done all of a piece, with no editing and no commercial breaks, you must remember to make it possible for an actor to get from one set to another.

---

[13]On NBC from October 7, 1951, to July 19, 1970, it often alternated its time slot with *The Catholic Hour* and *The Eternal Light*.

Months later Gene sent Gunn a splash of reality in an Air Mail Special Delivery letter.

> I've only now gotten to the material you sent. I'm
> still involved in winding up the show I produced in
> San Francisco last week, and it looks like another
> ten days or two weeks before we get it into the
> can. Which means it would be a least that long before
> I could prepare any sort of story line for your approval.
> Meanwhile, however, I'll go through this very
> carefully and see what comes to mind.
>
> As I mentioned once before, I am fascinated by the
> philosophical challenge your show presents—the
> opportunity to grapple with some strong and real
> ethical paradox. But you must understand that I am
> a complete pagan, and consume enormous amounts
> of bread, having found the Word more spice than
> nourishment, so I am interested in a statement
> couched in dollars and cents of what this means
> to the Roddenberry treasury. Not that I am unwilling
> to considerably lower minimums in your case.

A bit later, in February 1960, Gene again wrote to Gunn:

> You will shortly be receiving a letter from Don Ingalls,
> formerly Story Editor of *Have Gun Will Travel*. Don
> is very interested in the moral challenge indicated
> in the stories you sent me and should be able to
> turn you out an excellent script.
>
> Just finishing up a picture I have been laboring on
> these many weeks, and hope to get a note off to
> you in a couple of days.

Although there is no letter in the file, by March 11 the following response suggests that Gene learned that his letter about money had offended Gunn in some way. He writes to Gunn again:

> I'm really sorry now that I bugged you (humorously,
> I hope) about a statement on money for writing your
> show. My intention was to develop one of the
> themes last week, shoot it to you. I really do want
> to write one, and what I have to say now may sound

like money was actually in the back of my mind all the time. Unfortunately, despite the continuing strike, Screen Gems has elected to put my agreement with them into immediate effect, a marriage which includes a clause similar to the one my wife insisted upon some nineteen years ago. So, for better or worse, I'm bound-up exclusively theirs. For a year, anyway.

There is no record of any further correspondence.

Simultaneously, Gene played a bigger game, the result of which was obliquely reported in the letter above. Sometime in mid- to late 1959, Gene had been approached by England's Sir Lew Grade, later Lord Grade, owner of Associated Television (ATV) and the international distribution company, International Television Corporation (ITC). Grade was a showman in the grand style. By the time he contacted Gene, he had been in the television business less than three years but was expanding aggressively. The correspondence between Gene and Grade's top man, Ralph Smart, explored the feasibility of a deal where Gene would develop stories, scripts, and pilots for Grade, ultimately ending up with his own production company. More than that, it indicates part of Gene's philosophy and hopes for the future of television.

On July 27, Ralph Smart wrote:

I talked with Lew Grade again this morning about the possibility of your coming with us. We quite understand that you do not want to give us your energy, talent and invention just to make us rich. He is quite prepared to start a new production company and give you a part of it.

On August 7, Gene replied:

I was much pleased to have this letter of yours expressing faith in my ability and ideas. As you must know, the feeling is warmly reciprocated. The friendship implied here makes the possibility of our working together doubly attractive.

The other evening, I brought up the idea of life in England to Eileen and the children. Eileen was, of course, delighted. But our two girls were a bit

shaken, seeing it as a thinly disguised plan to do them
out of our winter vacation in Hawaii. That is, until
we mentioned England is also an island. (I swallow
a purple comment on our local school system at this
point.) At any rate, we've somehow gotten into a
situation where the youngest, at least, thinks of
London in terms of breadfruit trees and surf-riders.
I know this is asking a lot but if we come there, could
you possibly arrange to meet us wearing a grass
skirt and strumming a ukulele?

Please tell Lew Grade that an ownership in a new
production company does sound interesting. I would
like to hear further details. I assume these would
include expenses and a salary in the area of my
present earnings. In return, I would expect to invest
time, energy and ideas into the full creation and
production of *Freelance* (or alternate property),
with series profits to be shared on the basis of
company ownership.

The only drawback I see in such an agreement is
that it may employ only half a man. My interest
in ITC goes considerably beyond some loose
alliance as an independent producer. Your organization-
complex apparently plans expansion into a leading
position in world-wide television. I would suppose
this means the eventual and continuing creation of
a large number of television shows, including not only
the rather stereotyped filmed-drama currently popular
but also reaching out to conceive new areas and
new levels of entertainment. I'm certain your people
constantly remind themselves, as I do, that this television
thing is still relatively new; that the shows which
dominate the tubes today are not necessarily the
ones which will be most profitable three or ten
years from now. I'm certain, therefore, that the future
of your organization demands it do more than merely
duplicate the kind of things which have already
become a highly efficient pattern of Desilu, ZIV,
Four Star and others.

If this is true, it happens to coincide with certain
desires of my own. During your trip here I spoke
of an interest in creating on a broad spectrum and,

perhaps, even demonstrated in a small way some such ability.

I would like to take some space here to suggest some such areas of creativity which could be mutually profitable. Hollywood is currently hemmed-in and blinded by a frenzied attempt to duplicate and re-duplicate the successes of the past few seasons. Much of the industry's thinking here is cluttered with incredibly bad copies of the recent cowboy and private-eye successes. The mortality rate on these new shows is bound to be high, everyone is worried, but very few are really yet ready to seek the new ideas which the buyers will shortly demand. It seems to me to be an opportune time for a company outside Hollywood's charmed (or bewitched) circle to analyze tomorrow's market and create new and profitable entertainment patterns.

Secondly, although Hollywood does seem to have a monopoly on the kind of writers and directors who excel in the current slickly executed styles, certainly England and other countries do produce artists who themselves excel in areas of their own. And there may be some solidly profitable wisdom in seeking some television shows in these areas instead of battling American television producers on their home ground.

During your trip here I mentioned the *Controversy* example, a show which could very well capitalize on the new willingness of countries to exchange ideas and criticism. The recent taped Nixon–Krushchev debate brought a satiated American audience flocking back to their television sets. Someday, American television is going to wake up to the fact that *Controversy* isn't really a nasty work and that it actually can provide dramatic and highly exciting entertainment. At that time, I'd like to be sitting ready with the season's hit show in my warm little hands.

Another example, Ralph, which we didn't get into during your visit is *history*. It has always seemed remarkable to me that although history has been a mainspring of entertainment in every other dramatic medium, television has made strangely little use of it. For one thing, I would like to talk very seriously with your people about the possibility of a series embodying a panoramic treatment of history, very much in the same type as *Victory At Sea*. Combining stock footage from motion picture libraries, actual location shooting, miniatures and diagrams where necessary, all tied together with a [sic] filmed dramatic episodes highlighting the historical characters who made that period exciting. Certainly not a deep or exhaustive treatment, but researched and narrated by competent people, symphony scored as befitting the power and sweep of the subject. All with accent on the excitement and suspense which a good writer can extract from the subject—as found in some of the better passages of Wells' *Outline of History* which, coincidentally, breaks down into about thirty-nine chapters.[14]

There are other areas of history which come closer to television's current style. I think these possibilities are worth talking about too.

Another simpler example is a low-budget show which takes advantage of something current—expanding world-travel. The United States like other countries, is in the grip of travel fever. People who never before journeyed beyond the city limits are now embarking for Europe, Asia and South America—a large majority of these travelers not quite certain how to handle the thousand and one little details which can make such journeys comfortable and rewarding. Without going into further detail, I think we might do something interesting with a show called *Traveler*—factually narrated filmed series combining both the glamour of far-off places with the professional traveler's know-how. A "how to" show—where, why, when, how much, etc. Some tie-up with people like Cooks, American Express or Pan American Airways seems a distinct possibility.

Please excuse the random quality of all this, Ralph, since it's from notes made on the back of a theater bill last night during a dull third act. I'll let

---

[14]Then the standard number of episodes comprising a television season.

you off the hook at this point although there are five
or six more ideas scribbled there which I'd like to discuss
with you. Plus a drawer-full of the more usual
dramatic-type filmed shows with continuing lead
characters.

By January 1960, the mutual ardor between Gene and ITC
must have cooled a bit as Gene sent Ralph Smart a final letter:

Don Ingalls[15] has several times relayed greetings from
you and I hope you have received my return best wishes
as promptly. From the scripts I've read, it appears
he did an outstanding job on the *Whiplash* project,
certainly a collection of stories up to the quality of
the very best adventure shows being made hereabouts.
Good luck on the production of them. Hope the
company is wise enough to allot plenty of rehearsal
time since they'll no doubt be working with actors
who have little experience with TV's frantic schedules.
Just concluded a long term exclusive deal with
Screen Gems, the type of thing we once discussed,
in which I'll be creating new properties for them,
producing the pilot and getting the show off the
ground, then moving along to the next one.
Hesitated a long time since I value freedom
considerably, chewed it over during a month in Hawaii
with the family. Meanwhile they made the thing so
palatable I finally had to forget my fears.
No particular message to impart, just wanted to
stay in touch, let you know where I'll be working.
Please be sure to call when in town and reserve some
time for drinks with me.

In the short time Gene had been in the business, he
learned how to play one company off against another. Would
Gene have left Hollywood and moved wife and children to
another country, especially a country with currency restrictions that would make taking money home difficult? Would

---

[15]Gene's friend and office mate from LAPD, former story editor on *Have Gun
Will Travel,* then working in England for Lew Grade and ITC.

Gene have put all his eggs in one basket, so to speak, cutting, or at the very least distancing, contacts with everyone he knew in Los Angeles and the television industry? Finally, in contrast to what Gene wrote to Ralph Smart about his girls being excited about possibly moving to London, Darleen Roddenberry, Gene's oldest daughter who was twelve at the time, remembers nothing of her father discussing any sort of move to London. Gene used Lew Grade's interest to boost his value with Screen Gems, ultimately cutting a very lucrative deal.[16]

Gene's deal with Screen Gems was worth in the neighborhood of a guaranteed $100,000 a year plus profit participation with any successful series. Gene celebrated by buying two cars—a 1959 Black Coupe de Ville for himself and a 1960 Gold Fleetwood (formerly owned by the mayor of Beverly Hills) for Eileen—a dozen suits, and taking the family out to a big dinner at one of their favorite restaurants, The Luau.

Gene's contract with Screen Gems brought forth a flurry of creativity, including his first go at producing. It was called *The Wrangler*—and a summer replacement program for the *Tennessee Ernie Ford Show*.

Gene was ever on the alert for information he could incorporate into a story or series ideas. On December 20, 1960, he sent Bill Dozier, head of Screen Gems, a memo about a series idea with more than a little personal interest on Gene's part.

Dear Bill,
    At a party the other evening, someone asked why
nothing has ever been done with Michener's book
Tales of the South Pacific. I was about to reply,
mentioning the stage play, the motion picture, and
Twentieth-Century's television series. Then it struck
me that this was a hell of a good question. One,
single short story from the book has been used.
Over and over again. And it was the weakest and most
undramatic story of the entire book.

---

[16]Lew Grade and ITC went on to do well during the sixties and seventies with *This Is Tom Jones, The Saint, Secret Agent, The Prisoner, The Muppet Show, The Julie Andrews Show, Whiplash,* and others.

The bulk of this great book, one of the all-time best sellers, is a collection of unusually well-written, small and varied tales of Pacific war camp life. As you know, it is *not* a collection of war stories. Rather, it tells of the old Tonkinese woman who sold souvenir shrunken human heads, of the savage whose dream was to parachute from an airplane, of heat itch, of bootlegging, of the admiral who caught his zipper in his underwear, of the weird escapades planned to relieve their endless waiting, of gigantic poker and crap games and their humorous aftermaths, and of *". . . reef upon which waves broke into spray and inner lagoons lovely beyond description . . . the sweating jungle, the full moon rising behind the volcanos, and the waiting. The waiting. The timeless, repetitive waiting."*

In short, I am suggesting a half-hour, network-quality television series unlike anything which has been done. The title: *The Wild Blue* [later renamed *APO 923*]. Not "Tales of the South Pacific;" no deal with Michener, but involving the same area of story, emphasizing quiet, ordinary and identifiable men caught up in the extraordinary background furnished by this most romantic, bizarre, and flavor-filled backwash of World War II. Let me emphasize these would not be combat stories. We would stay a mile away from the phony war tales of "hack" heroics of television. Rather, think in terms of *Mister Roberts* and the first half of *Caine Mutiny*. I'm not suggesting a "patriotic" or "hate" series; the enemy is rarely, if ever, seen. The State Department and policy makers need have no worry on that score. Our antagonists are boredom, OD's, the censorship officer, hunger for small civilized pleasures, "Dear John" letters from home, and defeats, both humorous and tragic, in the personalities of the men themselves.

It has been almost sixteen years since I left the South Pacific myself. In the interval, I've felt winter-pangs about certain experiences down there, a certainty that there are wonderful stories hanging undeveloped, which could contain that wonderful melding of humor and tragedy which has characterized all truly great stories of men in conflict with themselves and their surroundings. Michener's book comes close. Although it is not exactly right for a television series, it *does* have the right feel, and has proven the audience's interest in this story area.

Specifically, our series has two continuing characters. Phil Pike, middle-thirties, seeming older, experience in matters of war and woman, father of the "fifty missions" crush, a "Pappy Boyington" character. This contrasts nicely with Eddie Jellicoe, early-twenties, just out of college, as intent regarding life as he is ignorant of it. They are pilot and co-pilot in a half-assed, ex-recon squadron, flying rickety B-17's in the early days of the Pacific War. We pick them up stationed at Guadalcanal, move with them through assignments, both routine and unusual, playing locales ranging from a tent in the coconut palms, to Naval Headquarters, a trip to a French Island town, a rest cure in New Zealand, an episode in the nurses barracks, a "raid" on a navy cruiser, a lonely radio shack on Munda, an episode with a PT flotilla, etc. Thinking in terms of "Don't Go Near The Water," we will include a fabulous "golf tournament" played in the jungle. This will contrast with a grim camp episode where Pike meets the man behind his "Dear John" letter. A love story too—the time the inexperienced Jellicoe wins the only white girl on an island against impressive odds. And the defeat of the Air Group's boxing champion, the wild dedication of a thatched officer club, the episode of an entire bakery stolen from a Marine regiment, the formation of a "one-arm bandit" syndicate by an enlisted mechanical genius, the case of the missing CO's jeep, the mix-up with a USO troup, the arrival of a "Hollywood" war film producer, the capture of a Navy LST, etc. Of course, the war will always be present. Air raids and the leaving and returning from missions will remind us of this. We will play sad episodes— the times planes and friends do not return. We may even play our continuing characters on an occasional mission. But the war will serve as in interest-loaded background, not main story line.

Alternate episodes of *The Wild Blue* would emphasize Pike and Jellicoe respectively, a la *Maverick* with occasional stories featuring both. More or less stat characters would be the Squadron Commander, the Flight Surgeon, a General and an Admiral, several enlisted men, a particularly weird and tricky B-17 named "The Beast," and so on. Essentially, we would treat our B-17 squadron in much the same manner as a number of novels and motion pictures have treated naval vessel units.

As you consider this, I am anxious for you to skim through Michener's book, re-read portions of it which might recall to your mind the unique flavor of the South Pacific during these campaigns. This period (as with the "Western") compares with no other time or place. A language of its own, a different point of view, a time and feeling unique. All this, subtly affected by the exotic sea, and landscapes, and the strange uses to which they were being put. It is important that one aspect of this be completely understood by anyone with which you discuss this. The series will aim at a certain "timeless" quality; de-emphasizing the fact this is a specific war in favor of a feeling that these same stories probably happened in other wars, and, in fact, happen also in peacetime. The war serves us only as catalyst and flavoring ingredient (again, as it served the same purpose in *Mister Roberts, Don't Go Near The Water,* and *Caine Mutiny*), *The Wild Blue* would make potent use of something important in *The Untouchables* and several other current television successes— *nostalgia* for a period now gone. The clothing of the early Forties, the expressions, all the sights and sounds we remember with a foolish lump in our throats. Music also; songs like "Rosie the Riveter," "Don't Sit Under the Apple Tree," "Coming In on a Wing and a Prayer," and the ditties soldier sang then such as "I've Got Sixpence," "P'Riley's Daughter" (cleaned up), "Roll 'em Over" and others.

Suggesting the rich story material available, within an hour of settling upon this as series potential, I came up with two pilot stories, one emphasizing each character.

The Wild Blue has been discussed with Bob Sparks.
He is of the opinion the physical requirements of .
such a project can be met. More than ample stock footage
is available for the occasional airplane flight and battle
scenes. A number of promising camp, jungle and
island locations are locally available. B-17 mock-
ups and interiors are, of course, obtainable also. He
concurs with me that the *approach* is all important,
that too sketchy a presentation to sales staff or
networks might see the specialized quality and
freshness of the idea lost in a summary rejection on
general grounds as it is a "war" series.

Respectfully yours,

Dozier liked what he read and gave the go-ahead. On May
5, 1961, Gene sent the following memo:

Dear Bill,
Keeping you posted on things—am in the process
of delivering to Bill Sackheim a very detailed sales
presentation and format on the World War II Pacific
Campaign series (originally suggested to you by memo
"The Wild Blue," December 20, 1960). Incidentally,
it has been a real pleasure to work with Sackheim
on this. His vigor and creativeness really sparks
a writer. We both feel we could have the "grandaddy"
of a new television cycle in this.
Have written a memo to Cruikshank [reprinted
a bit further on], explaining why I began this project
at such a late date in my contract—specifying the
guarantees you have agreed to afford me. He has also
been made aware of my cordial relationship with
you and my desire for a separation agreement which
will see that friendship not impaired in any way.

Gene sent another memo to Dozier on May 17:

Have in hand the mimeographed presentation of *APO
923,* dated May 15th, 1961, which will go to New York.
Wanted you to know I am pleased it credits Bill Sackheim
for his part in designing this presentation. While working
on it, I had wondered many times why such things were

never done and it seemed unfair to me that his name was not included.

The pilot episode was called "Operation Shangri-La," with three main characters: Air Force Captain Phillip Pike, the strong, in-charge captain (who would surface again with a different first name in the first *Star Trek* pilot); Navy Lieutenant Edward Jellicoe, the character whose emotions were in the forefront; and Army Lieutenant James T. Irvine, the "smart" character who early in the episode had built an ice machine out of spare parts. The plot concerns Lieutenant Irvine's conflict over whether he can kill again. He disappears when he is ordered out on what will probably be another bloody mission. Pike and Jellicoe search him out.

The pilot was not a success but, in Gene's mind, the character interplay was; Gene would remember, refine, and bring back three characters for a future series, renaming them Kirk, McCoy, and Spock.

Even though the pilot was made with love and care, the network did not buy. With *APO 923* Gene was, again, well ahead of the industry and network executives. Ten years later, the idea of sophisticated, comic/tragic, people-oriented stories of men and women in war found a home in the hit series *M*A*S*H*, set during the Korean War. *M*A*S*H* had been a highly successful book, then a smash-hit film directed by Robert Atlman, and *only then* a television show. Without the book and film, it is questionable that *M*A*S*H* would have ever made it to the CBS lineup.

Another memo to Dozier gives further insight into Gene's thinking, his ethics of television production, and his humanistic philosophy. Dated April 6, 1961, it reads:

Have had a couple of long chats with Joe Naar regarding the possibility of a Youth Corps Series. Unlike shows which are offered purely as escape entertainment, this one involves certain moral and philosophical issues on which I have strong feelings.

In my opinion, any shallow treatment of the subject, hemmed in with the normal sponsor, agency and network continuity restrictions, could be disastrous to the reputation of the personalities involved and for Screen Gems.

This is a show which would have to be done right. By that I mean deep, sometimes provoking, often shocking, inquiries into the customs, needs, prejudices, beliefs and aspirations of people in many foreign countries. To do the "syndicated" route, treating people in the Middle East, Africa and South America as mere curiosities, living in exotic places with strange irrational customs, doing the usual melodrama of good guys and bad guys, with little or no attention to the economics, politics, and history which prompts unrest in the world today, would defeat the whole aim of our Nation's effort. Worse, it would be viewed all over the world as another example of the United States' inability to understand other people. If this would be the direction of the show I could not under any circumstances let myself become involved in it. On the other hand if there were some way to do a completely honest series, fictional or documentary, with all the usual dramatic-television restrictions and convention eliminated, I would be quite interested in doing anything I could to advance the project.

In the space immediately below the body of the text, Dozier had written a simple, "I agree. B."

Something else happened during Gene's tenure at Screen Gems that would have much greater effect on his life than a successful series. One afternoon a tall, beautiful, and new-in-town actress walked in his door. Her name was Majel Lee Hudec and her business was acting. Unlike most of the thousands of other young women who had come to Hollywood, she was approaching her career in a businesslike way. Gene was impressed. She wrote letters of introduction to every producer in town (an unheard of practice then) and followed up with a personal visit to as many producers as she could meet, introducing herself and giving her credits, selling herself rather than relying on the usual procedure of a photo and list of credits submitted by an agent. Gene became a producer whom she regularly saw on her rounds. They became friends, absent the producer-starlet casting-couch routine. Gene was not happily married, but Majel's recollection is that he did not start in with the standard "my wife doesn't understand me" routine, something she had heard numerous times before and would not have bought in any case. Like most solid friendships, theirs grew slowly, Majel only seeing him every few months. They were business friends, nothing more, and would remain at that level for two years or more.

Gene's time at Screen Gems ended in mid- to late 1961. Beginning to tie up loose ends, he wrote to his agent, Lawrence Cruikshank, in May. Gene's level of creativity for the year at Screen Gems was extensive, and he was concerned about how his intellectual property should be handled.

Dear Larry,

Spoke to Art Frankel this morning and said you would be contacting him shortly to agree upon terms covering certain properties left here. So that you can get cracking on this, here are my thoughts:

Defiance County will be left at Screen Gems by giving them some reasonable period of time in which to make and sell a new pilot. After this reasonable time the basic property should revert to me. My attitude is this—I have no intention of playing "sea-lawyer" with Bill Dozier, of whom I am very fond. He has treated me well during my stay here, and I think there is a moral obligation to let them have a shot at *Defiance County*. Business demands, however, we arrange certain guarantees for my protection—that my pilot will be the one used to sell the show, or that, in any case, I am guaranteed full royalties as set forth under my contract. In other words, I want no future changes in format, etc., as might be dictated by CBS or some unforeseen changes in program structure to deprive me of the royalties. This is a shifting, changing business, and I want iron-bound provisions in this area which supersede the language of my basic contract. I think this is fair and affords me protection which costs Screen Gems nothing.

Bill Dozier wants me to stay with *Defiance County* in some capacity, naturally needing the original creator and writer connected in some way with the package he hopes to sell. I told him that I could not make any agreements at this time which might interfere with contracts I could be considering upon leaving here. Conceivably, I might accept any one of the exclusive arrangements which have been offered me at other places. I did tell him, however, that I would try and hold enough freedom to do some *Defiance County* scripts. This is my show, I have a stake in it, naturally will want to do everything possible to make it a success. Also told him any agreements as associate producer or story editor, or etc., are definitely out. I would consider agreeing to act as "script consultant," assuming they offer a reasonable fee which would cover the time and effort spent on such a job. But we should make it clear I do not intend to be aced into a position where I would be rewriting every show under such an arrangement.

Now, to the subject of the property *APO 923*— before the decision to leave Screen Gems occurred, I selected Bill Sackheim as the Executive Producer with whom to work on this project. It was a happy choice, we see pretty much eye to eye on the project, both of us have great enthusiasm for it. When the *Exodus* question arose, I told Dozier I would go ahead with this project only if certain agreements and protection were agreed upon. These are: 1) I would do the pilot or, under any eventuality, will be guaranteed full royalties per my original Screen Gems agreement; 2) regardless of the eventual shape of the project (considering the possibility of alterations made after my leaving) I will have exclusive billing as series creator; 3) Property will revert to me after giving Screen Gems a reasonable time to make and sell pilot; 4) I will have the option to act as script consultant at a reasonable fee. The thinking behind all of this is simply I believe this property to be extremely valuable, a good bit for beginning a whole new television cycle.

Would like to be as reasonable as possible with Screen Gems in these areas, maintaining basic protections, but cooperating everywhere else as much as possible. The reason is simple—I consider it vital at this time to get a first-class television show on the air. We should not discount the value of such a credit— out of a successful show, dear agent, many other things flow. Let's be wise, careful, but not greedy.

My verbal agreement with Dozier, putting it in horsetrade terms, is that I will give them back *Defiance County,* and in return take certain properties away with me. The point being there are several in which Screen Gems has no current interest, and I see no reason for them to lie in file drawers collecting dust. These properties are:

Kapu—Hawaiian Islands action-adventure, circa middle 1800's. There is a pilot script on this.

Freelance—A pilot script has been written on this under the title "Telegraph Hill." Action-adventure-detective type show with the lead a free lance writer.

The Centurion—Roman Empire period series with the lead a Roman Army Commander acting as agent for Caeser. There is a pilot story outline on this.

Caravan—"Sea Hunt" type action-adventure utilizing the mysterious desert instead of the mysterious sea. There is a pilot script on this.

Courtroom—Actually, this might be considered my property anyway since I never went to format, merely sent in a detailed memo. Worked with Ackerman a short while on it. However, since the memo was detailed and the point might be argued, we should clear this up before I leave. This project is a weekly hour show which utilizes two "name" actors (or conceivably more on a rotating basis), acting as prosecutor and defense counsel in a series of exciting trials.

The Olympians—Northwest Canadian-American police type show. Again, this should legally be my property since there was only a memo on it, not a format. But let's have it spelled out. This project contemplates an American and Canadian law enforcement team located in the Puget Sound area, specializing in international cases involving mixed jurisdiction.

Of this list, the ones I am most interested in retaining and would fight hardest for are *Courtroom, The Olympians,* and *Caravan.* I believe that *Freelance* and *Kapu* might be considered mine anyway since they were brought into the shop with me.

So you will have the whole picture, here's another item. Two weeks ago, I suggested to Dozier that

Screen Gems Foreign Sales investigate the possibility of purchasing a West German television show entitled *The Third Reich,* now being televised in that country. The thought was that Shirer's book and the current Eichman trial would see Screen Gems scoring a real coup if they could quickly obtain this negative (mostly the story of news and German government footage) translate and rewrite the narration, rescore it, and get it on American TV fast. Dozier and I merely agreed that I would be guaranteed some sort of "finder's fee" if the project should work out, i.e., a royalty or etc., and would have the opportunity, at my option, to cooperate in planning and writing the project. Merely a verbal agreement . . . Screen Gems may not even be able to obtain the rights, but wanted you to be aware of what's going on.

Would appreciate it if you would go over all this carefully, plot your comments so that we can have a detailed discussion and quickly arrange an inclusive agreement. Please keep in mind this agreement should specifically state it supersedes all points in the original GR-SG agreement with which it conflicts, without limiting items of advantage to me in any other part of the contract.

Defiance County produced a rift between Gene and Erle Stanley Gardner. The misconceptions and miscommunications over this property illustrate the fragility of relationships between creative individuals in Hollywood's charged atmosphere and the result of the all-pervasive presence of lawyers in the business. The letters exchanged regarding this property reflect the core of each writer's personality.

In the first week of January 1962, Gail Patrick Jackson, the wife of Gardner's close friend Cornwall Jackson and the producer of the Perry Mason television programs, got a memo from Jackson Gillis, their story editor. Gillis was calling Jackson's attention to the script of *Defiance County,* which he had just read. He understood that CBS was about to finance and produce the show, dropping Gardner's program *Doug Selby.*

"*Defiance County,*" he wrote, "can scarcely be considered

a mystery of any sort, let alone a whodunit. It's an action-detective story, I suppose, though some action-detective writers might throw rocks at me for hanging the classification on it. Actually, the intent of the show seems to be to combine some detective double-talk with a dash of legal double-talk—but lightly, and not to interfere with the latter-day Western atmosphere with Gary Cooper's nickname added so that all bases may be covered. Poor television."

Gillis further tore apart the script and its concepts, saying that he "didn't know whether Mr. Gardner will feel there is actual infringement here. But I certainly think the script comes close to it, since *Selby* has been in wide circulation for a very long time. That's a matter for him to decide, of course." He further wrote, "For considering how long the Gardner books have been sitting on CBS desks, I'd say they've certainly violated something here!" Gail Jackson sent the memo on to Gardner.

Gardner and his associates' were highly concerned, as Bill Dozier, then head of Screen Gems, had been an executive at CBS and had also been Gardner's agent for years, going back to at least 1938. Gene, the writer of *Defiance County,* was also Gardner's friend of many years, yet Gardner contacted neither man to inquire about the matter. Within a day or so of receiving Gillis's memo, he turned the matter over to his attorney, a partner in a large and prestigious Los Angeles law firm. The lawyer called Screen Gems and was told that *Defiance County* had started shooting. According to notes in the Gardner Archives, Gardner's attorney says he told Screen Gems's attorney, "I thought you ought to know you're starting a show which is very comparable to a show Paisano owns." The note further quotes the Screen Gems lawyer saying, "Bill [Dozier] remarked he'd never heard of a character, Doug Selby."

Then it got complicated. Gardner's lawyer decided that "since Bill [Dozier] had been the head of CBS for 5 years he should have known what was in the works, and the writer [Gene] knowing Gardner, couldn't have missed your character." He further thought that "CBS's involvement with Bill could be similar to conspiracy. Also, Bill, having been your agent, should have known about your characters."

Since it was now in the hands of the lawyers, it became clear that old friends would not be able to iron things out by talking to one another. On February 9, Gene wrote to Gardner at the ranch.

Dear Erle,

A couple of weeks ago I called your secretary upon receiving a telephone call which had annoyed me and, hearing that you were to be back in the bushes for a few more weeks, put off this follow-up letter until now.

Simply stated, I have created a format and written a pilot film, produced last month and now in cutting stage, which has as its central character a prosecuting attorney in a Midwestern town. Not an entirely new idea, I suppose, understand several other studios have tried similar things, but my hope was to come up with something rich in mid-America flavor, capturing the spirit of a portion of our country neglected by those who see drama as strictly East or West Coast big city. It occurred to me that a county prosecutor would make an ideal character to catapult us into the type of highly personal stories which could achieve all of this. Again, making no claim for particular "freshness" in concept, the format, character and pilot story were wholly my original creation.

The show was sold to Screen Gems since, at the time of creation, I was under contract to this studio. At about the time the show was being produced, the Screen Gems attorney called me to say he has just received a telephone call from a lawyer representing Paisan Productions or Mrs. Jackson there (exactly which was unclear), claiming my show was a copy of a property owned by yourself. The implication was, referring to our friendship of long standing, that I had somehow gained access to your files or had been told of your creation in this area and had rushed into production with my own version. There was some talk also that a similar creation by yourself had been submitted to William Dozier who happens to now be in charge of Screen Gems Production, with the inference that perhaps Dozier had given me a copy of your property. But this, of course, did not happen and I need not assure you you would have heard from me immediately had any property of yours been in jeopardy.

The purpose of my immediate telephone call was to request you straighten out the complainant. I bear no one over there any grudges as it may be since it is well known we are friends they assumed we must have many times discussed television formats and stories, and I suppose the fact we have never done so is a little surprising. Actually, other than keeping you informed of whatever progress I may be making in the writing field, I have tried constantly to avoid the subject, having that sort of foolish pride which requires me never to use my friendship as a crutch in establishing myself in any new venture. As with you, I am tremendously proud of my reputation and I certainly did not want any rumors affecting it flying around this strange little town.

Let me make it clear, Erle, I never for a moment assumed you had any knowledge of this accusation.

Gene finished off the letter with a paragraph about his personal life, new house, and other details, ending the letter:

Sorry to bother you on the above but since it touched on both my personal and professional reputation it was a matter of some importance. Hope to see you soon.

A week later Gardner wrote to his attorney enclosing a copy of Gene's letter, and, staying true to his legal training wrote:

This letter is very friendly and informal, yet has everything in it. It could well have been plotted by an attorney and then paraphrased.

Gardner suggested writing a letter to Gene saying he had been busy and that his complaint was with CBS, that he was unhappy with the situation, but since it was now in the hands of his attorney he knew that his attorney wouldn't want him to comment on it.

Gardner then wrote his attorney:

CBS wanted to put *Doug Selby* on television. Gail [Jackson] is a good businesswoman who, as she admits, has dollar signs in her eyes. Looking at it from our standpoint, we get a lot of money out of CBS that would otherwise have gone down the drain. Looking at it from their viewpoint, they have probably decided that we are a pain in the neck, with our auditing of their books, etc., etc.

I wouldn't be too surprised if at about this time some lawyer didn't advise them 'Look here, Erle Gardner doesn't own the character of a rural district attorney and there's nothing to prevent us from dealing with someone else getting virtually the same sort of an opportunity we would have with the Gardner property, without having any of the headaches and getting a more favorable setup.'

I just don't like to take things lying down. I am different from Gail in that I always believe in giving the other man the breaks wherever possible, but when he tries to slip something over on me I don't like it.

Three weeks later, on March 9, Gardner wrote Gene essentially the letter he had described to his lawyer, adding:

I was, of course, disappointed when CBS elected not to proceed further with my property *Doug Selby*. However, on the basis of all the information that we have, I am not taking the position that either you or Bill Dozier, or Screen Gems has committed any actionable wrong. I instructed my attorney, who made a preliminary investigation, to refrain from making any claims against either you, Dozier or Screen Gems.

Gardner then conveniently left for Baja California where he wouldn't be readily available by correspondence or telephone.

Gene did not like the tone of the letter or the phrase "actionable wrong" Gardner had left hanging in the air. In a letter that clearly reveals his straight from the shoulder approach, he wrote to Gardner on March 15:

Dear Erle,

I was not writing for Wm Dozier, or for Screen Gems.

I was not asking what legal position you were taking.

A thief is a thief, "actionable" or not. Either I stole something from you and my last letter is a lie—or neither is true.

I sympathize with the fact you are busy, and so am I. But this happens to be very important to me. I can't very well find out who is fucking who without a straight answer from you.

Gene Roddenberry.

On March 20, Gardner sent a memo to his attorney and Gail Patrick Jackson just before he left for Baja in response to Gene's letter. Gardner noted he "did not have the time to look up prior correspondence and see what Gene Roddenberry is talking about but I am enclosing a copy of a letter which I have received from him and think it should be answered in a straight-forward manner."

Gardner continued, "He [Gene] evidently feels that I said he had stolen something from me. This is exactly the position I didn't want to get put into."

Gardner then suggested that a letter be sent to Gene reminding him that he [Gardner] had been in Baja most of the time and that he never said Gene stole anything, never said he copied anything, never accused Gene of anything which was unethical and never authorized anyone to represent him in making any such statement to anyone.

Gardner further suggested the letter say that he was getting very much interested in this thing and would like to have the attorney for Screen Gems make a statement as to what his conversation was, what was said, and on what he based this implication, or on what Gene based his implication.

Then, writing to his attorney and Gail Jackson, Gardner commented:

Now, quite obviously Roddenberry's letter of February 9th and the statements contained in the third paragraph are so absurd as to be ridiculous. No one is going to imply that because of friendship he somehow

gained access to my files and rushed into
production with his own version because both my
lawyer and Gail Jackson knew that the character had
been exposed to public view for some twenty-five years,
had appeared serially in *Country Gentleman* and
in *Saturday Evening Post,* had appeared in book
published by William Morrow in hard cover edition,
by Detective Book Club, and in Pocket Books.

Therefore, if anyone had made any statement that
there had been an infringement it would have been
predicated upon the fact that the character was well
known and available to Dozier, Roddenberry and twenty
million other people.

Roddenberry therefore is either misquoting what
the attorney told him or the attorney has told him
something so downright absurd that it is ridiculous.

I'd like to find out which.

Now, in the very near future I have to do one
of two things. I have to adopt this position with
Roddenberry because I will meet him personally or
he will call, or I have to simply say that the matter
is now in the hands of my attorney, which I don't
want to do because that is asinine in view of the
statements made in his letter.

This letter is either a falsehood on his part, a
falsehood on the part of the Screen Gems attorney,
or an example of deriving an "implication" from
statements that would not support it.

Evidently Gardner never considered that his own attorney
might have been "overly enthusiastic" in his approach to the
Screen Gems attorney and overstated Gardner's position or
thoughts.

Gardner's attorney wrote to him three days later, doing little to settle the controversy.

Dear Erle:

I have read with amazement the copy of Gene
Roddenberry's letter of March 15th to you. Frankly,
my reaction is not to write him a letter going into
this matter in any detail at all. Rather, I would urge
you to simply write him and ask him to cease sending

obscene letters to you and that as far as you are concerned the matter is closed. You might say that you have never accused him of stealing anything from you and that you have not even read the script of his pilot film.

I think that Roddenberry is protesting too much and I see no purpose in getting into a letter writing contest with him.

Gardner sent a recorded letter to his secretary that was transcribed March 31, 1962.

Referencing his attorney's advice Gardner dictated: "Tell him that this is one time that I definitely do not see eye-to-eye with him; that Gene Roddenberry has made a specific accusation that I have instructed an attorney to advise an attorney for Screen Gems that the man is a crook and that he stole a specific plot from me. I am in a position where I absolutely have to deny this and deny it categorically and I want to do so. I want to tell him that I was in Baja California at the time, as nearly as I can find out; that I never instructed anyone to make any such statement; that no one representing me made any such statement; that I know nothing of any such statement being made, other than the statement that was contained in his letter, which contained some report of something that was supposed to have been said by an attorney for Screen Gems; that I want to know what this is.

"I think my letter represented about the best way of presenting this. If [our lawyer] doesn't think so I want him to write Roddenberry a letter stating that I am in Baja California and denying the charges emphatically and categorically. If we do not deny these charges and anything comes up later where Gene Roddenberry claims that I have damaged his reputation by slander, any evasive letters or any failure to meet the charge head-on will go against us. I feel very positive that there should be a denial. I think it is absurd to refuse to answer correspondence because of obscene or vulgar language contained in Roddenberry's letter. After all, we have all heard obscene or vulgar language and the man has made a charge that I have damaged his professional reputation in the community in which he is working. I want to deny that charge. I would like to get at the facts. I would like to have the attorney for Screen Gems come out and state when the conversation took place, with whom it took place and what the conversation consisted of."

Gardner then directed his secretary to call his attorney and read the foregoing to him as a memo. He finished the recording by saying: "I want some action on it and I feel that something should be done and I think that once [our attorney] looks at the thing from the standpoint of what is happening with Roddenberry he will understand the situation."

Gardner's lawyer heard the memo and said that he thought they should send the original letter Erle had outlined, rather than for him (the lawyer) to get involved in it.

Gardner's letter to Gene was dated April 2, 1962. After recapitulating the implications and the fact that he had been spending a lot of time in Baja, Gardner wrote:

> I never said you stole anything, I never said you copied anything, I never accused you of anything which was unethical. I never authorized anyone to represent me in making any such statement to anyone.

Gardner then went on to clarify his position, what his lawyer was doing and that:

> I certainly don't relish the idea of some attorney telling my friends that I have, by implication, accused them of this and that because some attorney representing either Paisano Productions or Mrs. Jackson—exactly which was unclear—made a statement in a telephone conversation from which certain implications were drawn.
> I have a contract with CBS. I have instructed an attorney to represent me in all matters connected with that contract. He has been representing me for years. I have never instructed any attorney to make any statement to you, to Screen Gems, or to Bill Dozier in connection with any show submitted by you.
> If there has been any misunderstanding about a telephone call, let's clarify it. If there has been any misrepresentation about a telephone conversation, let's find out who is making the misrepresentation.
> Will the Screen Gems attorney state to me that he

had a conversation in which there was any implication that you had somehow gained access to my files or had been told of my own creation of a rural district attorney and had rushed into production with your own version?

The idea that any attorney representing Paisano Productions or Gail Jackson would make any such statement is absurd on its face, but I would just like to find out whether a Screen Gems attorney was given this impression from a telephone conversation of this sort, and I would like to find out the facts on which he based such an implication or on what you base it.

You say this thing is important to you. It certainly is important to me. Now, let's find out about it.

Don't write to me telling me what some attorney told you and said the implication was. Let's get the attorney to state who was doing the talking and what was said, and let's run it down.

As nearly as I can tell I was down in Mexico when all this happened but I'd certainly like to find out about it and if anyone made any statements of that sort I'd like to get it straightened out just as much as you would.

Copies of this letter were sent to Gardner's attorney and Gail Jackson. On April 29, Gene responded:

Dear Erle,

Have just returned from a desert jaunt to get your last letter for which I am most grateful. Until then it seemed to me I had never gotten the point of my query across, i.e. simply word from you, signed or unsigned, by paper, disc or pony-express, did you believe the facts to be something that might destroy our mutual confidence and friendship? And I'm happy to accept the fact that your phrase "no actionable wrong" was something said in the haste of dictation, carrying no special meaning.

Except for that, the whole thing was of little importance to me. If the series sells, fine I'll loaf a little more next year. If not, maybe better, I'll work harder, try to improve my writing.

And so, having intruded enough on your vacation year, I wish you safe travels, exciting discoveries and peaceful vistas.

In friendship,

Gene R.

With or without concerns over similarities with *Doug Selby, Defiance County* was made and, like the majority of pilots, didn't sell. The only further entries in the Gardner Archives under correspondence with Gene is a copy of an article about Gene's production of *The Lieutenant* in the mid-sixties and a change of address note when he and Majel rented a house together in 1969. There is no further correspondence in Gene's files.

Gene's opinions and attitudes about race were consistent throughout his life, a remarkable achievement since he was raised in a household that held to the values of the "old South." Nothing more clearly illustrates his thoughts than this public service spot he wrote for the actor Jim Backus[17] in the early 1960's. It was submitted to the Anti-Defamation League of B'nai B'rith, but due to production costs was never made.

FADE IN:

EXT. DEPARTMENT STORE

1 ESTABLISHING SHOT OF WINDOW
where a crowd has gathered at the window to watch it being dressed.

INT. DEPARTMENT STORE WINDOW

2 MEDIUM ON TWO CLOTHING MANNEQUINS
male and female, the typical characterless, good-looking Caucasian, well-dressed. Suddenly JIM BACKUS sticks his head between the two mannequins, calling to someone at the side.

---

[17]The late Jim Backus was, for many years, a staple character actor in both films and television. He is perhaps most famous as irrepressible millionaire, Thurston Howell, III, stranded on *Gilligan's Island,* and as the voice of the cartoon character Mr. Magoo.

BACKUS
You've failed me again Rollo!

3 ANGLE ON HELPER
"Rollo," arranging decorations at the side. He turns, registers something he sees at about Backus' waist-level, points:

ROLLO
Mister Backus.........!

4 TWO SHOT BACKUS AND ROLLO
This and subsequent shots will be angled so that we do not see below Jim Backus' waist. Backus indicates the two mannequins.

BACKUS
I said dress this window with average Americans.

Rollo has moved in, disturbed, trying to get through to Jim, tell him something important.

ROLLO
MISTER BACKUS, PLEASE....

CAMERA DOLLIES with Backus as he moves down along the window decoration area to a second group of mannequins, Rollo protestingly following. Included are an Oriental in American street clothing, a Rabbi in beard and skull cap, a Negro mother holding her eight-year-old daughter by the hand, a Latin type in mustacho, and a Caucasian in "beatnik" attire.

BACKUS
This is what Americans look like, Rollo!

BACKUS
(indicates mannequin group)
A hundred-eighty million *individuals,* boy. Different backgrounds, colors, ways of looking at God....
(nose to nose with Rollo)

Haven't you ever wondered where our country's excitement and vitality comes from?

ROLLO
You're gonna get in trouble, Mister Backus.

BACKUS
Trouble? Out of our differences comes variety and greatness in music, art, science and everything else that matters. We're proud our system has room for every category of human being and we'll protect our neighbor's rights to be as different from us as we are from him. Americans welcome that kind of trouble, boy!

During the last sentence has come a TAPPING on the window glass. Jim Backus looks around, trying to find the sound. Rollo points at the window; Jim follows his indication

5 ANGLE THROUGH WINDOW
a Police Officer standing in front of the crowd, TAPPING on the window and getting Backus' attention, he points downward.

6 MEDIUM ON BACKUS
following the officer's indication, looks down below his waist. His face falls. He looks at Rollo, then turns and begins moving toward the window exit.

BACKUS
Think about it, Rollo boy, *Be proudly different!*
(quietly)
I'll see you in about thirty days.

CAMERA HOLDS as Backus exits, revealing, as he walks into LONG SHOT that he has forgotten to put on his trousers, has been working in the open window in shirt and undershorts.
FADE OUT

Gene was open to new and unusual ways of making money as a writer and was approached to be a spokesman/ad model for MONY, Mutual of New York, an insurance company. Naturally, Gene had some thoughts on the matter and wrote to Henry Hayden the account executive at the ad agency of Benton & Bowles in New York City. His conditions for being in the ad were: 1) a time limit for the use of his photo and suggested two years with options; 2) the specific right to approve all final copy directed toward the general public, specifically mass media advertising; 3) assumption by MONY of all liability with the publication and use of the photos; 4) limitation of the photos and ad copy to use by and for MONY.

Gene then went into a detailed analysis of the ad copy—a "bonus" the ad people certainly did not count on but that Gene found necessary. His criticism shows a great sensitivity to the ins and outs of a business he had been in for less than five years.

Now, referring to the story, specifically the copy given to me, dated April 4, 1961, I have the following comments: Some objections to the bold opening line which reads—*"I had to audition Life Insurance men too."* For one thing, "audition," "casting," and similar words have an unfortunate connotation in our industry. Moreover, it makes it appear that I consider myself too much of the big time producer. Actually, my duties concern mainly scripts, stories and series ideas, not casting. I do some casting, of course, but my fellow professionals are well aware of my primary job and I would not want to seem to be using personal publicity to create a false image. An alternate opening which suggests that a good insurance man is as hard to find as a good script (or story) would be more in line with what I do. This retains your hood of "selectivity." Of course, this is too long a caption and I leave it to your people to find better wording or an alternate opening.

Reference to myself should be as *"Gene* Roddenberry" since this is the name I use professionally.

I have some objections to the opening paragraph which identifies my background solely as police department. Police work was only one of several jobs I held in the past. Something which has served me very well in this industry is both the fact and reputation of a fairly exciting and varied past, including airline pilot and other occupations. A "cop" who has turned writer-producer is merely a curiosity, an interesting phenomena. In short, I would suggest we either delete the specific reference to police work or make the reference somewhat broader, more in line with the actual facts of my past occupations. These were all salaried occupations and MONY's point can still be made.

My agent has suggested that the initial reference to myself should be something in the order of "Gene Roddenberry, award winning T.V. writer. . . ." I have no strong feeling on this exact wording but he does make the point that this advertisement must serve me as well as MONY. The fact is I have been fortunate enough to have some success in this business. My work is respected by my fellow professionals, I have an excellent reputation for creativity and craftsmanship which publicity of this sort should support. I do not want this to be patently self-seeking, phoney in any manner, but it should represent an honest indication of my status in the television field. On the same subject, the copy might suggest that one of my problems was an elastic insurance program which kept up with a growing income, factual of course, again not phoney or obviously self-seeking, but suggesting the measure of success which actually exists.

Minor points—it has been suggested that the word "home" might be substituted for the word "house"—and I suspect this is pretty much in line with your own aims. Another suggestion is that "Hollywood" might be substituted for "Los Angeles." I have no strong feeling on either of these suggestions, merely sending them along for your appraisal.

Generally, I consider the whole project to be in good taste and was particularly delighted with the pleasant friendly and helpful attitude of your representatives on their trip here.

Gene's suggestions were adopted and the project moved ahead with the photography being done by Elliot Erwitt. According to Charron E. Fullerton, current director of Creative Services at MONY, the ad was part of a very successful five-year campaign that profiled actual MONY clients and their agents. The campaign was so successful that it was parodied in both *Mad Magazine* and *The Harvard Lampoon*. Gene's ad ran in *Life* Magazine, September 9, 1961; *Time* September 20, 1961; *Look* September 12, 1961; *Newsweek* September 6, 1961; and *Reader's Digest* September 25, 1961.

With his fortunes improving, Gene and Eileen bought a new house at 539 South Beverly Glen, Beverly Hills, moving from the old neighborhood.

CHAPTER 8

While Athena sprang fully formed from Zeus's forehead, *Star Trek* gradually developed out of Gene's imagination over many years.

Sometime in the early 1960's, Gene's friend and fellow writer Christopher Knopf was working at MGM. Gene dropped by and convinced Chris that the studio wouldn't fall apart if he played hookey and went to a baseball game. While both men enjoyed baseball, neither saw much of the game. Gene was enthusiastic about a new series idea that had its roots in the 1961 film *Master of the World*[1] and was excitedly pitching Chris on its potential as a series. With the Dodgers now relegated to the background, Gene described his vision of a giant dirigible set in the late 1800's manned by a multiethnic crew traveling the world righting wrongs and doing good.

Chris thought the series was a workable idea, but time constraints and other commitments made it impractical for him to write the story or do any development work.

Meanwhile, in direct contrast to the deterioration of his marriage, Gene's writing career flourished. He created the series *The Lieutenant* for Norman Felton's company, Arena

---

[1] American International Pictures, starring Vincent Price and Charles Bronson, screenplay by Richard Matheson. The film was a combination of two Jules Verne stories, *The Clipper of the Clouds* and *The Master of the World.* It was a variation of the theme explored in *20,000 Leagues Under The Sea:* a warped but idealistic scientist fighting against war and injustice. In place of a submarine, the central character, Robur (Price), had a flying clipper ship with propellers instead of sails.

Productions,[2] then headquartered at MGM. Broadcast on NBC from September 14, 1963, to September 5, 1964, *The Lieutenant* was part of the NBC Saturday night schedule from 7:30 to 8:30 P.M. It starred Gary Lockwood as the title character, with Robert Vaughn[3] as his wise and all-knowing captain, and was produced with the full cooperation of the United States Marine Corps. The program portrayed human drama in a military setting, examining social questions of the day.

There were several people in front of and behind the camera on *The Lieutenant* who later became part of the *Star Trek* family. In 1964, a young actress named Nichelle Nichols had her television debut on *The Lieutenant* in an episode that examined race relations in a remarkably open and frank manner for the time. The program was written by Lee Cronin, a pseudonym for Gene L. Coon, who would later write for and produce *Star Trek*. Both Leonard Nimoy and Majel Barrett also made appearances on the show.

The Lieutenant was the big break for Joe D'Agosta, who became its casting director—his first job as such. He later was brought on board the *Enterprise* when Gene needed casting help there. D'Agosta remembers that Gene was new at producing: "You presented him with a problem and he would say 'What do you want me to say?' you would tell him, he would say it, and you'd go solve the problem."

D'Agosta was a clerk in MGM's casting office. He was ordered to assist a veteran casting director who was replacing *The Lieutenant*'s sick casting director. The veteran director and D'Agosta went to the first casting meeting, but the veteran never showed up at another one. He was busy casting several other series, so the responsibility fell to D'Agosta.

"I was a real novice," D'Agosta recalls. "I would just bring people in and read them. Somebody would mention the name of an actor, I would mumble something and run into my office, quickly look up the actor's face in the various reference books we had.

---

[2] The production company that also did *The Man From U.N.C.L.E.*, and *The Girl From U.N.C.L.E.*

[3] Robert Vaughn was off NBC for approximately two weeks and then reappeared Tuesday evening as Napoleon Solo in *The Man From U.N.C.L.E.*

"When an agent would call me and say I *must* see so-and-so, I would ask if the client was right, was he good? And then I would have them brought in. I totally depended on my ability to judge the actor in whatever role they were going for. I'd been an actor and a director in theater, I had a sense of what was right and I trusted that.

"People who would normally play bit parts would end up playing leads. I got a reputation as a very creative casting director who was bringing in fresh people. They weren't fresh, I just didn't know any better."

Gene fired the other casting director and hired D'Agosta, giving him his first break.

Others noticed Gene's work. Quinn Martin, a fellow alumnus of Fred Ziv's "college of practical television arts and sciences," made an offer. On March 12, Gene sent him the following note:

> Meeting and talking with you again was a great pleasure to me. I was reminded all over again how closely we think and feel on a wide variety of subjects. And so, finding I could not go with your show next season was one of the most difficult decisions I've made in a long time. I think it is a fine product and would have been a pleasant and productive relationship.
>
> As Harold Breecher told you, it does appear more and more like *The Lieutenant* will be picked up for a new season. In the event we do lose out at the last minute, the studio has made certain commitments to me which more than cover the risk in waiting.[4] Despite my other inclinations, it added up to good business sense either way.
>
> Since you and I both intend to stay in this business a long time, we should make it a point to talk business sometime during the next season. And, whether anything comes of this or not, I think we now owe it to ourselves to pick up an old, tried and very sincere friendship.

Gene incorrectly judged the longevity of his show. It was not renewed, and by April 13, *The Lieutenant* was out of

---

[4] These promises evidently did not come through.

production.[5] Of course, even while *The Lieutenant* was in production Gene was at work on another idea. Gene had combined a number of his previous concepts—a ship as a "character" and integral to the story, from *Hawaii Passage;* the interaction between the ship's senior officers from *Hawaii Passage* and *APO 923;* the strong, heroic captain from C.S. Forester's Horatio Hornblower series[6]; the multiracial crew with a strong, idealistic bond—the "band of brothers and sisters" from his dirigible series idea; and a number of other concepts he found in the literary genre of science fiction[7]—to be dramatized and placed on a starship two hundred years in the future. Gene's series idea was something that had not been done on television to date: adult drama with a continuing cast of characters in a science fiction setting. By March 11, 1964, he had the concept down in sixteen pages, enough to show to industry buyers. He called it *Star Trek.*[8]

On April 24, Gene sent a check for two dollars and the required three copies of the series prospectus to Blanche Baker at the Writers' Guild of America, West, Inc. to protect the concept of *Star Trek* from theft.

Gene's level of respect in the business was reflected in the Writers Guild request that he stand for nomination to the guild board. Gene turned down the nominating committee,

---

[5] *The Lieutenant* lived on, quite unexpectedly, in another guise. As reported in *Field Manual for Collecting G.I. Joe 1963–1969* by Harold Fowler, "Don Levine (creative director of new products at Hasbro Toy Co.) was invited to view a prescreening of *The Lieutenant* in Manhattan. The show turned out to be a soap opera with no toy potential from Hasbro's point of view." Inspired by the show and the idea, Levine "pursued his instincts" and created a working model of a moveable figure to sell to boys: G.I. Joe.

[6] Without question, Gene's favorite literary character, he read Hornblower when it was first published in the United States in 1939 and continued to reread the novels until a few weeks before his death. Ironically, Forester wrote several science fiction stories and at least one SF novel. He died the same year *Star Trek* went on the air.

[7] Gene was also influenced by Robert A. Heinlein's early work from the 1940's and 1950's, especially stories from Heinlein's "Future History" series. Gene picked up some ideas from Arthur C. Clarke's *Profiles of the Future* (1962). Of course, he was also influenced by Isaac Asimov's entire body of work.

[8] Contrary to sworn testimony by his ex-wife, Eileen, she did not help Gene name *Star Trek.* It is Darleen Roddenberry's distinct memory of helping her mother look up the word "trek" in the dictionary when she first heard it. No one in the family knew what it meant.

citing the press of business and "two personal reasons, aged 10 and 16."

While Gene pitched the *Star Trek* idea around town, another opportunity presented itself. Ivan Tors, whom Gene knew from Ziv, had contacted Gene concerning a series he was developing about a veterinarian who ran an animal study center in Africa. It was to be called *Daktari*[9] and Tors wanted Gene to write the pilot, but there were delays. Early in May, Gene sent Tors a letter telling him that he had waited as long as he could "hoping the matter would be resolved but am told little or no progress has been made toward a resolution of a Tors-MGM agreement. Accordingly, and with considerable regrets since I did look forward to working with you at this time, I have had to instruct my agency to enter into other negotiations."

Gene returned the *Daktari* files and notes that Tors had loaned him and closed his letter with a typically generous offer: "Best of luck on this show. It is an exciting concept and I am certain it will be a highly successful series. If I can assist by passing on to you various thoughts during the study of this material, I will be glad to meet with you and explain them. Again, best of luck."

On the same day as he wrote the letter to Tors, Gene also wrote an in-house memo to Alan Courtney, an executive at MGM:

In the event I do not reach you by telephone today, I thought it best to get this note to your attention.

Because of the delay in the negotiation of an Ivan Tors-MGM arrangement, which was necessary before either party could negotiate a pilot writing contract with me, I have had to write Ivan Tors with some regret that I could no longer remain available for the assignment at this time. Perhaps we can get together on it later.

During the same time, although I have been gratified at the interest you have shown in my science fiction series presentation, *Star Trek,* and have received similar comments from others at MGM who have read it, my agency Ashley-Steiner has received no indication of MGM interest. In the meantime, interest has developed elsewhere

---

[9] *Daktari* eventually made it onto CBS in January 1966. It was on the air for three years.

and Ashley-Steiner, as they properly should do in such a case, has begun discussions there.

I thought it only proper to let you know that these discussions are moving so rapidly that I may very quickly have to give an answer to some firm offer.

Two weeks later Alan Courtney responded:

Dear Gene:

Thank you for your gracious note. I too enjoyed our brief association and look forward to a longer one somewhere in your bright future.

Regretfully I am returning your material on *Star Trek*. You know my opinion of this property, so you can understand why I feel like the man who is watching his mother-in-law drive off a cliff in his brand new Cadillac.

Kindest regards.

Sincerely,
Alan

While several people at MGM thought *Star Trek* was a winner, the studio wasn't interested. The "elsewhere" Gene alluded to was Desilu, and it was there that a unique combination of interests and events came together.

Desilu was owned by Lucille Ball and Desi Arnaz and was originally created to produce their television program, *I Love Lucy,* which burst onto the television scene in 1951. It ended its first season as the number three rated show and then rose and stayed at number one for the rest of its run on CBS, except for the October 1955 to April 1956 season, when they were number two, just behind *The $64,000 Question.*

Unlike other stars of early television, Lucy and Desi profited handsomely from their creativity. *I Love Lucy* was photographed on film rather than CBS's preference of being broadcast from the East Coast, where eighty-five percent of the nation's sets could watch it live, and then rebroadcast by kinescope[10] to the rest of the country. Film union regulations

---

[10] Kinescopes were 16mm films of a television screen. It was never a satisfactory process and did not produce a high-quality picture.

forbad the show being shot at CBS facilities, so additional costs were incurred. Neither the sponsor, Phillip Morris cigarettes, nor CBS would come up with the additional monies needed. Desi, through his agent Don Sharpe, used this impasse to cut one of the most lucrative deals in show business history.

Sharpe suggested that Lucy and Desi take a $1,000 a week cut, reducing their weekly combined salary to $4,000 a week and fifty percent of the profits. Desi wanted complete ownership of all the shows, figuring that the $39,000[11] he had just given up actually represented four or five thousand dollars net, given their tax bracket.

Hubbell Robinson, in charge of business affairs at CBS in New York, agreed, giving Lucy and Desi complete ownership of their shows after the network run.[12] Desi's creation would be *very* profitable for them and, in perhaps the most ironic of situations, even more profitable when they sold the 180 episodes of *I Love Lucy* back to CBS in 1956 for $4.3 million.

In addition to producing their own show, Desilu produced other programs, the wildly popular *Untouchables* being one. They also rented out studio space.[13] Lucy and Desi were unique in that they (perhaps more than any other creative individuals at that time) were able to earn serious money for their talents. Most other creative people, even high-priced performers, did not.

While Lucy had a genius for performing, Desi's genius blossomed behind the cameras. He became a formidable executive, with a near photographic memory for production details, who added successful touches to many of the shows Desilu produced. The company became so successful that

---

[11] Programs were usually produced in 39 episode cycles.

[12] As reported by Coyne Sanders and Tom Gilbert in their well-researched book, *Desilu,* "Desi had, in effect, at that moment, created the television off-network 'rerun' market."

[13] In the early 1950's, motion picture studios looked askance at television, seeing only that it kept movie audiences inside their homes watching free television when they should have been out paying money to see films. Consequently, few if any movie lots were willing to rent their studios to television production companies. As they had plenty of extra space, Desilu was one of the few rental studios in town and was always busy.

they eventually bought the old RKO lot on Melrose Avenue, right next door to Paramount Pictures.[14]

Unfortunately, the success of their business did not spill over into their marriage. Lucy's insecurity and Desi's drinking, gambling, and womanizing were a fatal combination, and the marriage failed in 1960. In spite of a divorce, Desi stayed on as the president of Desilu with Lucy as vice president. Each owned twenty-five percent of the stock and secretly held options to buy each other out should the opportunity arise.

This arrangement continued for two years after they divorced, but Desi's excesses had their effect on the company. After dozens of denials and refusals to sell, the industry was stunned when the announcement was made on Friday afternoon, November 9, 1962, that Desi was out as corporate president and Lucy was in. She was the first women president of a major telefilm company, her only distant predecessor being Mary Pickford, who had been president of her own independent theatrical film company. Lucy, with the assistance of CBS, had bought out her exhusband.

Lucy decided to bring in Oscar Katz to run Desilu's programming. Twenty-six years at CBS, first in the research department and later in programming, few knew the business as well. Lucy displayed her respect for Katz by allowing him to move into Desi's old office, which she'd kept closed since he had left the studio. Katz, used to the more austere furnishings at CBS headquarters in New York, was overwhelmed. The office was richly panelled in mahogany, with a fireplace, dining room, bathroom, and shower. "It was a real Hollywood mogul's office," Katz would later say. And no wonder. Before Desi, the first occupant had been Howard Hughes, when he owned RKO.

Katz hadn't warmed the rich leather of his executive chair before he encountered two problems. First, floating around on the Hollywood rumor mill, an unspecified talent agency was telling people "not to buy shows from Desilu—they're

---

[14] Many years later, when the standing sets of *Star Trek* were dismantled after the show had been cancelled, a small, forgotten trap door was rediscovered under one of the sets. In the small room beneath the stage floor was a pile of old models carelessly thrown in the corner who knows how many years before. They were the articulated brontosaurus and stegasaurus from the 1933 RKO production of *King Kong* and are now in the possession of a noted collector.

really an extension of the CBS programming department." The unfounded rumor warned that "Oscar Katz was put in the job as a protection for the CBS loan to Lucy to buy the studio. Anything they pitch to you has already been turned down by CBS."

Then there was Katz's other problem. Over the years, Desilu had developed a poor reputation for their high overhead charges. The charge is a percentage of the program's cost applied only to in-house productions.

"This is very important to the creative people of the world," Oscar Katz remembered, "the Gene Roddenberrys of this world. You make a deal with Desilu to develop a program for Desilu, that percentage may reduce the profit, and if you're on some definition of sharing the profit or gross, it may reduce your participation if they are taking too much out.

"Here's how this works against creative people. Let's say that Gene made a deal for *Star Trek,* for example. Let's say the deal specifies that he would get X percent of some definition of profits, in addition to his producer's royalty and fees for services performed. Now, Desilu is spending X dollars on cast, X amount of dollars on directors, etc. That's understandable. On top of all that, before they get to whatever it is that Gene Roddenberry's profit is going to be based on, they add a fourteen percent overhead charge. That makes it less likely that Gene Roddenberry is ever going to get to the profit position.

"When I took over Desilu there were shows that had been on the air for years, had been in syndication for years and hadn't reached profit.

"The creative guys thought that Desilu was charging too high an overhead charge. It kept changing, depending on the union deals but I think it was around fourteen percent."[15]

Several standard practices in Hollywood—one of which was the definition of net, which can be unique to each profit participant—would effect Gene's life for years.

Katz was known as a very particular buyer with high standards when he was at CBS. In that position you can, as he said, "Go for one show and reject ninety-nine." As the

---

[15] Katz stated that in his two years at Desilu he was never able to have anyone explain to him how the overhead charge was determined or justified.

head of programming at a studio, it was strongly suggested to him that he reduce his standards.

Lucy had a number of unique perks, and one of them was a way of funding program development at Desilu. Lucy was only signed with CBS for a year at a time. Every year, beginning in the early 1960's, she would draw out the signing of a new contract. One year she announced that she was too tired to continue with her popular show. The appeals of sponsors and network president Jim Aubrey were to no avail. It took the intervention of William S. Paley, founder of CBS and chairman of the board, who flew to Los Angeles to deliver his message personally, to get Lucy to change her mind. Inside each new contract was "development money," money that Desilu could use to develop new series.

As Oscar Katz remembered the deal: "There was money for at least five scripts and one of them had to be piloted, or filmed as a pilot, but there was no guarantee that the pilot would go on the air. We're talking maybe $500,000."

Alden Schwimmer was in charge of the West Coast office of Ashley Famous and, as Oscar Katz recalls, second in command overall of the talent agency. He was someone whom Katz respected. He suggested Katz "take one guy from the action field and one writer or writing team from the comedy field and make an overall deal with them." This would send a favorable signal to the creative community, helping to overcome the problems mentioned earlier, and thereby attract talent to Desilu. Katz followed Schwimmer's advice. Conveniently, Schwimmer had just the person in mind for the action-adventure producer, since Ashley Famous represented a successful writer-producer who had just become available. Gene was signed to a long-term, three-project deal.

As one-time head of CBS programming, Katz knew everyone in the business to one degree or another. Gene was no stranger.

"When I spoke to Gene I told him that I didn't want to know his program ideas now. We had respect for him as a talent. We asked him to come to Desilu and make it his home base. We gave him office space, a secretary, and guaranteed we'd do a certain number of his projects. We'd at least go to script on them. I considered Gene to almost be on staff and with him it wasn't a project deal, it was a person deal. Gene and I developed a long, personal relationship and we always liked each other."

Gene had been clever and lucky. Instead of trying to sell Katz on a one-project deal, Gene's agent had gotten him a situation which gave him more latitude, power, money and, possibly, longevity. Gene would be around the studio long enough to build relationships and, with luck, he would last long enough to see one of his series ideas become reality. Gene had several, one of them being *Assignment 100,* which was later made as a half-hour pilot that failed to sell, called *Police Story.* He also presented Katz with his idea for a science fiction series called *Star Trek.* Oscar Katz remembers:

"When I was head of programming at CBS I was responsible for twenty-five or so shows on the air and perhaps fifty or a hundred in development. I was always running late for meetings and when someone came into my office I was immediately thinking about how I could get him out. One of the luxuries I had in my position at Desilu was having a limited number of projects. At the most I would have five projects going to pilot. So I could have Gene come into my office—this luxurious office that had been Howard Hughes's and then Desi's—where I had a chair that rivaled anything a Supreme Court justice has. Gene would sit in one of the overstuffed chairs and we would kick ideas around for hours.

"At Desilu the creative process worked much differently than at the network.

"At the network you start out with four thousand submissions. You or your staff pick out a hundred or so that go to development which might mean a detailed outline and/or a script. At each stage you have a better idea of what you've got. There's more meat on the bone, so to speak. You make a judgment from the outline or the script and from the script you pick twenty-five or thirty projects to be piloted. Now you have even more meat on the bone. This is what we call the 'step process' or a 'step deal.'

"From the twenty-five or thirty projects, you pick six or seven or eight to go on the air. It's not much different than what you have in the art world. Look at how many pictures you have to paint to get one masterpiece."

Katz immediately began to develop strategies to sell *Star Trek* to the networks. Comfortably sequestered in Katz's opulent office, he and Gene developed the sales pitch they would use on the networks to sell *Star Trek.*

"First we went to CBS. We sat at a big table in the CBS

executive dining room. Their head of development, a guy named Hunt Stromberg, Jr. who had worked for me, was there, as was the network president, James Aubrey, although it was Hunt who asked most of the questions. I think Alden Schwimmer was with us as well.

"The CBS guys questioned us in such detail and for so long that I thought we had real interest from them about the series. They later passed on doing the series and we found out that they had questioned us thoroughly because they had a science fiction project called *Lost in Space* in development and they wanted to know what the hell we were doing.

"Up to this point, nobody would go for science fiction in the true sense of the word. It was too esoteric for them. The only guy who had science fiction on television was Irwin Allen, a very creative guy in another sense."[16]

Having been burned by CBS, the pair next went to NBC with a more careful sales pitch. Oscar Katz remembers:

"When NBC asked us what the show was about we did our best to get it away from its esoteric, science fiction background. We said there were four kinds of stories on *Star Trek*. First, the spaceship is out for a five-year mission on some sort of 'police action.' It gets word that on some planet where there's some rare mineral being mined there is some claim jumping. So we go to the planet and settle the dispute, whatever. We said, 'That's very much like *Gunsmoke*. The sheriff or marshal settles the problem.'

"The second kind of stories has us on the spaceship. It's five stories high, has five hundred people on it, it's huge and the story takes place entirely on the ship. There's a girl who has a problem, she's in the crew and the two leads find out she has an emotional problem with her boyfriend or her parents or whatever. The two leads are the catalytic agents who push her into solving her own problem. Once she solves her problem you never see her again. We said, 'That's very similar to *Wagon Train*,' which was a very big hit then on the air. The wagon train had eight hundred wagons so there would be no difficulty in finding people with problems.

---

[16] After his tenure at Desilu, Katz spent a few years as an agent. Ironically, one of his clients was Irwin Allen, who produced the SF series *Voyage To The Bottom of the Sea*, ABC 1964–1968; *Lost in Space*, CBS 1965–1968; *The Time Tunnel*, ABC 1966–1967; and *Land of the Giants*, ABC 1968–1970.

"We always compared it with current hit shows before we got into the more esoteric parts of the format.[17]

"The third type of story, that still related to this country and what was going on then, is that the spaceship visits a planet where they are very much like us because the atmospheric conditions are the same. The locals are lagging behind us. The story is that their Al Capone is about to take over their Chicago or their Civil War is about to break out and our leads use their knowledge of what happened on Earth to help these people. Or, and we just mentioned this in passing, we come to a planet where the natives are two hundred years ahead of us. We didn't get into that too much.

"Finally—only the last story type we pitched would be considered real science fiction by the *Star Trek* fans—they land on a planet where the atmospheric conditions are different, people don't look like us, and things are very different.

"NBC gave us some 'story money' and Gene developed three outlines. NBC selected the last story type to be done as a pilot. That's how 'The Menagerie' got made. The two guys who ran NBC, Mort Werner and Grant Tinker, were both very honorable guys. I was friends, or semi-friends with both of them. I knew what they had selected would be a tougher sale to Advertising. I tried to convince them that they were wrong and to do one of the first types of stories, but they wouldn't budge.

"I also knew that the pilot was going to cost a lot more. I think NBC gave us $435,000 for the *Star Trek* pilot. We spent $500,000 to $600,000 on the pilot and deficit-financed the difference. A good part of the additional $150,000 spent wasn't cash, it was studio services, studio overhead. Today it would cost $2 or $3 million."

Meanwhile, Gene and Majel's relationship had progressed to a full-blown affair. It had started about the time Gene had moved over to MGM, or shortly thereafter. A man of tremendous appetites, Majel was not Gene's only girlfriend,

---

[17] Nimoy, in *I Am Not Spock,* recounts a series pitch. "I was present when a writer presented an idea for a TV show to a major studio executive. The writer was eloquent and enthusiastic. He told his story in right language, filled with historical and social references. The executive's response was, 'That sounds great, but give it to me in a line that I can use in the *TV Guide.'* "

but certainly his main one. Because of his irregular hours, Eileen apparently remained unaware of Gene's extracurricular activities.

One Writers Guild awards dinner stands out—not for any award given Gene, but for the little drama that played out at one of the tables. Even in as liberal a town as Hollywood professes to be, it was considered bad taste to bring your mistress to a business function if you were still living with your wife. Gene brought Eileen but arranged for Majel to attend, escorted by noted character actor Ray Walston.[18]

What neither Majel nor Walston knew was Gene's little plan to have some fun at their expense. He had made arrangements for a series of surprises to be delivered to Majel at her table. Shortly after everyone was seated and the appetizers were being served, a messenger arrived with a small bouquet of flowers for Majel. There was no card and the messenger did not enlighten her as to who had sent the gift. Walston was amused but paid little attention.

Next came a bottle of good champagne and Walston began to notice what was going on. Then, twenty minutes later, a bottle of expensive perfume, then a box of expensive chocolates, then another gift, and another—gift after expensive gift all delivered without a card.

With each gift's arrival, Walston was becoming more insistent on knowing the identity of the mysterious philanthropist. Majel's increasingly strenuous denials of knowledge were only exceeded by Walston's increasing skepticism. Majel's acting skills were taxed that evening, as she knew full well who was sending the gifts but could not tell her irritated escort.

As Majel had driven, she took Walston home. Getting out of her convertible, he looked at the backseat, stuffed with anonymously delivered loot, and declared that since Majel didn't know who had sent it, she wouldn't mind if he helped himself, which he did, quickly filling his arms and vanishing into his house.

Gene found the whole situation funny and laughed about it for years.

* * *

---

[18] Twenty-five years in the future, Walston, who had played a Martian in the sitcom *My Favorite Martian*, would play Boothby, the groundskeeper at Starfleet Academy in *Star Trek: The Next Generation*.

Majel had her own life, and while she was becoming emotionally involved with Gene, she occasionally saw other people. One afternoon, she was invited to a barbecue at Jack Webb's house. Webb was between wives and Majel was single, but Gene learned of her "date" and decided to have some fun.

Majel had only just arrived at Webb's home and was being given the tour of the house when the doorbell rang. Webb's houseman answered and found a deliveryman with two dozen long-stemmed roses. They were for Majel Barrett, the deliveryman announced, but there was no card and no indication who had sent them. Like Ray Walston before him, Jack Webb was curious as to who had sent the flowers, especially to a woman he thought was single and on his turf.

As with Walston, Majel relied on her acting skills and professed complete ignorance. She minimized the gift by leaving the flowers in a corner of the room and excusing herself and going to the bathroom. When she returned, she found that Webb's houseman had put the flowers in a vase and placed them on the fireplace mantel, the most conspicuous place in the room. The flowers, a huge bouquet, dominated the room. Majel was as uncomfortable as Webb was curious for the rest of the afternoon. When she left, Webb made certain she had her flowers in the backseat of her convertible. Of course, the flowers had their effect. Webb understood that they were from another man, "marking his territory," as it were. He never asked Majel out again.

Years later, Gene ran into Webb at Paramount. The two men had been friends for years, from Gene's days at LAPD Public Affairs, and when Gene told him he was the sender of the flowers those years before, Webb had a good laugh.

Television programs are a variation on the old-time medicine show principle: draw a large crowd with a free show and then sell a product to those gathered.

These forms of entertainment (like all advertiser-driven attractions) have another commonality: a strong devotion to the bottom line—the cost of producing the show versus how much product is being sold. The cost of the show is first, last, and always a primary concern. Art, aesthetics, and literary merit, have always been secondary. Write a show too expensive to produce, and it will never be on the air. Shows have to attract a mass audience and be produced on a reasonable budget—"reasonable" being a word that often has different meanings to the creative people and studio bosses.

From the time Hollywood began making silent films, there had been a continual battle between the individuals who create the product and the studios who financed and distributed the product. It had to do with making the highest quality product at the lowest possible price and then keeping as much of the earned money in the studio's pocket. Television was no different from film in those regards. Gene had learned that at Fred Ziv's knee, but what Gene wanted to do hadn't been done on television—yet.

NBC was not sure that a novice producer with a short track record working at a small studio could deliver a profitable product. There was one other major consideration: could a serialized, one-hour science fiction television show with continuing characters be filmed in six days? Gene was very careful with his idea, as this letter to his close friend, Don Ingalls, shows.

> Dear Don:
> Enclosed are the series presentations you requested.
> One is *Whirlwind,* a Western I am currently
> rewriting, and the other is *Star Trek* which must
> be held very, very confidential.
>
> >   Best regards,

Gene wasted no time in writing the outline. On July 9, he sent a memo to Oscar Katz:

> Enclosed is the final draft of *Star Trek* pilot outline
> "The Cage."
> Whether this should be sent to NBC now or held
> to be included along with the two other story
> outlines, I leave to your discretion.

NBC selected "The Cage" to be filmed as the pilot episode. Gene began working on the script and, as producer, on a multitude of other fronts as well.

Science fiction presents different and additional problems for television production. Unlike a Western or any other period setting, Gene's series was to take place 200 to 300 years in the future. To look "futuristic," everything that appeared on screen had to be designed and specially made.

Gene expressed his frustration some months later in a letter to a friend at MGM.

> Dropped out of sight because of the enormous work involved in this science fiction pilot. Fun, but also very time consuming when every set and location has to be created purely out of imagination. Am beginning to long for the old Westerns where you could simply write "Dodge City Street" and everybody knew exactly what it and everybody looked like.

Gene's thoughts of the look and feel of the bridge were spelled out in a memo to Pato Guzman, designer, on July 24, 1964.

> More and more I see the need for some sort of interesting electronic computing machine designed into the U.S.S. *Enterprise,* perhaps on the bridge itself. It will be an information device out of which April and the crew can quickly and interestingly extract information on the registry of other space vessels, space flight plans for other ships, information on individuals and planets and civilizations, etc. This should not only speed up our story telling but could be visually interesting.

There was yet another hurdle Gene had to surmount at the network: would *Star Trek* be filmed in color or black-and-white? On the last day of July 1964, he sent a letter to Grant Tinker at NBC. Typically, Gene made his argument with care and in great detail in the following short essay, stressing the economic factors involved.

> Further research and preparation on *Star Trek* has so convinced me of the necessity of color photography that I felt I owed you this early note on the subject.
>
> It is important to effectively meet the challenge of giving continuing variety to the new planets we visit from week to week—plus that extra "something" which suggests the mystery and excitement of other worlds. Color solves many problems here. For example, the occasional converting of our blue sky to violet or other hues can be accomplished via filters, mats, and other methods. Along the same line, color can also convert even common vegetation into

something new and exciting. Whereas fabricating entirely new vegetation can be quite a budget factor, the spraying of an occasional bush and tree to a new tint can be economical and highly effective. Costumes which might seem rather Earthly in recognizable colors can take on an entirely different identity in the same way. And without expensive changes in form and configuration, a vegetable-dyed green woman can be at once very attractive and still highly alien. It also permits the occasional use of such effects as "black light" and other unusual luminescence. I am told also that color consultants can come up with shades of makeup for our Earth cast which will keep their skin tones normal while camera filters are creating unearthly effects in the set or location around them.

Still another plus—the art designer and I have been puzzling over such problems as creating the illusion of the remarkable speeds necessary to the U.S.S. *Enterprise.* A significant portion of our audience (including the space-wise younger generation) will know that rocket engines are too primitive for our galaxy travel concept. But, without the roar and fire of rockets, how do you create the illusion of spaceship speed? One answer is suggested in the *Journal of the British Interplanetary Society,* an article by Dr. I.E. Sanger, "Some Optical and Kinematical Effects in Interstellar Astronautics." (Impressed? I wasn't kidding about research.) The point being, speeds exceeding light can be suggested by graduated changes in colorations of the ship and of space bodies ahead and behind. This, along with some appropriate new sound, could create not only an illusion of extraordinary acceleration but also give our series vessel an imaginative and completely unique effect.

In short, in science fiction where credulity is a key factor, color can actually create and support believability, and materially increase our choice of routinely available locations, props, costumes, etc.

Let me make it clear I certainly do not suggest by the above that we will be doing a series about colors, any more than we will be doing stories about interstellar physics. Like any good tool, color would be used selectively, never allowed to interfere or become too obvious. But used properly, it could add the decisive dimension to the imaginativeness and believability we want to bring to *Star Trek*. And, I suppose always in mind is the fact that I would hate to put this much labor and love into a project in black and white and have an imitator come along in a future session and swamp us simply because he could see better than we the unusual potential of color in a space show.

Sincerely yours,

In the 1960's, filming in color or black-and-white was a major decision that affected the show's bottom line. The first episodes of *Lost In Space* were shot in black-and-white, as was *Voyage To The Bottom of the Sea*.

In an August 10, 1964, memo to designer Pato Guzman, Gene expressed early agreement about ancillary merchandising:

Let's give some thought to a *distinctive emblem* for our ship and the uniforms of our crewmen. You may have been the one who suggested a week or so ago that this would have the side advantage of giving us a merchandising "trademark."

On the same day, he sent a memo to Herb Solow, Oscar Katz's assistant, with a copy to Guzman:

You may recall we saw MGM's *Forbidden Planet* with Oscar Katz some weeks ago. I think it would be interesting for Pato Guzman to take another very hard look at the spaceship, its configurations, controls, instrumentations, etc. while we are still sketching and planning our own. Can you suggest the best way? Run the film again, or would it be ethical to get a print of the film and have our people make stills from some of the appropriate frames? This latter would be the most helpful. Please understand, we have no intention of copying either interior or exterior of that ship. But a detailed look at it again would do much to stimulate our own thinking.[19]

---

[19] The charge had been made in some circles that Gene had simply copied *Forbidden Planet* (which itself was a retelling of Shakespeare's *The Tempest*). It is hoped this memo will finally put that charge to rest.

Gene also sought input from a variety of sources to stimulate his own creativity: books, magazines, members of think tanks such as the Rand Corporation, and friends. Sam Peeples was a fellow writer, longtime science fiction fan, owner of a huge collection of old science fiction magazines, and an old friend of Gene's. The two men had known each other since 1958, when each had been nominated for best Western script in the Writers Guild annual awards. Gene's nomination was for an episode of *Have Gun Will Travel,* and Peeples's was for an episode of *Wanted: Dead or Alive.* Their friendship firmly established by the mid-1960's, Gene now took the opportunity to presume upon their friendship for some design help. On August 25, 1964, Gene asked a not-too-subtle favor via a letter to Peeples's Woodland Hills home.

It's time I sent you another note of sincerest thanks for the most helpful information you keep providing on science fiction for my *Star Trek* series. I don't want to become a burden and hope I'll have opportunities to repay the kindness.

Things seem to be going well. It's exciting and I'm enjoying every minute of it. Hope this finds *Tarzan* progressing smoothly too. If you want to try any ideas on a fellow writer, always feel free. Although I can't pretend to be an expert on the jungle or Burroughs, I can promise always a frank and honest opinion.

One item is troubling us considerably at the moment—the configuration of our spaceship. Our problem is simply we're too far ahead of what scientists are now planning, or even speculating. After many days of wasted research, even with Rand in Santa Monica, I've decided I've got to go back to science fiction in this area too. Have you any idea of a best source of sketches and drawings of ships of the far future? I probably anticipate your answer here by guessing that the best probably would be simply thumbing through stacks of science fiction magazines, looking for something that strikes the eye as meeting our requirements.

I hesitate asking permission to go through your magazine library. Can you suggest some other source of a considerable number of science fiction magazines? What it may come down to is the art director and myself sitting down and thumbing through magazines and books until a configuration or some area of configuration begins to jell for us.

Warmest regards,

There wasn't any other source of cover art available, so Peeples happily invited Gene and his designer over and turned them loose in his collection. Gene took somewhere between fifty and a hundred photographs of old science fiction magazine covers, searching for ideas for the design of the *Enterprise*.

Exactly what inspired the final design is left to speculation, but Richard Kyle, writer, publisher, bookseller, and expert on the pulps and science fiction, has always held the opinion that the *Enterprise* looks like a spaceship of the 1930's designed by Hugo Gernsback's favorite illustrator, Frank R. Paul.[20]

Near the end of August, Gene wrote a memo to Jim Paisley, his production manager, setting forth a series of questions he needed answered.

... in addition to the multitude of production and budget planning and analyzing it thrusts upon you, script delivery schedule demands I begin an immediate rewrite. In order to cut it to length and polish it properly, here are some areas and specifics on which I need fairly immediate answers or estimates:

• Can we afford to miniaturize something close to the action indicated in the opening? It would help, I assume, if I devised this "spaceship traveling through the galaxy" opening so that it would be the format opener for every show, possibly even the title opening.

• Comments on the ship interior, specifically the bridge. Can we afford the large overhead "bridge viewing screen"? Once established, it would have to be a regular feature of our episodes. I think we can safely estimate a

---

[20] In going through Peeples' collection, Gene could not have missed Paul's work, as he had done all the cover and interior art for *Amazing Stories* between 1926 and 1929. Paul became Gernsback's chief illustrator on *Science Wonder Stories* and *Air Wonder Stories*, painting more than 150 covers in all.

heavy percentage of the ship interior scenes in future episodes will continue to take place in the ship's bridge interior.

• Not too important in the rewrite, but allied in the above—what about windows or viewing ports in the spaceship? They have some importance to us via opening up scenes, giving illusion of space, motion, etc. But what area of episodic costs are we getting into by adding windows to the ship?

• Space travel hyper-drive and time-warp effect. Specifically here the transparency "double exposure" effect. Here, as with many other effects, I'd like to establish something we can afford as format.

• Regarding the surface of planet Talos IV, does the present description of the planet seem practical as regards available locations? Is the description and action presently in the rough draft suited for matching set construction, i.e. stage shooting of the more complicated dialogue portions of these Talos IV planet surface scenes.

Gene's questions and concerns continued for several single-spaced, typewritten pages.

The script was shaping up, with the first draft not expected at NBC until the first week of September. In spite of the myriad details that occupied his every waking moment, Gene was on schedule.

As part of his production team, Gene brought Robert Justman on board. Justman was a television veteran, having been an assistant director on the 1950's *Adventures of Superman* show as well as on *Star Trek*'s most immediate science fiction predecessor, *The Outer Limits*.[21] Urbane and affable, with a sharp and ready wit, Justman was a rare find in television production. His value as a production executive was evident on many levels, but perhaps his most useful skill

---

[21] Justman was responsible for changing the tone and setting of a Harlan Ellison script for that show. As originally written, it would have been too expensive to film. Justman revamped the original concept and filmed it almost entirely in the famous Bradbury building in downtown Los Angeles. It became one of the finest *Outer Limits* episodes, "Demon with a Glass Hand," with Robert Culp and Arlene Martel who would later play "T'Pring" in the original *Star Trek* series episode "Amok Time."

was his ability to give a script a quick read-through, and determine how much time would be needed to shoot it and if it could be produced within budget. Justman was also a stickler for details and minute planning, talents and skills that made Justman invaluable. Nothing is worse than an unforeseen problem or an expensive emergency. Justman was always prepared.

By September 14, there was a special effects budget. A few items have been extracted and are listed below.

Int. Space Ship	$2,850
Ext. Talos IV Planet	$6,400
Set No. 4 Underground	$9,500
scene 48 laser effect	$300
scenes 125 & 127, Vina grows old	$900 each

Three pages of details gave a total of $36,200, plus a 20% lab charge and 4% sales tax, for a total of just over $45,000 for special effects.

Red Smith, the famous sportswriter, once said, "There's nothing to writing. All you do is sit down at a typewriter and open a vein." Gene knew that full well and poured his life-blood into this pilot, as evidenced by the number of drafts and revisions "The Cage" went through. At the UCLA Archives, the following draft notations are on file:

Pilot story outline—First Draft	7/8/64
Final Draft—	7/22/64
Revised	7/29/64
Script—Rough Draft	8/4/64
Next version	8/31/64
Revised	10/6/64
Title changed to *Star Trek Voyage One*—"The Menagerie" and revised	11/16/64
Captain's name changed from James Winter[22] to Christopher Pike	11/25/64
Act 4 partially revised	11/27/64

---

[22] There is no specific date when Robert April changed to James Winter, but Winter was used only briefly.

Act 4 partially revised	12/4/64
Act 4 partially revised	12/8/64
Act 4 partially revised	12/9/64
Finally, five pages, scenes 56	12/11/64
through 61, were revised	

As if creating, writing, producing, and making certain it was filmed in color weren't enough to keep Gene busy, there was handling the network people who would have their say, requested or not. Beyond the executives who bought the show, and had an opinion, there was the network's Standards and Practices Department.[23] As the late November date for the beginning of filming grew closer, Don Bay, in NBC's S & P Department, the network's censor, sent his comments on the script. For ease in reading, the page and scene references in the following have been eliminated.

Bay wrote:

Please delete April's "My God" and substitute something such as "Great Scott."

Please exercise extreme caution in make-up of the various grotesque monsters. The NAB[24] Code states "The use of horror for its own sake will be eliminated; the use of visual or aural effects which would shock or alarm the viewer . . . are not permissible."

Caution must be exercised in Vina's seductive behavior in April's presence. Avoid dialogue and movement that would have too specific a sexual inference.

Please exercise caution when showing the characters writhing in their telepathically produced agonies. As before, please avoid elements that would shock or alarm the home viewer. Caution on the screams. Avoid sensationalizing.

Caution on costuming of Vina. The torn dress should not go beyond the bounds of propriety.

Please delete the underline and substitute the bracketed in Vina's speech: "*For God's Sake*

---

[23] Each network had such a department, which was responsible for clearing all material to be aired, in accordance with the National Association of Broadcasters' codes and the company's own level of acceptability and good taste.
[24] The National Association of Broadcasters.

(Please), stop him! Don't you know what they do to *women* (us)?" In addition, caution on the wound on April's forehead. Avoid excessive bloodiness.

Please avoid camera angles that would feature the lance protruding from the giant creature's back. When April swings the shield to drive the lance home, we must not see the shaft plunge deeper into the flesh (i.e. we may see the shield hit the shaft but not see where the shaft is embedded in the creature). Please exercise caution when the creature falls to the compound below.

Caution on costuming of the green woman. Please stay within the bounds of propriety.

Caution on the woman's movements to the barbaric rhythm. The NAB Code states "The movement of dancers . . . shall be kept within the bounds of decency . . ."

Due to the masochistic sexual inference in the dialogue, please delete the underlined from Vina's speech: "Don't let me hurt you. *Take the whip . . . tame me!*" In addition, caution in handling of Vina's clawing of April. We must not see the actual lashing of the woman with the whip.

Please exercise caution in the references to April and a woman being needed for breeding purposes. In addition, please eliminate the underlined from The Keeper's speech: "The factors in her favor are youth and strength, *plus an unusually strong mating drive which . . .*"

Please delete April's speech: "As in 'all ship's scientists are dirty old men!' "

Gene had his own thoughts on Bay's memo, and on October 8, he fired off a memo to Herb Solow, assistant to Oscar Katz.

Reference Don Bay's memo, I can accept all these points but the following:

April's expression "My God" is said in a context and manner which could have no feeling of profanity.

Reference the Talosians and monsters, dream sequence "punishment," etc., although these may have some shock effect for legitimate dramatic value, we do not intend ever to use "horror for its own sake."

Reference Vina's speech "For God's sake, stop him!" I feel this is unprofane also but will accept your judgment on this. However, in the case of the rest of the speech "Don't you know what they do to women?", I see no sexual connotation in this and cannot understand why they want it eliminated.

Perhaps strongest of all, I simply cannot agree with their thinking regarding April's speech "As in all ship's doctors are dirty old men!" This is a humorous line, has no connotations at all which could by any stretch of anyone's imagination make it objectionable.

While the battle for the integrity of Gene's vision continued, so did his search for actors. Gene was fastidious in finding the right actors to play his "children."

The central character, the ship's captain, was originally named Robert April. This was changed to James Winter and finally to Christopher Pike.[25] The captain was the heroic character on which the show depended. Every leading man and leading man type in the business was examined. One casting consultant submitted a list of forty names. Included in the list are people we still recognize today: Nick Adams, Jack Cassidy, Cameron Mitchell, Ray Danton, Peter Graves, Efrem Zimbalist, Jr., Jason Robards, Jr., Rod Taylor, Earl Holliman, Robert Loggia, Sterling Hayden, Steve Forrest, Howard Duff, Jack Lord, Robert Stack, Leslie Nielsen, Mike Connors, Hugh O'Brien, William Shatner, George Segal, Frank Converse, Guy Stockwell, Liam Sullivan[26], Warren

---

[25] Later, in the animated *Star Trek* series, the first captain of the *Enterprise* was noted as being Robert April in "The Counter-Clock Incident" broadcast 10/12/74. As a tribute to Gene, the husband and wife writing team of Denise and Michael Okuda (also brilliant graphic designers on *Star Trek: The Next Generation* and *Star Trek: Deep Space Nine*), in their exhaustive history of the *Star Trek* universe, *Star Trek Chronology* (New York: Pocket Books, 1993), computer-blended a contemporary photograph of Gene's face with that of a previously unpublished still of Jeffery Hunter from "The Cage." They published it without explanation as a photo of "Robert April, First Captain of the *Enterprise*."

[26] Liam Sullivan guest-starred as Parmen in "Plato's Stepchildren," by Meyer Dolinsky, which aired 11/22/68.

Stevens[27], Skip Homeier[28], Rhodes Reason[29], and, ironically, Ed Kemmer, who played Commander Corry in *Space Patrol*.

Gene went through this list and several others submitted by other consultants and sent a number of names over to NBC for their comments. Included in this shorter list are Tom Tryon, Dan O'Herlihy, Patrick O'Neal, Jeff Hunter, and James Coburn. Coburn's name was there because of Majel. She remembers strongly suggesting James Coburn to Gene and a group of men sitting in a smoky room, only to have her suggestion rejected because Coburn, in their considered opinion, "wasn't sexy enough." Majel's only comment: "A lot they knew!"

The next day, Gene was informed by Herb Solow that NBC was "very much against" Jeff Hunter and two others on his list. NBC suggested Patrick McGoohan, Mel Ferrer, and several others. The memo closes with: "There was a strong reaction for both James Coburn and Patrick O'Neal."

By November 4, the first two actors were set for the pilot as Gene sent the following memo to Ed Perlstein in Desilu Business Affairs:

> Please make a deal on Magel (sic) Barrett to play "Number One" and Leonard Nimoy to play "Mister Spock," as per our previous conversations.

The role of "Number One," the ship's emotionless executive officer, had been written for Majel. While Gene may have gone through the motions, no other actresses were considered for the part.

For the role of "Mr. Spock," several actors were on the short list, including Leonard Nimoy, Rex Holman[30], DeForest Kelly, and Michael Dunn.[31] Majel had reminded Gene of Nimoy, an actor they both knew from a guest appearance on

---

[27] Warren Stevens would guest star in "By Any Other Name," by D.C. Fontana and Jerome Bixby, aired 2/23/68.

[28] Skip Homeier would guest star in "Patterns of Force," by John Meredyth Lucas, aired 2/16/68.

[29] Rhodes Reason would guest star as Flavius in "Bread and Circuses," by Gene L. Coon and Gene Roddenberry, aired 3/15/68.

[30] Holman appeared as Wyatt Earp in the original series episode "Spectre of the Gun."

[31] Dunn was a dwarf and later starred as Alexander in "Plato's Stepchildren."

The Lieutenant. Once Gene saw the thin Nimoy with his narrow face and sharp features, no other actors were given any consideration.

On November 17, Gene was still looking for someone to play "Doc" and sent a memo to a casting consultant saying that he would like to consider David Opatoshu[32] for the part. He had also asked director Bob Butler to look at some film of DeForest Kelley as a possibility. This memo closed with, "I have the name Mike McDonald. Is this anyone you suggested? Same on Carol (sic) O'Connor."

At about this time, Gene turned to his old friend Joe D'Agosta, the casting director he knew from his series at MGM, *The Lieutenant.* D'Agosta had gone his own way after *The Lieutenant* and ended up at Fox. One afternoon he got a call from Gene telling him he had sold a pilot called *Star Trek.* They did not have a casting director and they had been calling people in on their own and were not happy with the result. Gene wanted him to come over and be the *Star Trek* casting director. Unfortunately, D'Agosta had a steady job and couldn't leave it for one show. He told Gene he would be happy to do consulting by phone, happy to do his friend a favor. D'Agosta remembers:

"At this point I knew what I was doing and I gave Gene lists of actors for various parts. Jeffery Hunter was already cast before I came in. That was a network-producer-Desilu decision, prior to my involvement. Later, I was shocked when I got a check for $750. I didn't ask for it or expect it and one day it just showed up.

"After the show sold and was going into production Gene went to Herb Solow. At that time Desilu was producing *Star Trek, Mission: Impossible,* and *The Lucy Show.* Gene told Solow that they needed a casting department and that I ought to run it.

"Desilu felt they couldn't afford a separate casting director for each show so they went to Bruce Geller, the producer of *Mission* and asked if he knew Joe D'Agosta? By sheer timing and luck I had cast *Rawhide* for him earlier. Geller said, 'There's no one else,' and I got the job. I eventually became Casting Director at Paramount when they bought out Desilu."

---

[32] Opatoshu made it to *Star Trek* as Anan 7 in "A Taste of Armageddon." He was cast for a role in *Star Trek: The Next Generation* but fell ill and the part was re-cast.

Because of the need for dance skills, the role of Vina was proving to be particularly elusive. On October 30, Gene sent the following memo to Herb Solow and others about actresses to play Vina along with comments.

Have the following information from Kerwin Coughlin on actresses we were interested in considering as "Vina":

Janice Rule—available.

Anne Francis—probably available. Doing TV pilot November 11, a *Burke's Law* spinoff.

Elizabeth Ashley—not available, currently in a motion picture.

Stella Stevens—not available, currently in a motion picture.

Barbara Eden—available—an excellent dancer.

Jane Fonda—unavailable—does not want to do TV at this time.

Diana Millay—available—no information yet on whether she can dance.

Piper Laurie—available.

Maggie Pierce—available—considered a good actress but not of the name value we presently hope to attract.

Anne Helm—available—same as above.

Yvette Mimeaux—available—might do television if it is a great part.

Carol Lawrence—unavailable, pregnant.

Susan Oliver—available—her agency says she is an excellent dancer.

Dyan Cannon—available. Played "How To Succeed" for 16 months.

Yvonne Craig[33]—available—excellent dancer.

Suzanne Pleshette—available can move well and would cost top of show.

Joan Blackman—available, danced in "Blue Hawaii" (Presley film).

Jean Seberg—not available.

Gene kept searching for his Vina.

---

[33] Yvonne Craig made it to *Star Trek*, ironically wearing the same green makeup she would have worn as Vina, playing the green Orion slave girl, Marta, in "Whom Gods Destroy."

The Spock character was another dilemma. Originally conceived as a red-hued Martian, Gene decided that if the show were a success, explorers might actually land on Mars during its run, so Spock's origin was moved to another, unnamed planet. The idea to have him ingest energy through a plate in his stomach was also scrapped after an intense discussion with Sam Peeples, who argued that Spock should share more human traits, making him a more interesting character and able to comment on the human condition more believably. Even after Spock was more fully formed, NBC was against him. It was his satanic appearance that bothered NBC, a visage that had been designed by Gene, drawing on his half-hidden memory of the caricature of Emmanuel Schifani from his flight cadet days.

Oscar Katz stepped in to mediate.

"We had trouble with NBC, I can't remember who, but I know it wasn't Grant, about the guy with the ears who was going to scare the shit out of every kid in America. Having sat with Gene in my office and discussed almost every detail of the show, I knew what he [Spock] stood for. I told NBC that they didn't understand. Spock was Gene's counterpart of the half-breed. Everything was based in reality and in the old Westerns there was often a character who was part-white and part-Indian. Spock had the ears to show that he was from a different planet and not human. What he represented was another aspect of 'peace on Earth.' We not only had blacks on board we had aliens working cooperatively with their shipmates. We won that battle, easily as I now remember, and Spock stayed in."

The industry got a brief glimpse of what was happening at Desilu through Army Archerd's *Variety* column, "Just For Variety," on the morning of November 5. In addition to letting the industry know how busy the studio was, Archerd's column also helped squelch rumors of a Desilu sellout.

Meanwhile, Desilu is prepping five pilots, "Star Trek," "Police Story," "April Savage," "Recruiters," plus "His Highness O'Hara." . . . In case it isn't obvious, Lucy has no plans for selling the place—"But," she adds, "I listen to every offer. Most are merger opportunities—but they always want me to put up the money, do all the work, and still run the place! No, I've got no desire to get rid of it. I've learned a lot in the last three-four years. I can rely on my own judgment now." Thus it also follows she has no intentions of retiring. "What would I do? There's a lot of work to be done, a lot of challenges. And if there isn't a challenge—I make one up!"

On November 6, Project Unlimited, Inc., a prop construction house, sent a memo listing their prices for the unusual props Gene wanted.

Spider Man
1. (Using existing chimp suit) create new head, hands; overlay chest area with new character

$350.00

In the left margin Gene wrote "maybe."

2. Create new upper torso to combine with existing lower costume, create new head, re-work existing hands.

$450.00

Gene wrote "too much."

Ear appliances:
First set   80.00
ea. pr. thereafter   8.00

In the left margin GR wrote "ok."

Laser Cannon
(To mount on existing tripod and connect to existing control box) with glowing coils & blinking lights.

$450.00

Gene wrote "no."
On November 13, Project Unlimited sent an additional Prop List Budget:

I. Musical Flowers *3 quotes*
(1) 6 plants w/avge of 6 leaves each with built-in vibration, battery operated. $350

(2) If less than 6. *Each*	$80
(3) 3 practical & 3 dummy	$275

II. Communicating Devices (6)
(1) Practical blinking lights*   35.00
*(If we can get battery operated self-blinking Xmas lights.)
5 Dummies 15 each[34]

                                   75.00

III. Laser Cannon New Design 11/13/64
with radar antenna   225.00

The last two items and the $80 musical flowers were noted "ok" by Gene.

Problems can be expected to crop up in such an involved and complicated project, but no one could have guessed there was such a thing as doing one's job *too* well. Vina's green Orion slave girl makeup was a case in point. Majel was on payroll, so she stood in for the color tests of Vina's coloring. Makeup artist Fred Phillips would apply the tint to Majel, she would be photographed, and the result would be examined a day or so later. Unfortunately, the green color wasn't coming through. Majel looked her normal self with each test. Something was clearly wrong. The makeup men applied greener, heavier makeup each day, but Majel photographed just like always, a normal, healthy Earth woman.

Finally, someone figured out that the color technicians hadn't been told the purpose of the tests. They had been correcting the color, thinking the lighting was off. Another test was done, and everyone learned just how well the Orion slave girl makeup photographed. Majel was relieved. The next level of makeup would have to have been applied with a trowel.

By the middle of November, the search for Vina was over. Oscar Katz remembers:

"Gene wanted Susan Oliver to play Vina. She was a pilot

---

[34] A communicator from the Bill Theiss costume collection, used in the original series, sold at a December 1993, memorabilia auction for $4500.

who flew her own plane. She had just finished a movie and was going on a one or two-week flying trip and doing the pilot would have interfered with that.

"I said to Gene, 'Bring her to my office and I'll talk her into it.' So he brought her to this luxurious office that I've previously described and although I'm usually not that charming with women, I talked her into taking the part. Part of the appeal was that it was going to be very easy—she could knock it off just like that.

"Well, the pilot was shot at Desilu Culver on a very large stage, one of the largest in the world at the time. We built the planet sets there with the control room set off in a corner.

"When she found out that she had to be painted green and that the part wasn't as easy as I'd described, she was pissed off at me. I knew that she would not be kindly disposed towards me and so I had to forgo my usual visit to the set on the first day of shooting. I'd made it a habit to attend the first day of shooting of a pilot to show that the head of the studio was with them. On *Star Trek* I stayed away religiously even though it was just a fifteen minute ride away from my office.

"Susan kept saying, 'Where's Oscar?' Finally, she went to Gene and told him that he had to get me down to the set. Gene called and said there was some sort of emergency on the set and I got into my car, reluctantly I must say, and drove over to Desilu Culver. I was greeted on the set by Susan and two other girls in scanty outfits holding a sign saying 'Oscar Where Are You?' There was also another scene where the three women who played the natives on the planet were also holding a sign saying the same thing. This cost a fortune having these people in full makeup."

Susan Oliver's contract had her working from November 23, 1964, through December 14, 1964. She was to receive guest star billing in the main title in the same size type as that afforded Jeffrey Hunter, the star.

The cast budget and amount of time contracted was as follows:

Jeffrey Hunter as Captain Pike	16 days	$10,000
Susan Oliver as Vina	16 days	$7,500
Leonard Nimoy as Mister Spock	16 days	$2,500
Majel Barrett as Number One	16 days	$2,250

Laurel Goodwin as Yeoman Colt	15 days	$2,000
Peter Duryea as Jose Tyler	16 days	$2,000
John Hoyt as Dr. Phillip Boyce	9 days	$1,500
Adam Roarke as C.P.O. Garrison	5 days	$750
Meg Wylie as The Keeper	3 weeks guaranteed at $400 per week	
Edward Madden as the Geologist	one week guaranteed—$650 per week.	

The voice of The Keeper was not her own. While he did not receive billing, Malachi Throne was paid $350 for one day's recording of The Keeper's lines.

Hunter was well paid for his work. By way of comparison, in 1964 it was possible to buy a new Southern California tract house for around $15,000.

Finally, the day after Thanksgiving, November 27, shooting began on Desilu's Culver City facility on production #6149, "The Cage." The production reports list the following—Producer: Gene Roddenberry; Associate Producer: Byron Haskin; Director: Robert Butler; Asst. Dir: Robert H. Justman; Prod. Manager: James Paisley.

Shooting on stage 16, the first scenes shot were the interior of the Transporter Room scene 15 described as: "Group gets ready for trip—transporter Chief works controls—group disappears." In the "group" are the captain, Spock, Tyler, Boyce, first crewman, and geologist. On stage 14, they were rehearsing the dance number in scenes 86 through 91.

The industry was notified through "the trades." On the same day that shooting began, the following appeared in *The Hollywood Reporter*'s "On the Air" column by Hank Grant:

> Producer Gene Roddenberry draws a fat two-weeks rolling sked for Desilu's Star Trek pilot starting today at Desilu Culver. Stars Jeffrey Hunter & Susan Oliver trek to Arizona locations for three of those days. NBC's the bankroller . . .

While the production was shooting, Gene was still looking for someone to do the music. A note on December 8 listed some of his options and their status:

Jerry Goldsmith—Not Available

Elmer Bernstein—Interested—likes pilot wants to read script.

Harry Sukman—MGM—available

Les Baxter—available

Dominic Tronteri (sic) [Dominic Fronterie who did the music for *The Outer Limits*]—available

Franz Waxman—available

Sy Coleman—suggested by Oscar Katz

Alexander Courage—young composer—up and coming

Hugo Friedholder—did some of the original music on *Voyage to the Bottom of the Sea.*

David Raxton—wrote *Laura.* Works closely with the producer

Johnny Green—would love to do a series, did music for Empire

Leith Stevens—Doing Novak—did the 1st few shows for Empire, scored a feature with a science fiction theme

Johnny Williams[35]—did *Checkmate,* presently doing music for "Baby Makes Three" pilot for Bing Crosby Prods.

Jack Elliott—suggested by Oscar Katz, feels that he has great potential

Will Markowitz—being checked out

Lalo Shiffrin—recommended by Wilbur Hatch and Herb Solow

Nathan Van Cleave—being checked out.

Gene settled on Alexander Courage to write the music and conferred with him on what he wanted.

Things were busy at Desilu. A number of independent companies had rented space. During the second week of December, the main lot saw the filming of *The Lucy Show, My Favorite Martian, My Living Doll, My Three Sons, Ben Casey, The Bing Crosby Show, And Baby Makes Three* (a pilot), *The Andy Griffith Show, Gomer Pyle, USMC, The Joey Bishop Show, The Dick Van Dyke Show;* and at Desilu Culver *Frank Merriwell* (a pilot that didn't sell), *Lassie, Kentucky Jones,* and the *Star Trek* pilot.

---

[35] Williams did theme for *Lost In Space* and later did *Star Wars, E.T.,* and became conductor of the Boston Pops.

Principal photography of the *Star Trek* pilot was completed on December 11 with the shooting of the picnic scene between Pike and Vina, but this had not been anything near a picnic for Gene. Records at the UCLA Archives show that he was constantly rewriting sections of the script. Act 4 seemed particularly troublesome with revisions on November 27, December 4, 8, and 9. Finally, five pages of the script, scenes 56 through 61 were revised overnight for the last day of shooting. "The Cage" went into post production, but this did not mean any respite for Gene. By December 28, he had seen a rough cut and dictated a critique that ran to three single-spaced typed pages.

Generally in the opening of the picture, would like to see a greater feeling of urgency. And specifically, this urgency should center around the Captain. Something happens, others look to him for his reaction. When he does nothing, they eye him and then each other nervously. That sort of thing. In other words, making it very clear from the first that Christopher Pike is Captain of the Enterprise and our strong central lead for a television series.

Having set the Captain up as central figure in this little opening drama of something unknown approaching the ship, when we find it is a radio wave we should have some reactions, i.e., that Captain Pike was right after all in doing nothing. While everyone else was tempted to panic, he calmly sat there and now it has been proven that calmly sitting there was the right thing to do.

Before Pike tells Number One he's leaving her behind, is there some way we can get some indication she would like to go and some indication he is hesitating and feels badly [sic] over having to tell her she's staying behind? We'd like to feel she is as eager as Jose and Spock and would also like to feel the Captain recognizes this fact and thus feels some small tug in having to single her out as the one who stays.

For our next cut, just so as not to throw the music man, can we lose the bells on the surface of Talos IV? After all, Christmas is over now anyway.

And so on for two more pages.

* * *

Work progressed on the pilot through January 1965. It was finished by January 18, when Gene expressed his thoughts in a letter to Sam Gold, a friend and film editor who was recuperating in a convalescent hospital. As usual, Gene mused philosophically about the business.

You may not believe this, but I have missed you considerably these past two weeks. In other words, the pilot was over length, controversial, and complex—needing the Sam Gold touch. Not having that, all we could substitute was time, so worked a daily schedule averaging from 9:00 a.m. to 1:00 a.m. the next morning. Finally got it done on time. I think.

Why don't they ever give you enough time in television? The problem is always that by the time a final cut is achieved, everyone connected with it is so groggy that it's impossible to make a decent evaluation of what you've done.

Or maybe that's good. If we could evaluate it, we'd probably recut it again.

Strange how you leave the stage the last day, loving the director—and a week later in the cutting room you're cursing him out savagely. And, I suppose, the sound people a few weeks later are cursing the film editor. And so along the line. It seems to me that the greatest miracle of our business is that we ultimately end up with something that makes sense, and sometimes with something that is entertaining and great.

In fact, it seems that our business violates the one basic rule of all businesses, i.e. that committees can never accomplish anything. In almost any other work, creativity always ultimately reduces itself to one man doing the job. Here we have a half dozen or more creators, all contributing. The producer can guide them but he dare not do much more. I'm beginning to realize the problem of the producer is knowing the dividing line past which his attempts to guide begin to stifle creativity.

Got into special effects a lot with the *Star Trek* pilot. Among the most fascinating were the optical effects. Spent considerable time in Anderson Company, the optical house here at Desilu, watching and learning. This pilot, as you undoubtedly noted when you read it,

is full of scenes and transitions which require opticals.

We were lucky in having an excellent artist[36] for our
mattes as well as great talent in set design. Thus, a lot of
things which might have been unbelievable actually seem
quite real on film.

Still, sometimes the simplest of tasks do not go smoothly,
as evidenced by the following memo to business affairs
dated January 28:

> This is to verify that Malachi Throne returned a second
> day (January 15) to complete his looping at Glen Glenn
> Studios for the *Star Trek* pilot.
>
> As I mentioned to Bill Heath, a good part of the reason
> he came back was due to faulty Glen Glenn equipment
> which made it impossible for Throne to complete his full
> day's looping chore. It seems to me we should have some
> redress from Glen Glenn for this, at the very least a waiv-
> ing of charges for the second day.
>
> > GR

The pilot was shown to NBC executives, who both liked
it and didn't like it. Rumors abounded, and there was talk
that NBC was going to slot *Star Trek* on Fridays at 8:00 P.M.
By the second week of February, the program had been
tested before an adult audience. As Oscar Katz explains:

"The pilot was finished and it was everything we hoped it
would be. NBC audience tested it. I paid close attention to
the test results because that was a field I knew since I started
in Research. I went to the audience test—or I think I sent
Herb Solow. Anyway, the pilot didn't do well in testing as
the procedure was flawed. They showed a test picture to establish a 'norm,' then a test cartoon, then they showed two
hour shows, and in between them, commercials. Then they
showed *Star Trek*. I don't think it did too well in the test, but
a lot of shows didn't do well in audience testing, like *All In
The Family*.

"I screamed at NBC and they agreed with me and retested
Star Trek in first position instead of second position."

The results were mixed, one source saying that there was

---

[36] Albert Whitlock, an Academy Award-winning artist.

a difference of twenty points in each test. NBC management took their time deciding what they wanted to do.

Hanging in limbo, Gene poured out his thoughts and feelings in an unusually candid letter to a business associate and friend dated February 12, 1965.

Have just talked to Oscar Katz in New York about present indefinite sales status of *Star Trek*. I felt that all sides had been heard from but me and I owed it to Oscar that he understand my feelings clearly. And of course I want you to be in on any such conversation, so therefore am repeating it here in this letter . . .

First, about the *Star Trek* pilot itself. Whether or not this was the right story for a sale, it was definitely a right one for ironing out successfully a thousand how, when and whats of television science fiction. It did that job superbly and has us firmly in position to be the first who has ever successfully made TV series science fiction on a mass audience level and yet with a chance for quality and network prestige too.

We have an opportunity, like "Gulliver's Travels" of a century or more ago, to combine spectacular excitement for a mass group along with meaningful drama and something of substance and pride.

This particular story, whatever its other merits, was an ideal vehicle for proving this point to ourselves. And if the network wants to be partners in such ventures as these, they have to share some of the pain, responsibility and risk of this type of planning. Or they can have copies of other shows, or parallels, breaking no new ground, without any pain or risk at all. I'm quite willing, and I think capable, of giving it to them either way. In a sense, this has been sort of a test for me whether any brave statements I've heard are true.

Now, about the length of the pilot, etc. I agree it should be shorter and should be paced differently. It's my fault that it wasn't since I let myself be swayed by an arbitrary delivery date and did not take a day off and then look freshly at the whole picture before it went to negative cutting. This will not happen again. In future, of the two risks, I will risk violating contract provisions rather than sending out product readied only through weeks of sixteen hour a day fatigue. Where the agency can help here is early in the planning of a pilot, leaning hard on the network in those primary stages where they waste three, four, and five weeks getting back to you with approvals on this and that. This plays a very large part in ending up with production dates which are bound to create problems.

Let me say about the foregoing, I was under no undue pressure from either Katz or Solow. Unlike most studio executives, they stayed off my back, contented themselves with merely pointing out the obvious contract delivery dates. Solow, whom I worked with most directly and intimately, was enormously helpful. One of the most pleasant and talented men I have ever had the pleasure to work with in this business.

Now, summarizing attitudes on the pilot, I think even as it now stands, certainly with many things I'd still like to do with it, it is good quality product.

For those at NBC who honestly do not like it, do not understand or dig it, do not believe it has audience potential, no complaints from me if they turn thumbs down. I have learned to applaud people who make decisions. But I have no respect or tolerance for those who say things like "If it were just a couple minutes shorter . . ." or "Yes, but if it were not so cerebral . . .", and such garbage. And I respectfully suggest to you that tolerating or compromising with this kind of thinking could only lead to us making a bad show out of what could have been good. In other words, am wide open to criticism and suggestions but not from those who think answers lie in things like giving someone aboard a dog, or adding a cute eleven-year-old boy to the crew.

I'm not saying anyone has suggested the above. Or that you would stand still for it. But having been around television for some time, I do know that shows sometimes reach frantic sales moments in which things like that have been known to happen. And it's only fair to let you know I'm not that anxious to sell the show.

Which, I guess, is my central point. There seems

to be a popular delusion that networks do people
a favor by buying shows. I happen to think the truth
is somewhat nearer the other direction—that a man
who creates a format and offers integrity and a large
hunk of his life in producing it, offers much more than
networks or advertisers can give in return. Therefore,
it logically follows, that side has a right to some
terms too.

Mine have not changed. And no matter how difficult
or tenuous any negotiations for sale may become, they
will not change.

We must have an adequate budget to do a show
of this type—otherwise the labor involved is foolish
and meaningless.

Network *must* give early notification that they
are buying the show, or at minimum an early story
order so scripts can be put into work.

Network must agree that any notifications of pickup
or cancellation must be made early, or additional
story orders must be made early enough to permit
proper continuation of schedules.

Without the above, a sale would be completely
meaningless for me. Have no desire to risk heart
attacks or ulcers without at least a fighting chance
to make entertainment I can be proud of. If terms should
turn out different, I will cooperate with all involved
to find a producer who feels otherwise.

Incidentally, I've told both Oscar and Herb Solow
I've had it with the audience testing thing. The fact
there was this enormous twenty point difference between
the two *Star Trek* tests so far certainly must indicate
to any sensible man these people are capable of
gross error. And since they are obviously capable of
this, I insist that this final test be run in number one
position so it is at least a fair comparison with the
last test. And no amount of statistical rationalization
will budge me from this position. It's make or break
with me. If they are going to use these tests (and we
both know they give great weight to them despite
anything they say), then they've got to at least give
us the benefit of an even chance.

Although I've been nervous about *Star Trek* for this
couple of weeks of decision, actually it's been a

good thing for me. Like a fever reaching a crisis
point and then breaking. For the first time I think
I see our particular and peculiar medium exactly
for what it is. It has been and can be very good—and
if someone proves to me they want me to try for that
level, I gladly will. On the other hand, without that
proof, I intend to aim for safe copies and parallels
of existing successes—settle for doing it just two or
three percent better than the next guy so that job and
profits are always there, and I eat dinner every night
at 6:00 p.m. with the children and have two days
at home out of every seven to play horseshoes and
putter in the garden. And do everything possible to
move on into another medium.

Sorry, didn't mean to make this an epic poem.
Maybe it's just catharsis. But I think it's more.

Sincerely,
Gene

By the end of February, NBC was still testing the pilot
and hopes at Desilu were dimming that it would be on the
fall broadcast schedule.

The majority of the television industry learned *Star Trek*'s
fate through "the trades." The March 15, *The Hollywood Reporter,* "On the Air" column with Hank Grant noted:

Fickle scrapping of pilots that don't make a specific
Fall chart may be a thing of the past if the other two webs
follow NBC's new line of reasoning ... Fully realizing
that they couldn't slot 'em all, NBC has invested coin in
a record number of 31 plots projected for Fall '65, half of
which (a surprisingly healthy percentage) are now firmly
slotted for action. Usually, the rejected pilots either slide
into oblivion or find an airing on a summer anthology series, but NBC's not letting either of the two alternatives
happen this time. Instead, the network will hang onto the
rejects on the sound and sensible theory that what was
good enough to offer as sponsor bait for Fall '65 may
have a better sales chance for Fall '66 and even as mid-
season replacements come next January. Thus, the web
has a second-string team on the bench to replenish first-
string casualties—a lot more sensible than having just a
first-string and, when one of 'em falls, pushing a panic

button for almost anything available to replace the casualty ... So, don't count as dead such fall drop-outs as "Kissin' Cousins" "The Good Old Days," "Star Trek," and "The Ghostbreakers." They'll live to fight another day!

How right Grant was, and "another day" came sooner than anyone expected. NBC told Katz they would not buy the series because they didn't think they could sell the program to enough sponsors. The "too cerebral" excuse was put out to save network face.

Katz said:

"NBC looked on the pilot as the kind of episode you'd have every five or six weeks, but not as the sample episode.

"It wasn't the quality of the program that they objected to, they didn't like the type of story we told.

"I think they selected this type of story to test Desilu on the hardest kind of story to produce because of the reputation Desilu had. Then, when they saw it they were satisfied that Desilu was able to produce quality material, but it was the wrong kind of episode to take around to advertising agencies and sell. It was too off the beaten path. They didn't see it as a typical episode.

"This gets back to a) the Desilu reputation, b) how they selected stories to turn into pilots and c) how programs got sold then.[37]

"So I said, 'Hey, fellas,' and you have to remember I'm

---

[37] Katz was referring to how sponsored television began, repeating the same pattern seen in network radio thirty years before. Early TV advertisers would buy a block of time from the network and then supply a program they purchased through their advertising agency from an independent producer, like Desilu or Bing Crosby Production or Danny Thomas Productions. Network schedules were always tentative when announced: a combination of already purchased time slots—sponsored shows—and those that were being offered by the network. If announced shows did not sell, even at deep discounts on the price, they were taken off the schedule and others substituted.

This system worked as long as the price of producing programs remained low. As costs rose, advertisers were less inclined to spend large amounts of money buying hour or half-hour blocks of time. Soon they were buying every other show, sharing the cost with another sponsor. Finally, as costs, salaries, and the value of advertising time escalated, the system evolved into what we have today, with the networks selling 30-second and one-minute commercial space and the advertisers having no responsibility for the content of the programs.

talking to honorable guys, 'I urged you against this, and you're the guys who picked this.' They said, 'We know, and because of that we're going to give you an order for a second pilot for next season.' "

On Friday, March 26, 1965, NBC made television history by ordering a second pilot.

While that drama was being played out on the two coasts, another little play had been acted out the day before in a Desilu project room. Gene had invited Jeff Hunter, his wife, and a few other people to a screening of the pilot. In his invitation to Hunter dated March 19, written before NBC ordered the second pilot, Gene said:

> Strangely enough, network interest continues and it sometimes seems they're caught in the dilemma of being a little afraid to do something this unusual and equally afraid of letting it drop and get away from them. Good. I like to see executives tormented.

The screening was not successful. As Oscar Katz would later remember, Hunter's wife hated the pilot and, dutiful husband that he was, so did Hunter. Within two weeks, Hunter made his feelings officially known, and Gene, who still hoped to salvage Desilu's large investment, responded in an April 5 letter, keeping the door open.

> I am told you have decided not to go ahead with
> Star Trek. This has to be your own decision, of course,
> and I must respect it.
>   You may be certain I hold no grudge or ill
> feelings and expect to continue to reflect publicly and
> privately the high regard I learned for you during the
> production of our pilot.
>   I do have one request. As you learned from your
> own experience during production, I stinted nothing
> in time or money to do the best for you and the show.
> You will recall I mentioned to you during shooting
> that I felt there were things more important to both
> of us than budget. One result of this is we have an
> enormous investment in a project which can now be
> recouped in only one of two ways: (1) expansion
> of current footage via stock and long cutting into

an "acceptable" motion picture, or (2) one day or two of shooting an additional action opening which can result in a fast, tightly cut, exciting film release. Again, the second choice seems best for all reputations involved. Certainly, assuming the extra production can be arranged, it would be best for the people who have invested considerable money on our expression of intentions.

This is a personal note; I am not sending copies to agencies or Desilu offices. I don't even know if the expense of an extra scene will make sense to the business people involved. But should the subject of reasonable additional filming come up, I am hoping you can cooperate within reasonable limits, in the interests of protecting both an investment made in good faith, and performances. As the intermediate cut runs now, I would much like to trim the scenes into something taut and exciting rather than be forced by motion picture running time requirements to extend them into something none of us would consider our best.

I don't know what the various legal rights and situations are in this, nor do I really care. I'm sure we share one identical belief—that the first and most important interest is always professional pride and obligation.

Best of luck in your plans for the future.

Sincerely,
Gene

Gene wasted no time in laying the groundwork for a successful second effort. Almost immediately, he directed his production assistant, Morris Chapnick, to assemble critical comments from the production office, crew, and various Desilu departments. The report was quickly completed and delivered. It is dated April 6, 1965. It was not intended as a criticism of any individuals or Desilu departments and itself states that more than a fair share of the comments are concerned with the functions of the production staff. Everyone solicited for a comment was asked to speak freely and all comments were anonymous.

The critiques ranged from the sound department—"Due to the slope of Stages 15 and 16, platforms had to be built up to give us level sets. Unfortunately, the platforms and sets were not floored with an insulator nor did we have a double-layered floor construction, and every movement of men and machinery, no matter how slight, was picked up by sound. We might consider a form of carpeting on key set, perhaps a metallic-colored rug"—to seemingly small details such as steps—"Instead of the present two widely separated stairways leading down into the Command Module, there should be four. This would eliminate having the actor cross half the set before he can step down into the Module." This went on for thirteen pages and helped smooth the way for the production of what was then known as "Star Trek No. 2."

The day after the report was delivered, Gene sent a memo to Bob Justman.

Here is the situation on *Star Trek*—we plan to begin photography July 5.[38] Therefore, in order to bring you in with plenty of time for preparation, would like you to plan tentatively to report on June 7. That's a week more than planned in the budget and if we add some post-production time to it, it could create difficulties. However, these could be resolved by your working as associate producer overall plus first Assistant Director during actual filming. In other words, taking the budget allowance for both and applying it to your overall cost. Does this create any problems?

At any rate, we should get together again soon and discuss all this, plus get an idea of salary and other terms for me to present to the business people here. Also, as quickly as I get some basic stories into work for myself and the other two writers, would much appreciate getting your comments on dangerous production and cost areas.

The second pilot would be a different type of story, one both Desilu and NBC management felt was more apt to sell the series. NBC would be given a choice. Gene wrote outlines for two stories, "The Omega Glory" and "Mudd's Women," writing the script for the first and passing the sec-

---

[38] Later moved back ten days.

ond on to Stephen Kandel. For the third story and script, Gene called on his old friend Sam Peeples. Peeples was currently receiving more money to write scripts than the *Star Trek* budget could afford, but this was an opportunity to write adult science fiction, a genre Peeples loved, and for a good friend whose program format he had helped develop. He took a cut in pay.[39]

Peeples remembers sitting down with Gene in his office and kicking around a number of story ideas, one of which was entitled "Where No Man Has Gone Before." Gene liked both the title and the brief story idea and told Peeples to go ahead with it.

On June 10, Gene received a memo from Herb Solow detailing Solow's conversation with NBC executives that morning. Stephen Kandel had been sick, delaying his completion of "Mudd's Women." Solow had made a decision that avoided further delay and submitted only the Peeples and Roddenberry scripts for NBC's consideration.

Solow explained that it was his opinion, based on his reading of Kandel's first draft, that as a pilot episode "Mudd's Women" was "a little too light and frothy and would not be a good example of the overall series."

NBC preferred Gene's script, but from "the point of view of doing a more straight-line adventure show, they felt that the Peeples script as a finished film would better compliment the first pilot and would also show the different ranges in which the series can go. As you know, this was also our feeling."

Solow finished by telling Gene that NBC was aware that Gene would be polishing the script and altering the story to get the characters on the planet surface earlier. He closed by saying that Gene should "get into preparing Sam Peeples' script just as soon as you've had a chance to rewrite it."

Gene responded the next day.

As I have said before, no sensitivity here at all over which script they choose and this office is now proceed-

---

[39] At that stage in his career, Peeples was getting a minimum of $7,500 per script, often with bonuses that kicked the price up to $12,000. He wrote the second pilot for $5,000 and feels he was fairly treated.

ing full speed into casting and preparation. And with enthusiasm. Our aim is to make an episode which will sell *Star Trek*.

Among our first steps will be the preparation of a *production revision* of the current script. By this we mean a quick rewrite aimed to bring photographic effects, special effects, sets, and shooting time into something that approaches practicality from a production point of view.

While there will be some dramatic revisions too, we feel it necessary to get the production revisions into mimeo[40] as soon as possible.

Hopefully, we will have that in mimeograph very early this week next.

With the subsequent success of the Peeples's script, there later arose one of the most vicious and persistent rumors in *Star Trek* mythology: the allegation that Gene stole *Star Trek* from Sam Peeples. Sam has a simple reaction to this:

"Since Gene died, I've had calls from people in Hollywood who have said, 'Well you know that bastard Gene, you know what he did to you,' and my reaction has always been to say, 'Hey back off, this is a close friend to me and he didn't do anything to me and if he did it was unintentional, and if I did anything to him it was also unintentional. The man is gone, he can't stand up for himself and I'm sure as hell not going to be a part of anybody who is going to take a slam at him.' "

There was no legal action of any kind brought by Sam Peeples with regard to *Star Trek* and today he is happy and proud to say that Gene was his friend and he Gene's. Peeples is also quick to say that *Star Trek* was Gene's creation and that he was brought in to write a script based on Gene's format, created years before.

There is no question that Sam Peeples contributed to the creation of *Star Trek*, as he was an expert on science fiction and, more importantly, was a friend whose opinion Gene valued. The two often had heated discussions over the definitions and limitations of hard science fiction as opposed to

---

[40] This was in the days before Xerography. Multiple copies, beyond those that could be made by carbon paper, were made by cutting a stencil and making multiple copies by the mimeographic process.

fantasy, but these discussions were on the same level as the arguments Gene had with Chief Parker—vigorous intellectual battles, never anything personal.

Peeples remembered a book that was instrumental in the development of the *Star Trek* format: *Last and First Men* by Olaf Stapledon. First published in 1930, it was difficult to find. Peeples remembers how Gene got a copy:

"I had been working at 20th Century Fox on a theatrical feature. That was in October of '63 and it seemed to me it was around that time or possibly a little after when he came to look at the magazines. I knew about the project [*Star Trek*] sometime before because Dorothy Fontana had called and asked me if I had a copy of *Last and First Men*. I said I did. I was a little reluctant to loan it out because it's not a very easily accessible book. Gene called me and asked if he could borrow it and I said yes. As I remember it, I sent a cover letter pointing out the idea of future history, as in *Last and First Men*, was a standard in Science Fiction. Robert Heinlein for example, had his future history. I knew both of these men very well, so I'm speaking of friends. I don't think any of them including Gene Roddenberry were indebted to old Stapledon, although probably the very basic idea came from his *Last and First Men*. That's future history, not the details."

Sam Peeples also happily worked with Gene in the early 1970's, writing the pilot episode of the animated *Star Trek* series, and again, later in the 1970's, when he collaborated with Gene on *The Tribunes*, a pilot that did not sell, and *Spectre*, a fantasy story filmed in England and shown as a "movie of the week."

Without a star, Gene had to find a new group of actors for his second pilot. The search for the captain began all over again. Additionally, NBC had raised objections to the "Number One" character, so she was eliminated, but many of her traits were transferred to Mr. Spock, still played by Leonard Nimoy, the only actor held over from the original pilot. NBC objected to his character, too, but Gene, backed by Oscar Katz, held firm, and both Spock and his ears stayed.

Which is not to say that Leonard Nimoy was at all thrilled with the prospect of appearing on television with pointed ears. Gene made him a promise that if he really hated the ears they would, in a few episodes, work out some way to "bob" them.[41] Nimoy was a serious actor, dedicated to his craft, as shown in his 1977 autobiography, *I Am Not Spock:*

> For many years, Hollywood publicity men sold the public on the idea that stars are found at bus stops and soda fountains. It was very good publicity. It led every young male and female to fantasize about the possibility of being "discovered." That was good for the box office. But it made a mockery of acting as an art.
>
> Tracy and Cagney were able to give very simple answers to the "how do you do it" question. That simplicity was beautifully visible in their work. Behind the simplicity were years of effort, study, trial and failure until all the rubbish that most actors start with was stripped away and only the clarity of finely polished work remained.
>
> Of course, there's "luck" involved in any career. Many very fine and well prepared actors never get the opportunity to achieve wide recognition. It usually comes when the proper role in the proper vehicle finds the right performer.

It seemed that Nimoy found the proper role in the proper vehicle, however reluctantly he came to accept it. Perhaps more than any other actor on *Star Trek,* Nimoy would be firmly joined at the hip to his Vulcan alter ego for the rest of his life.

The most important role, that of the new *Enterprise* captain, James T. Kirk, was given to Canadian-born actor William Shatner. Shatner had status with the studio and network heads, and for good reason. His acting credits prior to *Star Trek* were very impressive. Shatner was part of a group of actors who had worked solid stage roles, films, and prestigious, dramatic television. His first film in 1958 was the role of Alexi in *The Brothers Karamazov.* His television credits included *Playhouse 90, Armstrong Circle Theater, Goodyear Playhouse,* as well as a number of guest staring appearances on television's better dramatic programs, including *The Twi-*

---

[41] NBC didn't wait for that and issued at least one publicity still with Spock's ears and eyebrows airbrushed to "normal."

light Zone.[42] While he did not have widespread public recognition that could be converted into an instant audience for the show, he had the next best thing: recognition by the studio brass. Getting Shatner to star would be a coup for *Star Trek*. Coincidentally, Shatner's series, *For The People* had just run its only thirteen-week cycle. Though highly acclaimed, the show had not been picked up and he was available. Joe D'Agosta remembers that "Shatner had the same thrust going for him that Clint Eastwood and Steve McQueen did."[43] Shatner also had one other advantage: he was represented by the Ashley Famous Agency, the same agency that represented Desilu and Gene.

Shatner's agency used his cache to maximum advantage, working out a healthy salary and one side benefit that would ultimately pay handsomely: the first year's deal got Shatner $5,000 a week plus twenty percent of his original salary on each of the subsequent five reruns plus the bonus; twenty percent of the net profits should the series ever go into net.[44] Should the series be successful and continue, Shatner would receive yearly increases of $500 a show.

The other actors hired were lesser known, didn't have Shatner's reputation, and consequently were paid as little as the studio could get away with. A production memo dated May 31, 1966, shows the disparity of compensation.

Leonard Nimoy, the supporting actor who was far from being a household word, but who would quickly become a national sensation, was paid $1,250 a week. His reruns were SAG (Screen Actors Guild) scale plus ten percent. DeForest Kelley was paid $850 a program and his reruns totaled fifty percent of his initial payment. Grace Lee Whitney got $750

---

[42] Ironically Shatner played the passenger in *The Twilight Zone* episode, "Nightmare at 20,000 Feet." The pilot of the plane was Ed Kemmer, the actor who played Commander Corry on *Space Patrol*.

[43] D'Agosta was also of the opinion that unlike *Wanted: Dead or Alive* and *Rawhide,* which boosted McQueen and Eastwood's careers respectively, *Star Trek* stopped Shatner's career. McQueen and Eastwood were just remembered as being good, while Shatner became permanently identified with his character.

[44] The full division of the net was to be 26⅔ percent each to NBC, Desilu, and Norway Corporation (Gene's personal services corporation), and the remaining 20 percent to Shatner. Of course, as the joke goes, The Eleventh Commandment in Hollywood is "There Shall Be No Net." Shatner's 1968 divorce from his wife, Gloria, ultimately cut that extra bonus in half, but when it turned a profit years later, it was still worth a considerable amount of money.

a program and SAG scale on reruns. George Takei got $600 per program and SAG scale, and James Doohan made $850 a program plus SAG scale plus one-ninth percent for reruns. Nichelle Nichols made between $600 to $800 per program.

As any producer, Gene was cost-conscious, watching every penny, trying to stretch his resources as far as they would go. On July 6, he sent a short note to Alexander Courage, who was producing the music.

> Enclosed is a script of our new *Star Trek* venture, "Where No Man Has Gone Before."
>
> There has never been any question in my mind that you are the man to do this one too—and I have hopes this episode will put us over the top and into a long association together.
>
> As you probably know by now, one of the primary things we must prove in this episode is that we can bring *Star Trek* in on budget. As a result, budget and cost is very important to us on this one. My hope is that we can use at least fifty percent of the music from the previous show and devise the rest with an eye to doing the best possible job at the least in men and time. Because this is so important, it is probably wise that you have this script well in advance so that you can begin to do some thinking on it.

With delays of various sorts the second pilot, "Where No Man Has Gone Before" did not begin production until Thursday, July 15, 1965. Gene was producer, James Goldstone, director, Robert Justman, assistant director, and James Paisley, production manager. Actual filming began on the following Monday the nineteenth at Desilu's Culver City facility on stage 15 with interior scenes of the ship's briefing room, corridors, and transporter room being shot. The second pilot, using sets already constructed, cost just under $300,000.

Star Trek was not the only project occupying Gene at that time. *Assignment 100,* with a title change to *Police Story,* was shot in August. The pilot was directed by Vincent McEveety, who would later direct six episodes of *Star Trek.* DeForest Kelley, Grace Lee Whitney, and Malachi Throne as the chief of police were used in the ultimately unsuccessful pilot about a modern police department. While the pilot was unsuccessful it did not come from a half-hearted attempt by Gene. He had put a great deal of time and energy into that pilot as well, pulling a few strings to expose Throne to a real chief of police in the hope that would give the show a solid air of reality. On the twelfth of August Gene wrote a letter to Chief Parker thanking him for his help. As usual, to a friend, Gene exposed part of the thought process he used in writing.

> As I indicated to you in our telephone conversation the other day, we had no intention of portraying "William H. Parker" in this role, but I am anxious that his office reflects the multiple burdens and tasks of a real Chief of Police and that his portrayal reflect a man with the kind of emotional and intellectual strength which you typify. Incidentally, I'm told that today marks your fourteenth year in office. I'm sure you remember much better than I do the news articles which gave you six months at most. Am unsure whether to offer congratulation or condolences since, having for a while worked close to you, have some understanding of how grueling it has been.
>
> About the police show, hope to discuss it with you someday at your convenience. Although we differ in philosophy on some matters, as you know, we are closer together on others than you may suspect. And either way, I like to think of myself as a thoroughly professional writer whose many characters can reflect many ideas and whose manuscripts are not a medium of personal propaganda but rather examinations of many things from many points of view.

As if the pilot of *Police Story* and *Star Trek* weren't enough to keep Gene occupied, he had promised his good friend Sam Rolfe, the creator and producer of *Have Gun Will Travel,* that he would produce the pilot of Rolfe's latest creation, *The Long Hunt of April Savage.* That meant two weeks of location shooting in the mountains around Big Bear in the Angeles National Forest ninety miles outside of Los Angeles.

With all of that going on, Gene managed to take time to do a favor for Leonard Nimoy. The two men had discussed

Nimoy's ambitions to move into directing and producing. To further that goal, Gene sent a letter to his old friend at MGM, Norman Felton, producer of *The Man from U.N.C.L.E.*

> Dear Norman:
>   Leonard Nimoy, I believe you know him and have indicated some respect for his ability and potential, has very serious aspirations about moving from acting into directing and producing at some later time. He has great regard for you and for the fact you and David Victor have so often taken an interest in young people with potential and ambition. And so, while asking me for permission (granted) to audit[45] one of our shows, he also asked would I send this letter of recommendation to you on his behalf.
>   Please, feel under no obligation to me personally on this. I know, like and respect Nimoy but I'm referring him to you strictly on a professional basis as someone who shows indications of more than average talent in the direction indicated.

A similar letter was sent to David Victor, another producer friend on *U.N.C.L.E.*, who responded with a short, pleasant note saying that he would be delighted to have Leonard Nimoy audit one of their *U.N.C.L.E.* shows. Victor added, "I hope someday he will be a very successful director."

In October, Gene commented on the NBC publicity presentation of the first *Star Trek* pilot.

> One of the things we found on all our *Star Trek* scripts so far is we tend to get a bit complex and science-fictionish. Certainly, I was guilty of that on my series description. And in the first pilot we have had to leave a lot of science fiction gobbledegook on the cutting room floor to keep it a story of people and not of theorems and gadgets.
>   I've made a few pencil line changes in your NBC pres-

---

[45] Essentially, an unpaid apprentice who watches and asks questions but does not participate.

entation along those lines—probably you will find more yourself. Just suggestions, born of our own experience, and I hope they are helpful.

Otherwise it looks exciting and helpful. Good luck.

Best regards,

GR

In early December, Gene finished the lyrics to the *Star Trek* theme and sent them to Ed Perlstein. The lyrics would be a small source of income, but it cut the royalty in half for the writer of the music, Alexander Courage, and engendered some bitterness on his part. Two and a half years later, on October 3, 1967, Gene wrote to Courage in an attempt to straighten things out:

Dear Sandy:

After the telephone conversation with you, I sat down and spent some time going over old notes and jogging my memory regarding our conversation so long ago regarding *Star Trek* music. Perhaps this will help refresh your memory—in my old office, the small bungalow across the lot, you and I sat down one afternoon and discussed sharing the credits on the music. I recall very distinctly that you shook your head and stated you would naturally prefer not to split the money on the theme but, on the other hand, since this was the way it was and since we were working so closely together on the concept you would go along with it. You may recall that shortly afterwards I assigned you to do the theme on *Police Story,* unfortunately not sold, and did not ask for a similar arrangement since I had no strong notions about that music and did not expect to work as closely with you on it.

I think you know it has never been my way or policy to be unfair. On the other hand, I have always considered handshake agreements not only to be as binding as written agreements but also more important. I am certain you feel the same way and intend no effort to violate such agreement.

I am sending the enclosed to you in all hopes that a reference to your old notes on the subject will recall to your mind that conversation.

Sincerely yours,

The second pilot was sent to NBC, who saw that it delivered the promise of the action-adventure story Gene and Desilu had promised. By February 1966, NBC informed Desilu that they were buying the show. NBC thought they could sell it to advertisers and penciled it into their fall schedule.

CHAPTER 9

Gene now had roughly six months to put together a production team and produce a continuous product, one a week, at the level of quality he had delivered in the pilot. It was an impossible task.

He did not like to fly blind in picking his production staff, preferring to work with known quantities, and so he set about gathering intelligence. As a writer himself, Gene knew that any good program began with good writing. Without the solid foundation of a good story and good dialog, the best production team in the world could not make up for all the deficiencies.

Morris Chapnick, Gene's Production Assistant, spoke privately with a number of producers, story editors, and associate producers around town, getting their opinion of writers. A partial list and the general comments follows:

Robert Culp	Excellent writer who says something
Peter A. Fields[1]	Excellent—A comer
Dean Hargrove	Excellent—A comer
Ken Kolb	Excellent
Alvin Sapinsley	Excellent—a poet

and on for several pages.

Gene contacted a friend who gave him the following opinion:

---

[1] Wrote the *Next Generation* script "Half A Life" and now writes for *Deep Space 9*.

Robert Sheckley—very good.

Ray Russell—former Playboy editor, currently at Warner Brothers. Talk to him regarding science fiction writers.

Harlan Ellison—odd but talented

Pohl [sic] ("Poul") Anderson—very prolific

George Clayton Johnson—recently did a *Mr. Novak,* lives in Pacoima.

Robert A. Heinlein, Isaac Asimov, Richard Matheson, and Arthur Clark (sic) were also listed with no comments after their names.

By March 15, Gene had written another Writer-Director Information Guide to send out to people he wanted as writers for his series. He moved forward with his plans to use noted science fiction writers for his stories but was concerned over possible repercussion. On March 22, 1966, he wrote to Bernie Weitzman in Business Affairs.

Dear Bernie,

Brought this up at the *Star Trek* production meeting the other day and wanted to again here emphasize my definite feeling we should review and analyze our plagiarism insurance setup.

The point being, I have been warned by a number of science fiction writer friends that the whole SF field of writers is "up in arms" against what they view as being a wide-spread theft of their SF stories and situations by TV and motion pictures. Some are really quite emotional about this. And I think we must accept the fact that science fiction is a rather unique field in which certain themes and situations occur and reoccur constantly—for example, my own "man in a menagerie" situation of Star Trek #1 [first pilot "The Cage"] has undoubtedly been done a dozen times in science fiction. It is a rather strange thing that similar situations from one Western to another never seems to offend anyone, while even basic non-copyrightable situations in SF do create trouble.

Obviously we intend to purchase SF originals wherever they are usable and ride herd on our writers in this area as much as we can, but we could still *under the very best of circumstances and control* end up facing more than an average number of law suits. Again, let me emphasize, sf is a very strange breed of cat and may turn out to be quite different than our insurance and legal experience in other types of series.

Gene Roddenberry

By March 22, Gene had assigned the following writers:

John D.F. Black	Richard Matheson
Robert Bloch	Jerry Sohl
Oliver Crawford	Adrian Spies
Harlan Ellison	Barry Trivers
Lee Erwin	A.E. Van Vogt
George Clayton Johnson	Shimon Wincelberg
Norman Katkov	

The most famous science fiction writer in that group was Van Vogt, one of the original writers who helped create the Golden Age of Science Fiction that began in the John W. Campbell-edited magazine, *Astounding Science Fiction,* in 1939. Van Vogt was a master of intricate and metaphysical space opera and was one of the several noted SF writers unable to adapt to the medium of television. His involved plot ideas, which could carry a reader to vast and unexplored realms of the imagination, simply could not be translated to the small screen and hammered into television's narrow budget and time requirements.

While the writers worked on their individual story ideas, Gene had thoughts for other aspects of *Star Trek,* one of which he explained in an April 14, 1966, memo to Bob Justman regarding the captain's yeoman.

While trying to work out additional duties for the Captain's Yeoman, fill out her role a bit, plus give her actual things to do which make believable being a part of some landing parties where we need her, it has been suggested that she carry as a part of her regular equipment (and she's got some pretty good equipment already), some sort of neat, over-the-shoulder recorder-electronic camera via which she can take log entries from the Captain at any time, make electronic moving photo records of things, places, etc. Haven't given much creative thought to what this would look like, but it seems like it could be also a potential toy item for female-type children.

On April 20, 1966, Gene sent a long, detailed memo to "all concerned" finalizing the running characters. It added and supplemented his earlier Writer-Director Information Guide of March 15, 1966. In the memo, Gene had solved the problem of the yeoman's device, describing it as "a small over-the-shoulder case, a 'Tricorder,' about the size of a small handbag, which is an electronic recorder-photographer, an instrument of the future whereby wherever the Captain is, he can make log reports or records of any kind or type, which later are fed into the ship's computer system as a part of the Captain's regular log." Gene also changed his mind, dropping the term "transicator" for the simpler term "communicator" to describe the handheld device used to talk from person to person or ground to ship.

Even though the earlier guides and memos seemed detailed and inclusive, Gene realized that he had not covered enough ground in his Writer-Director Information Guide. On May 2, 1966, he sent out a number of supplementary pages with the note, "After a number of weeks of story outlines and early script drafts, it became obvious there are some important questions we failed to answer." First among those questions was "What was the *Star Trek* script format?" which the supplement explained thusly:

a. Teaser, preferably three pages or less. Captain Kirk's Voice Over opens the show, briefly setting where we are and what's going on. This is usually followed by a short playing scene which ends with the Teaser "hook."

b. Main Title

c. Four Acts. Captain Kirk's Voice Over, while not mandatory for act openings, is recommended. Not only does it give *Star Trek* a "trade mark," but also helps us get past exposition *fast* and into dramatic action. *Note:* Our most important act break, the one which outline *must* indicate, is at the half hour mark ending Act II. It appears our critical competition will come at that point and a suspense "hook" is definitely needed here. Captain Kirk's Voice Over can also be useful within acts where it speeds and helps to bridge a considerable change in time or situation.

d. Epilogue. Optional. If used, it should be kept short, not more than a page or two.

Several more questions were asked and answered. The text then continued:

In your early stories and outlines, have any general areas of problem shown up?

a. *Unbelievability in characters or motivations.* Somehow, in the process of putting characters into the future, some writers tend to leave credulity behind. Science fiction is no different from tales of the present or past—*our Starship central characters and crew must be at least as believably motivated and as identifiable to the audience as characters we've all written into police station, general hospitals, and Western towns.*

b. *Illogical situations.* For example, it is swallowing quite a bit to believe a present day naval cruiser would be full of renegades and mutineers. Or that a present day U.S.N. Captain would imperil his vessel and crew over a philosophical disagreement with some foreign country. We want the exotic, the inexplicable, the terrifying—but *not* in the U.S.S. Enterprise, its organization and mission. *The ship and characters are our audience's tie to reality.*

c. *Intellectual rather than physical or emotional conflict.* It's hard to get a good story out of philosophical conflicts. We've had some interesting analyses of possible alien civilizations, socio-economic speculation which seemed brilliant to us. But the characters were "sitting and talking" rather than "feeling, moving and doing." They fail what we call our "Gunsmoke-Kildare-Naked City Rule"—would the *basic story,* stripped of science fiction aspects, make a good episode for one of those shows? Don't laugh. Try it.

Do the science fiction pro's have any helpful hints for us?

Two: Beware getting too wrapped up in The Wonder of It All, keep the story tied to people, their needs, fears and conflicts; remain a story-teller at all times—the quality of an SF tale is always inversely proportional to the pretensions a writer brings to it.

And finally:

Then must the Starship crew be perfect humans?

No, you can project *too* optimistically. We want characters with any believable mixture of strength, weaknesses, and foibles. Credulity is the key here. What kind of men would logically and believably man a vessel of this type? Obviously, they'd be better selected and trained than the wild enlisted short leave group in *Mister Roberts*. On the other hand, we hope they're not too stuffy to enjoy themselves on liberty in an exotic alien city filled with unique pleasure. (Possibly not a bad story there.)

On the same day the supplement went out, Gene sent along his character analysis of Mr. Spock. It is interesting to note Spock's level of development at this early date.

Mr. Spock is the ship's Science Officer, in charge of all scientific departments and personnel aboard the U.S.S. *Enterprise.* As such, he is the ship's Number Two ranking officer.

There follows a detailed description of his duties and workstation and then his background:

Mr. Spock's mother was human, his father a native of another planet—unnamed as yet.[2] This alien-human combination results in Mr. Spock's slightly alien features with the yellowish complexion and satanic pointed ears. Thus he is biologically, emotionally, and even intellectually a "half-breed."

We do know a few things about Mr. Spock's planet and will develop others as the series continues. For example, the somewhat larger and more cupped ears come from the physical fact that the atmosphere on his home planet is somewhat thinner than on Earth—lighter sound waves and thus more hearing sensitivity required. Because of this, all his sensory organs are slightly better developed than ours. And since his home planet is also dryer and hotter than Earth, Spock can withstand greater temperatures, go longer without water.

---

[2] This is a bit misleading given the date on the memo and the fact that another set of correspondence, beginning with a Bob Justman memo dated May 3, 1966, makes an extensive discussion of names from Spock's home planet, Vulcan.

Playing in contrast to his satanic physiognomy, Mr. Spock is a devout vegetarian. The idea of eating animal carcasses, cooked or not, is revolting to him. Even his vegetable diet is restricted, limited to the simplest of vegetable life forms.

Hypnotism is an everyday tool on Spock's home planet, deriving from the intellectual intensity of the culture there. It forms a part of their economic, social, and sex life. He has this capacity—and when we play it, we stay accurate, never get into hypnotism-fantasy. But he uses this ability rarely since this is one of the many compromises Spock has had to make in the past in order to rise to his present position and live with humans.

More about Spock's home planet—the background of the culture there is *stoic,* possibly something akin to the direction which was being taken at one time by our own Greek civilization. But over the centuries Spock's planet developed it even further—repressing emotion further and further until emotion became a thing evil, even sordid, and finally reaching the point where no one would admit to emotion and indeed even took great pride in the fact that they had no feelings at all. This probably led to a need for hypnosis as a part of the sex act, and we may gather from time to time that love on Spock's planet has a somewhat more violent quality than Earth's aesthetics permit mankind to enjoy. (Unless NBC changes its policies somewhat, we probably will not do a script directly dealing with this subject.)

However, the above does bear on our series since even Spock's "hypnotic" look strongly affects Earth females and he goes to great pains to avoid too much contact with them. There is a back-story on this—many years ago when Mr. Spock first joined the service, he was careless on this score, perhaps even enjoyed this strange ability over Earth women. But it quickly created both personal and professional troubles. His own "love" action and reaction goes far beyond what men would accept and the effects on Earth females lasted far too long for comfort. Thus celibacy became one of the many compromises he would have to make to stay in service.

Mr. Spock's mixed blood led to his science and starship career. On his home planet he was half-Earthman, on Earth he was half-alien—uncomfortable in either place.

While Spock's planet and Earth generally respect each other, the strong emotional differences limited closeness and intermixing. Science was a legitimate occupational choice, Science Officer on a vessel even better. He could make some sort of life for himself in the artificial society of a semi-military organization.

Even at this early point in character development, Gene defined the relationship between Kirk and Spock, laying down certain parameters and limitations.

There is a kind of friendship between Kirk and Spock, although our Science Officer would be quick to deny an "affection." He rationalizes that his interest is solely the fact that Captain Kirk is an unusually good commander and the odds are against getting a better replacement. Actually, we will understand that Spock does "feel" but, conditioned since a child to deny it, he thrusts it aside and finds a "logical" rationalization for any emotional feelings that bother him.

He also defined the relationship between Spock and Dr. McCoy that played out so successfully over the years.

There is something of dislike between Dr. "Bones" McCoy and Mr. Spock. The Doctor, like most cynics, is at heart a bleeding humanist. And so Spock regards McCoy as an archaic, bumbling, country doctor, usually achieving cures through luck. On the other hand, McCoy regards Spock as little more than a sometimes useful piece of computer equipment. But, while disagreeing constantly, they do work well together when it becomes necessary and we're never sure but what there could be some affection hidden behind the dislike for each other.

One aspect of the character that was never carried forward followed:

About the only person on the ship who can joke with Mr. Spock at all is the Captain's Yeoman, Janice Rand. Perhaps beneath her swinging exterior is a motherly instinct for lonely men—at any rate, Yeoman Janice can mention things few others would dare to say to Spock's face. And in return, guessing logically at some of *her* secrets, Spock will give (if you'll excuse the expression) tat for tit. But if the conversation has him looking at her too intently or too long, she will feel the hypnotic quality and beg off—and Spock will look away. They have an unspoken agreement that the joke will only be carried so far."[3]

The memo concludes with further definitions of Spock's personality.

Spock's weakness is an intellectual's superiority complex. He finds it hard to hide his look of smugness when others decide questions on the basis of anything less than cold logic. Perhaps Spock's torment over his "half-breed" background and his "half-life" necessitates a need to feel superior about at least something. There is a loneliness in all this, akin to the Captain's loneliness of command but without its concurrent advantages.

Spock's strength is his courage and his absolute loyalty to Captain Kirk, the starship, and its crew. There is never any question but that he will at any moment, logic not withstanding, give his life to accomplish any mission.

In none of the early guides and supplements is the name of Mr. Spock's planet mentioned. It appears on a memo from Bob Justman to Gene Roddenberry dated the day after the date on the character analysis. Justman remembers that the name "Vulcan" was Gene's and that they had been using it for some weeks before his memo of May 3. Justman explained that the additional pages for the Writer-Director Guide and supplementary character information was cobbled together from notes and previous material that may have been several weeks old.

The development of the Spock character and his background, once thought unnecessary by Gene, illustrates the unique form of "creation by committee" that exists in television production. The process that Gene would use in the formation of the details of *Star Trek* was to pass everything through one filter, himself, deciding whether to include or

---

[3]None of this made it into any scripts, as the Yeoman Rand character was written out of the series.

exclude the idea. One writer commented that Gene had spent so much time in the twenty-third and twenty-fourth century that he would argue with you about the merits of an idea as if he had been there.

Gene had developed his sense of "future logic" to a fine degree. As he would later say, "Who says it's *Star Trek*? I DO!" And he did, which is how he got the committee process to work.

Gene read and commented on every outline and script. On May 19, 1966, he sent a memo on the first draft of the episode that became "Miri."[4]

A good first draft, one of the best we've received. With the potential of being a most unusual and exciting episode. But, as normal in first scripts of a new series, lots of minor points to be corrected, some pulling and tugging necessary to bring the story and characters into line with where we are going.

The new planet should be much more than 4,000,000 miles from Earth ... probably more like "hundreds of light years away."

Page 5, McCoy's guess of a "global epidemic" is hard to believe.

Selection of landing party should be routine, give us the impression of a highly trained, disciplined group who has been through this many times. Having Kirk explain why he is taking our Principals down only calls this more than ever to the audience's attention.

Dialogue. Gets a little "1966" at times. For example, Rankin's Page 2 line using the word "kookie." In several other places with various people through the script.

Also re: "1966" dialogue, we might carefully examine the lines of the kids. Understand Adrian is aiming for a child-talk and he handles it very well, but it does stray often into highly contemporary terminology, which hurts believability in that even though the planet is like Earth, it is hard to believe the colloquial expressions would be *exactly* our own contemporary time period. Just a caution ... please examine carefully.

Yeoman Rand-Captain Kirk Relationship. Suggest we

4"Miri," written by Adrian Spies and directed by Vince McEveety, was aired on October 27, 1966.

have Adrian review the mimeographed information on Janice Rand. She comes off much too "chummy" with the Captain. We've decided our direction should be completely opposite, i.e., she plays it highly professional with him and he plays it pretty cool in return.

If they are to find a rapport in the story, it should come only when it can be well motivated by considerable tension and crisis . . . and even then it should be only a temporary rapport with both of them realizing they must fall back into their original professional relationship.

Gene's comments, observations, and analysis continues for five more single-spaced, typed pages.

Gene wove some of his own early history into *Star Trek*. As previously mentioned, part of Mr. Spock's personality grew out of Chief William H. Parker's taciturn personality (albeit transferred over from the first pilot character, Number One). But there was more.

"Scotty" came from a crewmate on his B-17, Harry Scotidas, as well as from the seafaring tradition of Scots as engineers.

In the original series episode "The Return of the Archons," the name "Archons" came from a service club that Gene had belonged to at Los Angeles City College. In his collection of photographs and memorabilia is a small award presented to him for school service by the Archons, the Men's Honorary Service Society, April 1, 1940.

Gene also found himself a handy source for last minute needs. In the episode "Charlie X," the lyrics to the song sung by Uhura in the rec room were written by Gene.

In that same episode, about twenty minutes into the story, Captain Kirk receives a call from the ship's galley on the intercom. The voice, presumably that of the ship's cook, says somewhat excitedly, "Sir, I put meatloaf in the ovens. There's turkeys in there now, real turkeys!" The voice is clearly identifiable as Gene's pleasant tenor. When Richard Arnold, then the *Star Trek* Archivist at Paramount, approached Gene about his discovery, he was greeted with an enigmatic smile and his acknowledgement that this was his "little bit of Hitchcock."[5]

---

[5]Gene also did a hidden voice-over in the TV movie *Spectre*.

* * *

As a producer, Gene received hundreds of pieces of mail, many from agencies soliciting work for their actors. As a sign of the times, a few of the agencies submitted lists of actors with the designation "negro" in parenthesis next to a few names. None of the other actors were designated "white," but not all agencies represented black actors, either.

On a less serious side, Gene had to concern himself with the most trivial of details and a memo from late May 1966, indicates the depth of detail a producer must be willing to go to be successful.

> Per conversations with most concerned, the problems of too modern hairstyles on male actors in *Star Trek,* regulars as well as both SAG and SEG, has been resolved. Rather than requesting altering of the basic contour favored by the actor, a simple and easily adjustable change is being made in the sideburns, i.e. pointing the bottom of them rather than wearing them square across.
>
> For those doing single jobs on our show, it is easily adjustable via hair growth in a few days, or touching with a makeup pencil. In the case of far background extras, it may be necessary only to point the sideburns with makeup pencil actual shaving unnecessary. Where possible, however, even on such extras, we would prefer the proper job.
>
> This is mandatory for *all* actors appearing in our show.[6]

---

[6]This would not be the last time Gene would be concerned with hair. On February 5, 1968, he received the following memo from Justman:
Gene:

If you haven't already heard about it, we are missing some wigs and hair pieces.

Bill Shatner borrowed all four of his hair pieces when we finished shooting. There are two new ones and two old ones. The new ones are worth approximately $200 apiece and the two old ones are worth approximately $100 apiece. Should "Star Trek" go again next season, this no doubt means that we will have to construct new hair pieces again for Bill because he will have used both the old ones and the new ones to such an extent that they will not be photographable. This I guarantee, since it has happened to us before.

Majel Barrett's wig has disappeared. Nobody, including Majel, knows what has happened to it.

Nichelle Nichols' wig has disappeared. She borrowed it when she finished

In addition to actors and their haircuts, Gene had to ride hard on writers. Stories were being approved and were being turned into teleplays, but the science fiction format of *Star Trek* was something that was frustrating a number of highly regarded writers. In mid-1966, Gene wrote to an agent friend who represented a writer with whom Gene was not happy.

We like what we have here from this writer, but frankly he is dogging it. I've been at the game of being a writer myself too long not to know the symptoms of one who is trying to con the producer into doing his thinking for him. Usually it comes out of having too many assignments all at one time, understandable to some extent because of the pressure the Writers Guild strike is putting on everyone. But time and time again in our initial conference the writer kept hinting broadly that since "science fiction is so impossibly foreign to him" that perhaps it would be better if we paid him his *full* fee for a generalized first draft and we should do most of the revisions and polish in this office. Naturally we refused.

Now, we have here his revised draft. Understand, despite his earlier attitude, he has worked hard and given us a revised script. Fine, up to that point. But he has not done his homework, he has not read and digested the information sheets we have sent him, he has obviously not studied the other script we sent him for a sample so that he could properly use our sets, our people, our various characterizations, etc.

Here's where I need your help. We are asking of the writer no more than any other new show asks or must have, i.e. study what is available on the lead characters, his attitudes and methods, the secondary characters, the inter-relations, and those basic things you would have whether this was the beginning of a Western, hospital drama, or cops and robbers. One of two things—[the writer] has either "frozen up" in some imagined fear that SF is bigger than him, or he is simply using it as an excuse to avoid doing

working and claims that she returned it, but neither Freddie nor Pat Westmore know anything about it being returned.

That takes us up to here on missing hair goods.

the homework and thinking every writer on a new series is expected to do, in fact *commits* himself to do. You've got to help us get this fact to him somehow.

If it were merely penciling in the correct scene descriptions, nomenclature, terminology and so on, we are willing to do that, in fact anxious to help out. *At this point, we are not asking [the writer] to write science fiction!* We are asking him to give us quality in how he draws his characters, in making our regular people act and interact per our format with which he has been amply provided, to give them the "bite" of their individual styles, to have the Captain (like Matt Dillon or Dr. Kildare even) *act* like what he is, and above all, *again forgetting science fiction,* have everybody use at least simple Twentieth Century logic and common sense in what they look for, what they comment on, what surprises them, how they protect themselves, and so on.

For example, as you will see in the script, we are in an Earth-like city which stopped living some centuries ago. And yet, as they land there, no one comments on the strange ancient aspect of it. For God sakes, if Matt Dillon[7] came upon an Indian village which had been deserted for even three or four years, he or Chester or someone would at least be aware of that fact, especially if it were an important story point as it is here. And if Matt Dillon and a posse were searching through a mysterious area for some mysterious danger, at least the writer would indicate some intelligent use of the number of people in the posse, some people being sent out to do this, some to look into that, etc.

Again, [this writer] has given us an honest rewrite insofar as listening to some comment and suggestions and trying to use them. But he seems totally blanked out as far as approaching this with the characterizations and common sense I've seen him use a dozen times on hospitals, police stations, and Western saloons.

I'm much too fond of him to bitch about this to anyone

---

[7]Central character of the television Western, *Gunsmoke*. The other reference to "Chester" also comes from the same series.

but you. And I respect him too much not to use
every available tool in order to challenge him into doing
the kind of prize-winning work this script deserves
and his talent should make possible.

> Respectfully,
> Gene Roddenberry

Then there was the ego tightrope Gene walked. He had received a letter from a writer complaining that he had been
"frozen out." Gene took the time to write an honest letter,
explaining his situation, soothing the writer's bruised ego at
the same time.

> Nobody "froze you out." With only money advanced
> for a certain number of episodes at this point, and with
> the good fortune of practically all the top television
> and SF talent wanting to write for us, we had our
> assignments locked in much sooner than expected. Many
> excellent people that we wanted to use were never
> called in simply because stories came quicker and
> faster than normal.
>
> Assuming, and hoping, that we later get a pickup
> for more film and more episodes, then we'll be seeing
> some of the rest of these people. In what order?
> First, we'd be damn fools if we didn't give second
> assignments to those writers who really came through
> for us on the first group. Then, a number of writers
> have submitted one paragraph or one page ideas
> and some of these seem so interesting and likely
> that we'll probably go to these people next. Then there
> are short stories already published which have been
> submitted to us for possible adaption by the writers.
>
> Finally, I do my damnedest to do what seems
> wisest during a very hectic twelve-hour a day schedule.
> I don't intend to let myself tailspin over the fact I may
> miss some people, make some mistakes, lose some
> opportunities.
>
> Meanwhile, the show is represented by Ashley Famous
> Agency, our personal contact man there is Eddie Rosen.
> The studio Legal Department and insurance require
> that all submissions be made through him. He reads,
> comments, forwards things. I don't know that this is

the best way, either. But that's the way this game is played.

Thank you for your good wishes. Hope I'll see you at the sci-fi convention this fall, if not before.

At last all of the long hours of preproduction work ended, and on May 24, 1966, *Star Trek* went before the cameras as a regular series. In order to insure a certain smoothness of operation, Gene sent the following memo to "all concerned." Pay particular attention to paragraphs two and four. Even though Gene stayed in the front office most of the time, his presence was never far from the set and his "child."

On starting this first day of production, I think it wise we establish certain routines of value to us during the shooting year:

1. Assistant director should convey to my office, or in my absence to the office concerned, at noon and at late afternoon before our office closes, a simple verbal report of pages completed and any problems or information pertinent.

2. John D.F. Black should establish a routing of visiting the set once morning and afternoon, establishing that the tenor and mood of the scenes being photographed are generally in keeping with the script and our discussions with the director. If this is found not to be the case, he and I should confer on the subject immediately.

3. None of the above is meant to replace or supersede R. Justman's normal production responsibilities and routine.

4. Cameramen and script supervisor have been alerted to flash this office should the director depart appreciably from dialogue, characterizations, etc. In my absence or unavailability, John D.F. Black will handle the matter as appears best.

5. Notification from set of deviation from production planning and routine will be handled by R. Justman.

6. Where possible, in order to insulate us from actor problems and maintain our friendly relationship with cast, complaints from actors, unusual or special requests from them, etc, should be passed on to Morris Chapnick of Herb Solow's office.

In short, for best efficiency and a minimum of anguish,

let us of the *Star Trek* staff start along with the show and the crew with a planned routine and division of responsibility which will have us all drinking champagne and feeling smug a year from now.

Gene Roddenberry

That afternoon Gene received a telegram.

Have a successful liftup, the best to you for a long and successful trek to the stars.

Majel

In early August Shatner was recording the opening lines that would become world famous: "Space, the final frontier ..." only they didn't start out that way. One of the early versions went like this:

"This is the story of the United Space Ship Enterprise. Assigned a five-year patrol of our galaxy, the giant starship visits Earth colonies, regulates commerce, and explores strange new worlds and civilizations. These are its voyages ... and its adventures."

On August 2, a memo from Justman to GR with his ideas:

Dear Gene:

Here are the words you should use for our standard teaser narration:

"This is the story of the Starship Enterprise. It's [sic] mission: to advance knowledge, contact alien life and enforce intergalactic law ... to explore the strange new worlds where no man has gone before."

Regards,
Bob

At the bottom, in Gene's penciled scrawl, is a variety of words, some scratched through:

Where no man has gone before. Space, ~~this is the USS Enterprise~~ Continuing ... new planets, exotic life forms, strange alien civilizations.

This is the story of the ~~USS~~ Starship Enterprise ... these are its voyages ... its adventures.

John D.F. Black sent a memo to Gene on the same day with his thoughts.

> Gene ...
> Think the narration needs more drama.
> Follows an example of what I mean ... at about 15 to 17 seconds
> KIRK'S VOICE
> Space ... the final frontier ... endless ... silent ... waiting. This is the story of the United Space Ship Enterprise ... its mission ... a five year patrol of the galaxy ... to seek out and contact all alien life ... to explore ... to travel the vast galaxy where no man has gone before ... a Star Trek.
> Or ... at about 11½ second length
> Would you believe:
> KIRK'S VOICE
> The U.S.S. Enterprise ... star ship ... its mission ... a five year patrol to seek out and contact alien life ... to explore the infinite frontier of space ... where no man has gone before ... a Star Trek.
>
> JDFB

Finally, on August 10, 1966, Gene wrote:

> Space ... the final frontier. These are the voyages of the Starship Enterprise, its five-year mission
> ... to explore strange new worlds
> ... to seek out new life and new civilizations
> ... to boldly go where no man has gone before.[8]

Other deals were shaping up. About a month before the show went on the air, early in August, Ed Perlstein sent a letter to the Licensing Corporation of America informing them that he had concluded two separate deals with the AMT Corporation in connection with toy models.

The first deal consisted of monies paid by AMT to LCA, and the second was that AMT would construct, at its own cost, a full-sized exterior and interior of the *Galileo* shuttle

---

[8]As times and sensitivities change, so did *Star Trek*'s opening. "Man" was replaced with the non-sexist "one."

craft, the estimated cost being $24,000.[9] The memo detailed amounts of royalties to be paid, but basically, AMT would build the large mock-up for Desilu's use as a set in return for the model rights. It was built in Arizona and trucked to the Desilu lot.

While the shows were being filmed, behind the scenes analysis was taking place. The supporting running characters were carefully scrutinized and a memo sent to Gene from D'Agosta. Each actor had a contract that specified how many days they worked and for how much money. Extra days meant the actor was paid more money. Additionally, each actor was guaranteed a certain number of shows out of each cycle of thirteen. For example, Nimoy and Shatner had guarantees of thirteen out of thirteen shows. For the others, the deal was leaner.

DeForest Kelley was contracted for $850 for five days work on seven of thirteen shows. The consultant recommended, "DeForest has become enough of a valuable member of our group that I feel his contract should be re-negotiated so that we may have him for more days per show at an agreed salary. This would give us a break on overtime and protective days. This can be done by guaranteeing him more shows per cycle at a higher salary for more guaranteed days per show."

Grace Lee Whitney[10] was contracted for $750 for four days on seven of thirteen shows. The performance analysis showed that on the seven shows she appeared on, she was used nine extra days and three days under her guarantee. The recommendation was, "Grace for the most part has cost us a lot of money for the little that we use her in each show. The character is one that if cast with a free lance player would cost less and would hold as much value. I suggest that we drop her option and use her on a 'when and if available' free lance basis. An alternate way of going would be to either re-negotiate her contract so that it would be more in

---

[9]It was later reported that the cost was $65,000.

[10]Along with DeForest Kelley and James Doohan, Grace Lee Whitney was one of the most experienced actors on the show, having been in the business for years. One early credit was the mermaid for Chicken of the Sea brand tuna. While she had a great deal of turmoil in her personal life, no one remembers it affecting her work. She was always most professional.

line or to re-cast the character with an actress that doesn't command this kind of salary."

George Takei was paid $600 for five days work on seven of thirteen shows. The recommendation: "George is a good actor well used and a good balance that fits well in our group. However, in that we use him chiefly on the bridge, we are paying him, in most cases, for more days than we need him.

"I suggest that we drop his option and use him on a 'when and if available' free lance basis. An alternate way of going would be to re-negotiate his contract on a 'sliding scale basis' similar to the handshake deal that we have with Nichelle Nichols, with the exception that we would have him tied to the series. With this deal we would still guarantee him a minimum of 7 out of 13 shows and pay him according to the amount of days that he works. In many cases this would cost us more money for 6 and 7 day periods. However, it would cost us less for the 2 and 3 days that we use him."

James Doohan had no contractual agreement, but the consultant noted that they had fulfilled their handshake agreement and guarantee of five shows at $850 per show. The recommendation was, "We can either tie Jim to the series on a sliding scale basis as illustrated with George Takei or negotiate a sliding scale non-contractual deal similar to the one we have with Nichelle Nichols."

The consultant concluded by saying, "In order to pursue any re-negotiation stipulated above, we must be prepared to lose the actor."

The consultant's recommendation regarding Grace Lee Whitney, along with the direction the show was taking, sealed her fate. By September 8, 1966, a memo was sent from Business Affairs to Legal directing them to inform Whitney's agent that her Memorandum of Agreement was being terminated. Gene expressed his thoughts in an October 28, 1966, memo to Gene Coon.

Bob Justman and I both think we should look for an opportunity to bring Grace Lee Whitney back as "Yeoman Rand" in some upcoming episode. We might discuss at that time the possibility of trying some slightly different hairdo, something more on the order of that she wore in *Police Story*. It actually made her look much younger and softer.

So, rumors and innuendo aside, the real reason Grace Lee Whitney left the show was financial. The character cost too much and she was eliminated. A reality of Hollywood life.

Although the show was not yet on the air it was getting publicity, of a sort. On August 21, 1966, the Los Angeles *Herald-Examiner TV Weekly* magazine ran a "Fall Preview" article. It covered two pages with around 200 words and four photos—two small photos of "Len Nimoy, scientist," "Grace Whitney, yeoman," "William Shatner is the captain." And a two column, half-page shot of the *Enterprise,* printed upside down.

Another publication ran a two-part column on the upcoming show. Gene wrote to thank the editor and take exception to what he had said.

> However, may I take friendly issue with your preface in italics in which you say, " ... *Star Trek* ... strikes TV Week as a *Lost In Space* for adults ..." Sir, of all things *Star Trek* is, it is *not* in any way a "Lost In Space."
>
> Am certain you did not mean this comment to be caustic. However, we are naturally anxious that it not be thought we are a copy of any show. *Star Trek,* in fact, was conceived long before "Lost In Space" and was in script form a year earlier than that show. We do not criticize that series, it does what it sets out to do, but *Star Trek* is as different from "Lost In Space" as "Gunsmoke" is from "Lassie."
>
> There are a great number of talented and dedicated people involved in the production of *Star Trek,* and we all believe we *do* have something proud and new for television.
>
> Sincerely,

There was good publicity, of course, and Gene received a tremendous boost when he was a guest at the 24th Annual World Science Fiction Convention in Cleveland, Ohio. It was five days before the show premiered on NBC.

As described by author Allan Asherman, a participant at the convention:

> "A tall man appeared at the front of the room. Although he looked formidable, his voice was contrastingly gentle. He sounded almost timid when he introduced him-

self as Gene Roddenberry, a lifelong science fiction fan. He told the audience that he had produced a new television pilot which had already been accepted by NBC for a series called *Star Trek*. The series would debut the following week with a 'sneak preview' episode, but our opinion was still extremely important to him. Having sold his series Mr. Roddenberry was undoubtedly busy, and yet there he was; he had brought his film to us himself, just to ask our opinion."[11]

Gene left the stage and "Where No Man Has Gone Before" was shown to the 500 people in the audience. Some in the audience weren't certain Gene had said this was for television.

When the film was over, Gene returned to the stage. The general silence was broken only by excited whispers from the audience.

"Finally, Roddenberry broke the silence. He asked for our opinion; we gave him a standing ovation. We came close to lifting Gene Roddenberry upon our shoulders and carrying him out of the room."[12]

Finally, after two pilots, into which Gene poured two years of his life and nearly a million dollars of studio money, it all came together on Thursday, September 8, 1966, 8:30 P.M., when NBC broadcast "The Man Trap."[13]

Gene watched the program with his wife Eileen and two daughters in the upstairs living room of their Beverly Glen home. The two girls, then about twelve and eighteen, had never been allowed to see horror movies and so were transfixed by the salt monster character. Gene, in the practical joker tradition of his father, saw an opportunity to have

---

[11]*The Star Trek Compendium* by Allan Asherman. (New York: Simon & Schuster, 1981).

[12]Ibid. Asherman also relates that Gene had a black-and-white copy of "The Cage" with him and, by request, showed that as well.

[13]Written by George Clayton Johnson and directed by Marc Daniels. Actually, the sixth episode filmed—or fourth, not counting the pilots. Daniels was a Desilu institution, having directed the first year of *I Love Lucy*. He directed Lawrence Olivier on stage and was highly regarded.

some fun with his two daughters. He snuck up behind them as they stared at the television set and grabbed them just as the action was reaching a climax on the screen. Taken by surprise, Darleen and Dawn screamed their lungs out. Years later, Darleen was surprised the neighbors hadn't called the police.

While the Roddenberry girls were being scared, science fiction fans were beginning their love affair with the program. Unfortunately, the critics were less than impressed.

The *Daily Variety* review was particularly ironic since one of the complaints about the original pilot was that it was "too cerebral." The reviewer wrote that the show was "not for the common herd who prefer less cerebral exercises," and that the premiere episode offered only violence for excitement "and very little of that over the hour spread." The reviewer concluded that the series would not be able to hold an audience.

Louise Sweeney, writing in the *Christian Science Monitor,* was a bit more perceptive, even though she got the name of the ship wrong—*Explorer* instead of *Enterprise.* She thought that the show would be successful in the sense that *The Green Hornet, Time Tunnel,* and *Love on a Rooftop* were, its longevity depending on what direction it took in the future.

The *Chicago Tribune* observed, "Producer Gene Roddenberry vowed this NBC science fiction hour would specialize in adult plots scripted by fine writers. From the premier, he has considerable distance to go to attain that objective."

Bill Ornstein in *The Hollywood Reporter* was the most upbeat: "There's quite a bit of suspense and tricks with gadgets that will please the sci-fi buffs no end." He further described the premier episode's director as having "an eye for building suspense; people running in and out of rooms and passageways excitedly." Ornstein was also the most direct when it predicted that the show "should be a winner."

Later in the season, Cleveland Amory expounded his opinion in the pages of *TV Guide.* After watching a number of episodes, Amory wrote, "The Enterprise has plenty of fun places to go, and make no mistake abut it, it has fun people to go to those fun places." His favorite episode was "Shore

Leave,"[14] which contained the line delivered by Captain Kirk, "Face front. Don't talk. Don't think. Don't breathe." Amory suggested this was "the best way for an adult to watch this show."

For more stinging criticism, Gene did not have to go very far. His father did not like the futuristic drama and remarked to neighbors that his son would be getting back to writing "real" television soon; real television being Westerns. Gene's mother admits that she never much cared for *Star Trek*, and his brother Bob liked the show only when it was more action oriented.

There was one important person who appreciated what Gene and crew had done. On October 5, a small note was delivered to the production office. It had no return address and only one first name in script across the top that matched the single signed name at the bottom. There was no confusion over who had sent it.

> Dear Gene and the rest of you hard-working people . . .
> Just heard the good news, and want you to know how proud and happy I am.
> Looks like you really have a hit on your hands, and we all appreciate your efforts.
>
> Love,
> Lucy

Gene had figured out a way to use the first pilot as part of the series, even though it had a different crew. At his direction, several writers had attempted to write what he called an "envelope" or "wrap-around" story that would encompass the previously shot story, with careful editing, into a larger, more complex storyline. They were unsuccessful, so Gene sat down and in a weekend wrote the needed script. It was named "The Menagerie" and was the original series's only two-part episode.

On October 18, a memo was sent to the Desilu Legal Department advising them that arrangements had been made with the participants in the first pilot.

The directors were cooperative. Bob Butler, who directed the first pilot, only wanted sole credit for part two because

---

[14]"Shore Leave" by Theodore Sturgeon, broadcast December 29, 1966.

he felt that it was his exclusive effort and Marc Daniels, director of the envelope show, wanted credit for part one, which was principally his sole effort.

Jeffrey Hunter was paid an additional $5,000 for the use of the footage from the first pilot and his residuals were minimum. The other supporting players were paid $750, except Susan Oliver; there is nothing in the files indicating what sort of a deal was worked out with her.

The envelope was tricky. To make certain it worked, Gene sent a memo to Ed Milkis on October 24:

Dear Eddie,

Because of the peculiar nature of "The Menagerie" beast, certain very definite ideas I had in mind when writing a show within a show, please see that I get a look at *every reel* of this show before the final dubbing. Regardless of what is going on, I'll depend on you to remind me of this message and bully me into going over there.

Regards,

The envelope show was shot in five days and aired on November 17 and 24, 1966.

Gene was quick to capitalize on what he perceived as a movement. On September 28, 1966, he sent the following memo to "all concerned":

It appears we may have a useful catch-word deriving out of *Star* Trek in our title. For example, star base, for command bases on various planets, star cut describing the style of our pointed sideburns haircuts, starship, of course, is a generic term for the *Enterprise,* Star Command for fleet headquarters, and so on. Undoubtedly other examples will occur to you. As with "Batman," "Batmobile," clever use of it may create a kind of terminology for our show.

Gene Roddenberry

The next day Gene dropped a note to composer Wilbur Hatch regarding his thoughts on Uhura's song in "Conscience of the King," keeping even the music believable.

Dear Will:

As I told you at the time, I thought the music
you did for Uhura was exceptionally good! However,
taking into account all we know of the music and art
appreciation of our basic audience, I must agree
with Gene Coon that perhaps we'd be safer if we
were not so far "out," giving them a tune they could
conceivably hum or sing along too.

The fact we've had considerable letters requesting
more information on Uhura's "Spock and Charlie
X" song reinforces this belief with both us and NBC.

Really, it's my fault for not thinking ahead. We found
consistently through trial and error that *Star Trek*
reaches more people when we let the "way out"
business of all kinds stay in the background and reinforce
audience identification with familiarity and terminology
(Naval), food (no SF pills) [concentrated food],
emotional reactions (essentially Twentieth Century
man), et cetera. We've had much of the same problem
in designing costumes and find when we go too high-
fashion futuristic there, we begin to lose
identification and believability.

I'm sure you realize this is no criticism of your talent
or excellent job.

Gene Roddenberry

Gene lived and worked in a business that often seemed
unnecessarily paranoid, yet years of experience had shown
the studio legal departments that what may have appeared to
be unnecessary caution often wasn't. Lawsuits by people
who submitted unsolicited manuscripts were a reality and a
strict prohibition against accepting scripts and stories from
unknown sources was vigorously enforced.

On October 4, Gene dropped a note to Bernie Weitzman
in Business Affairs regarding an unsolicited book. The book
came in a package that had been opened since Gene had no
idea what it was. The book had a proposal for a television
series attached to it. Gene sent it to Weitzman to handle in
the proper legal manner. Gene closed the memo by saying,
"Incidentally, we don't like it and see no value in it."

A week later Gene got a memo from one of the lawyers
in Legal requesting that all such items be sent directly to

them. The lawyer pointed out a number of legal distinctions and problems that could arise if the procedure was not followed precisely and correctly. He did not like what Gene wrote in the memo. "I cannot determine whether your last sentence was written seriously or in jest. In either case, it reflects a cavalier attitude towards something which we must all take seriously. Please DO NOT READ unsolicited manuscripts; if you have not read them, please do not write internal documents which imply that you have read them."

The lawyer concluded by saying, "Gene, I have seen a television producer lose control of a major series in the middle of the year because his insurance coverage was cancelled; it was all the result of one foolish act on the part of a man who worked for him. It could happen to us. Please cooperate, and instruct your staff accordingly." Gene didn't argue and followed instructions.

Star Trek was Gene's baby. He was quick to respond when public information was incorrect. On October 25, he sent a letter to the *Herald Examiner TV Weekly*—the same people who had printed the upside-down picture of the *Enterprise.*

In your October 23rd edition a letter writer inquired how Mr. Spock could have a Vulcanian[15] father who married an Earthling. Your reply that "it was an emotionless marriage" is incorrect.

Actually, marriage to an Earth woman seemed the *logical* thing to Mr. Spock's father at the time. And it is a well-known fact throughout the galaxy that Vulcanians are immeasurably attractive to all females, but most particularly to Earth women. Regarding Mr. Spock's own emotions, we quote from his biography: "On his own planet, to show emotion is considered the grossest of sins . . ." But he will sin a lot during upcoming *Star Trek* episodes.

Sincerely,
Gene Roddenberry
Executive Producer
Star Trek

---

[15]This term for the natives of Vulcan was later abandoned.

Regardless of how much the science fiction fans loved the program, there just weren't enough of them to push the ratings up. *Star Trek* was not a resounding success in the overall ratings. Gene was nervous that NBC might pull the plug before the program could become firmly established, so he began a hedge against, if not the inevitable, the highly possible specter of cancellation. While much credit has been claimed by others as to having organized the protest and "saved *Star Trek*," the truth is that it was principally Gene's plan from the beginning, with him working behind the scenes through cooperative individuals.

Gene had contacted Harlan Ellison to see if he would be willing to use his name in letters sent out to save the show. Harlan was willing and contacted other writers as well. On November 18, 1966 Gene sent a memo on Desilu Productions Inc. letterhead to Howard McClay in Desilu Publicity—Subject: Attached Letters—Publicity for *Star Trek*.

Dear Howard:
This is my final revision. Harlan Ellison will be in touch with you via Dorothy [Fontana] regarding any polishing you and he may want to do on this version.

As it stands now or with whatever changes you two make on it, I think we should get it immediately into the works. Dorothy is enclosing a revised copy of the basic plans and directions I drew up, which list places where we could start an immediate mail out.

You'll notice there is an "A" and a "B" form, one for magazines and publishers, the other for fans and fandom.

There were five enclosures with Gene's memo: a letter to Lloyd Biggle,[16] revised plan and directions—publicity, Letter "A", Letter "B", and mailing instructions.

The letter directed to publishing houses and science fiction magazine editors read:

Dear _____,
We need your help. The undersigned, representing also a large number of other professional writers,

---

[16]Lloyd Biggle, Jr., secretary-treasurer of the Science Fiction Writers of America, the originator of the Nebula Award.

are interested in and concerned about the future of a television program called *Star Trek* which is showing signs of opening up an entirely new and mass audience for science fiction. Made with considerable difficulty and pride, designed for true science fiction, it is receiving a steadily growing volume of mail from not only professional people and college students but also a surprising number of wonderfully ordinary people who never before realized science fiction existed.

I doubt if I have to point out just why this is good for all of us. Obviously, any mass medium effort which breaks through the "limited audience barrier" is bound to create new purchasers of SF books and magazines. Further, it can create more resales of published stories to other media, hopefully even large motion picture sales and a further audience increase this would create.

In short, *Star Trek* is not competition to any of us. It is a highly welcome break-through and it could be an important one.

The problem—we've learned that the "Nielson roulette" which goes on at this time of the year makes the future of this program doubtful. Unless something happens, it will either be cancelled or that threat will be used as a lever to throw it into a "kiddie show" category, either of which can be used to "prove" that real science fiction is not a very marketable commodity and actually constitutes an unimportant branch of literature.

We need your help in reaching fans, instituting not a "form letter" campaign, but rather statements in their own words, embodying their own feelings about *Star Trek.* Television, like it or not, is a mass media and highly sensitive to audience reaction. Letters should be directed to: local television stations which carry *Star Trek;* to sponsors who advertise on *Star Trek;* local and syndicated television columnists; *TV Guide* and other television magazines.

The situation is critical, next month is too late. This is not only a worthy project, supporting fellow professionals who are making a sincere and not too undistinguished efforts in our field, but also a

successful letter campaign at this time could eventually
mean dollars to both of us. Can we count on your
help?

Sincerely yours,
Harlan Ellison

The letter to fan club presidents and fan magazine editors
was as follows:

Dear Mr. _____,
   We need your help. For some time our field of science
fiction has needed a vehicle to take it to the mass
audience, establishing it in its rightful place as a
legitimate, highly entertaining, and important branch
of literature. The television show named *Star Trek* has
begun doing that for all of us. Made with enormous
difficulty and with considerable pride, it has begun
to attract a new audience to our field. It's beginning
to happen, it's good for all of us, but we've learned
that even its very healthy growth has been much
too slow for nervous network executives playing
their game of "Nielson roulette."
   We've learned that unless something happens *fast*,
Star Trek will face either year-end cancellation or
have this used as a lever to try to force it into a
"Lost In Space" format. It would be catastrophic if
either of these happened since such action would lend
credence to those voices which, despite all the
lessons and evidence to the contrary, have long
scoffed at SF as an "unimportant and limited" field.
Worse, the result will be to demonstrate the "failure"
of real SF, or to force all future mass audience
attempts into a "kiddie show" mold.
   We need letters! From leaders in the field such as
yourself, *plus* from every fan and TV viewer we can
reach through our publications and personal
contacts. Not form letters, they should be in the
writer's own words and express honest attitudes. They
should go to: local television stations which carry *Star
Trek;* to sponsors who advertise on *Star Trek;* local
and syndicated television columnists; *TV Guide* and
other television magazines.
   The situation is critical; it has to happen *now* or it

will be too late. We're giving it all our efforts; we hope we can count on yours.

Sincerely,
Harlan Ellison, Chairman
Theodore Sturgeon
Richard Matheson
A.E. Van Vogt
Robert Bloch
Lester del Ray
Phil Farmer
Frank Herbert
Poul Anderson

Less than a month later, Ellison was sending out letters on a letterhead designated "The Committee," with the above listed writers' names prominently displayed. Of course it came as no surprise that five of the eight signers were people who wrote for the program. Ellison's letter was dated December 1, 1966, and was four paragraphs long. The first paragraph was almost entirely in his own voice, but did use some of Gene's phrasing from his two sample letters, specifically "Neilson roulette," and "made with enormous difficulty and with considerable pride." The third and fourth paragraphs are Gene's writing.[17]

While an unknown number of letters were mailed out and some fan protest to NBC resulted, the general reaction of the science fiction community was less than enthusiastic. One fan who received a letter explained her reaction by saying that the letter she received seemed to her to address the needs of the small percentage of professional science fiction writers who wrote for television and that it did nothing to inspire a fan to write.

The program was renewed, but the network took a dim view of the letter-writing campaign. As reported by Sheila Wolfe in the *Chicago Tribune* in May 1967, "Reports that *Star Trek* was going to be grounded triggered a lot of mail but the writers needn't have bothered. NBC said it never planned to scrap the program in the first place."

---

[17]As late as 1987, Ellison failed to mention Gene's participation or his formulation of "the basic plans and directions" for the letter-writing campaign when he wrote about this moment of television history in his magazine column, "Harlan Ellison's Watching," *Fantasy & Science Fiction*, May, 1987, pages 109–115.

One well-placed individual who was around the *Star Trek* office at the time said she thought it was part of the poker game that was played between producers and networks. An outpouring of letters might put Desilu in a better negotiating position for the second season.

Regardless of where the truth lies, the show was renewed and Gene kept writing, rewriting, and producing for another season.

CHAPTER 10

During its first season *Star Trek* had attracted the attention of the SF community. Isaac Asimov wrote an article that appeared in *TV Guide* and Gene responded late in November, 1966, sending his letter to Asimov through *TV Guide*. The two men had met briefly at a science fiction convention before *Star Trek* went on the air. Gene had great respect, if not outright reverence for Asimov, but that did not stop him from sharing his thoughts with Asimov on his article. It was the second time Gene had put Asimov "in his place," but the first time he had done it intentionally. At the convention where Gene showed "The Cage" to an eager audience, as the film was starting a man in the row ahead kept talking. Gene spoke up saying, "Hey, fellow, stop talking. That's my picture they're starting to show." The fellow quieted down and Gene's seat companion quietly whispered in his ear that he'd just chewed out Isaac Asimov. Gene attempted to apologize, but Asimov knew he'd been in the wrong and said so.

Gene's letter is a model of a civilized "taking to task."

Dear Isaac:

Sorry I had to address it in this round-about way since I did not have your address and Harlan Ellison, who might have supplied it, is working on a final draft for us and is already a week late and I don't want to take his attention away from it for even a moment.

On second thought, I believe he is a month or two late.

Wanted to comment on your *TV Guide* article, "What Are A Few Galaxies Among Friends?"

Enjoyed it as I enjoy all your writing. And it will serve as a handy reference to those of our Star Trek writers who do not have a SF background. Although, to be perfectly honest, those with SF background and experience tend to make the same mistakes. I've found that the best SF writing is no guarantee of science accuracy.

A person should gets facts straight when writing anything. So, as much as I enjoyed your article, I am haunted by this need to write you with the suggestion that some of your facts were not straight. And, just as a writer writing about science should know what a galaxy is, a writer writing about television has an obligation to acquaint himself with pertinent aspects of that field. In all friendliness, and with sincere thanks for the hundreds of wonderful hours of reading you have given me, it does seem to me that your article overlooked entirely the practical, factual and scientific problems involved in getting a television show on the air and keeping it there. Television deserved much criticism, not just SF alone but all of it, but that criticism should be aimed, not shot-gunned. For example, *Star Trek* almost did not get on the air because it refused to do a juvenile science fiction, because it refused to put a "Lassie" aboard the space ship, and because it insisted on hiring Dick Matheson, Harlan Ellison, A.E. Van Vogt, Phil Farmer, and so on. (Not all of these came through since TV scripting is a highly difficult specialty, but many of them did.)

In the specific comment you made about *Star Trek,* the mysterious cloud being "one-half light-year outside the Galaxy," I agree certainly that this was stated badly, but on the other hand, it got past a Rand Corporation physicist who *is* hired by us to review all of our stories and scripts, and further, got past Kellum deForest Research who is also hired to do the same job.

And, needless to say, it got past me.

We do spend several hundred dollars a week to guarantee scientific accuracy. And several hundred more dollars a week to guarantee other forms of accuracy, logical progressions, etc. Before going into production we made up a "Writer's Guide" covering many of these things and we send out new pages, amendments, lists of terminology, excerpts of science articles, etc., to our writers continually. And to our directors. And specific science information to our actors depending on the job they portray. For example, we are presently accumulating a file on space medicine for De Forest Kelley who plays the ship's surgeon aboard the USS *Enterprise*. William Shatner, playing Captain James Kirk, and Leonard Nimoy, playing Mr. Spock, spend much of their free time reading articles, clippings, SF stories, and other material we send them.

Despite all of this we do make mistakes and will probably continue to make them. The reason—Thursday has an annoying way of coming up once a week, and five working days an episode is a crushing burden, an impossible one. The wonder of it is not that we make mistakes, but that we are able to turn out once a week science fiction which is (if we are to believe SF writers and fans who are writing us in increasing numbers) the first true SF series ever made on television. We like to think this is what we are doing. Certainly, that is what we are trying to do, and trying with considerable pride. And I suppose with considerable touchiness when we believe we are criticized unfairly or as in the case of your article, damned with faint praise. Quoting Ted Sturgeon who made his first script attempt with us (and now seems firmly established as a contributor to good television), getting *Star Trek* on the air was impossible, putting out a program like this on a TV budget is impossible, reaching the necessary mass audience without alienating the select SF audience is impossible, not succumbing to network pressure to "juvenilize" the show is impossible, keeping it on the air is impossible. We've done all of these things. Perhaps someone else could have done it better, but no one else did.

Again, if we are to believe our letters (now mounting into the thousands), we are reaching a vast number of people who never before understood SF or enjoyed it. We are, in fact, making fans—making future purchasers of SF magazines and novels, making future box office receipts for SF films. We are, I sincerely hope, making new purchasers of "The Foundation" novels, "I, Robot," "The Rest of the Robots," and other of your excellent work. We, and I personally, in our own way and beset with the strange problems of this mass communications media, work as proudly and as hard as any other SF writer in this land.

If mention was to be made of SF in television, we deserved much better. And, as much as I admire you in your work, I felt an obligation to reply.

And, I believe, the public deserves a more definitive article on all this. Perhaps TV GUIDE is not the marketplace for it, but if you ever care to throw the Asimov mind and wit toward a definitive TV piece, please count on us for facts, figures, sample budgets, practical production examples, and samples of scripts from rough story to the usual multitude of drafts, samples of mass media "pressure," and whatever else we can give you.

Sincerely yours,

Asimov had second thoughts on what he'd written, possibly prompted by the strong criticism he'd received from a close friend who was a fan of the program. He immediately wrote Gene a letter with the two letters crossing in the mail. Gene received Asimov's letter a few days after he mailed his own.

Dear Mr. Roddenberry,

In a recent issue of *TV Guide,* I had a high old time pointing out scientific errors in the current crop of TV science fiction shows. In doing this—and enamored, as I always am with my own purpose—I completely neglected to say that I liked *Star Trek* very much. Actually, I hinted at that in passing but I didn't make it anywhere near strong enough.

Some friends, who are fans of *Star Trek* (I have intelligent friends) have pointed out my failing in

extremely forceful language and on re-reading my
article I feel very ashamed at having lost a chance
to support good science fiction before a large
audience merely because I was so intent on being
funny.

I am trying to get a sentence into the letter column
of *TV Guide* to point out my opinion of *Star Trek,*
but even that may not be enough. Is there anything
I can do that would usefully express my appreciation
of the sterling efforts you are making to produce an
adult science fiction show of high quality?

                                                    Asimov

A few days later Gene received a second letter from
Asimov.

Dear Gene,

Two days after you wrote me your letter of
29 November via *TV Guide,* I wrote you a letter,
also via *TV Guide.*

I hope to goodness you have received it. Just in case
you did not I will here repeat my letter which (once
again) I mailed to you *before* I received your letter.
Here goes:

[The full text of the first letter is repeated. Asimov
then continued.]

Now—Your letter to me was far milder and
gentler than I deserved. Mr. Samuel Peeples wrote
me a much stronger one, which I answered with vigor
myself, but in a second exchange I believe we ended
friends.[1]

As for what to do, I would *love* to be able to
boost *Star Trek* anywhere, and if you think you would
like it, I would ask *TV Guide* if they would like me
to do an article on *Star Trek* for them. Better still,
it might be a good idea if Ted Sturgeon were to
try. He knows the program and he knows the Hollywood
system now, and he could do it far more authoritatively
than I could. (But I am not trying to get out of my
own personal penance for my own personal sin.

---

[1]Asimov and Peeples had been friends for some time, and the friendship continued after their exchange of letters.

I will give *Star Trek* favorable mentions every chance
I get and do whatever I can to help it. In fact,
there's a new sf show coming in next January and *TV
Guide* has put out a very feeble feeler about an article
on that—which may not come to pass—and if I
do such an article, it will go hard, but *Star Trek*
will get into it, and favorably.)

I might say that you are perfectly right in thinking
that I know nothing about the practical aspects of
TV writing and producing and of course when I
started the article, it was merely my intention to be
lightly (rather than mordantly) humorous—but it ran
away from me.

I could almost wish I were in Hollywood so that
I could see a program in the process of being produced—
but that will never be. I don't travel and I will never
see Hollywood.[2]

> Yours,
> Isaac

In spite of a grueling schedule, Gene found time to write
to fans who wrote intelligent letters. On the sixth of December,
he explained the star date system used on the show, the
internal arrangement of the *Enterprise* and continued by
sharing his thoughts about the person who was becoming the
show's central character.

Mr. Spock is meant to be a study in contradictions.
Being half-human as well as half-Vulcan he undergoes
a constant struggle between what he was taught was
the "immoral" emotionalism of his Earth blood and
the "moral" and acceptable logic of his father's Vulcan
blood. He is very fond of his fellow crewmen and terribly
ashamed of that feeling. Yet at other times it pleases
him strangely.

Spock's blood is green because of *traces* of nickel
and other metals which our blood does not have.
However, the difference is minor and it is
compatible with Terra blood when the conception

---

[2]Asimov would travel short distances outside of New York City but no further.
He once admitted that he hadn't walked on the balcony of his New York apartment
in the many years he'd lived there.

and pregnancy is properly planned and controlled by techniques of the highly advanced Vulcan school of medicine—just as our own present Earth school of medicine is learning to beat the RH factor. There is actually no inconsistency in having a pulse rate of 242 beats per minute and practically no blood pressure by our standards. The average diameter of his arteries is larger than Terran, more efficient, and the faster, lower pressured hydraulic action of his "slightly different heart" results in about the same volume delivered as our slower higher-pressured system.

We depict humanoid aliens because we (along with Cal Tech studies and others) do believe that parallel evolution is a distinct possibility. Natural laws govern life development just as other natural laws govern time, space and atoms. There are no "accidents" in nature, probably not even in social development. Every effect has a cause. It is our misfortune on Earth today that our understanding of cause and effect in life and social evolution is almost nil.

Again, thank you for a most interesting letter.

Sincerely yours,

In Hollywood's verbal shorthand, Gene was a hyphen: a writer-hyphenate-producer. While a writer's duties are self-descriptive, a producer's aren't well known. While directors and writers come and go it is the producer's responsibility to maintain the overall vision and continuity of a show, its characters and storylines. Gene was a double hyphen in that he created, wrote, *and* produced *Star Trek*.

In addition to his regular responsibilities of writing and producing, Gene, in moments of exasperation, added yet another hyphenated duty to his title—suckle pig or wet nurse to actors' egos.

With his program established, Gene faced the inevitable metamorphosis of actors-grateful-to-have-a-job into actors-who-want-more: more money, more lines, more camera time, more close-ups, more credit, more something, more anything.

Motion picture and television studios are small war zones with individuals and groups jockeying for power, influence, money, and prestige. Even though the time of *Star Trek* was set in Gene Roddenberry's utopian future, the day-to-day reality of *Star Trek* was firmly set in mid-twentieth century, where it was every man, woman, or alien for themselves.

While most actors know that their character is the result of many people's contributions—the writers, who create the character and give it words; the costume designer, who puts the right clothes on it; the makeup artist, who makes the character look right; the lighting director, who brings it out of darkness; and the camera man, who photographs it properly—there are a few actors who would like the public to think that they show up at the studio, perform in front of a camera, record their golden words for posterity, and somehow, magically, then appear on television to delight their fans. While they may acknowledge the others, they know in their hearts that it is their performance and their performance alone that makes the true difference in the success or failure of a show. Some don't like the public to think of directors, producers, craftspeople, or writers as being important or even necessary.

Sometimes they are right—their performance is the difference between a show's success and failure. Conversely, sometimes the characters are so well drawn, so powerful, that they resonate with the public's basic needs and are larger than any one actor; the character is so strong that any competent performer would be a success playing the part. Henry Hathaway, the 1940's director, once said, "It's never the actor, it's always the role." Perhaps the truth lies somewhere in the middle.

Art and craft aside, studios are first, last, and always businesses that want to get the most out of their employees, creating the most attractive product for the widest possible audience at the lowest price possible. Actors and others live under a simple rule: the most money they would get is the lowest they will accept. Thus, actors, writers, producers, and studios continually thrust and parry, threaten and bargain to get the best deal they can. It is out of this maelstrom of conflicting interests that television programs are created, produced, and marketed.

Studios are, by their very nature, not generous (which is not to say that individual executives cannot be and haven't been extraordinarily generous and thoughtful). Studios are very careful with money and do not part with it willingly or easily, but when circumstances change, so do perceptions of value and compensation.

Leonard Nimoy became a case in point. A sensitive and intelligent man, Nimoy was and is deeply committed to the craft of acting. Only someone as deeply committed as Nimoy would have suffered through the privation of his early years, when acting jobs were few and far between and one took what one could get to feed the family. An early biography on file in the *Star Trek* archives lists a number of early Nimoy credits, but leaves off his appearance in the Republic serial *Zombies of the Stratosphere*—now endlessly playing on cable's Sci-Fi Channel, where Nimoy is given billing out of proportion to the part he played. *Zombies* was a minor role, which in thirteen episodes only gave him a few lines and one or two close-ups.[3] Also missing from this early bio was his first probable television appearance: he played a young thug with no lines on *Dragnet* in 1953 and was listed last in the credits. Nimoy played a variety of parts on television, including a gunfighter/tough on *Gunsmoke* and the acclaimed Kid Monk Baroni. He first came to Gene Roddenberry's attention when he played a guest role on *The Lieutenant.*

From all reports, Leonard was happy to have a job, yet his serious commitment to acting and perhaps his memory of playing a Martian in the aforementioned Republic potboiler, caused him some pause in agreeing to the role of Spock, as he thought the ears might damage his budding career.

Still, the role was a big step for Nimoy. It was a chance at series television and serious money. In spite of critical notices for several roles, a big night on the town for the Nimoys and their two children was going to a Chinese restaurant and ordering two dinners, which were shared among the family. With the second pilot a success and Leonard signed for five years, things began to look brighter.

As he wrote in the autobiographical *I Am Not Spock*[4]:

---

[3]Nimoy may have had second thoughts about Spock when he remembered his other SF experience, *The Brain Eaters,* a low-budget opus produced by American International Pictures and released in 1958. According to *Fantastic Cinema Subject Guide,* by Bryan Senn and John Johnson, (North Carolina: McFarland & Co., Jefferson, 1992), the film was an uncredited "adaption" of Robert Heinlein's *The Puppet Masters,* over which Heinlein sued.

[4]*I Am Not Spock,* by Leonard Nimoy, New York: Ballantine Books, 1977, page 80.

When the Spock character became as successful as it did, I felt I was a son who was doing his share to carry the family load. The studio legal department saw me as a menace. "He's getting popular and he's going to want more than he contracted for. That's trouble."

In his book, Nimoy then goes into a description of what he characterizes as "interesting games" with regard to him obtaining supplies for answering his fan mail, but there were other "fun and games" that he did not delve into.

Approximately five episodes into filming the first season's shows, before the program was even on the air, Leonard's agent, Alex Brewis, called for a meeting. Present at the meeting was Gene, Brewis, and Morris Chapnick, who had been Gene's production assistant on *The Lieutenant* and the first two *Star Trek* pilots. Morris now worked as Herb Solow's assistant and remembers the meeting clearly.

From the scripts they were filming, it was clear that Spock's importance to the storyline was nearly equal to that of the captain. Spock was not just a minor supporting character, and consequently Nimoy wanted more money. Chapnick's memory of the meeting is that Gene was inclined to agree, but Morris—then working for Herb Solow, the executive in charge of production—thought differently. At that time, Desilu had the *Star Trek* and *Mission Impossible* casts, thirteen actors, under contract, and Chapnick reasoned that if the studio gave a raise, however meritorious, to one actor, they would face the probability of the other twelve demanding the same.

Morris rejected Nimoy's agent's demand, which created a mild schism between Morris and Gene. Gene at first thought that Chapnick was disloyal to what he, Gene, thought was fair, but later realized Morris was just doing his job. Brewis was told to bring the subject up again at the appropriate time, after series renewal but before the start of the second season's filming. Brewis did just that.

At least one person has made the observation that Nimoy probably made more in the first three weeks of the first season of *Star Trek* than he earned the previous year as an actor, but his demand for more money should not be taken as a characterization of greed. Spock was pivotal to the series and Leonard saw an opportunity to better himself, doubtless feeling his work was worth more, especially since he was

Gene at eighteen months, 1923.
(Courtesy Caroline Glen Roddenberry)

His mother, Caroline Glen Goleman Roddenberry circa 1926. *(Courtesy Caroline Glen Roddenberry)*

Gene's father Eugene Edward Roddenberry, circa 1926. *(Courtesy Caroline Glen Roddenberry)*

High school graduation portrait. *(Courtesy Caroline Glen Roddenberry)*

18-year-old Gene proudly displays his Los Angeles City College Associated Men Students sweater. *(Courtesy Caroline Glen Roddenberry)*

Gene and Eileen's engagement party. (*left to right*) Gene, Eileen, Pat MacDonald, and Bob Atchison. (*Courtesy Bob Atchison*)

Gene and Eileen, 1945.
(*Courtesy Bob Atchison*)

Gene in the South
Pacific, 1943.
*(Courtesy Caroline
Glen Roddenberry)*

Remains of the June 19, 1947, Pan Am plane crash in which
fourteen people died. Gene helped rescue a number of the
nineteen total survivors. *(Courtesy Anthony Volpe)*

Mutual of New York Insurance advertisement which appeared in *Life* magazine 1961. *(Photographer: Elliott Erwitt. Courtesy Mutual of New York)*

Gene looking suave in a Guinness Stout advertisement. *(Photographer: Victor Skrebneski. Courtesy Guiness Import and The Marketing Centre)*

December 1964: Talosians with Gene (*left*) and Bob Butler, director of first *Star Trek* pilot (which later became "The Cage"), with gag sign looking for the head of Desilu, Oscar Katz. *(Courtesy Oscar Katz)*

Famous, but little seen 1966 photo of Leonard Nimoy as Mr. Spock with rounded ears. NBC, nervous about his satanic appearance, airbrushed his ears and eyebrows. *(Courtesy Richard Arnold)*

January 1968
torchlight
march/protest on
NBC Burbank.
*(Courtesy Wanda
Kendall-La Vita)*

Gene at party after
torchlight march.
*(Courtesy Wanda
Kendall-La Vita)*

Gene and Majel in private Shinto-Buddhist
ceremony in Japan, August 6, 1969.
(Courtesy Majel Roddenberry)

Isaac Asimov with Gene at the first Star Trek convention, New York, 1972. *(Courtesy Majel Roddenberry)*

Roddenberry with original *Star Trek* cast at the naming of the U.S. space shuttle *Enterprise*, September 17, 1976, Edwards Air Force Base, California. *(Courtesy NASA)*

Rose Parade float sponsored by Nestlé Food Company entitled "Space . . . the Final Frontier"—January 1, 1992. The shuttle craft was named *Roddenberry* in tribute. *(Photo courtesy the Pasadena Tournament of Roses)*

Quietly at work in his office. *(Courtesy Majel Roddenberry)*

A candid shot. *(Courtesy Majel Roddenberry)*

Gene, son Rod, Majel, late 1970s.
(Courtesy Majel Roddenberry)

A few Roddenberry family members: (*left to right*) brother Bob Roddenberry, sister Doris Willowdean, their mother, Caroline Glen, and Gene, early 1980s. *(Courtesy Majel Roddenberry)*

Gene and his oldest daughter,
Darleen Roddenberry, late 1980s.
(Courtesy Majel Roddenberry)

Gene and Majel at Palm Desert, 1990.
(Courtesy Majel Roddenberry)

Gene receives his star on Hollywood's
walk of fame, September 4, 1985.
(Photo by Buzz Lawrence)

At the helm of his boat *Star Trek*.
(Courtesy Majel Roddenberry)

being paid one-fourth what Shatner was making. This was all part of how the game is played in Hollywood, but the studios knew how to play, too.

On March 17, 1967, Alex Brewis requested and received a meeting with Ed Perlstein at Desilu Business Affairs. Before the meeting, Perlstein had informed Nimoy's agent that it was Desilu's intention to bring Nimoy's fee up an additional $250 a week over and above the $500 a week advance in salary that was in his contract. Plus, Perlstein informed Brewis, the studio would provide Leonard with an additional $100 per program to handle secretarial costs for his fan mail. At that point, Leonard was making $1,250 per program for the 1966/1967 season for up to seven days work per show. His contract called for a $500 increase for the 1967/1968 broadcast season to $1,750 per program, and then $250 escalations per year thereafter for up to seven days work. The original contract had Nimoy earning $1,750 per show for the second season. The studio's offer would jack that up to $2,000, plus the secretarial allowance.

Nimoy's agent had a counter proposal: Leonard would get $4,500 per show for six days work, not seven; Leonard would get all of his original salary for reruns spread over five program repeats (the same level as Shatner); and there was more. Leonard wanted to direct a minimum of one out of each thirteen programs—the first at minimum and the rest at the top pay scale of the show[5]; if any of the shows were released theatrically,[6] Nimoy wanted to be paid five times his applicable program compensation or $25,000, whichever was greater. On personal appearances he wanted first-class transportation and accommodations for both him and his wife. He wanted a permanent dressing room large enough to serve as both his room and his office; he wanted a telephone installed at studio expense (he would pay for long distance calls); he would accept the $100 per show secretarial allowance and expected the studio to continue to

---

[5] *Star Trek* directors were paid a flat $3,000 for up to thirteen days work—six days of preparation and seven days shooting. Today, *Star Trek: The Next Generation* pays $22,500 for approximately the same schedule.

[6] Some television programs, such as *The Man From U.N.C.L.E.*, would have two hour-long programs edited together and released as feature films in foreign markets.

supply him with stationery and photos with which to answer his fan mail; if he was to be away from Los Angeles overnight in connection with the production of the program, personal appearances, or any other program requirements, he wanted his *per diem* to be the same as the highest *per diem* paid to any actor on the show. And there were a few other minor requests.

Of course, as any good negotiator knows, initial demands always exceed what one will settle for, and Perlstein reacted as any good studio executive should: he was furious. Everyone played their parts as expected. Perlstein told Nimoy's agent that Leonard's demands were outrageous but that he would pass them on. Perlstein also informed Leonard's agent that all the studio had to do was exercise the existing option under Leonard's current binding five-year agreement and he would *have* to perform. Of course, every studio wants its employees, especially those who are its public face, to be happy, but happy is not defined by studios as giving actors everything they want, when they want it.

Perlstein discussed the matter with Gene and other Desilu executives and on March 29 again spoke with Brewis. He told Brewis that the studio agreed to a telephone for Leonard in his dressing room, subject to Leonard paying the long distance charges, a few other minor concessions, and the studio would adjust Leonard's salary to $2,500 per program for the 1967/1968 broadcast season.

Perlstein announced that this was as far as the studio would go, that there would be no renegotiations, and that the studio had extended itself much beyond their previously agreed-to terms. Then he drew a line in the sand when he delivered the studio's final word: if Leonard did not accept these terms, the studio felt free to continue under the terms of the original contract for the second year—Leonard would be paid $1,750 per program to play Mr. Spock, like it or not.

If this example of studio hardball intimidated Brewis, he didn't show it. He conferred with Nimoy, then called Perlstein and told him, "Everything that you offered is no good!" He had a counteroffer. Perlstein said he was not open to a counteroffer, would not accept it, but would listen and write it down. A copy of the memo still exists in Gene's old files, along with notations that appear to be in Gene's handwriting next to each of Leonard's demands. The following is the exact language of Perlstein's memo, relating Nimoy's agent's demands, followed by Gene's notes.

1—With regard to directing, Leonard insists that he was promised that he would direct in the second year and he wants to direct, and insists upon directing, at least one, and preferably two or three, *Star Trek* episodes during the year.

[*There is a large penciled "X" in the left margin next to the first paragraph.*]

2—Leonard wants $3,750 per show for a maximum of six days work for the 1967/1968 season; $4,500 per show for up to six days work for the 1968/1969 season; $5,000 per show for up to six days work for the 1969/1970 season; and $5,500 for the 1970/1971 season for up to six days work per show.

[*Gene has written, "2500 7 days" in the left margin.*]

3—On reruns Leonard wants 35% for the first rerun, 25% for the second rerun, 20% for the third rerun, 10% for the fourth rerun and for each rerun thereafter without stopping at the end of the fifth rerun.[7]

[*In the upper right margin where there was more room Gene wrote, "50% / 17, 12½, 7, 6¾, 6¾."*]

4—Leonard wants specific language in the contract that the billing he is currently receiving cannot be changed without his approval.

[*Gene wrote, "OK, no change in his credit without approval."*]

5—Leonard wants the contract to specifically indicate in writing that the dressing room will consist of two rooms with a bathroom, a telephone in the permanent dressing room and a telephone in the dressing room on the set.

[*Gene wrote, "My word—2nd floor, Bldg E."*]

6—With regard to off-camera voice commercials, Leonard wants unlimited rights subject only to conflicts of sponsorship.

[*Gene wrote, "No program or commercial conflicts, no Mister Spock."*]

---

[7]This endless rerun residual was unheard of in those days. It was something not even program creators got and had he received it, Leonard Nimoy would have become a wealthy man much sooner than he did.

7—In connection with guest appearances in addition to or as part of the three out of each 13 permitted in each cycle and if *Star Trek* finished before the other one-hour Desilu shows, Leonard wants to be a Guest Star, at the top of the show, on the shows that are still shooting.

[*Gene wrote, "No! But will go out of way."*]

In other words, Gene would do what he could to get Leonard what guest shots he could, but it would not be part of his contract. Ironically, the other big Desilu show being shot at the same time was *Mission Impossible*, whose cast Nimoy would join shortly after his travels through the galaxy ended.

Perlstein finished the memo by describing his out of character behavior: "Usually I am a very peaceful and serene man but I must tell you that I told Alex off at each request and not only do I think that Leonard is sick but I think we can include Alex and Leonard's business manager in this observation as well."

Perlstein was fully prepared to enforce the studio's standing contract if Leonard did not show up for work on April 27, as he had been notified to do.

Sometime during that same day, March 30, Joe D'Agosta, the casting director for *Star Trek*, delivered a memo to Gene. Its subject was "Vulcan Possibilities." It was divided into three categories: an "A" List, a "B" List, and a "C" List. The memo was D'Agosta's suggestions for new Vulcans for the program.

The "A" list had such names as John Anderson, Michael Rennie, Edward Mulhare, Lloyd Bochner, and David Carradine. The number one name on the "A" list was Mark Lenard.

Whether he was aware of the list or not, the next move was Nimoy's, which came in the afternoon of March 30 when he called Perlstein and heated things up a bit.

Perlstein described the call in a memo the following day.

Yesterday afternoon I received a telephone call from Leonard Nimoy directly in which he indicated that since we weren't interested in further negotiations and that we intended to exercise his option pursuant to our contract, he was officially advising me that he would not report for work when required notwithstanding the consequences that we may bring against him. Leonard was very arrogant in indicating that being an actor was not the only employment or source of income available to him in his life span. I told him that if we sought the recourse of SAG in suspending him permanently for willful disregard of his contract, he would never be able to work again as an actor. Leonard again indicated that he would take that chance.

I told Leonard that if he had any thoughts of other avenues in the theatrical industry, Desilu will exert all pressures to other producers and members of the entertainment industry to make known to all in the entertainment industry what he has done and what he contemplates doing.

Perlstein observed that he thought Leonard was still willing to negotiate but that he [Perlstein] told him that Desilu was not renegotiating "but had reconsidered previous increase requests and had come to a final conclusion of the $2,500 per program fee plus $500 escalations for each year thereafter for the balance of the original five-year term."

There was a second purpose to Nimoy's call. He wanted to know if Desilu still wanted him to attend the National Association of Broadcasters' convention in Chicago. Leonard was keeping the door open. Perlstein thought he should go, and the game continued.

On April 6, Nimoy sent a certified letter with a return receipt requested to Perlstein explaining his position. He told Perlstein that he did not feel he could perform the services the studio called for. His representatives were ready and willing to discuss any further ideas Desilu may have in the matter but made clear he was ready to reap what he was sowing. He wrote:

Since the studio has chosen to take a "freeze" attitude, I am prepared to deal with whatever "consequences" may arise from my action, if in fact there should be any.

This was not the first time Perlstein had to handle a recalcitrant actor and he quickly made his next move. On April 10, Perlstein sent a copy of Nimoy's letter to Chet Migden at the Screen Actors Guild. Perlstein's letter was short and to the point.

I would appreciate it very much if you would call upon Leonard Nimoy and discuss his intended breach and tell him the facts of life.

We have no record of what Migden may or may not have said to Nimoy or how Nimoy took it, but the next entry in the files is a memo from Perlstein to the legal department dated April 14, four days after his letter to Migden, detailing the terms for Nimoy's new contract, instructing Legal to prepare it for his signature. Nimoy would receive $2,500 for the 1967/1968 broadcast season for up to seven days work, with $500 per year raises through the 1970/1971 season. Further, his residual payments were 20%, 15%, 7%, 4%, 4% with no further residual after the fifth rerun, for a total of 50%. Nimoy got the $100 per program secretarial allowance for the 1967/1968 season; a *per diem* equal to the highest paid actor if he was required to be away from Los Angeles overnight; his billing would not be altered without first securing his approval; and he received the right to do off-camera voice commercials subject to sponsor, time, and network restrictions without utilizing the voice of the character portrayed in the *Star Trek* series. Nimoy also got the larger dressing room, which turned out to be stifling, but an air conditioner was not part of his contract, so he resorted to subterfuge. Nimoy explained in his autobiography that he had to have his secretary fake a faint and be attended by the studio nurse before management would install the air conditioner.

Shatner may have been satisfied with his money but he had a healthy opinion of himself, his talents, his place on the show, and his future in Hollywood. The crew quickly came up with a nickname one person who was a regular visitor to the set remembered years later.[8]

Regardless of whatever personality shortcomings Shatner may or may not have had, he played one of the central characters in *Star Trek,* and Gene worked hard at keeping him that way, in spite of the growing popularity of Spock. Gene realized how easily the show could tip out of balance, favoring one character over another. In June of 1967, Gene broached the problem in a letter to Asimov.

---

[8]"Shat," she explained, "and it wasn't an affectionate shortening of his name."

Dear Isaac,

Wish you were out here. I would dearly love to
discuss with you a problem about the show and the
format. It concerns Captain James Kirk and of course
the actor who plays that role, William Shatner. Bill
is a fine actor, has been in leads on Broadway, has
done excellent motion pictures, is generally rated as
fine an actor as we have in this country. But we're
not getting the use of him that we should and it
is not his fault. It's easy to give good situations
and good lines to Spock. And to a lesser extent the
same is true of the irascible Dr. McCoy. I guess it's
something like doing a scene with several business
men in a room with an Eskimo. The interesting and
amusing situations, the clever lines, would tend to go
to the Eskimo. Or in our case, the Eskimos.

And yet *Star Trek* needs a strong lead, an Earth
lead. Without diminishing the importance of the
secondary continuing characters. But the problem we
generally find is this—if we play Kirk as a true ship
commander, strong and hard, devoted to career and
service, it too often makes him seem unlikable. On
the other hand, if we play him too warm-hearted, friendly
and so on, the attitude often is "how did a guy like
that get to be a ship commander?" Sort of a damned
if he does and damned if he doesn't situation.
Actually, although it is missed by the general audience,
it is Kirk's fine handling of a most difficult role that
permits Spock and the others to come off as well
as they do. But Kirk does deserve more and so does
the actor who plays him. I am in something of a quandary
about it. Got any ideas?

Asimov responded immediately, the date of the letter suggesting he wrote on the day he received Gene's letter.

In some way, this is the example of the general
problems of first banana/second banana. The star has
to be a well-rounded individual but the supporting
player can be a "humorous" man in the Elizabethan
sense. He can specialize. Since his role is smaller and
less important, he can be made highly seasoned, and
his peculiarities and humors can easily win a wide

following simply because they are so marked and
even predictable. The top banana is disregarded
simply because he carries the show and must do
many things in many ways. The proof of the pudding
is that it is rare for a second banana to be able to support
a show in his old character if he keeps that
character. There are exceptions. Gomer Pyle made
it as Gomer Pyle (and acquired a second banana of
his own in the person of the sergeant.)

Undoubtedly, it is hard on the top banana (who
like all actors has a healthy streak of insecurity and
needs vocal and constant reassurance from the audience)
to [not] feel drowned out. Everybody in the show knows
exactly how important and how good Mr. Shatner
is, and so do all the actors, including even Mr.
Shatner. Still, when the fan letters go to Mr. Nimoy
and articles like mine concentrate on him, one can't
help feeling unappreciated. (Andy Griffith had to
face it when Don Knotts got the Emmies, and Sid
Caesar when Carl Reiner got them and so on.)

What to do? Well, let me think about it and write
another letter in a few days. I don't know that I'll
have any magic solutions, but you know, some
vagrant thought of mine might spark some thought
in you and who knows—

A few weeks later, Asimov sent another letter.

... I promised to get back to you with my thoughts
on the question of Mr. Shatner and the dilemma of
playing lead against such a fad-character as "Mr.
Spock."

The more I think about it, the more I think the problem
is psychological. That is, *Star Trek* is successful, and
I think it will prove easier to get a renewal for the
third year than was the case for the second. The
chief practical reason for its success is Mr. Spock.
The excellence of the stories and the acting brings in
the intelligent audience (who aren't enough in
numbers, alas, to affect the ratings appreciably) but
Mr. Spock brings in the "teenage vote" which does
send the ratings over the top. Therefore, nothing can
or should be done about that. (Besides, Mr. Spock

is a wonderful character and I would be *most*
reluctant to change him in any way.)

The problem, then, is how to convince the world,
and Mr. Shatner, that Mr. Shatner is the lead.

It seems to me that the only thing one can do is
lead from strength. Mr. Shatner is a versatile and
talented actor and perhaps this should be made plain
by giving him a chance at a variety of roles. In other
words, an effort should be made to work up story plots
in which Mr. Shatner has an opportunity to put on
disguises or take over roles of unusual nature. A
bravura display of his versatility would be impressive
indeed and would probably make the whole deal a great
deal more fun for Mr. Shatner. (He might also
consider that a display of virtuosity would stand
him in great stead when the time—the *sad* time—came
that *Star Trek* had finished its run and he must look
elsewhere.)

Then, too, it might be well to unify the team of
Kirk and Spock a bit, by having them actively meet
various menaces together with one saving the life of
the other on occasion. The idea of this would be
to get people to think of Kirk when they think of
Spock.

And, finally, the most important suggestion of all—
ignore this letter, unless it happens to make sense
to you.

Isaac

A couple of days after receiving Asimov's advice, Gene
responded.

Your comments on Shatner and Spock were most
interesting and I have passed them on to Gene Coon
and the others. We've followed one idea
immediately, that of having Spock save his
Captain's life, in an up-coming show. I will follow
your advice about having them much more a team,
standing more closely together. As for having
Shatner play more varied roles, we have been
looking in that direction and will continue to do so.
But I think the most important comment is that of keeping

them a close team. Shatner will come off ahead
by showing he is fond of the teenage idol; Spock
will do well by displaying great loyalty to his Captain.
In a way it will give us *one* lead, the team.

While "the Team" were working together on the screen,
Nimoy was the only actor who had his bags of fan mail delivered to him once a week on the set in front of Shatner and
the other actors. Nimoy may not have made nearly as much
money as Shatner, but he would be certain Shatner knew
how popular he was on the program.

Creativity in Hollywood is a sellable commodity, but attendant with that is attaining credit for creativity. The more
credit you have, the more people know your name as a
writer, the more in demand you can be, the more money you
make, the more people know your name, the more you are
in demand . . .

Getting credit isn't always easy or simple. In Hollywood,
the path to writing success is a maze without a plan, as this
September 19, 1967, letter from Gene Coon, producer of
Star Trek, to the Writers Guild attests.

Re: "Bread and Circuses"
    First of all, a few words of explanation about this
matter, for it is involved and complicated.
    Gene Roddenberry and I sat down and developed
the story idea, which you have in your possession at
this time, included among other pertinent material. We
then called in John Kneubuhl, gave him the story,
which, while not completely developed, was
considerably developed. John added a few pages to
the story, we had it approved and then he went into
First Draft; then into Second Draft. But he had
many personal problems and his health failed him,
and one day John called me and told me that he simply
could not finish the screenplay and requested that he
be withdrawn from the project.
    This was granted. At this time, I went back to
the original story, the one written by Roddenberry and
me, and wrote a brand new First Draft, with different
structure, dialogue, character development, and so

on, which you will see in the first mimeographed copy of the script. When I had finished with a First Draft, Re-write and a Polish, Gene Roddenberry stepped in and contributed a complete Re-write, with new structure and character, based upon NOT THE KNEUBUHL SCRIPT, but upon my script, which was, in its turn, a complete original and not a simple Re-Write of the Kneubuhl effort.

Ordinarily, I would not go to such length, but since John Kneubuhl gave up completely on the script and returned the job to us, not only unfinished, but, in fact, unstarted-upon, since he had done no writing at all on his Re-Write so far as I know, I want to be sure the arbitration panel knows the full story.

Strictly speaking, I do not see why arbitration is called for, since "Bread and Circuses" is a completely original story with the producers of the program to begin with, and the final product was completely written ... not re-written, but written ... by the two producers of the show. Roddenberry and I are certainly not competing for credit.

After serious thought, being as fair as possible, we feel that since all aspects of the Final Draft are original with us, credit should go to no one else. Despite the fact that John Kneubuhl withdrew from the project, he did indeed receive full pay as per contract, even though he did not in the strictest sense fulfill the terms of his contract.

We are not asking for arbitration between Gene Roddenberry and Gene Coon ... We have made equal contributions to the script, and since we are both production executives, and since we do not, unlike many writers, regard each other as enemies, we hope for a calm, rational, and sensible adjudication of the issue. We would be most pleased to see the credits established as suggested. Due to the circumstances, we are not even sure that it is necessary to submit this package for arbitration, but we would not like to break any of the Guild's rules.

Sincerely,
Gene L. Coon
Producer
Star Trek

When the process of arbitration was completed, the broadcast credit for this episode read: "By Gene L. Coon and Gene Roddenberry, story by John Kneubuhl."

Sometimes it was difficult to be generous, though Gene was not afraid to give credit where he thought credit was due. On June 3, 1966, Gene sent a memo and three copies of each version of a script to the Writers Guild, proposing that the credits on "Mudd's Women" be as follows: "Story by Gene Roddenberry; teleplay by Stephen Kandel, John D.F. Black, Gene Roddenberry."

On June 21, 1966, Mary Dorfman, credits administrator at the Writers Guild responded with the following:

> The Writers Guild Credit Arbitration Committee, after carefully considering all of the material submitted to it in the case of "Mudd's Women" has decided the writing credits shall read as follows:
>
> Teleplay by Stephen Kandel
> Story by Gene Roddenberry.

Gene did a great deal of work that, while paid for, was uncredited. Buried in the files at UCLA is a memo that Gene sent to the Desilu front office regarding rewrites and polishes. There was some debate with the front office over when such rewrites should be authorized.

In the files there is also the second page of a memo from Gene, specifying some of his work:

Polish on "Catspaw"—$750.
Complete rewrite on "Friday's Child"—$2750.
Furnished the story for "Who Mourns for Adonais?" (credit on film reads "by Gilbert Ralston and Gene L. Coon.")—$750.
Furnished story on "Amok Time"—$750—Polished script—$750. (Film credit reads "by Theodore Sturgeon.")
Polish on "Wolf in the Fold"—$1,000.
Furnished story for "I, Mudd"—$750—polish—$750. (Credit on film reads "by Stephen Kandel and David Gerrold.")
Furnished story for "Bread & Circuses"—$750. Complete rewrite—$2500.

Complete rewrite and a new script for "A Private Little War"—$3,000.

Rewrite on "Obsession"—$2500 (credit reads "by Art Wallace.")

In mid-April 1967, Gene sent a memo to "all concerned" regarding bridge efficiency and disciplines on the set. It was the sort of memo that could have only been sent by someone who had military command experience such as Gene. It is a further example of Gene's close attention to detail, which gave *Star Trek* much of its believability.

Late last season and in many first draft scripts coming up this year, we are not seeing the "trained group efficiency" that should characterize even a 20th Century Bridge much less one of the U.S.S. *Enterprise* in our Century. For example, far too often someone reports to the Captain that something is approaching the ship. The Captain asks how far away it is and gets an answer. Then the Captain must ask if they can make out the size of it, and he gets an answer. Then he asks Mr. Spock for an opinion, gets an answer. Hardly the kind of smooth trained, and experienced coordination one would expect in a group of future day astronauts aboard something like the U.S.S. *Enterprise.*

Kirk should never have to ask these questions. Sulu should know what information from his instruments should be immediately transmitted to the Captain. Same with everyone else aboard the Bridge. Just as even a co-pilot aboard a present day airliner knows he should be constantly be making verbal reports to his Captain on the reading of this instrument or that radio marker, or etc.

Why it this important to us? Believability again! Our audience simply won't believe this is the Bridge of a starship unless the characters on it seem at least as coordinated and efficient as the blinking lights and instrumentation around them. And we're not going to believe our characters either unless there is a constant reminder they are indeed the trained kind of individuals who would have these posts of responsibility. The same comment might be made about their inter-actions while on landing party duty. We get an added advantage from all this, i.e., the fact they can go casual off duty away from emergencies only makes them more multi-dimensional.

Admittedly it is first a script/dialogue problem and we will certainly try to keep an eye on it there. But we will miss and need the creative assistance of our directors in giving us movement and pace which helps keep the Bridge and routines efficient and believable.

Gene Roddenberry

Gene was fortunate in that he had tremendous energy and needed only five or six hours of sleep a night, giving him additional time to write. During the middle of 1967, Gene wrote a *Robin Hood* script, dated August 25, 1967. Two weeks before, he had written a friend about his project.

By a strange coincidence your letter came at a time in which I was preparing a pilot in the "Robin Hood" area and was at that moment wrestling with the problem of hero and anti-hero. I realized that Robin Hood could not succeed in today's market if he were the wimpy "St George And England!" type hero and yet how far could I go in the other direction without completely destroying the value of the legendary figure? I think I have the problem solved but it would be fun if you were here so I could sit down over coffee and discuss all the questions involved.

A writer who creates strongly emotional characters and situations can be a great success, but can also be extremely difficult to deal with in the traumatic business of producing a weekly television show within the limitations of a specific format. Some understood the problems; others did not and developed a lifelong enmity toward Gene. The ability to write a science fiction short story or novel did not automatically translate into an ability to write for the visual medium of television, with its need for acts, pauses for commercials, simple stories that could be told in a specific amount of time, and financial limitations. Gene was also adamant that the principles and honor codes, the "logic" of the universe he had created, be followed. Whatever was written *had* to be *Star Trek*. Several big names in science fiction tried and failed, finding the restrictions of time and budget too confining for their kind of storytelling.

Some confusion and more than a little hostility has arisen over one specific *Star Trek* episode: "The City On the Edge of Forever." The original story was written by Harlan Ellison[9] and concerned drug dealing and extortion by a member of the *Enterprise*'s engineering staff.[10] It also had elaborate aliens, and while the overall story was good, it was not filmed for two reasons: 1) it wasn't *Star Trek* and, 2) it would, according to Bob Justman, cost at least $100,000 over the normal budget. Ellison was told to rewrite it, but was unable to produce a script that met the show's requirements. One or two other writers were assigned the project, and when they failed to deliver Gene rewrote it himself. To further the irritation process, all this occurred within a couple of months of Ellison's help in the previously mentioned letter-writing campaign and his work on "the Committee."

Ellison has written and spoken at length about this episode over the years. At one point, he demanded that his name be removed and substituted with a WGA registered pseudonym, Cordwainer Bird. This demand was later withdrawn and his name stayed on the script.[11] Harlan Ellison's name is the only writing credit that appears on this script.[12]

The show won several awards. The Writers Guild Award was accepted by Ellison for his original script, not the final shooting script, as was the usual custom.[13] This episode also

---

[9]The original story outline has either been stolen or misplaced in the UCLA Archives. It was replaced with a copy from this writer's files.

[10]Over twenty years later, Gene had forgotten the precise details and inadvertantly said in an interview that it was Scotty who was dealing drugs. This was not accurate and he corrected himself when it was brought to his attention, saying that it had been many years since he had read the original story.

[11]In addition to the original story outline, three letters from Ellison that appear in the UCLA collection index are missing from the folder they were assigned to. They were not available to this writer in the preparation of this book.

[12]This happened around the beginning of February 1967. By the end of February, at least one fanzine was reporting that Ellison was "quitting Hollywood." The editor ventured his own thought by saying, "It is the opinion of this editor that either Harlan has overreacted tremendously, or he became burdened with a surplus of book contracts and decided to pull out of one area, Hollywood, in order to devote his entire time to writing for publication, and do so in a manner which would suggest a sudden impulse. With Harlan Ellison it's difficult to decide which is more plausible."

[13]Bob Justman, sitting at a table with Gene, remembers Ellison shaking the award at them as he walked off the stage.

won the 1968 Hugo Award, and thereby hangs the tale of one of the few public comments Gene made about this matter.

In late 1968, Gene received a letter from Alan E. Nourse, then president of the Science Fiction Writers of America. Nourse reminded Gene that they had spoken briefly at the Baycon Science Fiction Convention in Berkeley over the Labor Day weekend regarding complaints "various SFWA members had made to him on account of promotion and sales of copies of *Star Trek* scripts in which they believed they had a royalty or fee interest."

Nourse then got to the real reason for his letter:

> I now understand from one of our members, Mr. Harlan Ellison, that copies of *Star Trek* scripts authored by him have been on sale under this arrangement in excess of 12 months, but he has received no reports of sales from Paramount, nor any compensation.

Gene rarely discussed his rewrites, or justified his actions with anyone, but in this case he made an exception and responded within a day of receiving Nourse's letter.

> Thank you for bringing the delay to my attention. However, please be informed that the delay has not been twelve months but more on the order of six, since any actual sale of scripts began. It may also interest you to know that Mr. Harlan Ellison has no scripts authored by him being sold by Lincoln Enterprises. You might find it interesting and even amusing to ask him about his "authorship" on the recent Hugo he won on that basis.
>
> Lincoln Enterprises is currently preparing a report on the subject for Paramount Pictures. No doubt they will be contacting Writers Guild of America West who represents writers on such subjects.

Being Gene's friend did not guarantee escape from his rewrite gauntlet. Even Don Ingalls, close to Gene since their days at LAPD, felt the point of Gene's pencil. His first *Star Trek* script, "The Alternative Factor,"[14] was rewritten only a

---

[14]Aired 3/30/67, guest-starring Robert Brown as Lazarus A & B.

bit, but his second, "A Private Little War," written specifically as a critique on the Vietnam War, was heavily rewritten; so much so that Don was thoroughly irritated with Gene. He stayed mad at him for a year. Further, he insisted on a pseudonym for his credit on that particular show. He chose "Judd Crucis," a variant on Latin for "Jesus Christ," which he said was emblematic for having been crucified on the show.

Even as executive producer there were certain responsibilities Gene could not escape. One was chastising writers who did not deliver. Theodore Sturgeon was once described thusly: "He had, one might say, a binary career: either he was writing nothing or he was writing at a high pitch."[15] Asimov used to tell the story of Sturgeon making a deadline by having friends drive him in a car to the publisher while he wrote furiously in the backseat to finish the assignment.

While he was a good writer, Sturgeon's temperament was not well suited to the time demands of writing for television. In short, he was slow to deliver. On April 3, 1968, Gene sent a memo to Fred Freiberger and Bob Justman.

> Talked to Ted Sturgeon long distance today and informed him in no uncertain terms that our new Producer, Fred Freiberger, will not hesitate for a moment to make use of the WGA Minimum Contract Regulation regarding promptness of delivery of material. Freiberger no monster, but a very, very practical Producer and businessman and Sturgeon had better get with it and stay with it, or he's going to find himself delaying story, script or revision to a place where he gets cut off and no payment made.
>
> Gene Roddenberry

Small wonder that even though he wrote two of the better episodes, Sturgeon only wrote two episodes.

With two daughters, Gene had become aware of a trend in popular music that became known as the "English Invasion." Other television producers and networks also noticed and

---

[15]*The Encyclopedia of Science Fiction* 1993, edited by John Clute and Peter Nicholls, Orbit, a Division of Little, Brown and Company, London, UK.

were quick to jump on the bandwagon. Inspired by the Beatles' 1964 film, *A Hard Day's Night,* NBC launched *The Monkees,* a "manufactured" musical group that featured two actors and two musicians in a series of fast-paced skits and adventures. *The Monkees* debuted on NBC September 12, 1966, the Monday after *Star Trek*'s Thursday debut. Ten days after *The Monkees* first broadcast Gene sent the following memo to Joe D'Agosta regarding a needed crew type.

> Keeping our teenage audience in mind, also keeping aware of current trends, let's watch for a young, irreverent, English-accent "Beatle" type to try on the show, possibly with an eye to him reoccurring. Like the smallish fellow [Davy Jones] who looks to be a hit on *The Monkees.* Personally I find this type spirited and refreshing and I think our episodes could use that kind of "lift." Let's discuss.
>
> Gene Roddenberry

The "needed crew type" ultimately had his English accent replaced with a Russian one in order to kill two birds with one stone, as a copy of an October 10, 1967, letter from Gene to Mikhail V. Zimyanin, Editor of *Pravda,* the newspaper of the Central Committee of the Communist Party of the Soviet Union reveals:

> Dear Mr. Zimyanin:
> About ten months ago one of the stars of our television show, *Star Trek,* informed us he had heard that the youth edition of your newspaper had published an article regarding *Star Trek* to the effect that the only nationality we were missing aboard our USS Enterprise was a Russian. We were certainly most flattered to even have mention from so far away and wondered if perhaps you could confirm that there was such an article and if so could we possibly presume upon you for a copy of it.
> Incidentally, as soon as we heard of this article we added that Russian character. His name is Chekov, and he is, we feel, a great addition to our show.
>
> Very sincerely yours,
> Gene Roddenberry

We have no record if the story actually appeared in *Pravda* or if Gene ever received a reply from the editor, but Ensign Pavel Chekov found a permanent assignment on board the U.S.S. *Enterprise* beginning with the second season episode "Amok Time," broadcast September 15, 1967. Chekov would appear in nineteen of the second season's twenty-five episodes and thirteen of the third season's twenty-four episodes.

A myth has grown around one specific *Star Trek* episode. "Plato's Stepchildren" made television history, but in a less spectacular manner than has been previously described.

The story began in outline as "Sons Of Socrates," written by Meyer Dolinsky. Dolinsky's story had the *Enterprise* encountering a small group of beings living on the planet Platonius. The beings had modeled their society on that of Plato and ancient Greece. Humanoid in appearance, they possessed psychokinetic power—all except for their dwarf jester, Alexander.

The Platonians were cruel, arrogant, and unable to easily recover from wounds. Their leader was suffering from an infected cut and in his delirium damaged the *Enterprise* with his uncontrolled psychokinetic power. The dwarf shows the only spark of "humanity" and risks his life to help anesthetize Parmen, the delirious leader.

When Dr. McCoy treats him, Parmen is grateful and decides to keep him as part of their community against the possibility of someone being injured again. Kirk, Spock, and the rest of the landing party have no choice because of Parmen's willful use of his mental abilities. Ultimately, they are made to act like marionettes controlled by Parmen and the others.

The landing party is divided equally with three men and three women, and among other forced actions, Kirk and Uhura are made to embrace and kiss.

Much has been written about who was to kiss whom, with frantic discussions by and with management in the front office, ending with Gene dramatically standing fast, demanding that Kirk would kiss Uhura. Nothing could be further from the truth.

Dolinsky's first story outline dated June 10, 1968 (five

months before the episode aired),[16] clearly shows the author's intent from the beginning. On page 20 of the outline, Mr. Spock is paired off with Nurse Chapel (in keeping with the show's continuing storyline), Captain Kirk with a young and pretty yeoman, and Dr. McCoy with Lieutenant Uhura, being "made to play toesies with each other. Nurse Chapel, meanwhile, lies dreamily against Spock's chest."

Spock kisses, caresses and embraces Nurse Chapel. The yeoman is pulled away from Kirk and Lieutenant Uhura is tossed into his lap. "The Lt. is starting to bend Kirk's head back in a violent kiss when he suddenly gets the psychokenetic power,"[17] is how the original outline described the action.

In the teleplay's first draft, dated July 9, 1968, Uhura ends up on Kirk's lap after Kirk kissed the yeoman. In the final draft, the script the show was shot from, we find Kirk and Uhura kissing—only he is kissing her, not as the author originally had it in outline.

Just how much noise did NBC raise over this, how much concern did they display? The answer is found in the one letter and two surviving Broadcast Standards and Practices memos in the Roddenberry Archive.

The letter is from Stanley Robertson, manager of Film Programming at NBC. His letter was sent the Tuesday following a conversation he had with Fred Freiberger (who had taken over as producer) the previous Friday, June 21, during which Robertson had approved the story outline with certain reservations.

In his letter, Robertson notes that he had read every *Star Trek* submission since the inception of the series and comments that Dolinsky's outline was "one of the very, very few instances in which I have not been able to truly and fully understand the story which was being told by the writer."

Robertson followed his line of thinking and made a strong case for the story's lack of believability. Finally, he analyzed the story's resolution, ending his letter by saying: "In conclusion, I again remind you that as I advised you, any inference or reference to the point made by the writer that our

---

[16]Currently in box 23, file folder 7 of the Roddenberry/Star Trek Archives at UCLA.

[17]Ultimately, the power develops in Kirk, Spock, and McCoy from an element McCoy has found in the water.

heroes would be 'forced to make love to one another' as a form of sport for their captors, is unacceptable to NBC. Also, that great care should be utilized in the dramatic use of the dwarf, Alexander, so as not to make light of, or ridicule, his physical deformities."

Not a word about the famous interracial kiss, coming, ironically enough, from a man who was the highest-ranking African American then working in the NBC hierarchy!

The following two memos are from Jean Messerschmidt, NBC's Broadcast Standards and Practices's representative: the NBC censor. The first is dated June 27, 1968. Ms. Messerschmidt writes that she had read the story outline for "The Sons Of Socrates" and had the following comments:

> The enforced love-making will have to be deleted, and since the plot will be clarified and otherwise revised according to Mr. Robertson's letter to Mr. Freiberger dated 6/25, the handling of conflict resulting from use of psychokinetic power will be reviewed upon receipt of the script.

When she received the script, Ms. Messerschmidt sent another memo dated September 4, saying:

> Please exercise care throughout to make certain that Alexander, the dwarf, is treated subserviently only as required by the plot, i.e., by his masters, the heavies, so that those viewers similarly afflicted will not be offended. Caution also on costuming to be sure it is within the bounds of television propriety, and on the selection of such items as statuary, so there will be no embarrassment to the viewer.
>
> Please make certain the sight of Parmen's infected leg is not shocking or alarming.
>
> Here and wherever else the psychokinetic force is evident, normal restrictions on reactions to the blows and impacts would apply just as though there were visible blows and impacts, and will be judged accordingly. Please make certain also that reactions such as twisting, choking, and back bending are not grotesque or shocking to the viewer.
>
> Please delete the underlined in McCoy's speech, "Fe-

ver's broken and *Lord,* what incredible recuperative powers!"

All source music should be checked for clearance.

Kirk's bruises must be minimal if shown at all and, of course, there will be no blood.

Extreme care must be exercised when staging these scenes, so it is obvious the Platonians' intention is to humiliate; there may be no hint of voyeurism. Caution on the postures and actions of our four principals so that no impropriety can be suggested. The embraces must not be such as would embarrass a viewer, and there must be no open-mouth kissing. Further, it must be clear there are no racial over-tones to Kirk's and Uhura's dilemma.

That is the sum of NBC's concern: one line at the end of a typically pedantic Standards and Practice's memo, whose main concern was that there be no open-mouth kissing and nothing to shock the viewer.

Finally, in October, Gene, as executive producer, wrote to Fred Freiberger, commenting on "Plato's Stepchildren," concerning himself, as usual, with the story line and its believability, and not at all with interracial hanky panky.

It should make an unusual episode and an excellent one. I thoroughly enjoyed viewing it even without sound effects and music. Speaking of music, I do not think this episode can be tracked or partially scored. Agree completely with Bill Hatch that it must have an original score since it is a totally unusual piece of film.

As usual, although I like the episode immensely, I will concentrate on the negative.

My greatest criticism of "Plato's Stepchildren" is that the first reel comes off rather *Lost in Space.* Now, that should shake you up since you have got to be asking yourselves how can anything done with taste and talent compare with that particular kiddy show? The reason is that in our episode we haven't *in the slightest* given the audience any reasonable explanation of who these humanoid people are, how they got here, why they so much fancy Greek philosophy and the clothing of the small era in Earth's history, etc. The way the episode begins now we sort of get the feeling that Captain Kirk and the others are saying, "Oh yes, here we are on another one of those

Greek philosophy planet places." Remember how *Lost in Space* would be in a planetary Chinatown one week, Greece the next, a western setting the next, etc., without even a logical explanation of why or how?

To keep *Star Trek* in its proper perspective and to keep Kirk, the ship and crew, and Earth in their proper intelligent perspective, we must constantly keep in mind that Earth is only one of tens of thousands of inhabited planets. Although Earth is a principle factor in the Federation, it is still only a speck of matter in the vastness of space. Earth's history and its customs and costumes are only an infinitesimal fraction of the enormous variety of life and society and customs found throughout the galaxy.

If, as this particular episode, our Starship on a far-off planet should come upon some people that have adapted Plato's philosophies so completely, it would be a source of considerable surprise and not a few questions.

In other words, in this particular episode as in recent others, I fear that we are losing our sense of wonder about space and the strange things we find out there. Our captain seems to be saying, "Oh yes, another one of these places" rather than, "Wow! This seems impossible on the surface; let's get to the bottom of it."

In still other words, we have an excellent show here but it could have been made even better if our audience could be made to *believe* in this place and the people. One way to make them believe is when it is an unusual occurrence, our captain and landing party also recognize it as unusual and comment upon it. Time after time in our best past episodes we said, "It seems impossible that it exists and yet it does, so there must be logic and reason behind it. It is probably that out of that logic and reason we will find an answer to the jeopardies in which we find ourselves." The public never gets tired of our characters trying to untangle that kind of puzzle.

Gene Roddenberry

The undramatic truth is the actors did what they were told, and "Plato's Stepchildren" was filmed as it was written with due consideration given to NBC's concerns. As Gene later remembered, they received surprisingly little negative mail from that episode.

Perhaps most telling is the fact that no one objected to the interspecies activity between Mr. Spock and Nurse Christine Chapel: television's first interspecies kiss.

As Gene moved forward with production of the series, the larger picture was changing. Paramount Pictures, Desilu's next-door neighbor, had been owned by Gulf + Western Industries, Inc. since October 1966. On February 15, 1967, the announcement was made that Desilu had been bought by G + W for $17 million in a stock exchange deal. Lucille Ball's sixty percent of Desilu stock netted her a tidy $10.2 million in Gulf + Western stock.

The new owners changed the playing field. Gone was the smalltown atmosphere that had characterized Desilu; in came the corporate mentality. A week after the merger, Charles Bluhdorn, Gulf + Western's owner, started seeing cost figures and called Ed Holly in the middle of the night.

"All I heard was 'What did you sell me? I'm going to the poorhouse!' Ed Holly replied, 'Charlie, you must be looking at *Star Trek* and *Mission: Impossible.* Those shows are costing almost to the dollar what our projections showed they would cost. You and your people made the judgment that that was all right.' "

Evidently Mr. Bluhdorn didn't think his people had made the correct judgment call and passed the word, which prompted the following September 20, 1967, memo from Gene to "all concerned."

The new Paramount-Desilu combine has made an exhaustive study of shows currently being produced here and has concluded, I think not unfairly, that television shows must be produced at a price somewhere near the long range revenue anticipated from them.

Our challenge, *and it does affect you*—shoot as fine a *Star Trek* as ever, but in less time and work with less cost. If I understand correctly the fact and figures presented in recent meetings on this subject, it appears we can meet these new goals without *significant* cuts into the quality of our show. Rather than making drastic format changes, the information given me makes it appear that we can accommodate the Paramount-Desilu management by simply tightening all along the line and most important of all, seeing that our final shooting scripts are within episode budget limits and the kind of show that can be shot in six ten hour working days. And then, shooting them in that time.

John Reynolds, head of Paramount-Desilu television, promises he will see that the studio meets us more than half way in seeking means of giving us increased efficiency from studio departments plus a double-check system that sees our charges are no greater than the industry norm.

In short, it appears that the studio is making a reasonable request and is willing to help us meet it. In return, we have committed ourselves just as reasonably to meet those requests. We will be needing your help. This is a dual commitment and we need (a) your efforts in helping us meet our commitment to them, and (b) your help in letting Paramount-Desilu know immediately about any area or items in which they are not meeting their commitment to us.

Just sending out a memo and keeping a more careful eye on the bottom line wasn't enough; Gene had to face a full frontal assault by the front office. At that time, Irwin Allen was producing *Voyage To The Bottom of the Sea* at Fox, based on his 1961 science fiction film. Someone in the Paramount front office had the bright idea to compare the costs of the two shows and show the comparisons to Gene with the attendant question, "Why can't you produce your show for less?" That the two shows were vastly different in concept, look, and feel, and that Allen had used many sets from his film were not taken into account. Both shows were science fiction and that was enough of a similarity to make a comparison.

Like others who have encountered Gene, Reynolds may not have been prepared for what came next: a detailed four-page, single-spaced document. Gene had directed Bob Justman to obtain budgets from *Voyage* and make a detailed comparison of the two programs. Gene added his own touches, and sent it off to Reynolds.

Dear John:
    This will include some budget facts I thought you might like to have.

Recently we had a meeting based on some budget comparisons between *Star Trek* and other shows in town, particularly *Voyage To The Bottom of the Sea.* The outcome of the meeting was that we on *Star Trek* would immediately begin to design our scripts and organize our efforts so that *Star Trek* could be photographed in six ten-hour days, meeting what seems to be the average or standard in the industry. As you know, we are aggressively pursuing this.

However, in comparing budgets on *Star Trek* and *Voyage To The Bottom of The Sea,* there are some additional facts you should have:

1. *Voyage* doesn't budget any money for its executive
producer. He exists and therefore he must receive a salary, but it is not on the budget.

2. *Voyage* never goes to another planet nor even to another time period far different from 1967. Therefore, they can use standing sets, local locations, and have few really difficult set design and construction problems.

3. *Voyage* spends more time aboard its submarine than *Star Trek* does aboard its spaceship. We intend to use more scenes aboard our USS *Enterprise* and will need your help against NBC who exerts constant pressure on us to visit new and different planets every week, to the exclusion of spaceship scenes.

4. Mimeograph charges at *Voyage* are much smaller than *Star Trek,* leading us to believe that Fox offers facilities or savings Paramount does not offer us in this area.

5. Fox does not charge for a studio generator operator. *Star Trek* is charged at least $90 per show.

6. *Voyage* uses contemporary costumes. Their uniforms, for example, are 1967 type gabardine shirt and trousers. Where they show people outside their vessel, these are generally contemporary costumes also. On the other hand, *Star Trek* must design and build special costumes for about every other show or more.

7. *Voyage* budgets one make-up man for six days and one hairdresser for three days. They do not budget any wardrobe lady at all. These are clearly missing

items and indicates Fox is spending money in areas which do not appear on the budgets. Keep in mind in that respect, also, that *Star Trek*'s make-up requirements are much more extensive because of the "other worlds" aspect of the *Star Trek* format.

8. *Voyage* does not budget any money for publicity expense. *Star Trek* budgets $1886 per episode for this item. No doubt, *Voyage* publicity is covered in studio overhead.

9. *Voyage* does not allocate any money for nearby locations in its series budget. *Star Trek* does.

10. *Voyage* does not budget any money for casting. *Star Trek* budgets $553 per episode for this service.

11. *Star Trek* budgets $75 per show for stationery. *Voyage* budgets nothing for this.

12. *Star Trek* budgets $600 per episode for telephone and telegraph. *Voyage* budgets nothing for this service.

13. *Star Trek* budgets $250 per episode for production mimeograph and multilithing. *Voyage* budgets nothing.

14. *Star Trek* budgets $175 for studio meals per episode. *Voyage* budgets nothing.

15. *Star Trek* budgets $25 for copyrights per episode. *Voyage* budgets nothing.

16. *Star Trek* is charged $220 more in insurance charges than *Voyage*.

17. *Voyage* budgets $2302 for amortization per show. *Star Trek* budgets more money than this for just preparation alone. The total is $3839 for preparation, plus $305 for lay-off amortization, plus $638 for clean up amortization, and $300 for unused scripts.

18. *Voyage* has no "all shows" account. *Star Trek* budgets $810 per episode for this item.

19. *Star Trek* pays 29½% on all I.A. Labor fringe benefits. *Voyage* is charged only 25.3% for the same item.

20. *Voyage* places no limit on stage space whereas this is not true of *Star Trek*.

21. *Voyage* is not charged for picture cars owned by Fox whereas *Star Trek* is charged.

22. On *Voyage* air-conditioning is furnished to the stages at no cost except for hook-ups or moving.

Where *Star Trek* has same available, it is charged for it.

23. *Voyage* operates under a Fox agreement which lists charges for transportation, cars, and drivers which are at a lesser charge than those established here at this studio.

24. *Voyage* has the benefits of a studio owned set, greens and shrubs department, is charged a wholesale rate less 33½%, compared with *Star Trek* paying the full market charge plus additional studio charges on same.

25. On items purchased for the show, *Voyage* is charged *exact cost*. *Star Trek* is charged retail cost (no discounts even though items may be obtainable at discount) plus a flat 20% override on same.

26. *Voyage* is charged a flat 15% on all direct costs which, in the instance of their budget, comes out of $21,715. *Star Trek* is charged $3,200 more in the case of an average show, even with the recent $10,000 reduction.

These are some of the most obvious differences. There are still others which work to the benefit of Fox companies and to the detriment of Paramount-Desilu companies and I will be happy to have them developed and passed on to you whenever you wish. It goes without saying that such items have a direct bearing on future profits, and open still further the question of whether or not Paramount-Desilu is taking out of the show in such charges what amounts to "advance profits" on the show. No doubt we will be discussing that in time but, in the meanwhile, these figures may be useful to you during any further discussions of show budgets with Paramount-Desilu management.

> Sincerely yours,
> Gene Roddenberry

By mid-October, 1967, Gene wrote to Asimov:

You haven't heard from me regarding the motion picture project because I have been in negotiations with Paramount (which took over Desilu recently) regarding how long I would stay on and under what terms and what projects etc. The typical miserable negotiating which this crazy business requires whenever a change in studios is made. I really don't know what the results of it all will be. If I stay on at Paramount, I will do some motion pictures. If not, should I go to NBC or another studio, then I'll have to present new projects to them.

Will let you know as it develops.

Star Trek is not doing too well on Friday nights. Can't say this surprises us much as we were very worried about this shift of nights. *Tarzan* is hardly the ideal lead-in for our show since the kind of audience that watches it almost certainly would not be interested in *Star Trek,* and vice-versa. For the second year in a row we have a failing show following us on the schedule, and then following that there is *Bell Telephone Hour* which is hardly a mass audience blockbuster. And against us, as you've seen, have been motion pictures like *The Great Escape, North By Northwest,* and so on.

Despite this, *Star Trek* bids to be NBC's high rated show for Friday night. But their Friday night line up is so bad that being high rated on that particular evening doesn't give us a great sense of security. We are presently agitating for a switch to another night.

Gene had more than "agitating" in mind as he prepared to persuade NBC to move him away from Friday night. As the second season approached its close, Gene was concerned that the show might not be picked up again. His first attempt at creating a grass roots support movement the previous year had not fared well, but a second try was in the works nonetheless. Again, Gene worked behind the scenes so he would not be publicly associated with the effort to save the show.

Gene had written a telegram that he wanted to send out with Asimov's name attached. He read the text to Asimov on the phone and received telegraphed permission shortly thereafter. The publicity telegram read:

Serving on committee to inform space industry leaders that television's Star Trek in danger of cancellation. Recent cutbacks make clear that space program desperately needs this type mass audience space exploration publicity. Urge you and associates make voices heard immediately at NBC or parent company RCA.

Isaac Asimov

Gene did use a few personal contacts. He wrote to SF writer G. Harry Stine, who responded that he would contact Fred Durant at the Air and Space Museum and marshal people in the aerospace community. Stine also called John W. Campbell, who promised to immediately contact NBC and RCA brass, sending them advance copies of his *Analog Magazine*[18] with Harry's article on *Star Trek* in it.

Stine also spoke with Trekker Bob Amos, account executive for Chevrolet who "moves among the rarified altitudes of 30 Rockefeller Plaza, and will lend a hand."

The students at the California Institute of Technology were also busy. In early November 1967, Clyde Chadwick, his girlfriend, Wanda Kendall, and a number of other "Techers" had been given a tour of the set during the filming of "A Piece Of The Action." They had been hosted by Gene, who made certain they were well taken care of. He had told them that the outlook was gloomy for renewal, planting a seed in their fertile minds. On the way home, the students explored the idea of a protest march. The word was passed to Gene, and he was supportive of their efforts.

This was the era of student activism and student protests over the Vietnam War, so a protest march for *Star Trek* was a natural for the students at the leading college of its type in the country. Andee Reese-Maddox, Gene Coon's secretary, knew Thom Beck, an announcer at the local Pasadena radio station. She called, and things quickly got organized. KRLA jumped onto the bandwagon by producing and airing announcements to attract a large number of people.[19] Coincidentally, the manager of the station was a fan of the show.

For several days prior to the march, listeners to KRLA would hear the announcer's stirring voice over a background of *Star Trek* theme music:

---

[18] Formerly *Astounding*.

[19] It was not the first protest march. Tim Courtney and a group from the Society for Creative Anachronism (including Bjo and John Trimble) marched on KRON-TV in Oakland earlier when they first heard rumors of cancellation.

"KRLA proudly joins the courageous scientists at the California Institute of Technology in their fight to save *Star Trek* from cancellation. Shoulder to shoulder we shall blend our many voices in a mighty chorus of protest to General Bob Sarnoff.[20] Save *Star Trek* from cancellation! Join the Save *Star Trek* Committee in a torchlight parade and march on the NBC Studios in Burbank this Saturday night. Armed with picketsigns and torches we shall overcome! Beginning our march at Verdugo Park at 8 P.M. Save *Star Trek* tonight."

At the time, Cal Tech was an all-male school. One of the ancillary attractions of the protest was to meet girls. In order to do that they would have to draw protestors from other schools, as the third announcement attempted to do. Finally, in case there was any doubt about the tongue-in-cheek nature of the protest, the following KRLA announcement should have removed all doubt:

"KRLA proudly joins the heroic young scientists at Cal Tech to save *Star Trek* from cancellation. What does General Sarnoff have against Mr. Spock? Doesn't he like the way he combs his hair ... or points his ears? Mr. Spock admittedly doesn't have a heart, but does General Sarnoff? Join KRLA and the Save *Star Trek* Committee from Cal Tech in a torchlight parade on the NBC Studios in Burbank tonight. Bring picket signs and torches to Verdugo Park starting at 8 P.M. Help save *Star Trek* tonight."

And finally, in an attempt to shame students at USC into joining the protest:

"Inspired by the leadership from Cal Tech other colleges and universities are now joining the campaign to save *Star Trek* from cancellation at NBC. From UCLA, Irvine, Pasadena College, from almost every campus (except USC of course) delegations are joining tonight's torchlight parade on the NBC Studios in Burbank. Help save this science fiction masterwork from the television graveyard. Join the Committee to Save *Star Trek* in tonight's torchlight parade and march. Bring picketsigns and torches to Verdugo Park at 8 P.M. Help save *Star Trek* tonight."

The announcements were a success and on January 8, 1968, nearly a thousand students from over twenty schools converged on Verdugo Park and marched the short distance

---

[20]Chairman of the board and president of NBC.

to NBC. Next to Cal Tech, the largest contingent was from USC, but participants came from all over, including three students from the University of Arizona and several from the University of Nevada, Las Vegas.

The protesters were orderly, reasonably well-dressed for college students, and courteous to the police who were there to keep order. A petition was presented to one of the NBC officials, who coincidentally was visiting from New York. He accepted it with somewhat strained grace, repeatedly saying that *Star Trek* had not been cancelled, perhaps not realizing that the students present had no intention of burning the building to the ground if they didn't hear what they wanted.

Little-noticed in the far rear of the crowd was a tall, bear-like man with shaggy brown hair. He was riding a motorcycle and observing the whole march. The next day, the tall man wrote a letter to a friend in New York.

Dear Isaac,

Thought you would be pleased and amused by the following. On Saturday night about 300 students from California Institute of Technology, supported by students from other local colleges, marched on NBC West Coast headquarters in Burbank.

Although we knew it was going to happen, it was the students' idea to do it and we very carefully stayed out of the picture. I did ride my motorcycle up, disguised by the hard hat and plastic face shield, watched from a distance. I was pretty safe since I looked rather like a member of "Hells Angels" and this is hardly the image NBC executives have of its executive producers. Almost froze to death during it since the march happened at 8:00 PM and it was getting down to freezing in Burbank at that time.

Rather exciting. They marched from a nearby park and they could be heard coming several blocks away as they chanted various slogans. It was a torchlight parade, extremely well ordered and mannerly. They had a parade permit from the Burbank Police Department who stopped traffic at the intersections for the kids. In fact, the Police were very complimentary. The students were, as one would expect from Cal Tech,

very clever in their signs, music, and proclamations
which was handed over to NBC Program
Executives in a nice little ceremony. Placards read things
like "We know Mr. Spock doesn't have a heart—but
do you General Sarnoff?" "Star Trek . . . si! . . .
Neilson . . . no!" and "Mr. Spock for President!"
We all felt rather complimented in that we've never
heard of another television show that has had its own
student march and demonstration.

The Asimov telegrams went out on schedule.
About 250 of them. As with the student march and
other things, naturally we have to stay out of the picture
and plead total ignorance if confronted by our
enemy the network. If they know we have any part
in any of this, then the whole value of it is immediately
lost. For some strange reason I don't feel at all immoral
about such protestations of innocence on our part
since the networks invented this silly game and
made up the rules for it. They may not suspect me
of being too deeply involved since they know I have
had a number of motion picture offers and by their
simple economic Robber Baron reasoning they
would assume I would be interested in the greater profits
in moving on to features.

While Gene was careful to keep his distance during the
demonstration, he did attend the party afterward, as did
Jimmy Doohan. Wanda Kendall[21] also played a part in making history. She had been brought in and made a vice president and spokesperson for the protesting committee. Gene's
office contacted her and asked her if she would like to go to
New York City and do some protesting there.

Gene's assistant, Rick Carter, met Wanda at the airport
with her ticket, some expense money, and a big box of "Mr.
Spock For President" bumper stickers.[22]

Wanda had no plan of action, and NBC wasn't going to
help her in any way. She was staying with friends and tried
to figure out ways of obtaining publicity.

---

[21]Now Wanda Kendall-Le Vita.
[22]Contrary to other reports, "Mr. Spock For President" was the only bumper
sticker they had at the time.

A shy young woman, Wanda felt, to use her words, that she had "a mission" and rose to the occasion. As Wanda remembers:

"I was handing out bumper stickers on the street, was interviewed by some newspapers while I was there, but thought I should be able to put these bumper stickers on cars that count, NBC executives. Of course, they weren't going to let me into the NBC parking lot so I watched to see what was going on. I saw that the limousine drivers would frequently stop, get out and talk to the guard at the gate before they went in and picked up their passenger.

"I waited until one of them did that and when the limo was empty I climbed into the back with all my bumper stickers and hid until he drove in. When the driver got out I jumped out and began plastering bumper stickers everywhere I could.

"Going in that way I was able to make my way to the Executive Parking lot. I walked past at least one guard, but once I was inside I was all right in their eyes, so no one bothered me. I acted like I belonged there. I spent a good amount of time in the executive parking area and probably decorated between 200 and 300 bumpers, almost all of them Lincolns and Cadillacs.

"Later, I managed to find a couple of *Star Trek* fans who got me into the executive offices. I was ushered into private offices where I left 'Mr. Spock For President' bumper stickers on desks. I laid them on desks, I didn't stick them on any desks. I also pinned them to office bulletin boards everywhere I could.

"I was very conservative with money, I was working my way through college at the time, so I was very careful. I think they gave me $300 at the time and as I stayed with *Star Trek* fans and friends I was able to bring home $225. I tried to give it back to Gene and he said, 'Do you realize the problems you'd cause for me trying to give that money back? I've already budgeted that and I can't put it back. Just keep it."

Gene did receive a few phone calls from NBC executives, who found the bumper stickers difficult to remove. Beyond the memories of the participants, a surviving one-page memo Gene sent to Emmet Lavery, Jr., an executive at Desilu, on March 12 links him to the campaign:

Dear Emmet:

Per our discussions, here is a list of expenses which I personally incurred in regard to the Save Star Trek Campaign.

1/68 Copy Master—5,000 Bumper Sticker—Mr. Spock for President $303.52

11/67 A.A.A. Glass Co—54 sets Star Trek Glasses— for publicity, fans, public relations, press. (Gifts) $263.00

12/67 Round Trip Air Fare—Miss Wanda Kendall LA-NY-LA (Save Star Trek Campaign plus cash for expenses.) $350.00

11/67 Pacific Athletic Company—Star Trek Tee Shirts for promotion purposes. $60.60

Total: $977.12

Gene Roddenberry

Ironically, as Gene was quietly moving behind the scenes to assure *Star Trek*'s third season renewal, he received the following memo from the Desilu publicity department.

I am happy to report that this year *Star Trek* is the leader of all Desilu shows in terms of volume of fan mail. As a matter of fact, it just about equals that of *The Untouchables,* which was one of our all-time fan mail champions.

In addition to the fact that Bill Shatner and Leonard Nimoy are getting a heavy share of this mail, it is interesting to note that thousands of viewers are writing in glowing terms about *Star Trek* as a program.[23] This mail is out of the general category of the "send me a picture" type request, but rather reflects a sincere and intelligent reaction on the part of the viewer to the production and entertainment value of the show.

In trying to break it down, I would estimate that the mail represents a wide age group, which would further indicate that *Star Trek* has something for all.

But not quite everyone, it seemed. Late in January, Gene responded to a fan who had written a letter chastising him

---

[23]While Nimoy and Shatner battled it out for fan mail supremacy, Gene used to chuckle that the *Enterprise* received the most fan mail of all.

on a number of subjects. As usual, Gene's reply went beyond a simple response.

> Thank you for your comments. We agree on most of your points. As a matter of fact, we retain the services of Science and Research Personnel and each script is subjected to careful scrutiny.
>
> Where do we miss on anything? Most often it is less of a "miss" than a deliberate choice. If our stories become ultra-scientific at the expense of Director and Drama, we would immediately lose mass audience appeal and, like it or not, we make our shows for a mass audience medium. I would like to make shows exclusively for people like you, but there are only about a million of you out there watching TV and unless our shows reach fifteen or sixteen million people every week, the whole thing becomes an exercise in futility. I don't defend that system; I merely point out that it exists.
>
> Carrying present-day scientific development to its logical conclusion would deprive *Star Trek* of a great deal of "identification" for the audience. It might, in fact, even frighten or repel the audience. For example, marriage, morals, food, economic systems, almost every aspect of life will be greatly altered during the next couple of centuries. It is possible that such vessels as the *Enterprise* will not only be more automated, but it is even conceivable that man might not even travel aboard them, preferring to remain behind at the relative safety of his own planet, receiving the sights, smells and physical sensations of travel via some form of communication directly to his own sensory organs. Much sounder than risking his own frail body out in space.
>
> The point is that in making a television show (and certainly in selling a concept to a Network) we must offer a certain amount of familiarity and identification to the audience. Instead of a compact and fully automated Bridge, we selected more of a "family group" environment, which allows us an interplay of character, simply because without character there is no drama. We have a large vessel with many crewmen because we needed the familiarity of a home base. Incidentally, we must limit the number of viewing screens and "windows" because of the

enormous cost of photographic mattes involved when seeing exterior views on or through them.

It may interest you to know these episodes must be made in six days, approximating one-half a motion picture per week. And keep in mind that even "B quality" motion pictures ordinarily take eight to sixteen weeks to shoot. When our error is an out-and-out mistake and not a question of choice, it is often the result of the time and pressure involved in maintaining this kind of schedule.

Thank you for your most interesting remarks. We hope ours have answered some of your questions.

Near the end of January 1968, *Newsweek* reported on the Caltech march, letters received by NBC, and the fact that twenty percent of the network affiliates preferred to show the *Grand Ole Opry* in *Star Trek*'s Friday night time slot. Gene was quoted as saying, "What frightens me is that what we see on TV depends only on whether it will sell deodorant."

More than one funny letter arrived at Gene's office. In early January 1968, an Air Force colonel who commanded an Air Force base, and who shall remain nameless, wrote to Gene inviting Nimoy and Shatner to visit his base and attend a graduation ceremony and presentation of awards. "The staff and students will be wearing their Air Force winter mess dress uniforms and we would be pleased if Messrs. Shatner and Nimoy would wear their Star Ship dress uniforms. If this is inconvenient black tie is proper."

Gene had the loyalty of a number of key, hard-core SF fans who liked him both for what he was writing and producing and because, up to that time, he was the only producer who had taken his product directly to the fans at science fiction conventions. He had solicited advice from fans who had become writers and generally made himself available. That acknowledgment of fandom's value earned him a solid following and was about to pay dividends. Aside from Gene's behind-the-scenes maneuverings, there was a genuine grass-roots movement to save *Star Trek* spearheaded by two longtime science fiction fans, John and Bjo Trimble.[24]

The Trimbles lived in Oakland and kept Gene apprised of what they were doing. While Gene wanted to become involved more actively, Bjo and John suggested that this campaign would be more effective if it appeared spontaneous. Bjo spent time canvassing the studio secretarial pool and a number of legal secretaries and executive assistants she knew to determine, as she described it, "what, of all the mail that comes in, makes you throw some of it away, put some in the nut file, and, finally, get that one letter to your boss?"

With that information Bjo wrote a detailed letter to fans that told them the problem and how to solve it by writing a letter to NBC, the sponsors, and Desilu. She gave instructions on how to write a letter and then instructed the recipient of her letter to copy and send it out ten times. This began the "fan pyramid." Of course, not everyone wrote a letter but, as Bjo said, "Out of the ten people you ask to write, four people actually get around to writing letters and asking other people. Of the six left, two will never do anything, and the others sometimes have enough guilt that sometimes, even though they haven't written a letter themselves, they will ask twenty people to write letters."

Bjo collected several mailing lists and Gene quietly supplied sacks of *Star Trek* mail from which Bjo, John, and their volunteers copied names and addresses, accumulating perhaps four thousand names altogether.[25] The Trimbles began the campaign by paying for the mailing out of their family finances, but soon after the word got out Bjo remembers receiving rolls of stamps from supportive fans.

The campaign grew and the fans began to write both to

---

[24]A true fan, even her name is a science fiction invention, created by her lifelong friend Forrest J Ackerman, literary agent, publisher of *Famous Monsters of Filmdom,* and the man who coined the term "sci-fi." Ackerman's invention, "Bjo," (pronounced "Bee-Joe") is a shortening of Betty Joanne, and Bjo much prefers it.

[25]There were at that time, perhaps 300 names on the Science Fiction Writers of America list. A couple of thousand names were obtained from the World Science Fiction Convention list, a small number were donated by a mail-order SF book dealer, and the rest came from fans who wrote to the show.

the network and the Trimbles. Bjo remembers the campaign's kitchen table beginnings:

"Our biggest expense was printing and postage. This was before there was a copy shop on every corner. We mimeographed the first letters on the machine that belonged to the Los Angeles Science/Fantasy Society. Since we had that at our house it was fairly easy, but as this grew we had to change over to photocopy because we just couldn't make that many mimeos.

"One of the great benefits of this campaign was that we got to meet people from all over the country. Many of them were sensible and interesting people who became our friends. One of the things that annoys me the most about the denigrating of 'Trekkies' is that these were not people who ran around and screamed 'Spock' like a bunch of demented flamingos. They were intelligent people who were saying they were happy that there was finally some intelligent science fiction entertainment on television."

The letter-writing campaign had an interesting and unexpected side effect that was to influence the popularity of the show for years to come. Bjo continues:

"Without planning on it, quite inadvertently, I began organized *Star Trek* fandom. To understand what I did you have to know that the average fan club works with a central core of three or five people. Many times the person who runs the club doesn't want to spread the powerbase very far. Everything comes back to that central core. This usually means that contact with the person who is the object of the fan club is through the president and rarely touches the average member.

"What I did, as the letters were being sent out, was put people in touch with one another. If someone wrote from, say, Pittsburgh, I would include with my letter a note saying, 'Did you know there are 8 other people interested in *Star Trek* in your area and here are their names.' The fans would get together, forming small clubs. Occasionally they would write and ask me how to find more people and I would give them ideas. The movement grew from there. Before we heard that the show had been saved, a matter of months from when we started, I knew of 25 clubs that had been organized.

"Trek fans learned from the science fiction fans how to

publish fan magazines, or 'fanzines'[26] and a number sprang up. The zines ranged in quality from crude to sophisticated, but all had the common thread of love for *Star Trek*. The clubs that started in colleges spread when the students went home and started clubs there.

"I don't care how many people give you numbers, nobody has a record of how many people there were in fandom and how many fan clubs there were then.

"Some clubs were wildly successful. The Basta girls in Michigan were very active. By the end of the third season there were about 300 members in their club. By the time the girls threw in the towel (it had gotten so big they couldn't handle all the paperwork), they probably had 1200 members. The paperwork just drowned them.

"All this is what blossomed into what we know today as *Star Trek* fandom.

"About the time the letter writing campaign crested we were running short on money so we went to Gene and told him we were running low. He asked us how much we needed and we told him $400. That was the only money we got from him, but we didn't feel it was our place to ask him for it. We never felt he owed us, we volunteered, and we saw it through.

"Now, I've never told anyone this, but I didn't think we were going to save the show. We thought we would just make enough noise to let NBC know we were mad as hell and weren't going to take it any more. We thought there would be a couple of thousand letters that would show them we were pissed and that would be it.

"About half-way though we realized we were on to something. Fans were sending us copies of petitions with hundreds of names and the letters they were sending to the networks, the sponsors, the holding companies of the sponsors, everyone. A notice appeared in the Kodak employees newsletter, a Mensa bulletin, and on and on. It was spreading."

At about this time NBC admitted to receiving around 6,000 letters a week, and since that consumed valuable office time, they began a search to find out who was respon-

---

[26]Or in the fan lexicon, "zines," pronounced "zeens." Zine publishers even have their own convention.

sible. Since he was the logical culprit, NBC focused on Gene, but because of his distance from the Trimbles, Gene was able to appear totally blameless.[27]

Bjo continues:

"There were a great many people around Gene who had no idea what we were doing. When we came to visit, Gene was always very careful to keep it 'fan visiting set.' We kept it that way, too. We all knew that we would become useless the minute our names became known to the papers.

"NBC kept accusing Gene and looking around Paramount to find out who was doing this, but no one really knew. Only Majel and one or two other people who were close to Gene knew.

"By now the news media had gotten wind of all this and NBC was steadfastly denying that they were receiving any amount of mail that would affect their decision.

"We learned about how many letters NBC really received in a round-about way. In my letter to fans my first tip on sending a letter was to use an ordinary #10 business envelope. If the sender had a legitimate reason to use a business return address and/or a meter, they were to use that so NBC could not differentiate between business mail and a *Star Trek* protest letter.

"NBC decided that they would correlate all the mail to come up with a demographically-perfect *Star Trek* fan. How they were going to do that with fans ranging from people with two Ph.D.s to ditch diggers to retarded children to grandmothers is anybody's guess, but they were going to use computers. It is important to remember that computers were a rare thing in those days and most big companies did not have one. They used special companies who had computers and rented time and services. NBC sent the letters to one of those companies.

"Months later I met one of the people who worked at the company NBC used. He revealed that they had processed a million pieces of mail! And they were counting petitions as one piece of mail! (I was told that one petition from a small town had almost 2500 names on it.) NBC was lying to everyone.

---

[27]Writer and editor Fred Pohl remembers NBC finally settled on him. While Pohl had signed a letter and encouraged others to write, he was not part of the plot.

"If you go back and look at interviews of network executives over the years you'll see that the number of letters changed drastically. It got as low as 10–15,000, 50,000 and went up to 150,000. They would never admit to anything over 250,000 pieces of mail. They thought they were putting us down when they used a small figure, but I thought, 'Fine. If we can change the world with 50,000 letters, that's great!'"

On February 1, 1968, Asimov wrote to Gene to cheer him up.

I am told *Star Trek* has been cancelled, but apparently the fight goes on. Two newspapers have already called me for an estimate of its worth and I gave them each an earful.

If the worst comes to the worst, I hope that all who have been involved with *Star Trek* made enough in money and reputation to be able to carry on without difficulty.

I feel certain about Leonard Nimoy, for instance, who must now be easily ten times as valuable a personality for any show business item as he was two years ago. You, also, have unmistakably proved your worth and so has Shatner.

I trust all the minor characters have also benefited and can feel that *Star Trek* has helped them not only in itself but for the future.

My major sadness is for the science fiction writers who see an adult market close for them. I'm sure they can write for other programs, but certainly not with equal satisfaction.

Please continue to keep me abreast of your own doings with *Star Trek* or anywhere.

Isaac

On the nineteenth of February, Gene wrote two letters, one to Asimov and one to a writer who had helped with a complimentary article on *Star Trek*.

Gene to Asimov:

Toward the end of last week we received ten thousand dollars advance story money for a third season of *Star*

Trek. While this does not mean definitely, we are on the schedule and it does make things look very much better. NBC is notoriously cheap and I can't believe they'd spend ten thousand dollars without a pretty fair intention of going a third season.

Latest rumor on this is that we are definitely back on the schedule (after having been firmly off it seven or eight weeks ago) and that our new time will probably be eight o'clock Monday, or seven-thirty Friday. The Monday time seems to be winning at the present moment.

Gene to his writer-friend:

We heard from a New York source that letters to the Network (probably counting two names on the many petitions received) passed the *one million* mark! It's hard to believe that figure and I'm trying to check up on it, but whatever the final tally, we do know the letters to NBC began to peak a couple of months ago and at one time I heard they received over two thousand a day. Whatever the final tally, it's obvious now it was the all-time-high fan response to any show, including the "greats" like *Playhouse 90, Robert Montgomery* and others. As a matter of fact, some think it has shaken the Networks' faith in the Neilsons and, indeed, I received some indication of that when I was back there a couple of months ago and talked to the Network's statistical and audience survey experts. We were off the schedule, wiped out, finished, about six to eight weeks ago. But the letters kept coming, increasing in volume rather than leveling off. It upset them enough that a committee was formed of six Network Vice Presidents to investigate the matter. Shortly afterward, we began to reappear on the schedule again.

On Friday, March 1, 1968, NBC announced, *on the air,* ironically at the end of the episode "The Omega Glory," written by Gene (his last script of the second season), that *Star Trek* was renewed and asked that no more letters be

sent. A note in a memo from Gene to Shatner and Nimoy on March 7, 1968, explains the rest.

> Incidentally, received a call from NBC today asking us to please ask the fans to "stop already!" It seems that in the last six days since the announcement was made that *Star Trek* would stay on the air, *they have already received over 70,000 letters thanking the network.*

The Man From U.N.C.L.E. had run its course and its 8 P.M. Monday time slot was open, but heeding Oscar Katz's caveat that network schedules were always first written in pencil, things could change, and they did. NBC decided on a new show for *U.N.C.L.E.*'s old time, *Rowan and Martin's Laugh In.* On January 15, 1968, *The Man From U.N.C.L.E.* went to syndication heaven, and one week later, *Laugh-In* started a phenomenon.

On March 29, 1968, Gene wrote to a friend, trying to put a good face on what he knew was a disaster.

> As you probably know by now, the network had slotted us at 7:30 Monday, then at the last minute shifted us to 10:00 P.M. Friday night. I fought the good fight, refused to produce the show under those circumstances but they elected to go ahead with it anyway at that night and time. I finally agreed to be Executive Producer since I did not want to abandon the show to the tender mercies of studio or whomever they brought in. This way, at least, I can guide the show, advise, read and comment on all scripts without undergoing the fantastic burden of actually line-producing STAR TREK. Also, this way I'll have time to write some scripts for the show.

Star Trek had survived once again, but this time they had been given what Gene thought was a kiss-of-death time slot. He was not happy. He knew that the show was doomed regardless of what he did, yet he was not willing to air his thoughts in public. There were a great many people whose jobs were on the line, so he put up a good front and sent the following letter to all *Star Trek* personnel on March 28, 1968.

Assume the Paramount production people have gotten in touch with you by now or will shortly do so. I look forward to working again with you on a third year of *Star Trek*.

You may have heard we were somewhat disappointed with our Friday 10:00 P.M. time slot but we have been disappointed before and have confounded the experts by coming out on top. With your help we intend to do this again.

We will have practically the whole team back with us as far as we know. My post on the show will be Executive Producer. Contrary to anything you may have heard, I intend to stay very much with the show and will give it close guidance and loving care. This will also give me some time to write some of next season's scripts myself—as well as develop new properties on which you and I someday may be involved.

This marks the third year of *Star Trek* and I have every hope that you and I will be together to celebrate its Bar Mitzvah.

Warmest regards,
Gene R.

Copies were sent to Mort Werner (NBC program chief), Herb Schlosser (vice president of programming, West Coast), and a number of other people. A copy of the letter came back to Gene a few days later. At the bottom were two words written in a bold and forceful hand—"Well done"—signed, "Herb S.[chlosser]"

On April 18, 1968, Gene sent a memo to "all concerned." Even though he had stepped back from the daily, hands-on life of a producer, he wanted everyone to know he was still there. The memo regarded Kirk, Spock, and other continuing *Star Trek* characters. It is interesting to note that much of what Gene said about the characteristics of command in Captain Kirk neatly dovetailed into those needed in a good producer.

The continuing challenge and sometimes problems to all of us is that of keeping our various characters growing, individualistic and orchestrated . . . *alive*.

KIRK

Even more so than in the past, Captain James T. Kirk should be a ship Captain, a strong leader of men. Too often forgotten in all our desire to emphasize comraderie of the nice people we have aboard, are simple truths of command—such as that a Captain simply cannot be too loquacious—once he explains one order to one man, he is liable to find a habit pattern growing in which his deck officers become a committee and all orders become the subject of discussion, and even vote. Let's see this problem—comment upon it in a script. Kirk must guard his tongue, guard even his affection for others. And although it sounds extreme, he must even guard his approbation of others, use it wisely. The trick is something akin to making Captain Kirk seem at times a bastard but keeping the audience in on the fact that he is really a good guy in a tough job which requires a certain amount of command "play acting." He knows that all eyes are on him constantly. The efficiency and indeed the very safety of the starship can depend on the crew's belief in him. He has any normal man's insecurities and doubts, but he knows he cannot ever show them—except occasionally in private with ship's surgeon McCoy or in subsequent moments with Mr. Spock whose opinions Kirk has learned to value so highly.

One of the most often heard complaints re: Kirk from fans is that he is too "jolly," and that he seems to be actively seeking friendship and approval of his subordinates. Our audience likes Kirk best of all when he is at his toughest and then they like contrasting cabin scenes where we learn in private that he is not as tough as he pretends.

We can use Kirk's voice over more effectively here—all our audience asks is he be willing to admit them later . . . if only to himself. Not because he is afraid of admitting to the world that he is fallible . . . but that he *is* afraid of what will happen to the ship and 430 crew members if the leader becomes anything less than The Leader. The best guide is still C.S. Forrester's "Captain Horatio Hornblower."

MR. SPOCK

In the beginning of *Star Trek* episodes Mr. Spock was a fellow who occasionally said "Illogical" and that was about it. We all worked very hard to build him into a fully dimensional character, and a lot of people, including Leonard Nimoy, deserve credit. But we should keep in mind that *he is difficult to write properly.* And our writers, like all others, do have that unfortunate tendency to avoid the difficult.

Spock needs our help and creativity again this season. We need to keep alert to constantly emphasize and make use of the fact that Spock is *second in command* of the USS *Enterprise* and also the vessel's *Science Officer.* This is no small job in a vessel which has a primary function of exploring the galaxy.

Spock's role should go far beyond merely providing the Captain with information on request. In our best scripts he has volunteered information, had opinion, pressured the Captain, argues with him ... and there is certainly no rule on *Star Trek* that Spock cannot occasionally be proved right and Kirk wrong.

Let's also get back to more of the colorful aspects of our Vulcan. For example—the continuing joke of his chess games with Kirk in which Spock invariably loses because of Kirk's humanly illogical moves. Spock guesses correctly what Kirk *should* do but Kirk invariably makes a "wrong" move which defeats Spock. Also, we established in an early episode that Spock plays an unusual looking Vulcan "harp" and plays it well. We have also established that Spock eats strange foods, is enormously lonely, involves himself in strange scientific computations in his cabin, and God knows what else.

There is no basic reason why giving scenes to Spock need necessarily reduce the number of Kirk scenes. Indeed, the more multi-dimensional the one, the more exciting the other. Unless it is a story point, Spock should never intrude upon Kirk's command prerogatives and Kirk should never intrude upon Spock's Science Officer Job.

MC COY

The single most numerous and most consistent complaint from fans of all age groups and levels has been the

fact that Spock and McCoy no longer "battle" as they once did. Again, no one dropped the idea, no one is at fault, we simply didn't realize how well it worked and how much the fans loved the bickering between our Arrowsmith and our Alien. No one believes for a moment that they do not secretly like each other but let them show it and we invariably are deluged with irritated fan responses. Another way, I suppose, of the fans saying they don't want an exercise in fellowship ... they want our characters to be proud *individuals* with differing points of view and perspectives. They want our people to be *men* who have the guts to differ without necessarily in the last act falling tearfully into one another's arms and apologizing for earlier harshly speaking to each other.

OTHER CONTINUING CHARACTERS

About the same comments on them. Let's keep Jimmy Doohan, the dour Scot who regards even the Captain's visit to the engine room as an unwanted intrusion. Jimmy Doohan is capable of handling anything we throw at him and the more protective of his engines and his prerogatives as Chief Engineer, the better the character seems to work. Nichelle Nichols and George Takei deserve more attention this year too. Let's develop them further as multi-dimensional individuals.

I suggest we find some additional mixed strength and flaws for them, especially some of the continuing joke idiosyncrasies which help so much in maintaining them as individual members of the "TV family" we have created aboard our starship.

CHEKOV

We may find our most important secondary character this season, certainly one which might give us our best entry to youth, is Chekov. The studio has been sufficiently impressed by the volume of Chekov fan response to sign him to a contract, one of the few secondary characters we have so optioned in our third season.

Most of us (because of our own ages) tend to forget that

Kirk and Spock and the others actually seem rather "middle aged" to the large youthful segment of our audience. We badly need a young man aboard the *Enterprise*—we need youthful attitudes and perspectives. Chekov can be used potently here.

Too often in the past Chekov has been simply the young man, who keeps saying "Russia invented that first!" This was never really a good joke anyway—in fact runs rather counter to the broad international philosophy we've always tried to build into *Star Trek*. If we do continue to use that as a continuing joke, let's make certain that it does come off as a good humored fun rather than appear to be a stupid chauvinistic attitude from the writer or producer of the episode.

Our original plan all along (and one we never really accomplished) was to play Chekov as an extraordinarily capable young man—almost Spock's equal in some areas. An honor graduate of the Space Academy. But even though verging on genius, his youthful inexperience and tactlessness, his youthful drive to prove himself, his need for approbation, his quite normal youthful need for females, and all of that, keep getting in his way. Kirk realizes his ability and can play something of the "father image" alternately slapping him down and lifting him up as wise Captains do when they have a young Ensign with the potential of someday becoming a fine ship Captain. Referring to something in the previous, an interesting continuing joke and one with which a youthful audience can relate could very well be Chekov's constant interest in young females, his continuing failures and frustration in that area—certainly a quite common experience for all young men at that certain time in life. It can have the double advantage of pointing out to the audience the existence of pretty yeomen and other attractive females aboard our vessel.

Gene Roddenberry

* * *

To prepare for the third season, Gene took Majel and eight scripts down to Palm Springs. He was becoming very comfortable with her company, a fact that would soon become significant.

CHAPTER 11

Gene was a successful producer, in as much control of his creation as possible, but that success only migrated to his personal life in material terms. He had the big house, the big car, plenty of clothes and fine furnishings. He had what other men dream of: a beautiful wife and two lovely daughters. Unfortunately, it was all on the surface. Gene was very unhappy at home. His personal life was becoming a shambles, and more and more of his time was spent at the studio attending to the thousands of details a complicated show like *Star Trek* produces. Eileen often brought the girls down to Lucy's El Adobe restaurant across from Paramount Studios just so the family could eat dinner together. Afterward, Gene would return to the studio and work late into the night.

The demands of continuous attention that came with the show had come at an appropriate time in his life. He had confessed to a few close friends that his marriage to Eileen had been over since the early 1950's, and by the mid- to late 1960's the strain of maintaining the facade of a happy marriage was beginning to show. His children were teenagers, beginning to lead their own lives and, simply put, Gene had outgrown the marriage. He had less and less reason to go home.

Pat and Bob Atchison were two of Gene's oldest friends, from all the way back at Franklin High School. They accompanied Gene and Eileen on their first date and double-dated many times after. They were more than friends, they were confidants. Pat Atchison remembers:

"Gene once said to me, 'You know, Pat, what Eileen wants is for me to be home at six o'clock, have a cocktail or two, then dinner.' She wanted a simple life, but Gene was the sort who'd call at midnight and tell her the guys are all coming, get sandwiches ready. That wasn't her routine."

On the Fourth of July, 1968, Gene and family spent the afternoon with Bob and Pat. Gene sadly confessed to Bob in a private moment that he and Eileen "never laughed any more." Things were coming to a head.

It is easy to characterize the failure of a marriage as the "fault" of one person or another, but those who have been through the process know it is far from that. People change, their needs change, they grow in ways other than their partners, and what was satisfactory, acceptable, and even necessary at one point is no longer the case later in life, or, as is often the case, they may find that they never had the same life goals in the first place. So it was with Gene and Eileen.

Friends and relatives describe Eileen as sharing many of her mother's traits: controlling, precise, particular in details, and certain about "how things ought to be done."

Gene was his father's son, a "man in control" with definite ideas of his own about marriage, sex, child rearing, and everything else, for that matter. In many of the ways where Eileen was precise, Gene was more free-wheeling.

Pat Atchison remembered a particular incident that illustrates the difference:

"I'll never forget one night—this is the way Gene was, and it's not the way Eileen was. We were sitting at the house at dinner, white linen tablecloths and all the china and everything, and red wine. I'm a little klutzy and I knocked my wine over, and Gene said, 'What difference does it make?' I was upset and Eileen looked like she was going to have a stroke.

"Gene said, 'Who cares!' And dumped his wine on the tablecloth.

"So this was the difference. I don't think Eileen thought it was very funny."

Adding to the basic incompatibility was the pressure of a mother-in-law who never liked her only daughter's choice of a husband. Maude Rexroat looked down on the Roddenberrys as common people, even though she had married a carpenter.[1] Gene's relationship with his in-laws was never warm and intimate.

His father-in-law, Frank Rexroat, was the polar opposite of Gene's father. Those who knew Frank describe him as a man dominated by his wife. Frank, it turned out, had serious problems, and one day those problems caught up with him, increasing the pressure on Gene.

Frank Rexroat was an exhibitionist and was arrested for exposing himself. The details of where and when are lost, but it happened after Gene had left the LAPD. Further, we don't know how Eileen approached Gene and convinced him to intercede on her father's behalf, but a retired officer of the LAPD, a good friend of Gene's, remembers that Frank was let off without charges being pressed only because Gene had the right friends in the right places. However, even well-placed friends had their limits, and Gene was told that if Frank was arrested again to not bother calling.

Most exhibitionists may suffer shame, but rarely show a great deal of guilt. They enjoy the shock they cause, it being a measure of control and power over women, something they don't have in their regular lives. Therapy is often without effect. We don't know how active Frank was in his illness, but we do know of one other incident that lives in the memory of a former close friend of Eileen's.

The friend and her husband were visiting the Roddenberrys at the Beverly Glen house. As it happened, Frank and Maude were making an extended visit, living downstairs in the maid's quarters. One afternoon, Eileen's friend, a naive and sheltered woman, was surprised in the hallway by Frank, a man she had known for years. As the woman vividly remembers, Frank was stark naked, stroking a full erection. He looked at her, smiled and said, "Look what I've got for you." Eileen's friend ran in the opposite direction as fast as she could.

One outcome of the ensuing tumult was that the Roddenberry girls were never allowed alone with Granpa Rexroat again.[2]

---

[1]Frank Rexroat was evidently quite skilled at carpentry. With Gene's help, he built the Temple City house, where Gene and Eileen lived during his time as a policeman. When television writing began to pay off, they moved to Beverly Hills in the late 1950's.

[2]Both Frank and Maude Rexroat are long dead, yet Eileen still maintains her parents' years-vacant condominium. Frank Rexroat is still listed in the phone book.

* * *

While time for the family was difficult to find, there was time for Majel, who often dropped by the studio late at night when Gene was rewriting scripts. Majel would help by reading dialogue aloud as he pounded away on the typewriter into the early morning hours. It was not unusual for Gene to work through the night, leaving the studio in the morning, dropping off the rewritten scripts for the day's shooting as the early-call actors were arriving.[3] It was also not unusual for Gene to have some chemical assistance in staying awake to do his work. It wasn't a desire to "get high." It was analogous to the long-distance truck driver wanting to drive the extra few hundred miles. While Gene was strong and healthy, this occasional amphetamine use, combined with smoking (he would not give up cigarettes until the mid- to late 1970's), would exact a price later. Gene's use of "uppers" was not unique in Hollywood's pressure-cooker mentality, where deadlines are severe and writers *must* produce material.

Gene's marriage to Eileen was over in everything but name and public appearance, but still he hesitated to make the final break. Gene had a sense of honor that did not keep him from having affairs, but seemed to prevent him from walking away from an unhappy marriage.

Years later, Majel offered the opinion that she had kept Gene at home for a couple of additional years, providing him an emotional outlet. She also remembered that Gene planned to leave Eileen between the first and second seasons of *Star Trek,* only to postpone the inevitable when the program was renewed, using the excuse of not being able to focus his attention on the show and on a divorce at the same time. This was, of course, the same man who just a short time before had created and written two pilots, produced them both *and* a third for a friend, all in the space of a year, while maintaining the semblance of a home life, a full-

---

[3]Bob Justman said he could tell when Gene had pulled an "all-nighter," rewriting a script. According to Bob, the first part was always superb and then the quality deteriorated as the hour got later, regardless of the amount of caffeine or chemical help Gene ingested. The last parts of the script, written in the early morning hours, weren't Gene's best, as Bob remembered, requiring that he rewrite that material later.

time mistress, and the occasional, opportunistic fling on the side.

Gene confided to a friend that he had made up his mind about Majel one evening at her home. They were very comfortable with one another. Majel wasn't anything like Eileen. She was impulsive and uninhibited, with a shrewd intelligence that was quick to size up situations. Further, she had an incisive and biting sense of humor that was a match for Gene's wide-ranging intelligence.[4] Finally, Majel was demonstrative, vocal, totally and completely in love with Gene, and demonstrated the sort of loyalty that Gene found most valuable in friends.[5] Gene confessed privately that he had been wishing how he could have this sort of relationship every night, when he suddenly realized that he could. The price was a confrontation with Eileen, but before that would happen, Gene had family duty to attend to.

On Saturday, July 27, 1968, Gene's oldest child, Darleen Anita, married William Luther "Bill" Lewis, II. It was a big wedding held at the Methodist-Presbyterian Church on Santa Monica Boulevard in Beverly Hills. While Gene was the proud father of the bride, the reception provided him an opportunity to embarrass Eileen, venting his frustration at the predicament he found himself in. It was the sort of situation Eileen was incapable of responding to and a rare example of Gene being unnecessarily cruel in public.

Gene had arranged for an old girlfriend of his to be invited to the reception. She came with a neighbor. Gene had known her when they were both young. The woman was in her early forties and stunning, with dark brown hair and large, expressive eyes. Her figure was still youthful and did not suggest that she was the mother of several children. She had a well-established professional career in Beverly Hills.

---

[4]Majel once confided that if she had been an intellectual, she would have lasted, perhaps, ten minutes with Gene.

[5]Years later, long after they had married, Gene and Majel were hosting a party. Something had come up, or been introduced, in conversation and Gene called Majel over. He ordered her to kiss his foot. In front of Gene's astounded friends, she immediately went down on her knees, bent over and kissed the toe of his shoe. She stood up, smiled, and walked away. Gene's friends were speechless.

When questioned by this writer, Majel's reaction was simple: "It made Gene happy and was nothing to me." While it may have been a private joke between the two of them, if anyone thought this behavior defined their relationship, they were sadly mistaken.

* * *

Gene had met the woman on the beach at Redondo in the summer of 1938. She had been a Medelin Kiddie, part of a dance troupe that supplied children to dance in the movies.[6] She and her family were spending part of their summer at the beach and she was out getting some sun, lying on a blanket reading when she saw Gene across the sand. He was seventeen, and she remembers clearly today what she thought of him then: he was gorgeous.

Gene walked over to the pretty girl and politely asked if he could sit down. She said he could, and while she was busy being impressed with his good looks, his quick wit came through with his second question: "Do you always read everything under the sun?" The two young people spent the next few hours talking about a variety of subjects, including their mutual love of books and poetry. She knew several poems by heart as did Gene, a side benefit of his study with Mrs. Church that she probably never envisioned.

The impromptu poetry recital came to a romantic end when she began *Invictus* by William Ernest Henley. She had completed the first stanza when Gene joined in reciting the remaining three with her. Looking into each other's eyes, they finished the poem together with Henley's famous words:

> It matters not how strait the gate,
> How charged with punishment the scroll,
> I am the master of my fate: I am the captain
>   of my soul.

Gene wanted to take her out that evening. She said she would have to ask her parents. The two young romantics parted company that afternoon with a promise to meet the next day. The young woman floated home, eager to get permission from her parents. In discussing this, her first date, her parents' first requirement was that she tell Gene her age. Because of her show business experiences, her physical development, and high intelligence, she was more sophisticated than the typical teenager of 1938, but still, she was only fourteen. Her parents also wanted to meet Gene.

The next day, the two met at the beach at the prearranged

---

[6]The most famous alumnus of the school was Shirley Temple.

time and Gene was informed how young this little beauty really was. The woman still remembers Gene literally taking a step back, but he recovered almost immediately and agreed to meet her parents. He was unflinchingly polite, told her parents where the theater was, how long they would be gone, and precisely what time he would have her home. She was so excited she could hardly contain herself.

The date went like clockwork, and while there was some romantic activity, it was not nearly enough for the young woman as she tells the story. "I'd have laid down on the beach in a minute if Gene had asked," she says today. But, put off by her tender years, he didn't and got her home on time, as promised.

She lived way out in the San Fernando Valley, without a phone, and her family's visit to the beach was over the next day. She gave Gene her address and he promised he would write . . . and did. He made the long streetcar and bus trip to see her once and then borrowed a car for the next visit months later. Between summers, Gene only made two or three visits.

Now sitting at a table at the wedding reception with Eileen and other members of the family, Gene launched into an involved and highly descriptive story of how he had spent a year preparing to seduce this woman decades before, how he thought of nothing but her body over the time between when he met her and when he could get her back on the beach the next summer, and how, when that happened, the great beach seduction scene had played out.[7] Gene neglected to relate any of the sweet, romantic details of the first meeting on the beach or their date. He immediately launched into how he had walked her to a deserted area, gathered firewood, started the fire and, with the two of them wrapped in a blanket how he had moved relentlessly towards the young girl's initiation into the mysteries of sex.

Gene built the story toward the expected ending when it suddenly veered left. He described how he had, with great responsibility that afternoon, purchased a condom and how he stood up and moved to the side in feigned or real modesty, to put it on. As a practiced storyteller, Gene went into

---

[7] In the interim, he had met and began dating Eileen, a fact he well remembered when he was telling this story.

careful detail, describing that when, in his hasty opening of the package, he fumbled and dropped the precious prophylactic. When he found it in the flickering firelight, it was full of sand, ruined. Gene ended the story with the frustrating line, "I was just a poor boy and it was my only rubber."

The woman who was the object of the story was somewhat embarrassed and didn't know what to think. In any event, she was not aware of the dynamics of the marriage. Regardless, she was irritated at being used as the "center of attention," or the "entertainment for Gene's friends" as she characterized it. She excused herself to make a phone call and left the table.

Gene followed her into the private area where the phone was and, without acknowledging his bad taste, tried to salvage the moment. He offered a tour of the *Star Trek* set for her and her son, which she accepted, but nothing further came from the relationship in spite of whatever hopes or designs Gene may have had.

Two weeks later, on Friday, August 9, Gene moved out of the house, officially separating from Eileen. He checked into the Century Plaza Hotel, called Eileen from the lobby, and told her he wasn't coming back. Majel joined him that night and stayed with him for the next twenty-three years.

The separation did not go easily for Gene. He was concerned that Eileen would not be able to take care of herself. A few days after he had left, he was having second thoughts when he learned what close family friend, Dorothy Parmenter, would testify to in court over twenty years in the future: Eileen had closed out their safe deposit boxes, removed gold bars and a number of sterling silver tea sets and other valuables to an undisclosed location immediately after he had left. From that moment on, any doubts Gene may have had that Eileen could take care of herself vanished. Also gone in that moment were any residual feelings of guilt Gene had over leaving.

Dorothy Parmenter had been a close friend of Eileen and Gene's for many years. Her husband had been in the military with Gene and the two couples remained close. When interviewed for this book, she was asked about Gene and Eileen's personal relationship as the two seemed to be, from friends' and relatives' descriptions, somewhat out of sync. Eileen had been described as something of a cold fish and Gene seemed to have a limitless sex drive. Dorothy did not go into detail, but remembered a comment Eileen made just after the separation that perhaps describes the relationship's more private moments: "I never said no to anything Gene wanted to do."

The divorce was not simple, and like so many before and since, it descended into pettiness. When Gene and Majel went to the house on Beverly Glen Drive to pick up some of his items, they found many of them on the floor under a pile of trash. On March 5, 1969, Gene wrote to his attorney Leonard Maizlish about Eileen withholding his possessions, not delivering lamps and linens and such. Almost two months later, he wrote again with many of the same complaints.

Dear Leonard,

This is the current status of the property division with Eileen, things missing, items not delivered as promised, etc.

First of all, if we go to trial, I think her conduct makes for some interesting comparisons. For example, she has yet to make any effort at all to share any of our belongings, even those which have an exclusive sentimental value to me and none to her. You may recall I had to make special efforts and finally appeal to both our lawyers in order to simply get my birth certificate. No sooner was I out of the house than she moved all her silver and valuable antiques to her parents' house. She closed out our joint safety deposit vault and moved the contained valuables to an unspecified location. Even on such small items as the family liquor stock, she simply took it all when she moved out, whether they were liquors she enjoyed or detested. She has yet to live up to the property division we agreed on one night at the house with our attorneys present. She has yet to make available to me the setting of silver which the judge ordered her to give me when we first appeared in court.

I am not writing in anger but rather, to give you information for a proper presentation of our side and for a proper rebuttal of any points she has. Also, I am getting tired of constantly giving and there

are some items she still retains possession of which
have a particular or peculiar value to me. I'd like
to have them back.

One of these is the large family Bible, a gift from
my mother and father. Eileen has her own Bible
from her family and there has never been any
question about the fact that this other Bible was really
a gift to me. In addition there is also a new-version
Bible, a gift from my brother and sister, which I
need in research comparisons in my writing work
and for which Eileen has no use whatsoever.

I would still like to have my ivory chess set.

Gene goes on to list his rock and jewelry-making materials and other household items. Gene continued with a reminder that even though Eileen had promised to provide him
with a fair share of linens, what he got turned out to be
"four old beach towels and two hand towels." He continued:

Phil's[8] records can substantiate that we made an
unusually large annual expenditure on jewelry for Eileen.
While I had no objection to her having a reasonable
or even generous collection of personal jewelry for
herself, we should keep in mind that a significant portion
of these acquisitions were agreed upon by she and I
[sic] as "family investments." For example, in the
case of the five carat diamond, we went to New
York with the intention of spending about $3000 on
her diamond. We ultimately spent $12,000 with the
thought that it was "money in the bank" anytime
we had to sell it. I have no list of her jewelry but
can estimate its retail value, including the five carat
diamond ring, as something in the neighborhood of
$25,000 or $30,000. It includes, for example, a
four-strand pearl necklace of extremely large sized
pearls which should be worth retail $3000 or $4000
in the current market. It includes rings, bracelets, broochs,
pins, all solid gold or other precious metal, almost
all set with precious or semi-precious stones. To
my best knowledge, Eileen owned no costume jewelry.

---

[8]Phil Singer, Gene's accountant.

Gene was particularly irritated that Eileen held on to the record of family memories and certain irreplaceable personal items.

> I would like to have an agreement regarding the family 16mm films and also the photograph albums and other still photos. I should like to have reasonable access to them and have a firm agreement they will be passed on equally to both children in any will.
>
> Another sentimental item, a scrapbook made up by my mother and presented to me. It contained school items from kindergarten onward, newspaper clippings, photographs, all manner of highly personal sentimental things that only a mother would think important. I would like to have it.
>
> Eileen still retains possession of my war medals.
>
> Sincerely,

Gene never saw his war medals or scrapbooks again.

Even though the divorce was very rough, Gene rarely made derogatory comments about his ex-wife, the woman he had been married to for over twenty-five years, the mother of this two daughters. An exception was a letter to an un-identified in-law in his ex-mother-in-law's family. She had written him a supportive letter, and he responded with frankness and candor on September 8, 1969:

> I want you to know that your letter is one of the most pleasant and welcome I have ever received. The way you have always kept your identity and refused to knuckle to "family" pressure has always pleased me. There are some exceptions in the family like you, but they seem to me in general to be as narrow-minded, petty and unintelligent a group of people as I have ever seen. You may not have known this, but there were many times when Frank and Maude were denied entrance to my home because of intolerant statements they kept making against other races and religions. I wouldn't let them back in until they promised to keep their mouths shut in front of my growing children. By the time I realized what an assortment of congenital haters I had married into, the children had been

born and I made the mistake of thinking I ought
to wait until they grew up before doing something
about it. If I had it to do all over again, I would
have divorced fifteen or twenty years ago.

It took a few years, but Gene thought a great deal about
his separation and divorce. In April 1972, he wrote to
Asimov, who had also gone through a divorce at about the
same time.

The separation and divorce after twenty-six years
of marriage, particularly with my Southern family
traditions and concerns over the sanctity of personal
contracts, was a traumatic experience. I realize now
it was much more difficult than it should have been.
Relationships, like people, can die and while they should
be properly mourned, it seems to me they also
deserve a decent burial at the appropriate time. I
wish I had realized all that sooner.

CHAPTER 12

Gene was always looking for other possibilities beyond *Star Trek*. One project that never passed the "high interest stage," but intrigued him greatly nevertheless, was discussed in a letter to Asimov in early 1968.

> I am currently going over the Robot[1] books for the third time, beginning to sketch out characters and story lines which seem to offer a melding of a number of the short story progressions into a longer, unified motion picture progression. As soon as we finish shooting our last show this Wednesday, I can spend even more time on this and get something drawn up quickly then. I'll present a sketch to you before I make up a final draft aimed at determining how serious motion picture interest is and on what basis for you as well as myself. I have talked it over with Paramount but until something is submitted on paper all they can or will do here or at any studio is to nod sagely and say "sounds interesting."

Gene also tried using *Star Trek* as a launch vehicle for a spin-off series, and he mentioned this to Asimov in the same letter.

> Oh yes, by separate cover I am sending a copy of the final script "Assignment: Earth" which is also a

---

[1]Asimov's *I, Robot*, and others.

pilot spin-off episode. In other words, it presents
a character and a story situation which suggests a new
series. If there seems to be interest in that direction
then it would be my job to cut a 15 or 20 minute
"Sales Presentation" out of the final episode and submit
it to the various networks. Also, sending you some
"Mr. Spock For President" bumper stickers. (I sort
of like "Dr. Spock For President" too.)

Assignment: Earth had been created by Gene and Art
Wallace. It featured a character called Anthony Seven, (later
renamed Gary Seven). Gene sent the format to Herb
Schlosser at NBC for consideration. In order to sell the program Gene used the same metaphoric device he and Oscar
Katz first used to sell *Star Trek*, referencing successful television programs familiar to the executives. Beyond selling
the format, the pitch letter turned into a mini-essay on television and the state of the times.

Assignment: Earth could also be called *Have Gun-Will
Travel, 1968!* Yes, I'm quite serious, and should know
what I'm talking about. As well as being co-creator
of *Assignment: Earth* I also was head writer of
Have Gun-Will Travel.[2] The prime dramatic ingredients
of the two shows are almost identical—both shows
feature a slightly larger-than-life main character,
who sallies forth weekly from a familiar "home
base" to do battle with extraordinary evil in an action-
adventure format. As top HG-WT writers were aware
(and you must have realized it, too), there were a
surprising number of "science fiction" ingredients
in the character of Paladin.[3] Certainly, for a person
living in 1872, his remarkable knowledge, attitudes
and abilities were very much that of a man from
"another place" or "another time." In fact, one of
Paladin's most effective dramatic tools and charms
was his detached and superior, sometimes almost
condescending, perspective from which he viewed

---

[2]Gene wrote 24 episodes over its five-year run but according to Sam Rolfe, creator of the program, there was no such position as head writer on the show.
[3]Paladin was the central character in *Have Gun-Will Travel*. He was played by
Richard Boone.

the fallible world about him. *Assignment: Earth*'s
Anthony Seven will have much of the same
perspective and charm. *And, because of what he
is, he also will have much of the same strengths.*

Will the audience "identify"? I was there when the
same question was asked about super-hero Paladin.
The answer was in a hit show, which ran with
extremely high ratings for many years. (I can't help
but add the same question was also asked about Mr.
Spock, who is now considered an American folk
hero.) Unless almost every current high-rated
action-adventure television show has it all wrong, unless
John Wayne has played it all wrong all these years,
the audience not only identifies with unusual and
superior lead characters, but shows increasing signs
of much preferring such heroes over the "slice-of-life"
variety which have failed in series after series.

Today's audience more and more seeks escape
and identification with "larger-than-life" characters.
Ordinary people are getting hemmed in by an
increasingly complex and frightening world and the
viewer finds that identification and escape are
possible only through characters who have unusual
strength and abilities. Example: "I Spy," "Mission:
Impossible," "Harper," "Our Man Flint," James Bond;
and we find the same factor in comedies such as
"Bewitched," "Get Smart," and others.

Time of Crisis. The late 1960's and '70's are the
most critical Earth is likely ever to face. Our audience,
from housewife to college draftee to scientist,
knows this and personally identifies. A public
figure was quoted recently as saying—*"I am only half
joking when I say I pray every night that somewhere
on earth there are visitors from an advanced race
who can help earth out of its growing dilemma."*[4]
If you don't think *that* possibility (or hope) isn't on
a lot of average audience minds, consider the recurring
waves of "flying saucer visitor" stories that flood
the newspapers every month or so. (*Look* ran a

---

[4]Gene used a variant of this theme in *The Questor Tapes* several years in the future.

special issue on this very subject and sold out their entire first printing overnight!)

If there was such a race somewhere who wants to help us, how would they do it? A logical way would be as in our story. In short, the *Assignment: Earth* lead character is not an alien, not a robot, but a human, raised and trained to find the sparks of Armageddon, extinguish them before the blaze engulfs us. It may be a large story, as in our pilot, or it may be as small a story as saving a highly necessary young scientist, who is about to wreck his life and career and deprive the world of something vital he must offer. The "enemy" can be the Mafia, a greedy politician, an overly eager agent operating inside the Pentagon, or even the Kremlin, or an honest mistake about to be made by a powerful Senate Committee. It can be university bacteriological experiment about to go awry, it can be, in fact, any *action-adventure about almost any interesting subject in almost any place.*

Is *Assignment: Earth* science fiction? *No,* if you mean by that strange planets, exotic aliens and science-oriented stories. Our time is *today,* our locales contemporary, our action-adventure takes place in recognizable story areas. *Yes,* it is science fiction, if you mean by that imaginative stories, lots of exciting gimmicks and devices and extra-ordinary challenges to an extraordinary man.

It is a matter of record that *Star Trek*'s most exciting and successful audience shows were those three in which Captain Kirk and Mr. Spock returned to 20th-century Earth and played out their story there. However interesting a science fiction device or weapon is when used on an alien planet, it is triply exciting when the same thing is used in a familiar earth locale. The word is "contrast."

Since the question is bound to come up, let's ask it. Is *Assignment: Earth* anything like "The Invaders"? No, quite the opposite. QM Productions made a basic error in their most important ingredient of the show—they picked the wrong villain. One-dimensional "bad guys from outer space" make for one-dimensional stories. Every successful dramatist should know that the only villain capable of supporting the main episodes of a television show is *man himself.* The list of man's possible villainies is endless, an extraordinary collection of vices, weaknesses, creeds, jealousies, hatreds ... you name it. There has never been a successful novel, screenplay, stage production or television series using any theme but *man against man, or man against himself.*

The idea went to pilot as a *Star Trek* episode— "Assignment: Earth" with Robert Lansing as Gary Seven and Teri Garr[5] in her television debut as his secretary, Roberta Lincoln. The show was directed by Marc Daniels and aired March 29, 1968.

Gene's plans for a fallback project did not work out. NBC did not buy the format.

As has been mentioned previously, one of Gene's great assets was Bob Justman. Justman's production expertise was valuable, but an added bonus was his sense of humor. Justman wrote memos that conveyed the twinkle in his eye. Near the end of the second season, before NBC had been beaten over the head by the fans into renewing the show, Justman sent out the following memo:

Dear Gene:

As you know, our season is rapidly drawing to a close. And now that we are already engaged in the production of our last episode, it is incumbent upon us to start terminating various personnel in order to effect necessary economies. Please understand that any terminations are made entirely without rancor and strictly in the pursuit of standard business practices.

Therefore, your employment is terminated as of tonight. I have discussed the situation with Gregg [Peters] and Eddie [Milkis] and we have determined that any decisions that have to be made with respect to the balance of this production can be handled very, very easily by any one of us on a moment's notice.

Gregg, Eddie and I wish to thank you so much for your unflagging efforts on behalf of the show

---

[5] Spelled Terri Garr, at the time.

and do wish you to believe that should we receive
a third season's pickup from the Network, we would
be more than pleased to have you back with us.

Affectionately,

PS. Feel free to come in tomorrow to clear up
your office.

A copy was sent to Herb Solow who sent his own response
to Justman:

Dear R.J.:

I must say that your attitude towards the
dispossessment of Mr. Roddenberry can hardly be
condoned. To treat in such a cavalier manner a man
who has given so much of himself is a prime example
of an overbearing negative mental attitude towards the
creative mind. Such a mind should be nurtured and
protected—not stamped out with cruel indignation.

Sincerely,

PS—Now that you've gotten rid of him, can I have
his desk?

Gene also had a well-developed sense of humor that expressed itself in elaborate practical jokes. One he regaled
visitors with happened a few years earlier and is recounted
by Gene's old friends, Nick Agid and Marta Houske:

"Gene anticipated the arrival of an out-of-town visitor
from the midwest, This guy had had talks with Gene about
what it was like to be a producer and he wanted Gene to
show him the ropes. Gene arranged 'a day' for him.

"The guy arrived to find Gene in his office, zipping up his
pants as his 'secretary' walked out. He got on the phone,
feet on his desk, swearing and using profanity on a series of
calls: 'Fuck 'em!' 'You'll never work in this goddamned
business again!' 'Piss on him!' 'Screwmover now, worry
about it later!', etc. All the time he was smoking *enormous*
cigars and blowing smoke in everyone's face, the secretary's
cleavage, etc.

"The 'secretary' was a tarted-up bimbette actress wearing
very revealing clothes, camping her role up to the max, calling Gene 'Sugar,' 'Honey,' etc. She leaned over to reveal
cleavage, pressed against Gene, jiggle walked, etc.

"Gene also had prearranged to have a bunch of 'celebrity'

calls come in—big-shot names that he was rude to or shmoozed, as well as babe-ola actress names that he made suggestive comments to, set up hotel rendezvous with, etc. By midmorning, the visitor's jaw was hanging down.

"The 'secretary' came in to announce that the 'actress' who's auditioning for a part has arrived. The 'actress' walked into Gene's office and Gene says, 'Okay, babe, show me some leg!' She lifted her very short skirt to reveal that she wasn't wearing underwear. By now, Gene's guest's eyes were absolutely bugging out!

"They went to lunch in the commissary. While all the pre-arranged fawning continued as they waited for the maitre d' to seat them, Linda Evans walked up with an urgent message for Gene. Ignoring the fact that Gene was with someone, she blurted out, 'Oh, Gene, I'm pregnant and it's your baby! What shall I do?' Gene countered with, 'Oh, gimme a break, babe. How do you know it's mine?' And with that, he brushed her off.

"The over-the-top show continued as a stream of 'cartoon characters' dropped by the lunch table. By late afternoon, Gene finally decided to 'fess up' to his guest. When told that the day had all been a prearranged joke, the guy refused to believe it. He ended up moving to Los Angeles and getting into producing.

"This last line may have been added by Gene as a punchline."

Like his father, Gene was a quick thinker and, with a twinkle in his eye, was always ready to have a bit of fun. For a short period of time Gene worked with Chris Knopf at Four Star Productions. Dick Powell had given over control to a new president who had redecorated his office with a lot of new, expensive furniture.

Working late one Friday, Gene looked around at the worn furniture in the writer's office and decided he wanted a change. He looked at Chris and, motioning him to follow, said, "Come with me." They walked down the hall to the new president's office and spent a bit of time moving several pieces of new furniture out of his office and into theirs, where they enjoyed the comfortable new decor as they worked through the weekend. Neither Gene nor Chris bothered to replace the furniture when they left for the weekend, but Monday morning the furniture was back in its proper place and no one said a word to them about it.

Gene voiced his opinions on where his characters should go in the third season. On February 19, 1968, he wrote the following to a writer who had supported *Star Trek* and submitted a story for the show:

Dear John:

Thank you for the copy of the article you wrote on *Star Trek* for the *Miami Herald Sunday Magazine*. Splendid! All of us here in the production staff really appreciate it, as we do your genuine enthusiasm for the show and all the other help you have given us . . .

I have the story somewhere you sent me and will get on it this week. I just couldn't bring myself to read stories during the period when it looked like we might not make it for a third season. On that score, your comments on Spock were most helpful, particularly that one that "Spock is the essence of cool," equating him with Youth rebellion against the Establishment.

Also, your comments on Spock's Vulcan Hand Salute brings to my attention we have not made near enough use of that and probably should let it become even more of a standard device during the third season.

Your statement, "Thus Kirk is torn between the two factors—cold logic (Spock) and humanity (McCoy)—and must take a stand somewhere in the middle" is exactly what we strive for and your comments on the subject remind me that I want to emphasize this ever more in a third year, too. I'll be getting together with the actors on that very subject.

Re: the third year, NBC insists that any pickup of *Star Trek* for a third season is predicated upon my functioning during that season as the working producer of the show. This in no way indicates they were not satisfied with Coon and Lucas and certainly we were happy with them; however, NBC feels that the originator of the idea should take the show now for the third season, critically appraise it and build on what we have there. This in no way indicates any basic changes, I fought to keep all our continuing characters, refused to put in a "space cadet" or a "Lassie" or anything like that. One of the new directions we *will* go is to do more *topical* shows, such as one which has to do with what if on a planet very much like ours, or exactly like ours, the police were selected like doctors and scientists and had every conceivable scientific device at their fingertips.[6] Since law enforcement is very much on the public mind today, this could be highly interesting and promotable. Similarly, I want to do a show on brain transplant,[7] since due to Dr. Christian Bernard's heart transplant, such things are very much in the public consciousness, and so on. This relates very much to your comments that "tomorrow is now."

Again, many thanks for everything.

From the beginning, there were plans to merchandise *Star Trek,* as a variety of memos indicate. AMT Corporation put out a successful line of plastic spaceship models that continues to this day. Books were a natural, and by 1967 James Blish was turning a number of episodes into novelizations.[8] Unfortunately, Blish had never seen *Star Trek* and did not write his novelizations from shooting scripts or finished programs. Consequently, Blish often included material that had not made it to the screen, and Gene was irritated that the stories often deviated from what was broadcast. At one point Gene issued orders that no licensees could get anything but final shooting scripts and not until after the program had been filmed. Gene was unhappy with Blish's work, and some years later told SF writer Hal Clement that had he been given a choice he would have been Gene's preference to do the novelizations.

---

[6]While this was never done on *Star Trek,* Gene kept it filed away and worked up a pilot script with Sam Peeples called *The Tribunes.*

[7]"Brain *and* brain! What is brain?!"

[8]*Star Trek,* by James Blish (New York: Bantam, 1967). Novelization of seven episodes from the original series. Blish then produced another book of eight episodes in 1968, one of seven episodes in 1969, six episodes in 1971, and four books of seven episodes each in 1972. The pace slowed down a bit, with two books of six episodes each in 1973, one of six episodes in 1974, with the last collection of five episodes not appearing until 1977 in collaboration with J.A. Lawrence.

Another project was a *Star Trek* novel aimed at children, written by Mack Reynolds.⁹ John Meredyth Lucas had sent a memo to Desilu Business Affairs with a carbon to Gene concerning his thoughts on Reynolds' work. Lucas was not pleased with what he had read.

> Mack Reynolds' novelization of *Star Trek* is not technically in bad taste, but it is extremely dull and even considering the juvenile market, badly written (if anything, one should write better for the juveniles). It does, moreover, contain some inaccuracies which, if possible, should be corrected. Spock's people are Vulcans, not Vulcanians. I understand this was pointed out and changed to the proper term in the Blish book (second collection).

There follow several criticisms of violation of General Order #1 (The Prime Directive) and:

> Page 10 of the summary: Mr. Spock *never* quotes poetry. This has been cut out of innumerable scripts. It is one of the character things that has been built into Spock. Anyone else could quote poetry, but not Spock.
>   In other places Mr. Reynolds refers to Sulu as a bland faced, small oriental; to Uhura as a negress and compounds this by having her break into a spiritual. We run a totally integrated ship in an integrated century and it would seem we should avoid these particular stereotypes for a juvenile market.
>
> J.M.L.

On November 14, 1967, Gene followed up with his own letter to Ed Perlstein in Desilu Business Affairs. It is one of the earliest examples of Gene's concern for items that carried the *Star Trek* name other than the television show.

> I agree completely with John Meredyth Lucas' comments on Mack Reynolds' novelization of *Star Trek.* I am particularly upset and made nervous by

---

⁹Writing name of Dallas McCord Reynolds (1917–1983).

some of the bad taste in it (Uhura as a "Negress" who breaks into a spiritual, etc.)

I think we must go on the assumption that *Star Trek* will continue on television for many years and is a valuable property worth protecting and I personally would rather blow a deal like this than see the property harmed.

I recommend strongly that in this deal and in all future book, magazine, or comic deals that we insist on enough advanced time for copy so that it can be checked over carefully. I further recommend that we pick someone like Dorothy Fontana who has an excellent and broad grasp of this show, demand that all such future deals include some reasonable payment to make it worthwhile for Dorothy Fontana (or someone else connected with the show) to spend some time going over the material and guiding the writer and publishers away from technical inaccuracy or outright bad taste.[10]

Ed, you have done an excellent and tasteful job of protecting us but now since you are leaving, who will be responsible for protecting the show as well as seeing to merchandising profits? I really feel very strongly about it since my name is necessarily connected with any by-product of *Star Trek.*

Respectfully,

In early February 1968, Gene sent in a five-page, single-spaced, typed critique of the reworked novel, which further illustrated how concerned he was with maintaining a certain level of quality in all *Star Trek* products.

Late in January 1968, Gene received a letter that began a friendship and closed a circle. It was a fan letter from the legendary John W. Campbell.[11] Campbell had started as a writer of epic space opera and was, for a time, the chief rival

---

[10]This was not implemented until the mid-1980s, when Gene hired Richard Arnold as the *Star Trek* archivist.

[11]John Wood Campbell, Jr. (1910–1971). Under the pseudonym of Don A. Stuart, he wrote his most famous novel, *The Thing from Another World,* originally published in *Astounding Science Fiction* as "Who Goes There." It was the basis for two movies entitled *The Thing.*

to E.E. "Doc" Smith. Campbell made his greatest contribution to science fiction as an editor. It was he who began the so-called "Golden Age of Science Fiction" in 1938, with his editorship of *Astounding Science Fiction*. Campbell invigorated written science fiction by an infusion of his concepts and encouragement of young writers such as Lester Del Rey, Eric Frank Russell, Theodore Sturgeon,[12] Robert A. Heinlein, Isaac Asimov, and A.E. Van Vogt. All of these were people Gene had read over the years; all had influenced him to one degree or another.

By 1968, John Campbell was still editing the magazine, only the name had been changed to *Analog* eight years earlier. Campbell had written Gene with support for the show and an idea for a *Star Trek* product.

Dear Mr. Roddenberry:
   I'm joining in the campaign to promote "Star Trek," naturally—it's the world's first and only true science-fiction program, and it averages really high in quality. (Of course you're bound to pull an occasional clunker! Who doesn't?) I'm writing a few letters—but also I thought of something that might help otherwise.
   Sorry I'm late on this, but it still may have time to do some good and get some fast action.
   For this noble idea, I'll charge a fee of $1.00—so it'll be legally and beyond question yours in full.
   Gimmick: Winter cap for boys, made of heavy black overcoat material (scraps and cutting can probably be used) cut to match Mr. Spock's skull-cap style hairdo. The usually winter-hat earflaps have appliqued pink felt Vulcan ears.[13]

Gene responded in typical good humor.

Dear John:
   You've got yourself a deal!
   I like the gimmick and have passed it along to

---

[12]Sturgeon wrote two *Star Trek* episodes, "Amok Time" and "Shore Leave."
[13]Campbell's idea was never put into production. The closest product was a baseball cap with Spock ears that came out during the time of the second or third film. For obvious reasons, it was not available for very long.

the merchandising people. Incidentally, I hope to get more deeply involved in merchandising for the show next year, since I think the last two years' attempts have been pretty shlocky and beneath the quality and image we've tried to project for ourselves. Too often they've taken old space toys and simply slapped a *Star Trek* label on them. But this idea of yours is good and to the point and would serve as great promotion for the show. Incidentally, what are the advertising rates for your magazine? Maybe I can talk the studio into doing some intelligent promotions in such directions.

Warmest regards,

By February 1968, Campbell had received his dollar and sent his next letter.

This is to acknowledge payment in full ($1) for the merchandising idea of caps for boys having Vulcan-type ears as ear-flaps.

Glad you liked the idea—my wife and I thought it would be fun.

And I'm glad indeed to hear that NBC is bucking the trend toward happy little shows for happy little morons who just *hate* thinking a new idea.

God knows there are plenty of ideas more-or-less standard in science fiction that have not yet been even touched by *Star Trek*.

Like several interpenetrating, mutually cooperating empires—one made up of oxygen-breathing inhabitants of Earth-size planets, one of chlorine-breathers, and one of ammonia-methane breathers who need gas-giant planets like Jupiter. Neither can use the kind of planets the other needs—and each type has minerals unique to its chemistry which would be of value to the others.

Gene became uncharacteristically candid in his letters to Campbell, and on October 30, 1968 wrote:

Embarked November 3 on something I've always wanted to do. Received an invitation to spend a week on the nuclear carrier USS *Enterprise* while it is

off the coast on air training maneuvers. Although
I was Air Force in World War II, I was always
rather envious of the Navy and rather wished I had
joined that service instead. Something about ships, old
traditions, mess etiquette, all that. For example, my
favorite fictional character is the not-too-admirable
Captain Hornblower. At any rate, the trip aboard
will be a chance to have a look at a way and a style
of life which promises to disappear soon.

I suspect that people like you and I will always
envy the "Hornblowers" whether real or fictional.
Why? Simply because we know it would be nice to
relax and enjoy a simplistic view of life—Bonaparte
(or communism) is bad; our people are good,
although this is not the best of all possible worlds
it is the best we can do during this imperfect time and
God help civilization if The Establishment falls; on
your feet as we toast the President and then a chorus
of "Anchors Aweigh." Don't we wish to Christ the
paths and the goals were that simple.

Well, for that week I am going to pretend they are.
I will not wear my Peace[14] medal, I will not mention
Vietnam and the Nuremberg trials in the same
breath, and when the mess boy brings me my coffee
I will be delighted the Philippine Islands produced
this race of pleasant little brown men for my
comfort.

A few weeks later, on December 3, 1968, Gene reported
the results of the *Enterprise* visit on National General Production, Inc. letterhead. He gave voice to his deepest
thoughts.

Dear John:

The *Enterprise* trip was a highly successful one from
a variety of points of view. Not particularly
pleasant, just successful. Like visiting San Quentin
can be highly useful to a dramatist; he can interpolate

---

[14]The symbol designed by Bertrand Russell in the late 1940's, who combined the
semiphore signals for the letters "N" and "D," which stood for nuclear disarma-
ment.

what he learned there into usable information relating
to a half-hundred other situations.

The *Enterprise,* however you cut it, as no doubt true
on any naval vessel, is very much a prison. I was
not particularly surprised when the Public Affairs
Commander commented on how wonderful it was to
live in this place where there are no strikes, no hippies,
and no problems of disorder. I supposed that was
his job. Although many cutting answers to his
comparison came quickly to mind, I kept silent. Most
hear the same comment repeated in one form or another
by practically every senior officer I met aboard the
vessel. All but the Captain and he's another story
which I'll get into in a moment.

I suppose that to rise to Field Grade rank or its naval
equivalent requires that particular peculiar
perspective on what is important in life. Or else
the man goes mad. Or certainly he becomes known
as a renegade or troublemaker and gets passed over
and discharged before he gets his gold or silver
oakleaf. If he's going to stay in and be a success
he must create a frame of mind in which he accepts
that kind of life willingly and even enthusiastically.
Or they'll find him out and get him the hell out
but fast. And granted the need for a Navy, it's
undoubtedly the only way to do it. But the whole system
of officer life aboard (and also of Petty Officer life)
reeks of "return to the womb." I'm not knocking
it, wombs are pleasant, secure, and safe. But wombs
or other kinds of this prison are not for me.

Captain Lee never used the foolish comparison of
the "perfect order" of this place as opposed to the
chaotic disorder ashore. As a matter of fact, his first
question was about Albert Camus, some obscure point
in the Frenchman's philosophy which I did not have
the answer for. We then spent several hours in most
stimulating discussion of "What is leadership?" Just
as I was interested in his job, he was very interested
in the techniques a producer uses in getting the best
men for the best job, keeping them there,
supervising them, and so on. We found that our
jobs were almost exactly alike and, indeed, he and
I used the same shameful tricks in creating the useful

and necessary image of ourselves, in creating and
maintaining employee loyalty, and in measuring not
just the current efficiency of a subordinate but in
making a useful guess of his potential if driven hard
enough with sufficient motivation. And we found we
shared the ever present problem of trying *not* to promote
your people too fast because that can be one of the
most deadly things to the organization; if you pick
people with high potential and then promote them as
fast as they deserve it or are capable of handling it,
you find yourself running an employee agency
instead of doing the job you're being paid to do.

In one letter, Campbell had previously described some
outlandish claims made by a paranormalist of his acquaint-
ance, and Gene commented:

I do believe we have something loosely and incorrectly
tagged a "sixth sense" and I do believe there exists
such things as clairvoyance and psychokinesis. But
as for a guy killing Japanese beetles from 500 miles
away just by looking at a picture of the field, in fact
doing it so selectively he can kill them off one leaf
and leave them alive on another, my life experience
adds up to a belief that this is impossible. In other
words, I've seen enough examples and read enough
documented reports concerning instances of telepathy,
clairvoyance, and psychokinesis to indicate that we
do indeed have latent abilities in these areas which
we do not yet understand or really know how to use.
Those instances which do happen are largely haphazard
or the "power" ebbs and flows to a point where
it is rarely controllable enough to produce any long-
term or meaningful results on a scientifically controlled
test. Thus, I find the ideas of a man looking at the
picture and saying "zap" rather hard to buy. If he
can do that with that control whenever he wants
to do it, and if he will do it twenty-six times for me,
once weekly on TV for a half-hour, I can get him about
a half million dollars cash. Or if he doesn't care
about that much money, we can use the bulk of
it to take care of wounded Vietnamese children or in
whatever charitable way he wishes.

Understand, I'm not saying all this is absolutely impossible. I'm saying rather that I've seen nothing yet to lead me to believe it is possible for any of us to exercise this power so regularly and on such a controlled basis. My father occasionally gets what he calls a "flash." For example, he *knew* what day Eisenhower would invade the continent. It "came to him" and came so certainly and effectively that he accepted it and had absolutely no doubt about it—and was right. I've played poker with him when it would suddenly hit him that the next card up is probably the jack of clubs, or whatever he happens to need. He is a good gambler and is firmly of the opinion that when he has "the power" he can make the jack of clubs come up to the top of the deck. He can "will" it into existence to fill an inside straight, say. And although the odds of filling an inside straight are something like 900 to 1,[15] when he announces he has "the power," he will fill every other one or at the least one out of every four. And damned if it isn't true that when he announces "the power's gone" his luck fades completely.

We suspect that the K-2 quotient I mentioned the other night is somehow tied into all this type of thing. It does seem that some people have a better than average ability to communicate, to transmit and/or receive, with whatever we are part of. Our ancestors recognized there were some who "were closer to God" than others. In India today everyone, whether religiously inclined or not, accepts the fact that Holy Men are a fact of life. Every experienced teacher, whether kindergarten or university, recognizes that out of every thousand students there will be a couple or six who are somehow "in tune" and a few definitely "out of tune" and ninety-six or seven percent who will accumulate sufficient practical information to

---

[15]Actually, the odds in filling a four-card straight in draw poker are 11 to 1 against making a straight open at either one end or the middle, and 5 to 1 against making a straight open at both ends. Gene's story is a good example of people who remember their wins and forget the times they were wrong. For there to actually be something to this, all poker games and all outcomes would have to be cataloged and a search made for deviations from chance.

eat and stay warm and live for a reasonable span of
years but who will never really think or understand
anything. They probably could be reached if man knew
when and how to reach them, but we don't. We give
them general information tests and upon
determining that they have a certain expertise in
not putting their hands on red-hot stoves and in reading
warning labels on medicine bottles and so on, assign
them a satisfactory IQ number. The two or three
percent of doers and thinkers are likely not to have
a higher IQ than many of those in the great mass group.
Obviously there is something we are not measuring
and must learn to identify and measure.

Campbell wrote back a letter in 1968, now lost, and Gene
again responded on the same subject.

I agree with you that mental-level phenomena *does*
occur, but I cannot accept that it occurs with any
consistent degree of control. Otherwise I must
wonder why slaves in Hitler Germany had to resort
to spitting in oxygen tanks in order to kill pilots. There
would be more subtle and effective ways to get at people
if a useful degree of control of mental-level
phenomena was presently possible.
Or maybe there are such things going on all the time
and this is why the good guys always win. They do,
don't they? And yet if Japan had won or even
gotten a draw out of World War II we would
probably have a very solid (and probably non-Fascist
by now) greater Asia Co-prosperity Sphere over there
now instead of Vietnam aflame and China in
torment and India falling to pieces, and so on.

Campbell had an opinion on slavery, which had come out
of a discussion he'd had with Gene. Campbell followed up
on the beginning of a conversation when he wrote:

Finally, neither of us had even a one-tenth chance
to discuss that business of what "equal opportunity"
really means, and what can, and should be done
about it. Something for you to consider that's
actually highly relevant in that connection is the comment

that Schwarzberg [another guest present] (and fits my own conclusions) that *slavery is many times beneficial to a people.* Lousy from the individual's viewpoint, sure—but it can be a hell of a benefit to a people. It's highly educational. Here's why:

A slave is a valuable possession; the owner has sunk considerable capital wealth into his purchase. He not unnaturally wants the most he can possibly get out of his purchase—which means he will tend to see that his slave is well-fed, well-housed, well-clothed, gets adequate medical attention, and is kept in reasonably good mental health—always within the limits of the technology and sociology of the time.

Now there has been one civilization in history which showed zero point zero zero racial discrimination. Black, white, yellow, or green-with-polka-dots made no difference. The man born a slave could become Chief Executive, and the son of the Chief Executive could become a slave. And since a trained, educated slave was obviously more valuable than a dope, the bright slaves were damned well educated. There was complete freedom of vertical movement in that culture—quite largely *because* there was slavery.

That was the culture of Islam. They practiced rigid segregation—and displayed marked discrimination, but purely on the basis of individual ability. What a man could earn, he could have—and what he refused to bother earning, he didn't get.

Gene gave Campbell his thoughts in the next letter.

Agree with your remarks on slavery, perhaps with the single exception that your tense indicated a belief that slavery is over while I can see no signs that the institution has vanished. If the measurement is happiness and contentment, while I do not believe that Nat Turner or his kin were at all happy or contented, neither do I see much signs of happiness or contentment in his descendants in Watts today. For that matter, although the material accumulation level of the white working man and clerk is considerably higher, the average one seems to me as bound to his employment category and social station as any

slave in more ancient times. I started to make this
comment in a rewrite of a *Star Trek* script which
had to do with finding an "Americanium 1968" but
found that to do it properly I might as well start a
whole new story and so left that episode essentially
as it was. My idea, which I hoped to dramatize,
was that economic fetters are much more efficient and
more easily manipulated than iron chains. By showing
a parallel planet in which Rome did *not* fall and
still had the institution of slavery, I had planned
to dramatize the thought that slavery fell simply because
it was an expensive and inefficient way of keeping
people in bondage. In this planned drama, we were
going to have slaves with social security,
workman's compensation, twenty-year pension, etc.
adding up to the rest of the populace working like mad
to keep the slaves in a manner to which they were
accustomed. I was even considering having a
Roman-type proconsul scheming to get out of his job
and *into* slavery. As is probably true also in the magazine
field, the ones we didn't do often sound better than
the ones we did.

Campbell must have responded in a letter now lost, for
Gene continued the discussion in a following letter.

I think you missed my point about slavery. What
is called "slavery" is just a given degree of domination
of our lives by others. Somewhere along the line,
if you can't choose your own woman or keep your
own children or hide a few coins in a mattress, and
if certain other restrictions reach a certain point, it is
recognized as and is called "slavery." But the truth
of the matter is many so-called "free" men actually
operate under greater practical restrictions than most
"slaves" of past eras. We'll always have one form or
another of "slavery" with us. It's just that we don't
do it with chains and whips any more. In our
complex society we have much better ways of keeping
the working class in line and punishing them when
they get out of line.

What outward and inward signs distinguish a
slave from a non-slave? Happiness? Laughter? How

much of this do we actually have in a typical
neighborhood in Encino or Des Moines today as
compared with the slave quarters in Greece or Rome
or Alabama yesterday?

Incidentally, my suggested Roman Consul
recognized that he was already a slave and didn't get
much happiness or laughter out of it, and had to work
seventeen times as hard for his food as the slaves
who worked for him, so he was thinking about
making a switch. His motivation was not cradle-to-grave
security.

And as far as studying and working and achieving
goes, a surprising number of slaves in history
studied and worked and achieved and *created* far more
than their masters.

To some extent or another everyone is a slave
and the amount of money you take home each year
seems to have little to do with the degree of slavery
you have been bound into. You can make a million
and be a complete slave whereas a one-horse farmer
in Montana may be almost free. On the other hand,
I do not subscribe to the theory that millionaires are
necessarily unhappy or in bondage.

In the last surviving communication is a Campbell letter
sent to Gene at National General Productions on February 20, 1969. Campbell thought he would be getting out
west to witness a rocket launch, but it had been scheduled
for Cape Kennedy and he was going there, instead. He was
happy that being at Kennedy would allow him to watch the
Apollo 9 launch, but he was irritated he would not be able
to visit with Gene.

As Campbell knew, Gene was less and less involved with
Star Trek by then, and commented on the last letter he had
received from Gene. Even though Gene had stayed on as executive producer, Campbell did not like what the new production team was doing to the content and direction of the
show. He wrote:

In my comment about not putting your name on the
new version of *Star Trek,* I was using hyperbole; I
know you have damn good reason for keeping the
title! But I'm afraid I can't use *Analog* to support

Star Trek again, as we did before—it's simply moved out of the field of science fiction in nearly all the shows.[16] (The one on Feb. 14 by Jerry Bixby,[17] was a return to science fiction ... but a leeetle slow-moving. It *was* a science fiction yarn, however. Leonardo as the multi-talented Rennaisance Man all-around genius makes a good idea.)

Campbell continued with his thoughts on what made a story a success, principles Gene knew full well, and his thoughts on "anti-heroes," which were then popular:

> Yet every great piece of literature Mankind has ever made its own is an account of heroes and heroic deeds.
> I repeat: The Odyssey has leapt every barrier of language and culture for some 3000 years. Originally composed by neolithic-Early Bronze Age barbarians, that hero's tale is on sale in pocket book in jet airports. A story of a "king" whose palace has a mud floor, with an olive tree growing up through his royal bedroom, is *still* enjoyed—because it's a tale of a *hero*.
> No anti-heroes have remained popular.

After a long and productive career that influenced hundreds of writers and the direction of all presentations of science fiction, John W. Campbell died in 1971.

Late in February 1968, Gene had been informed that *Star Trek* had won the Photoplay Award. Bill Shatner and Leonard Nimoy were going to pick it up on the *Merv Griffin Show,* so Gene brought them up to date on the latest fan response with the following memo:

> It is likely that while you are guests on the *Merv Griffin Show* for the Photoplay Award, the subject of fan mail, the intensity of it, the broad spectrum of writers, the total amount, the student marches, etc, will be brought up for

---

[16]If Campbell had watched every new show broadcast in the third season, he could have seen nineteen of them by the time he wrote this letter. There were only five unaired episodes left.

[17]"Requiem for Methuselah," by Jerome Bixby.

discussion. As a matter of fact, I'm sure you agree with all of us that the million letters NBC received and certain other aspects of this is highly exciting and reflects great credit upon the show and upon yourselves.

While most of the fan mail was supportive, occasionally a letter arrived that was the opposite. Nonetheless all letters, fan and critic alike, were answered. Unlike many shows, which might respond to a letter of criticism with a form letter, Gene often responded personally, and occasionally with some passion. In mid-April 1968, he received an intelligent and articulate letter from a fan who took him to task on a number of fronts.

It has just come to my attention that over a dozen of Hollywood's best scriptwriters, including such award-winning writers as John D.F. Black, Harlan Ellision, Don Ingalls, George Clayton Johnson, Boris Sobelman and Barry Trivers, have refused to write for any future episodes of *Star Trek* because of the treatment their past work has received at your hands.

I don't know just what you are trying to prove by this reworking of intelligent drama into some sort of maudlin freak show, unless it is that nothing in the industry is inviolable to the Hollywood mentality, even the loftiest ambitions of would-be innovators.

Three weeks later, Gene sent a forthright and candid response.

You have misinterpreted my intentions.

Reference the writers mentioned, unless you have seen samples of their *Star Trek* script drafts then it seems to me you have no foundation to make a value judgment on their ability. The only acceptable first draft of the group was Harlan Ellison's and it budgeted out nearly $100,000 over what we had to spend on an episode, plus his use of our characters was not according to format. When he couldn't do an acceptable re-write job, I re-wrote the script to bring it within budget and within line of our *Star Trek* format. The point of this is not that you deserve an explanation but that you should understand it is foolish to make broad generalization when you do not have all the facts.

I value you as a fan and as a supporter but I cannot promise you that we have, can, or will turn out week after week episodes which are "little gems." Television's time and budget restrictions simply do not permit this. Perhaps your list of "Hollywood's Best Script Writers" can accomplish what we have been unable to do. Perhaps it is time they stopped talking and began demonstrating.

And until somebody somewhere demonstrates they can do better, I think it is time some of our fans stopped listening to them.

While Gene was open and available to his fans, he also wasn't shy about sharing his thoughts with science fiction convention organizers. He sent a letter to one such person in May 1968. After several paragraphs about the convention, he got to the meat of his letter:

I must be quite frank in admitting I have been badly treated, insulted and embarrassed at past conventions and have little desire to undergo it again. I should say this was *not* by the fans at these conventions or by many fine friends I have made there but by the various organizers and staffs of these affairs. For example, I was awarded a plaque two years ago but have not received it. Last year I was not even informed I had won the Hugo and except for Isaac Asimov sending me a letter I would not have even known it. In both cases I provided film and every requested assistance and never received the courtesy of a "thank you" or any help or cooperation in setting up the things they asked me to do. I don't expect a diploma or a standing ovation every time I assist, but I do rather expect to receive the same kind of common courtesy I give them.

Yes, we like fans and are willing to help out with your convention where we can assuming there is some sort of *quid pro quo* in it which I can use to justify the time and expense to the studio business people who in the end give the final approvals on such

things and sign the checks. Paramount Studios
(formerly Desilu) is my partner in the *Star Trek* venture
and I am not permitted to make unilateral decisions
any more than they are. One thing we would like
at the convention is a table where *Star Trek* souvenir
items and such can be either on sale or orders taken
for them. Not that we expect to make a lot of
dollars on same, rather that the mail order souvenir
aspect has enormous publicity and promotional effect
on any television show.

And again, I sincerely and honestly dig our fans,
I think they are the greatest. I even dig our strongest
critics and I think you must know by now we that
circulate their comments among our staff. We're
professional people; we're proud of it.

Sincerely yours,

Then there were a few requests from peers, which Gene
enjoyed replying to. Roy Huggins was and is a most prolific
and successful producer.[18] In late April, he wrote to Gene
asking for assistance on a paper he was writing. In early
May, Gene replied, sending Huggins a mini-essay with his
thoughts and opinions on the business.

Dear Roy:
Good to hear from you. Mutual friends keep me fairly
well informed of you and your projects and I
continue to wish you every good luck in them. I
don't know how much help I can give you in preparing
your paper but I am willing to try.

I do believe that television has a significant
impact on the audience—a medium which
represents something like over a billion man-hours of
viewing per week can hardly escape affecting its audience
in some way.

First, has television done any good for anyone
or helped resolve any meaningful national problems?
Any answer to this question, like any other television
question, has to be divided into two parts, (a) news
and public affairs television, and (b) drama

---

[18]He created *77 Sunset Strip, Maverick, The Fugitive, Run for Your Life, The Rockford Files,* and several other fine shows.

television. Although I am something less than an expert on news and public affairs television, I am certain there has been a *significant* impact on the American people via quite a number of news and public affairs programs dating back to Edward R. Murrow's courageous stand against Senator Joe McCarthy. The Xerox and Purex specials, for example, have been significant pieces of television literature. Unfortunately, however, the dividing of television into these two branches seems to have given the networks a schizoid personality and they cling to a rather foolish belief that by doing good things in news programming they avoid responsibility for the foolishness and outright social immorality displayed in their drama programming. Also unfortunate is the fact that they (and few others) seem to realize that *drama* has by far the greatest impact on the audience. Just as in the written mediums where fiction (drama) has had probably a hundred times more impact on our world, perhaps thousands of times more impact, than expository writings.

Now to television drama. I think that although it is hard to find much to congratulate networks, agencies and studios for, we *can* be proud of TV writers. Although forced to compromise with commercial censorship since the beginning of television, they have always managed to insert into their scripts messages that "to be different is not necessarily to be evil" and many other similar concepts which historians may someday see as quite important in helping pave the way for the youth and social revolutions going on in America today. As bad as shows like "Mr. District Attorney" were, as terrible as the writing was, those ideas were always there—although usually disguised in order to get them past the businessmen and the censors. I'm quite serious about this—I cannot help but believe that these "messages" skillfully inserted even in the early Westerns we both wrote, skillfully hidden in the story, had over the years a cumulative effect on the attitudes of people like my own rather strange relatives in our small Georgia home town. This was done constantly by almost every writer I know and although most of them did not have your and my opportunities to occasionally force a pertinent theme story down the network's throat, the steady flow of these ideas could not have helped but soften prejudice and intolerance to a point where the current and larger breakthroughs became possible.

Other than that, and with the few exceptions we both know, I think the great majority of dramatic television has been a blot on our nation and will be a source of great shame in the future. On that subject, I think one could make a rather good case of the fact that commercial censorship is much more dangerous and insidious than government censorship, although I hate both.

I agree with you that a producer or writer cannot help make a statement of one type or another which influences his audience. Or, by trying to make no statement, a creator is committing a sin of omission and actually stating to the audience that there are no problems or issues which should concern the audience. This is perhaps the greatest evil which commercial television perpetuates upon our nation. The creative people in television have not permitted this completely to happen although it does happen enough to be a source of concern.

My attitude on television? Like almost every person I respect who is now in television, I want to get the hell out of the medium and probably will do so. But yet I have some nagging doubts about what happens to the medium if we all leave it to those who don't worry about its impact on people. It sounds trite to say that anything has to get worse before it can get better, and it may seem that television could not possibly be any worse, but I suspect that this is likely to be what must happen. I fervently hope that the television audience stops watching the tube in such great numbers that almost everyone in a position of power in the medium today is toppled from his executive chair and repudiated. I have a particular thing against the Television Academy for its grandiose posturing on the subject and its total failure to grapple with any of the issues.

The pity of the whole thing is that networks, agencies

and the like, represent some pretty well-educated, fairly decent people who make attempts, fail, then compromise and go along with the thing. They seem to find their shelter in the theory that they can escape personal responsibility in the fiction that a corporate entity has no social or moral responsibilities and thus they, as individuals, are relieved of same. This pleasant fiction is, of course, not limited to the television industry.

Gene was optimistic about his arrangement with *Star Trek* and Paramount. On May 7, he wrote to Asimov and for the first time gave him a true picture of the amount of his life he had given to making *Star Trek* successful. Paragraph six shows the extent of Gene's admiration and trust of Asimov.

Forgive the delay in answering you. We are presently up to our necks in trying to squeeze out enough finished scripts to get our new shooting season started on May 21 so that we will have the proper amount of film in the can for our starting date of September 20.

This year I am pulling back from actual line production of the show and will try to operate now as a real Executive Producer, confining myself to administration and policy. Our new Producer is Fred Freiberger[19] who produced "Ben Casey" and "Slattery's People" as well as other fine television shows, an experienced man who seems to have excellent taste and good ability. To assist him, I've raised our Associate Producer Robert Justman up to Co-Producer. Then for story editor we hired Arthur Singer who has served in that post for "Studio One," "U.S. Steel Hour," and many other fine shows. This team should be able to produce *Star Trek* if anyone can.

If they can't? I don't know Isaac. I had offered to

---

[19] According to Allan Asherman in *The Star Trek Compendium* (New York: Simon and Schuster, 1981), Freiberger's SF credits included cowriting the screenplay for *The Beast from 20,000 Fathoms* and *The Beginning of the End*. The latter effort was notable for its nonspecial effects of "giant" locusts walking across pictures of the Chicago skyline.

NBC to line produce it myself if they gave us a good
hour on a good week night but you know what happened
there. I had decided it simply was not worth the almost
crippling expenditure of time and energy if I could
not have a night and an hour which gave us at least
a fair chance of attracting a mass audience and staying
on the air. In the three years since I started the first
pilot, *Star Trek* came very near to breaking my
health—it's so much my baby that I couldn't
confine myself to ten or twelve hour work days, I had
some sort of compulsion that had me often working
through several nights in a row without ever going
home to sleep. Obviously, without some fair shot
at a good time slot I couldn't justify going into a fourth
year of that. Besides, the work load was so total that
other career projects and plans were suffering.

As Executive Producer I can now accept some
motion picture offers, work on some other projects,
get back into the mainstream of writing. And it is always
at least *possible* in the roulette game of television
that Friday night at 10:00 P.M. may work for some
strange reason or that we might get a mid-season shift
to a good time slot. I hope it works. I hope I can
supervise the new team into keeping the quality
of the show up, I hope *Star Trek* stays on for five
or ten years. Meanwhile, I think I can honestly feel
I have done my damnedest for the show and for what
I conceive science fiction to be.

Thanks for your ideas. I particularly like the
drama and entertainment inherent in William Shatner
as a Vulcan and Nimoy's comments regarding this.
Am passing it along to Freiberger and Justman in
the hopes that they can either use it or adapt it into
some story they have in work.

Your letter prompted me to inquire of the studio
people if there was any reason why you couldn't write a
Star Trek story for some publication if you wished
to do so. No one has ever written good *Star Trek* either
in novel, novelette or short story form, and I think
you could if you were so inclined and found it
profitable. The studio attitude, at my suggestion,
was that they would expect nothing back from you,
no part of your payment, since an Asimov approach

to *Star Trek* would have sound promotional and
publicity benefits for us. If the idea should appeal to
you, let me know and I'll see that the necessary
written permission is forthcoming.

I have talked to a number of studios about the
possibility of an "I Robot" motion picture and I've
gotten some favorable response but up until now
I have never really had the time to push it any
further. But now it appears I am on the edge of making
some motion picture deals and will get into it a little
deeper. Will of course let you know the moment
anything seems to be moving in that direction.
It would be fun if it could be arranged.

As executive producer, Gene had time for other projects
and took advantage of the opportunity to take a big step. In
1968, he made the move to features, the step many writer-
producers long to make. Regardless of what is said or how
much money is made in television, film is the medium of
prestige; witness the endless attempts by television actors to
make the transition to film. The power in the business, the
bigger money, the greater recognition from one's peers—it
was the next logical step, and Gene had offers.

National General Pictures signed him to a two-picture
deal. This was the door to even greater success. One or two
successful pictures, and Gene's career would take a much
different path, but even though he was making the move to
features, *Star Trek* wasn't out of his thoughts.

In June 1968, he went to Mexico to scout locations, and
when he returned he wrote to Fred Pohl, editor of *Galaxy*
science fiction magazine, outlining his then current situation.

I have been sort of out of action for a month while
trying to meet the deadline on a screenplay treatment.
I signed a two-picture deal with National General
Corporation, agreeing to do a Tarzan feature and
getting a contract for a second feature of my own
choosing by doing so. Actually, the Tarzan thing does
interest me since I have long felt the subject has
never been handled properly on film and that the
only right way to do it is to return as much as possible
to the original Burroughs concept. Whether successful
or not will depend upon a lot of things, including

the kind of budget they give me. More on that later
as it progresses.

Gene repeated much of what he had written to Asimov—
regarding his new position as "executive producer," stepping
back from the day-to-day responsibilities of producing, and
the problem with the slot on Friday nights at 10 P.M. and
then continued:

> I am sure some fans will not be able to understand
> the above and I suppose I must harden myself to criticism
> on this score. But I did prove that decent science
> fiction *can* be put on film not just as an occasional
> "accident" but on a methodical, professional basis.
> I believe that the outstanding success of *Planet of the
> Apes* and the unexpected box office returns on
> "Odyssey"[20] have been due in some part to *Star
> Trek* paving the way. I said at the beginning that if
> we were successful in the *Star Trek* venture, a new
> audience interest in science fiction films, books,
> magazines and other media might happen, and I
> hope these recent successful films are only a beginning
> of interest which will affect all who work in the field.
>
> > Sincerely yours,

Star Trek duties aside, Gene continued working on the
Tarzan script.

He had hired Morris Chapnick, who had not followed
Herb Solow over to MGM.[21] Morris enjoyed working with
Gene as much as he enjoyed working in the business.

Morris describes Gene's script:

"Gene wanted to do Tarzan, King of the Waziris, Lord
Greystoke, a diplomat speaking French, maintaining a man-
sion on the edge of the forest with the Waziries as his 'Pre-
torian Guard.' That's pretty much the way it was. We didn't
get into all that, as I recall.

"Tarzan was a racist and the way Gene points that out is
having Tarzan in the trees, watching a native being tortured,

---

[20]Referring to Stanley Kubrick's film *2001: A Space Odyssey,* released in 1968.
[21]At Oscar Katz's recommendation, Solow assumed his position when Katz left
Desilu to become an agent.

watching clinically. When he got bored, he would leave. Seeing natives being abused didn't bother him. Then, he comes across a white man and rescues him. The man was Belgian, spoke French, so that's how Tarzan learns to speak French. This is typical Gene."

One unanswered question is how much influence, if any, Gene's messy divorce may have had on the sexual symbolism in his Tarzan script. Chapnick continues:

"The story in the script as I recall, is that some woman comes to Africa, searching for her father. She goes to a temple where, once a year, the natives would sacrifice ten of the most beautiful women to a creature who came alive at that time. They had to be the most beautiful, the most exotic, the sexiest, and, of course, they had to wear very skimpy costumes. I'm sure this had to be Gene's thing—they would all be in individual cages. Gene's fantasy, I guess [laughter]."

Gene showed Tarzan's direct animal nature in the following scene, as described by Morris:

"Gene had a scene that has Tarzan, as he was bedding down for the night, rolling over and saying to the woman, 'Do you want to mate?' She is shocked and rebuffs him. Tarzan rolls over and goes to sleep.[22]

"The picture was going to be shot in Kenya. We were going to shoot interiors in Italy, using the Cleopatra sets—for the temple and that sort of stuff. This was the basic game plan.

"My job was to find Tarzan and ten of the most beautiful women in the world. Believe it or not, it got boring after a while. Some of the ladies who came in did not look at all like their photographs. We gave them their share of the time, but, for me, there was nothing worse than talking to someone you knew you weren't going to do anything with.

"We went to the Olympic Training Camp in Lake Tahoe, looking for Tarzan."

Gene wasn't the only person having personal upsets at the time. Morris continues:

"I was having some problems then with my marriage and

---

[22]Gene occasionally wrote from life. One man he worked with on the original series was told by his wife, years later, that once when Gene was sitting next to her at lunch, he smiled and quietly said, "I'd really like to fuck you." The approach occasionally worked for Gene, but not this time.

I had not learned how to say things to people without stepping on their egos. I remember saying to Gene, 'I don't think these people want to make this movie,' and he would sort of growl back at me. I thought this because we were not getting a budget from the front office, so I did a budget. If I could do a budget faster than the estimating office, what does that tell you?

"I don't know how good my budget was, but the people who were responsible for that sort of thing still hadn't delivered. Also, the head of production would take forever to return my calls. In the studio system you learn very early your status by how long it takes the guard to open the gate for you or how long it takes for people to return your calls.

"We turned in a budget, finally done by their estimating department. As best as I can recall, we were supposed to make the picture for $2 million. National General's front office said they couldn't do it for that."

Morris remembers that Gene's relationship with the studio deteriorated as the project moved on:

"He was, as I recall, being treated by the studio as a second class citizen. My understanding was that he had been promised certain things and then he was discovering that it wasn't happening that way.

"We had to cut the budget. I remember we had a huge forest fire in the script, that was gone. The shooting in Italy, that was gone. I think it bothered Gene. Then they brought in a production manager and another budget was done, and the front office thought that was too expensive as well.

"More cuts were made and now we're going to send a second unit to Africa to shoot the animal stuff along with a photo double for Tarzan, and the interiors would be shot here in Los Angeles. We were told that MGM had perfected their rear projection process so they could get a wider picture. We would build a jungle at MGM and combine the second unit material with film shot at MGM. At that point I checked out the Palace of Fine Arts in San Francisco as a possible location for the temple scenes.

"The budget kept coming down and things kept coming out of the script. It was not the movie Gene thought he was going to produce. It must have bothered Gene creatively as well as personally because I thought he had a lot of artistic integrity. He really cared about what he wrote.[23]

"Finally, the script came down to around $1.2 million. We tried to make deals with the studio regarding interest,[24] contingencies, all the things thrown into a studio budget. You'll have studio overhead, which could be ten to fifteen percent, then you have interest on the money, and then contingency, and so on. The studio wanted to put the interest on top of everything including the contingency and then to plunk some other stuff in as well."

Complaints and budget problems finally came to a head. "There was a meeting around the end of November 1968. We went over to the corporation's headquarters and met, not with the number one guy, but with the number two guy. When this guy walked into the room his jacket was off, his sleeves were rolled up and he clapped his hands together saying, 'Come on. Let's get this thing over with.' My heart went out for Gene. He really wanted this picture to go and had waited forty-five minutes for this guy to show up.

"Here is a producer of stature, a reputable individual who has the credentials, who, in my opinion, was being given short shrift by this guy. He was being treated as an employee rather than as a creative talent."

It is not clear now whether this project began as a theatrical feature—Gene seemed to think so—and then changed into a "made for TV movie," but Morris remembers the climax of the meeting:

"The essence of the conversation was that NBC was only giving them, the production company [National General], $750,000 for a television movie and they were going to pick up the difference, which I think was $250,000. Those two numbers stick in my head.

"I think a decision was made then, or Gene had his agent tell them later, that the picture could not be made for that price. Not with everything that would be tacked on since it was only leaving Gene with $700,000 to make the film. To get any sort of quality, forget it."

There was, perhaps, another reason why National General

---

[23]Morris' strong feelings prompted a letter to *TV Guide* in 1993, protesting statements made by William Shatner in an excerpt from his book, *Star Trek Memories*.

[24]On the money borrowed to finance the film.

did not want to film Gene's script, suggested by Tarzan's line of dialogue quoted above by Chapnick: Gene had made Tarzan sexual, very sexual. So sexual that the film could not have been made and broadcast on television in 1968. A short time later, a well-known writer was approached to "fix" the end of the script. He was offered $20,000 to rewrite the ending, toning down both Tarzan's and Gene's hormones. He was a friend of Gene's and passed on the assignment. The film was never made.[25]

Meanwhile, it was clear that there were different people running *Star Trek*.

In January 1969, Gene wrote to a friend thanking him for sending copies of a newspaper article, then continued:

> Situation at *Star Trek* is that we have finished shooting for the year and I have grave doubts that we will be picked up for a fourth season. As I indicated many months ago, the Friday night, 10 o'clock slot is an almost impossible one for a show like this and it hurt us badly. I understand the fans are mounting another "Save *Star Trek*" campaign and I am delighted, even if all it accomplishes is annoying the hell out of NBC.

Much has been said about this chapter in *Star Trek*'s history: Gene had "abandoned" the show, he didn't come back to "save" it, and other such things. As a fundamental part of his personality, Gene did not explain or justify his decisions and friends did not often ask. Fortunately, John W. Campbell did ask in a letter in early January 1969. The third season had run fifteen or sixteen new shows, and Campbell asked the questions people would ask for years to come. As Campbell was a friend and held a unique position both in science fiction and Gene's eyes, Gene responded with can-

---

[25]Majel's recollection is a bit different. It is her memory that the Burrough's estate killed the deal when they saw how sexual Gene had made Tarzan. Another person who was close both to Gene and Burrough's son says the estate did not have veto power over the film version. It is possible that Gene abandoned the project when it became a TV production, as he was trying to get away from television at that time.

dor, revealing his reasons and his private dealings with NBC in this January 27, 1969, response.

> Dear John,
>
> Yes, I am inclined by pride to remove my name from the program since it is being made by someone else now and comes out quite different in important ways from the way I envisioned the show. On the other hand, practical considerations like roof, car and food have kept it there since my only substantial income from the program attaches to the title "Executive Producer." The facts of life are that I simply needed a year of income like that to carry me over the transition from television to motion pictures.
>
> Yes, I feel sad about the perceptive fans and SF professionals who don't know that "Executive Producer" is a sort of honorary title and must assume I am still running the show but with remarkable changes in my ideas and attitudes. I want them to think well of me but, on the other hand, I don't want to publicly condemn or embarrass the man who is producing the show. He works hard and makes the kind of show he has been taught in television is a good show. Perhaps I should have dropped him mid-season but there simply wasn't anyone better in sight to replace him.[26] The kind of creativity and imagination you saw in the first year of *Star Trek* is hard to find. There are a few available who have it and have proven it but they have become impossibly expensive for television.
>
> I would like also to have had the chance to explain that my plan was *not* originally to use *Star Trek* as a way to leap to motion pictures. At the start of the third season I was committed to produce the show and planned to stay very close to it for many years. The network double-crossed me by switching

---

[26]Gene is referring to Fred Freiberger. When the twentieth anniversary of *Star Trek* was being planned, Gene balked at party invitations for only two individuals. If Fred Freiberger or Herb Solow were there, Gene explained, he wouldn't be. We have no knowledge why Gene and Herb Solow were on the outs. Solow will, perhaps, give his version in his book. Unfortunately, Gene died before he could explain his side to this writer.

it to Friday nights at 10:00 where I knew no possible effort would give it a sufficient rating. My only ammunition or lever against the network was to refuse to personally produce it unless they gave us a decent time. Big fight, complete with the network at one time intimating they'd see I never work in TV again. I held my ground but unfortunately they held theirs too. Apparently they had advertisers and talent at stake of greater total value than *Star Trek* and it stayed Fridays, 10:00 P.M. Many of our actors and crew think I should then have given in and agreed to produce it anyway, but most people I respect agreed with me that to do so would forever have weakened my bargaining power in this strange game of entertainment. And I feel much more comfortable myself knowing that I kept my word to them and to myself. The cost of doing so was high but I have to balance it against the many pleasures received from the series.

Enough of that. Time, I think, to wash *Star Trek* out of my hair, stop the habit of it playing a part in every thought, get on to start scaling the mountain top. I know many who have done in their life one interesting or fairly successful thing and they nourished themselves on that and really do nothing bright or brave or new again. I'm afraid of that and must be wary that I don't get sucked into something of the same trap.

Gene's letter to Campbell was written before NBC's official cancellation. We do not know if Gene had advance knowledge of the coming announcement or not, but for anyone in the business, a look at the ratings was a dead giveaway. The approaching inevitability was no surprise to Gene.

The last show, "Turnabout Intruder," was filmed in early January 1969. There were twenty-four episodes shot for the third season, as opposed to twenty-eight[27] for the first season (counting "The Menagerie" as two episodes), and twenty-six for the second season.

On Friday, September 20, 1968, at 10 P.M., the third season of *Star Trek* officially began with the showing of

---

[27]Number 1 and number 2 were pilots.

"Spock's Brain," written by "Lee Cronin" (Gene L. Coon) and directed by Marc Daniels. According to many fans, it ranks near the bottom as one of the least popular offerings of the entire three-year run.

Like an unwanted child, NBC would play fast and loose with *Star Trek,* preempting episodes on December 13 and 27, 1968, January 3 and February 7, 1969. After the broadcast of "All Our Yesterdays" on March 14, 1969, the last new show, "Turnabout Intruder" wasn't broadcast until Tuesday, June 3, 1969.

The world learned *Star Trek*'s fate in mid-February, when NBC issued a press release listing which shows lived and which died. Accompanying *Star Trek* on its trip to the NBC executioner were *Get Smart, Jerry Lewis, The Outsider, The Ghost and Mrs. Muir, The Mothers-in-Law,* and *My Friend Tony.*

An article in the *New York Times* quoted an executive at NBC as saying that none of the shows were doing "really badly" in their respective time periods, but that none of them had garnered the average thirty percent of the available audience "required to stay alive in prime-time television." Gene, of course, had done his best to point out to NBC's executive hierarchy that the decision to put *Star Trek* on at a time when most of its audience was out of the house, virtually guaranteed its inability to attract the needed percentage. As Gene had recognized from the start, the show was doomed.

Star Trek was replaced on September 19, 1969, by *Bracken's World,* a melodrama set in a movie studio whose gimmick was cameo appearances by real movie stars. It lasted for one year.

There was, of course, another letter-writing campaign, but it lacked the fervor of the previous effort. Those who wrote received the following from NBC's "Department of Information":

Dear Viewer:

We appreciate your loyalty to *Star Trek,* and want you to know that we too are disappointed that the program failed to develop the broad appeal necessary for maintaining it on our schedule.

A national network like NBC, as a program supplier for hundreds of stations around the country, must take into account nationwide program preferences, especially in its entertainment offerings. To ignore these preferences, as indicated to us by continuous research studies, would be unresponsive to millions of our viewers.

We are also obliged to refresh our schedule with program innovations, which we will do in replacing *Star Trek* in the fall. It was through this process, of course, that *Star Trek* itself came to our schedule.

Although we realize that a letter probably will not ease your displeasure, we do want to thank you for writing and giving us this chance to explain our point of view.

Star Trek was gone, labeled a failure, both by the network and by Paramount. As the show was sold to the network for perhaps two-thirds of its per episode cost, it was approximately $4.7 million in production debt and unlikely to ever show a profit, especially given studio accounting procedures. It was relegated to syndication, which was a Sargasso Sea of forgotten hulks of old series, living out their years in a fog of obscurity on independent stations and network affiliates' off-time. However, *Star Trek* was about to change that.

The program would become a pot of gold for Paramount, but not, as might be supposed, for Gene and the actors. They each received their residual payments for repeat broadcasts; all were paid off within two years. From then on, the only costs associated with *Star Trek* were the costs of striking new prints and the monies needed to sell it in various markets.

True, *Star Trek* had never won the ratings race,[28] but demographic surveys were not as sophisticated then as they are now. Then, the ratings were simply head counting. The truth about *Star Trek* was learned in the NBC executive offices, as Gene remembers it:

"This fellow from demographics comes into the office of an NBC vice-president and says, 'Congratulations, you've just gotten rid of your most important and successful program.' The vice president did not know what he was talking about.

---

[28]It never made it into the A.C. Nielson Company's "Top 20 Programs" for any of the years it was on the network.

"He told them that, demographically, the people who were watching *Star Trek* were the young people—the people who were buying new cars, building new homes, that sort of thing. The network was just counting heads, retired fireman's widows and the like. *Star Trek* was reaching an audience they had never considered as important, a narrowly defined group of consumers that accounted for a large percentage of the buying power in the country at that time.

"NBC argued for about a year and by then it was too late to bring *Star Trek* back. I would have appreciated them telling me about all this then. My ego was going downhill after *Star Trek* was terminated. I needed a boost."

Perhaps Leonard Nimoy summed it up most accurately when he wrote:

> The work on *Star Trek* lasted for three seasons: 1966, 1967, and 1968. I felt that the best work had been done during the first two seasons and that the scripts and production during the third year did not at all reflect the highest quality of the show, to say the least.[29]

Perhaps the most ironic twist happened just after the show went off the air. Forty-seven days after the last new episode of *Star Trek* aired, another televised "space program" attracted a larger audience: television sets all over the world broadcast Neil Armstrong taking the first steps on the moon. It was science fiction come true.

---

[29]*I Am Not Spock,* by Leonard Nimoy (New York: Ballantine Books, 1977), p. 121.

CHAPTER 13

Gene had left television for film. His first attempt, a Tarzan feature, had not gotten beyond the script and preliminary planning stages, but that is the nature of the film business. It is not unusual for a writer or producer to champion a film for years before it is made. Even after the film is completed, it may sit on a shelf while distribution is arranged, a process that has been known to take years.[1] According to stories published over the past few years, of every ten films made, seven lose money, two break even, and one makes money. It's a wonder anyone stays in a business with such poor odds, but when the odds are beaten and a film strikes the public fancy, the rewards can be astronomical: witness *E.T.*, *Star Wars,* and *Home Alone*—films made for modest budgets without major stars that all had phenomenal grosses.

Gene was now at MGM, the most prestigious studio in Hollywood, working for Herb Solow. At Katz's recommendation, Solow had taken his job as head of Desilu when Katz moved on. Later Solow moved to MGM as a vice president. Many thought he was the next Irving Thalberg and looked to him to save the studio from its decline.

In August 1969, Gene was in Japan scouting locations for a film project. In a country that can be a male chauvinist's dreamland, Gene was lonely. He missed Majel and decided to do something about it. He called her and proposed marriage. Actually, he told her to "hop on the next plane." Un-

---

[1] That is changing somewhat today with direct to video operations.

fortunately, Majel did not have a passport and had to go to the appropriate office in downtown Los Angeles.

There she spoke to an official she remembers as "a very nice man." Or, more accurately, she didn't so much speak to him as she cried out her problem when she learned that getting a passport normally took ten days. "But that's impossible. I have to leave tomorrow (sob) to get married (sob, sniff)." Majel got her passport that day just, she thinks, "to prevent his office from being flooded."

Gene's secretary, Anita Doohan (Jimmy Doohan's exwife), helped arrange the schedule and got her a seat on the first plane to Tokyo. The overly harassed, slightly hysterical bride-to-be was hustled onto the waiting flight at Los Angeles International Airport. Unfortunately, no one had bothered to tell Majel that this flight was not, as was the usual custom, by way of Hawaii; it was taking a different route.

After the plane was airborne and she was settling in, the pilot got on the intercom to welcome his passengers: "Good morning, welcome to flight so-and-so, we'll be flying at an altitude of thirty-one thousand feet and will be landing at Anchorage, Alaska, at approximately . . ."

"ANCHORAGE, ALASKA!" Majel screamed, certain she was on the wrong plane! Fortunately, the pilot continued, explaining that Anchorage was the first stop on the polar route to Japan before Majel could call the flight attendant and demand a parachute.

While the plane was refueling in Anchorage, Majel found a telephone and called Gene in Japan. She thought that if she had to "go through this hell, the least Gene could do is go through part of it, too." It was four in the morning for Gene.

The hotel woke him up, telling him he had a collect call from a Miss Barrett in Anchorage, Alaska. When Gene got on the line, Majel said, "Honey, I've gotten on the wrong plane," which was met by several seconds of dead silence. Then came a response in an awful German accent: "All right, vhat you do iss you get back on zee plane, go back to Los Angeles, und ztart all ofer again!"

Majel finally told Gene what the situation was and why she was in Alaska and, more importantly, when to expect her.

On August 6, 1969,[2] Gene Roddenberry and Majel Bar-

---

[2] Without planning it, this was the twenty-fourth anniversary of the dropping of the atomic bomb on Hiroshima.

rett, nee Majel Lee Hudec, participated in a Shinto-Buddhist ceremony. It was a traditional service with two priests, two maids of honor, and two musicians. To the strains of classical Japanese music, Gene and Majel in full, formal kimonos, took their vows. They observed tradition all the way, Majel carried a small knife to defend her honor should the anxious groom try something before the ceremony. A few years later, Gene explained:

"Well, perhaps, as you've seen in *Star Trek,* I believe that all people, customs, rituals and all that sort of thing, are equal. I can't believe that God favors my Southern Baptist setting more than he does a Japanese Buddhist, so it seemed like a foolish thing to do to bring in one of my own preachers when they had plenty of their own over there. Majel felt the same way."

They went on a honeymoon, touring Japan. On August 11, 1969, Gene wrote his parents from Kyoto expressing his innermost feelings.

Dear Mother and Dad,

Kyoto here is Japan's old capital city, before the emperor moved to Tokyo (Edo) in the last century. It was not bombed in World War II because of its art and historical treasures. Therefore, it is old and quite beautiful. Much of the other large cities were wiped out in 1945, therefore their buildings are relatively modern.

At any rate, Majel and I just arrived here an hour ago and are looking forward to two days of touring the temples and other historical sites here.

As you can see from the smeared ink above, it is hot and sticky. But we've got the room air conditioner on now and it's cooling.

Imagine you have a postcard or two by now but let me thank you again anyway for the wonderful cablegram which made my wife so happy. She really is nervous about you two and your love in the message has her feeling better.

Yes, we're on our honeymoon. Decided to stay an extra 10 days here and do it right. Herb Solow, VP of MGM insisted we do it, was so very happy since he is fond of us both and has wondered why we didn't do it long ago.

This is a precious as well as illuminating experience for me. I did not know it was possible to care that much for another person, and to be loved so much in return. It is not as if I were 21 years old and in love with love. I've had sex before, plenty of it. But affection like this, friendship like this, undemanding total love like this, I've never known. Yes, Majel has faults just as any of us do and we are quite capable of disagreeing like any married couple. And yet if I found someone more perfect I wouldn't trade Majel for her. And I know I can make mistakes, do foolish things, without changing her feelings for me either. With that knowledge, we are both learning to relax and enjoy this union of two imperfect halves into a blissfully happy whole.

I suppose the above reads rather love struck. Good! We're both very grown up, have seen a lot of life, and if we can still feel this way then we must be very fortunate.

Our room here in Kyoto is Japanese which is to say there are no chairs or tables, or even a bed. We sleep on futon mats rolled out on the woven reed floor. But it's very lovely with its sliding rice paper panels and natural wood decor. Very warm in feeling. In the bath, a deep tub where you can soak in hot water up to your neck.

We've been on a 120 m.p.h. train, will cruise on an inland sea steamship in a couple of days. This morning we prayed for each other's happiness at Ise Jingu, Japan's most sacred shrine.

Hey, yes! We ordered you a large color photograph of us in our wedding kimonos. I was dressed as a Samurai warrior. However, Majel carried the only weapon, a knife in her sash, with which to protect her honor, they explained, in case I should try to violate her before the ceremony was over. Japan's Toho film sent three news cameramen to shoot the wedding in 16mm color, plus MGM sent a still cameraman to shoot color transparencies. I think we were the most photographed wedding in Japan in years.

Majel has started writing her letter to you.

I suppose we'll cover some of the same
subjects.

At any rate, we'll have much to tell and show
you when we return.

I do so hope this finds you both well. Dad and Mom,
I am finally beginning to understand how you feel
about each other. You are very lucky too.

Love,
Gene

Gene would later write to the family historian:

> Typical of acting on our beliefs, when we found our-
> selves in Tokyo, Japan, wanting to be married, we ac-
> cepted as a proper thing to be married in the form and
> under the customs where we were living at that mo-
> ment. . . . we discovered our vows were not too different
> from those we might have taken in any Protestant or
> Catholic church in the United States, although they did
> include some "extras" having to do with responsibility for
> offspring of the marriage and toward the community and
> our relatives.

It was wonderful. It was romantic. It was not legal.
Gene's divorce from Eileen was not yet final. Their Japanese
"marriage" was a ceremony to formalize their emotional
commitment to one another. It did not constitute a legal
relationship, something Gene and Majel knew full well
when they did it. They would repair this minor technical-
ity on Monday, December 29, 1969, two days after his divorce became final and the first day they could get a
judge out to their house. There he performed a civil ceremony that was followed by a small reception for family and
close friends.

If a "wedding" is an emotional bonding, Gene and Majel
had a wedding in Japan. Even if it wasn't the beginning of
their legal relationship, August 6 was the date they celebrated as the anniversary of their formalized commitment to
one another.

On return, Gene caught up on correspondence. To a
friend, he closed by saying:

I think you'll like my new wife, Majel. We've been in love for some six or seven years and are now deliriously happy. My youngest daughter, Dawn, has elected to live with us, which pleases me very much, of course.

The honeymoon lasted. In April 1972, he wrote to Asimov:

At this moment, my marriage to Majel has brought me more happiness than I've ever known with a woman. She was in her mid-thirties, never married, a successful woman in her own work, and more than a match for me in ways I keep discovering every day. While she insists I was the Prince Charming she has always waited for, the marriage is built primarily and most securely on a great degree of friendship and mutual respect and it has made me realize that *friendship* is the most important ingredient of all. Out of that has come honesty and a number of other delightful things.

In late September 1969, Gene was returning from a fishing trip off Mexico when he ran head-on into Republican bureaucracy. Richard Nixon had taken a hard line on narcotics smuggling and instituted "Operation Intercept" through the Customs Service that supposedly tightened up the borders. Customs inspectors at Los Angeles International Airport were zealous in their duty, and in their zeal Gene felt he had been wronged. He sought redress and an apology and used the only weapons at hand—words. He wrote a number of letters. It became a battle to see who had the harder head: Gene or the government bureaucracy. On September 23, 1969, minutes after he arrived home, Gene let fly his first salvo to the District Director of Customs:

Let me put this in perspective by stating that I have been considered as somewhat knowledgeable in the narcotics field, years ago was head of staff research for the Chief of Police Los Angeles Police Department, also author of the study, *Youth and Narcotics* for years in use by California public schools and other organizations across the nation (perhaps even by your own organization). Also, I have traveled in

and out of about fifty countries in the last thirty years,
meeting customs procedures in a variety of conditions.

Including many visits to various forms of dictatorship
and other non-democratic countries, my treatment by
Mr. Carter [the Customs Inspector] in particular
and the customs group at L.A. International Airport
in general ranks as the worst example of
unprofessionalism, petty officiousness, and blustering
stupidity I have ever undergone.

The episode went something as follows.
Apparently under instructions to effect some kind of
"narcotics smuggling drive" the airport customs
inspectors were making a more thorough than usual
search of my baggage. This is always annoying,
particularly when carefully packed effects are strewn
about, but I responded in good humor at first and made
it clear that I would cooperate to the letter of the
law, although I did want to express my personal
belief that such drives were inefficient and a waste
of manpower. I was cautioned to silent my opinions
and responded that I understood the inspectors had
to follow orders and indeed sympathized with the
added labor imposed upon them, but they should
understand in return that it was the duty of citizens
in a free country to voice their beliefs wherever
appropriate, as long as they continued complying
with the law.

None of us can expect our political convictions to
be universally popular but mine in this instance saw
things quickly become more interesting. It is
evident that not a few inspectors and supervisors at
U.S. Customs consider political philosophy as something
which comes under their purview. I found myself
being quickly subjected to an ever more meticulous
baggage search and could see some annoyance
developing as no contraband was found. (I had been
marlin fishing from a small Mexican village with
little opportunity to make purchases of any sort.)
Finally in my shaving kit was found a vial of a few
pills which I identified as prescribed items which I
keep available under medical orders, particularly
when traveling a hundred or so miles from the
nearest doctor. They represented four Seconal sleeping

tablets, two Equinil, ten Cytomel (daily thyroid pills) and four hay fever pills. No, I did not know it was necessary to carry a prescription but doubted that this oversight plus the ridiculously small quantity of pills put me seriously in question as involved in narcotics or drug smuggling. Mr. Carter, who had been called in by then, became immediately loud and threateningly demanded to know where the rest of my smuggled drugs were, resorting to a low form of "beat cop bullying" which I had seen happily go out of style in the 1930's. He made no effort to ascertain my reputation, my community status, my business, perhaps because the nature of my trip had me in rather old clothes. This is, of course, hardly an excuse for Mr. Carter since all citizens should get equal treatment. When I asked him to return any pills which were not technically illegal, he retorted that "smart-ass remarks" like that would see me under arrest which he could do any time he had the whim to do so. In fact, he was seriously considering putting me in jail and wanted to know if that's where I wanted to go. He continued his abusiveness and threats of arrest as he ordered me carefully shaken down and personally searched.

Although I have not had the opportunity to observe your inspectors and supervisors at all entry stations, it still seems apparent to me that some form of educational program for U.S. Customs field personnel may be worth considering. It is apparent, in this instance at least, that training presently in effect is not properly indoctrinating your field representatives in proper attitudes in their admittedly difficult function in a free society. Also, it would seem that your screening process has failed in at least the instance of Mr. Carter.

I would much appreciate hearing from you whether my experience has resulted in any action in any of these areas.

Sincerely yours,

Gene followed by copying this letter to Senator Alan Cranston (D) California, along with yet another letter criticizing his unnecessarily "criminal" treatment.

The attached letter is largely self-explanatory.

I don't know if you recall, but I worked with Chris Knopf and other members of the Writers Guild of America in the support of your candidacy. I will undoubtedly do so again, regardless of your reaction or action on the attached but I do think it is probably the kind of petty, bullying bureaucracy which annoys you as much as it does the rest of us.

The real reason for Mr. Nixon's current "narcotics drive" on the California-Mexican border is in doubt to many of us who know something of narcotics and the drug traffic. I lean toward the belief that it is probably a great deal of relatively safe "sound and fury" planned to convince the electorate that our new president is "cleaning up the mess" as he promised to do in 1968. After all, it is about as hard to be for narcotics smuggling as it is to be against motherhood. Unfortunately for the American people, however, the current border comic opera will simply obscure the realities of drug traffic and addiction.

As for my attached letter, it recounts how I nearly went to jail for the "crime" of carrying with me on a fishing trip to Mexico a four-day supply of relatively ordinary medicine prescribed by my doctor. During the encounter, the U.S. Customs inspector angrily shouted at me that apparently I did not understand he was trying to protect my children. It seems to me that our children have had much more to fear from his type than from all the narcotics ever grown. It is probably fortunate I did not voice this thought since undoubtedly I would be writing this letter from jail.

A similar letter was sent to Senator George Murphy (R) California, an old Hollywood song and dance man turned politician, a conservative Republican who once said that Mexicans were good for stoop farm labor because they were "built low to the ground." Gene closed his short note to Murphy with:

I trust that my present reputation in the entertainment industry, as well as my past reputation in law

enforcement, will merit some action and a reply
by your office.

Gene was not a supporter of Murphy's and had never donated money to his campaign, so Murphy's form letter response was no surprise, but an insult nevertheless. Gene
angrily wrote back:

I cannot accept this answer to my letter of September 23, 1969.
Unless your staff is equipped to properly respond,
please save the taxpayers the cost of the reply and myself
the time wasted in writing you.

If a Republican senator was no help, a Republican-
appointee wasn't much better, as Gene's response to the letter from the Commissioner of Customs implies:

I cannot accept your suggestion that the existence of
Operation Intercept at that time in any way excuses the
officiousness and threats that I encountered from your
Los Angeles airport personnel as described. In fact, because of the very difficulty of law enforcement, an administrator with your responsibilities should be extremely
interested in any signs that a subordinate responds to
pressure in an emotional manner.
No one as yet has answered my question as to why
non-prescription medicines were taken from me and destroyed, nor why I was for the third time threatened with
prison because I insisted on some receipt or record of this
loss.
In all, it is apparent your staff has not provided you
with the facts which enabled you to "carefully consider
the report of the incident."

The last letter in the file was sent the following January
by the Acting Commissioner of Customs. He wrote that after
another review, the Customs Service was satisfied that Gene
"had not been treated in an improper or discourteous manner
by any of the customs officers involved in the performance
of their official duties."
While the Customs Commissioner refused to admit that

Gene had been improperly treated, there was a tiny bureaucratic crack in the letter that was the one crumb of victory Gene would see:

> However, the Bureau does appreciate the problem faced by you and others similarly situated in connection with the carrying of a small quantity of pills for medicinal purposes at the time of arrival at a United States port. We have issued appropriate instructions to our field offices to alleviate this problem.
>
> I appreciate your focusing the attention of the Bureau on this problem.

Gene made several more fishing trips but was never again bothered by Customs.

By October, Gene and Majel had moved into a house on Leander Place in Beverly Hills, where they would spend most of their marriage. At about the same time, Paramount began syndication of *Star Trek*.

A fatalist would say that all that happiness had to be balanced by a tragedy. It came on the fourteenth of December, when Gene's father died of cancer. He did not have a great amount of time to get to know Majel, but what he saw, he liked.

After the funeral, Gene wrote to a relative:

> Dad had very strong ideals and in his own way was a very honorable and even religious man, but he felt that religion was a thing of the heart and did not necessarily have to include fancy structures and involved ceremonials. He believed that people should be remembered for what they were in life and that it is foolish to spend great amounts of time, money and emotions on sorrowing over the remains.
>
> We're all extremely proud of Mother who handled herself with great dignity. As she told me, she had her tears privately, many nights of them, and she felt no obligation to display them to others. She loved him, he knew it, and she felt no obligation to prove it to anyone else by breaking down.
>
> It may help you some to know that Dad had reached the point where he wanted to die and

welcomed it very much like one who is very tired and
wants to go to sleep. He made us all understand
that death is as natural and normal a process as birth.
Or as marriage, the uniting of two people into one.
He was happy to have met my wife Majel and the
two of them got along famously. Both had a real
regret that they could not have actively enjoyed each
other for a longer period and in healthier circumstances.
She is a devoted fisherwoman and, as you know,
Dad was a great fisherman himself and the two of
them really wanted to get out on the ocean or on a
lake in competition with each other. Before he left
for the hospital, they spent many hours in the
bedroom alone together discussing life, love, small-
mouthed bass and God knows what else.

The Roddenberrys seemed fated to participate in endings.
Gene's father had been part of the search for Pancho Villa,
the last horse cavalry operation; Gene's combat duty was at
the end of the B-17 bomber's use in the South Pacific; his
creation and production of *Star Trek* happened when Desilu
was absorbed into the corporate mass of Paramount Pictures.
Now, in 1970, Gene was at MGM during its twilight years.
It was a sad time at Hollywood's greatest studio, a place that
once boasted "More Stars Than There Are In Heaven."

Kirk Kerkorian was selling studio property to finance a
hotel and casino in Las Vegas. The real estate was going to
be used to build condominiums, but before they could be
built there were seven warehouses—old sound stages,
actually—full of old studio "junk." They had to be cleaned
out before the sound stages could be torn down. The "junk"
was a collection unique in the world—decades of accumulated costumes, props, and memorabilia from hundreds of
the finest films ever made. While it is a cliché, it is appropriate to say that, "it was the very stuff of history." For
Kerkorian, it was an impediment to his plans and he wanted
it cleared out, so he sold it to an auctioneer for $1.5 million.[3]
In May of 1970 MGM was host to the biggest auction of its
kind. It made news all over the world, even in so staid a
newspaper as *The Times* of London. As Rhys Thomas re-

---

[3]For more details, see *The Ruby Slippers of Oz*, by Rhys Thomas (Los Angeles:
1989, Tale Weaver Publishing.)

ported in his book, *The Ruby Slippers of Oz,* reprinting a brief excerpt from the *Times* story, "Tatters of an Empire":

> Auctions are always melancholy: it is the speed and inevitability with which the evidences of a lifetime can be dispersed. Perhaps the reason why this sale is more melancholy than most is that in a way it is all our lives, the dreams which we have for so many years brought from Hollywood which can never be the same ... Once they sold shadows; and now they are selling the rags of shadows.

The project Gene had been scouting for in Japan was dropped or postponed, or an executive changed in his mind—the details are lost to us now—but MGM had a new project for him.

The studio had been on a downhill slide for some time, and Solow sought to revive it by buying unusual properties to be made into films. One of the properties he either bought or found at the studio was a novel by Francis Pollini called *Pretty Maids All In a Row.* As Gene was to tell a friend, the studio had poured some considerable monies into the book, first in acquiring the rights and then unsuccessfully trying to make it a script. It now fell to Gene to turn the book into a shootable script and then produce the film.

About that time, James Aubrey, the former president of CBS—one of the men who did not buy *Star Trek* from Gene and Oscar Katz—was brought in as president of the studio.

Over many months, Gene turned the novel, which he would later characterize as a "vulgar book," into a shooting script. At the beginning of the "Swinging Seventies," Gene wrote what he called a sex-comedy. The studio brought in Roger Vadim, whose marriage to Jane Fonda was just winding down, to direct it.

Gene hoped the film would be a turning point in his career. It would star Rock Hudson, Angie Dickenson, Telly Savalas, and Roddy McDowell, and would feature Jimmy Doohan, Keenan Wynn, and a host of pretty girls. As this was a film set in a high school, there was even a small part for Gene's teenaged daughter, Dawn.

The premise was straightforward: a high school male with exploding hormones is surrounded by a seemingly endless parade of teenaged females dressed by Bill Theiss in very mini miniskirts. Inexperienced, he learns about life and love from his high school gym teacher and counsellor, whose hobby is seducing high school girls. When one girl decides to tell about their affair, the teacher insures her silence by killing her. Several more girls are murdered.

While the sex would not be explicit, there would be nudity—something unusual for the time and certainly for a major studio. Everyone was in unfamiliar territory, except perhaps Vadim. He was French.[4]

Vadim, who had discovered and directed Brigitte Bardot, the "sex kitten" of the 1950's, had a little game he liked to play on the set. It was said he did not wear underwear beneath his tight knit slacks. When working with a young actress, he would sit her in a chair and talk to her while leaning against the back of a chair directly opposite, occasionally spreading his legs a bit. His crotch would be at her eye level. He would talk softly to her about the scene, watching her eyes working up and down. It was analogous to a well-endowed woman wearing a low-cut dress watching a man's eyes doing the same.

While Vadim had directed nude scenes in Europe, it was uncharted territory for MGM. The "pretty maids" were a group of eight young actresses who had been hired with the clear understanding that they would do nude scenes. There would be a *Playboy* photo spread as part of the film's publicity, and everyone understood from the start that nudity was required. Unfortunately, this was so new, no one bothered to get anything in writing. It is now part of the Screen Actors Guild contracts that nudity must be agreed to in writing at the time of employment.

One actress changed her mind and became the subject of a flurry of memos. The young actress had watched the dailies of some of her colleagues' nude scenes five days before her scenes were to be shot. She had a change of heart, conferred with her agent and lawyer at that time, but none of them bothered to pass on her misgivings to anyone at the studio.

Only after her death scene had been filmed, when she had been on the film for six weeks and her character fully estab-

---

[4]One individual who worked on the film related that Vadim was known on the set as the "Famous French fucker," and it was not a pejorative title.

lished, just before she was about to shoot the nude scene, did she voice her change of heart to the production team.

Films are made on tight schedules. Emergencies and "acts of God" can interrupt shooting, but nothing else had better. It is the worst sort of unprofessionalism for an actor to refuse to shoot a scene they had previously agreed upon, causing a production delay and a loss of shooting time. As one memo described it:

> Vadim was in the position of having to restate the scene, to change the conception of the sequence on the spot and coupled with conferences as to our rights and how much nudity she would consent to, led to one-half day of production time lost and to a different concept of the scene from what we intended and what she consented to.

The memo writer finished with the crux of the situation:

> The question here is not her moral thoughts on nudity but her lack of professionalism and the deception displayed that caused an unnecessary hold up in production resulting in high costs to MGM. If she had informed us at the time she had reservations—five days before the filming of the scene—we could have made adjustments at that time either by replacing her or accepting the situation and restaging accordingly.

Since Vadim was unable to change the young actress's mind it was left to James Aubrey, the president of the studio, to resolve the matter. Accompanied to the set by the casting director, Aubrey sequestered himself in the young woman's dressing room with her lawyer, her agent, and the actress herself. A short time later, Aubrey emerged and put the matter into perspective for the casting director who remembers him saying: "Have Vadim restage the scene. We can't win this one. How would it look for the mighty Leo the Lion to sue a twenty-year-old actress to see her tits?"

Filming proceeded and the young woman did not disrobe, but her acting career quickly faded.

Gene was always more than pleased to be asked for advice. Being a mentor was as natural to Gene as breathing. In response to a request for advice from a young relative, he wrote the following thoughts.

Responding to your interest in writing, I've arranged for a couple of *Star Trek* scripts and some other material to be mailed to you. I thought you might find it interesting, particularly the *Star Trek Writers Guide* which all professional writers had to read and absorb before we would hire them to do any episodes of the show. Keep in mind when reading this, however, that *Star Trek* like most science fiction was an unusual show and many of the special rules in the material you will receive will not necessarily apply to other forms of dramatic writing.

While I am on the subject of helpful material, let me recommend a book by Laos Egris titled *The Art of Dramatic Writing.* It is the book most used by professional writers around this town and its common sense approach to writing is remarkable, its rules worth practically memorizing. Unfortunately, in making its points by quoting drama, the book uses authors like Ibsen rather those more popularly known, but struggling through those parts is still worthwhile since what is true in Ibsen is equally true in novels, screenplays, and television, even down to shows like *The Beverly Hillbillies,* as ridiculous as that sounds.[5]

Also, before I get down to your more specific questions and concerns, I am delighted you were able to cut loose from that female that was giving you trouble. Too many men, young and old, let their inclination to be a "good guy" lead them into enormously complicated situations. There seems to be a rule that the better the individual, the greater his tendency towards making decisions on the basis of other people's needs rather than his own. As hard and harsh as it sounds, the fact a woman wants or needs you is totally secondary to a calm appraisal of what *you* need and want. Also, over the years I have observed that a surprising number of men get married out of sheer cowardice—they

---

[5]An interesting example for Gene to use, as Majel remembers that this was one of his favorite programs.

simply don't have balls enough to face the facts and tell a broad that it's over. I think men feel obligation much more than women do and the so-called "weaker" sex is skilled in making us feel obligated to them. What sheer nonsense to give half of yourself to someone on the basis of what are really trifling obligations, if indeed there is really any obligation in the first place. Anyone with serious creative interest or any real *joie de vivre* is in most cases an ass to get married before at least the mid-twenties. Nor would I advise anyone (including my own daughter) to ever get married without living with the other person for a trial period. Majel and I lived together, quite proudly, for almost a year before we took the step.

Now, let me comment on acting and the performer level of activity in this and related businesses. I find very few actors who are content with their role in life. The rest of them that I have met, the most interesting humans among them, have usually found it to be something of a dead-end street and are very much involved in shifting their major interest to writing or producing or some other thing which interests them. Except for a very fortunate few, the profession can be a miserable life since the actor is not truly a "creator" in that he cannot initiate projects on his own but is always dependent on the writer, director and producer to invite him in to a project. In other words, you can't go to your room and "act." The same is true of direction and to a lesser extent of producing, although producers do sometimes initiate projects by bringing together a literary property, writer, director, etc., and getting the ball rolling. Of the whole group, only the writer can truly go anywhere, even the privacy of his own room, and do his thing.

This is not to say that I think the writer is necessarily more creative than the director, especially in motion pictures where it is traditional for the director to be the strongest influence on the film. In a sense, he "writes" with his camera and actors. A strong director does this; a weak director merely interprets the written work he has been given. In television, the producer is more the central creative element since he stays with the show constantly while writers and directors generally check in and do their job and move on, leaving a need for the producer to supply the week-to-week creative continuity which keeps the flavor of the show and the direction the same in next week's episode as they were two or three weeks ago.

In talking about writing, directing and producing, I'm not suggesting that performing cannot be right for you. You have to decide that sort of thing for yourself. Performing can always be pleasant and indeed, rewarding on an amateur or supplementary income basis. But before you jump in full time, intending to make it your life's thing, let me suggest there are some traps there. The first and the one we in the industry see (and are plagued with most often) is the fact that performing attracts a surprising number of people with personal problems. Generalizing, they have very special needs which acting answers for them. Often, they have no identity of their own or faith in their own identity and, since everyone needs identity, they make out in life by assuming the identities given them by writers and directors in dramatic roles. Sometimes they perform because they are abnormally insecure and desperately need the direct contact with applause which comes from performing. Others are immature and do not want to get involved with real life and so they turn to the make believe world of Hollywood cinema or New York stage where they can put off all the harsh and immutable rules of life until at least middle or old age where, too often, it catches up with them in a frightening way.

And, of course, there are actors and entertainers who are true professionals in every sense of the word and they are most often charming and interesting people whether they happen to become great stars or not. But the number is few. I would certainly recommend to anyone thinking of entering the performing field as their life's work to be very, *very* certain that it, out of all other choices, whether ending up a star or a bit player, is exactly what they want out of life.

· This is not to say, of course, that some do not manage to become actors, directors, producers, and playwrights and many other things at the same time. Keep in mind their number is also few and those who do succeed have spent enormous effort preparing themselves for these diverse specialities. These things don't just "happen" to a person any more than one day a law student decides to become the new Clarence Darrow and suddenly the next day he is.

Keep in mind also that law, since you state you are still interested in it, is an excellent foundation for many pursuits. There are men with legal degrees heading universities, archaeological expeditions, involved in oceanography, and in a hundred other endeavors. In other words, if you do not want to be an attorney, the four years are not wasted. They've been an excellent settling and maturing time. Keep in mind, also, that you have a great advantage in your *youth* in that you can go ahead and pass the bar and spend a couple of years with some legal firm or endeavor and still go back to school and shift to whatever excites you then.

I think the most exciting aspect of this all is as long as you keep your head and your freedom and a healthy appetite for life, you have a hundred options and will continue to have them for some years.

With affection,

During early 1970, Gene became friends with Jake Ehrlich, the famous San Francisco trial lawyer. Gene wrote a letter in March that was a response to an earlier letter and small gift from Ehrlich.

This morning I came across a copy of your remarks "An American Message." It had arrived in the midst of a script deadline and I had put it aside because I want to thank you for it. I wish I could keep my desk as orderly as yours.

My first visit to Washington years ago had one moment of impact on my emotions and intelligence which I shall never forget—seeing that document which

began so proudly in giant letters "WE THE PEOPLE . . ."
Of course, no people could be expected to live up
to all the promise in this, but I am convinced we have
made a more than honest attempt. The question now
seems to be, can we continue to build and improve?
Or will our original revolutionary spirit be crushed
by size, complexity and fat?

If we have not lost our boldness, then we should
be able to find ways of capturing and using the
ardor found in the extreme factions of our several
races and age groups. I think we must recognize that
however much we regret the acts of violence by the
factions, it is not totally "senseless" violence, at
least to the degree that it does represent protest
against social or other conditions which the non-violent,
non-involved majority should have done something
about long ago. The incident of Watts,[6] for example,
troubles me. We simply cannot allow that sort of
thing! On the other hand, as a member of this community
for a long time as well as an ex-Los Angeles police
officer, I am certain that few of the things being
done now to remedy intolerable conditions in Watts
would have been done without the drama and the public
fear generated by the riot and fire.

I find myself, like many thoughtful citizens, on
the horns of the dilemma of being totally opposed
to violence but also as totally opposed to allowing certain
conditions in our society to continue. I don't want any
J.C. Penney branch store burned and looted, but
I deplore even more the original Watts in which
human dignity, aspiration, and often even life were
impossible! A contempt for law and resort to violence
will certainly destroy any social structure, but is
a discomforting fact that they are more often a
result of something than a cause.

Reducing it to personal terms, I want my bright,
thoughtful, sixteen-year-old daughter to respect our
laws. But I want her to do this not as a Pavlovian
response to conditioning and discipline but rather because
it is the intelligent thing to do. Thus I must convince
her that our system *is* viable and that there are ways

---

[6]The Watts riots occurred in August 1965.

within our system to accomplish the very decent goals she seeks. But in the face of Viet Nam, much less evidence of American massacres there, plus certain Black Panther raids, in fact an incredible continuing panorama of violence *on the side of law,* I find some difficulty in convincing her that the most dangerous and wicked violence is that used in what she sees as an attempt to retake Christ from the Romans.

Your friend,

On June 8, 1970, as work proceeded on *Pretty Maids,* Gene dropped a line to his friend Fred Durant, III, then the assistant director of astronautics at the Smithsonian.

Am at MGM at the moment preparing a motion picture called *Pretty Maids All In A Row* which started here as a sex comedy but which I hoped to rewrite so that it also has some meaning and some statement about the world around us today. Specifically, it concerns high schools and my opinion of the way we run high schools is pretty low. I think we may find someday we have been destroying creativity and dehumanizing kids more than we have been helping them.

I have tried to stay out of television since *Star Trek* closed. The commercial domination of the medium makes enthusiasm mighty difficult. So I've concentrated on motion pictures and have been pretty lucky there despite the industry depression ... What is happening is a new honesty in cinema. Having gone through the nudity thing, the industry is zig-zagging toward films which make statements pertinent to today. There's also more honesty in the way we photograph our films, edit them, etc. Films are now being made and controlled more and more by the talent and less and less by the businessmen and promoters. Much of the unemployment out here consists of marginal or sub-marginal talent, wheelers and dealers, etc. who are responsible for much of the trouble the motion picture industry has had. The new film makers are men who know how to put every dollar on the screen—or they don't last. In short, it seems to me that this whole branch of visual literature called cinema is finally growing up.

Back to television, you may be interested [to know] I

have recently had a meeting with Masters and Johnson in St. Louis to discuss ways of tastefully and accurately presenting certain areas of their work on television. They are two of the loveliest people I've ever met, immensely warm and yet totally devoted scientists. We got along well, even when I jokingly suggested I thought Tiny Tim might make an interesting commentator on the program involving their work. I was amazed to find Virginia Johnson is a *Star Trek* fan and so was the bank vice-president who is chairman of the board of governors of their foundation. The extent of this fandom continues to amaze me and makes me wish I had not had to grind those shows out one a week.

Larger battles were raging above Gene's head, and circumstances beyond his control would soon have their effect. There did not seem to be any great interest by Kerkorian to see MGM make movies. His interests lay elsewhere.

Gene had his differences with Vadim. Gene had written a sex comedy and in his view Vadim wasn't putting Gene's vision on the screen. Perhaps, as they say, something got lost in the translation. As one long-time participant in the film business said, "Vadim never could tell a story." Regardless of Vadim's shortcoming, film is a director's medium and the studio backed him. Gene walked out. He went south and stayed in La Costa, near San Diego. He left instructions with his secretary that no one was to know where he was. Things became so tense that whenever Gene's secretary had to go to the set, Vadim was heard to say, "Ah, we 'ave a leetle spy on zee zet."

Herb Solow called almost every day, demanding to know where Gene was, but Gene did not return until filming was complete or nearly complete. Gene was back for post-production and wrote to a friend in early January 1971:

The picture is approaching final cut and we are now getting into titles, music, looping and so on. Because of the way Vadim directed it, the cutting job was a terror and Vadim was in something of a panic that the whole thing was a total loss. But we cut the picture in something like six weeks hard work and now it is beginning to look like we might make something of it.

On the same day he also wrote to another friend:

> The director's first cut did not work very well and
> for a while it was panicsville until I got a new first
> cut edited into the direction I think the story should
> go. It'll not be a great film but I think now we have
> a good chance to come up with something amusing
> and entertaining.

Gene also mentioned what he would be doing in the near future, an idea for a film that never materialized, which would have been another platform for his commentary on social conditions.

> I'm not sure yet about my next project. I'm working
> on a screenplay which will be a contemporary comedy
> with just a trace of the science fiction element. It
> sets up a situation in which a new wave young film
> director and a short-haired police captain have their
> personalities accidentally switched into each other's
> bodies. A comedy potential is obvious ... there
> are some serious elements I hope to bring to the
> screenplay—the main one being the treatment against
> the continuing polarization of our society.

By March 19, 1971, *Pretty Maids* was complete and Gene wrote to another friend with whom he had worked at MGM.

> Yesterday (Thursday) I was told to vacate my office.
> New policy—as soon as you OK an answer print, out
> you go. MGM's way of building warmth and
> loyalty, no doubt. Then, that evening my agent
> called and said we're making an MGM deal for an
> original screenplay and, if they like it, producing that
> screenplay into a movie. So, I guess I'll be staying
> in an office here. I'm off the *Pretty Maids* premier ·
> in Atlanta ... If *Pretty Maids* does good business, then
> we can flex our muscles a bit. Out of 700 screen writers
> in town, I am probably one of maybe a dozen
> writers now actually working on a theatrical release
> film.

By late June, he wrote his thoughts on the film to a friend.

My picture did not turn out to my satisfaction but it appears to be making money for MGM which, in itself, is something unusual these days. I wrote it as a comedy but I'm afraid that much of the American quality of the comedy was not understood by the director. Am now deep in researching a new motion picture which will concern law and disorder in our society today. Am at present riding with police cars in the evening looking for interesting information.

Finally, in mid-summer, he wrote to another friend in Santa Barbara, making a candid observation of himself:

No, don't see *Pretty Maids*. There is nothing worse than writing something you hope is pretty witty and having the director not quite pull it off.

Answering your second question, *Pretty Maids* is making a profit for some reason; and this has encouraged MGM to put me on a second assignment. It is a take of the inner city, what is good and bad, fearful and brave about police work. At least, I hope that is something of how it [will] turn out as I am now only on the outline stage. Worse, at the moment, I am recently off diet pills after admitting to myself I have simply been using them as uppers; and I am now down so low that your salutation "Live long and prosper" elicited a chillingly bitter epithet.

I will return.

Really sincerely yours,

About a year later Gene did a mail interview with a group of Southern California high school students. They sent him their questions and he tape-recorded his answers. He talked briefly about his film experience:

"[*Pretty Maids*] involved a lot of naked high school girls and a high school counselor played by Rock Hudson who was trying to lead them into the paths of righteousness by manipulating their warm, young bodies rather than their minds. I had a lot of fun making it. It wasn't a great picture but did make some money at the box office.

"I think it was a better script than it was a movie. The script was really very funny.

"High school student counselors almost to a man, or to a

woman, hated me for suggesting that any one of them any-where could be that unprofessional. And perhaps they were justified. Although I would have preferred they watch it with the same sense of humor that I wrote it with. I consider sex not to be that awful.

"I think the ultimate pornography is the violent films, the war films. Those scenes of killing and maiming people. By some strange twist of mind, slaughtering people with machine guns seems to be acceptable while pinching a tit seems to be an awful thing."

Early in September, Gene wrote to a friend who was convalescing from surgery in Palm Springs. Gene's social consciousness came through in film projects, as well as television programs.

Having been rather in hiding while writing a tough film script, the news of your surgery came as a complete surprise.

This particular film script would interest you, I think. For some time I have been worried over the polarization of the police into a sort of "minority group complex" along with the polarization of blacks and browns into more and more violent directions. But hopefully, I'll come up with a film which illustrates the foolishness of both positions.

Darleen is pregnant, and I hope that this second grandchild will be a boy. [It was.] I think she is wise to have her family with no more than a year or two between children. Meanwhile, Majel keeps talking about helping me start a second family, which both frightens and intrigues me. But why not? I turned fifty last month, and it is probably time I started thinking seriously about what I will do when I grow up. I don't really mind that happening if I can retain a feeling of wonder, curiosity, love and other special qualities of youth which you have always exemplified so well.

Gene and Majel decided to have a child, but deciding was the easiest part. Pregnancy for Majel was an illusive goal. Having a child was to become an ongoing project.

* * *

Late in December 1971, Gene wrote to a fan with whom he had become friendly:

> Also, to be honest, I vary between regarding businessmen as sabre-tooth tigers and Builders of America. This usually depends on the status of my continuing fight with several studios over the difference between their gross and my net profits and my continued assertion (unique in this industry) that theft with a calculating machine is no less theft than that with a gun.
>
> I suppose *Star Trek* episodes carried something of both viewpoints since it is the dramatist's function to illuminate what he conceives to be *truth* and in the process of much writing he usually discovers that there are many *truths* on any subject. In fact, during the lives and works of famous writers it is possible to conclude that the worst possible thing for them is the belief that they have finally found it and need no longer search.

While Gene was writing and producing *Pretty Maids* and working on starting his second family, Paramount had been busy syndicating *Star Trek.* Though it had started slowly, momentum was gathering as people began to discover the show. Since syndication generally meant the program was run in a non-prime-time hour, often at 6 P.M., more people were able to see the program, often while they ate dinner. In some markets the program was shown five days a week. College students especially were "discovering" the program all across the country. In January 1972, *Variety* reported that *Star Trek* was airing in more than one hundred markets in the United States and seventy overseas.

January 1972 was also the time when the *Star Trek* fan phenomena manifested itself in a new guise.

CHAPTER 14

It was an event unique in television history: a convention devoted to celebrating a single program, and a failed program that had been off the air for three years, at that.

Science fiction conventions, of course, were old hat, events that had been held for years. The *Science Fiction Encyclopedia* states that "U.S. SF fans date the first convention as happening in 1936 when a group of New York fans spent a day with a group from Philadelphia," but "the first *planned* convention took place in Leeds, United Kingdom in 1937. The first . . . Worldcon, now the premier convention, took place in 1939. It is at the Worldcon that the Hugo Awards are presented."

The World Science Fiction Conventions, or Worldcons, (and awards) are principally for science fiction published in books and magazines. A Hugo for "Dramatic Presentation" was not awarded until 1958.[1] A large number of *Star Trek* fans had come into SF fandom, and there was more and more demand for *Star Trek* as opposed to written science fiction. (Some hardcore SF fans became irritated and suggested that *Star Trek* wasn't true science fiction and consequently not worthy of programming at an SF convention.)

As one of the 1972 convention organizers, Joan Winston, wrote, "*Star Trek* fans were always kind of 'tolerated' at the regular science fiction conventions, and we thought if a couple of hundred of us got together we could talk about *Star*

---

[1]*Star Trek* won Hugos in 1967 for "The Menagerie," and 1968 for "The City on the Edge of Forever."

Trek as much as we liked, with no one to sneer."[2] A core group was brought together, including Elyse Pines, Eileen Becker, Allen Asherman, Regina Gottesman, Joyce Yasner, Devra Langsam, Debbie Langsam, Steve Rosenstein, and Stuart Hellinger. Al Schuster became Chairman because "he had more convention experience."

With the energy, verve, vitality, and naivete of a Judy Garland/Mickey Rooney musical, the group got a barn and put on a show. A suggestion of the interest in the program came when a "talk session," held at Brooklyn College, was scheduled in a room large enough to hold 350. Over 700 people showed up—a portent of what was to happen at the convention proper.

Not knowing what they could or could not do, the group plunged ahead. Several people from Paramount were helpful, providing direction and suggestions. An article in *Variety* triggered an avalanche of calls from the media and more publicity than expected. Registrations were coming in from as far away as California and Canada—the momentum was growing.

They called NASA and asked if they could have a "little display." NASA sent them a one-third-size mock-up of the lunar module, a one-third-size mock-up of the LEM, and a full-size space suit with a model astronaut inside: four thousand two hundred pounds, packed inside seven huge crates, all delivered two days early with no storage facilities available in the hotel. A few hurried phone calls were made and NASA agreed to pick up the storage fees.

The New York Statler-Hilton and the convention organizers were prepared to handle a convention of up to 1,800. As a suggestion of how it would be, the committee received 800 advance registrations. On the day the con was to open, officially at noon, the hotel operators had been telling callers that registration opened at 8:30 A.M. By 9:00 A.M., there were 400 people waiting to register. Gene and Majel arrived around 11:00 and walked into the chaos.

Joan Winston remembers:

"Unfortunately, the kids at the reception desk were not familiar enough with their in-person appearances to recognize them. So, when Gene and Majel attempted to walk into the

Dealer's Room, one of the kids asked to see their badges. 'You can't come in here without a badge unless you are a member of the committee or connected with *Star Trek.*' Gene's response was classic. 'I *am Star Trek,*' he announced, sweeping theatrically past the stunned group.

"Gene did stop back to chat with the kids and prevent the hasty defenestration of the hapless fans."

After several hours of walking around, taking in the love fest for *Star Trek,* Gene's only comment was, "I just don't believe it. All these great people coming here to honor *Star Trek.*"

The event had attracted the media, and television news crews covered the event as best they could in the crush of people. While crews from ABC and CBS were in evidence, NBC, the network that had carried *Star Trek,* was strangely absent. In contacting them, Joan was told they were "completely disinterested."

Not completely, it turned out.

Joan Winston recalls:

"We heard later that they sent down some people to 'take a look.' They walked in Saturday afternoon, 'took a look,' turned ashen and left. I think that they were afraid that if anyone found out they were from the network that canceled *Star Trek,* they might have been lynched. You know, they might have been right."

The convention made history. On Friday, they registered 1,200 people and Saturday another 1,000 but, at times, they had over 3,000 jostling and jockeying for good seats. Sunday, before Isaac Asimov gave his speech, they registered another 500 or 600. After that, Joan remembers that they gave up and let anyone in, figuring it wasn't fair to charge full price for the remaining hours of a three-day program. Finally, three hours before the end on Sunday, 500 more people showed up, angry they hadn't heard of the convention earlier.

The organizers had accomplished far more than they had set out to do. In organizing a convention that might attract a few hundred people to celebrate a defunct television show, they ended up with the largest science fiction convention in history to that date, and a clear indication to Gene that *Star Trek* was alive and healthy in the hearts and minds of many people.

Gene had coordinated his visit to the convention with meeting network executives in New York City, so the convention organizers would not have to pay for his flight and hotel. When he returned to Los Angeles, he wrote to then *Star Trek* editor, Betty Ballantine:

> Discussing a horror series with CBS and some kind of sci-fi setup with NBC. My preference is the latter case. It would be something like doing *The NBC Sci-Fi Movie Of The Week* which could be used to pilot sci-fi series. At least it would be the kind of thing which would bring me back to TV with a glad cry and will let you know if anything materializes as you may have books you would like to suggest.

The next day he responded to an inquiry from the Reece Halsey Agency regarding an Alan Dean Foster script. Gene mentioned that "a deal for a possible *Star Trek* movie is being considered, but that interest could cool and the project could die." This March 1972, letter was the first mention of a possible *Star Trek* film, apart from contract considerations from the old Desilu days.

In mid-March, Gene wrote to a friend, bringing him up to date. Gene was regaining interest in doing television and had thoughts on other projects.

> I forgot to mention to you in past letters that my attorney checked out J.D. Salinger's *Catcher in the Rye*[3] and that it is available. Without giving any details he did mention that a number of people and organizations have been interested in the project from time to time but have had problems with it. It may very well be that you are the one who can come up with the proper approach. Meanwhile, I stand by my original belief that there is not an audience out there for it at this time.
>
> Things are beginning to move fast for me here. Most exciting of all, NBC has thrown in the towel and announced it wants *Star Trek* back on the air. Whether or not a deal with them and with Paramount (who own it with me) is possible is hard to say at this time, but it seems to me that the thing now

[3]Originally published in the early 1950's, Sallinger's masterpiece still sells 400,000 copies a year.

has a sort of momentum which will tend to push through
such obstacles. Also I am discussing a development
deal with NBC, doing a horror tale pilot for CBS, and
have two animation projects which look promising.
It's like all of a sudden everyone in town wants
me to do something, or so it seems.

Gene had spent time with Asimov while in New York and
wrote to him late in April:

It was so good seeing you in New York, and I hope
we won't stay out of touch so long this time. The reason
is both personal affection and business although
I will quickly settle for the first if nothing occurs
to make sense of the second.

The reason for mentioning business is that I am
convinced, *strongly* convinced, that both television
and motion pictures are swinging rapidly toward
an "imagineering" cycle in which the extraordinary
breadth of sci-fi literature may finally be appreciated
by investors and production people. For a long time
both *Star Trek* and *Odyssey 2001* were considered
freak successes. But now the great impact of things
like the film, *Silent Running, Clockwork Orange* and
others is being felt. Some are finally beginning to
realize that there can often be more reality and
meaning in science fiction, fantasy and allied literature
than in the rather dreary cycle of contemporary relevant
films and television programs. And much more
entertainment! I've already proposed to one studio
that a person such as yourself would make an ideal
host for a science fiction anthology hour on television.
This was, of course, with no indication that you
would even be interested but I think the point was
understood and appreciated. Certainly you would be
an invaluable advisor to a major science fiction film
project even if you were unwilling or unable to
become more deeply involved, something in the
way Clarke has served. I would appreciate your letting
me know the extent of your interest in such things
or whether you would prefer avoiding having your
name brought up but I suppose some of it comes
out of a genuine respect for the body of your work

and there's also ego in being able to say I know and talk to Isaac Asimov.

Isaac was flattered at being considered as the "Alfred Hitchcock of science fiction" and wrote back that he was "no less photogenic than Mr. Hitchcock, no less of an actor." Asimov then pointed out to Gene that he would not leave Manhattan, even to host a television program; the camera would have to find him in New York. He left the door open if anyone wanted to approach him on the idea, closing his letter by saying, "But let me make it quite clear that if it never comes to that point and if no one ever approaches me, I will hold you guiltless."

Also present at the New York convention was Harry Stubbs, who writes under the name Hal Clement. He and Gene had only a few minutes together at the convention. With no time to solicit his thoughts, Gene wrote Stubbs a letter framing several questions and then this observation:

> We did have one meeting with NBC after returning to the West Coast, and at least one comment from it will probably amuse you. The executives ventured the opinion "We probably cancelled *Star Trek* too soon." Is that what one calls a Pyrrhic victory? I think I would rather have the checks for the five year run.

Stubbs wrote back, gave his thoughts, asked a few questions, and closed with a question about the availability of the original cast. In his response, Gene made an interesting comment about Kirk for which no further details are available.

> Your comments were very helpful. Incidentally, we did take *Arena* from Frederik Brown's story and paid him accordingly. As for *The Doomsday Machine,* I think that was represented to us as the author's own original or, at least, there were no complaints so I guess it was handled properly one way or the other. We had a rather enviable record, which I wish someone would mention sometime, in that *Star Trek* was never sued for plagiarism in any form and I have always been rather proud of that (although I am knocking wood at this very moment). Not that everything used was virginal, but what items (transporter

chamber, for example) came from other places came
in the honest fragments that one picks up over a
lifetime of reading science fiction, and no significant
part was borrowed whole. In fact, some of the things
I did consider really original I later realized came
from as far back as childhood memory of some
piece of an. *Astounding Stories* tale I had read.

You will be interested to know that NBC has queried
me directly about putting the show back on the air.
Apparently the President of the network has ordered
the program department to look into it and do what
they can. The problem is that Paramount Studios
owns the basic rights to *Star Trek* (having bought
them as a part of acquiring Desilu Studios) and the
real question is whether Paramount would be willing
to put up the kind of investment necessary to put it
back on the air properly, and I think you understand
why I would insist on doing it right or not at all.

Will bear in mind what you say about the cast although
I guess at this time NBC would want a change in Kirk.
Nothing definite on that, but it is a feeling I get
when they discuss the findings of their research
people on audience attitude toward the various actors.
Also, I have an idea Bill would resist coming back
for various reasons, some of them personal and
beyond discussion by anyone but himself. I could
go either way on it. Leonard Nimoy is the one everyone
agrees would be the most help to a new *Star Trek* but
also he is the busiest of the actors, and that could
pose problems. However, I have had dinner with
Leonard recently, and his devotion to the character
of Spock and to the show is enormous and he went
out of his way to make it clear he would return
if there was any way it could be fit into his
professional needs and schedule.

Majel was a Dodgers fan, and she and Gene occasionally
took in a game. One friend sent them box seats and Gene
dropped a note, thanking him and giving insight why he
didn't go to more games with Majel.

Thanks again for the tickets. They cost me the usual
twenty dollar cleaning bill when my rabid fan-wife

showered beer all over us when the home team tied
up the score. My fault since I should have learned years
ago to always hold her drink when the Dodgers
come up to bat.[4]

By the early 1970's, the television piloting process had
grown so expensive that networks could not afford to finance a pilot just to see if the concept worked on film. They
sought ways to get a return on their investment, and shooting the pilot as a movie for television was a logical outcome.
It would become a permanent part of the industry.

In early May 1972, Gene checked into Warner Bros. studio where he was to create and develop television series. It
was a non-exclusive arrangement and he was free to develop
for other studios as well.

Gene's next project was more science fiction: *Genesis II*.
Set in the year 2133, Earth is slowly recreating itself after an
atomic war; human and atomically mutated societies existed
in independent city-states. The beginning of the show revolved around the resuscitation of NASA scientist Dylan
Hunt from 154 years of suspended animation. There are two
procedures to revive Hunt: injections of brain stimulants, or,
a typical Gene Roddenberry touch, sex. This plot device
shows Gene "pushing the envelope," something he did
whenever possible.

This was part of Gene's personality: when told he
couldn't do something, he figured out some way to do it,
partly from defiance, partly intellectual exercise, partly artistic integrity. Much of Gene's artistic career was one long
statement against authority stifling the free expression of
ideas and the artist's viewpoint.

We see glimpses of his independent nature when he was
at Four Star and his casting of Jeff Hunter as Captain Pike
when the network did not approve. Gene wrote a scenario
that allowed him to have his way and to satisfy the network
Standards and Practices people while thumbing his nose at
them at the same time.

Gene used aliens or "outsiders" in his shows to provide

---

[4]Another story Gene liked to tell was the one time he took her to a concert at the
Hollywood Bowl. While the music was playing, Majel had an earpiece firmly
plugged in, listening to the Dodgers through the concert.

conflict and as vehicles to make comment on the human condition. For *Genesis II* he created Lyra'a, a human mutant of superior physical and mental abilities. After years of network anatomy lessons where navels were never shown, Gene put two on his mutant creation.

Lyra'a, played by Mariette Hartley,[5] revives Hunt, played by Alex Cord, and while the audience is told she was able to revive him because her people have developed the medicinal uses of mutated plants, the audience is never quite certain that Lyra'a did not have to personally assist the plants in working their magic with a little magic of her own. Gene had gotten his idea past the network censor but little else.

As Gene related in an early 1976 interview:

"When *Genesis II* was introduced, I wanted Lloyd Bridges for the lead. The TV people went to their statistics file—the TV-Q list used by the advertisers to tell them who sells what and how they will sell it—and told me that Lloyd Bridges in a TV sci-fier was not what the advertiser thought would sell the toothpaste. In fact, all twelve of my choices were dumped out the same way. They chose a very capable actor—Alex Cord—but not for this series, as it turned out."[6]

The pilot was shot at the Burbank Studios in late 1972 and early 1973. Its last day before the cameras was January 18, 1973. Everyone thought they had something special: another adult science fiction show that worked and told human stories. Gene was ready for a series rollout and even had as many as fifteen additional *Genesis II* scripts prepared. The pilot, broadcast March 23, 1973, was well received. It was then undone by a bunch of talking primates.

Gene described *Genesis II*'s fate in a lecture at Stanford University:

"As a pilot for a potential science fiction series, I think it probably offered a range of stories and comment quite similar to *Star Trek*. We had the series tentatively sold to CBS. Then the network ran a high budget, very well made motion picture called, *The Planet of the Apes*. It was tough competition. Until then we had been the highest rated Thursday

---

[5]Ms. Hartley also played the character Zarabeth in the *Star Trek* original series episode "All Our Yesterdays," broadcast March 14, 1969. *Genesis II* also had another *Star Trek* alumnus, Ted Cassidy, who had appeared in "What Are Little Girls Made Of?"

[6]*The Monster Times*, May, 1976.

night television movie of the year. *The Planet of the Apes* went twelve Neilson points higher.

"The public went ape. The network programming office cried, 'Apes!' I said, 'Wait! I thought we agreed that we were talking about science fiction.' They said, 'Roddenberry, you dummy, science fiction IS apes!' And there was considerable panic at Warner Brothers where we'd made my pilot. They said, 'Roddenberry, you've got to save *Genesis II*. Isn't there some way you can add apes to *Genesis II*? Or baboons or orangutans, or something?!'

"At that time, a junior executive came up with one of those great front office suggestions. He suggested that we consider the possibility that man's best friend had evolved into a hind-legged species of talking dog. And intending to be sarcastic, I said, 'No. I have something much better. I have in mind a turtle-man creature and it may turn out to be even better than apes because it will give our show an underwater dimension.' I knew it was all over when they were taking that suggestion seriously."

So the literate science fiction of *Genesis II* was done in by network executives. Gene warned the network executive that monkeys acting like people is not a format, it's a joke—a "one joke show." The executives wanted apes; they got apes, and *Planet of the Apes* debuted on CBS September 13, 1974. Fourteen programs later, the apes had not evolved into higher ratings and quickly became extinct.

Gene tried again with the *Genesis II* format in a retooled version called *Planet Earth*. Alex Cord was replaced by John Saxon, but that didn't sell either. Gene had his thoughts on that version as well:

"In *Planet Earth,* the second *Genesis II* attempt, the casting was just a horror. They turned down all the names I suggested. They were so far into the production date they didn't even run screen tests on my people."[7]

The studio or the network took a variation of the format and did one other version without Gene's name and called it *Strange New World.* It was undistinguished in every way or, as Gene characterized it, "too far gone at that stage." His concept, chopped up and broadcast without his name, was an ignoble end to Gene's dream of a new adult SF format.

* * *

---

[7]*Ibid.*

Gene's energy was high; there was another project going on, almost simultaneous with *Genesis II*.

In mid-May of 1972, Gene had written to Asimov:

> I have just invented for use in a TV series presentation something called "Asimov's Rule" since I am too modest to attribute anything so clever to myself. It goes: "The innovative quality and entertainment potential of any sci-fi outline is inversely proportional to the number of learned persons who insist it won't work."
>
> In other areas, you have let me down sadly. At the request of Universal Studios, have started to work on something with a robot as the lead character but have found little to steal out of the two books you gave me other than the fact he can't hurt a human being, which I actually stole from someone who stole it from you. Someday someone will invent a human being who can't hurt a human being, but who would believe it?
>
> Had hoped to be back to New York by now but the contract came up at Warner Bros. and it looks like we have a deal, so will spend the next couple of weeks checking in and getting some projects rolling plus hopefully picking up a pay check so we can get off this diet of hog jowls and hominy grits.
>
> Write when you get a chance.
>
> Gene R.

Before Asimov could respond and point out the error in Gene's formulation, Gene quickly wrote:

> In my last letter I should have said "directly proportional," not "inversely proportional." I said it right in the format presentation, and you have no idea how many people are going around Hollywood today quoting you.
>
> Recommended to Universal Studios the other day they should look at *I, Robot* as a movie idea, and they seemed intrigued, but you can never tell for sure about studio heads.

By August the series idea with a robot as the lead had evolved into an android named *Questor,* whose original title had been *Mister Q*. The story and series concept were by Gene, but he'd brought in his friend Gene Coon to write the teleplay. Then it became a teleplay by Gene Coon and Gene Roddenberry with revisions. And revised it was: one script listed nine revisions between November 1972 and early February 1973.

Questor Series Projections are dated March 1, 1973 and March 5, 1973, but there may have been more as the files are incomplete. Important story concepts were explored in this show, concepts that would surface again with Data, the android character in *Star Trek: The Next Generation*.

The story begins with the titles projected over Michaelangelo's *Creation of Adam,* which suggests one of the story's underlying themes. Instead of God creating Adam in his own image, we have man creating Questor, an android that was the perfect replica of a normal human male, but with extraordinary powers and abilities. Questor had been built by multiple Nobel laureate Dr. Emile Vaslovik through a five-nation conglomerate,[8] but Vaslovik had disappeared before the beginning of the story and the completion of Questor.

Vaslovik's assistant was Jerry Robinson, a shy and somewhat introverted "gadgeteer" who was really an unrecognized genius—unrecognized except by Vaslovik. Robinson is strongly moral, with intense feelings about human suffering.

In an unsuccessful attempt to decipher Questor's programming, scientists from the five nations accidentally erase some of the start-up tape. Questor is activated, but he is incomplete. He does not have emotions and cannot make moral judgments. Further, he does not know who he is or his reason for existing. With Robinson to tutor him in emotions and human interaction, Questor sets out on a journey to learn who he is and why he exists by finding his missing creator. Questor is searching for answers to humanity's fundamental questions.

In their search for Vaslovik, Questor encounters a friend of his missing creator, whom Gene named Lady Helena Alexandria Trimble, after his friend and *Star Trek* fan, Bjo Trimble. Misinterpreting her motivations, Questor thinks he may have to make love to her to extract the information he needs. Gene reportedly had a battle with the network censors

---

[8]The U.S. representative was played by Majel Barrett.

on this, but this may have been publicity hype. It is unlikely, given the tenor of the times and the conservatism of network executives, that Gene ever thought he could get a human-android love scene on the air.

However, Gene had sufficiently pushed the envelope: fourteen years before Data on *Star Trek: The Next Generation,* utters his now famous line, Questor states to Lady Trimble, "If vital to an exchange of information, I am fully functional." As a sign of the times, Questor's functionality was not brought into use, as was Data's with Lieutenant Tasha Yar.

There is also a gambling scene in *Questor* that was reused by Gene in *The Next Generation* episode, "The Royale." Both androids are able to use their extraordinary abilities to throw whatever number is needed when playing craps.

When they find Dr. Vaslovik hidden in a cave on Mount Ararat, they learn that he too is an android, one of a long series of guardians placed on Earth by an unnamed race millennia ago. As Vaslovik nears the end of his lifespan, having laid on a table, waiting for Questor for over two years, he recites the essence of Questor's basic mission:

"Since the dawn of this world we have served this species, Man. We protect, but we do not interfere. Man must make his own way. We guide him, serve him, aid him. But always without his knowledge."

Questor was to be the last of his kind, his lifespan to run two hundred years. By then, Vaslovik says, humanity will be ready to live on its own.[9]

It was a series with a number of directions available to it. Universal gave the go-ahead for the two-hour pilot/TV movie and swiftly cast it without Gene's input. Robert Foxworth, under contract at Universal, was cast as Questor, and Mike Farrell, also under contract at Universal, got the nod as Jerry Robinson. While Gene always said Foxworth and Farrell did a fine job, he was angry that he was not consulted about casting: he had written the script with Leonard Nimoy in mind as Questor.

With costs in mind, the original setting of *Project Questor* was moved from Geneva, Switzerland, to Pasadena, Califor-

---

[9]That two hundred year timespan would have brought them into the time frame of Gene's *Star Trek* universe.

nia. The California Institute of Technology served as the background.

While shooting the exteriors at Cal Tech, some of the students stole the sign that identified one building as the home of "Project Questor." Gene thought it funny, and when the sign was not located, he called the studio for a replacement. Unfortunately, the sign-maker at the studio didn't get the correct title and sent over a sign that said "Questor Project." It was not used.

In a previously unpublished interview conducted at the time of filming, Mike Farrell saw as the theme of *Questor* "that there is hope for mankind—that mankind need not be doomed to futility, to blowing himself up; whether it be being helped by this master race which sends down its androids, or whether it be being helped by ourselves."

While Farrell saw parallels between the character of Questor and Mr. Spock, he made an observation that turned into a prediction:

"I think the series has tremendous potential. The question is whether they will allow us to exercise, realize, the potential. We have two ways to go, I think. One is we can, if it goes into series, we can continue to say things that need to be said about mankind, humanity and man's relationship to machines and vice versa; or we can be another simple adventure story which is *really* going to be a tragedy if it happens."

Robert Foxworth was not sufficiently familiar with the Spock character to venture an opinion, but had an equally prophetic answer when asked about the possible future of the show as a series:

"I think if it went to a series, if it does, it could be ground into hamburger meat by the powers that be."

The pilot was finished by the end of the summer of 1973. Everyone from network to studio to performers seemed to like it and it sold. NBC placed an order scheduling it for Fridays at 9 P.M., right after their new series, *The Rockford Files.* They ordered a dozen episodes, and Gene drafted a "bible" or *Writers and Directors Guide.* The show concepts were more fully fleshed out and new characters were added, new possibilities were explored, and then—something happened. Someone, somewhere in the great machinery that is network television decided they had to have *their* ideas impressed on the show. These "suggestions" came down about changing the format "just a little bit."

By November 7, 1973, there was a "New Questor Series Format." On the first page of the "new format" is the parenthetical note: "We ignore the ending of the pilot in which [Questor] did find Vaslovik and got a full explanation of his identity and purpose." Perhaps only a network executive could tell a series creator to ignore fifty percent of the previously broadcast storyline, the denouement to the entire drama's problem, and the setup for the continuation of the concept as a series.

If the dismissal of half the pilot and original story line weren't enough to swallow in one memo, the character of Jerry Robinson, the half of the partnership who would provide the emotional counterbalance to Questor's cold and precise logic, was eliminated. This would have eliminated dramatic situations where Questor could make the type of insightful social comments and criticism Spock became famous for and Gene loved to write.

As the "new" format detailed, *Questor* was to be a "one-star series." The Robinson character was disposed of with the sentence, "It is conceivable we could one day find a story which legitimately would use Jerry Robinson but this would depend wholly on the value of such a story."[10]

The network wanted an android *Fugitive/Run For Your Life/Six Million Dollar Man* franchise. Gene would have none of it, but his protests fell on deaf ears. He walked out. The project collapsed and *Questor* was shelved, ultimately shown as a TV movie on January 24, 1974, to respectful, but by then, meaningless ratings. The final exploitation of the idea was a mass-market novelization. Like so many potentially delicious meals, *Questor* was ruined by too many would-be cooks. It was an expensive meal, too—Majel believes Gene walked out on something that could have generated a million dollars.

Another project occupying some of Gene's time in the early 1970's was as executive consultant to the animated *Star Trek* series. It wasn't big money. He earned a straight

---

[10]Farrell was given his release and was free, in 1975, to take the role of Capt. B.J. Hunnicut, M.D. on *M*A*S*H*.

consultant's fee of $2500 per episode. Dorothy Fontana, who had been story editor and writer on the original series, was brought in as story editor and associate producer for the animated series. Other writers from the original series wrote scripts, and Sam Peeples, who had written the second original pilot episode, was hired to write the animated series pilot episode.

The animated series almost didn't happen, as Gene told an interviewer for *Show* magazine in the early 1970's:

"There was, for instance, talk of an animated *Star Trek,* but Paramount refused to give me complete creative control. I refused to give them *anything.* The project was pigeonholed until recently when they capitulated. Now, the animated version will be on the air this fall. I just didn't want space cadets running all over the *Enterprise* saying things like—'Golly gee whiz, Captain Kirk'—you know, like Archie and Jughead going to the moon. And with this animated version I have a decided advantage. If a script calls for a three-headed being, we have one at the same cost as a two-headed or a one-headed being. It's just paint."

When asked about the maturity level in the animated version, Gene responded:

"That was one of the reasons I wanted creative control. There are enough limitations just being on Saturday morning. We have to eliminate some of the violence we might have had on the evening shows. There will probably be no sex element to talk of either, but it will be *Star Trek* and not a stereotype kids cartoon show."

Seven years to the day that *Star Trek* debuted on NBC, the animated series bowed in with Peeples's episode, "Beyond The Farthest Star," except in Los Angeles.[11]

Episodes were written by Marc Daniels, an original series director, as well as Walter Koenig, the actor who played Chekov, and noted science fiction author Larry Niven. All of the original series actors supplied the voices for their char-

---

[11]There, George Takei was running for elected office and his opponents had complained to the FCC, citing the equal time rule. The FCC, apparently concerned how exposure to thirty seconds of George's dulcet tones might effect the voters who watched Saturday morning cartoons, required the substitution of another episode in Los Angeles, where viewers watched "Yesteryear," by Dorothy Fontana. The pilot episode was broadcast on December 22, 1973, after the election.

acters except for Walter Koenig.[12] Unfortunately, the dialogue was not recorded in a studio in ensemble. Individual actors would take two or three scripts and read their lines into a tape recorder. The animation studio would then mix the lines from the various actors together into a finished episode. While convenient to the actors, it did not produce the interaction between the characters that was a hallmark of the original series.

To fans of animation, there was no chance of mistaking this Saturday morning cartoon for a finished feature: they usually had far fewer cels per second than quality animation. There were enough to give a feeling of movement and action, but not the smooth quality other animators were famous for. Fortunately, the animated *Star Trek* was generally a well-produced product, but the quality was principally in its writing rather than in the animation, even though it had a reported budget of $75,000 per half-hour episode. Another downside to the series was a standardization of character pose and costume: Lieutenant Uhura wore the same earrings for all twenty-two episodes.

One clear benefit of animation was its limitless possibilities. No expensive costumes to make, guest stars to hire, or photographic effects to pay for. Just ink and paint on celluloid. With that freedom, two new crew characters were created: Lieutenant Arex, with three legs and three arms, whose voice came from the talented vocal chords of James Doohan; and Lieutenant M'Ress, a female cat creature who appeared in four of the animated episodes. M'Ress's voice was supplied by Majel Barrett.[13] The rest of the cast played themselves, with Doohan supplying the needed voices for a host of characters. A few actors did reprise their original series guest roles, including Stanley Adams as Cyrano Jones, Mark Lenard as Sarek, and Roger C. Carmel as Harcourt Fenton Mudd. In addition to the original cast playing themselves, there were seventy-five artists who produced 5,000 to 7,000

---

[12]Reportedly, rules limited the number of actors allowed to work as opposed to voice-over actors. Gene is supposed to have felt bad about Chekov's exclusion and hired Koenig to write one episode, "The Infinite Vulcan," broadcast October 20, 1973.

[13]Majel Barrett is the only actor to play in all dramatic incarnations of *Star Trek:* the original pilot, the original series, the animated series, two of the theatrical films, *Star Trek: The Next Generation,* and *Star Trek: Deep Space Nine.*

separate drawings per show, plus a host of other support personnel.

It received a variety of reviews. Cecil Smith, writing in the *Los Angeles Times* on September 10, 1973, thought it was out of place on Saturday morning and likened it to "a Mercedes in a soapbox derby." Smith suggested that NBC move the show to prime time and commented that the network "never understood the appeal of the live program" and probably wouldn't do it. He described the animation as above the usual quality found on TV with "magnificent effects which could never be achieved on a sound stage."

On the other hand, a critic writing in the *Chicago Tribune* suggested "fans" of *Star Trek* be referenced correctly as "fanatics," and mentioned they were in "full cry nationally" complaining that the animated *Star Trek* was being called a "kiddie cartoon."

To complete the confusion, Tom Zito, in *The Washington Post,* who had reviewed a number of Saturday morning children's programs, found the animated *Star Trek* "fascinating," but questioned whether the target audience of four- to eight-year-olds would be able to understand the program's themes.

Filmation produced twenty-two episodes.[14] It won an Emmy for children's programming and was shortly thereafter cancelled by NBC. The last new episode, "The Counter-Clock Incident"[15] aired October 12, 1974. Paramount Home Video released all episodes in June 1989, the same weekend as the release of the feature film *Star Trek V: The Final Frontier.* It was arguably the second series Gene had created that had been killed because of a bad time slot. Gene would later say that had he thought that there would be a live-action *Star Trek,* he would never have permitted the animated series. He did not consider it part of the "canon" of *Star Trek.*

* * *

---

[14]A bit of trivia. According to *Star Trek* archivist and consultant, Richard Arnold, there was no episode thirteen. When the cartoon episodes were put on video, they were numbered 1-2, 3-4, 5-6, 7-8, 9-10, 11-12, 14-15, and so on.

Richard Arnold: "I called up Dorothy [Fontana] to find out what happened and she said there was one that [Filmation] bought that just never went anywhere. It must have been scheduled and they never got back to it. So that one was never done. It's just one of those puzzles."

[15]Written by Fred Bronson (as John Culver).

His movie career had not taken off, but Gene had learned a lesson: television is the producer's medium because the producer is the one constant through episodic production; directors and writers come and go, but the producer guards the vision. In film, it is the director. Regardless of the brilliance of the writing or the possibilities in the script, it is the job of the director to realize that potential.

Gene still had an ace in the hole: *Star Trek*. Though the production debt was being paid off at an abysmally slow rate and profit, if it ever came, would be in the far distant future, the popularity of the program continued to grow—and so did Gene's reputation. In addition to fan clubs for the various actors, there was the Gene Roddenberry Appreciation Society, doubtless the first "fan club" for a writer-producer.[16] Through a friend, Gene learned how to use this popularity to help support himself and Majel.

Arthur C. Clarke is one of the world's preeminent science fiction writers. He was a radar instructor with the Royal Air Force during World War II and earned a Bachelor of Science degree in 1948 from King's College, London. He has always had a fascination with science, evidenced both by his writing and his chairmanship of the British Interplanetary Society from 1946 to 1947 and 1950 to 1953. His first professional science fiction story appeared in *Astounding Science Fiction* in May 1946. The *Encyclopedia of Science Fiction* indicates why he and Gene became friends.

With "The Sentinel"[17] came the first clear appearance of the Arthur C. Clarke paradox: the man who of all SF writers is most closely identified with knowledgeable, technological hard SF is strongly attracted to the metaphysical, even to the mystical; the man who in SF is often seen as standing for the boundless optimism of the soaring human spirit, and for the idea . . . that there is nothing humanity cannot accomplish, is best remembered for the image of mankind being as children next to the ancient, inscrutable wisdom of alien races.

---

[16]The book, *The Making of Star Trek,* published during the run of the show, had added to his reputation, educating fans to what a writer-producer does.
[17]The short story that formed the basis for the film *2001 A Space Odyssey.*

Gene had attended a lecture on astronomy given by Clarke. During their visit afterward, Gene told him things were slow and that there was a possibility of losing his house. In addition, Gene's divorce from Eileen had saddled him with a monthly alimony bill of $2,000, and Eileen did not like to be kept waiting for her check.[18]

Clarke introduced Gene to his lecture agent, Bill Leigh. Gene visited Leigh's office in New York City, recalling the meeting, years later, to Neil McAleer, Clarke's biographer, "I had the feeling that television was not something that Leigh was close to. The feeling I got was 'If Arthur recommends you, of course we shall try to handle you.' "

As Gene wrote to friends in late 1974:

> I took Arthur Clarke's advice and signed up with
> his lecture agent. They are the Leigh Bureau. Beginning
> September 4, I have about forty appearances
> scheduled around the country, mainly at
> universities. Students, for whatever their reason seem
> to want to see and hear me and I get the double advantage
> of staying in touch with youth and what is going
> on outside Hollywood, plus fees which about
> balance out the writing income lost during the trips.
> Since Paramount has yet to pay me the rerun or
> merchandising profits, claiming *Star Trek* is still
> a couple of million in the hole, income is still a
> consideration.

As *Star Trek*'s popularity grew so did Gene's, especially on college campuses. More and more college students wanted to hear what the man who created *Star Trek* had to say. Starting slowly, Gene made lecture appearances on campuses all over the country. He talked about *Star Trek,* he showed the famous "blooper reel" (showing mistakes that happened during the shooting of the show), he talked about his career, and he talked about the future—the place where he spent much of his waking time. Gene's message to the college students he encountered was one of hope and faith— hope in the future and faith in humanity, trust in ourselves.

---

[18]In perhaps one of the most incredible propositions of all times, Gene offered Eileen his profit interest in *Star Trek* for half of one month's alimony bill. She turned him down.

In June 1973, he received an honorary doctorate in Humane Letters from Emerson College, Boston, the first of three honorary doctorates he would receive in his lifetime.

An old travel slogan said, "getting there is half the fun," and so it was, most of the time anyway, with Gene and Majel's attempts to start a family. Fun, yes, but ultimately frustrating. After dozens of tests by a series of fertility doctors and three miscarriages, they gave up, disappointed but knowing that they had done all they could, or at least all they thought they could. It just didn't seem to be in the cards. Then when Majel missed two periods, she did so without concern; she had missed periods before, without being pregnant. Suddenly, one day she started to feel "different." She immediately thought "cancer" and went to the doctor.

They couldn't find a problem until someone suggested she be given a pregnancy test. The test came back positive. No one was certain when she had become pregnant, so the age of the fetus became an educated guess.

Unlike earlier times, this pregnancy was relatively uneventful, except for one unusual circumstance: movements by the baby triggered instantaneous nausea and vomiting. There was no warning. Without any preliminaries, Majel would simply erupt. Gene complained that he would appreciate some warning when they were driving somewhere, but she was never able to give any. This made for an interesting social life and adventurous car trips.

One night during Majel's pregnancy, Gene had a very realistic dream that he later described as exactly like someone vomiting on his back. Waking up, he felt wet, and looking over his shoulder, found Majel had thoroughly soaked him. She had slept through the entire episode.

Even though they did not know the exact age of the baby, the doctors eventually concluded that Majel was nine days overdue and decided to induce labor. Gene, about to be a proud father of a baby boy—as amniocentesis some time earlier had identified the sex—went out with a friend and got, to use Majel's words, "shitty-eyed snockered" the night before. Gene was to drive her to the hospital the next day and insisted before he went out that he would be up for the job. Majel knew better and prepared her own bag for the hospital stay. Gene swore up and down he would drive her there.

The next morning, Gene slept through the alarm. Majel got up, dressed herself, got her bag, kissed him on the cheek, and drove herself to the hospital.

Gene awoke later, confused and hung over, upset that Majel wasn't there. He stumbled around and ordered a cab, knowing her car would be at the hospital for him to drive home. He ordered the cabbie to drive him to the Queen of Angels Hospital. Moments later, a large, hung over, un-shaven, disheveled television producer stormed the admit-ting office, demanding to know where his wife was. When the hospital said they had no Mrs. Roddenberry registered, Gene became frantic, demanding they find his wife. Sud-denly Gene realized he should be at Cedars of Lebanon, not Queen of Angels. He had ordered the cabbie to take him to the wrong hospital.

Meanwhile, Majel was on medication to induce labor and a device monitored her progress. Every few moments, the needle would rise and she would have a major contraction, but she had not dilated enough to give birth. This went on for over nine hours. She was in considerable pain and not happy with the situation.

Finally, the doctor decided to perform a C-section and gave her a spinal block. Whether it was the sudden release of pain or the type of medication given, Majel became very talkative, watching the operation in the reflective surface of a chromed light just above her. By her own description, she chatted and yakked almost nonstop through the entire oper-ation.

As the nurse held the baby in front of her, Majel smiled, happy it was all over. Drenched with sweat, exhausted from her long ordeal, Majel looked at her newborn child, and with the tenderness of a new mother said, "Well, he certainly is well-hung!" and promptly passed out.[19]

---

[19]Of course, she didn't realize virtually every infant's genitalia are larger than av-erage due to the mother's hormones during pregnancy.

CHAPTER 15

The return of *Star Trek* was a long and convoluted journey. The first convention in 1972 had spurred interest in bringing the show back, but as Gene later revealed, there were roadblocks along the way, and in fairness to all concerned, nothing like the *Star Trek* phenomenon had ever happened before. It was uncharted territory for everyone, including studio executives. They had seen fads before and had not recognized that *Star Trek* was becoming a phenomenon, part of American culture. It was not a fad, but there was always some fear lurking in the minds of some executives that the "fad" could peak and any monies invested in new projects would be lost. Everyone wanted to be protected. No one wanted to risk a job or a career on a wrong decision.

In one interview in the mid-1970's Gene revealed that "NBC requested a new pilot show be submitted. Paramount replied that the rebuilding of the sets and replacement of the costumes and props would cost $750,000. At this price, they would proceed only if NBC would order *four* shows. NBC nixed the whole thing, and I went on a vacation to dream up something new."

There was another, purely economic, reason the studio was reluctant to have a new *Star Trek* series. A new series would mean negotiations with actors who were now far more valuable than they were a few years before, and Paramount was rightfully hesitant to pour money into something that might not show a return for years.

Further, Paramount reasoned that any new *Star Trek* show would diminish the value of what some executives called

"Paramount's 79 Jewels," which appeared to supply an end-less flow of income with little monies needed to keep them going, except an occasional new print.[1]

As *Show* magazine reported in 1973, "Surprisingly enough, the show's following is growing even though it is not on the NBC web anymore. The reason is that local stations have been buying all three seasons of it at a phenomenal rate—and at a phenomenal rental fee."

As Gene told his *Show* magazine interviewer in a fit of candor: "Now *that's* what is holding up any further talks about the new live episodes. The people at NBC have come to the point of being ready to put up the money for a new pilot—a two hour film—but the brass at Paramount are reluctant to take it. They say that if they produce new shows, the old ones won't be worth the high rental fees they are charging and the demand will drop off. So we're stalemated again."

During the next few years, Gene's correspondence reflected his thoughts on a new *Star Trek* program, as well as thoughts the original program had brought to the surface.

On his birthday in 1974, Gene wrote to Margaret and Laura Basta, two of the most active and supportive fans, bringing them up to date on *Star Trek*'s return and how he thought the process would work.

> The status of the *Star Trek* theatrical film has gone from fair to good. Perhaps very good! Negotiations are currently underway between our attorneys and if we discover we are indeed talking about the same kind of ball game in the same kind of ball park, I will soon begin writing the motion picture story. Briefly, my major consideration is that we do it right with a film budget adequate for the proper rebuilding of sets, props, costumes, and so on. Also, we have agreed that the acquiring of all these things out of a film budget makes more likely a possibility of *Star Trek*'s return to television. With the sets and

---

[1] Even that became a marketing tool. Years after the show had been syndicated, Paramount struck new prints and trumpeted the fact across the country. Yet another reason to watch *Star Trek:* better quality pictures. Local stations and advertisers loved it.

everything already paid for, we could make good episodes even at today's higher production costs. In other words, we would not have to spend a big hunk of the television episodic budgets on amortizing the heavy cost of rebuilding everything. We could spend it instead on important things like stories, writers, good actors, good directors and so on.

The next hurdle will be the story outline or possibly the full screenplay, at which time Paramount would then estimate the cost of making the film and determine whether or not anticipated revenues merit the risk of that amount of money. They seem to be becoming more aware all the time, fortunately, that there are quite a few fans out there who will almost certainly buy tickets to see almost any movie *Star Trek*. Naturally, I would hope to make it as good as possible but Paramount has to consider the possibility that a motion picture can sometimes turn out to be something less than you hoped for regardless of how hard you worked on it. My answer to that has been that the fans will still go to see the picture so long as we made an honest effort to give them *Star Trek* without cheating or cutting corners. Especially, if we give them the original actors too, or as many of them as are available.

If the budget is approved, of course we would then set a production date and begin to prepare to roll cameras at that time. If all went well, then Paramount would consider several possibilities. First, I think, would probably be the pros and cons of making a series of *Star Trek* motion pictures as was done with *Planet of the Apes*. I think Paramount television would also, at that time, be considering whether *Star Trek* should return to television in its original hourly form or whether it might best return as several ninety or one hundred and twenty minute television Movies of the Week each year. Of course, all of this is speculation at this time and it is difficult to guess what the final decision might be.

In early March 1975, Gene wrote to his cousin, John, in Honolulu, thanking him and his wife Iko for gifts and hospitality.

As for our plans, I finished the Twentieth Century Fox movie, first draft of it at least, [either *Battleground: Earth* or *Spectre*] and will start soon on the *Star Trek* movie which will go into theatrical release if all goes well. Which means, barring complications, I should finish the story and the writing of it in May and I should be able to rationalize flying over and doing some of the work there while Mom and Majel and Rod generally get into trouble all over the island. I promise I will take some time off though to pick up my expenses at the crooked poker table your gang over there runs.

A week later, he wrote to another friend:

As for the motion picture, it appears we have now completed an arrangement with Paramount and from all signs it also seems they want it to be a major picture with ample budget and plenty of "name" stars in guest or cameo roles. The principal characters, of course, will be the original actors from the television series.

As the *Star Trek* and Twentieth-Century Fox projects moved forward, Gene continued his interest in ESP and psi "phenomena" by becoming acquainted with Andrija Puharich and a group of people at "Lab Nine" in Ossining, New York, while doing research for a pilot/series idea. On April 2, 1975, Gene wrote to John Whitmore at Lab Nine:

I do not reject the possibility that other forms of intelligence can be in contact with humanity or with certain humans. Nor do I reject the possibility that another life form or forms might even live among us. It would seem to me rather extraordinary if this were the only place in the universe in which intelligent life happened to occur. Neither do we know the real nature of *time* and whether it and space are always linear and constant.

On the other hand, I've never seen any proof or at least anything I recognize as proof that other intelligent life forms exist or are or have been in

contact with us. Nor have I ever seen anything I
recognize as proof that other laws of physics exist.

Two weeks later, Gene's high school, Franklin, had a
small convention hosted by the school's Science Fiction
Club. Gene attended and later wrote to the club's sponsor,
teacher Bill Lomax:

> I wanted to let you know I was most impressed with
> the FHS Science Fiction Club Convention. The whole
> atmosphere of the school seems tremendously
> improved since I attended some seemingly useless
> Vocation Day talks there six or eight years ago. I have
> no doubt that much of this new feeling of excitement
> in learning comes out of imaginative programs such
> as yours and imaginative instructors such as
> yourself..
>
> I never considered Franklin a very good school. At
> least, there seemed little to stimulate the minds of
> students when I went there. Those who had
> imagination and a desire to learn were considered a
> little odd by most, unfortunately including a great number
> of the teachers. Particularly if they questioned the
> existing order of things. Here and there was a
> teacher who treasured these students but they were
> considered rather "odd" themselves.
>
> Thus, I was delighted with the whole new feel
> of the place and you can count on my support of
> such programs in the future.

Gene bore down on the script. In early June, he wrote to
another cousin, thanking him for information on the
Roddenber(r)y family and continuing:

> The *Star Trek* motion picture script goes as well as
> can be expected during the pulling and tugging of first
> draft. Hope to have that part of it completed in
> about a month. Meanwhile, I have suspended all
> traveling and lectures and probably won't get out and
> around much until sometime this winter. Find myself
> even turning down dinner dates and having my
> secretary handle a lot of correspondence I would

otherwise be doing personally. But a motion picture is really the same size chore as doing a novel and it must be done in much less time.

Gene heard from another cousin, Julien Roddenbery of Cairo, Georgia. Julien was slightly younger than Gene's father and Gene treated him with respect.[2] He replied to Julian's letter on his personal typewriter, which had a distinctive script font.

> My present situation is being in the midst of a motion picture script which will necessarily occupy almost all my full time for the next two or three months. It involves a pressing deadline and will require a considerable output of energy and time. I've even had to temporarily discontinue the university lecture tour which brought me to the pleasant meeting with Ledford Carter [the cousin mentioned above]. I mention these things only so you will understand why you are not getting a more complete letter at this time. I am in a sort of "feast or famine" business with a lot of "hurry up and wait" situations. At the moment it is all "hurry up." But at least, times like this keep beans on the table and carry us through the "wait" periods.
>
> The most exciting Roddenberry family member (in my eyes, of course) is Eugene Wesley Roddenberry, Jr. now 6 months old and probably capable of tearing down a Roddenbery Plantation[3] cane patch in record time. Will bring him down to Georgia some day when it appears the State may be ready to handle a small hurricane.

Though deeply immersed in the *Star Trek* script, Gene always found time to write to Asimov and share his thoughts. On October 6, 1975, he wrote to Isaac on his personal typewriter:

---

[2]Gene's first choice for Captain Picard's name *(Star Trek: The Next Generation)* was Julian.

[3]The Roddenberys—one "r"—were a well-known family in Georgia, and their "down home" products were local legends.

Someone sent me a copy of your "Space 1999" review
from *The New York Times,* and I wanted to write
and say that I think it one of the most reasoned and
knowledgeable analyses of television science fiction
I have ever read.

Have you ever written any articles on this general
subject? If not, I wish you would consider attacking
the whole subject of translating science fiction to cinema
and television. It would be a great service to the
sci-fi community of writers and ultimately to
the fans. There seems to be fairly general agreement
on what makes science fiction work on paper but, it
seems to me, far too many of our best sci-fi writers
do not understand that translating it into film or
tape words and images is a monstrously difficult thing
with vastly increased problems in maintaining
believability.

I really think I am still too close to *Star Trek* and
its formats to do the above job properly. If it is ever
to be done right, it's going to take an observer like
yourself.

Gene lectured in the San Diego area in October. He was
always ready to trade philosophical thoughts. In early November, he received a letter from Bernard Rimland, Ph.D.,
director of the Institute for Child Behavior Research in San
Diego.

I tend to ruminate, and I have been ruminating over
several remarks that you made during your visit here.

I don't remember your exact words, but in
discussing the throngs of college students who
come to hear your talks, you remarked with a trace
of annoyance that what the kids were looking for was
some kind of a god, and in effect you weren't
interested in filling that role. That started a train
of thought that has intrigued me. Why not let others
think of us, or even treat us, as though we were gods?
Why should we not think of ourselves as deities?
And why should we not treat everyone else,
including the college kids, as though they were deities
as well? A case could be argued from a number of
viewpoints, not only that each of us is a god, or

is at least god-like in a number of respects, but also
that if each of us thought of ourselves and of each
other as somewhat of a god deserving at least a
little reverence, respect and awe, the world might be
a much more pleasant place to live.

On November 20, Gene wrote back:

About being treated as God, I do share your belief
that we are all a part of the basic creative force of
the universe and if it can be described as a "deity,"
certainly there is deity in all of us. I believe that
many of our world's problems would be resolved if
we did treat ourselves and others with the reverence
appropriate to that concept. Perhaps we will begin
to do so as our race approaches adulthood. I do
believe that at present we are in something of a racial
childhood filled with all the pushing and shoving and
mistakes and aggressiveness which seems to be a
part of the process of experimenting, learning and
growing. We should learn to view these things with
the same kind of patience and affection felt by good
parents watching their children going though these
stages.

I suspect that if there is such a thing as extraterrestrial
life watching us during our present stage, they probably
view us with exactly that attitude and feel that we
probably will amount to something when we reach
maturity. If this is true, I hope that while they let us
make our mistakes they will also gently intervene
whenever our lusty young aggressiveness takes us
to a point where we may injure ourselves. I think
it not impossible that they actually do intervene now
and then, perhaps without us realizing it. I would hate
to think that we are all alone here.

Rimland also likes to recount another experience with
Gene that had a strong influence on him.

"A local university invited John Ott to give a lecture
about his discoveries on the profound effects that prolonged
exposure to different light sources have on the health and
behavior of plants and animals—including people. John is a
pioneer in the development of time-lapse photography, and

his films clearly reveal the kinds of effects he lectures about. Gene was interested in John's work and accompanied John and me to the campus.

"On our way to the lecture hall, we encountered a faculty member I knew, so I introduced John as the guest speaker. The professor had read the announcement about John's talk, and immediately began to express his skepticism, asking impertinent questions and in other ways giving John a hard time.

"Gene listened quietly, then finally had had enough. Then he said, 'Listening to you gives me the impression that you divide everything into two parts—the things you believe, and the things you don't believe. I look at the world differently—there are a few things I firmly believe, and a few things I don't believe at all, but in between there is a vast range of things I wonder about, and that's what makes life interesting.'

"Gene's remark shamed the skeptic into silence and Gene, John, and I continued on toward the lecture hall."

On January 14, 1976, Gene dropped a note to Dick Adler at the *Los Angeles Times*, gently correcting the reporter's characterization of *Star Trek*.

Many thanks for your mention of *Star Trek* in your recent *Times* newspaper article "Break in Space: 1999." Sometime we must get together and discuss whether or not *Star Trek*'s attitude was "optimistic, recklessly liberal." You make a valid point there but not when you categorize it as worried about America's role in the world. Our show postulated that mankind did indeed make it into an era of world peace by the 24th century although we made many references during the series about harsh realities which occurred between our century and then, including references to a "Dark Ages," "Genetic war," and such. The optimistic point we did make is that during all this mankind finally learned the foolishness of petty nationalism and political and racial hatreds and finally discarded them. There was no USA in our series, nor was the Earth planet in any way the "head planet" of the Federation. True we did see mostly humans in the series, but this had more to do with budgets

and casting options than any chauvinism about any
one of our present systems.

At any rate, I wanted to respond. And this
response in no way indicates any feeling that our show
was perfect science fiction or anything like that.

By the beginning of the new year, the motion picture project Gene had been working on had evolved into a series development deal, referenced in his files[4] as *Star Trek II*.[5] One
of the earliest memos on *Star Trek II* is dated January 16,
1976, and details a number of steps to be taken in the development of the new series.

Establishing five planets of the Federation, their
inhabitants and their physical qualities.
Establish: Kirk, Spock, others have dispersed, still
friendly.
Kirk returns from mission to Planet Z. McCoy detects
changes in character. Under hypnosis (other means?)
elicits vague sense of threat from Planet Z. Exact
nature of threat and of Z Race to unfold gradually.
Much inform'n to be withheld here.
Spock sent as Ambassador: Seeks live-and-let-live
accommodation. Unsuccessful. (Endangered?
Captured? To be discussed)

Gene had kept in touch with his distant relatives and enjoyed meeting with them whenever travel took him near by.
On February 6, 1976, Gene wrote to a cousin, seeming to
talk about a motion picture project as opposed to a series.
He may have been referencing the two-hour pilot film; there
may have been plans to sell the pilot as a theatrical release
overseas.

---

[4]After Gene's death, Paramount retained approximately fifteen boxes of material
stored at the studio under Gene's name. None of this retained material was inventoried, and when some of the boxes were turned over to Majel after Paramount's
lawyers combed through them, there was no way of knowing what Paramount
retained.
[5]As opposed to the feature film *The Wrath of Khan,* also known as *Star Trek II.*
The first series return project was called "Star Trek II." To add to the confusion,
the second pilot, the Peeples's script, was called *Star Trek 2.*

The *Star Trek* motion picture situation is muddled as usual. We have a July 15 shooting date set but I'm having some trouble getting together with Paramount on the selection of a script. Most of our problems are the same old ones that film has always had, i.e. interference by business types in artistic and entertainment areas. I believe we will ultimately get a good movie underway but I doubt if we'll get into production as soon as they think.

On the same day Gene corresponded with George L. Thurston, III, who was about to become the editor of the Roddenber(r)y Family History project. Gene supplied biographical information—children's births, wedding and divorce dates—also expounding on his personal beliefs and those expressed in *Star Trek:*

My second wife Majel Lee (Hudec) and I were both raised Protestant but well before ever meeting had both left the Protestant Church in favor of non-sectarian beliefs which included respect for all other religions, but emphasizing the concept of *God* as too great and too encompassing to be explained and appreciated by any single system of belief. Upon meeting we found that we both believed in the brotherhood of all life forms, human and otherwise. Some aspects of Buddhism express some of our beliefs but also do some aspects of the New and Old Testaments as well as other books and philosophies.

It may also interest you that the "name giving" of our son was accomplished by a Jesuit priest, a rabbi, and a Protestant minister on the basis that this represented the religions and beliefs of most of our friends and families and those three gentlemen each conducted a ceremony, one after the other, emphasizing we are all of one family under one creator.[6]

Perhaps some of the above thinking found its way into *Star Trek* in the philosophy of tolerance and respect for life which I tried to include in the episodes. Attached to this letter is a xerox of an article on the "Vulcan

---

[6]"Rod's" godfather is former California governor Edmund "Pat" Brown, his godmother is old family friend and noted attorney Lillian Finan.

religion" which I wrote about during the series and
which includes many aspects of our above
described beliefs.

Later in the year, Gene dropped a note to his cousin, a
Catholic nun in Atlanta, Georgia. They had just met.

> . . . am sending off notes to both you and Andy so
> you'll know what a pleasure it was for me to meet
> you and all of the relatives. It is a good feeling
> to find that one has kinfolk and that they are such
> fine people. You all make me very proud of being a
> member of the Roddenber(r)y family.
> It was at Denver that someone wrote a question
> "What is your religion?" My answer was: "I do
> not belong to any church but I *do* consider myself a
> religious man. I believe that I am a part of you and
> you are a part of me and we are a part of all life
> . . . also a part of the creative force and intelligence
> behind life. Therefore, if we are a part of God then
> our lives are not brief meaningless things, but rather
> have a great importance and significance. All of
> us and each of us."

In addition to shepherding and supervising the film, there
was another aspect of the *Star Trek* universe which concerned Gene. He expressed himself in a memo to an executive at Paramount on February 27, 1976:

> Since my last memo to you on *Star Trek* conventions,
> the situation seems to have quickly gotten much worse,
> and may pose an even greater potential danger to
> promotion of the film. We now hear of a *Star Trek*
> "circus" being planned in June or July for Chicago,
> a series of *Star Trek* "stage reviews" in planning
> stage, still another convention this year for New
> York, a mammoth convention in Denver, in
> Washington, etc.
> Additionally, I have received a number of telephone
> calls from members of the press in which there have
> been intimations that the entire *Star Trek* fan
> phenomenon is beginning to look like a "milk the kids"
> racket.

Without this taking valuable time away from finding the film version story and getting into preproduction phase, I believe it to be vital that someone determine which of these affairs are licensed by or encouraged by Paramount or, if not, determine what controls and guidelines can be imposed over them by Paramount. There is nothing quite so cold or old as "yesterday's mania" (witness Batman) and the rush of entrepreneurs cashing in on *Star Trek* may put us in that category.

In April 1976, Gene was honored at the Count Dracula Society Awards Banquet. He is introduced by his friend Forrest J Ackerman by the following speech delivered in Forry's notoriously punny manner.

The Remarkable Roddenberry

My text this evening is from the First Book of Bradbury, Chapter 3, Verses 6 thru 9.

Fiends ... Romans ... Countrypersons—

Lend me your fears!

We are gathered here this evening, in the sight of these multitudes and the Divinity of Dr. Reed, assembled of one accord: not to bury Roddenberry but to praise him. For once the wasteland of television was barren of weekly sci-fi fare, of space opera to compare with the best of the Golden Age of science fiction, and there was a vacuum and a-void and a great lamentation in the hearts of the true believers. And there rose one among us, an ex-policeman who looked upon this distressing situation and in his infinite wisdom observed:

"You can police some of the people some of the time and you can police some of the people all of the time ... so better I should devote my time to *pleasing* ALL of the people ALL of the time on primetime TV." And before another Halloween had hallowed the ground with an autumnal spread of leaves of brown, this seer, this sage, this Saint of the Starways had devised a format at first called *Trek or Treat* but eventually evolved to what the world came to know and love as ... STAR TREK.

And the Great God Nielson looked upon the ratings and saw that they were good. And there was rejoicing thruout the land. And the talents of Robert Bloch and Theodore

Sturgeon and George Clayton Johnson and Harlan Ellison and Dorothy Fontana and David Gerrold were wisely employed by the Great Bird of the Universe to tell stellar tales of interstellar derring-do and men and women of tomorrow boldly splitting not only infinitives but infinities to BOLDLY GO where no PERSON had gone before: to the Network Executives to *demand* a third season when all reason fled from the tele-moguls and they threatened in an excess of madness and abysmal ignorance to throw televiewers back to the Dark Ages by egregiously illogically cancelling STAR TREK.

Yea tho I walk thru the valley of the Shatner of death I shall fear no evil for thou art with me, thy Rod and thy Berry, they comfort me—Thus Spock Zarathustra.

So much for the serious side of this introduction.

We are honored to have with us tonight the man who could work miracles: he let us have our Kirk and eat it too. His creation lives long years after its origin. His brainchild has spawned clubs, conventions, pocketbooks, toys, games, manuals, models, costumes and things that go bumperstick in the night—a veritable way of life for his cast of characters ... and the characters who cast themselves before him. The Count Dracula Society is proud tonight to pay homage to an eternal Questor after ever better science fiction fare on television, to recognize and reward the immeasurable contribution to the field of visual fantasy by one of its most popular popularizers.

In the immortal words of Isaac Asimov, "It's all in the Genes."

Forry signed it: "For Gene Roddenberry who almost turned this into the most fiery speech I ever made."

O King,
Live Forry-ever
24 April 2076

In mid-1976, Gene thought that doing a spoken record album would be a good way to answer questions he was frequently asked at conventions and through the mail. He worked through Columbia Records and a producer there named Ed Naha.

Naha remembers the project:

"Everyone in my department thought that was the worst idea they'd ever heard, so I went to the president of the company, Bruce Lundvall. He was a really nice man who had an affinity for spoken word albums. He had released a couple of W.C. Fields albums based on old radio shows.

"He gave me the go-ahead for this project. At that point it was known as 'Naha's folly' because no one could understand why a rock-and-roll guy wanted to do this. I thought it could be fun.

"I enlisted the aid of a wonderful engineer named Russ Payne. We had worked together on audio presentations before for CBS conventions. I spoke to Gene on the phone a few times and it was agreed that I would meet him at a *Star Trek* convention that was in New York.

"I went down there early in the morning and Gene was totally haggard. It turns out the night before, while Gene and Majel were down at dinner, someone had broken in and roughed up their maid-nanny and demanded to know where their jewelry was and stole all their clothes. The only clothes Gene had at that point were the clothes on his back. Gene just looked at me, as we were going down in the elevator, and he scrunched down a bit and said, 'Maybe if I act short no one will notice me.'

"We went and talked about this album. It was decided that Gene would answer a lot of questions that he'd gotten about *Star Trek* and would try to assemble as much of the cast as possible for little vignettes that would explore the characters they played. In terms of science fiction he would talk to someone along the lines of Ray Bradbury or Isaac Asimov.

"Then we begin the nightmare known as logistics. Gene was on the West Coast, I was on the East Coast, and half the time when he was on tour, he would be in colleges that were not accessible to set up sound equipment. Finally we came up with a suitable college not too far from New York and taped one of Gene's lectures from start to finish. Little did we know that we'd be mixing it in three different studios across America!

"Now it was time to get the cast and various participants together. Leonard Nimoy gave us a flat 'No.' Shatner was free, but tracking him down was hard.

"Each little segment, which Gene had done, had a three or four-page script that, depending on how the take was going, you could either stick to it or vary a little bit if you got on an interesting topic, and then pull back and get back into the script.

"Gene was very meticulous about arranging all of this. He left all the technical things to me, such as getting the mike the proper way, which is very difficult in a sit-down situation. For a more relaxed atmosphere, we had a table and two chairs set up with table mikes. The nice part of that is you're relaxed with the script in front of you. The downside is, if you bumped the table, or moved the mike, suddenly you have the soundtrack of *Godzilla*.

"Mark Lenard and DeForest Kelley, Mark especially, were at home with this format. With Shatner, it was another matter.

"We were waiting and waiting for Shatner to show, and the dollars were building up on our studio time. Finally, he showed up in his tennis whites and racket. Gene asked him if he had his script or looked at it, and Shatner just said, 'Oh, no. We'll just chat.' Gene's eyes were slowly growing to the size of grapefruits and his cheeks were getting beet red.

"I had a script for Shatner and we got the tapes rolling and he went into a five-minute monologue on Zen, out of the blue. I was sitting in the control booth thinking, 'I don't need this. I went to Catholic school. I should have gotten brownie points for all those rosaries and stuff!'

"Gene didn't know what to do.

"I stopped the tape and suggested we try to get a bit more of the script in there, something about *Star Trek*. We finally did and got the tapes back to New York.

"We did Mark Lenard's segment and it came off without a hitch.

"DeForest Kelley was just wonderful, but he had just had some dental work done. It usually takes a while for you to get used to that kind of change. So the reading was fine, but he had a tendency to sometimes hiss and sometimes pop. We didn't know what to do, because you can't say it to the guy. You can't just say 'Could you take out your teeth?' Gabby Hayes made a career out of that, but ...

"We wound up going line by line.

"The most hellacious aspect of the whole record was that we wanted to use the *Star Trek* theme music as recorded in the show. We did get to use some effects because they were basically public domain, and we used some synthesizer music from an existant Columbia album. But Paramount, at the time, was not one of Gene's biggest fans, and there was no way they would let us use the tape.

"After about a month they said we could use it if we paid them a fee that was more than the entire budget of the album. I think it was fifteen to twenty thousand dollars.

"So Gene managed to get the sheet music to the theme, since he had written the lyrics. My boss brought in an arranger named Charles Collela. He had worked on a lot of Columbia albums. We had almost no money left from the budget, so we got half a day in a studio with about fifteen musicians and a vocalist to record the theme song.

"We were in Columbia's real old studios and they were tearing down the buildings next to us. So while we're trying to record, we have one of those big metal balls swinging through walls fifteen feet away and we have four hours to get this down. Most of the musicians had been around since *The Jazz Singer,* and were looking at this cold, and they didn't know *Star Trek* from foot disease. There were a couple of hip guys who said, 'Yeah. I watched that and *The Man from U.N.C.L.E.*'

"We had guys on the chimes who'd whack them and it would sound like a doorbell from hell. I'm sitting there, almost in tears. Thank God we had an engineer who worked the lot in the classic days of Columbia Big Band music.

"We got it done and then mixed it in the old rooms at Columbia no bigger than a closet. We took the best stuff we could and used the sound effects to bridge everything. Gene was lecturing down south somewhere, so I had to fly in with the tape and hire a studio down there so Gene could listen to it and approve, which he did.

"So now all we had to do was get the cover designed, get a lot of publicity done, write the liner notes and we'd have this out in a couple of months. There was no money for liner notes, so I wrote them myself. For the cover we used some artwork that shows the *Enterprise* as if it's on a draughtsman's table.

"When the first box of albums arrived, I looked at the cover and it says 'Inside *Star Trek*' and in the lower right-hand corner it lists the producer's names, the engineer's names, and Gene's name is the last one listed. I had a fit.

"I had the press packages ready, I had the eight-by-ten and the different masks of *Star Trek* and the bio, and now I couldn't show this album to anyone, and I couldn't ship them out. I went nuts. I had some stickers made and we had to take every album back to the plant and have people put them on individually. It was a Gene Roddenberry album featuring William Shatner, Mark Lenard, DeForest Kelley, and Isaac Asimov. Otherwise people would have looked at it and thought, 'Oh, look. The new Ed Naha album is out!'

"When the albums were finally released, we had cardboard displays made that were supposed to be put on a counter by the register of the music stores, but they all came back. It seems no record store wanted to have a spoken word album near the register when they could have the top sellers there. The albums ended up in the spoken word sections of the music stores. These are the places that have 'Boris Karloff Reads From Thriller.' They're just dead.

"There was no money allocated for television advertising and we had to rely on word of mouth. Eventually we broke even on it. I think my royalties, when it had been out there for three years, came to about twenty-six dollars."

By late July, 1976, the project was a feature and Paramount had hired Chris Bryant and Allan Scott to write the screenplay. They were to begin on August 16, 1976, and write an outline of eight to ten pages. For that they would be paid $12,500, plus more for the first draft and revisions. Jerry Isenberg was to be executive producer and Phil Kaufman would direct. The film was to have a budget of $7.5 to $9 million.

In an interview published a year later in *Starlog,* Allan Scott talked about their problems. One was defining the "difference between what is television and what is movie." He confirmed that all the regular characters would return with a few new ones to "augment and supplement." Scott explained a lesson Gene had learned years before: one of the difficulties in writing SF is that a writer often has to spend a great deal of time writing background for a character who may be in a scene for four lines and never be seen again, but unless the character's history is understood "he's going to look like he wandered off twentieth-century Earth in a funny disguise."

In another magazine article published in late 1976, plans for ten cameo roles were in the works, but there was no mention of a proposed plot, although there was talk about a sequel if the film did well.

Bjo Trimble, the fan who, with her husband John, was the principal organizer of the grass-roots push to keep the original Star Trek on the air, received a call one day from two men who still prefer to remain nameless. They'd had an idea to name the first space shuttle *Enterprise* and wanted Bjo's help. As she remembers it, within a week her "help" turned into running the project as the two men walked away leaving her to carry it through to completion.

Bjo remembers that it took about a month to get fandom informed. Meeting with a core group at the Los Angeles Science Fiction and Fantasy Society, she put together a mailing that comprised over twelve thousand letters to key individuals and fan club leaders. Within a month, the avalanche of mail began.

Reporters started to call, more publicity resulted, and the mail to the White House increased appreciably. There is no clear figure on the number of letters received at the White House. Most accounts put it between 400,000, and 500,000. Whatever the true figure, it was impressive enough to convince President Gerald Ford.

When he held his news conference to announce that the first shuttle would be named *Enterprise,* he stunned a number of NASA officials, who had not been privy to the process and had thought the name was to be *Constitution.* There were, of course, any number of people both in NASA and the space industry who were delighted at the choice. Bjo remembers that at the cocktail party before the official rollout, several dozen engineers and aerospace officials had buttons pinned underneath their suit lapels. When they saw her and learned who she was, they would flip over their lapels, exposing the button with the words "Closet Trekkie."

On September 17, 1976, at Edwards Air Force Base, shuttle orbiter 101 was officially rolled out and named *Enterprise.* As the giant craft came out of the hangar, the Air Force band played the *Star Trek* theme. The entire original cast was present, as was Gene. The dedication was moving as Walter Koenig would later write:

I can't remember seeing a group of people so moved as those in the row beside me. I felt myself close to tears and wasn't the least embarrassed by it.[7]

It was a surreal meeting of fiction and reality, capped near the end of the ceremony when across the crowd Gene spotted the arch-conservative senator from Arizona, Barry Goldwater, known in political circles as "Mr. Republican." Goldwater was a charming and gracious man, but his politics were the antitheses of Gene's.[8]

Goldwater, spotting Gene, waved at him and shouted, "I'm a Trekkie, too!"

On October 26, 1976, Gene sent a memo to Allan Scott and Chris Bryant, giving them his comments on their story to date. He was giving copies to Jerry Isenberg and Phil Kaufman but to no one else, as it was what Gene characterized as "writer talk." He wanted to feel free to

... make every question or criticism, large or small, that comes into my mind. While we understand this level of early story communication, I don't want it in the hands of those who might read more problems into it than really exist.

You two writers are almost too good! Your fifteen page story was styled so excitingly that the holes and discrepancies which worried you and us were hardly visible. Many of them are fixable in script, of course. But a great number of them, at least in my opinion, are not and the time to tackle them is now. If some of what follows sounds trivial or picky-ish, I know you will accept it in the spirit of my simply wanting to get everything discussed. I know that neither you nor Phil will have any hesitation about coming back to me where it appears my opinions are too much influenced by "television *Star Trek*" concepts.

There followed nine and a half pages of detailed analysis of what Scott and Bryant had written, asking questions and trying to solve problems and potential problems.

---

[7] *Chekov's Enterprise,* by Walter Koenig (Longwood, Florida: Intergalactic Press, 1980), page 16.

[8] Goldwater's positions on a number of issues seem to have mellowed with age.

In early November 1976, *Starlog* reported that the feature originally set to begin filming July 15 was not ready to begin production because there was no script. Part of a Roddenberry story that had been submitted to and rejected by Paramount was quoted. The reporter characterized the story as dealing with the meaning of God and wrote that "Roddenberry thinks Paramount executives were bothered by a 'little sequence on Vulcan in which the Vulcan masters, the people Spock studied under, were saying 'We have never really understood your Earth legends of gods. Particularly in that so many of your gods have said, "You have to bow down on your bellies every seven days and worship me." This seems to us like they are very insecure gods.' "[9] The article said shooting of the film was to begin in January 1977.

That start date was unlikely because Gene had, in addition to the *Star Trek* feature, or whatever it was going to be, two other projects in at Twentieth Century Fox. One he handled personally, the other he turned over to a trusted colleague, Cy Chermak,[10] a highly respected series producer with a reputation for quality.

Gene had sold the *Battleground: Earth* concept to Twentieth Century Fox. They liked what they saw and started series development. It was science fiction with a different twist. *Battleground: Earth* was not set in a utopian future or a distant time after an atomic war, like Gene's previous efforts. It was set roughly ten years in the future right here on Earth. Invaders from another planet were slowly infiltrating society, taking over key individuals. This was to be the continuing saga of the fight against alien takeover.[11]

Gene liked Chermak and gave up a percentage of the program to bring him in as producer, while Gene was in England producing a script he had written with Sam Peeples. Chermak had an order from the network and time was of the essence. Stories needed to be turned into scripts and, as

---

[9] Presumably this came from *The God Thing,* a novelette by Gene, submitted to Paramount as the story for the first film. Paramount rejected Gene's effort as too antireligious, yet this writer can find no such line by Vulcans in his copy of the manuscript.

[10] Cy Chermak was the executive producer of *Ironside* and took over as producer of *Kolchak—The Night Stalker* in the middle of its 1974–1975 season.

[11] If this sounds familiar, it is the central plot thrust of *V,* first broadcast as a miniseries on NBC in 1984 and then as a short-lived series.

Chermak recalls, he put out ten script assignments to different writers. Costumes were being designed, and the thousand details that make up the creation of a television series were attended to.

The network wanted the pilot rewritten, so Chermak took on that responsibility. Gene liked what he did to the work and approved. With the pilot script completed and accepted by the network, actors were being considered for roles, but only one actor was ever actually hired; while he was to play an alien on the show, he was brought in early so that makeup designs could be tested.

Cy Chermak remembers one actor in particular, whose career was just getting started:

"A young man who had just gotten a little hot as the Marlboro Man was looking for work. He was going to a lot of interviews. I interviewed him for the lead in our show. He was very depressed because he'd been meeting a lot of people and nothing had happened.

"I remember telling him that it was going to happen for him. If not on my show it would happen on *some* show, but it *was* going to happen, so he should buck up.

"He was my choice, but he had no experience. I couldn't say it was going to happen because that's not the way leads got cast in pilots in those days. Everybody had their fingers in the pie. The actor's name was Tom Selleck."

Rumors of network executives' opinions of the show filtered down to Chermak:

"I heard that the then president of CBS thought the show was too realistic, too frightening. It was too near for being science fiction as opposed to being twenty, thirty, or forty years away. He felt that, much like *War of the Worlds,* it might frighten people and he didn't want to do that."

The end of *Battleground: Earth* came suddenly and abruptly. Chermak remembers:

"I was making the show and then one day they told me the network decided to cancel it. They gave me the reason I had already heard, the one from the president of CBS. Nobody else had any more information. I was the best man at the wedding of the head of the television division and he didn't have any more information. I never talked to Gene about it because when he got back from London it was all over."

* * *

While *Battleground: Earth* was going through its brief lifespan at Fox, Gene had packed up Majel and Little Rod and shipped out to London. The script he had written with Sam Peeples was an occult thriller called *Spectre*. While it was promoted as a movie of the week, its original inception years earlier had been as a series format.

The earliest record is a seven-page format written by Gene and dated March 14, 1972. He later credited Majel with inspiring him by her suggestion that he write a story about "the power of supernatural forces which could be present in today's society." While neither of them believed in such forces, Gene recognized a good story idea when he heard it.

The format's central character was William Quentin, a "skilled amateur criminologist, disliked by just about everyone." Quentin was a financially independent genius with a photographic memory and a disdain for social interaction. His one consuming interest was battling the supernatural. Gene closed out his character description by saying, "The concept clearly calls for an actor with balls and *style*, as contrasted with the pretty young men with Sebring hair styles cast as leads in so many series today."

The final collaborative result toned down Quentin's character a bit in range of idiosyncrasies, but true to Gene's casting requirements, Robert Culp was hired to play Quentin.

Quentin's sidekick and assistant was Dr. Peter Hamm, originally described as having a "huge Falstaffian frame, beard, and the eyes of a shrewd GP-type who makes up in human warmth for what he lacks in highly modern specialized medical knowledge. He and Quentin hate each other on sight."

This character was changed a bit, too. Gone was the Falstaffian girth and beard—the part was played by clean-shaven Gig Young—and their relationship was played as old friends who know each other too well.

There was another character in the original format: Lace, Quentin's housekeeper. Gene dropped this character and created, Lilith, especially for Majel. Majel did not play a simple housekeeper. Lilith seemed to be Quentin's resident witch, preparing potions and spells. The filmed version opens with Lilith preparing a spell that she will use to cure Dr. Hamm's alcoholism. Seconds after she opens the front door and he walks in, she snips off a lock of his hair and walks out of the room with a knowing smile on her face. Gene later said it was a mistake not to have written the character into the rest of the film.

Also appearing in this film was the noted British character actor Gordon Jackson a few years before he became the butler in *Upstairs, Downstairs.* Another fine British actor who appeared was John Hurt (before *The Elephant Man*). *Spectre* was shot in Hertfordshire, using the All Saints Pastoral Center, an old abbey, as one of the main locations, and broadcast in 1977 as an NBC Movie of the Week.

The family spent three months living in London while the film was shot; by the time they returned to Los Angeles, Gene became occupied with another large project.

Based on the strength of the *Spectre* script he had written for Twentieth Century Fox, they commissioned another. Gene returned to science fiction and pulled out all the stops. He wrote *Magna I,* a mature story of the Earth in the near future. Humanity had divided into two groups: land dwellers, dehumanized by overpopulation, governed by strict laws; and ocean dwellers, a tiny fragment of humanity who had adapted to living in harmony with and in the sea. The breakdown of the land-dwellers' life values was represented by Magna I, a gigantic atomic-powered strip mining machine.

There was intrigue, a murder mystery, plenty of social commentary and philosophy from Gene's pen, and a heartstopping duel between the hero and the gigantic machine that would have filmgoers on the edge of their seats. But only if it were made into a film, "if" being the operative word. The studio brass took one look at the story and told Gene how it was one of the most magnificent and exciting stories they had ever read. They also told him they weren't going to make it.

What Gene had written would have cost $50 million in 1976. The special effects alone wouldn't be invented for years. *Magna I* was a great story decades ahead of itself. Today, computer graphics and special effects have developed to the point where *Magna I* could be made with full justice to Gene's vision. The script sits in Majel's files, waiting for a filmmaker of hefty imagination and hefty wallet to find it and realize its potential.

* * *

Adding to the public confusion over the revival of *Star Trek* were often contradictory newspaper articles or announcements seemingly out of context.

On February 15, 1977, the *Washington Post* reported that Paramount had announced a feature film to begin filming by summer. It would have an $8 million budget and be directed by Phil Kaufman. The article quoted Harlan Ellison as saying he felt that the *Star Trek* phenomenon "is dead."

Star Trek wasn't dead, only breathing hard as Paramount executives changed their minds about the best use of the property. They had greater ambitions than a feature film. On April 18, the *San Francisco Chronicle* reported that although the studio had scrapped the film, *Star Trek* would return to television in the spring and launch Paramount's great adventure: a fourth television network. The resurrection of Gene's creation would be the centerpiece of the new network's initial offering: one evening of prime time programming per week. The show was scheduled to premiere in April 1978.

Ten days later, the *Los Angeles Times* ran a story saying that the script, being written by Bryant and Scott, needed a "significant overhaul," although the basic storyline would remain essentially intact. The film was being postponed again. Gene was quoted as saying, "If it had been just another sci-fi film, it could have been done immediately." Gene also said he was expecting a new series of ninety-minute or two-hours shows to come out of a successful film, and that he would come back on the condition he be allowed sufficient time to polish these episodes. He concluded: "The whole problem we face is that people have made more of the series than it really deserves. It has sort of become larger than life. If we just came back and tried to do one episode every six days people would be disappointed. The way to come back would be to do a number of specials."

On the third of May, Gene wrote to Asimov on *Star Trek: The Motion Picture* letterhead.

Dear Ike,
    I whipped into and out of New York a couple of times recently, and last being the IEEE Conference where I went to meet with Dr. Hal Puthoff and Russel Targ of Stanford Research Institute on the book *Mind Reach* and other papers reporting laboratory experiments in telepathy, etc. I am sort of a

practicing disbeliever in all this sort of thing, but
I keep running into aspects of it and then reports
from advanced physics theoretical people which
seem to explain why the "impossible" may be a lack
of our fully understanding all of the true nature of time
and dimension and so on.

Would dearly love to get your point of view on
such when next we can sit down together. I wanted
to see you during the last trips but they had me scheduled
so I could hardly get to the bathroom. (Not that
I place visiting you anywhere near the same
category.)

Always when I'm on these speaking things, someone
in the audience will ask the question "Who are your
favorite science fiction authors?" I think it will
please you to know that without exception whenever
your name is mentioned it results in at least a minute
of sustained applause.

The *Star Trek* movie? Next week I celebrate my
second year since having moved onto the Paramount
lot to do the movie. It has been an incredible exercise
in patience.

Rumors ... innuendo ... wishful thinking ... the final
word seemed to come on June 7, 1977, when *The San
Francisco Chronicle* reported the cancellation of the film after nine months of preparation and $500,000. Phil Kaufman
was stunned at the decision. The studio was definitely working on a "new programming concept to compete with network programming."

On May 25, 1977, a relatively low-budget science fiction
film without major stars was released. It quickly made history. It was called *Star Wars*.

On June 18, 1977, the *New York Times* reported that Paramount Pictures had announced that *Star Trek* would return
to series television with Gene Roddenberry as its executive
producer. The short article also noted that *Star Trek* was currently on 137 stations across the country and had never been
off the air since it went into syndication.

Gene plunged forward. By July 12, 1977, he had hired
several people, including Bob Goodwin as co-producer, Joe
Jennings, art director, and Matt Jefferies as a part-time con-

sultant. In a memo of the same date, Gene listed a number of other people he was about to hire, including a story editor, post-production supervisor, special effects, cameraman, and the like. Gene was gearing up, getting back into the swing of producing.

He noted in the same memo:

Pilot script should go to work soon. Recommend three stories be assigned to three writers per my memo of July 8, 1977. Writers currently being considered are:

Arthur Heinemann
John T. Dugan
Dick Nelson
Ted Sturgeon
Alan Dean Foster
Jerome Bixby
John Meredyth Lucas
Don Belasario

Star Trek lead actors availability within our budget limitations should be determined by Paramount as early as possible. Obviously, the *desirability* of Shatner and Nimoy depends very much on whether one or the other or both can be obtained. If we are faced with a choice of anywhere near equal terms, it is my opinion that Shatner is the most essential. He provides title narration, familiar voice over, and a direct "command tie" to all of *Star Trek*'s past.[12]

Per my memo of July 6, I believe that keeping Shatner as Captain allows us to cast a *new-young lead,* possibly a lieutenant commander or commander (second in command) who becomes more and more our series central character in command of landing parties, etc.[13]

Leonard Nimoy as the sole returning lead actor would work. It would mean choosing a new "Captain Kirk."

DeForest Kelley was billed in second and third season as one of the three more or less "equal" leads. (Discuss problem this could create.)

---

[12]While several executives, both studio and network, mistakenly believed the stories hinged on Spock, Gene knew that Kirk was the character charged with the exposition of the story. It harkened back to the letters Gene had exchanged with Asimov years earlier. Asimov's advice was still valid, and Gene knew it.

[13]This idea was incorporated into *Star Trek: The Next Generation* ten years later.

For the final paragraph of the memo, Gene made a recommendation that reflected his vigor as a creative individual as well as a series producer; it would have changed the face and history of *Star Trek* had this series gone forward.

> Recommend on all other actors we employ them on a seven out of thirteen basis and use this as our opportunity to promote many or most of them off the bridge and replace them with young new faces.

> GR

On July 13, Gene dropped a note to Greg Bear,[14] who had written an article in the July 10, 1977, issue of the Calendar section of the *Los Angeles Times*.

> Much enjoyed your very interesting and well written article. I really came alive when I read your statement "And while an individual might pull it off, sitting alone at a typewriter, it's almost impossible for a committee to do so." Which was, of course, our problem in trying to get a *Star Trek* motion picture off the ground. At the thought of spending eight or ten million dollars, the studio suddenly got very nervous and began second guessing every decision I tried to make.

> Things seem to be going a bit better with the project of returning *Star Trek* to television. Your overview of film and television science fiction is comprehensive and interesting. I would read or listen with great care to any comment you might have on the return of *Star Trek* to television. Obviously, many years have gone by since we made the original shows, many things have changed and we will have many very interesting decisions to make regarding continuing characters, present ages of the original group, scientific improvements in instrumentation, readouts, controls, also original theme music and many other things.

> Again, I did enjoy the article.

---

[14]Gregory Dale Bear, son-in-law of noted science fiction writer Poul Anderson, started writing SF in 1967, going full-time in 1975. The *Encyclopedia of Science Fiction* references him as "one of the dominant writers of the 1980s" and "hard to overrate in importance to the realm of hard SF and SF in general." He wrote at least one *Star Trek* novel for Pocket Books.

There was a *Star Trek* production meeting held August 3, 1977. The synopsis of that meeting gives a unique look into the development of a new series:

Roddenberry expects within the next two weeks to have 8–10 writers working on episode stories. Presently 4 writers working on the two hour concept.

Our prime concern must be the two hour show for two reasons: (1) the opening of the series; and (2) enormous amounts of worldwide potential in the first return of *Star Trek*. February 1st answer print date is vital, and the film must be superb.

Roddenberry's feeling is that the more story ideas we can get in work, including series episodes, the more we will have to choose from to include in the two hour feature. For this reason all writers are working on cut-offs, with intention to give best material to top established writer.

MDE[15] not concerned about writing costs, agreeable to whatever is necessary to insure best possible script "even if it takes a hundred or two hundred thousand dollars."

MDE stressed February 1st delivery date and concern that story must be firmed up quickly to allow sufficient pre-production. Fellows reports pre-production already under way, construction in progress but subject to delays for lack of competent personnel.

Roddenberry at this point cautioned, "We'd be kidding you if I didn't say we have some problems on the February 1st date, but we're hoping to overcome them," to which Eisner responded, "If the two hour script is good enough, three million." He made clear he is not encouraging extravagance but concerned that we meet target date and the film be "visually fabulous," with a writer who can make the characters come alive, with a terrific director and a terrific story.

Kalcheim negotiating for Shatner. Roddenberry talked with Shatner today and he does want to be in the film.

Roddenberry concerned over tailoring script to fit Shatner and Nimoy, would prefer to eliminate Nimoy to-

---

[15]Michael D. Eisner, head of the studio, later became the *wunderkind* who revitalized Disney, boosting their company value from $2 billion to $22 billion and making several hundred million for himself.

tally. MDE very strong on necessity for having both actors in the film (too great a fan following worldwide; both are *essential* to this film) and we must sign them, even at unreasonable figures. Roddenberry disagreed, based on his experience can almost promise us the excitement generated by the return of *Star Trek* with most of the original crew, aided by a publicity campaign to hype excitement over the "new, different type of Vulcan," would cancel out any disappointment over Nimoy's absence.

Eisner insisted Nimoy must be signed, even if only to appear briefly in opening scenes. This is acceptable, and even preferable, to Roddenberry and Goodwin, as a brief appearance will satisfy audience demand while allowing freedom to work with the new story and character concepts.

Nardino has an offer in to Nimoy which includes the two hour film, selected episodes, and settlement of his lawsuit against us.[16] Nardino will now place a deadline on this offer, and then return with a new offer next week separating the items and negotiating only for the two hour film at whatever price we must pay (up to triple) but the deal with Shatner must be closed first to hold his cost down. It was also understood there is no interest in Nimoy for the series, although we may have to make a pay or play PTS commitment as incentive for the two hour film. MDE feels Nimoy would accept $100,000 for 2 or 3 days work, and he would be agreeable to this figure if it becomes necessary.

MDE enthusiastic about story concept as described. (see attached)

Roddenberry again questioned February 1st urgency; at which Eisner revealed he is trying to make commitment abroad to generate money on this property before it goes to TV; date is crucial, as is quality of the film. He made clear there is only one priority at Paramount: *Star Trek* February 1st, big time movie; and has given full approval on money needed to move quickly to attain the goal. Specifically he will approve up to $3 million budget "on

---

[16]Richard Arnold, the *Star Trek* consultant, remembers that this was over merchandising and the lack of royalties from the *Star Trek* blooper reel, which was being widely disseminated on 16mm without the actors, or Gene, receiving a penny.

these conditions: terrific director, terrific writer, Nimoy and Shatner." Consideration must be given to series (projected deliver in March) but cautioned against allowing series problems/deadlines to affect the two hour film. Approval given to put 13 scripts in work now.

Discussion of Magicam process and quality relative to theatrical film. Gene Roddenberry will view and make decision. MDE will accept Magicam if it "looks good at Radio City Music Hall."

There was a small crisis in fandom that Gene had to attend to: the persistent rumor that Nimoy would not be back and Spock would not be in the film. Coupled with Paramount's vacillation on deciding what the *Star Trek* project would actually be, Nimoy's desire to get on with his life and career (Nimoy's stage acting schedule often conflicted with film shooting dates), and the lack of money coming forth from *Star Trek* merchandising, Nimoy was in no hurry to commit himself.

On October 22, 1977, Gene sent a letter to fan clubs and organizations addressed to "Fellow Nimoy-Spock Fans." Gene told them that he liked Nimoy, enjoyed working with him, and wanted him back as Spock. He made his case by stating:

Has Leonard Nimoy been offered the Spock role in *Star Trek II?* Discussions and negotiations with Nimoy to play Spock in a *Star Trek* movie and/or television show have been going on for over two years! The best evidence of my sincerity in wanting our original stars back is that I voluntarily reduced my movie profit percentage so that it could be given to Nimoy and Shatner to further induce them to do the *Star Trek* film.

In late August, Gene wrote a thank-you note to Franz Joseph Schnaubelt. He may have had a bad day at the studio when he wrote this letter, pulling no punches in his thoughts about Paramount.

Thank you for the advance copy of the *Star Trek Technical Manual.* Have only had a chance to give it a quick scan so far but it does look impressive and I wish you good luck with it.

I do have some objection to being listed with Lon Mindling and a dozen others in the "grateful appreciation" paragraph. In fact, although I have great respect for many of the names listed, I do have great objections to the creator of the basic *Star Trek* concept being acknowledged in a committee-like way. I still say this in all friendship. It may reflect a little bitterness at never having seen dollar one from any *Star Trek* merchandising, and indeed, never having even been able to get the studio to get me a list of what has been sold or any accounting on it.

As far as handling public enthusiasms or being greeted like a "celebrity," I still have so much trouble handling that whole area myself that I hardly feel capable of giving good advice. Perhaps one fact will help—*Star Trek* fans are almost always friendly, gentle, warm people. I found that you can talk honestly to them, tell them when you're tired, explain why you will do this or can't do that, and they generally are quite understanding. They will rebel if they think they are being conned, but they respond with equal fervor to honesty.

Warmest regards,

The basic *Star Trek* concept for a pilot film, as of August 3, 1977, was as follows:

Kirk is aging, and the *Enterprise* is being totally rebuilt after many years of service, incorporating the latest technological advances and designed to serve as a model for future Star Fleet ships. Kirk has been assigned a desk job in charge of the project.

At the far edge of the galaxy, approaching fast, an enormous spaceship threatens Earth—it's already destroyed several ships in its path. The new *Enterprise* construction finished but only in the initial testing stages, is the only ship with the capability of meeting this threat.

The new, younger Captain of the *Enterprise* (now the youngest Captain in the Star Fleet) is reluctant to take up an untested ship, and insists that Kirk be in command, by

STAR TREK CREATOR 481

virtue of his experience and intimate knowledge of the ship and crew.

Spock is sought and found, but is incapacitated or otherwise unable to actively participate. Kirk insists he be replaced by another Vulcan, as he has accustomed himself over the years to the unique thought processes of the Vulcan and feels this could be of critical importance in emergency situations.

A young Vulcan is found (introduced by Spock?) and subjected to much criticism and resentment from the crew, who are under the impression he has usurped Spock.

The *Enterprise* goes up, with the young Captain second in command to Kirk, and finds itself unable to control the intruder. Not until the story is half over do we become aware that this is not an invasion by aliens but by a totally new and unique life form, actually a machine—an intelligent entity with the capacity to synthesize biological forms (swarms of poisonous bees which turn out to be mechanical, etc.) possibly to the extent to synthesizing a humanoid adversary.

At some point the *Enterprise*'s computer joins forces with the machine but this is not understood—crew thinks it is malfunction of the new system, to the point of extreme jeopardy.

By some brilliant quirk of the Vulcan thought processes, our new Vulcan saves the day, the *Enterprise,* and Gene Roddenberry's reputation.

The new Vulcan was Xon, to be played by David Gautreaux, who signed a Test Option Agreement for Pilot and Series. For the pilot he would get $10,000 for four weeks, and if the show went to series, $2500 a show the first year with healthy raises thereafter. In the agreement is the standard Paramount merchandising clause stating Gautreaux would receive "5% reducible to 2½% of net profits after Paramount fees and expenses of 50%."

Persis Khambatta was to appear as Ilia for the same deal, but it was the old crew that received a pleasant increase in their salaries over the old days. Nichelle Nichols, whose name was spelled "Michele Nichols" on the agreement, would return to play Uhura and received $8000 for four weeks for the pilot, and then $3,000 a show for seven out of thirteen shows. It was a long way from the $600 a show of the first year and her day-player status of the second and third years. Nichelle, like the other regulars, would be signed to a six-year contract. DeForest Kelley also received better compensation: $17,500 for the four weeks of the pilot and then $7500 a show for the first year of the series, with a guarantee of ten out of thirteen shows. The deal memos were dated September 26, 1977. They probably looked good to the actors during the two months they remained unchanged.

By the last week of November 1977, the reincarnation of *Star Trek* had gone through yet another metamorphosis. This time it would be a feature: a big-budget feature with a big-name director, and all the bells and whistles a major studio could provide.

The late Bill Theiss,[17] Gene's friend and costume designer on the original series, remembered that the TV movie was about ten days away from going before the cameras when the word came down: "Stop!" This order would prove to be expensive.

A memo was sent on November 23, 1977, outlining financial commitments with respect to the following actors:

DeForest Kelley—We currently have a deal for a Television Pilot at a guaranteed compensation of $17,500 (for four (4) weeks services) with a November 15th start date. Attempts to convert this into a theatrical feature deal with additional series option hold money and a delayed start date have been unsuccessful.

Recommendation—Since we are now doing a feature, we probably could not hold DeForest Kelley if he objected. Further, he could also claim we did not have a series option since it is a feature. I think we should pay off the $17,500 and attempt to make a new deal to commence between March 1 and April 1 (with 30 days start notice).

---

[17]Bill Theiss was Gene and Majel's friend for twenty-five years—part of the family. Gene hired him for *Pretty Maids, Genesis II,* and *Questor*. Gene credited his friendship with Bill for helping to get him past his homophobia. Gene was one of the very few people Bill trusted with his secret, telling him in 1985 that he had AIDS. Despite this, Gene hired him to do the costuming on *Star Trek: The Next Generation*. Bill Theiss died on December 10, 1993.

I believe this will cost $40,000 (for six weeks services plus one free week) plus $2,000 for the series hold. (These sums are in addition to the $17,500 payoff.)

James Doohan—Our current deal is the same as DeForest Kelley, except the guaranteed compensation is $10,000. The problems are also the same.

Recommendation—I think we should pay off the $10,000 and make a new deal with the same start date as proposed for Kelley. I believe this will cost $17,500 for five (5) weeks plus $2,000 series hold money. (This is in addition to the $10,000 payoff.) Because the new amount of money is less than $25,000, we would have to obtain a Guild Waiver for the spread date, which I am hopeful of getting.

Persis Khambatta—The same as Doohan, with the same problems.

Recommendation—Pay off the $10,000 and attempt to make a new deal, which I believe will cost $20,000 for six (6) weeks, plus $2,000 series hold money. Same waiver problems as Doohan.

David Gautreaux—Exact situation and recommendation and anticipated new compensation as Khambatta.

George Takei, Nichelle Nichols, Walter Koenig, and *Majel Barrett*—I had originally made a deal for a television film for $8,000 guaranteed compensation for four (4) weeks with a November 15th start date. Pursuant to earlier discussion with management, I converted each deal to a theatrical deal calling for $15,000 guaranteed compensation for five (5) weeks commencing November 22, plus $2,000 in series hold money. I recommend trying to reconvert the deal to $8,000 guaranteed compensation each, paying off each, and entering into a new deal with the same start date as the other above-named performers. I believe I could make each such a deal on the same terms and conditions as the now theatrical deal (i.e., $15,000 plus $2,000 series hold).

If all these payoffs are made it will cost $79,500. The new estimated guarantee will be $157,500 plus $16,000 series hold, for a total of $173,500.

Majel remembers that the actors were paid off three times—every time the executives changed their minds—all of which would, ultimately, be charged to the feature's budget.

The variety of conflicting newspaper reports and a number of interviews done by Gene before and after the film confused many. Here is a synopsis of the history of the *Star Trek* movie project:

1. Paramount decides to make a medium-budget feature film. With sets already built, a new TV show would be the next logical step.

2. Paramount hates Gene's script and other attempts at scripts by other writers meet with no success. Paramount has doubts about the film's ability to attract an audience.

3. Fans react to news and bombard Paramount with letters. Conventions get good publicity, there is a permanent display of the *Enterprise* at the Smithsonian and the first NASA space shuttle is named *Enterprise*. Paramount becomes convinced that a movie would do good business.

4. New feature film project with Phil Kaufman as director and a bit larger budget. Problems: Gene is told he has creative control, Jerry Isenberg is told he has it, and Kaufman is told he has it. After nine months and $500,000, project gets cancelled.

5. Paramount wants to create a fourth television network using *Star Trek* as lead in, with two-hour TV movie as pilot for a series—which might be a series of ninety-minute or two-hour films, or a weekly series of one-hour programs. Discussion on both possibilities. Paramount pours lots of money into this project.

6. (a) Paramount can't get enough advertising to launch fourth network. Project collapses.

(b) *Star Wars,* followed by *Close Encounters of the Third Kind,* become huge hits.

(c) *Star Trek* would suffer in comparison as only a TV movie. Paramount commits to big-budget, wide-screen feature with major director.

There is a sharp line of demarcation in the studio world. On one side, you have features: the movie people and those who are in film—the big screen. On the other side are the, well, you know, the television people—those who make entertainment for the mass audience, the commercial market—the little screen. It is not an easy line to cross. Having done film is not enough. You have to have done film successfully, and then you can play on the adult side of the street. Gene's experience in *Pretty Maids* didn't win him any points, plus what he was doing was science fiction. Gene was aware of all this, as he said in a 1980 interview:

"George Lucas fought the same fight. He had the good fortune to have a hit motion picture behind him, and he could say, 'I'm sorry, this is the way we'll do it,' and make it stand. I could do that on a television show; I could not do that on what was, essentially, a first science fiction motion picture. I had several pictures behind me, but I never had any hits."[18]

The big director the studio wanted was Robert Wise. Wise had begun his career at nineteen as an assistant editor at RKO in 1933. By 1938, he was editing movies such as Charles Laughton's *The Hunchback of Notre Dame* (1939) and Orson Welles' *Citizen Kane* (1941). His first directing job was when he replaced Gunther von Fritsch on *Curse of the Cat People* (1944), the sequel to *The Cat People* (1942). He directed one of the classic films of cinematic science fiction, *The Day The Earth Stood Still,* as well as *West Side Story* and *The Sound of Music. The Haunting,* which he directed, is considered by many to be the finest ghost story ever filmed.

Gene was slowly moved into the background. A memo he sent to Jeff Katzenberg on March 2, 1978, suggested another executive who was negotiating with Wise thought Gene was "involved in the discussions and has been fully consulted . . ."

Gene wrote that he had not been in on any discussions regarding Wise's deal nor had he received any memos "regarding the nature and details of a proposed Wise deal. My sole information has come from three telephone conversations which you and I have had on the subject."

March 28, 1978 was a big day on the Paramount lot. The original crew of the *Enterprise* were together for the first time since the end of the series in early 1969. Gene was there, Robert Wise was there, Charles Bluhdorn, chairman of Gulf + Western was there. Chasen's, the famous Beverly Hills eatery, catered the food.

Michael Eisner, president and CEO of Paramount, made

the announcement: *Star Trek* was to return as a major motion picture with a $15 million budget. Robert Wise would direct and Gene would produce, and Leonard Nimoy would be in the film. Nimoy had found that, for a variety of reasons, he could be persuaded to don the ears once more. He had signed his contract the day before the press conference.

In an interview published after the film was released, Gene called the hiring of Nimoy a "comedy of errors." He detailed that at one time the only way the studio wanted to do the film was as a two-hour movie special and pilot of the new TV series, but that Nimoy had rightfully refused because of Broadway commitments. There never was any truth to the rumor that Nimoy had been thrown off the show. Gene always thought that Nimoy and Spock were "very important to the show;" but, with that said, Gene also thought that "none of us were absolutely essential." The casting decisions, Gene said, were "really much more sensible, businesslike decisions than rumors make them out to be."

With all his credits, talent, multiple Oscars and knowledge of movie-making, Robert Wise had one small defect that had to be corrected before he could start the film: he had never seen the original *Star Trek*.

A few weeks before, as Wise was just coming on board, the studio prepared a *Star Trek* fact sheet based on data from the November 1977 Arbitron rating service. It showed that *Star Trek* was:

> Licensed in 134 U.S. markets and 131 foreign markets.
>
> Playing 308 times a week across the U.S.
>
> In its ninth year in U.S. syndication still the #1 off-network program for men 18–49.
>
> Has increased in popularity in recent years. Since 1973, its national syndicated rating has improved 77%.
>
> In Los Angeles alone, *Star Trek* is delivering audience shares 33% higher than its initial 1969 appearance.
>
> In New York alone:
>
> More adults 18–34 watch *Star Trek* than watch *M.A.S.H.*
>
> More men 18–49 watch *Star Trek* than watch *Monday Night Football*.
>
> More teens 12–17 watch *Star Trek* than watch *One Day At A Time*.
>
> Last November, according to TVQ, the nation's largest

television popularity poll, *Star Trek* was the most popular dramatic show on all of television for men 18–49, beating all of the current network dramatic series.

Star Trek had been making money for the studio since it went into syndication. Nine years of cash flow. The studio, in its generosity, offered to screen a few selected episodes for Wise. They would only charge Gene $150 *per episode* for the cost of the projectionist and projection room. Gene was furious. He called Richard Arnold[19] and asked him to locate 16mm prints in the hands of collectors, who would be happy to help Gene for nothing.

By April 10, 1978, Gene was sending detailed analyses of the script to Wise.

The happiest decision you and I have made is that of restructuring the ending of our story. The last twenty minutes of our film, our drama and special effects climax, will take place inside V'ger.

There follows sixteen pages of Gene's thoughts on Acts 2 and 3 of the script as it stood at that moment. He ends these early comments by saying:

It is fortunate for Spock (and us) that our story involves his exorcism (really *repression*) of all but a fragment of his humanity. Machine logic communicates with machine logic—V'ger's consciousness does come close to destroying Spock. But Spock, once recovered, will slowly come to the realization of a certain barrenness in V'ger. Despite V'ger's incredible intelligence and logic, something is missing. (Helping us set up the need for a poet Decker to provide what Spock, sans his human half, could not provide.) And a slow understanding in Spock that exorcizing his human half could result in the same barrenness within himself. Is it too late? Is that capacity for passion (beauty)

---

[19]Richard Arnold was a fan who volunteered his time and expertise to Gene. Later, when Gene convinced the studio for the need of a *Star Trek* office, he hired Richard Arnold as his resident expert. Arnold's knowledge of *Star Trek* is encyclopedic.

totally gone or can he breathe [sic] spark of it into life again?

The Spock-V'ger mind-meld is the "Open Sesame!" of our story. Spock's Vulcan logic has allowed communication—and the existence of Spock's machinelike Vulcan logic allows him to convince V'ger that the *Enterprise* and the organics aboard it are integrally connected with planet Earth which Tasha has identified as the home of V'ger's "creator."

The principal problem, that of changing what was a television script into a film script, took some doing. Gene acknowledged their partial success a year after the film was released: "We had a two-hour television script, which that story was right for, rather than being given the time to ... really get the major motion picture story." Wise had his view of how the film should be made, Paramount executives had theirs, and Gene, of course, had his own vision of *Star Trek.*

Isaac Asimov was brought on as a Special Science Consultant for a fee of $5,000. Gene would later say that it was because Paramount's executives were convinced his ideas were nonsense that they wanted an outside authority to bolster their view. Asimov was sent the script and surprised the executives with his analysis. Within a month, Gene wrote to Asimov:

Dear Isaac,
  Thank you! I think they were rather flabbergasted when you saw the same elements in the story that I have been arguing about and fighting for all these months. I told them that it wasn't at all surprising since a great deal of my science fiction ideas from the beginning have come out of my reading Asimov in both science fiction and science.

  You've really eased a major burden I was carrying, and I am deeply grateful. It was a fairly rough draft you read and needs considerable improvement and clarifying, but at least now we have management accepting the direction we're going.

  I'll do more than keep an eye on them—I'll threaten them with the wrath of fandom if they break their agreement with you. I doubt they're quite sure what *fandom* really is, but with this film coming out they certainly don't want to risk offending it.

Will send you further script polishes as they come out. I wish selfishly that you were sitting here in the next office.

Warmest regards,

The Washington Post noted that Republican Senator Strom Thurmond had begun campaigning throughout South Carolina in a red, white, and blue camper named "Strom-Trek."

It is well known that the special effects were a disaster, costing the film six to nine months production time, perhaps more. The April 7, 1979 release date was moved to December after a marketing study, but that didn't ease Gene's fears. He refused the date, thinking he would not have the time to finish the film as he had visualized. With his opinion voiced, Gene was "outvoted" or overruled by the studio brass. The December date was set.

The opticals were rushed, and one former Paramount executive stated that the studio had "every special effects company in the world working on double, triple, and in some cases quadruple overtime, to get the opticals done for the December release." The $15 to $20 million film was reported to have cost $42 million. Part of that huge expense was the optical debacle, but part of it was that all the development costs for all the previous movie and TV projects were dumped into the movie budget barrel.

Adding to Gene's problems, the script was constantly being rewritten throughout the last quarter of the shooting schedule. Above all, there were additional fingers in the pie. As described by Walter Koenig:

Not only must the work be compatible with the esthetic tastes of Paramount, Robert Wise, and Gene's co-writer Harold Livingston (no doubt all of whose tastes are at some point in opposition to each other), but he must now consider the preferences of Bill [Shatner] and Leonard [Nimoy]. Due to contractual stipulations based in part on the length of the shooting schedule, the two actors now also have script approval.[20]

---

[20]*Chekov's Enterprise*, by Walter Koenig, pp. 163–164.

Script revisions were so numerous that not just the dates on the revisions were noted, but the time of day as well.

Gene and Wise worked on the film until the last minute, perhaps not finishing the film so much as simply doing as much as they could in the time permitted and then stopping. Wise flew to Washington, D.C., for the December 6 world premiere with a print fresh from the lab.

Everyone connected with the film had flown in on the morning of the sixth. Gene and DeForest Kelley had flown in earlier. The special premiere was held at the MacArthur Theater with a reception at the Air and Space Museum afterward.

Before the film was shown, Paramount personnel were gathered together and told that when the press saw them after the showing there was to be no discussion of the Robert Abel special effects fiasco; Paramount would make some statement about all that later. Everyone was ferried over to the theater in a caravan of limousines, in ascending order of cinematic importance. Gene's limo was last. It was raining.

Only Wise had seen the finished cut—none of the actors, none of the producers. As one person who attended the screening, and requested anonymity because of continuing contacts in the *Star Trek* world, related:

"The movie started up and the audience was blown away by that first scene of the Klingon ship that sort of goes under you and then the camera turns around. There were 'oohs' and 'aaahs' in the theatre. It was great! No one had seen *Star Trek* on the big screen before. It went downhill from there. After it was over there was a lot of applause for all the names as they scrawled by and then we all piled back into the limos and went over to the National Air and Space Museum.

"As we arrived at the museum a band was playing the movie music, not the original theme but the new movie theme. We went inside and they had a great spread. Everybody was being very polite, but I could just sense that people were holding back. No one really said anything that I can recall. It was a wonderful party and went on very late. Then we went on back to the Four Seasons for one final gathering and then back to our hotels and back home the next day."

If everyone was polite at the party, the critics weren't. Vincent Canby in the *New York Times* said the film was "like attending your high school class's 10th reunion at Caesar's Palace. Most of the faces are similar, but the decor has little relationship to anything you've seen before."

Charles Champlin in the *Los Angeles Times* thought it more a phenomenon than a film, "a space family reunion, fan club meeting and Thanksgiving Day parade under the same spacious roof." He did note that it was, in his experience, the only time a producer's name had drawn applause when it appeared on the screen.

David Denby in *New York* was disgusted that the producers had "spent $42 million and aimed low." He didn't like Wise's work either, saying he did not display that kind of ironic awareness or a love of the fantastic necessary to make the film more intriguing.

Harlan Ellison reviewed the film in *Starlog,* saying the film wasn't bad, but that "it is also not a good film. The saddening reality is simply that it is a dull film: an often boring film, a stupefyingly predictable film, a tragically *average* film." He ended his review saying that he hoped the film would serve as a bitter lesson to Hollywood executives, encouraging them to let the *human* adventure begin.

Gene was philosophical. For public consumption he wrote:

> I think that while the film failed in a number of areas where I would have liked it to have succeeded, it was a successful adaptation of the television story to the screen. We could have done more—and we could have done a lot less, but we did what we could under the time, conditions and circumstances—and the fact that God double-crossed us by making us fallible.
>
> I think, considering the way it all happened, we came out with a remarkably good film and I'm very pleased to have been a part of it. It could have been better—yes! I don't ever expect to make a film where I don't look back and say to myself, "Ah, I'd like to change this and this . . ."[21]

Gene was also philosophical about the critics. He wasn't upset with those who disliked the film. He thought that many of the criticisms weren't well-reasoned. As he had been friendly with Ellison, he was asked about his review.

I thought that it was an excellent review, except that Harlan, as usual, would like to escape dealing with the fact that motion pictures, like television and most entertainment today, is a blend of art and commerce. I wish Harlan's adolescent wishes . . . that money would cease to be an influence . . . I wish they would come true. But [that wish] is not the real world that we live in.

I had many, many opportunities on *Star Trek* to say, "If you keep doing it this way, I will take my name off the picture and I will walk out mad." And I would have walked out very early in the thing had I done that. But you can't get things made that way. You don't walk because investors need to know that their money is being used in some way they can relate to. I wish this were a better world, in which people pressed money on artists and said, "Go out and be an artist, I'll invest in that." This just doesn't happen that often. Everyone can't take this adolescent attitude, which makes it very easy to be bold and brave and right.[22]

Privately, Gene exchanged thoughts with a few friends. In early January 1980, Gene heard from Asimov who had just seen the film:

Janet and I were unable to see *Star Trek: The Movie* on the night for which the tickets you sent us were good.

However, we finally saw it yesterday on our own and enjoyed it very much.

I must tell you that however much it pleased me to see all the old friends of the *Enterprise,* the character who won me over was Baldy.

I came in with an invincible prejudice and told Janet there was no way I would find myself sympathetic with a billiard-ball female Kojak, and long before the picture was over, she was all I was waiting for. She was beautiful.

So was my name, correctly spelled, moving up the screen. I applauded wildly.

Isaac Asimov

Gene responded a few weeks later.

---

[22]*Ibid.*

Dear Isaac:

As you have discovered with "Baldy" I am much shrewder than you vis-a-vis the human female and what makes her excite us. I bow to you in all other areas of science and art.

I still chuckle when I remember Paramount going secretly (they thought) to you in order to get expert proof that Crazy Gene was talking nonsense by insisting that machines could be alive and that there might be more dimensions to the universe than those we presently know. It was all made doubly funny by the fact that so much of my thought and theory on such things came out of reading Asimov. I'll never forget the day that one of Paramount's young vice presidents came to my office with an astonished expression on his face as he reported that you agreed with most of the story points I had been fighting for. Ah, I'd like to have back all the energy wasted on such fights during the last four years of trying to get this film started and completed.

It seems to be going well at the box office. I was not completely happy with the final cut of the film as I thought some of the optical effects went on too long at the expense of character things which were deleted in order to accommodate them. On the other hand, Robert Wise, Doug Trumbull, et al. did a remarkable job in the time they had, and I suppose I should be content. In fact, in newsprint I do report myself content, but between you and me there remains the wish that they had let STAR TREK'S creator have a final look at the film before it was rushed to theaters.

Gene's uncle on his mother's side, Albert Golemon, sent him an article from the *Houston Post,* showing the gross receipts of the film at $17,060,837 for the first week of release. Gene wrote back:

We had mixed reviews across the country, some hating us and some loving us, which is about the way *Star Trek* has always gone. Fortunately, the audience makes up their own minds, and we have set box office records across the country, and much the same

is happening overseas. Let's hope it continues on into
a net profit situation. At about $100 million I should
begin to see something back.

It has taken me about five weeks since our Washington
premiere to begin to unwind a bit. I was on the
picture for so many years that it seems strange to sit
around and feel rested.

Early in February Gene answered a letter from a friend
with whom he was comfortable.

Lately, have found myself wandering more and more
often to my desk and making a note about this or that;
my reading appetite is beginning to turn from light
fiction back again to more thoughtful things; all
the other signs of wanting to go back to work are
returning too.

My next move will probably be a novel or maybe
even a couple of them, perhaps one Star Trek
(designed for a sequel movie) and the other something
else entirely different. I am a storyteller who has gotten
a bit tired of having to always tell my stories
through directors, actors, studio policy decisions,
and etc. Not that I intend at all to give up television
and film, and I may be into one or the other within
a week of two if certain offers get too good to
resist. But a change would be nice.

Most criticism Gene just shrugged off or paid little attention to. An exception was an article in an early February issue of *The Christian Science Monitor*. Their daily religious
article of February 11, 1980, commented on *Star Trek: The
Motion Picture*. The column said, "Something in us does
want to transcend the restrictions of space-time and matter.
Something does want to expand and know without limitation. Can this yearning be fulfilled by supertechnology and
unlimited material knowledge, as the movie implies?"

Gene wrote, saying simply, "It seems to me that your
writer missed the point of the film's comment: 'The Human
Adventure is Just Beginning.' "

Three years later, Gene wrote the most insightful and candid letter we have regarding his thoughts and feelings about
the film. The letter was to Jungian scholar Karin Blair, liv-

ing in Switzerland. She was the author of the book, *Meaning in Star Trek*. On May 10, 1983, Gene wrote the following:

I never responded properly to your unusual and perceptive *Meaning in Star Trek* book. Oh, I'm sure I said proper nice things when it appeared, and I had given it two fast readings. Unfortunately, never did I find the leisure in those days (or, more importantly, the inner peace) to give your book the kind of study and thought and hopefully creative responses that it richly deserved.

You have spoken or written sometimes of having to struggle through periods of adjustment or readjustment to this or that and I really never knew fully what people meant by such statements. I think my personality probably features a high degree of adaptability and therefore I never felt much stress in life as I went from combat aviation to commercial airlines to amateur writer to cop to pro writer, to producer and quite a number of little byways during all that. I have always sort of expected exciting good things to happen and even felt that way about *Star Trek*'s success and then its fan phenomenon. I still feel that way and am wondering which among several new things is going to be *the* new excitement in store for me.

However, it probably will interest you that a considerable and very nearly traumatic "period of adjustment" began happening to me some time after your *Meaning In Star Trek* came out, and it accounts for my seeming to drop out of yours and almost everyone else's sight.

My producing of the first Star Trek movie, *Star Trek: The Motion Picture* was not a happy experience. The main problem was probably that I did not see clearly how different my relationship with the property would be in making it a motion picture film. As you know, in a television series like ours it is the writer-producer or executive producer (which in TV usually means "supervising producer") who is the *creative* head of the project. Directors come and go in TV and at most can only do one out of four or five episodes and creative leadership naturally becomes the provenance of the supervising writer-producer (whatever his/her title) who is there on the show constantly and can maintain continuity of the characters and the show's style and format.

Although I had produced motion pictures before, and knew that the director has creative control in them, I had problems with "my" *Star Trek* being placed into someone else's hands. Even then our director Robert Wise was experienced, four Oscars, quiet and gentlemanly, and I think we probably would have eventually worked it out, even though theatrical films and television are *very* different animals from which the audiences expect surprisingly different kinds of satisfaction. Free from interference I think our combined abilities would have resulted in quite a picture.

Paramount Studios made this impossible. We found ourselves stuck with an optical house through which Paramount was draining millions out of our budget for God knows what future optical arrangement with the—[sic] and it was unfortunately an optical house which never ever turned in an optical within a year of its due date. Clearly, in someone's eagerness to make an arrangement with this optical company, the usual routine check on that company's delivery history was neglected.

Paramount by then had accepted over $20 million in advances from theaters by promising a delivery date which the optical effects hassle made impossible. Worse, that first *Star Trek* movie was actually never really finished. The director even had to deliver it without even the usual trial audience screening, something which is unheard of in our industry. Meanwhile, optical experts from all over the world had worked around the clock into golden, double golden, even quadruple golden time, adding [millions] to the picture's cost—and even at that the ticket grosses have by now paid it all back.

As I said earlier, an unhappy experience. Wise and his people somehow got the picture together with sufficient surprise effects and big screen excitement and gloss for the audience to believe they had seen a finished motion picture, maybe not the *Star Trek* they had hoped for but with enough familiar faces

and excitement cleverly whipped together to make
the film at least "acceptable."

People now and then ask me why I wrote that particular
story or why I had or had not written this or that into
the script, oblivious to the fact that the story and the
script were written by other people at Paramount's
insistence that we use "experienced screenwriters"
rather than a mere television writer for a project of
that size.

So, as well as an apology for not responding to
your book as deserved, you have the "behind the
scenes" history. It did not live up to the *Star Trek* you
knew. As for whether this story is confidential, I ask
only that you refrain from quoting me or indicating
I am the source of your information. The reason
for this is simple and understandable—I will soon be
going into court against Paramount on many issues
which date back to the original television series
and their continued insistence that the television
show has never made a profit, from which I was supposed
to have received one-third share.[23] My attorneys want
nothing said that indicates I might be questioning
their bookkeeping.

Re the "period of readjustment" which started this
story, it became clear after the experience of the first
movie that I could not allow myself to be so closely
involved with the making of new *Star Trek* movies
and I will confine myself to a not unprofitable Executive
Consultant role in them.

Realizing then that I had to get *Star Trek* "off
my back" having been with it a couple of decades,
it was difficult not to be fiercely protective and worried
about what might happen to it in strange hands
representing different attitudes and values. Finally,
I did manage to adjust to that and my energies are
now centered on new things.

---

[23] Actually 26⅔ percent of the net.

CHAPTER 16

The years of working and battling to see his vision on screen had taken their toll. It took some months for Gene to decompress. Early in February 1980, he dropped a note to his friend, producer Eugene B. Rodney. For years, he and Rodney had shared laughs over the confusion brought about by the similarities of their names.

Dear Gene,
 Glad you were able to see the movie and please take all the credit you can get. After all, I spent years living off of your reputation. Now and then a friend will still come up to me and ask if I would be offended by knowing that they liked my *Father Knows Best* better than *Star Trek*. I invariably tell them that I also enjoyed it the most.
 I was fairly well pleased with our "Star Trek" film, although I never did get a chance to put my own touch on the final post production of it. Our schedule was simply too tight and I knew that Bob Wise would give me a good film even though it might not be exactly how I would have done it in every way. In fact, the schedule was so tight that we never got a chance to get it in front of a preview audience—if we had, a couple of fairly dull optical sequences would have been trimmed down considerably. Perhaps we'll do a recut and re-release late this year.

At the same time, he wrote to his longtime friend in Scotland, Janet Quarton, with whom he had corresponded for years and whose opinion he valued.

> . . . I consider the new uniforms a bit too "militaristic" and, indeed, talked Bob Wise out of using a lot of the highly military uniforms that had been prepared. The short-sleeved white top and some others were invented after I had complained that the whole thing was getting to look a bit Prussian.
>
> At least it remained *Star Trek*. However, I think we would have had a better film if schedules had been arranged so that the originator of *Star Trek* had had a chance for a final look and some final comments.

Gene had written the novelization of the motion picture and it was well received, appearing on the *New York Times* bestseller list for six months. He sent a copy to Robert A. Heinlein, then the dean of science fiction writers. Heinlein wrote back:

> I have read only the two prefaces, the first chapter, your most warmly pleasing inscription, and your note. But I do not agree that "one book doth not a novelist make." It is possible that you may never again take the time to write a novel, since you are deeply involved in another form of storytelling.
>
> 24 hrs later—I have now read your book. Whew! Gene, it's terrific! Above, I was about to say something to the effect that a novelist hardly ever becomes one gradually, etc. But all that is now academic; this yarn speaks for itself. It hooks on the very first page and the tension mounts throughout to the very last page . . . and there, with the plot fully solved, you play us out with music and the knowledge that the action still continues, on and on, out and out farther, to the end of Time. I am delighted.
>
> (And I have never before seen "deus ex machina" used literally.)
>
> Congratulations,
> Robert

Star Trek: The Motion Picture had grossed nearly $180 million worldwide, including $5 million paid by ABC to televise it. That was enough to convince the power structure at Paramount that a sequel was mandatory.

In mid-1981, a taped message from Gene was played at a New York convention. Gene laid it on the line, saying that he was not given creative control so would not ask for executive producer credit to which he was contractually entitled. He would become an "executive consultant." It was a nice title—a way of associating his name with the film project.

The studio was still smarting over the massive costs of the first film. Rightly or wrongly, a large portion of the responsibility had been dumped on Gene. *Star Trek* was Gene's child and, perhaps, he was overly protective and overly concerned about the quality of the final product, at least in the studio's eyes. *Star Trek* was a product to the studio, a very profitable product, a product that should be produced at the lowest possible cost in order to maximize earnings.

They brought in a new producer: Harve Bennett. It was a slap in Gene's face, as Bennett was a *television* producer with no feature experience. An article in the *San Francisco Examiner and Chronicle* in June 1982, reported that Bennett would understand how to find "economic shortcuts" and still produce a successful product.

He was publicly disdainful of the first film, "My kids kept asking to go to the bathroom and to buy popcorn,"[1] but did watch all seventy-nine episodes of the original series.

Bennett would later say about his contribution to the *Star Trek* franchise:

> In those days, in order to succeed with a series, you had to deliver 20 million people. "Star Trek" never did that so it got canceled. But it delivered fifteen, fourteen, ten. Well, that was enough to support it in syndication during the seventies. You could find your favorite "Star Trek" on every channel off network. Great. All the same people who loved it stayed with it. *Star Trek: The Motion Picture* almost killed it. It depressed the syndication, it depressed

everything. So if I have made a contribution, it was to have resuscitated a beached whale.[2]

To put things in proper perspective, Bennett was once characterized by a writer friend of Gene's as someone "who always had to take credit [by saying] 'I saved this or we wouldn't have that if I hadn't done this.'"

Nicholas Meyer was signed as director. In an article in the *New York Times,* Meyer was described as someone who had never seen the original series, was not a science fiction fan, and knew nothing about special effects. He did, however have one thing: the producer was confident in his abilities.

Gene remained true to his word and stayed in the background, giving his opinion, as was his prerogative as executive consultant.

Gene's files tell the story. There are several storage boxes holding material from the first film. The amount of material generated by his consulting diminishes with each successive film. By *Star Trek VI: The Undiscovered Country,* there was less than half a small storage box of material, mostly scripts and script revisions.

A memo sent from Gene to Bennett on September 29, 1981, regarding consultant duties and script comments may suggest the level of their relationship.

Responding to your note received yesterday, your language seemed to imply that I am being somehow delinquent in my *Star Trek* Consultant duties. I find this rather puzzling. I received the script only a week ago, accompanied by a buckslip saying simply: "Please get back to me." I have received no information of any kind from you or your people on production schedules, shooting dates or on anything else pertaining to the show. Having gone so many months without any news and with no requests for any kind of advice, I thought I could safely take a week to study the script and to prepare my comments.

Having been further surprised today by the arrival of the revised script, I am now hurriedly comparing white page notes against blue page revisions which means that only part of my comments can be appended to this memo.

[2]*Captain's Log: William Shatner's Personal Account of the Making of Star Trek V,* by Lisabeth Shatner. (New York: Pocket Books, 1989).

Most of the rest of them will be sent tomorrow. A few will have to be sent later in the week because I am awaiting advice on what my position should be if certain areas of advice are rejected. Let me add that I am not seeking problems and see no reason they cannot be easily avoided.

I don't want to quarrel with you, Harve, and in fact am much pleased by the very considerable improvements made in this script version. I have also heard how diligently you have studied the old television episodes and I think such effort is praiseworthy. But let's be honest with each other by not letting it be even implied that I have shirked any advisory responsibilities. You have never requested nor even made it possible for me to act in any way as "Executive Consultant" on this movie. Or even as "Infrequent Advisor." You did not ask for my comments on the story, always a critical stage in science fiction production; neither did not ask for my comments on the writer selected, although I have had long professional experience with him; we never discussed the director other than your calling me the day before his name was announced. Although I may have sometimes wondered if you could not have profited from at least some of my experience, I am neither embarrassed nor annoyed over the way you clearly preferred for it to be. You are the man running the *Star Trek II* movie and I accept your right to run it your way.

As to the responsibilities that go along with all that, I do believe you have inherited certain obligations concerning the effects of the show's philosophies, particularly on young people. My position is that I consider certain things in the script to be fairly unimportant, for example starship terminology, using the established names for shipboard things, and so on. Nice if you could keep that continuity going, since it pleases people who know the show, but it won't destroy the movie if you decided not to do these things.

Then there are the more important established things which probably *will* affect the film's success, since they were part of what made *Star Trek* so successful. Examples of these are things like the fact Starfleet was always very clearly a *paramilitary* organization, and you may remember that both our title narration and our story plots placed great emphasis on exploration and seeking new life and new civilizations as the starship's *primary* functions.

If *Star Trek* slides into becoming just a routine "space battle show" (an SF form which the critics now consider "tiresome"), then I have no doubt but that *Star Trek* will slide downhill rapidly. In this case, I am doubly concerned because I have an interest in this property remaining valuable.

However there are some areas of script comment which I consider the most important of all—examples of these are things like *Star Trek*'s avoiding the use of violence in story solutions, maintaining the importance of the Prime Directive, continuing our reminders that to be different does not mean something is ugly or to think differently does not mean that someone is necessarily wrong.

It seems to me that there is something very decent and very necessary in saying such things to people, especially today. It is especially in these areas that I wish we had more opportunities for discussion.

Again, I am neither angry nor offended and sincerely wish you the best in producing an entertaining and successful *Star Trek II*. I hope our script comments will prove helpful.

Gene and Bennett's relationship was not helped when Gene's longtime secretary, Susan Sackett, revealed publicly at a convention in England that Spock was going to die in *Star Trek II*,[3] and die in the film's first fifteen or twenty minutes. Everyone had been under strict orders to say nothing about the film's plot when Sackett spilled the beans to the fans.

Bennett was furious. He called Gene, and as one person who was privy to the exchange described it, "read Gene the riot act." Bennett wanted Sackett fired immediately, but Gene was not the person to take orders from someone like

---

[3]The film was first called *The Undiscovered Country,* which was changed to *The Revenge of Khan.* At that time, Twentieth Century Fox was preparing *The Revenge of The Jedi.* The two studios battled over the two "Revenge" movies, threatening each other with lawsuits. Eventually titles on both films were changed.

Harve Bennett, especially orders to dismiss part of his staff no matter how well deserved or justified the order might have been. Gene did have a rancorous discussion with Sackett moments after he hung up from Bennett.

The information disclosed by Sackett in England circulated in the *Star Trek* community close to the speed of light. A group known as Concerned Supporters of *Star Trek* came into being overnight. They conducted a survey to determine the fans' opinion of Spock's death and how much money Paramount would lose if it were carried through. A quarter-page ad in an industry trade paper was taken out, and Paramount was publicly informed that should Spock die it would cost them $28 million. This story made the front page of the *Wall Street Journal* in early October.

The fans and the media would not let the story die any more than they would let Spock die. On the twenty-third of December, *Star Trek* fandom had the ultimate "fanzine" for a day when the *New York Times* ran a brief editorial pleading the case for Spock's life: "The cool and deliberate Mr. Spock is a man of peace and we can ill afford to lose him."

Gene understood that actors do not like to continue in roles forever. In the *Wall Street Journal,* he said that there were alternatives, and "in science fiction there are ways of handling things like this to make it appear Spock is dead, but still leaving some future options . . . It's a bit unfair for someone to kill off a character I created."

Gene was forced to write a letter sent in response to protest letters addressed to him.

Dear Friends:

    I cannot imagine what gave you the idea that I have anything to do with the idea of killing off Mr. Spock of *Star Trek.* The truth is that I am doing everything in my power to prevent it. . . .

    In this second movie, we have had to face the fact that Leonard Nimoy no longer wants to play Spock. Our information is that Nimoy believes that the admittedly powerful Spock image interferes with his career, and he will play Mr. Spock in this movie only if the Spock character is destroyed and permanently eliminated from *Star Trek.* Paramount and the producer of the movie appear to have granted Leonard Nimoy's request, and the latest script still shows Spock being killed. I am making an effort to secure a rewrite in which the Spock character is not permanently destroyed, and my recommendation, in deference to Nimoy's wishes, is that Spock can seem to have been killed but with a science fiction possibility left that he may still one day reappear. Although I can understand how the Spock image troubles Nimoy, I believe that it is foolishly wasteful to permanently destroy this key character (and a bit unfair to me as Spock's initial creator).

As you may know, I have elected not to be the producer of this new *Star Trek* film, but am serving as consultant. In that role, I can only recommend to Paramount and the producers that they do *not* destroy the character that has become *Star Trek*'s "trademark." Even if Nimoy never plays Spock again, I think it would be wonderful years from now to see *Star Trek* come back with an equally talented new cast playing Spock and Kirk and Bones and Scotty and all the rest as they say tomorrow's things to tomorrow's generations.

The plans were redone and Spock did not die until the end of the film, leaving the possibility open for his resurrection in the next film.[4]

There was a small inside joke in the final filmed version shared at the time by only two people. Gene's old friend Sam Peeples wrote an early script of *The Wrath of Khan*. While his work was completely rewritten, there was a tiny bit of him left in the final version.

Sam Peeples:

"If you see the *Wrath of Khan*, when we go toward the other galaxy the name of it is *Mutara*. What we've done was pay tribute to Edgar Rice Burroughs by pulling a unique fictional name out of his work and planting it in a new story."

---

[4]What was written in an original draft, as reported in *Starlog* of March 1983, had Spock killed in the first third of the film. Meyer had suggested that Spock die in the film's opening sequence, and Bennett had considered total annihilation of the crew. Public pressure was brought to bear and Bennett helped rewrite the script.

On July 30, 1982, Gene dropped a line to Janet Quarton, discussing *Star Trek II*.

> As you have no doubt seen by now, many of the problems you and I found in the script were hidden or quickly glossed over in the film, which has become quite successful and has many fans comparing it favorably with the original television series. Whether or not you and I completely agree with this, it is a fact that the film is making lots of money, and that fits in neatly with the value systems of Paramount and those involved in the film.
>
> I think they did a pretty good job. A brilliant job? In making *Star Trek* work in a motion picture, possibly yes. In finding a way to stay true to *Star Trek* values, definitely not. It will be interesting to see what happens on *Star Trek III*.
>
> Meanwhile, while your letter includes a number of points I would like to discuss with the producers of any new movie, I will try to be patient since no one will hear a word I say so long as the box office keeps yielding dollars. Unfortunately, that is what rules most people in this industry. On the other hand, films like *E.T.* do happen, and so all is never completely lost, and anything is always possible.

Well after *Star Trek II* was released, Gene wrote to Julien Roddenbery, telling him that he had given firm instructions to his lecture agent to book him near Cairo, Georgia, so he could visit. He also supplied Julien with the answer fans everywhere wanted to know:

> Yes, you are right that I did win my battle concerning "Mr. Spock" of *Star Trek*. Although he seems to die in the last movie, you can be certain he will be revived in *Star Trek III*. It was not too difficult to do this since neither the actor nor the studio were able to turn their backs on the rich profits they could expect to derive from that character in the future. The almighty dollar is the sole ruler in Hollywood, as unfortunately it is in so many other places. Since I believe otherwise, most studios tend to consider me some kind of dangerous radical.

From whom can I order some Roddenbery peanut butter? *Please,* this is not a hint for some free samples. It is simply a fact that the stuff I get from the store shelves here is not nearly as good as what comes from down in the Roddenbery home area.

Since early 1981, Gene had been sporadically working on a new novel. He had been heartened by Heinlein's comments on his first book, which spurred him into the second effort.

In February 1983, after spending a relaxing ten days in La Costa working on the book, Gene wrote to his friend Rupert Evans in England. In his letter, he explained how, with the help of his novel, he had managed to put *Star Trek* into proper perspective.

I have been enjoying my solitude and some very heavy writing down there, including diet, regular exercise, and things like that. The last few times I checked my head, it seems to be sitting up there as if it's finally set firmly and straight.

1982 was not the best of all possible years. Nor was it for a lot of friends although we probably should be grateful for the good things interspersed with difficult times. For me, it was a year of finally and definitely exorcising *Star Trek* from my life. Oh yes, I admit to having been the father and am delighted when an "Executive Consultant" movie credit replenishes the old bank account, and I'm still delighted when it gets me an invitation to some event at Jet Propulsion Lab, or an extra airlines cocktail, or a good seat in a restaurant. What I mean about "exorcising" it is that the show is simply a remembered thing now but no longer forms any part of my day-to-day planning or work.

It wasn't easy since I had, after all, been intimately connected with it for some 17 years. Now, finally, I can contemplate Paramount and others creating some horror out of it without feeling the slightest chill myself. Or, equally important, I can also wish them all good luck (as indeed I do!) and hope they

find a motion picture format formula which makes
it a bigger than ever success—I feel absolutely no
jealousy at that thought. My *Star Trek* is in the past
and I feel terribly good about that, realizing that
putting it there has also lifted a heavy weight from
my shoulders.

Gene called his novel *Report From Earth,* and the form it
took illustrates a method of creation in which Gene had
great proficiency. Every writer of fiction has his or her own
way of creating characters and plot: some writers meticu-
lously outline, others simply begin and let their characters
carry them forward. Asimov's wife once walked into his
study and saw him staring off into space. Asking him what
he was doing, he replied that he was "listening to his characters talk."

Gene could become the characters. In working out Spock,
he was able to pose questions and "Spock," lurking somewhere in Gene's subconscious, would come forward and answer.

The central character of Gene's novel was Gan (later
changed to Gaan), an alien who had come to Earth and taken
human form in order to study humans and their culture.
Gaan had a completely different chemistry and so was not
connected to earth in any way: he was totally alien.

As Gene explained in a letter to Janet Quarton:

The hardest part about the book is probably the final
decision to accept no TV or movie assignment till I
got into it and got it done. There *is* a bit of a
financial risk because I have no guarantees that
anyone will publish it or want to buy a copy of it,
but it very much *feels* like the right thing to do.

I spent the first month or so getting to know the
character, where he (I should say "it" since they
are not a bisexual species) came from, what kind of
planet it was, what type of society, what other creatures
live there and so on, much of which will probably
never appear in the manuscript.

Gene described, through the facility of his well-trained
imagination, how Gaan saw our world, seeing it without the

millions of little prejudices and assumptions we all carry. It was the perfect platform for Gene to use for one of his favorite exercises: social commentary.

Gene expanded on his thoughts to Rupert Evans:

> Because of the opportunity to comment on major questions, I first thought of the book as sort of a collection of essays by him on various things he runs into here. But the value of spending that time analyzing it and working formats out, is that you also have a chance to think it through to the end and realize that essays are really dull stuff, however clever one thinks himself. So the direction finally decided upon is adventure—and can thereby make things much more adventurous than putting one's consciousness into the dominant life form on a planet somewhere without really knowing very [much] about the dangers there, the customs, or even the kind of food they eat. In comparison, Robinson Crusoe's island adventure was a Sunday picnic, or at least that is how I hope to make it seem through using suspense, mystery, humor and all the things that help any adventure work.
>
> My aim, then, is to follow Gan's adventures here which begin with such moments as his learning that life form nourishment on this planet is a process of *everything trying to eat everything else!* There's another little shock due for him when Gan (a unisexual creature) learns that in the human reproductive system here it takes *two* of them working in very strange and frantic cooperation. Also, having a perfectly duplicated body, he begins to discover that he has inherited certain of its drawbacks too.
>
> ... My only feeling now is one of absolute enchantment over the fact that I can write this any way I wish, without any thought of meaningful censorship or production budgets, directors, actors, or anything else like that. Just me and my thoughts and my word processor.

The Wrath of Khan had done well at the box office; *Star Trek III: The Search for Spock* was under development. Gene wrote to Janet Quarton on January 5, 1983:

> Also, finding and agreeing on the right story for *Star Trek III* is demanding a lot of time now. And we have some very complicated acting demands to work out.

Leonard Nimoy would direct the film. Gene sent a letter to Nimoy on May 20, 1983.

Dear Leonard,

Wanted to get this to you before a ST III second draft arrives. At that time, as was my practice on ST II, I will feel obliged to channel communication to you through the producers.

I'm writing this mainly to make your job easier by removing any possibility of doubt over how I might see my role. So let me assure you that I have no intentions or desire to be anything but consultant. Interesting that we both have had a similar struggle, you with Spock and me with *Star Trek*—and apparently we have both shaken our individual monkeys off our backs and into reasonable perspective. I see our TV-ST relationship as having happened on a different project in another era, a past which should not be allowed to affect our present roles and relationship. I see it as only sensible for me to want ST III to become as great a success as possible, and within the limits of my consultant role you will find me committed to helping make that happen.

As you probably know, I was not enthused at the proposal that you become the director. Another reason for this letter is to assure you that my attitude had nothing to do with our past disagreements or misunderstandings, whatever they were. My concerns were whether you had sufficient experience for a project of this size and whether your special relationship with our show, plus your very intimate struggle with the Spock character, and your deep friendship with Bill might create too many difficulties—all this in the face of problems that Paramount executives can sometimes cause in artistic and creative areas.

Now that you are the director, I accept it fully. In fact, as usually happens between professionals in our strangely wonderful business, I see many reasons to be enthusiastic over your being there. My only feelings toward you now are those of a hearty congratulation and every good wish for a great success which will establish a high reputation for you in the field of film direction too.

My Executive Consultant role, as I understand the agreement, is not complicated. I am supposed to be shown as early as possible every step in making the film from story outline to final cut which could have any effect on the *Star Trek* format and image. I will also make myself available any other time that you or the producers believe my experience or knowledge may be helpful. My comments will be made in written form and I will ask Harve to make all my memos immediately available to you. In turn, you and the producers are free to accept or reject my advice, presumably after having given it reasonable consideration.

In return, I would appreciate being informed as soon as possible whenever any major recommendation has been rejected so that I can adjust my comments accordingly. I do not want to seem to be nagging away at items which have ceased to be applicable, but neither do I want any good advice to go down the drain because my point was made so unclearly that it was misunderstood.

. . . I believe it is important for you to know that my present Executive Consultant position is of my own choice, reflecting my discovery on *Star Trek: The Motion Picture* that my only interest in our business is in having or sharing some meaningful control of the creative process, and that to acquire this as a producer requires more maneuvering and strife than I care to go through all over again a second time on *Star Trek*. Although my original and basic ST contract gives me the unconditional right to produce and write any *Star Trek* theatrical films that are made, I prefer this present arrangement and hope it remains permanently the best alternative.

This new ST film should be thought of as the director's, actors', producers', and key production specialists' show. I have no need to use it for increased personal credit or visibility and would prefer most of that to go to you and your people. I expect only the reasonable respect and credit which equates with my smaller and different contributions to the film.

... It is my hope that on this one everyone will finally lock in on a proper ST film format and make by far the best one of all.

Very sincerely,

Gene had become friends with a few fans with whom he corresponded on a regular basis. One was Maria Muhlmann of Hawaii, who sponsored a series of lectures at the university. In the early part of 1983, he spoke his mind in a letter to her.

Please don't feel sad about my pulling back a bit from *Star Trek*. I will still be there on every film as Executive Consultant, and, as a matter of fact, only a few days ago did a rewrite for them on an hour Leonard Nimoy special which will probably be titled: *Leonard Nimoy—Memories of Star Trek*.[5] Although he has given me little reason to be fond of him personally, I never withhold help and assistance from that part of him which is the "Nimoy who is Mr. Spock in *Star Trek*." I deal with that part of him as a separate entity which is important to *Star Trek*.

The above one hour special is not a bad job, and I think you'll probably enjoy it if it gets shown over on your television stations there. I was brought in to rewrite it because in the first draft he tended to ignore contributions of the production office and me, and was not entirely honest about whose idea it was for Spock to die. I gave him a rewrite in which he did not have to confess that it was his idea but had him merely admit that an actor gets tired of continually playing the same character and that he was "tempted" when he saw the powerfully written death scenes. Then I have him refer to the fact that Bennett and I rewrote it so there was a possibility that Spock might come back alive and have Nimoy say: "And the Mr. Spock in me was greatly relieved at this." Not the whole truth, but close enough to the truth to satisfy me and to keep the "Nimoy who

---

[5]Ultimately named *Leonard Nimoy's Star Trek Memories*.

plays Spock in *Star Trek*" from being called a liar
by his fans. *Compromise* is, after all, much
recommended by the great Ben Franklin as a handy
lubricant in keeping human affairs moving smoothly.

In late March, Gene wrote to his granddaughter Tracey
Lewis:

You have been born in an *absolutely wonderful time*
in which females are considered absolutely equal with
males (which they always have been but a lot of
people didn't notice), and you can go out into this
world and be anything you want to be—and you will
discover you want to be a lot more than just beautiful,
embraceable, danceable, etc. etc. etc.

I am writing a book, a novel, about an
extraterrestrial visiting here from another planet although
it is based on something I did years before the movie
"ET" came out and am afraid my character isn't
quite that cute. In fact, my character has a human
body since he belongs to a life form who is able to
"manufacture" any kind of body on any kind of planet
they want to visit. Once it is manufactured, they
simply put their *consciousness* into that body's
brain and use it just like it was their own. Maybe that
does not sound too exciting but believe me it is pretty
exciting for my character who knows nothing at
all about human bodies or Earth or our civilization
and anything else about this place. It will take me at
least the rest of this year to get it finished—*if* I work
hard at it.

In mid-April, Gene wrote to a friend then in France:

Your "no strings" story idea was very interesting
but Paramount and their Executive Producer Harve
Bennett were already deep into a story going other
directions. They were not even interested in the fact
that I had one. I endure those things because of having
put Star Trek behind me—something I did in another
portion of my life—something that will go on in

a slightly different form because slightly different
kinds of people are in charge of it now.

I will continue as "Executive Consultant" which
I wrote you, this means simply that everything that
is written or filmed or edited will have to be run past
me for my comments but it does not obligate them
to follow any of my suggestions. As far as my
suggesting a scientific advisor, they feel no obligation
to listen to me in these areas either. In fact, they have
made it clear they would go out of their way to
avoid using anyone whom I endorsed for any aspect
of *Star Trek.*

If the above has done nothing else, it has at least
freed me from *Star Trek*—at least from the current
Star Trek.

In May, Gene was off lecturing on a schedule that wore on
him, as he noted in a letter to Lois Roddenberry in Berkeley,
in response to her request for tickets to his talk at San
Francisco's Jung Institute.

As far as any other free time goes, the Jung Institute
people have a couple of prominent science fiction writers
who are hosting me and have set such a tough
schedule already that I have asked to be relieved
of some of it in order to get badly needed rest between
appointments and interviews. Lois, I am exhausted!
My agency sent me on too much touring this year
and I am counting the seconds to get home from
this one at which time I plan to disappear into my
hideout for a Spartan regime of diet, exercise, rest and
just a couple hours a day work on my novel. Ain't
gonna see nobody! Not till I get that old bounce
back in my step.

In early July, Gene was sick and took the time to write to
Julien Roddenbery in Cairo, Georgia:

I retreated here last month to fight off a stubborn
influenza bug. Treated myself successfully it seems,
with diet, exercises and hot baths and am now a

bit trimmer and feeling fit again. The thing most hateful about being sick is that when I feel "blah," my writing looks that way too.

The bug also fouled up my schedule and it appears I will have to spend the summer months catching up with obligations here. My wife Majel has our son Rod in camp, hoping it would free us for a trip there (Cairo) and we're both sorry we have to delay it. However, a good date appears to be coming up. Am scheduled to give the keynote address to a computer corporation convention September 9 and a very convenient time to drop in on you would probably be a few days later. The convention is in New Orleans which delights Majel who loves the food and the city—so it should be easy to seduce her into a trip at that time.

As for golf, I have given up playing while sick and will probably stay away from it until my novel gets back on schedule. Majel, however, can hardly be kept off the courses and you had best warn male and female alike that she's a tiger—although she will insist almost tearfully that her handicap is impossibly low and that she *never* plays as well as that. Or maybe you shouldn't tell any of the men so that you and I can watch her sucker them into some five dollar Nassau bets. Perhaps the men down there don't believe in golfing with women. I suspect the South may not be quite that "liberated" yet. Maybe I'm not either— Majel insists I *talk* full sexual equality but don't really practice it in my own home. Strangely, it sometimes sounds as if that pleases her—but only in my case. From other men, she wants full equality, although it pleases me that she remains polite enough to refrain from mentioning those feelings to others who might feel otherwise.

It appears to me that in the end, the "sexual revolution" will probably change the country more than freeing the blacks or any other social change. It can be seen happening very rapidly in New York and on the West Coast. Paramount Pictures, for example, now has a dozen female vice presidents of this and that and I must admit that I find them at least as competent as males I've dealt with in the same jobs, perhaps

even better than most. Explained, I suppose, by the
fact that females generally have to be better to get
the same chance at promotion. Not that it doesn't bother
me now and then, although I find it gets steadily easier
as I become more and more accustomed to it. In
fact, I now find myself feeling a bit ashamed of
some of my past attitudes and action on the subject—
perhaps much as others have been ashamed of their
past attitudes about the blacks. Some, of course,
will feel that they have never been wrong about
anything and I suppose they are put here so that people
like you and I can learn patience and tolerance toward
them too. I find myself being less and less
judgmental about others with every year that goes
by—but within reason. Just as we will also find things
that deserve admiration, perhaps we must always have
the strength to speak up against what we believe
to be truly evil.

On the sixteenth of August, he wrote to Rupert Evans in
England.

Cameras began rolling yesterday on STAR TREK
III. Sometime today after posting this letter we will
have a look at the first day's dailies. Doubt that
they will tell us much—it will probably take a week
or so before we get a feeling as to how the film is
going. I went on stage 9:00 yesterday morning and
gave Leonard Nimoy a handshake and best wishes
for a good film. Even went to a "kickoff" party
at Harve Bennett's house on Sunday so that the cast
and crew would know that we're all together in wanting
this to be a good film. I wish I felt better about
the script but have done all that I can do. They
accepted some of my suggested changes and ignored
others which, I suppose, is about all one can expect
unless he wants to shoulder the burden of producing
it himself.

Gene evidently forgot to answer a question Rupert had
asked, and two weeks later remedied the situation.

Oh yes, I am reminded now that you said something
in one of the letters about wishing to be able to "repay"
or some nonsense like that and I wanted to remind
you of our agreement that *friendship repays
friendship* with riches that accountants can never put
on a ledgerbook.

We are now finishing up the second week of
photography on the film and the dailies continue
to look quite good, although Nimoy has been unfair
and annoying a number of times, I am pleased to see
him doing a good job of direction so far and wish
his efforts the best. Nobody wins if we end up with
a bad film.

The work on the novel was going slower. On August 26,
1983, Gene wrote to Dr. Charles Muses:

Interesting you once considered a novel to be called
Diary of a Martian. My *Report From Earth* is a similar
attempt to create that kind of objective *platform.*
It goes more slowly than I like for several reasons,
a principal one being that I am writing it in first person
style and thus he is initially limited to what he knows
of Earth. This means that although he has a
complete knowledge of the English language, his
limited Earth background prevents the use of many
of the adjectives, similes, analogies and so on which
pepper our own speech and makes it flow easily.
My intention is that this will change how he lives
here a bit longer because his considerable intelligence
and acuity lets him pick up on such things very rapidly.
Still, I doubt I can ever have his first person
narration ever totally human in form.

On the above, do you know that Mr. Spock was
identified as coming from Mars on one of the early
series drafts? Fortunately, I was optimistic about
the space program and decided to move his home
a bit further away just in case.

One other thing I remember gratefully is that in those
days of television cigarette commercials I had the
sense to fight off NBC's insistence that the
Enterprise bridge crew smoke—even though most of

us making the show were hooked on nicotine at that
time. NBC even suggested a "compromise" solution
in which I would invent some kind of "futuristic
cigarette."

About your question of control, I suppose I did not
have to lose control of *Star Trek* if I had been willing
to go back on the old ten and twelve hour a day schedule
and oversee every aspect of the films, keeping up
a constant battle with the front office. You see, I
never had any *contract* control over the show—such
things just weren't given in the days it was conceived
and written. The way I maintained control during
TV was waging that constant and wearying battle
until sheer *force of will* won out for us. Not only did
I not want to do this again, it seemed unlikely that
it would work this time in which I did not have a *film
background.* I finally concluded that even
if won it would not be worth what it cost.

Yes, it is annoying to watch it being changed but
I've become fairly comfortable about that now and
am content I took the right path. Also, I feel a
twinge of annoyance like when I watch the first *Star
Wars* and find them using my concepts like "tractor
beam" and "photon/proton torpedoes" and weapons
that "stun" in the same flash of blue light that we
used—not that others haven't a perfect right to borrow
things like that (we all do) but I would feel better about
Lucas and some of the others if they would in some
way acknowledge our having been first in such
areas, including that of stars drifting past the POV
which has become TV and film's space trademark.
Fatherhood!

In early October, Gene wrote to the son of one of his relatives. The details of the referenced incident are not available, but obviously Gene was giving fatherly advice and
candidly admitted his own drug experiences:

About the drug "bust," I knew something about that
already and hope you have not let it grow in your
thoughts to anything out of proportion. It is easy
for something like that to happen when a man is

trying to help a friend. Although I wouldn't want you
to mention it to [your father]. I have gone even
further myself and have tried a sniff or two of it [cocaine]
several times. Fortunately, it did me no harm and my
main feeling was one of disappointment that it was
no more exciting than swallowing an "upper" of
some sort. I don't recommend it as something to do
although I suspect most everyone I know has tried
it once or twice with almost all of them shrugging
it off as "nothing special." The main danger is for
the occasional poor devil who does find it certainly
becoming a necessary crutch. The same can happen
with marijuana and tobacco and alcohol. The real
narcotics such as morphine and heroin are deadly
dangerous and experimenting with them is a form of
insanity.

In mid-October, Gene communicated his fatherly pride to
Rupert Evans in England, including a progress report on the
current film.

Star Trek III seems to be coming along nicely. As
before, I read scripts, see dailies, and so on. This time,
it is a much happier arrangement with Harve
Bennett and the studio acting strangely friendly,
even to the point of introducing me at the beginning
party as "the man who started it all." They even insisted
that my name be included as one who invited the
cast and crew to the Wrap Party. As you know, this
is 180 degrees off the way it was handled last time
and I keep wondering what they really have in mind.
Or, is it possible everyone is getting older and tired
of name calling and battling? I much prefer it this
way.

At about the same time, Gene wrote to Janet Quarton:

Have just returned from stage where we are on our
last few days of shooting Star Trek III. The arrangement
has been a bit happier this time with producer, cast,
crew, and studio seeming to have noticed that I did

have quite a bit to do with *Star Trek* and presumably its success, and suddenly they are going out of the way now to make their respect clear. Nice. Some of it, I'm sure is genuine. Some of it, show business being show business, is doubtless based on the realization that any unhappy comments from here could cost them dollars. Which is about the best one can count on anywhere in life, right? And my reaction in return (the only proper and intelligent one, I believe) is to accept it all in good spirits as if it had never been any other way.

The filming was on schedule, as Gene reported to his cousin, Sister Madeline Roddenbery:

We shot the last scene of *Star Trek III* just two weeks ago and now our fingers are crossed that the film will edit together in proper style. Also, we will now begin to add the optical effects in and ultimately sound effects, music and all the rest of those things needed for a complete movie.

Leonard Nimoy directed this film and it seemed to go well. He was a good director and much liked in that role by the rest of the cast. As for the question of whether or not Mr. Spock is found and whether or not he becomes a science fiction "Lazarus," I am sworn not to say anything—except that I will hint to this relative that director Nimoy probably won't let actor Nimoy end up too disappointed.

Gene had had a battle with his waistline for some time and had embarked on a personal self-improvement odyssey he described to Janet Quarton in February, 1984.

Got dissatisfied with my weight and my general physical condition last mid-December and checked myself into Pritikin Longevity Center for four weeks over the holiday season. Don't much enjoy Christmas and New Year's parties anyway, and studio work is usually fifty percent efficiency or less during that time, so I bailed out of the season's obligations.

The Center is in Santa Monica, only a short drive
from home, so I was able to be with my son
Christmas Eve and Christmas Day and have a
couple of father/son get-togethers during the time. I
wasn't sick or anything but so many people I know
have had heart attacks or heart bypass surgery that
I got interested in the reasons for this "epidemic"
and the Pritikin system seemed to be the most logical
answer. Living there was like checking into boot camp—
strenuous exercise and strenuous diet, a literal
reshaping of one's life style, and came out twenty-
three pounds lighter and with a blood pressure of a
nineteen-year-old. Am still losing about a pound a week
and hope I can keep it up so as to be maximally
trim and ready for whatever you island pirates
throw my way in August.

There has always been a small but vigorous controversy
in *Star Trek* fandom concerning Starfleet's military standing.
In a number of letters and personal appearances, Gene had
addressed that question, but took the time to explain it again
in this letter to a teacher who wanted to reproduce a few
pages of the Writers Guide. Gene granted permission and
then added:

Do other shows have "bibles" of this type now? Ours
was the first that I had known of, prepared mainly
because there had never been a real science fiction
show on television before, or at least not one that
required any knowledge of space and starships and
the kind of details key to our format. Interesting to
recall how hard we worked in those days to keep
our series *un*military (the various ranks being used
mainly as job titles) whereas almost all film and TV
science fiction today has gone the direction of being
more rigidly structured militarism. God, what an
awful vision of the future!

Gene was stimulated to expound on the state of the world
because of an article sent to him by his cousin Julien. In
early 1984, Gene wrote back:

A most interesting article from the Thomasville newspaper and one that brings back many memories of my own. Saddest among those memories is the comparison between Lebanon 1947 and today. That earlier Lebanon was a tranquil place filled with warm and friendly people whose religious differences and disputes seemed very well under control or at least were generally expressed non-violently. I dealt with Moslems who obviously considered me a bit "odd" but the majority I met shared my own viewpoint that the other fellow was rather unique and different and worth getting to know.

At the risk of shocking you, it seems to me more and more with each passing year and each new massacre (as many perpetrated by Christians as anyone else) that the real villain is *religion*—at least, religion as generally practiced by people who somehow become sure that they and they only know the "real" answer. How few humans there are that seem to realize that killing, much less hating, their fellow humans in the name of their "god" is the ultimate kind of perversion.

At any rate, I've elected to believe in a God which is so far beyond our conception and real understanding that it would be nonsense to do anything in its name other than perhaps to revere all life as being part of that unfathomable greatness.

Events in Central America bother me even more than those in Lebanon. Perhaps it is because my wife and I have made friends of a succession of domestics from Central America who have worked for us over the years. A couple of them became especially close, both of which I helped obtain driving licenses and one of them assisted her in obtaining a high school diploma. In the course of that, we heard and saw in their letters from home a great deal about how the ordinary working people of El Salvador and others of those countries feel about the tiny group of families who have ruled their countries for centuries. Few Americans realize that the U.S. has militarily intervened in Central America over 50 times since the year 1900 and always on the side of our business interests and the wealthy of those countries.

I can write that way to you since you know I am not
and cannot be a "commie" or anything that ridiculous.

On the bright side, all of this is probably only part
of our adolescent human race being still in process
of "growing up." All this may even be necessary.
Perhaps we need problems, difficult problems, to solve
in order to prove that we're worthy of whatever lies
in the future for us.

Nimoy and his crew had worked hard on *Star Trek III,* and
Gene seemed pleased with what he'd seen, as he said to Maria Muhlmann in this March 21, 1984, letter.

Just wanted to get this off to let you know that *Star
Trek III—The Search for Spock* has so far been tested
twice in surprise preview showings (still with some
sound effects, opticals and other things incomplete)
and it has scored *the highest of any Paramount movie
in a year or so.*

The exciting thing about this is that these were
not "Trekkie" audiences but rather "you are invited
to a major science fiction movie preview" invitation
given to people on the street. I saw the last (intermediate)
cut and predicted it would end up very, very good.
Paramount brass sent over a note recently saying
they had used every cutting suggestion I sent to them
and one of our (unnamed) *Enterprise* crewmembers
called the other night and asked how I'd feel about
a petition from them that I take over the show
again. I replied: "Thanks, but no." I like this executive
consultant role. If they want more of me, then let them
attend more carefully to what I write and say and
consult with me earlier at each stage of production.

The franchise moved forward, as Gene informed his
cousin Julien in Georgia on January 14, 1985.

We should begin making our new film *Star Trek IV*
either Spring or Summer in this new year. Fortunately,
our *Star Trek III—Search for Spock* was profitable
enough to keep Paramount Studio's new

management (as of last Fall) interested. My book *Report from Earth* has not been going as easily as hoped, partly due to travel diversions no doubt, but perhaps even more because the direction I've gone has not led to the drama and excitement I want. May have to back up and take another run at it in a different direction—which happens in this profession (or should happen when the author is unhappy. Like a mountain climber, he must always be willing to face up to having led himself up to an impossible precipice.) Much of my time lately has been in making certain I've been facing the impossible rather than merely fatigue and difficulty.

Somehow I'm certain that you have faced similar lonely battles and frustrations in creating the things that build a future for the ones you love.

The novel had served its purpose as a therapeutic device. *Star Trek* was in proper perspective and Gene was moving forward with his life. *Report From Earth* would never be completed, and there is scant evidence that he worked on it past early 1985. The mountain climber analogy was apt. He had written himself into a rocky corner with little or no conflict in the character's adventures to move the story on.

In early February, Gene wrote to Rupert Evans in England, bringing him up to speed on the new *Star Trek* film.

As you may have heard, we've gotten a "go ahead" on *Star Trek IV* from Paramount and I doubt that pre-production will involve me very heavily during any of that time.

Yes, it does appear we are going to make IV. Nimoy will direct and I believe he's probably a good choice for that. Suspect he has learned now that it pays to listen to me a bit more carefully when I point out the advantages or problems which might attend this or that particular story direction. In fact, Nimoy and I have graduated back into the kind of mutual respect I prefer. Bill Shatner, on the other hand, has become a perfect shit in almost every way. He is still a good actor and still should do a good job,

but almost everyone on or off *Star Trek* finds it
more than a little worrisome to deal with him.

We celebrated Rod's 11th birthday Feb 5th and
on Feb 8th tomorrow I'm taking him and five of
his 11-year old boy friends down to La Costa. We go
on the train, which includes a junk food dinner, and
then to Sea World the next day, and other
adventures, ending with a train ride back to Los
Angeles on Sunday evening. I'm still wondering how
I got into all that, but am sure it will be fun—almost.

Gene could be vulgar, but charmingly so. He was, for the
most part, unflappable, as the following illustrates.

One afternoon he and a female friend were having lunch
in the busy Paramount commissary. Gene had gotten a bit
deaf and as is often the case with people who have a small
hearing loss, he boosted the volume of his own speaking
voice. He was telling this friend of a girl he was having a
passing fling with.

Conversations and room noise have their ebb and flow
like the movement of tides. Just as the flow of the room's
conversation reached a low point Gene said quite loudly, "I
like her cunt." The entire room fell instantly silent as everyone absorbed what this famous writer-producer had just
said. Gene's luncheon companion, a producer-director who
is capable of drinking and swearing with the best of them,
slowly turned beet red and tried to shrink down in her seat.
Gene only smiled and laughed.

As his guest slowly regained her composure and the room
got back to normal Gene said, "Well, it could have been
worse."

To which his friend said, "How do you figure that?"

"I could have said I liked *your* cunt."

In mid-February Gene wrote to his cousin, Sister Madeline:

Enclosed is a certificate making you an official member
of our *Enterprise* crew. Don't know what the regulations
say about having nuns aboard, but am sure the
vessel will be only better for your being there.

I was thinking of you only a couple of months ago
when I was invited to Jackson, Michigan, to give a

community lecture about the human future and had three Catholic fathers invite me to stay with them at their house out on one of the lakes. They were great guys and we stayed up late a couple of nights discussing us and the universe and our connection.
They seemed to find me not as much a heathen as some believe me to be.

The latest here is that we have been given a "go ahead" on our next movie, *Star Trek IV,* and are presently trying to settle on a writer and story. Leonard Nimoy will direct, and we've gotten Bill Shatner down to a price where we can afford him. Hope we make something that you like.

In mid-1985 Gene received several letters from fans that alerted him to the new directions *Star Trek* novels seemed to be taking—directions opposed to what Gene originally intended. As a result, a new area of battle opened.

CHAPTER 17

There was one subject that Gene definitely wanted included in his biography, a subject for which he had particular irritation: they were "the damn books!" as he characterized them. From the earliest days, books had been a prime conduit for the exploitation of *Star Trek*. At first the books were nothing more than novelizations of episodes, but their steady sales showed there was a market for *Star Trek* in print. In early 1970 a new factor entered the picture with *Spock Must Die* by James Blish, a 118-page Bantam paperback. It was an original work, "based on the television series created by Gene Roddenberry," not an episode novelization. The book's sales showed that there was a healthy appetite for new *Star Trek* material, too.

Blish's novelizations of the television shows continued, as did the later novelizations of the animated series by Alan Dean Foster. Along with the authorized novels, there was a small amount of fan-published material—the "fanzines"— that ranged from cheap mimeo jobs to sophisticated layouts with professional touches. They were nearly all created out of love of science fiction and love for the show. The "zines" as they are called, ran fact, rumor, hope, convention reports, fan letters, fan debate, and fan-written fiction. Most zines were usually break-even operations with the life span of a mayfly. Few, if any, could be called commercial operations. Small and unthreatening, Paramount ignored their existence.

Hidden away in a few zines were stories that appealed to a narrow spectrum of fans; homoerotic fiction featuring a speculative relationship between Kirk and Spock. It became

known as "K/S material" or "K/S stories." As long as it remained on the fringes, Gene didn't care, although he once
wondered why anyone would have a sexual relationship with
someone who only became sexually active once every seven
years.

For the most part, Gene paid little attention to the printed
exploitation of *Star Trek*. In the early 1980's, as Gene was
distancing himself from *Star Trek,* becoming more philosophical about his creation, he wrote the following to Janet
Quarton:

> There is no sadness for me in the way *Star Trek*
> has gone and will continue to go. Yes, I dream of how
> nice it would be if I had been able to own it wholly
> and control all rights. Many of the present *Star Trek*
> novels would never have appeared and probably none
> of them without some really extensive rewriting. On
> the other hand, by giving the property my sole
> attention there would have been many novels I
> would have written, keeping the entire *Star Trek* property
> more cohesive. Certainly it would have been fun to
> see Earth and Federation civilization of that century
> better explained. But none of this was possible, and
> my attitude now is that it has probably worked out
> as well as it could have happened in this real world
> that I must live in. And I *am* grateful for the talent
> of those who did write those books and stories.
> Indeed, I am not past hoping that the entire experience
> is leading me toward something more important, even
> more more fulfilling.

Slowly, more original novels began to be published, each
meeting with good sales. Over time the schedule was increased and with nearly guaranteed sales, the expected revenues could be factored into the financial picture and treated
almost like money in the bank. While much attention was
given to the acquisition of manuscripts, there was less and
less concern over *Star Trek* continuity, character integrity,
and allegiance to Gene's philosophy. Occasionally, information contradictory to what Gene had said in the past was
issued by lower-level Paramount employees that caused
projects to go in the wrong direction.

In the mid-1980's Gene's attitude toward the books

changed when Pocket Books, a division of Simon and Schuster, owned by Paramount Communications, published a novel with elements of K/S as part of their continuing series of *Star Trek* novels. Gene received a few letters from outraged fans. He investigated and became livid. Printed *Star Trek* was taking a much different course than the one originally plotted by its creator.

Gene was not a homophobe—anyone who knew him knew that, but these were *his* characters. *He* created what they were and they weren't going to be changed *that* much without his permission. He threatened to raise hell publicly and the offending edition was withdrawn and rewritten with thirty pages excised. Oddly enough, several years earlier, in 1980, in an exchange of letters with the author, Gene had written:

> As you may have seen by now there is a footnote in the novel,[1] . . . Kirk comments that he and Spock were never physical lovers although not due to any aversion by either to any non-harmful form of love or pleasuring.

Gene took a closer look at all the proposed stories from then on, as well as how *Star Trek* was used in other outlets, including comic books. Getting those stories into the *Star Trek* format often created problems, although it should be noted that of sixty or so novels published during this time frame, only perhaps a dozen were a source of problems.

Gene's irritation grew out of authors who wanted to push their own characters and not the *Star Trek* regulars; authors who wanted to feature themselves in the story (the so-called "Mary Sue" stories); and authors who wanted to change *Star Trek* history or format, or deviate from Gene's philosophical underpinnings. This should not suggest that most or all *Star Trek* books are poorly written. Many are of excellent quality by professional writers, who looked to Gene for advice and direction, and many of whom Gene liked both as people and as writers. What Gene objected to was the writers who tried to use *his* universe for stories that clearly weren't *Star Trek.*

While Gene may have eschewed battles in his *Star Trek* universe, he didn't when it came to protecting his vision of

---

[1]Gene's novelization of *Star Trek: The Motion Picture.*

his creation. Most of the problems stemmed from what one former employee characterized as a "lack of familiarity" with the product by many of the executives in Paramount's marketing department and the continuous pressure to push through *Star Trek* product to feed the bottom line.

As the number of books published each year increased and Gene became involved in the *Next Generation* and other projects, he found it more and more difficult to manage oversight, so he brought in *Star Trek* expert Richard Arnold to read the books, look over licensed products, and make appropriate commentary. This was done under Gene's direct supervision. A careful reading of the material in Gene's files shows that each memo went through him as they are signed with authentic signatures. In 1990 alone, there are nearly seventy memos from Gene on some aspect of *Star Trek* in print. It became the classic battle between art and commerce with Gene determined to win.

Richard Arnold remembers:

"Between the stress of the show and fighting with the studio over the merchandise, I felt bad that he put me in the position of watchdogging that stuff and dealing with it. I would bring the problems back to him, which fed fuel to the fire, and he would go over there and throw flame all over them.

"He enjoyed the fighting and being right, because he had been right so much lately, in those few years. He proved himself to be so right that it empowered him and he just wanted to keep proving that, if he told them to do it this way, and it succeeded, he'd be right."

Working with Gene every day, Arnold was able to see aspects of Gene's personality not seen by outsiders.

"As the books based on the new series suddenly started to sell very well, instead of five or six books a year, there were thirteen or fourteen books a year, and they were selling more and more of them. He was right again—that there was not a finite amount of *Star Trek* merchandise that you can put out.

"[In the early days of *Star Trek* merchandising] they were writing little deals with little companies[2] and suddenly they have AT&T and Hallmark and all these major corporations coming in and spending millions of dollars on licenses to sell legitimate *Star Trek* merchandise—Franklin Mint, and

---

[2]In the early 1970's Arnold, as a high school student purchased a license from Paramount to print and sell *Star Trek* bumper stickers. It cost him $25.

all of that, which *Star Trek* had never had in twenty-five years of merchandising. And he was right.

"The more right he was, the more determined he was to let them know and to make it even better.

"And they fought him every inch of the way."

Gene fought his battles with words. A few examples follow of memos sent by Gene on a variety of projects. The names of the memo's recipients and the subject novels have been deleted.

April 12, 1990
Subject: POCKET BOOK's novel
By now you will have seen the memos sent on this novel, which is typical of what I was talking about in last week's meeting with you. My comments are: [this] novel is unacceptable, as it does not focus on our characters, but those of the author.

This novel could work, but it would need considerable rewriting. In the cover letter that came with the manuscript, [Paramount employee] outlined some changes, but in my opinion none of them will improve the story. These suggestions did not come from me.

This type of thinking is at the heart of our current difficulties. The changes needed to make this novel acceptable as a *Star Trek* story should not come from other but from my offices.

Gene did make compromises with what was done to his creation.

May 29, 1990
Subject: Pocket Books' manuscript [different from previous memo's subject]
This is something of a disappointment after such a strong proposal. The authors have written an excessively long novel and have used far too much "non-*Trek*" source material for their background (constant references to other Trek novels and the terminology from the wargames).

There is excessive techno-babble, the book is too often scientifically implausible, some of the sequences are excessively violent and more *Star*

Wars than *Star Trek,* and Starfleet and our twenty-third century descendants are painted in a very bad light. No matter how terrible the incident at [named location], Kirk and crew would never face treatment like this, from their colleagues or the general populace.

However, it is very likely that once again it is too late to ask for a complete rewrite of this novel, and Richard informs me that in order to make this acceptable, a major overhaul, including hundreds of changes in technology, terminology and historical references, would have to be made. This due, for the most part, to the fact that the authors were not given the proper guidelines on writing an acceptable *Star Trek* novel, guidelines that we have insisted on for more than a year and a half now, and long before this book was "fleshed out."

In view of the above, and with the understanding that we will very likely not have the time to turn this into an acceptable *Star Trek* novel, I am going to request a disclaimer once again be printed in this book, distancing it from the *Star Trek* that we consider acceptable.

Hopefully this will be the last time that this is necessary.[3] I trust that the authors of other novels in the works are aware of what I will and will not accept.

Gene also did what he could with story lines in the DC Comics edition of *Star Trek,* especially when it was clear his philosophy and format were not understood or followed.

June 8, 1990.
Subject: DC Comics' proposal for our 25th anniversary

Robert Greenberger needs more than my opinion before he can proceed with this project . . . he needs my approval.

I wrote "Assignment: Earth," and the alien race that trained Gary Seven was far more wise and advanced than suggested here (they would certainly not hunt down nor punish members of their race for

---

[3]It wasn't.

STAR TREK CREATOR   533

having differing opinions, and members of their
race would not kill those they had trained to prevent
them from fulfilling their missions).

Once again Kirk is being portrayed as some kind
of god, who knows far more than this advanced race.
This is unacceptable.

This is not approved ... do not proceed.

June 22, 1990
Subject: POCKET BOOK's novel [first memo subject] revised manuscript

This now works as a *Star Trek* novel, although I am still
not satisfied that it was at all necessary for the author to get
rid of Spock for the entire book. This will not be acceptable
in the future. Our characters cannot be shoved aside so that
an author can star their own characters.

There is also the problem that, although this now contains
no format problems, this novel is boring. The author spends
too much time on technical details that do nothing for the
plot, and *Star Trek* has never been about hardware ... it is
about people.

The good news is that her characters are believable, and
she has captured our established *Star Trek* characters well.

This is approved ... please proceed.

Not all Gene's memos were stinging and not all his advice
went unheeded. On July 10, 1990, he sent the following regarding *Exiles* by Howard Weinstein.

Howard is to be congratulated on a highly entertaining
very socially relevant story, and for writing what is probably the best *Next Generation* novel to date.

Attached are Richard's notes on this novel, which once
again are not meant to be critical, but are suggested improvements on an already excellent work.

Please proceed.

Gene fought for consistency in his universe and against
"in-jokes" by writers. He directed that one such comic story
have all the material removed obliquely referencing *Lost In
Space*. There seemed to be a continuous battle on the part of
some authors to make Starfleet a military organization rather

than an organization loosely based on military lines, or "paramilitary," as Gene often said. Several militaristic novels slipped through, regardless of Gene's opinion.

> July 17, 1990
> Re: DC Comics' material
>
> This proposed story line does not work. Again
> we are introduced to a new race of "bad" aliens, and
> again we are introduced to a romantic story line (this
> time with Scotty, who has never been established
> as teaching at the Academy during the *Enterprise*'s
> refit, which he would have been too involved with
> to do any teaching). This story line is far too militaristic
> in nature, and will feature one battle after another.
> Again, not much of a tribute to our *Star Trek*
> philosophy. This is not acceptable at this time.

The comics and novels weren't the only publications to get careful scrutiny. When various magazines published story synopses, Gene insisted they be written from broadcast episodes, not scripts. In one memo on the subject he made his expectations clear:

> I expect all *Star Trek* merchandise to be created with
> accuracy and with respect.

Gene's oversight extended to all *Star Trek* products he could see and occasionally fans informed him of improprieties. He was quick to respond.

> February 21, 1991
> Subject: Columbia House release of *ST:TNG*
>
> Just thought you should know that we have had
> a couple of calls from fans unhappy with Columbia's
> release of our new series on tape.
> The first tape, "Encounter at Farpoint," was not
> our premier version, but an edited, strip syndication
> version, and now it appears that the second tape has
> problems as well.
> "Code of Honor" has the bumpers that are added
> in for the stations, but these should not be included

in these merchandise tapes (they aren't in "The Naked Now" or any of the original series tapes).

The battles raged on, memos were sent and resent, and little changed except that Gene grew older and more tired. Slowly it developed that some of the authors and licensees thought Richard Arnold the gray eminence behind Gene's criticism, but it was just the opposite. Arnold was sometimes given his memos back for rewrite using stronger language, as Gene did not feel his points had been made forcefully enough. Nonetheless, many memos continued to go unheeded. Paramount had the choice of an angry Gene Roddenberry or a slowdown of merchandising revenue. They accepted the former as a condition of doing business and the merchandising profits kept rolling in. Merchandise that Gene did not approve was published or manufactured over his objections.

Ernie Over, Gene's personal assistant, remembers Gene having it out with a Paramount executive via car phone one afternoon as they were driving home. Over's memory illustrates the extreme frustration Gene felt because, as with the movies, he was being moved into the background. Gene became livid that the man simply ignored him, shouting "fuck you" into the phone before hanging up.

Richard Arnold continued to supply format continuity and character criticism after Gene started working more from home. Every memo was still run past Gene for his approval, but much of his energy for battle was drained. The old warrior was approaching seventy and trying to pull back from the show.

Less than a month after Gene's death, Arnold left his office to deliver mail to the actors on the set. When he returned he was stopped at the front of the building and told not to bother trying to return to his office. The locks had been changed and Richard Arnold was told he no longer had a job at Paramount. Under guard, he was allowed to retrieve his jacket and personal items, and then, still under guard, he was escorted to his car and shown off the lot.

Arnold called his lawyer and instituted proceedings on a variety of issues. After five-and-one-half months of discussion with studio attorneys, one highly placed executive was apprised of the circumstances of Arnold's firing and an amicable resolution was reached. Ironically, within weeks of his dismissal the studio called him for photos they needed for a project. Today, he is still used by certain divisions of Paramount and other official licensees as the premier *Star Trek* expert. Only in Hollywood!

CHAPTER 18

Wednesday, September 4, 1985 was a happy day for Gene. He was the first hyphen—writer-producer—honored with a star on Hollywood Boulevard. The Walk of Fame uses five different symbols for the five categories of show business it honors: motion pictures, television, recording, radio, and stage. The Writers Guild had proposed a sixth, which was rejected by the Hollywood Chamber of Commerce who runs the walk.

It was principally the fan clubs and their supporters who pushed for Gene's star. The fee at that time was $3500—it was a dollar a fan and fans from all over the world sent money. But a fee alone wasn't enough. The Walk of Fame Committee had to vote you in. It was suggested that the ceremony be as close to the anniversary of the show (September 8) as possible.

Gene wrote to a friend a few weeks before the ceremony:

> Our La Costa sojourn will be broken up for a couple of days by a quick trip up here to look properly pleased when they dedicate a Hollywood Blvd. "star" to me. I suppose it will be kind of fun since I am the first writer[1] to be so honored, and the Los Angeles City Council will be making it officially "Gene Roddenberry Day." My mother is so pleased she can hardly talk.

---

[1] Actually writer-producer: there were other writers on the walk at the time.

The ceremony was simple and straightforward. It was the 1,810th star installed on the walk, located in the 6600 block near the corner of Hollywood Boulevard and Las Palmas. The sky was cloudy and hundreds of people showed up to share the moment with Gene. Almost the entire cast from the original show was there: Leonard Nimoy, DeForest Kelley, Walter Koenig, Nichelle Nichols, George Takei, Jimmy Doohan, and Grace Lee Whitney. Standing at Gene's side was Majel. One guest star even attended: Roger C. Carmel, the infamous "Harry Mudd."

It was a bit nostalgic for Gene, as it was the same area where he had served his sergeant's probation supervising radio patrols and foot beats.

The Los Angeles Police Pipe Band—bagpipes and drums—played several numbers, which inspired Jimmy Doohan to find his Scottish accent and say a few words in character. Nichelle Nichols said her "hailing frequencies were always open for Gene," and Nimoy thanked Gene for "talking me into the ears."

Gene introduced his family, which included his mother, brother, and sister, in order to share his success with them. Everyone who had donated had their name inscribed on a scroll, which when presented to Gene unrolled down off the small stage. According to Richard Arnold, the look on Gene's face when he saw all the names was "typically Gene. He was appalled that so many people cared so much."

A few days later, Gene wrote to Rupert Evans in England:

Well, the great STAR ceremony is over and it has taken me all the weeks since to properly thank everyone. Everyone except you—and you must know I did appreciate the contribution and the telegram.

If anything, the day (for me) was almost too exciting. Leonard Maizlish called it "a triathlon event" with first the star ceremony on Hollywood Blvd. with not only fans from here but people flying in from all over the country and from a couple of foreign locations too; then *second* the studio party with all those hundreds and more gathering here on one of the stages where Susan and her "assistant" Richard put on a fine party, even an extravagant one, including great food and drinks and a band and displays, etc; then *thirdly* the Bel Air Country Club party where

Majel had arranged a party for intimate friends ("just a couple hundred of my most intimate friends") where I was "roasted" from the platform by quite a number of friends who are comics plus ex-Govenor Brown of California and assorted others.

It went on a bit too long for my personal taste—I remember thinking that one runs out of things for which to praise God after 20 minutes. I also thought several times "Thank God I didn't become an actor." But everyone else seemed to enjoy every moment of it. I suppose the one thing that did reach me during this busy day was a sense of surprise and wonder that I indeed have so many friends who seem to care about me and want to celebrate their feelings on that score.

Gene wrote to his friend, science fiction and fantasy writer, Ray Bradbury thanking him for sending flowers to mark the day.

As you must know, I am much like yourself in being a "private man" and I was hiding a lot of discomfort and nervousness during the entire day. Also, I have many reservations over what a Hollywood Blvd. STAR really signifies. The really wonderful thing that happened to me that day was a growing realization at the event and at the parties that I have an amount of respect from associates and friends that I never realized existed, and these things make the memory I'll carry.

Much like Jack Webb's attitude towards his star, (he kept a picture on the wall of his star after it had been "graced" by a dog), Gene kept things in perspective. A writer friend had written and teased him:

Congratulations! I always thought it would be fun to hire someone to install a star with my name. Do you think anybody checks? Half of those people I've never heard of, and I'm pretty good at Trivial Pursuit.

Now, in years to come, people can gaze down at your star and say in hushed tones, "Who's that?"

"Gene Roddenberry? I think he was Hopalong Cassidy's sidekick."

"Oh yeah. I remember."

Gene responded to the jibe:

Of course people notice! I have it on good authority that several fellow members of Writers Guild of America have already gone out at night and peed on my star.

CHAPTER 19

In September 1986, Gene wrote to Janet Quarton, summing up the year so far:

> It has been a much busier year than I expected with it being the Twentieth Anniversary (September 8) of the showing of the first *Star Trek* episode, which in turn made the preparation of *Star Trek IV* more important and more time consuming, which created great Paramount interest in the first pilot and Paramount's plan to issue it as a TV cassette special, which in turn got me finagled into doing an 8-minute introduction shot on the Enterprise stage sets. Am only now getting to the golf course with some regularity. Am very, very tired of studio parties and conventions and other celebrations of *Star Trek*'s success. Paramount Studios threw a big party on September 8th, [with] 2,000 people crammed into two stages, in the midst of which I sat thinking, "It was more fun to fight for this than to actually win it."

After a series of financially rewarding films, tens of millions of dollars in revenues from merchandising, and the endless syndication of the original series, by mid- to late 1986 Paramount had changed its mind about the viability of a new television series. Marta Houske, a close friend of Gene's from the late 1970's until his death, remembers how he became involved:

"To the best of my memory, Paramount asked Gene to do

a new *Star Trek* series. He told them 'No way, I owe it to the fans to maintain the integrity of the series, etc.' So, a while later he and I were having a drink at Nuclear Nuances on Melrose and he said, 'You won't believe it. They're doing it on their own.'

"I didn't know Gene's legal position and said, 'They can't.' To which Gene replied, 'Yes, they can and they are.' He was disgusted."

In early August, 1986, *USA Today* reported that Paramount was close to selling the series to the Fox network when they decided to scrap the deal. The article had Madison Avenue executives speculating on Paramount's decision, thinking that a new series would hurt revenues from the films. Several ad executives thought that a new series wouldn't attract a large audience, so it wouldn't be of interest to advertisers.

On September 12, 1986, John Pike, president of Paramount Television, sent Gene an overview of "the preliminary conceptual work on the new show." Pike described it as "developed principally by Greg Strangis after meetings with Jeff Hayes, Rick Berman and myself."

This "preliminary conceptual work" was done without any consultation with Gene, even though Paramount apparently tried to interest him originally. On September 19, 1986, he wrote back to Pike.

Gene said at the beginning he did not believe that Paramount could proceed with any new *Star Trek* TV series "without my approval, or without a new contractual arrangement relating to that series." Gene further told Pike that with regard to a new series he had not decided what role, if any, he would take. Because of their friendship, he was passing along his comments, which he characterized as "not comprehensive." There followed a five-page letter of Gene's views on the new *Star Trek* format.

A few selections include such comments as:

I do very much appreciate your providing me with what has been written to date on the proposed "Star Trek: The Next Generation." It shows the considerable effort your people spent in studying the *Star Trek* format and characters. However, I believe I see some difficult problems in it as presently conceived.

It seems possible that too much time was spent

in making up a cast and too little in considering what kind of stories would be told.

Gene did not like the idea of cadets manning the ship.

I am very uncomfortable with the concept of any starship manned heavily by Starfleet Cadets. Yes, I know cadets were used in one of the *Star Trek* movies. Unfortunately, here we have our starship embarked on a *highly important, highly delicate* mission of great consequence to Earth and the Federation.

Cadet story characters rarely do very well in military or quasi-military stories except when played against the confines and restrictions of the cadet world.

These are *not* "nitpicking" comments. One of my first *Star Trek* battles was with some NBC executives who wanted cadet characters in the original *Star Trek* series. However, good science fiction must be built on *believability*. That's partly why none of the half-dozen copies of *Star Trek* have ever succeeded—one just can't get away with saying "It seemed okay to put it into the script because this *is* science fiction, isn't it?"

Gene was also concerned about militarism.

Only a small percentage of the original TV episodes were about space battles and the like. We never saw the inside of Starfleet Headquarters—and for many reasons beyond budget limitations. Once a space science fiction series becomes too militaristic, featuring stories about high command and interplanatary politics, and Space Admirals pontificating, that series is in danger of becoming Buck Rogers childishness.

As gratified as I've been with the *Star Trek* movies, I've also been very concerned with the increasing militarism reflected there. They've gotten by with it because of the difference in what works in movie and TV formats—and also because they're talented people. But still the costumes, for example, have some of the movie scenes looking like a STUDENT PRINCE operetta. *Star Trek* was *never* a military

show originally and a new television version will
probably not succeed if we try to make it that now.

Gene ended his letter by opening the door wide to Pike, a
person well aware of the subtle nuances of what Gene implied.

> John, I do hope the above will be somewhat helpful.
> In none of this do I mean to say that a new series
> must be done exactly the way I did the original.
> Because of our friendship and what I believe is an
> excellent relationship with Paramount, I will make myself
> available for discussion on any of the above. I do feel,
> however, that Paramount has no right to go ahead
> with any press conference regarding a new series
> until arrangements with me are concluded.
>
> Warm regards,

Later it was reported that he called the new format "Animal House in outer space." He thought it would damage
Star Trek as he had created it. Gene was protective of his
creation, but now it was even more important to be protective. After fourteen years of worldwide syndication, after being shown almost continuously in every North American
market, the original series had gone where almost no one
had gone before with a television series: into profit. *Star
Trek* was again exploring uncharted territory.

True, it had taken a legal expedition mounted by Gene and
Bill Shatner (another net profit participant) to make the studio own up. Gene had hired one of the most respected, and
feared, show business lawyers to threaten the studio with an
independent audit. His presence on the case told Paramount
that Gene and company were serious. Paramount took a
good look and found that *Star Trek* had gone into profit. After fourteen years of studio-style bookkeeping, the $4.7 mil-
lion production debt had finally been paid off. Gene was
sent a check for $851,000. Shatner, with a lower share of the
profits, presumably received proportionately less. Gene was
delighted and knew that more checks would follow, along
with seemingly endless legal problems.

Fox hadn't been the only potential buyer. According to
published reports, Paramount had offered the series to the
three major networks as well. The networks had balked at

Paramount's conditions of purchase: a guarantee of the purchase of a full season of episodes (twenty-six episodes at $1.5 million each, probably reduced in cost, but still a large commitment), plus a set time that would not be preempted or an intensive promotional campaign advertising the series. None of the four networks were willing to commit to such substantial expeditures. Paramount executive Mel Harris said, "We came to the conclusion that nobody was going to give it the same kind of attention and care that we could give it." That "attention and care" was distributing the show through the concept of first run syndication.

It was a simple concept: give the program to independent stations around the country on a first run basis. Don't charge the stations for the program, just reserve seven minutes of advertising time for the studio to sell and give the remaining five minutes to the station. Propelled by *Star Trek*, the concept took off like a rocket. When the program hit the air in 1987, the *Los Angeles Times* reported that it was broadcast in 209 markets, which included 108 network affiliates, twelve of which were going to preempt network programming. The *Chicago Tribune* reported it was being carried by 150 stations. That meant Paramount had 1,050 minutes of time that blanketed the country. For an hour a week, Paramount had a fifth network and could sell national advertising time.

Gene dropped a short note to Janet Quarton on November 6, describing his reasoning for ultimately working on the new series:

> I am an independent artist to whom Paramount has laid down the challenge of a lifetime. They very carefully made it clear "No one thinks it can be done again." Could you turn your back on that? I certainly can't. I've never begun a morning's work without wondering if I'd win or lose artistically on that particular day—I know of no other way to work or attitude to have.

Behind the scenes, Gene was battling for creative control. As he would later say:

> I found myself in a fat cat position. The only way the studio could get me to do the series was to give me creative control over it. But why *should* they send an exec-

utive to look over my work in advance? I've been in television a hell of a lot longer than any executive they could get; I've fought the wars of television. It's not that I wouldn't listen to somebody who had something to say and a background to say it. But if he's just someone who's been appointed the office with the bathroom ... then no.[1]

When the matter of creative control was solved, Paramount announced the return of *Star Trek* almost immediately, on October 10, 1986. Gene faced the press with no characters, format ideas, stories, or support staff. The only question Gene could fully answer was when one reporter asked why the program would not be seen on a network. Gene explained that his wounds of twenty years before had not yet healed.

While the first run syndication concept would be a success, the inception, development, and birth of the program that would propel it were not easy. Gene was sixty-five years old, a time when most men are seriously contemplating retirement—something he had previously announced— but this may have been a negotiating ploy suggested by Leonard Maizlish, his lawyer. With the new series Gene saw an opportunity to finally earn serious money for his creativity, enough to leave his family well cared for after he was gone. Also important, however, was the opportunity for him to show that the first *Star Trek* wasn't an accident, a fluke of good timing and good luck. As Gene said, "I loved the idea of taking a show and making it a hit for a second time—it had never been done before."[2] While Gene's lawyer Leonard wrestled with the studio over compensation, Gene moved forward.

Publicly, Gene explained what made him take the job:

The first *Star Trek* took years out of my life, separated me from my family and I really didn't want to go through that again. And there was a career consideration. I was saying to myself, "Why rock the boat? You're ahead. You've got a show that's a success. Suppose you go in

[1] "Gene Roddenberry—The Tommorow Person." Interview by Stephen Payne and David Richarson, *Starburst,* Vol. 13, No. 7, March, 1991.
[2] *Ibid.*

and the thing nose-dives?" No television series had succeeded in coming back again.

Put yourself in my place. You think that you did it all, that you're really basically responsible for the first *Star Trek* but so many years have gone by.... Success has many fathers, and for twenty-two years there have been a collection of people coming out and saying, "He really didn't do it; it was me, or my brother, or this or that person." I found myself thinking, "They could be right." The first sign of insanity is everyone's out of step but you.

The result of all of this is it made me mad. It made me very angry. *Star Trek,* I said to myself, may be an ego-fed dream, and the rumor mongers may be right, but at least I'm going to have the courage to say, "Fuck you" as I go down. I thought to myself, if *Star Trek* could be done so easily, why didn't more people do something like it in the twenty-two years since we did the original series? I finally got angry enough to try it.[3]

Paramount officials, who would say that they thought Gene's participation to the return of *Star Trek* was vital, quickly forgot about the first Roddenberry-less format. Gene's name on the show was, they thought, critical to its success, and now they had it, one way or the other. The studio couldn't lose. If Gene actually created something that was acceptable, great—but Gene was in his mid-sixties and had been out of the daily grind of creating and producing a television program for years. If he couldn't come up with anything, they could bring in script "doctors" and make it right, and they would still have his name on the show. No matter how it went, Gene's magic name would be out front for all to see. In spite of his age and less than perfect physical condition, Gene would surprise them all.

Gene assembled his team: a group of people who had *Star Trek* experience and could provide expertise and input, ideas and concepts that would add to his own creativity. While Gene would not create everything that would be in the new show, any more than he created every single thing that was in the original show, he was the single person who could say, "It isn't *Star Trek* until I say it's *Star Trek.*"

---

[3] From a tape of Gene's remarks at a June 1988 *Star Trek* convention.

Back on board was Bob Justman, who had worked on the original series; veteran Dorothy Fontana; Eddie Milkis, another veteran from the old show; Bob Lewin, a well-known writer-producer who was new to the genre; and writer David Gerrold, who was hired as a consultant.

Gene had not taken good care of himself over the years, and his closest friend, his lawyer Leonard Maizlish, sought to protect him and conserve his time and energy. Susan Sackett, Gene's secretary, also became protective of access to Gene.

The first 22-page "bible" is dated November 16, 1986, forty-seven days after the official announcement. The creation of *Star Trek: The Next Generation* would not be simple or easy. Bob Justman remembers:

"We had a lunch every day, which Gene organized, where we were just to kick ideas around. In the beginning there was Gene, Dorothy, David, Mike Felt, Ed Milkis and me. That was it. We would sit in the private dining room at Paramount, next to the commissary, and boot ideas around."

Bob Lewin was suggested by Justman. Lewin knew Gene in passing from their days at Desilu: while Gene was doing *Star Trek*, Lewin had been a writer on *Mission: Impossible*. Gene interviewed him, telling him what he wanted. Lewin truthfully told Gene that while he loved *Star Trek*, he didn't know much about science fiction. Gene did not see that as a problem. Lewin describes the beginnings of the series:

"The characters were being set. The basic story of the pilot, the idea of the pilot was set. It was a rewrite of an old *Star Trek* episode. Dorothy and David were working on it.

"Everything would go to Gene with a copy to me.

"Gene was Executive Producer. I was the first producer hired. Even though I was working on the literary end, not the production end, I was a producer. [Rick] Berman was not yet on the show."

Stories, as in the original series, were the most important and frustrating part of the production. The word got out, and veteran *Star Trek* writers started coming in to pitch ideas. Bob Lewin remembers:

"They had ideas that were really not twenty-fourth-century ideas. So, Dorothy would type up the results of the meeting if it was worth submitting to Gene. A paragraph would go to him and he would yes or no it, depending, or he would say, 'See if you can improve this, and here's what the problems are. . . .' The general procedure was always the same.

"The pilot material I would also get from Gene. Whatever Dorothy gave him and whatever David gave him he gave to me. I would read it and make comments."

The show was sold and an air date loomed ahead in the fall. The preproduction development was not going smoothly.

Lewin continues:

"Little by little we began falling behind. We had a schedule. We knew what airdates were supposed to be. We knew when we would have to go into production and postproduction and all of that.

"So Gene said, 'Listen, I think I'd better hire another producer or two. How do you feel about that?' It was okay with me, providing the material would still go through me and I knew what the traffic was and who's doing what, so there was no overlap or conflict.

"He then hired Herb Wright, and a month or more later, Maurice Hurley came in. The problems became complicated because we couldn't clear with each other exactly what the other one was doing, and Herb and I had different attitudes about stories and they had different texture to them.

"So everything would go to Gene and the way I learned about what Herb was doing was I would read Gene's memos to Herb and he would read Gene's memos to me, and that way we finally began to know more and more."

Gene explained how the process differed from the "old days":

"What we've discovered is that this is much more complex than the old system of shooting a pilot and laying out your format and then having time to study what you've done while you wait for the pilot to be sold to the network. We're doing a two-hour opening show but we have no time to see how it works. We have to go right into the making of our episodes. It's a hard, hard thing. I'm working seven days a week, eleven or twelve hours a day."

Bob Lewin remembers the pressure:

"During those early years Gene was extremely busy. He was writing pages of the actual pilot and he was falling behind, because in addition to that, he was going to the stage to see the sets, he was looking at the drawings for the ship, he was away from the office doing other things, I think he was talking to Asimov and Clarke all the time, and he was involved a great deal with Leonard Maizlish over legal matters with the studio.

"There was never an easy moment in his relationship with the studio that I knew about. He was always on edge about it and Leonard was helping him be defiant."

The stress was bound to spill over onto the production team, especially the writers. Bob Lewin recalls:

"Gene was difficult in working with writers because he was impatient, but he was impatient because he saw the twenty-fourth century very clearly. Probably more clearly than anyone in the world. He lived in the twenty-fourth century. He knew what was happening and how it was happening. He had this whole structure in his head. So if you came up with some technical thing in the show, he would say, 'Now, come on, that's absolutely stupid! You cannot do warp speed with dadadada . . .' as if you should have known that. But you didn't know it! *He* knew it.

"Gene was just beset all the time. On edge. So it was tense. He was a counterpuncher. You'd give him something and he'd shoot it down. In my opinion, he was not a really original story mind. He took material and would change it and put it into a shape that he could use. There are many producers and executive producers like that.

"He was great on rewrites with dialogue. He could take a scene between two people discussing drugs, or whatever, and do four or five pages that would just jump off the page, it was so good.

"He could have done a *Star Trek* with two people for an hour and made it interesting. Nobody else could do that. There was one long speech he did in one of the shows that was absolutely brilliant.

"Now, he never took credit on any of those scripts, but on a lot of them you will see his mind in the dialogue.

"His irritation was impersonal. I think he was in physical pain. I think he was in mental pain. He was being sued by his ex-wife, he wasn't getting along with the studio, the pilot wasn't coming along properly, the episodes were too expensive. I mean, it was just madness!

"On the old show he had one guy he really depended upon, and that made things really easy for him. Here, he had three producers, he had a developing relationship with Dorothy, and his relationship with David flip-flopped. There were times when he loved what he was doing and then he hated what he was doing. Sometimes he'd kick him [David] out of the room. Sometimes he would lose his temper with Dorothy, and he also had the three of us. He had fights with Herb, then he was generous, and the same with Hurley, and the same with me. We were always on edge.

"Gene's relationship with Dorothy went from acceptable to terrible. I found her work always helpful to me. It wasn't always as passionate, but it was always incisive. She knew the show very well, she was resourceful and fast and reliable."

Bob Justman spoke on Gene's ability to write:

"Gene was a good leader. I certainly found no problems working with him until *The Next Generation,* when I think part of the problems were engendered by physical problems on his part.

"Gene . . . always rewrote these things, but I have to say that we never had a perfectly good script. We would have liked to have had. We had good scripts that he rewrote and made better. That's the way it always was. But it wasn't just Gene who always did that. I've worked on other shows and that was the situation. Gene also took terrible scripts and rewrote them and made them better, so it's all, 'beauty is in the eye of the beholder.' There were hardly any scripts that I read that could not be made better or that were not replete with many flaws.

"The one that I had the least amount of notes on were the ones Gene wrote himself as originals."

Out of this situation arose two major controversies. The first concerned Fontana, as Lewin recalls:

"I was the producer and she was, I thought, my story editor. I would say to her, 'What about this . . .' and she would say to me, 'I really can't do that.' I said, 'Why not?' She said, 'I'm not paid to do that.' I said, 'Aren't you the story editor?' She said, 'No. I am the Associate Producer.' I said, 'Then you're not covered by the Guild.' She said, 'No, I'm not.' I said, 'You have to be. Otherwise, I can't use you!' 'Well,' she said, 'that's the situation.'

"I went to Gene and said, 'Gene, you've got to get her the title of story editor or assistant story editor or something so that she's covered by the Guild and she can get this, and she can get that, and it would mean a raise for her. I know, it's going to cost a little money, but it's absolutely essential. I can't work without Dorothy,' He discussed it with Leonard and he dragged his feet. I don't know why."

Perhaps Fontana supplied the answer in a three-part interview published in the British fan magazine *TV Zone,* Fontana remembered that ". . . Gene wanted me to come aboard as story editor and I said I would rather be associate producer. There were some problems, but I finally got my associate producer title."[4]

Lewin found it difficult to continue developing the show with Fontana not covered by the Writers Guild:

"I could not use her to write up the meeting and advise me on things. I was handicapped there. But I did it anyway, because she wanted to do it. I would say to Gene, 'I'm doing this, but it's really sub-rosa. I'm only doing this because you say you're going to get her the money that she needs and get her the story editor title.' So they kept promising that they would do it, but they didn't raise her salary. She was working for very little.

"Eventually, she did get it, but there was resentment. They felt they were blackmailed, or sandbagged, or something, why, I don't know, because Dorothy was also working on the pilot, too."

Fontana recalls working on the pilot in her interview in *TV Zone:*

> . . . in late November, Gene asked me if I would like to be involved and I said, "Sure, I'll come and pitch some stories." The stories I pitched were fine but Gene had this other idea. He asked why didn't I do something about a mysterious station that has suddenly been presented to the Federation?
>
> Although the characters were changing quite a lot at that point, I developed the story that became "Encounter At Farpoint," which was to be the premiere episode. Unfortunately, the length of the episode was like an accordian! First it was two hours, then ninety minutes, then it dropped back to an hour, then they said, "Can you make it two hours again?" I turned in a first draft script which was actually about ninety minutes. Gene took it over and added all the Q stuff and I never got my hands on it again.[5]

---

4 *TV Zone,* Issue 51, February 1994.
5 *Ibid.*

Bob Justman commented on Dorothy Fontana's writing:

"Dorothy has a certain talent that works very well for her. In that regard, she was better than most of the writers we had working on the show. Her talent was for airtight construction. It was always constructed so there was an introduction, development, and conclusion. It proceeded clasically in its construction. I can't say that there was much fire in her writing, and I think that's what Gene did when he rewrote her.

"Gene rewrote most of the two-hour premiere of *The Next Generation* and he put life into it. You know, excitement.

"[Dorothy] did a terrific job, but it wasn't sufficient unto the task as far as Gene was concerned, and I must admit, as far as I was concerned. I was responsible for bringing her back in the fold, and I'm glad that I did it, if for nothing, [other than] that two-hour show.

"Once we started making it, we knew what it was to be, but the writing of it, it was really a bone of contention. It was one of the reasons why Eddie Milkis was so angry at the studio, because he felt that they were jerking us around. My feeling always was that they didn't come out and tell us what they wanted in the first place because they weren't sure themselves."

Dorothy would write several other episodes, but her relationship with Gene was going downhill quickly. Publicly, she was supportive. In the November 1987, *Starlog* she was quoted by Publisher Kerry O'Quinn in his editorial:

Absolutely nothing is written, bought, or done without his final approval. I think I can say without any reservations that this show is Gene Roddenberry at his best.

There were creative differences. In the same British magazine interview, Fontana revealed that she had written a first season show with an appearance by Spock. Gene turned the story down because "Leonard Nimoy would never do television again." In season five came the appearance of Spock in "Unification," a two-part episode. Fontana states, "It does prove, once again, however, that I did have the right take on *The Next Generation* and I didn't have many opportunities to prove it."

Perhaps, but this does not coincide with Gene's vision of

the new show in an interview published late in 1989.[6] Talking about the two crews, he said:

> They are different people. They are essentially apart. I think we should be happy that we have Kirk, Spock, and McCoy who do their things so well and we're now lucky to have Picard and Riker and Data, too, doing their thing so well. I think that if you start mixing them together it's like having two great soups that people love. If you take those two soups and pour them into the same pot, they don't taste the same, and, most likely, they taste bad together. So I don't think it would be wise to mix our two crews.

Bob Lewin remembers:

"Eventually, Gene was so caustic to her [Dorothy] that she would not talk to him without a tape recorder. She said to him, 'Gene, you're treating me badly. I'm going to bring in a tape recorder to our meetings.' He said, 'Bring whatever you want to! Good! Fuck you!'

"You know it was bad. So she recorded everything he said to her. Eventually, they developed a long-term arms-length relationship."

Dorothy Fontana eventually left the show and filed a Writers Guild claim. The second major battle would be fought with David Gerrold.

Bob Lewin remembered David Gerrold's work on the new series:

"David's very emotional, determined, apparently sure of himself, but not really, and very dedicated to the show. Of course, he was involved, to a lesser degree, on the old show. He acted like he was very deeply involved, and he was very familiar with it, but I think he only wrote one show that created any degree of real interest.

"He had an interesting imagination so I always listened to him. I enjoyed what he had to say. It was very hard for him to change his mind. Once he'd thought of something and thought it through, he locked into it, and you can't be a writer in television with that attitude. You're constantly beset with other people's opinions, [people] who are more

---

[6] By Dan Madsen; *Star Trek the Official Fan Club Magazine*, Oct/Nov 1989.

powerful than you and frequently right when you're wrong. You don't always see it, but you may five years later.

"David wasn't an archivist, but he was kind of a resource, because he knew so much about the original show. He was used as a reference point on a lot of stuff.

"He got involved with me fairly early, and he had an idea, and it went through an enormous amount of changes. Gene kept throwing it back to him. I wasn't really directly involved in it, because I really couldn't be. He was doing it over and over and over. He was dying to have a solo credit on the show. He wanted a homosexual man on the episode and he wanted it clear that that was what he was, and he wanted it clear that he was accepted on the ship as such.

"I think Gene was willing to do that, but the studio had a fit. They went nuts. Gene spoke to David about rewriting it and David resisted and then rewrote it several times. Herb helped him with it. Finally, he left the script behind and went on a vacation on a ship somewhere. Gene read the script and sent him a wire that said, 'Ecstatic about the script. It's one of the best things you've ever done. I really love it.' I don't know if he read it, because a few days later, Gene hated it.

"So, David came back expecting to have a wreath put around his neck as a hero, but it was like getting hit in the face with a fish! Gene hated the script. Maybe Gene didn't read it but gave it to someone else to read. I don't know. That was the beginning of the deterioration of his relationship with Gene."[7]

Gene was not the only person with whom Gerrold fought, Bob Lewin recalls:

"David and I got into one bitter argument about something, I don't remember. We were in a story conference. I got very angry at him. We broke for lunch and I asked him not to come back. I said, 'I don't want you in the meeting. It's too difficult. So, cool off and we'll discuss this situation

---

[7] Gene was asked about this in an interview in *Starburst,* March, 1991. He said:

"David was treating a futuristic show as if it were dealing with homosexuality in the present day, in which they are secretive and use code-words and so on. Homosexuals are not going to be like that once we get out of these generations. Homosexuality is normal, natural and it's perfectly wonderful for someone to seek gratification that way. David was keeping it in its twentieth century guise; it was silly. That was the only reason."

tomorrow. Don't come to the meeting.' Everyone was upset. . . .

"Disruptive, yes. I think I put that in a memo. It took us about a day to get over that, but we became friendly again."

Gerrold had been writing a column called "Generations" for *Starlog* magazine, stirring up interest in the upcoming debut of the new series. In it, he gave little glimpses of the show's development.

In the July 1987 issue, Gerrold wrote on the necessity of preparing a guide or "bible" for the writers and directors: "A preliminary guide was written by Gene Roddenberry and distributed last November.[8] This gave us a good sense of who our characters would be and let us begin the job of telling stories about them. The first bible was 22 pages long."

Gerrold then told about the need for a larger guide with biographies, terminology, and much more: "Head Writer David Gerrold (yours truly) rough drafted some sections for Gene Roddenberry who then wrote and rewrote most of the bible's pages until they represented his vision of what the new *Star Trek* was going to look like. The new bible was finished on March 23 and put into distribution to writers and agents. It was more than 50 pages long."

Bob Justman, when asked about Gerrold's claim of being head writer, responded: "What head writer? You don't have a head writer on this show unless you're the writer/ producer. . . . No, he wasn't head writer, nor was Dorothy, nor was anyone else for that matter. That certainly was not his job description or what his contract specified."

David Gerrold's contract ran out, and was, as Richard Arnold remembers, extended for a month, and then not renewed.[9]

---

[8] The earliest we have in hand is dated November 26, 1986. Characters included: Captain Julien Picard, William Ryker, Lt. Commander Data, Lt. Commander Macha Hernandez (security chief), Lt. Deanna Troi, Ensign Geordi La Forge, and Leslie Crusher, who underwent a gender change in later formats.

[9] In his October 1987 column, Gerrold explained his exit from *Star Trek:*

"My contract with Paramount expired at the end of May and I asked Gene Roddenberry to please not renew it.

"Why?

"In April, I was offered the opportunity to write and produce a four-hour science fiction mini-series for CBS and Columbia Television . . . If the mini-series is a hit, then a regular weekly SF TV series would be developed from it."

After he left *Star Trek,* Gerrold filed a claim with the Writers Guild, claiming nothing less than co-creator status on *The Next Generation.* He also made a demand for compensation as story editor.

David Gerrold's first script sale became one of *Star Trek*'s most popular episodes, "The Trouble with Tribbles." The tribbles—small, round, furry creatures that purred when you stroked them—were hungry all the time and bred profusely. Tribbles were clearly evocative of Robert A. Heinlein's[10] creation, "Martian flat cats," as they appeared in the SF juvenile book, *The Rolling Stones,* published in 1952. In the chapter "Flat Cats Factorial," Heinlein has a flat cat named "Fuzzy Britches" begin breeding on a long space voyage.

The first flat cat has eight kittens. The kittens were small, round, furry creatures that purred when you stroked them, were hungry all the time and bred profusely. As Heinlein's story progresses, the flat cats multiply to the point where the next round of births would fill the spaceship with over 4,000 small, purring and hungry creatures. Heinlein does not enumerate this final round but had one of his characters describe it as "too much."

In his 1973 book on the history of that episode, David Gerrold explains that he learned of the similarity of his story to Heinlein's through the clearance process.

Gerrold writes:

The first ones to catch the resemblance were Kellam-DeForest Research. They noted almost offhandedly in their regular research report on the script that several chapters in Heinlein's book revolved around the same premise. They suggested that Heinlein could conceivably make a good case that the future value of his book as a film property would be damaged by *Star Trek*'s use of the gag, and it might be a good idea to purchase the rights from him.[11]

---

[10] Robert Anson Heinlein (1907–1988). One of the original members of SF's "Golden Age" in *Astounding Science Fiction,* Heinlein was prolific, imaginative, and essentially in a class by himself. His juvenile stories started many a reader on a lifetime of enjoying SF.

[11] Gerrold, David. *The Trouble With Tribbles: The Birth, Sale, and Final Production of One Episode,* Ballantine Books, New York, 1973, pages 252–253.

"Almost offhandedly" is not offhandedly and the situation was serious. The "gag" Gerrold referenced was the central premise of his story. Gerrold wrote that the problem was solved with a phone call from either Gene Coon or Gene Roddenberry. While Gerrold does not know who called Heinlein, he manages nevertheless to quote that person verbatim and then to characterize Heinlein's response. Gerrold quotes Heinlein as saying that "he didn't see that there was any kind of a problem at all. But he would appreciate a copy of the script."

Gerrold describes what he wrote when he autographed the script that was sent to Heinlein. He also says to have later received a letter from Heinlein which he quotes in his book:

[Heinlein wrote,] "Let me add that I felt that the analogy to my flat cats was mild enough to be of no importance—and we both owe something to Ellis Parker Butler[12] ... and possibly to Noah."

In reading Gerrold's quote of Heinlein's note, it is important to remember that from all accounts, Heinlein was a gentleman in the Old-School-definition of the word.

Heinlein's widow, Virginia, remembers this incident clearly. It was Gene Roddenberry who called and spoke with Robert. She remembers that the call came in the afternoon, and is most clear that the call came *after* the episode had been filmed, but before it was aired.[13]

Mrs. Heinlein remembers that she and her husband stopped what they were doing and discussed the matter thoroughly, deciding not to pursue it, letting the show go forward. She states that the reason why her husband permitted the show to be aired was because Gene had called *before* the show was broadcast, the only time in Heinlein's long writing career that this courtesy had been given.[14]

---

[12] Heinlein's reference to Butler was to cite his story, "Pigs Is Pigs," in which a shipment of two guinea pigs overpopulate a post office while the recipient and the tax collector argue over whether or not the livestock tax should be paid because "pigs is pigs."

[13] This would mean that Gene called sometime between August 1967, and December 1967, when the show was first aired.

In November 1968, Heinlein made a consignment of items to the University of California Santa Cruz Library. The inventory is typed on Robert A. Heinlein's letterhead. Itemized is a television script with the following notation listed:

Items to be filed with number 92 *The Rolling Stones*.
This is a TV script for *Star Trek*, "The Trouble with Tribbles." It was purchased by *Star Trek*, then someone in their story department noticed a strong resemblance to the chapter "Flat Cats Factorial" in number 92 *The Rolling Stones*. The executive producer telephoned me. I waived any possible redress for possible piracy and/or plagiarism. It was produced and broadcast. Ten years earlier I might have sued, but I have learned that plagiarism suits are a mug's game even if you win. Time, trouble, worry, and expense.

This is the only copy of the script for "The Trouble with Tribbles" found by the archivist for the Heinlein Archive and it does not have David Gerrold's signature, but does have a short, penciled notation in Heinlein's hand:

("I condoned the possible literary piracy. R.A.H.")

To ascertain the facts regarding the claims Gerrold made in the Writers' Guild arbitration, an executive at Paramount was contacted. Not an official company spokesperson, the executive did not wish to be named but reviewed the file and provided the author with the following quote for this book:
"David Gerrold was hired by Gene Roddenberry as a consultant and compensated as such. The arbitration filed by him claimed that he was co-creator of the series and also

---

[14] This may have been a misunderstanding on Heinlein's part if Gene used the term "pre-production" or "in production" to describe the story's status, as an interview with Gene Coon's old secretary, Andee Reese-Maddox suggests. Her memory was that the script had been put on the schedule (in pre-production) which was why it had been sent to research for clearance. Both Gene Coon and Gene Roddenberry were concerned that the conflict would hold up production as they had no finished script to replace it.

It is doubtful Paramount's legal department would have permitted filming with the conflict unresolved.

claimed that he should have been paid as a story editor for his time on the series.

"There had been a lot of preparation for this arbitration, even to the extent of hiring outside counsel, anticipating that the process would be centered on the co-creator claim. We felt this was completely erroneous.

"After two days of sworn witnesses examined by lawyers for both sides the Guild withdrew the claim for co-creator credit. What precipitated that, I don't know. All I know is that it occurred.

"The only claim left was for money: Gerrold claiming that he had been a story editor and had not been compensated as such. He was asking for the difference between his consultant's fee and story editor's fee. Once this became just a money issue, just a matter of differences in payment, we decided it was not cost effective to go forward. There was some difference over the number of weeks worked as story editor but we were able to resolve this and we settled the claim."

Gene related that Gerrold was paid $25,000, and Richard Arnold remembers the amount as $35,000. David Gerrold has publicly disputed both these figures, but says that he is restricted from further comment as he is bound by a confidentiality agreement.

Also on the table was Dorothy Fontana's claim that she had performed as a story editor. The Paramount source said that Dorothy's claim was settled equitably.

Bob Justman remembered the creative process Gerrold was a part of after the lunch meetings:

"I would go home at night and I came up with a scat of ideas which I presented. If anyone co-created *The Next Generation* it was me, it certainly wasn't David. I can't think of very much that David came up with that was very useful.

"I don't think he deserved anything because, in the end, I don't think he was that important to the writing process of the show."

In June of 1988, Gene appeared at a Star Trek convention in Los Angeles. Arbitration was behind him but some of the irritation was not. He was asked about the conflict during the question and answer portion of the program.

"As I understand it, David Gerrold wanted to have co-credit for creating *Star Trek The Next Generation,* which is absolute bullshit and I refuse to talk about it. He was hired like five or six other people. . . . My way has always been to bring people in and say, 'What do you think?' 'Comment on that.' That is the way I work. This is the first time someone has said, 'Oh, because you asked me what I think, suddenly I'm a creator.' It's a very annoying thing to me. He is saying that 'You have lied in taking the credit.' I am not a liar. I kept him on for longer than the people there wanted because I thought they were being unfair to him. I believe I've done more than the honorable thing with him and I've put it behind me now."

On Tuesday, July 9, 1991, Gene received a letter from Gerrold in which he apparently tried to make amends or re-establish the relationship. Gerrold wrote that people had told each of them "bad things" about the other and that "a lot of falsehoods were spoken on both sides." Gerrold quoted advice Gene had given him about a script Gerrold had, apparently, written when he was working on the show: "Do you know what this story is about? It's about hate. Hatred is wrong. It diminishes the person who hates. It takes away his own humanity. That's what this script should say."

Gerrold thought the advice was good for both of them, ending the letter by asking Gene if he agreed.

Gene wrote back three weeks later on July 24:

Dear David:

I enjoyed your letter and agree with it too. The days you spoke of were traumatic ones and indeed there were people around us who enjoyed creating a feeling of hatred between us. But actually I have never hated you and I feel certain the same is true about you.

Let's do meet someday when the opportunity presents itself. However, I don't want to meet on the subject of past work you have done on *Star Trek: The Next Generation*. Let's let that past stay buried.

Anyway, this is the way *Star Trek* is running itself now. Stories are done solely under the guidance of Michael Piller and Rick Berman. It is their responsibility now, and I could not possibly step in and violate that arrangement.

Exactly three months later, Gene died.

* * *

In creating *The Next Generation,* Gene repaired what he perceived as a flaw in the storyline of the films. Earlier he had written his thoughts to a Paramount executive, who was a friend.

Klingons were invented by an episodic writer when he ran into "last act problems." They were never considered very imaginative but those of our writers who tended toward bad guys/good guys "hack" scripting loved them dearly. At that time I was rewriting so many of our stories and scripts that I could never get around to providing new villains—and anyway painting a beard and a scowl on an actor's face was within our limited budget requirements. (Spock's ears, simple as they were, had almost bankrupted us.)

But Klingons were never a key element in the original TV format on which *Star Trek*'s phenomenal re-run success was based. In fact, all in the original writer/producer team considered them rather clumsily drawn "bad guys" whom we planned to replace the moment we got a little time in which to invent more imaginative villains. But with producing a TV series being what it is, we never found that extra time. The Klingons stayed available . . . and years later when the *Star Trek II* production team signed on and began seeking bad guys for their film story . . . the Klingons volunteered. Having by then adopted a policy of rarely interfering with the film producers and directors, I simply made my feelings known but never carried my belief beyond that.

In the succeeding movie, *Star Trek III,* the Klingons stayed on and many people, including some right here at Paramount, began assuming that was what *Star Trek* was basically about. By the time of release of *Star Trek III,* I had become alarmed that over-emphasis on Klingons might be harming the property. These movies turned too often to "tried and true" (read *simplistic)* Klingon villainy rather than making use of the myriad alternatives that science fiction offers. Soon, interest in *Star Trek* was visibly declining and my office was encountering statements of disappointment from the most respected of fans and sf writers, their

concern being that *Star Trek* seemed to be
deteriorating into a two-dimensional "good guys vs
bad buys" space opera.

The movie *Star Trek IV* changed the whole
picture. That very talented production team (many
of which also made *Star Trek* movies II and III), sensed
the stagnation induced by Klingon over-emphasis and
came up with an entirely different kind of story
which ignored Klingon villainy in favor of a story
closer to *Star Trek's* origins ... and the difference this
has made is already visible. Unfortunately, however,
the proposal for a new *Star Trek* TV series reflects
not the lessons of *Star Trek IV* but rather the
outdated preoccupation with the Klingons.

Gene partially solved the problem in *The Next Generation*
by making the Klingons allies and putting one on the bridge
of the *Enterprise*.

The android character, Data, came directly from Questor,
and was originally described as having the appearance of
"an Asian or Eurasian human in his mid-thirties. Until the
role is cast, Data can be defined as representing any racial
group between Pacific Oceania to the Middle East." Data
was originally conceived as having been built by "advanced
and never seen aliens" to save the memories of a doomed
Earth-Asian colony. Counselor Deanna Troi was an out-
growth of the Counselor Ilia character introduced in the first
film.

As with the original series, the search for the actor to play
the captain was all-important. Bob Justman found him.

Patrick Stewart was known in England as a solid, depend-
able actor who knew his business. He had performed as Shy-
lock, Henry IV, Sejanus in *I, Claudius,* and the notorious
Karla, head of the KGB in *Tinker, Tailor, Soldier, Spy* and
Smiley's People. In spite of a long and busy career, he was
virtually unknown in the United States. Hanging on his
dressing room door reads a sign that says it all: "Beware,
Unknown British Actor."

Justman was attending a lecture at the University of California at Los Angeles on "The Changing Face of Comedy."
Stewart was demonstrating scenes for his friend, who was
giving the lecture. By the time Stewart had gotten from

Shakespeare to Noel Coward, Justman turned to his wife, Jackie, and said, "I just found our captain."

Gene did not warm to the idea immediately, and only after meeting Stewart did he see the possibilities of giving command to this unlikely individual.

When asked why he made the Captain French, he replied:

> I decided to make Picard that nationality because the French have had a marvelous civilization and yet, everything we do is usually based on the English. I love the English, but I can't help noticing in history that the French explorer Louis Antoine de Bougainville got to Tahiti before Captain Cook. Bougainville was an enormously witty man and a great adventurer. He once stated that "five Tahitian men could be clothed with one glove and a pair of scissors."
>
> I also made Picard French because I love the image of oceanographer Jacques Cousteau. He's a little older than Picard but he's a marvelous man. And he's a wonderful philosopher. I wanted that type of individual to come through in Picard.[15]

For die-hard fans there was only one crew for the *Enterprise,* but they would not be back, and Gene faced a hard sell. He explained the problem in a letter to Janet Quarton:

> Wish us luck on replacing the old cast. Please make certain everyone knows we'd love to keep all or most of them, but the practical realities of television production and distribution make this impossible. We would not be able to sell it without one or more of the present lead actors plus the majority of the others, and all but a few of these would either be unwilling to go back to the old 12-hour production days of television or are at a place in their lives where they would simply have to charge more for their work than a new television show could afford.

Some fans were irate that the old crew wasn't coming back and said so publicly.

---

[15]*Starlog Star Trek: The Next Generation* #1, interview by Dan Madsen and John S. Davis with Dan Dickholtz.

* * *

Besides the new series, the thousand and one details that required attention and the myriad details that needed decisions, Gene had one more major problem to which he would devote not a little of his time and attention.

On December 18, 1986, an article in the *Los Angeles Times* gave a small suggestion of the trouble brewing on the horizon. Bill Shatner wanted to write and direct films. The article, "Embattled Enterprise," focused on whether or not Shatner would direct the upcoming *Star Trek V* film. *Star Trek IV* had been released a few weeks before and was doing well at the box office—$20 million in its first three days and $50 million in less than three weeks. The article said that Shatner had a secret contract with Paramount apparently guaranteeing him the director's chair for the next film. There were "a series of red flags raised by Roddenberry, who says that any future *Star Trek* director (including Shatner) must pass his muster."

After the press learned of Shatner's guarantee, the article reported that Harve Bennett "was suddenly tapped as the studio's official spokesman. 'If there is a *Star Trek V* and I think there will be, then Bill Shatner will direct it. But I do feel that it is premature of him to set himself up as the sequel's writer.' "

"Shatner bristles about his right to direct the sequel," the article continued. "I *will* direct and am searching for a screen writer to fashion a script from my story."

Bennett was given the last word in the article: "Roddenberry will oversee, Shatner will direct, and there will be a happy ending."

Getting to Bennett's happy ending took some doing. On June 3, 1987, Gene sent the following memo to Bill Shatner.

Bill, as you undoubtedly know, I expressed to Harve Bennett at lunch last Monday my deep disappointment in the proposed *Star Trek V* film story. I simply cannot support a story which has our intelligent and insightful crew mesmerized by a 23rd Century religious charlatan.

I had thought from our discussion that you were going to reconsider using religion and God as subject matter, particularly with what has been happening to public attitudes in that area.

I had also thought that we had a clear understanding,

man to man, that I would be consulted *before* any story
went to screenplay. Thus, I was both shocked and surprised when a member of my staff learned from your office, later verified, that David Loughery was already
working on a first draft.

Bill, you are just two floors above me. If you want my
detailed objections or want to discuss alternative story
lines, all you have to do is call.

Can we talk?

On that same day, Gene sent a memo to Harve Bennett.

Dear Harve,

It has been two days since I told you how terribly
troubled I was by the proposed *Star Trek V* film
story. I did not know then, as I do now, that without
first consulting me you ordered a first draft screenplay.

I cannot support the proposed story. It is *not Star
Trek*. In my opinion, a film made to this story or
anything similar to this story would destroy much
of the value of the *Star Trek* property. I cannot understand
your ordering up a screenplay before getting my input.

Harve, we have had a decent relationship which
I hope can be maintained.

I want you to know that I have contacted Frank
Mancuso's office to set up a meeting upon his return
from New York.

                                        Gene Roddenberry

Gene also wrote to his attorney, Leonard Maizlish, and
brought him up to date.

Let me record here some of my thoughts on the *Star
Trek V* film story so that I have them on record and
so that you can be prepared to discuss it from my
point of view in your dealings with Paramount.

I received the May 18, 1987 version of this from
Harve Bennett on May 27. I met with Bennett the
following Monday, June 2. The story is not *Star
Trek* and thus was not in accordance with our
agreement concerning the movies. We spent about two
hours discussing it during which time he tried to
convince me that it was a "tongue-in-cheek" approach

to God. I responded that I really didn't know what he meant by that.

I object to this story on so many levels that it is hard to know where to begin. Perhaps the value of the *Star Trek* property is a good place to start. I have no doubt that to film this story or anything similar to it would gravely damage the *Star Trek* property, both the "old" *Star Trek* and the "new."

Examining this from the point of view of the mass audience, it would be hard to imagine a more inappropriate time to do a story about a real God or a fake God who has mesmerized our usually intelligent and experienced crew into accepting its authenticity. How can Bennett and Shatner and Loughery have missed the considerable shift in public attitudes which have accompanied the Jim and Tammy Bakker hijinks and Jerry Falwell's semi-shady interest in their ministry and Oral Roberts' plea for a God-ransom to save his life, and so on.

It is important to understand that much of the value of the *Star Trek* property and its mass audience reputation come out of the fact that it has been kept scrupulously clear of religion and political theory, a path which has won *Star Trek* a broad affection which has been not a little bit founded on the affection of the "best and brightest" people in our land for *Star Trek*. An example of this is the Smithsonian Institution. Another is *Star Trek*'s reputation with NASA, with MIT, with Cal Tech and with a host of distinguished thinkers, not the least of which are Isaac Asimov and Arthur C. Clarke who I predict would feel betrayed and would almost certainly say so loudly if *Star Trek* takes this course.

The errors of property format, science, and fact in this movie story are nothing less than shocking. Do the people involved actually suggest that the "center of our universe" is located on the edge of our tiny galaxy? Are they suggesting that the proudly logical Vulcans who foreswore emotion somehow are plagued at the same time with a Roman-like collection of deities? Will Bill Shatner actually wrestle with God?

Come on, Paramount, you're putting me on.

The next day, Gene sent a similar memo to Frank Mancuso, head of the studio:

> To avoid possibly causing indigestion at our scheduled Wednesday lunch and in all fairness, I think you should have in advance some of my thoughts on the *Star Trek V* film story.
>
> First, I received this story just days ago, May 27, 1987, from Harve Bennett. I met with Bennett the following Monday, June 1, 1987, to discuss it. I told him that the story is *not Star Trek*. It is totally out of character and in no way conforms to the image or reputation of *Star Trek*.
>
> One day later, June 2, 1987, I learned that *before* I was even consulted, this horrendous story was ordered into first draft screenplay. Although the sequence of events was outrageous, I don't want the substance to be overshadowed by the procedure. I want to stay focused on this incredulous story.
>
> Second, *Star Trek* over the past two decades has generated over $500,000,000 in gross revenues from films, TV, animation, merchandising, book, records, cassettes, etc. The new TV series using only my name and that of *Star Trek* has already produced approximately $75,000,000 in sales. This property is truly a studio treasure and one that should not be treated lightly or with ridicule. I have no doubt but that to film this story or anything similar to it would gravely damage the value of *Star Trek*. I cannot support such an action.
>
> Third, succinctly stated, the unbelievable storyline concerns a charismatic Vulcan named Zar, "the Messenger of God." Although the *Star Trek* series establishes Vulcans as without emotion, this Zar is described as a "Vulcan theologian" who was Mr. Spock's "hero and mentor" while Spock studied under him at "the seminary" (all news to me and *Star Trek* followers), who first converts peasants to his God-beliefs by "laying on hands" (shades of Oral Roberts); then travels by Unicorn to convert a Klingon and Romulan; and finally and unbelievably mesmerizes members of the *Star Trek* crew (initially Sulu, Chekov and Uhura and ultimately two of film history's certified cynics, Mr. Spock and Dr. McCoy). Only Kirk somehow escapes the blandishments of this charlatan Messiah. Zar is too light a foe for Kirk; Kirk wants God

and he battles him in a struggle in which the Deity hurls thunderbolts at our Captain. In the end, Kirk overcomes "God" (Las Vegas had Kirk the 8 to 5 favorite), who it turns out is actually a "devil" of sorts.

I didn't make this up. It's all there—unfortunately.

Fourth, from the mass audience point of view, it would be hard to imagine a more inappropriate time to do a story with religious and cultish overtones. The Bakker hijinks; Falwell's dirty laundry list; Oral Roberts' plea for a God-ransom to save his life; Robertson and Jackson running for President are all affecting and will continue to affect in 1988 public attitudes.

Bennett says this story is a "tongue in cheek" approach to God. I don't know exactly what he means but if he means this is a spoof on religion, I think in actuality it appears to be more a spoof on *Star Trek*. And that is dangerous.

Much of *Star Trek*'s mass audience reputation comes out of the fact that it has been kept scrupulously clear of religion and political theory. *Star Trek* has been honored by, among others, the Smithsonian, NASA, MIT and Caltech. I have no doubt that distinguished scientist-thinkers in this field like Isaac Asimov and Arthur C. Clarke who have publicly supported *Star Trek* would feel betrayed by this story and undoubtedly say so strongly and publicly.

Fifth, Bennett has made valuable contributions to *Star Trek* II, III, and IV. So have I. For example, the idea that Spock "die" in such a way that he could be resurrected originated in my office and led to *Star Trek* III and IV.

Sixth, as the Paramount-proclaimed "conscience of *Star Trek*," I must disassociate myself from this story. It is not fixable. Do we drug the crew? Do we let the secret out before the last reel? Does God turn out to really be "God" and Kirk walks out into the sunset saying, "Lord, I think this is the beginning of a beautiful friendship?" All nonsense, of course. Just like the story.

Seventh, I will not prolong this memo with a recitation of the shocking errors of science and fact, i.e. the "center of our universe" is located on the edge of our tiny galaxy, etc. Hopefully those problems will never have to be addressed.

What is needed is a redirection of energy, time and

money to a new and exciting story (Bennett says he has
others) so that *Star Trek* can get back on course.

Gene R.

On June 8, Bennett sent a memo to the writer, David
Loughery, with a copy to Gene.

... Through an inadvertent sequence of time, Gene
Roddenberry's notes of response to our story outline for
Star Trek V were not received prior to the studio's "go-
ahead" to script.

Bennett asked Loughery to stop working on the draft and
wait for Gene's notes, explaining that "Gene's notes have always been of enormous value to us in the time between
story and first draft."

Bennett apologized for the mixup, citing a "combination
of events, enthusiasms and unusually fast responses which
pushed us along before you could respond as you have done
so eloquently in the three prior features."

On June 15, Gene sent the following to Shatner and
Bennett:

I took a few days in responding to your memo and
telephone conversations so that I could reread again
the proposed story to see if my initial reaction that
the story is without redeeming value was a fair
evaluation. And although, as noted below, there are
some minor things that are either acceptable or fixable,
I still believe that the basic story has no saving
grace.

I take no pleasure in writing this. I do not want to
strain my relationship with either of you and I certainly
recognize that some effort and money has gone into
this story. In my very firm opinion, however, it
would be far worse to continue with this story which
I regard as a prescription for disaster.

I have no objection to the Yosemite scenes at the
beginning and end of the story. I suppose those
could be transposed to any appropriate main story.

While I would prefer using other "black hats"
taken from the vastness of space, the continued use
of the Klingons as villains is something I can live with,

although Buck Rogers-type scenes showing the Klingons as "bad" simply because they're "bad" should probably be avoided.

There are some glaring science flaws in the story—one being that Zar appears to have no mode of transportation other than Unicorn. If true, this is *fantasy* which the *Star Trek* format has always avoided. Also, there is no way in which the *Enterprise* we've created can get to "the edge of the universe," especially since Starfleet has explored only 11% of just our own galaxy—and even high school science students are taught that there are as many *other* galaxies in the universe as there are stars here in this galaxy. Also, calling some place in our own small galaxy "the center of the universe" is the kind of nonsense that even bad science fiction avoids.

At the risk of repetition, allow me to restate my position.

Yes, I have commented on past film projects saying "this isn't *Star Trek*" and as you note we worked to make it the real thing. This eventually led to the success of movie IV. But it is quite another thing to begin with a story which demeans and degrades *Star Trek* with subject matter that it has assiduously avoided in the past and which is particularly inappropriate at this time.

Let me explain. Our stalwart and bright *Star Trek* crew, excluding Kirk, allows itself to be hoodwinked and converted of its own free will by a religious charlatan posing as "the Messenger of God." In the past, only an external agent such as alcohol or a virus could induce aberrant behavior in the *Star Trek* crew. Especially demeaned is Mr. Spock, who has been given an entirely new background as a former seminary student and disciple of this "messenger of God" and who acts totally contradictory to his character by betraying Kirk. Along the way Vulcans, always played as a logical race which has rejected emotion, become worshipers of "many gods." Then, despite the awesome power of our and other starships, "peasants" are converted and armed (shades of *Viva Zapata*.) Finally Kirk emerges as a Homeric hero who

shrugs off thunderbolts while conquering "God"—
perhaps it is the "Devil." Tell me you're kidding.

Finally, Bill, I ask you especially to rethink Kirk's
position as a sole hero, an implied insult to the other
cast members (who were an important factor in *Star
Trek IV*) and which is certain to become a sensitive
matter with audience and critics given your triple capacity
as star-director-writer. As a matter of courtesy and
common sense, I think a copy of the story should
be sent to Leonard Nimoy right now if I do not
convince you and Harve and Paramount to trash this
terrible story.

Harve, you have said that you have other story
ideas that are good. I believe that because I have
many times seen your fine imagination and creativity.
I ask only that you now make use of all this so that
the *Star Trek* audience, which you so ably cultivated
in *Star Trek IV,* can be entertained again.

Please abandon this story laden with mesmerization,
pop psychology, flim flam betrayal, a lack of power,
a lack of humor. Please do something with the
ingredient that is the hallmark of *Star Trek* . . .
believability.

Gene R.

PS I invite you to solicit the views of Isaac Asimov or
Arthur C. Clarke or any other respected science fiction
writer if you feel I am way off base.

Three days later, Gene wrote to Asimov:

Dear Isaac,

This involves a subject that I know to be close to
beliefs you hold. The same here. However, if after
reading this you'd rather not be involved, I'll think
none the less of you since I know something of how
busy you are.

On the surface, the matter will appear to be about
Star Trek but actually concerns more important
things. I believed it affects you somewhat since you
have publicly praised *Star Trek* at times.

The enclosed confidential story outline for the *Star
Trek V* motion picture tells much about what concerns
me—and my enclosed reaction to it tells the rest.

Without consulting me, contrary to my agreement with
Paramount, it was submitted to the studio by
William Shatner (to be director), producer Harve Bennett,
and by a writer whom I do not know. In fact, it
was then ordered into script also without my seeing
it—that script now said to be "on hold" because of
my strong objections to its subject matter.

I don't know whether I'll win this battle, or
whether I'll continue with the new series *Star Trek:
The Next Generation* if I lose the fight. Or whether
Paramount will want me here if I contest the matter
further, especially if I take it to court. They're much
concerned with the dollars involved in starting the movie
again from scratch, even though they violated the
agreement to let me see and approve any changes
in the basic format.

At this time, I don't want Paramount to know I
submitted this confidential studio information to you,
yet I badly need your advice on the matter.

Warm regards,

A week later, Asimov wrote back:

Dear Gene,

I have your letter of 18 June and am appalled. With
your track record, you should not be subjected to
this sort of back-stabbing.

I agree with everything you say about the mis-
characterization, the story flaws, and the ludicrous bit
about "the center of the Universe." The Universe
has no center or (which is the same thing) is all
center. If it had a center, the odds would be enormous
against it being in our Galaxy.

You might stress also that the God-Devil picture
as presented is childish in the extreme and will
offend any theist with more than a grade school
education. Naturally, it will be laughed at by rationalists.
Also Zar, as a picture of our contemporary TV
evangelists, is too dumb to please the evangelist-lovers,
and far too noble to please the rationalists.
In short, the picture, if it is made, would displease
everyone.

Isaac

That was a private letter. On July 14, Asimov sent a letter to be shared with others.

Dear Gene,

I will be glad to give you my opinion of the *Star Trek V* treatment.

I am sorry to say that I think it breaks with the rationalist tradition of *Star Trek*.

To bring in a charismatic preacher who seems to be all-powerful and ends up being ludicrously wrong is going to move the more educated and sophisticated end of the audience to embarrassed laughter. If there are any sincerely religious people in the audience they will be offended by so primitive a conception of God and be puzzled over the fact that the supremely intelligent and rationalist Spock can fall for it for even a moment. And, of course, those who are religious in a more primitive sense are going to object to the portrayal of the preacher, either as a fanatic, or as a dupe, or both. Then, too, remember that *Star Trek* appeals to a world-wide audience and there are several billion people in the world that do not share the Judeo-Christian view of God. A great many will be horrified and a great many others will be totally puzzled. Why on Earth should *Star Trek* meddle with such things and seize upon a subject that will be treated in a way that offends nearly everyone.

Then, too, there seems to be a lack of scientific intelligence that is wholly foreign to *Star Trek*. There seems to be no clear distinction between the Galaxy and the Universe, which is roughly equivalent to seeing no distinction between Wichita, Kansas, and the planet Earth. To place God on a planet of any kind is ridiculous to most intelligent theists who quite understand that God is immanent in the Universe, existing equally everywhere. To have the planet "at the center of the Universe" is sheer nonsense, for there is no center of the Universe any more than there is a center to the Earth's surface. Even if there were a center, what are the chances of its existing in our

Galaxy when our Galaxy is only one of a hundred billion galaxies all told. This is really childish.

Other points would puzzle any *Star Trek* devotee. What are these unicorns? Where do they come from? Why bring them in?

Why should Spock's mother be revolted by his partially Vulcan characteristics when she is in love with his father who is all Vulcan?

Why should McCoy have to wear a cast, considering the futuristic medicine of the day?

In short, I consider the treatment an out and out disaster.

Isaac Asimov

Gene sent essentially the same letter to Arthur C. Clarke in Sri Lanka. Clarke's response was shorter, but he was no less dismayed. The give and take, pull and shove between Shatner, Bennett, and their writer, and Gene continued for some months. At the end of August, Gene sent the following to Bennett and Shatner:

Thank you for the August 21, 1987, script *Star Trek V: The Final Frontier.* Your co-writer David Loughery is clever, obviously talented, and I enjoyed many of the things he appeared to bring to it.

Let me begin it by being very clear that I have no objection to an alien antagonist who is so powerful that he claims to be "god" and produces many of the superstitious and other accouterments which back this claim. We all know that strong, colorful villains can lead the way to strong, colorful films.

It is obvious throughout that you have made a strong effort, Harve, to deal with some of my objections to the original story. The fact remains, however, that we proceeded into script on a story which I did not have an opportunity to evaluate and comment per our agreement, with the result that my core objections about format flaws remain.

It seems to me dangerous to the property to make a film in which our regulars act far out of character. . . . Harve, you said that Asimov has been your science advisor and your friend, and you have an excellent relationship with him. If you don't wish to heed my views on this subject, I plead with you to listen to his.

It sincerely pains me to be negative about this. I like your new writer. He cannot be expected to have our fix on the details of the *Star Trek* format but his skills are obvious. Of course, I am forever grateful to the things you have done and that Bill Shatner has done to realize the highly valuable *Star Trek* property we have. But I cannot be less than honest about my views on what we have here so far.

By mid-November, *Star Trek: The Next Generation* had been picked up for another year, and Gene wrote the following to Frank Mancuso:

Clearly, the credit for that belong to a lot of talented and hard working people, but I want to note at this time that the success of the show is due in no small measure to the support, input and approach furnished by Paramount. Such support always begins at the top, and so a special word of personal appreciation is due. I thank you.

A few words are also due on the subject of the *Star Trek V* movie. I have deliberately not written a memo on the second draft script because I had already informed you and others of what my thoughts were on the first draft script, and despite some cosmetic changes, they remain the same on this present second draft script.

. . . Beyond that, the script has become filled with many moves reminiscent of *Star Wars* rather than *Star Trek,* examples of that being shock troop "marines," "machinegun phasers," and other items which are bound to puzzle our audience.

It seems to me that Leonard Nimoy's unavailability could be put to good use in giving us time to develop a story that will not diminish the value of our *Star Trek* property as I believe this one most certainly will do. I am willing to do anything I can to help, but, Frank, I just can't lend my name to the present script. Please, believe me that I do not want to be an obstructionist in any way, but neither do I want to deceive you regarding my true feelings about this. I suppose I'm saying that I need your advice on how to proceed with this.

Very sincerely,

Gene said what he could, but the film proceeded. One of the last memos is dated September 13, 1988 to Harve Bennett—"Subject: Star Trek V: The Final Frontier, Revised shooting script, August 24, 1988":

Many improvements in this version. The story moves along at a nice pace.

In my opinion, most of the problems left are in the last half of the script.

Re Sybok's control of Sulu, Uhura, Chekov, etc., we have always played all of our *Star Trek* characters as a superior kind of human. Thus, our audience would be surprised at having Sybok control them as easily as shown in the script. Our *Enterprise* continuing characters have gathered a hell of a lot of knowledge and conditioning all these years we've travelled through space with them. They are anything but "ordinary" people, and they will remain much more valuable as a part of the *Star Trek* format if Sybok has to work particularly hard to take control of them. He now takes control of them almost as easily as he does Act One's simple farmers.

The script must protect McCoy even more if he is to retain his format value to us. It is simply unbelievable that the hard-nosed, highly realistic McCoy would swallow this God nonsense so easily to the point he actually acts shocked when Kirk questions the identity of the Being. This is simply not the McCoy who has worked so well for us these last 22 years. By all means, make Kirk bold and brave enough to question this Being, but do not destroy McCoy's strength and value in the process of doing it.

How can Sybok control people as he does? Simply because he "relieves them of their pain"? This seems too thin to satisfy the kind of believability that the *Star Trek* format has always required in the past.

It also requires answers to other questions. Does Spock have similar powers? Or does Sarek? Or, if Sybok has power beyond that of other Vulcans, the reasons for this should be explained.

McCoy is right when he describes Sybok's methods as "pop psychology." But his saying it doesn't take the curse off it. Can't we do better?

I have great problems with Paradise or even a fake Paradise being a planet and *enormous* problems with any of our continuing characters believing it could be true. This doesn't hurt our story at all because if it turns out they are wrong, all the more exciting our finding this planet becomes. And it detracts not at all from our people that they don't believe it. It should *not* exist, and the fact it does tells us that the Being must have extraordinary powers in many ways.

Harve, we long ago got rid of the idea of our dealing with anything suggesting the traditional Judeo-Christian God. It is vital to *Star Trek* that we deal properly with the attitudes of our crew regarding this question. As I predicted, once I got a copy of this in script form, *Star Trek* will be in a difficult position regarding our characters' attitudes toward the question—a situation of being damned if they believe and damned if they don't.

It seems to me the only possible answer to this is throughout the script to stay a mile away from revealing or even hinting at what our people believe about God. I was generally successful in doing this in the original *Star Trek* series. A few things did slip by, but not many, at least not many serious variations of my policy to keep *Star Trek* free of serious religious themes.

In my opinion, the only possible way to protect the *Star Trek* property in this production is to make it abundantly clear to our audience that this is a story of the *Enterprise* and crew versus a super-alien—and our continuing characters must react accordingly. Suggest we emphasize even more strongly that this Alien Being is one which hopes to pull the old "God" trick on the life forms of this galaxy. It tried to do this once before and was stopped by more powerful Entities in the distant past and left "bottled" up on this unusual planet—but now it sees a chance to break free.

Turning now to scientific believability, does our story need the Great Barrier in Space? Have never heard a reputable scientist state a belief that this kind of thing exists. Here, as with the previous "God" question, we must remember that a highly vocal percentage of our audience is college trained and would see the Great Barrier as a fantasy approach to *Star Trek*. Caution that we do not risk our format's reputation on an obscure or misunderstood theory about the galaxy's center.

Perhaps the answer is simply to not call it that. Why

not play on the Center of the Galaxy as a most unusual place to go, then have the *Enterprise* go there and meet the things described in the script? Blame the things we find on the "titanic" struggle that once went on there between the alien super-Beings. That way we don't risk making ourselves look foolish.

Incidentally, getting to the Center of the Galaxy, even at the highest warp speeds, would take months or even years at the velocities established for the *Enterprise*. You'll have to deal with that somehow.

Again, compliments on the improvements that have been made so far. More comments later, if necessary.

On April 30, 1989, the "Outtakes" column of the *Los Angeles Times* Calendar Section reported the following:

Not all the news from the summer pic fronts is upbeat. Reports put *Star Trek V: The Final Frontier*—due June 9 from Paramount—back in the editing room following recent test screening.

A Paramount rep said the film that was screen tested "was really a work in progress," and promised "a blockbuster."

A test-viewer we talked with reported "a lot of laughter and snickers" through a recent screening at the Paramount lot, attended by a recruited audience of more than 200—along with star/director William Shatner, star Leonard Nimoy and producer Harve Bennett.

"There was only a little applause at the end," said our source. A sequence that looked "real fake" was set in Yosemite National Park. "There's this little tiny figure shown from a distance—scaling a massive, sheer-drop cliff. Then the camera zooms in real close, and you see it's Shatner. And he's sweating, and climbing free hand! No ropes, no nothing! The audience just cracked up."

Special effects got mixed marks. Some time warp scenes "are really neat." But there were also snickers, said one source, for "some real tacky effects," including one in which the *Enterprise* "looks like a cardboard cutout" as it hovers against a planet.

The film was released in June 1989, and was met with almost universal scorn by the critics. (*The New York Post* entitled their review, "Live Long and Wither.") Roger Ebert, writing in the *Chicago Sun Times,* said ". . . pretty much of a mess . . . crowded with loose ends, overlooked developments and forgotten characters." He also thought that the film lacked the "trademarks of the *Star Trek* sagas," and the subplots that featured the other characters. David Denby in *New York* dryly observed that the film was "the most Californian" of the five films, especially in how the Vulcan Sybok behaves like a group therapy leader. Director Shatner, Denby thought "mismanages the climax of what is mostly an amiable movie." The fans voted with their wallets, but instead of supporting the film, as they did with the first effort, they stayed away in droves after a strong opening weekend. The studio could no longer put the *Star Trek* label on anything and expect the fans to turn out. *The Final Frontier* is the lowest grossing of all the *Star Trek* films.

CHAPTER 20

While the studio paid a premium price for his name and creativity, the development of the show was not without cost to Gene. He was under a huge pile of problems: the pressure from the studio to create something that would justify their investment of millions of dollars, the ongoing problems with the movies and merchandising, and the ceaseless tension brought about by a workaholic-style of writing propelled by an overwhelming desire to prove himself right by "capturing lightning in a bottle again." This fueled by a nagging fear that he couldn't rise to the occasion one more time, his knowledge that all the chips were riding on this one play, combined to put him into a severe depression. What would have been difficult for a man in his forties to handle took their toll on the sixty-five-year-old: Gene became depressed, more so than any other period of his life. While he was a regular, social drinker, he began to drink more. Things that were natural and normal for him became problems as he began to bend under the ferocious pressure. Gene started to drink in the morning, a deviation from his normal pattern of unwinding in the afternoon and evening.

Like his trips to the Pritikin Longevity Center to control his weight, Gene opted for the fast fix and checked himself into the Schick-Shadel Hospital in Santa Barbara on September 21, 1986. He would stay for ten days.

Schick-Shadel defines sobriety as "total abstinence from any mind-altering substances." Given that definition, even one drink would be forbidden and cause you to slip from "sobriety." Gene often drank every day, socially at lunch and in the evening with dinner.

Gene's attending physician was Donald F. Sweeney, MD, who was also the medical director of the hospital and a person who had a financial interest in the facility. He took a detailed medical history of Gene that covered his substance abuse history. Dr. Sweeney wrote:

> He has used marijuana in the past, has used cocaine/snorting only a few lines earlier in 1966, he has never considered it a problem. He used Dexamil in the past. He has used Valium and Seconal, none regularly.

The file also had Gene's past medical history, and under the heading "Para-Illnesses" we find the following:

> Patient states that he feels that depression might be a problem. He took Dexamil and he felt that it made him much more alert and creative in the past.[1] He has not used it in many years. He feels, apparently as does his physician, that the "depression" may be responsible for his drinking and that the Desyrel[2] that he takes is helping him.

Gene went through Schick-Shadel's aversion therapy[3] during his ten-day stay and then returned home. The aversion procedure did not work and Gene began drinking again, but in moderation—a couple of drinks with lunch or a glass of wine or two in the evening. No more drinking in the morning.

Eight days after checking out of the hospital, Gene was part of the drama and excitement of a major press party when Paramount announced *Star Trek: The Next Generation*.

The depression lifted but did not go away completely, nor did the relentless pressure. It got worse with the conflicts

---

[1]During the original series, when he did the all-night rewrites.

[2]A prescribed antidepressant. The majority of drugs listed in Gene's patient history were prescribed at various times over a period of years.

[3]The patient is given a drug that makes them react strongly to alcohol. They then ingest alcohol and become violently ill. The treatment is supposed to kill the desire for alcohol. Schick's own advertisements claim a 70% success rate, defined as staying away from alcohol for a year.

with his colleagues in the creation of the *Next Generation* format. And the writing was slower. It was just as good, if not better—only slower. Gene was finding that one of the things he could not control was the relentless passage of time. He was growing old.

At the suggestion of his regular doctor, Gene visited Dr. Robert Podell, a psychiatrist and neurologist. Gene first visited Podell in early July 1989, and then a few more times after that.

Podell was later deposed in the course of the will contest brought by Gene's daughter, Dawn. During the deposition, Dr. Podell was asked by Dawn's lawyer about Gene having any "cognitive impairment whatsoever." Dr. Podell testified:

"Well, yes that in the sense when he was depressed, he had very negative thoughts about his future. He felt that if he couldn't write, that his life wasn't going to be worth very much. That's a cognitive impairment. That's a cognitive distortion.

"I tried to help him correct that, that if he couldn't write that does not mean your life is no good or your life is only good if you can produce scripts for this show. That's part of a cognitive distortion, overgeneralization and negative thinking that depressed patients exhibit. That he had."

The studio finally quit vacillating on the length of time for the pilot and settled on two hours. Gene took what Fontana had written and rewrote it, performing a feat similar to what he had done with "The Menagerie" all those years before. He wrote an envelope story, surrounding Fontana's work and adding a new character, whom he named "Q" for his friend Janet Quarton.

Quarton wasn't the first friend to be included in *The Next Generation*. Another longtime friend of *Star Trek* was given a posthumous tribute. George La Forge had muscular dystrophy, a disease that stopped him from attending school in the ninth grade. He continued to study at home and eventually graduated from high school, receiving his diploma in a special ceremony in his room.

"A prisoner in his own body it was *Star Trek* that took his mind away," said his mother, Sue. George attended *Star Trek* conventions in Detroit and California, ultimately meeting writers, producers, and Gene himself. Gene liked him and remembered. Twelve years after George died, George La Forge became Geordi La Forge on the show.

On August 4, 1987, shortly before the new show debuted, Gene wrote to friends in Hawaii and gave them some insight into the new show:

Yes, I'm still working a bit too hard—have personally rewritten every new *Star Trek* episode we have so far—but it is also exhilarating. First, because I love challenge—and second, because good things are happening.

The Paramount brass saw our first regular hour episode this morning—a rough cut, yet—and they've been calling all day. My favorite call came from the rather surly president of Paramount television who said: "I didn't think it would be this good." Faint praise, but he did follow it up by approving a budget increase for the show. Strong praise from others—I'm told the rumor around the industry is that *Star Trek: The Next Generation* is the most exciting series in town, including the network shows. The two hour premier show, due for final editing tomorrow, will go on the air October 3.

So, things are going well for the moment—the next test being how much the audience will like it. Some good news there. Our people who have attended sci-fi conventions are reporting that even the die-hard Kirk/Spock fans are beginning to applaud news of the new series. To me it is not a case of replacing one group of characters with another. They're all my children. And I know, of course, that the odds are astronomical against pulling off a similar phenomenon a second time.

Paramount must have thought so too and hedged its bet. The series regulars had *three* contracts: one for the pilot, one for the first thirteen episodes, and one for multiple years. The studio could bail out if it became necessary, with no long-term financial obligation to the actors.

The show was difficult to write for and the level of stress

was high.[4] There were additional problems. Gene's longtime friend, attorney, and agent, Leonard Maizlish, in an attempt to conserve Gene's time and energy, began "helping out" with the scripts. His assistance was not appreciated by the members of the Writers Guild, who made a complaint to their union. Maizlish was told to quit "helping" and was asked to vacate the lot.

The new show was met with mixed reviews and perhaps the most vocal critics of the new show were some of the cast of the old show. However, DeForest Kelley provided a bridge between the old and the new *Treks* with a brief appearance in the pilot episode as a 137-year-old Admiral McCoy, for which he accepted only SAG scale as payment. Doohan would return in an episode, as would Nimoy in a two-part episode that was part *The Next Generation* and part advertisement for the then upcoming *Star Trek VI* film.[5]

The concept of first run syndication was a success. Writers, producers, story editors came and went. Some enjoyed themselves, others did not. So few people understood the 24th century, anyway.

At a *Star Trek* convention in Los Angeles in 1988, a number of items came up for discussion and the old fire returned once more. Gene's secretary, Susan Sackett, for whatever reason, let it be known that Gates McFadden would not be back for the second season. Gene was not scheduled to talk for several hours, so a number of fans organized a protest complete with chanting and quickly copied handouts. When Gene was introduced and walked out on the stage, there were some chants of "Bring Back Gates." During the question-and-answer part of the program, he was asked about bringing her back. Gene's response gave them some insight into his thoughts on creativity:

"I like Gates McFadden, too. I think she's a charming lady and a good actress; however, you're talking to a past

---

[4]Bob Justman left after the first year after watching his blood pressure spiral upward.

[5]In addition to not liking the Spock episode, Gene had made the comment he thought it was a "two-hour ad for the film." The ultimate irony was that it was the first new episode run after his death and the tribute slide, "Gene Roddenberry 1921–1991" was run at the beginning of the program.

master of forcing people to do things. There's no way any amount of talk about Gates McFadden will do anything more than the fact she is liked will already do for us. As far as it being a vote; are we going to have Gates McFadden [back?], you all move 'For'; I say, 'Nay.' The nays have it.

"I am actually not the one who said 'nay.' The whole staff looked over the thing and said, 'We do want to try another image.' You have to accept that because if I were to listen to your voice, I could have listened to the network voices, and other people saying, 'Do this. Do that.' *Star Trek* would have been shit. Really. There is such a thing as telling the artist what you want and like and then leave it up to him to do what he does. That's the only way it can be."

Gene continued to give occasional lectures on his vision of the future to colleges, associations, corporations, and institutes. One lecture was most memorable for the small drama that preceded it.

On October 14, 1989, Gene was scheduled to speak to a group from the Jung Institute at Mount St. Mary's College. It would be the easiest talk he ever had to get to, as it was less than a mile from his home.

As he was being escorted to the front, he passed by an attractive woman, who looked up at him, smiled, and asked how his mother and sister were doing. Gene stopped, returned the smile, said they were now living together and responded with a question of his own, "How is your son?"

The woman was surprised at Gene's apparent recognition. She hadn't seen him since he'd arranged for her and her son to visit the set during the third season of *Star Trek*. There had been that awkward episode at Darleen's wedding reception during which Gene had related his unsuccessful teenage beach-seduction scene, and then no contact for twenty years.

She managed to answer that her son was doing well. Then, like a trained boxer, Gene moved in and landed the knockout punch. Fixing her with a steady gaze he said, "Are you still reading everything under the sun?"

The woman was stunned. Chills ran down her spine as she heard Gene's seemingly innocent question and realized its import. Fifty-one years before, when she was a young girl spending the summer at Redondo Beach, Gene had used it on her as his opening "line."

He smiled and was pushed forward by one of his hosts,

who was completely unaware of the emotionally loaded mini-drama that had just happened in front of him.

By the third season of *The Next Generation,* Gene had stayed longer than he had planned, but there were one or two producers who had come along that he thought he had to watch since they thought they had been brought in to "fix the show," as Gene described them.

By the fourth season, he was withdrawing. Michael Piller and Rick Berman were in place, they knew their jobs, and it was time to leave. Gene was organizing his life more and more to operate out of his home office. By this time he was still maintaining his office at the studio, but only coming in a few days a week. The first signs of normal pressure hydrocephalus, a difficult to diagnose disorder, were beginning to show. Gene's health was slowly failing.

Essentially self-effacing, Gene often found himself a little self-conscious at honors' ceremonies. That said, it did not prevent him from being thrilled and excited when something big came along. Frank Mancuso, head of the studio, decided that the newest building on the Paramount lot should be named for Gene and told him so at a lunch. Gene was delighted. It was a huge honor, given only to Paramount's most important stars, current and historical.

Paramount did it right, with all the hoopla and fanfare of a Hollywood premiere. On June 6, 1991, Gene's family, local dignitaries, studio brass, and almost all members of both *Star Trek* crews, along with the men and women of the Paramount family celebrated the dedication of the Gene Roddenberry Building.

Gene had no prepared words, but that did not put him at a loss. Leaning on his cane, he smiled broadly and said, "Paramount paid me more money that I deserve," and then, with a dramatic pause, finished his thought, "and they've been paid more than they deserve."

Sometime later Gene reflected on the building dedication to Richard Arnold who remembered:

"[Gene] needed to be loved, and I think that Gene, probably in his later years, knew that he was loved by millions, but that gives you nothing. He pretty much said as much when we were talking about the building being named for him.

"He said that when he'd been eating at Nickodell's [a restaurant near Paramount Studios], shortly after the original series got on the air, some people at the next table were discussing the episode of the night before. Whoever these people were, they were raving about how wonderful it was. [Gene] was absolutely blown away by that. He said, for him that was *the* single most incredibly flattering thing to ever happen to him.

"Then they named this building after Gene. He said to have a studio name a building after you, that topped that."

At core, Gene was a shy man. His friend of over a decade, Marta Houske, remembers several incidents:

"I remember crossing the lot one day with Gene, and I saw him get this kind of shy, introverted look on his face, which by then I knew. I looked up to see who was coming. It was some studio bigwig, I think the head of marketing and promotion at Paramount. I could see from his body language that Gene was feeling shy about even saying 'hi.' The guy suddenly saw that it was Gene and came up and said, 'Hey, Gene! Howya doin?' Then Gene became his affable self, like he was relieved that the guy remembered him. He wasn't doing this gladhanding-Hollywood-producer-hustle-bullshit number. I never saw him do that. I never once saw him put on pretentious airs.

"We would walk into Lucy's El Adobe, [a famous restaurant across the street from Paramount] and it wasn't 'Here's Mr. Roddenberry. Let's give him our ringside seat.' It was more like 'Hey, Gene! Howya doin?' and he would say, 'Hi, Frank. How are you?' And they would plop him down at any old table. It was just the naturalness of the way he related to people."

There was yet another film planned, *Star Trek VI: The Undiscovered Country*. Nick Meyer was to direct. Richard Arnold and Ernie Over were privy to two meetings between Gene and Nick. At the first meeting Meyer got up, reportedly after five minutes, and walked out, leaving a surprised and insulted Gene Roddenberry sitting behind his desk.

Richard recalls: "I was outside the office during that meeting. Meyer must have gone out the door to the hallway because I didn't see him leave; I just knew that the meeting suddenly ended. Afterward, Susan went in and I went upstairs because there was enough tension in the air that you could cut it with a knife. Susan told me later that Nick had left. In the meeting there was someone from the front office, Ralph Winter, Leonard, no more than half a dozen people. Gene was not happy."

Right after that Ernie drove Gene down to La Costa. Within hours, the latest script was delivered by messenger and Gene went through it. Gene had asked Ernie and Richard to comment on the previous draft and now Ernie would compare that to the newer script. Ernie Over remembers:

"There were very few changes. Gene had me make up a list of all these things; some were minor and he was willing to let them go; but some were substantial and he wanted to deal with those.

"We came back up to Los Angeles specifically for this meeting with Nick Meyer, Ralph Winter, John Goldwyn, David Kirkpatrick, Leonard Maizlish, Gene, Susan Sackett and myself. Susan brought everyone into the office and had a notepad and sat down on the couch. I also had all of Gene's notes, and Gene told me, 'Ernie, I want you to stay and remind me in case I forget anything; I want to make sure to go over all the points.'

"I was sitting behind and to the left of Gene, who was at his desk. The others were on the chairs in front of the desk, except for Susan, on the couch. When we got going, one of the men asked Gene if he thought it was appropriate for a secretary to be here, so Gene dismissed Susan. She looked at me and said, 'What about Ernie?' and Gene said, 'I want him to stay.' Susan turned crimson and slammed the door. We could hear her yelling and screaming in the adjoining office.

"Nick Meyer said a few words like, 'I apologize for our misunderstanding at our last meeting. That's why we're all here today, to go over these concerns.' Ralph made a few introductory remarks and Goldwyn and Kirkpatrick mainly listened. It was mainly a dialog among Gene and Ralph and Nick. Gene went down his list, point by point, of all the things that he was concerned with. Winter was taking notes. Then Gene and Meyer would square off about some of them.

"For example, there was a comment about taking the *Enterprise* out of dock. Meyer had made a reference in the script to a very nineteenth-century nautical thing, like, 'right standard rudder.' Gene was saying, 'Starships don't have rudders! We need to think of a more appropriate term.' That sort of thing.

"Meyer was very concilliatory on most things. He stood his ground on a couple of points, where he said, 'I'll take a look at that.'

"As a matter of fact, they made all these grandiose promises at that meeting, and almost none of them were incorporated into the script. They ignored him. It was obvious from the tone of the meeting that they were giving him the opportunity to say whatever he wanted to say and everyone was all very pleasant about it; but nothing happened about it.

"There were a few things that ultimately stayed in. Gene objected to the reference of the Klingons saying, 'As the Americans would say, 'Only Nixon would go to China!' Gene thought that was the most ridiculous thing he'd ever heard."

Gene died two weeks before the film was released. During the film's first showing, when theaters were filled with Trekkers, reports came back that when Gene's name flashed on the screen, the applause was loud and prolonged.

CHAPTER 21

Gene was gone, and the ebb and flow of emotion washed back and forth over her. She would struggle for control and then the enormity of the situation would overwhelm Majel. She drove home listening to KNX Newsradio, hearing the announcement of Gene's death, released by the studio just moments before. It was surreal. Driving was an exercise in self-control, a demonstration that she could handle what was thrown at her. There were a thousand things to consider, a hundred decisions to make—where to bury Gene, what to do about a memorial service.[1] When she came into the house, her mother was there, quietly sobbing. Majel sat on the white leather couch in the family room and, speaking to no one in particular, said, "I feel lonely already."

The day after his death, Gene's body was cremated at Forest Lawn, Hollywood Hills. Four people were present: Majel, Leonard Maizlish, Ernie Over, and this writer. Gene's body was in a wooden coffin finished in a highly polished dark cherry stain. Because of the cremation, all the metal, handles and adornment, had been removed from the casket.

Majel spent several private moments beside the casket while the three of us stood a respectful distance away. Leonard moved up, placed his hand on the casket and quietly

---

[1]Leonard Maizlish had prepared for the inevitable. A month before Gene's death, he had Ernie call a number of mortuaries and get information on facilities. Forest Lawn Hollywood Hills had a large hall that could accommodate the number of people Leonard expected.

said, "So long, pal." Ernie and I each then had a moment to say our good-byes as well.

We stood together quietly; no one moved, no one wanted to say the final word. After several quiet moments, at some unseen signal from the Forest Lawn director, the two men who stood nearby silently pushed the casket over to the crematory door. The casket was gently, reverently pushed inside, and the stainless steel door slid down, cutting off our view. We turned and walked out. No one said anything. It was a somber ride home.

The Saturday after Gene's death was to be Majel's annual Halloween Party. She agonized over cancelling it, and then, after discussing it with several friends, she decided Gene ought to have a party, so she modified the plans. The entertainment was cut down to only Brian Gilles, a magician. All the guests were called and told it would not, as was the custom, be a costume party. There was a mix of studio colleagues, Bel Air Country Club friends, a large contingent of the old guard Hollywood writers, and veterans from *Star Trek*'s original series. The party guests were a perfect reflection of Gene's love of diversity. It was a wake, a celebration of Gene's life with endless numbers of people telling each other "Gene stories." Even a few people who had originally approached the party with opinions that it was in bad taste were swept up in the love of Gene and the feelings displayed by those there. Near the end, Majel stood up, thanking everyone who had come, saying she had not known how many friends she and Gene truly had and how glad she was that everyone had come. The sharing of stories went on for hours, with the last guests not leaving until well after 1 A.M.

The memorial service was coordinated by Leonard Maizlish, a final duty for his longtime friend. Leonard had taken a lot of criticism from various sources, but one thing was clear—his devotion to Gene was unmistakable. He put together a memorial tribute befitting Gene.

Driving up the winding road to the Hall of Liberty at Forest Lawn, Hollywood Hills, the family saw hundreds of people walking up the road. Many were fans, a few in *Star Trek* uniforms; one woman in a wheelchair had traveled by public transportation from San Bernardino. People who had been touched by Gene in one way or another had flown in from all over the country. They were all there, united in their desire to give a tribute, to say a final farewell to a man who had influenced their lives. Even though the announcement had erroneously been made that the service was private, over 1,200 people showed up.

Before the service, Majel had gone through the family album, selecting a number of photographs that would be turned into slides and projected during the first minutes to a background of Gene's favorite music. Photographs were selected that showed the range and breadth of his life, aspects that many of his friends and colleagues had never seen. The nearly fifty photos were well received.

Nichelle Nichols sang two songs; one was a special tribute called simply "Gene." Ray Bradbury's tribute was the introduction to this volume. Whoopi Goldberg came next. Her thoughts were short and heartfelt.

"What to say about a man whom I didn't know well for twenty-five years, but I knew him well spiritually. He was a man who was able to reach out through my television and explain to me that I had a place in the world and in the future. For me, I guess, Gene Roddenberry is Thoreau. I always wanted to meet a visionary. I didn't realize it until I was on my way over here that that's exactly what he was.

"I sat with him and Rick [Berman] as I begged to be on the show. They thought I was kidding. I said, 'No, you don't understand. We're talking about *Star Trek*. I really need to be part of this.' And they just kind of mused at me. They thought it was very interesting and Gene wanted to know why.

"When I explained to him that his was the only vision that had black people in the future, he thought that was very bizarre. I guess he didn't realize that nobody else saw us there. This is what drew me to this show and to this man.

"He always had something nice to say to me, always something really fun. I'm not going to mourn. I was lucky. As Mr. Bradbury mentioned, it's time to celebrate this life that changed the entire face of the world. Everywhere you go, no matter what country, they all know *Star Trek*. They all know that somehow, the world can actually be better, because of this one man's vision.

"What an honor to have been able to meet someone who changed the world without screaming, or yelling—or that cursing out the presidents, like some of us do. He just said, 'No. This is my vision.' And for once, people who were in charge listened. And twenty-five years later a kid from the projects, and kids from all over the world, all over the country, are sitting here to celebrate Gene Roddenberry. Thank you."

Chris Knopf, a well-known writer-producer and friend of Gene's, was next. He told the story about his participation in the early invention of *Star Trek*, when Gene told him the idea at a Dodger Game. He continued:

"It was six years earlier I first met him, indirectly, at first, through a phone call from Sam Rolfe, creator and producer of another memorable series of its own era, *Have Gun, Will Travel*. 'Do you want to read a helluva writer?' he asked. You didn't hear that from Sam very often. I read. I recall two emotions: excitement and envy.

"I said I met Gene indirectly at first. Not true. He leaped out at you off the page. You could picture the man through his words, all the while keeping his reader transfixed with his characters and style. Through Sam and Hilda Rolfe, I got to know him and there started one of the countless friendships Gene nourished in his lifetime. 'Hey, where are you?' he'd say when we hadn't spoken in months. 'We haven't heard from you!'

" 'Gene,' I'd say, 'you've got thirty thousand things to worry about!' 'Thirty thousand and one,' he'd say. The war years, his flying in the army and for Pan Am, his desert crash, the years on the police force—he loved adventure. And you'd better be ready to go along for the ride, as I found out one rainy night.

"We'd been to dinner, celebrating something-or-other, as we pulled up the steep driveway leading to Gene's house then on Beverly Glen. The headlights played off a motorcycle, glistening wet. It was Gene's newest toy, and he prized it as he prized none other. 'Ever been on one?' he asked. 'No,' I answered, 'and it doesn't start now.' In our blue suits, shirts and ties, rain beating us to death, down the driveway we went on that Harley, onto Beverly Glen leaning into a turn up Lynbrook, lots of leaning, way over leaning, traction suddenly history, The bike and its sides spinning on the asphalt.

"We picked ourselves up off the pavement, our suits torn to shreds, blood pouring out of our knees, the bike, what was left of it, plowed through a hedge. We sat on a curb trying to decide whether the wiser course was emergency hospital or hot shower. Gene turned to me with that sudden, marvelous laugh of his. 'Do you realize,' he said, 'you'll probably never do anything like this again?' You gotta love it!

"Then, *Star Trek*. Most of us would have made a mess out of that: the eternal debate between good and evil, standing for justice and equality. Except that his choices, his words, the poetry and rhythm with which he used them, his philosophy and ideas, were so many levels above what most of us as writers knew how to achieve. Never mesmerized with the sound of his own voice, he was a spectacular learner, providing insight, charm, compassion, humor—infusing his work with qualities of self-searching. Putting us on paper—himself on paper. And the result you know: a seemingly ordinary man with extraordinary vision, the greatest gift of all.

"The younger of us, who know no better, and the older of us who do, grow lost sometimes in ridiculous dreams of a better future. Gene never did. On the contrary, he brought them to life, for millions of us. Nor did I ever see him squirm at a negative reaction to an idea of his. No using his shoetip to test for landmines—he knew enough never to let impossibilities plague him. He was so confident.

"Most of us can hear ourselves say, 'Damn it! I'd better hurry up! The thing's starting without me.' Gene led the parade. And few things carry more pain, disturb more, than watching a great man lessened. But over the past few months it was happening. The times I saw him or talked to him, he never made allusion to it. Not at Sam and Hilda Rolfe's home, where I first saw him in his struggle, nor the Halloween or back-to-school or Christmas parties Majel gave that seemed to so buoy his spirits.

"It couldn't have been a month ago that Sam and I had lunch with Gene at the house. It was the last time we would ever see him, though he seemed to be improving. He was as gracious as he'd ever been, wanting conversation, though it was difficult, coming at you with that grin on his face, excited about joining Sam and me and Jack Neuman and Dick Simmons at lunch someplace. 'Can you make it?' I asked him. 'Of course I can make it!' he said.

"Somewhere there is a great squealing and grinding. The wheel of humanity has lost a bearing."

Next came E. Jack Neuman, a writer of both radio and television, who had known Gene since his days at Ziv.

"Majel, Rod, family, friends, fans, Trekkers: I'm sure you've noticed in recent years that a great many folks have been making a great deal of fuss over Eugene Wesley Roddenberry. And rightly so. Gene's been awarded, cited, nominated, honored, dinnered, luncheoned, pedestaled and Beverly Hiltoned. Even the people at Paramount Pictures got excited and named a building after him. And three or four years ago, the star-street crowd implanted his name on one of their stars on Hollywood Boulevard. Gene Roddenberry's right up there with the Gloria Swansons, the Marilyn Monroes, and the Rin-Tin-Tins.

"Go over to Musso's one day. Have a bite of lunch. Then take a stroll and see for yourself. I don't suggest this facetiously, reverently would be a better word. Gene is the very first writer to be cemented there. In a way it's the first time the film industry has openly admitted that someone has to put that stuff down on paper before it gets up there on the screen.

"Anyhow, that's in Gene's public life. Privately, he liked to play a little golf and he was a fairly decent golfer, so I've been told. I never played golf with Gene (or with anyone else for that matter) it's just one of the few vices I've resisted. Aside from the fairways Gene's expertise was in a little-known, very obscure, track and field event called self-effacement. In Hollywood it's practically extinct. Gene was the hands-down champion of self-effacement, unequaled, unrivaled, unchallenged. Gene owned the gold, the silver and the bronze without even competing. He invented the event.

"1956. The flight was from New York to Los Angeles. A big man in a big black overcoat (wearing a bow tie) fastened himself into the seat next to mine. We grunted at each other and once we were airborne we ordered drinks. No in-flight movies and no jet engines in those days and it was no sin to have a second drink. Then a third one. Then a fourth. I don't remember what big black overcoat and I were talking about but I do know that round number five was en route when I said, 'Why are we doing all this drinking?' 'Because I'm scared,' he said. By that time I had enough brave-maker under my belt to say something real encouraging like, 'Hey, what's to be scared about?' Black overcoat lowered his eyes and sort of mumbled: 'I used to fly one of these things.'

"You've probably guessed that big, black overcoat and

bow tie was Gene Roddenberry. What you couldn't guess is that it was the first and only time in all the years we were friends that he ever mentioned he had a life before film. Three lives, actually. Three careers. Gene flew for the Army Air Corps before it was the Air Force; he flew for Pan American Airways before they went broke; he was an officer with the Los Angeles Police Department before Jack Webb finished re-inventing. Today if someone told me he had been an ordained priest or even a neurosurgeon I don't think I'd be surprised. But right here and now I want to tell you that I'm glad, I'm very glad that he discarded all of those frivolous, irresponsible pursuits and became a member of a dignified, honorable, long-respected profession with an assured future. He became a writer. A writer is a guy who gets up in the morning, puts on his or her pants, sits down at his or her desk, looks chaos squarely in the eye, and gets busy putting it into some kind of order. When he or she fails and the bad reviews pile up, the writer is a guy who cheers himself or herself up by telling himself or herself that the audiences are becoming less and less talented. (And if you can parse those last two sentences, you're a better man than I am.)

"Every writer has to have a patron. William Shakespeare had the queen of England. Bach had the elector of Brandenburg. The Prince Esterhazy sponsored Haydn and the network subsidized Gene Roddenberry. The spontaneous judgment of the public is always more authentic than the opinion of those who set themselves up to be judges of what is written, but after three seasons the network un-subsidized him. The man who invented self-effacement took personal affront—not because of the cancellation since that is a natural hazard always lurking in the background of commercial television—what peeved him was the casual way a network spokesman announced that Star Trek was too cerebral for the audience. Fighting words. You don't say things like that within earshot of a relentlessly decent man in a big black overcoat brave enough to wear a bow tie, whose respect and consideration for the audience was always uppermost in his mind. As far as he was concerned the audience was composed of one hundred million Ph.D.'s. Consequently, he had no alternative but to correct that network spokesman's thinking. He went from one end of this country to the other, crisscrossed the nation, telling his audiences that even though our future lies in space, our own big, beautiful, blue planet is worth saving. He provoked an avalanche of protesting mail that could not be ignored. The man in the black overcoat pulled it off. *Star Trek* came back. Bigger than ever. As you might guess I never heard Gene mention the miracle he had wrought. Not once. Not ever.

"Another airplane. Another time. Heading for London on this one. Black overcoat materialized along with Majel and Rod, who was a frisky three-year-old. A fun-filled flight. A little longer than the usual ten hours because of weather and a bomb scare at Heathrow. We sat on the ground in Manchester for five hours, but eventually we were in London. Customs. Cabs. Luggage, wrinkled and weary we all landed at the same hotel, notorious for soft beds. Gene was signing the register when he noticed the check-in date and turned to Majel. 'I don't know how to tell you this,' he said, 'but I have to be in Austin, Texas, tomorrow morning.' Bone-weary, beat, he took his bags, crawled in a cab, went back out to Heathrow and Texas. Something he wouldn't sidestep. A little speech for some Texas Trekkers. He'd promised them he'd be there.

"What I've been trying to do is pay my personal tribute to Gene Roddenberry, as one writer to another. We all know that whatever we may have done we always start from scratch. We never know how good we are—we may think we are better or worse than we are—but we never know exactly. We just do our best. Eugene Wesley Roddenberry did rather more than his best. That's the man I knew. I'm going to miss him and his big black overcoat.

"When my Prince Hamlet spoke of his father the king, surely, most surely those words were meant for our friend: 'He was a man, take him for all in all, I shall not look upon his like again.' "

Finally, Patrick Stewart, stately of bearing, eloquent of diction, spoke the last tribute.

"These addresses have merely been in alphabetical order, Leonard informs me. I just got lucky for the first time in my life to come low in the alphabet. It's always been a handicap in the past.

"The first impression of Gene Roddenberry was size. Bulk, stature, bigness. Gene dominated by the space that he filled and when Gene opened his arms, not only were the dimensions involved impressive, but he suggested dimensions that went on, beyond his fingertips. The next, unexpected, impression, when he spoke, was of gentleness. A surprisingly light, tenor voice with a rising inflection that gave a lilt, an airiness, an almost whimsical tone to his statements. And only in the past few days, when reading the obituaries, the appreciations, the editorials, did I discover that, had he lived there longer, I might have heard the sound of Southwest Texas, because Gene was born in El Paso.

"I wish I had known that, because for a short time I lived in a neighboring city across the Rio Grande: Juarez. And I stood under those skies and felt the heat, and looked at those hard, bare mountains. Considering the impact that Gene Roddenberry was to have on our culture and the culture of the world, what a perfect location El Paso was for him to draw his first breath. Straddling the old world and the new. A meeting point of people and cultures: Aztec, Olmec, Tigua, European, Oriental, African. On the banks of a great continental river, this place of diversity, a mixing, a flow of challenge and space. How appropriate!

"There are many people here who are much more qualified than I to speak of the life of Gene Roddenberry that followed since his first appearance in 1921. I have known Gene for only five years, and though we were always promising each other lunch or dinner, times of quiet away from the set, when we can exchange thoughts and experiences and ideas, we only in fact found them twice. Two lunches. Of course, had we really wanted to, we would have found those times more often. But I never called and Gene never called and the seasons went by.

"It seems to me that I sensed why. Gene had launched *The Next Generation* and now he expected us to get on with it. He had other pressing matters to absorb his attention: living, for one thing. And dying.

"Dying. Gene certainly thought about that, and he wrote about it. It has become a standing joke on our sets that whenever the good captain begins to philosophize, the crew and cast will burst into universal groans. Eventually somebody will cry out, 'Give us the death speech, Captain!' Well, Jonathan, Marina, you're going to get it. Lavar, Gates, Brent, Michael, here it comes: that speech that we've so often laughed about.

"It occurred very early, in the start of the second season. It was written by Gene in an episode, I believe, mostly written by another writer, and once again, the good *Enterprise* was in peril and all of us were convinced that we were going to die. The android, Data, paid an unexpected visit to the captain's quarters and asked him, 'Captain, what is death?'

"Picard replied, 'Well, Data, some explain it as our changing into an indestructible form, forever unchanging. They argue that the purpose of the entire universe is to then maintain us in an earthlike garden which will give us pleasure through all eternity. At the other extreme are those who prefer the idea of our blinking into nothingness, with all our experiences, our hopes, our dreams, only a delusion.'

"And Data asks, 'And which do you believe, sir?' 'Well,' says Picard, 'considering the marvelous complexity of our universe, its clockwork perfection, its balances of this against that, matter, energy, gravitation, time, dimension, pattern, I believe that our existence must mean more than either of those choices. I prefer to believe that what we are goes beyond Euclidean and other practical measuring systems and that, in ways we cannot yet fathom, our existence is part of a reality beyond what we understand now as reality.'

"I wonder how many popular television series would have the guts to place a speech like that in the middle of a prime time broadcast? The Old Testament, atheism, Euclid! And a few weeks ago, a fifth season episode described the legend of Gilgamesh and spoke of the Homeric hymns, and in a letter to Rick Berman, a fan, thrilled and amazed by these references, reflected that in the one week of that show's transmission, more people were probably made curious about that literature than at any time since their creation!

"Even at its most frivolous, which sometimes *The Next Generation* is, it is concerning itself with ideas, with issues. . . . That is Gene's gift to us, which we actors and producers and crew and technicians and staff strive to sustain.

"Gene's gift to me was this job, and that endowment will last a lifetime—sometimes as a curse, but much more as an unexpected, life-transforming, life-bestowing blessing. Five years ago, first in his home, then twice in his office, he looked at and listened to a middle-aged, bald, opinionated, working-class British Shakespearian actor and he said, 'He will be captain.' Inexplicable!

"Gene at the beginning was challenged on all these counts. Our American icon played by this, this . . . ! How to describe him? Even my hairline was subject to heated questioning. When a journalist remarked that 'Surely, in the twenty-fourth century there would be a cure for male pattern baldness,' Gene responded, 'But why? In the twenty-fourth century nobody will care!' With that remark, millions of men stood taller. Even without hair.

"That is what Gene did. He readjusted our view. He corrected our vision, our vision of where we were going and what our values were. What our values will become. And the view wasn't always consistent, especially where it concerned women. Infuriatingly, *Star Trek* remains simultaneously liberated and sexist. Maybe even in that, Gene remains, sadly, a visionary. We discussed this particularly contentious issue, Gene and I, and he reminded me that before we began shooting the pilot he had said to me, 'Patrick, if you have something important to say about this show, say it to me.'

"Gene always made it easy to be honest and frank with him. He never intimidated, though he could impress. I was reminded of that this week when A.C. Lyles spoke of an incident when President Reagan visited the set in the spring. He and Gene stood side by side, and somehow Gene's stick got knocked to the ground and at once, the president bent on one knee to pick it up. When this was referred to later, Mr. Reagan said, 'You know, in that moment, I felt I was about to be knighted.' In one way or another, Gene graced all of us while he was alive and he will go on doing so.

"Almost a year ago I was here, taking my farewell of another friend who died too soon. I'm going to repeat some words of a British doctor on the subject of dying:

" 'To walk we have to lean forward, lose our balance, and begin to fall. We let go, constantly, of the previous stability, falling, all the time, trusting that we will find a succession of new stabilities with each step. The fullest living is a constant dying of the past, enjoying the present fully, but holding it lightly; letting it go without clinging and moving freely into new experiences. Our experience of the past and of those dear to us is not lost at all, but remains richly within us.'

"Gene, I have something important to say about the show. Thank you!"

The memorial closed with a dimming of the lights and a spotlight playing on a picture of Gene while he, as usual, had the last word with a recording of some of his thoughts.

Leonard had the whole operations timed to a thirty-second tolerance. Everyone stepped outside.

It was an exceptionally clear day as we stood on the side of the hill just outside the Hall of Liberty, the San Fernando Valley spread out at our feet like an urban carpet. We heard a low buzzing in the distance, off to our right. Four planes approached from the east, flying in a slight V-formation. Our position, elevated from the valley floor, gave us a unique perspective, looking off at the planes rather than directly overhead. As the planes passed slightly above and in front of us, the plane second from the right peeled off in the famous "Missing Man" maneuver, aviation's honor to a fallen flyer. As it ascended into the clear sky, I remembered the words that were used at the end of the memorial, Gene's response when I asked him how he wanted to be remembered:

That I had great patience with and great affection for the human race. What we humans are is really a remarkable thing. How can you doubt that we will survive and mature? There may be a lot of wisdom in the old statement about looking on the world lovingly. If we can, perhaps the world will have time to resolve itself.

Like the memory of Gene, the image of the plane persisted in the mind's eye long after it was out of sight.

EPILOGUE

"Space. The final frontier . . ."

On September 24, 1992, eleven months to the day Gene died, a letter was sent to Daniel S. Goldin, Administrator of the National Aeronautics and Space Administration on Mount Wilson Institute stationery.

Dear Mr. Goldin:

We would like to add our endorsement to the nomination of Gene Roddenberry for the posthumous award of a NASA Medal for Distinguished Public Service.

Gene Roddenberry's creative genius opened the imaginations of hundreds of millions to the fact that the remarkable achievements of NASA are only the first step in an advancing technology that will carry humankind away from humanity's birthplace and out to the stars—perhaps to join the even larger and more diverse community of intelligent life in the Cosmos.

We respectfully urge that NASA consider the award of the Medal for Distinguished Public Service to Gene Roddenberry coincident with

the first anniversary of Gene's death on
October 24, 1991.

Sincerely,
Hugh Downs
ABC News

Robert Jastrow
Director
Mount Wilson Institute

Schedules did not permit the award to be given on the
first anniversary of Gene's death, but shortly thereafter, on
January 30, 1993, Majel accepted the Distinguished Public
Service Medal for Gene from Daniel Goldin at a ceremony
held at the Smithsonian's National Air and Space Museum
in Washington, D.C.

The citation accompanying the medal read: "For distinguished service to the Nation and the human race in presenting the exploration of space as an exciting frontier and a
hope for the future."

There was another honor NASA accorded Gene, but of a
more private nature. This tribute brought to light the true
faces of NASA's people, revealing the poetry hidden in their
hearts. It was something they all knew was right in the
doing.

In October, 1992, a year after his death, Gene's ashes
were sent to Houston to the care and keeping of astronaut
Jim Wetherbee. The ashes were transferred from the canister
they were shipped in and sealed in a slightly larger, ma-
chined, stainless-steel cylinder. Accompanied by a $5'' \times 7''$
American flag, the cylinder was carried on board the space
shuttle, inventoried only as part of the several pounds of personal property each astronaut is permitted.

On a giant column of fire and smoke, the space shuttle
Columbia rose into the sky above Florida, taking a small
part of Gene along with it. Gene Roddenberry had made it
into space, if only symbolically. He was a part of our evolution into a space-faring society, and his contribution was being honored by the people who had turned imagination into
reality. It was a unique tribute for a man whose vision inspired many of the people whose creativity and skills took
him into space that day. By their actions, their generosity of

spirit, with this quiet, simple tribute, NASA showed that Gene's optimistic vision of humanity's future, his *Star Trek* dream, lived on.

Gene would have loved the adventure.

A P P E N D I X   I

A GENE RODDENBERRY FILMOGRAPHY

This is as complete a listing of Gene's output as is possible to compile from credible sources to date. Those sources include Gene's personal files, the CBS broadcast archives, the Ziv archives, the Sam Rolfe archives, and Gene's credits on file at the Writers' Guild of America, Inc. (WGA), which he joined March 1, 1954.

Broadcast dates of network shows have been listed where possible. Syndicated programs were shown at varying times in different markets, so the dates listed are those on the script.

Gene began his career writing under the pseudonym of Robert Wesley, his brother's first name and Gene's middle name. The following scripts were written under that name. Since the bulk of Ziv programs were syndicated, the dates listed are those on the scripts.

As Robert Wesley:

Mr. District Attorney—1954—Ziv Productions—Syndicated.

"Defense Plant Gambling" 2 March 1954
(First recorded script sale—written and sold in late 1953—filmed and broadcast in 1954.)

"Wife Killer"	26 April 1954
"Police Academy"	15 July 1954
"Court Escape"	14 January 1955
"Patrol Boat"	5 April 1955
"Police Brutality"	1 July 1955

I Led Three Lives

"Radioactive"	9 January 1956
"Discredit Police"	6 February 1956

Highway Patrol

"Reformed Criminal"	23 August 1955
"Human Bomb"	24 October 1955
"Mental Patient"	7 December 1955
"Prospector"	7 February 1956
"Oil Lease"	28 June 1956

The following scripts were written for Ziv under the name Gene Roddenberry:

The West Point Story

Broadcast: CBS Fridays 8:00–8:30, October 1956–September 1957; ABC Tuesdays 10:00–10:30, October 1957–July 1958.

Episode	Broadcast
"The Operator"	unk
"Home Folks"	unk
"The Brothers"	11 Nov 1956
"Double Reverse"	28 Dec 1956
"Man of Action"	7 Dec 1956
"Manhunt"	11 Jan 1957
"One Command"	22 Feb 1957
(Story by Gene Roddenberry and Jack Bennett, Screenplay by Gene Roddenberry.)	
"Jet Flight"	8 Feb 1957
"Guest of Honor"	unk
(Gene took over a script from Sam Rolfe and finished it.)	
"Drowning of The Gun"	unk
(Written by E. Jack Neuman and Gene Roddenberry.)	

Dr. Christian—Ziv—Syndicated.
"Bullet Wound"
(Written by Gene Roddenberry. Date on Ziv script 5 July 1956. Reg. with WGA 11/56.)

Harbor Command—Ziv—Syndicated.
"The Psychiatrist"   12 February 1958
(Written by Gene Roddenberry and William Driskill.)

Bat Masterson
Broadcast: October 1958–September 1959, NBC Wednesday 9:30–10:00; October 1959–Sept 1960, NBC Thursday 8:00–8:30; September 1960–September 1961, NBC Thursday 8:30–9:00
"Pecos Shootdown"[1]   7 November 1958

In at least one resume, Gene listed the programs *King of Diamonds* and *Science Fiction Theater,* both Ziv productions. Research shows that, technically, he did write for *SFT.* He was commissioned to write assignment #1614, "Undersea Canyon," for the producer Ivan Tors from a story Tors provided. The production was cancelled by Tors after delivery of the first draft, but because of Tors' difficulties with the production company, not with Gene's work. If Gene wrote for *King of Diamonds,* the script does not survive in the Ziv archives. One damaged script in Gene's files seems to be a *King of Diamonds* script. It may not have been bought and Gene remembered writing but not selling it.

Jane Wyman Theater (Name changed in 1955 from *Fireside Theatre*)—NBC—5 April 1949–23 August 1955—Revue Productions.

"The Perfect Alibi"
(Teleplay by Gene Roddenberry, story by Patricia Highsmith. Reg. with WGA 10/57.)

Chevron Hall of Stars—Syndicated—Gene's episode broadcast in Los Angeles 6 March 1956—Four Star Films.

"The Secret Weapon of 117"
(Written by Gene Roddenberry as Robert Wesley. Reg. with WGA 2/56—actually written late 1953, early 1954.)

---

[1]This script is in the Ziv Archives but not listed in the WGA printout.

Kaiser Aluminum Hour—NBC—3 July 1956–18 June 1957 hour-long dramatic anthology alternated with *Armstrong Circle Theater* on Tuesdays, one of the several shows which comprise television "Golden Age."

"So Short A Season"
(Written by Gene Roddenberry. Reg. with WGA 2/57.)

Boots and Saddles—Syndicated—1957–1959—California National Productions.

"The Marquis of Donnybrook"
(Written by Gene Roddenberry. Reg. with WGA 11/57.)
"Gatling Gun"
(Written by Gene Roddenberry. Reg. with WGA 11/57.)
"Rescue of the Strangers"
(Written by Gene Roddenberry. Reg. with WGA 11/57.)
"The Prussian Farmer"
(written by Gene Roddenberry. Reg. with WGA 11/57.)

True Story or ***General Electric True***—NBC—Saturdays at noon—16 March 1957–9 Sept 1961—Dramatic anthology series.
"V-Victor Five"
(Teleplay by Harold Jack Bloom, story by Gene Roddenberry. Reg. with WGA 7/62.)

The Dupont Show with June Allyson—CBS—Mondays at 10:30P.M.,—21 September 1959–12 June 1961.—Four Star Productions.—thirty-minute dramatic anthology series.
"Escape"
(Teleplay by Bruce Geller, story by Gene Roddenberry. Reg. with WGA 2/60.)

Have Gun Will Travel
Scripts by Gene Roddenberry are listed according to those on file in the archives of CBS Entertainment, New York, and the WGA list. As this was a network program, the broadcast dates are supplied by CBS Entertainment archives from final shooting scripts.
Broadcast history: CBS—Saturday nights 9:30–10:00, September 14, 1957–September 21, 1963.

Title	Air Date
"The Great Mojave Chase"*	9/28/57
"The Yuma Treasure"*	12/14/57
"The Hanging Cross"*	12/21/57
"Helen Of Abajinian"*²	12/28/57
"Ella West"*	1/4/58
"The Hanging of Roy Carter"*	10/4/58
"Road to Wicksburg"*	10/25/58
"Juliet"	1/31/59
"The Monster of Moon Ridge"	2/28/59
"Maggie O'Bannion"	4/4/59
"Episode in Laredo"	4/19/59
"The Return of Roy Carter"	5/2/59
"Les Girls"	9/26/59
"The Posse"	10/3/59
"The Golden Toad"	11/21/59
"Tiger"	11/28/59
"Charley Red Dog"	12/12/59
"El Passo Stage"*	4/15/61
"Alice"	3/17/62
"Taylor's Woman"	9/22/62
"The Marshal of Sweetwater"	11/24/62
"Trial At Tablerock"	12/15/62
"The Cage At MacNaab"	2/16/63
"The Savages"	3/16/63

* Indicates scripts not in the CBS archives.

The following are Gene Roddenberry *Have Gun Will Travel* scripts adapted for radio and the dates of their broadcast.

Name of Show	Date
"Food To Wickenberg" adapted by John Dawson (E. Jack Neuman)	11/30/58
"Ella West" adapted by John Dawson	12/7/58
"Indian Christmas" adapted by John Dawson	12/21/58

---

²Gene won the Writer's Guild Award for this script.

"Shotgun Marriage"	1/4/59
adapted by John Dunkel	
"Monster of Moonridge"	3/8/59
adapted by John Dawson	
"Maggie O'Bannion"	4/5/59
adapted by John Dawson	

Jefferson Drum—NBC—Friday nights from 7:30–8:00, April 1958–April 1959—Screen Gems.
"Stagecoach Episode"
(Written by Gene Roddenberry. Reg. with WGA 7/58.)
"The Poet"
(Written by Gene Roddenberry. Reg. with WGA 5/58.)
"Madam Faro"
(Written by Gene Roddenberry. Reg. with WGA 4/58.)
"Law and Order"
(Written by Gene Roddenberry. Reg. with WGA 3/58.)

Naked City—ABC—Tuesday nights at 9:30—30 September 1958–29 September 1959; Tuesday nights 10:00–11:00—12 October 1960—11 September 1963—Screen Gems.

"The Rydecker Case"
(Written by Gene Roddenberry. Reg. with WGA 5/62. This story was originally conceived for *Studio One*.)

In 1960, Gene went to work at Screen Gems to create and develop pilots. He also wrote scripts for Screen Gems shows. While at Screen Gems, Gene produced *The Wrangler*, seen on NBC, Thursday nights 9:30–10:00, August 4, 1960 through September 15, 1960. It was a replacement for *The Ford Show*, starring Tennessee Ernie Ford. There is little documentation in his files regarding this program.

The Detectives (Also known as *Robert Taylor's Detectives*)—ABC/NBC—16 October 1959–22 September 1961 (ABC); 29 September 1961–21 September 1962 (NBC)—Four Star—went to an hour from 30 minutes in 1961 when it shifted networks.

"Blue Fire"
(Written by Gene Roddenberry. Reg. with WGA 1/60.)
"Karate"
(Written by Gene Roddenberry. Reg. with WGA 1/60.)

Target: The Corruptors—ABC—Friday nights 10:00–11:00—29 September 1961–21 September 1962—Four Star.

"To Wear a Badge"
(Teleplay by Harry Essex, story by Gene Roddenberry. Reg. with the WGA 9/61.)

Shannon—Syndicated—1961—Screen Gems (not to be confused with the CBS show of the '81–82 season).
"The Embezzler's Daughter"
(Teleplay by Gene Roddenberry, story by Ward Hawkins. Reg. with WGA 5/61.)
"The Pickup"
(Written by Gene Roddenberry. Reg. with WGA 4/61.)

Two Faces West—Syndicated—1961—Screen Gems.

"The Lesson"
(Teleplay by Gene Roddenberry, story Eustace Cockrell. Reg. with WGA 2/61.)

Dr. Kildare—NBC—28 September 1961–30 August 1966–MGM Arena Productions.

"The General"
(Written by Gene Roddenberry. Reg. with WGA 4/62.)

The Virginian/The Men from Shiloh—NBC—19 September 1962–9 September 1970—16 September 1970–8 September 1971—Revue.
"Run Away Home"
(Teleplay by Howard Browne, story by Gene Roddenberry. Reg. with WGA 2/63.)

The Lieutenant—NBC—Saturday 7:30–8:30—September 14, 1963–September 5, 1964.

"Pilot episode, untitled"
(Written by Gene Roddenberry. Reg. with WGA 1/63.)
"To Kill A Man"
(Written by Gene Roddenberry. Reg. with WGA 4/64.)
"A Very Private Affair"
(Written by Gene Roddenberry. Reg. with WGA 7/63.)
"The Alien"
(Written by Gene Roddenberry as Robert Wesley. Reg. with WGA 11/63.)

The Long Hunt of April Savage (pilot 9/65)—produced for Sam Rolfe.

Star Trek, The Original Series.

Wrote "The Cage" first pilot—did some rewriting on second pilot, "Where No Man Has Gone Before."
Episodes credited to Gene Roddenberry:
"The Menagerie" written by Gene Roddenberry.
"Return to Tomorrow."
"The Omega Glory" written by Gene Roddenberry.
"Mudd's Women" teleplay by Stephen Kandel, story by Gene Roddenberry.
"The Return of the Archons" teleplay by Boris Sobelman, story by Gene Roddenberry.
"Bread and Circuses" written by Gene Roddenberry and Gene L. Coon.
"Assignment: Earth" teleplay by Art Wallace, story by Gene Roddenberry and Art Wallace. Attempted spin-off from series.
"The Savage Curtain" teleplay by Arthur Heinemann and Gene Roddenberry, story by Gene Roddenberry.
"Turnabout Intruder" teleplay by Arthur Singer, story by Gene Roddenberry.
"A Private Little War" teleplay by Gene Roddenberry, story Jud Crucis.
"Charlie X" teleplay by Dorothy C. Fontana, story by Gene Roddenberry.

In addition to these fully credited scripts, Gene rewrote major portions of the first two seasons of the show.
For a variety of reasons, much of his rewrite work was never credited to Gene. During the production of *Star Trek: The Original Series,* Gene sent a memo to the front office noting that he had done the following and made the appropriate charges.

Polish on "Catspaw"—$750.
Complete rewrite on "Friday's Child"—$2750.
Furnished the story for "Who Mourns for Adonais?" (credit on film reads "by Gilbert Ralston and Gene L. Coon")—$750.
Furnished story on "Amok Time"—$750—polished script—$750. (Film credit reads "by Theodore Sturgeon.")

Polish on "Wolf in the Fold"—$1,000.

Furnished story for "I, Mudd"—$750—polish—$750. (Credit on film reads "by Stephen Kandel and David Gerrold.")

Furnished story for "Bread & Circuses"—$750—complete rewrite—$2500.

Complete rewrite and a new script for "A Private Little War"—$3,000.

Rewrite on "Obsession"—$2500 (credit reads "By Art Wallace.)

Gene wrote at least three theatrical features; one produced, two not.

Tarzan—1968—unfilmed theatrical feature for National General.

Pretty Maids All In A Row—MGM—1971—reg. with WGA 11/70. Screenplay by Gene Roddenberry based on the novel by Francis Pollini. Gene also produced this film. The film starred Rock Hudson, who later said that it was one of the few pictures that he had a financial interest in that actually paid.

Magna I—1975/1976—grand scale script for $50 million film before studios made $50 million films. Years ahead of its time.

Television listing continued:

Alias Smith and Jones—ABC—21 January 1971–13 January 1973—"The Girl in the Boxcar" #3 Jan 1971—teleplay by Howard Brown, story by Gene Roddenberry.

Star Trek: The Animated Series—NBC—1973–1974—Saturday mornings—Gene was executive consultant for the 22 half-hour shows.

The Questor Tapes (television pilot, made for TV movie for Universal)—teleplay by Gene Roddenberry and Gene L. Coon, story by Gene Roddenberry—air date 23 January 1974—ABC. Original titles: "Questor", "Mr. Q."—story conceived much earlier.

Spectre (pilot, made for TV movie) aired in 1977—filmed in England—teleplay by Gene Roddenberry and Samuel A.

Peeples, story by Gene Roddenberry—conceived in early 1970's.

Genesis II (made for TV movie/pilot)—Warner Bros.—air date 1974—reg. with WGA 2/73—writer: Gene Roddenberry.

Gene wrote 16 episodes for *Genesis II,* including "Robot's Return," the uncredited core story for *Star Trek: The Motion Picture.*

Planet Earth (made for TV movie, pilot, same premises as *Genesis II*)—Warner Bros.—teleplay by Juanita Bartlett and Gene Roddenberry, story by Gene Roddenberry.

Star Trek: The Next Generation—1987–1994—Syndicated. Creator and Executive Producer for the first five seasons. Writers Guide written by Gene Roddenberry.
"Encounter at Farpoint"
(Teleplay by D. C. Fontana and Gene Roddenberry— two-hour pilot episode.)
"Hide and Q"
(Teleplay by C.J. Holland (Maurice Hurley) and Gene Roddenberry.)
"Datalore"
(Teleplay by Robert Lewin and Gene Roddenberry, story by Robert Lewin and Maurice Hurley.)

Unsold Concepts, Scripts, and Filmed Pilots

Battleground: Earth—in preproduction and then cancelled before it was cast—1975—similar in general concept to "V," which later made it to NBC.

The Nine—script for psi lab drama—1975—unsold.

Defiance County—Screen Gems—unsold pilot.

Police Story—Desilu—August 1965—unsold pilot (30-minute pilot written by Gene Roddenberry, with a "created by" credit as well.)

Robin Hood—August 25, 1967—date on unproduced pilot script.

Sam Houston—Screen Gems—unsold pilot.

"The Man From Texas"
(Written by Gene Roddenberry. Reg. with WGA 4/58.)

Nightstick—Screen Gems—unsold pilot.

"The Big Walk"
(Written by Gene Roddenberry. Reg. with WGA 2/59.)
Pilot episode
(Written by Gene Roddenberry, Clarence Green and Russell
   Rouse. Reg. with WGA 1/62.)

APO 923—Screen Gems—unsold pilot.

Pilot episode: "Operation Shangri-La"
(Written by Gene Roddenberry. Reg. with WGA 1/62.)

A P P E N D I X   I I

Terrance Sweeney's "God and Roddenberry"

Gene had been lecturing for several years, elevated, as it were, to the position of First Electronic Philosopher. He had given a lot of thought to the major questions of life, at least as far as they pertained to him. While he addressed his answers to these questions in a variety of formats—lectures, interviews, television scripts—in the late 1970's he had a unique opportunity to express himself. Terrance Sweeney, a Jesuit priest, was conducting research for a book.[1] The book's premise was disarmingly simple: Sweeney asked a variety of prominent individuals—Ray Bradbury to Phyllis Diller, Eugene McCarthy to Joe Pasternak, Willie Shoemaker to Frank Capra—three questions: Who is God to you? How has your relationship with God changed in your life? Who are you to God? The respondents were invited to approach those three questions however they wished.

Sweeney published Gene's response second, right after Ray Bradbury.

Gene: I presume you want an introspective look at this. I think I've gone through quite an ordinary series of steps in life. I began as most children began, with God and Santa Claus and the tooth fairy and the Easter Bunny all being about the same thing. Then I went through the things that I think sensitive people go through, wrestling with the thoughts of Jesus—did he shit? Did he screw? I began to dare to believe that God wasn't some white beard. I began to look upon the miseries of the human race and to think

---

[1]*God &,* by Terrance A. Sweeney, (Minneapolis, MN: Winston Press, 1985).

God was not as simple as my mother said. As nearly as I can concentrate on the question today, I believe I am God; certainly you are, I think we intelligent beings on this planet are all a piece of God, are becoming God. In some sort of cyclical non-time thing we have to become God, so that we can end up creating ourselves, so that we can be in the first place.

I'm one of those people who insists on hard facts. I won't believe in a flying saucer until one lands out here or someone gives me photographs. But I am almost as sure about this as if I did have facts, although the only test I have is my own consciousness.

Sweeney: What's the primary plot that comes to your mind when you say that we are becoming God?

Gene: I think God is as much a basic ingredient in the universe as neutrons and positrons; I suspect there is a scientific equation in matter and time and energy, and we'll ultimately discover the missing ingredient. God is, for lack of a better term, clout. This is the prime force, when we look around the universe.

I think God—we—(the equation of the universe) created time—our own beginnings and ends—so that we could exist. Let me explain what makes me think so: I think it's the very fact that I am the center of the universe, which is obviously so because everything in the universe comes to me via my sensations and impressions inside. And I hope it does to you, too. I hope you're not a trick someone is playing on me. I hope you have the same views. In that case, the universe is not really as simple as one universe, with one time sequence. It is a marvelously complex thing.

The very fact that though this thing I loosely describe as "thought" all this comes to me—my own experiences and also your experiences—this must mean that as certainly as two and two is four, God is the basic force behind creativity of life, and so on.

Sweeney: Is is fair for me to summarize your thinking on God in this equation—God equals thought?

Gene: God equals consciousness, yes.

Sweeney: To take that one step further, can I conclude from this that in your life, when you have had an experience of God, it has been in terms of your increased consciousness, your increased exhilaration at being able to think?

Gene: No. My experiences with the loose term "God"

have not been a total sweep of understanding, but rather a slow putting together of a bit of this and a bit of that. God is a very personal and selfish concept to all of us, because we have no total certainty. Yet putting together these small pieces is the beginning of the feeling of Godliness.

Sweeney: There are some people who have divided human experience into mind, body, and spirit. When you say the word "thought," are you excluding for it feeling and emotion?

Gene: I'm including it, completely. I think this Godliness that we're talking about is part of pain, ecstasy, longing—all of these things which we only imperfectly realize and categorize.

Sweeney: Can you point to one or two or three experiences in your life where you were able to say, "Ah, I think I have experienced God?"

Gene: The first major experience of my life came rather late. I envy people who had it earlier. I went to a Baptist young people's Christian association, BYCU, which is about the ugliest title you could have for anything. They had by mistake invited a Scottish ex-minister who turned out to be, in the 1930's, a left-wing radical. He talked of new and exciting things, such as, wars were not just. And he said—this was World War I—the Germans were not Godless; God was not on our side. He really ridiculed the whole war. He introduced me to—I suppose not a very great book, but it was a revelation to me in those days—Pierre van Paassen's *Days of Our Years*. And that was the first revelation in my life that things are not as they are said to be.

I met with him later. He took me to his apartment, in a hotel. My father was deathly afraid that I was being lured into a homosexual relationship, because what kind of man would invite a young boy to his apartment? He had a copy of the Koran there. To hear him say that this book was as holy as the one next to it, which is called the Bible, was a shocking and exciting thing. Yeah, that was a moment of taking a faltering step toward Godliness, I think.

Sweeney: Is that *the* moment in your life, or are there others?

Gene: Well, that was *the* one. It just caught me at the right time, the right moment of glandular secretions or whatever. I wanted to read everything on earth because this was such an exciting discovery. What there must be out there in all the libraries and bookstores!

I don't think I can remember any other experiences that were quite that huge. I suppose adolescent experiences must always have a hugeness about them.

Sweeney: How old were you?

Gene: Fourteen.[2] I suppose the only experience similar to that came when I was creating the show *Star Trek* and thinking maybe I could do what Jonathan Swift did. When he wanted to comment on the English political system and do a satire on it, he had it happen to little people. Somewhere it occurred to me that I could make my comments, and if they happened to little purple people on far-out planets I could get it by my censors. And the idea began to grow in me that *Star Trek* adventures could be about many different "creatures" and events, so that I could get many different ideas by the censors on religion, on sex, on unions, on management, or on Vietnam, which was big on their minds at that time. There was in creating it—a moment of—shit, man, hey! I can do it! I can really think some things out and really say them.

Sweeney: The experience that you relate is different from other things that I have read and other people I have talked to. They relate their experiences of God in terms of a person rather than in terms of an idea or an insight. How much of your experience of God has been related to a person as opposed to a heightening awareness, an idea, increased knowledge, and, of course, affection?

Gene: I tend to ignore what I think you might want to hear.

My own feeling is that relation to God as a person is a petty, superstitious approach to the All, the Infinite. I remember as a young man being in Mexico City, at the Lady of Guadalupe Cathedral, I think it was. I watched the people

---

[2]It is more likely that Gene was seventeen when he read the book, as he was fourteen in 1935 and the book was not published until January 1939. It was a popular book, going through six more printings by September 1939. The flap copy reads, in part, " . . . [van Paassen] bring to his material a deep compassion and love for mankind. Here is humanism at its best, the revelation of a free spirit and a belief in the fundamental dignity of man. The impact of this book is unforgettable, and its reading a genuine emotional and spiritual experience." One can only imagine its formative influence on the youthful Gene.

crawl from ten miles away, from the city, with bleeding knees. I felt and understood that—at least to me—this was as foolish as the things I'd always laughed at on television when I saw the African tribesmen do the same thing. God is not a person, not a simple thing like that. I wish I could simply bleed or flagellate myself to get closer to him. But unfortunately it's not that easy. In fact, for many years I was bitterly angry about people hurting themselves, and I categorized anyone who believed this way as stupid. I think that those who find pleasure and relief in being at that—I was going to say level, putting myself above them, but I don't mean that—if this is the way they want to believe, and it gives them some understanding of themselves, then fine. God—whatever you are—bless them, make them happy. For me it's not that simple. It's not an individual. It's not even as simple as categories of good and evil, because all we have to do is look in our backyard to find that all of our systems of good and evil are denied by nature. It's a more complex thing.

Sweeney: Do you . . .

Gene: I'm afraid of my answers. You ask me a simple question and I go into a whole field.

Sweeney: No, give me a direct answer. Don't worry about whether it's contrary to my belief. But concerning what you believe, do you communicate with God at all?

Gene: I don't know. I see no reason to believe in, and I don't believe in, psi factors, and cults, and things like that. But it does seem that sometimes in the process of writing, in making things happen, that sometimes you seem to get tuned in with things. It's almost as if your receiver or transmitter were working better. And ideas begin to come out of you that you're almost not capable of. And certain things begin to happen that you somehow know are right. Without for a moment equating myself with Einstein, he said that in laying out relativity, certain things came to him that he had to spend fifteen years working to prove, and yet when they first came to him he knew they were right. Perhaps, I think, the odds are slightly in favor that there is a mass consciousness, a transmitter somewhere that some of us occasionally tune in to and get information that we have to spend many years verifying.

Sweeney: What difference does God make in your life?

Gene: I would have to say, the concept of *being* God in my life ... It's not anything to do with religion ... it's the sense that I belong ... that I'm part of it. And I cannot treat that casually. I must try to become more a part of it and to understand what my part of it means. It's much too important to just discard by junking up, drinking whiskey, and smoking cigarettes—all of which I do. But in between there's the feeling that I am a part of something as important as the molecules that make all this up. And I ignore that at my own peril.

It's too marvelous, too. It's too marvelous to ignore and get tossed aside.

Sweeney: Does your being God or your participating in God, whatever term you find appropriate, make a difference in such things as whether we drop bombs in Cambodia and drop bombs in Dresden? Does that make a difference?

Gene: Oh, yes. It makes a great difference, and yet it doesn't make a difference. Let me try to explain that: I deny the bad logic, the stupidities that make ... that create these things. I hate the fact that people who do it never thought of Godliness or obligation; or the fact that they are growing powerful and comfortable, while people who are more worthy of being part of this are dying and living in torture and pain.

At the same time, having worked in science fiction, which I think in some ways is a more interesting field than it has been given credit for, I've learned to take a longer perspective of all these things. I see a lot of this as the probably natural excitement and aggressiveness of an infant race growing up. If you're actually in Vietnam and flesh is burning up around you from napalm, it's got to be a horrible thing. But if you can take a few steps back from it—as indeed we do when we look at the story of the Roman Empire—I think you begin to see it as part of an infant God, an infant race, growing, lust, shouting, slapping at each other in kindergarten. And I think that God or those nearer to God, another race, another intelligence slightly higher, looks at us and says, "Well, the marvelously aggressive, healthy child is coming along." I think that races grow up the same way as children grow up. It can become something.

Sweeney: How do you see us in the adult stage?

Gene: That's—I was going to say that's the *one* thing, but I have to correct myself—that's one of *many* things that I haven't been able to resolve. In an adult stage will we achieve, or have thrust upon us, a oneness in which we are all cells in a great organism and a great mind, a great organism which is lofty and mature and wise and never does anything wrong? I'm afraid that might be rather dull. For me, at my level anyway, the sign of wisdom and maturity is being able to take delight in someone who says, "I disagree with you because." I think the worst possible thing that can happen to us is where all of us begin to act and talk and look and think alike. So I can see us moving toward that infinite oneness which is full of wisdom and peace and so on. And I find myself drawing back and saying, "Better we should have the loveliness of disagreeing." I don't want to play Monopoly if my dice are perfect every time. I want to be able to say, "You're wrong. You prove to me you're right." At least I'll have the joy of proving that you're wrong. What loveliness!

It seems to me—it's likely that heaven's here right now. If you could take life with its pain and misery, where you fail and you sometimes win, and if you package it into a game, people would pay a fortune to have this game. And I don't know that I'd want it to be resolved so peacefully that the game would be all over.

Sweeney: In several traditions of the world, people as Christian, or Hindus, or Buddhists, have a vehicle which they consciously direct to contact God—meditation or prayer or lifing up one's heart. Now, you did mention the act of writing, where sometimes you feel that some of the ideas are falling into you mind, coming from outside of you. This seems to be a bigger experience for you than any other to date. Is there any activity in your life that is a *conscious* attempt to be more of what you want to be, to get closer to this God ideal? Is there some vehicle that you use? Writing seems more of a passive thing. You were writing, then it was as though the muses were illuminating, or God was illuminating. . . .

Gene: Writing takes you into a confrontation of self.

Sweeney: Is there any other form, any other vehicle that you use?

Gene: I tried Transcendental Meditation once and it didn't work particularly. It's very relaxing, but that's it. It was just a pleasant, floating lull. Like having pot. But you don't get busted for it! But as far as having lightning strike and saying, "Wow! I see it all!!"—no.

No, there are not things I use. For the last fifteen or eighteen years, my own way to get in touch, if indeed I do get in touch, has been to train myself to wake up around five in the morning. Strangely enough, you can do it without an alarm clock. I read for two—two and a half hours—before the family wakes up. The books I've read recently range from trashy literature to a new Oxford study of the life of Alexander the Great, *No Time to Die, Attica, Helter Skelter, The Study of Cromwell*—and just whatever reading happens to come along. I always read *Playboy* cover to cover and wish I were younger and could try some of those things. I read every morning, and it just sort of gets my engine going, so that by the time I get outside, and walk around, and take a swim when the weather's right, and get to my desk, everything is going and I write better. The only other thing I use is going out and lecturing at colleges. Kids ask me embarrassing questions and you really have to—I'm sure the same thing happens to you—you have to ask, "Did I give the right answer?" I never really reexamined my whole thinking because wow, that was tough. And that's good for a writer.

Sweeney: What do you think of one of the documents in history which is the New Testament?

Gene: I think there is almost clearly a divinity, a concept which is in these things. But I think that this is probably true of almost all serious writing. I think that the Bible is probably no more divine than Shakespeare or *Naked City* or anything. You have to search for divinity. You have to find it and analyze it. I can't conceive of whatever God is, going down and pointing the finger and saying, "Okay, for this particular publisher you've got divinity." I think that you see it in *Walden Pond* and *Leaves of Grass* and no doubt in Oriental and Indian and other things that we're not even familiar with.

Sweeney: What about the Bible's explicit claims of Christ's divinity?

Gene: Well, my feeling about Jesus, which has gone from the things I talked about in boyhood in a church which probably held Jesus as more divine than the Catholic Church hold him—you know, "Sweet Jesus," "Jesus wants me for a sunbeam"—it has gone from that to almost an affirmation for me that I am God. It seems to me that everything he said is, "I am, and you are." He did a better job of it than I've done. But, you know, many people do better things than I do. Yes, I think he was in closer contact. I think, to me the whole joy and glory of Jesus is the fact that he is one of us. It seems to me that the whole statement of the New Testament is, "Hey, man, you can too, because I was born like you. I died like you. There's nothing special about me that's not special in you. And I'm offering you both." And I think this divinity thing is bullshit because they've taken away from the glorious, divine message that he kept saying over and over again. Divine, yes. But so are we. I think that's what he was saying: "So are you."

Sweeney: There's a book by Alan Watts called *Beyond the Spirit.* Have you read it?

Gene: No.

Sweeney: If you ever have the chance . . .

Gene: I don't read religious things very much because I got burned by them so badly as a child. I think this is true of many people. I know it doesn't make sense, but it is getting burned. And you sort of turn your back on it, and if they can sneak you religious stuff without your really knowing that it is, like I read a beautifully religious book on my last trip called *The Kapillan of Malta* or something like that. A story of a priest—oh, yes, it's a beautiful book. I'll loan it to you before you leave if you like. The story of a simple priest who turned out to be not so simple because of his inner strength. It took place in the days of the blitz and all that, and showed how he led his people, these villagers that lived in the catacombs. The hierarchy of the church hated him because there was the shit and smell of shit soup and the people lived on the ledges where they had taken the saints' bodies away so that these people could live, sleep, and make love. And he was saying, "This is life. This is how it is. I cannot change my people. All I can do for them is live with them, find them when they bleed." And finally as he was dying people began to realize, "Hey, wait a minute. This is more Christlike than any of the high bishops that look down their noses at him." It's a lovely book.

Sweeney: This lobster dinner was terrific. So was the interview. I'm really grateful.

Gene: Me, too. It's been fun.

INDEX

If you and/or a friend would like to receive the *ROC Advance*, a bimonthly newsletter featuring all the newest and hottest ROC books and authors, on a complimentary basis, please fill out this form and return it to:

ROC Books/Penguin USA
375 Hudson Street
New York, NY 10014

Your Address

Name _____

Street _____ Apt. # _____

City _____ State _____ Zip _____

Friend's Address

Name _____

Street _____ Apt. # _____

City _____ State _____ Zip _____